Harry Potter

AND THE HALF-BLOOD PRINCE

J.K. ROWLING

6

英汉对照版

哈利·波特与"混血王子"[上]

Harry Potter

〔英〕J.K. 罗琳 / 著

马爱农　马爱新 / 译

WIZARDING WORLD

人民文学出版社
PEOPLE'S LITERATURE PUBLISHING HOUSE

著作权合同登记号　图字　01-2024-1008

图书在版编目（CIP）数据

哈利·波特与"混血王子"：英汉对照版：上下/(英）J.K.罗琳著；马爱农，马爱新译. —北京：人民文学出版社，2020（2025.7重印）

ISBN 978-7-02-015072-4

Ⅰ.①哈…　Ⅱ.①J…②马…③马…　Ⅲ.①儿童小说—长篇小说—英国—现代—英、汉　Ⅳ.①I561.84

中国版本图书馆CIP数据核字（2019）第040996号

责任编辑　翟　灿
美术编辑　刘　静
责任印制　苏文强

出版发行　人民文学出版社
社　　址　北京市朝内大街166号
邮政编码　100705

印　　刷　三河市龙林印务有限公司
经　　销　全国新华书店等

字　　数　1500千字
开　　本　640毫米×960毫米　1/16
印　　张　60.25　插页6
印　　数　100001—110000
版　　次　2020年10月北京第1版
印　　次　2025年7月第9次印刷

书　　号　978-7-02-015072-4
定　　价　129.00元（上、下册）

To Mackenzie,

my beautiful daughter,

I dedicate

her ink and paper twin

献　给

我美丽的女儿麦肯琦

愿她喜欢这个散发着墨香的孪生妹妹

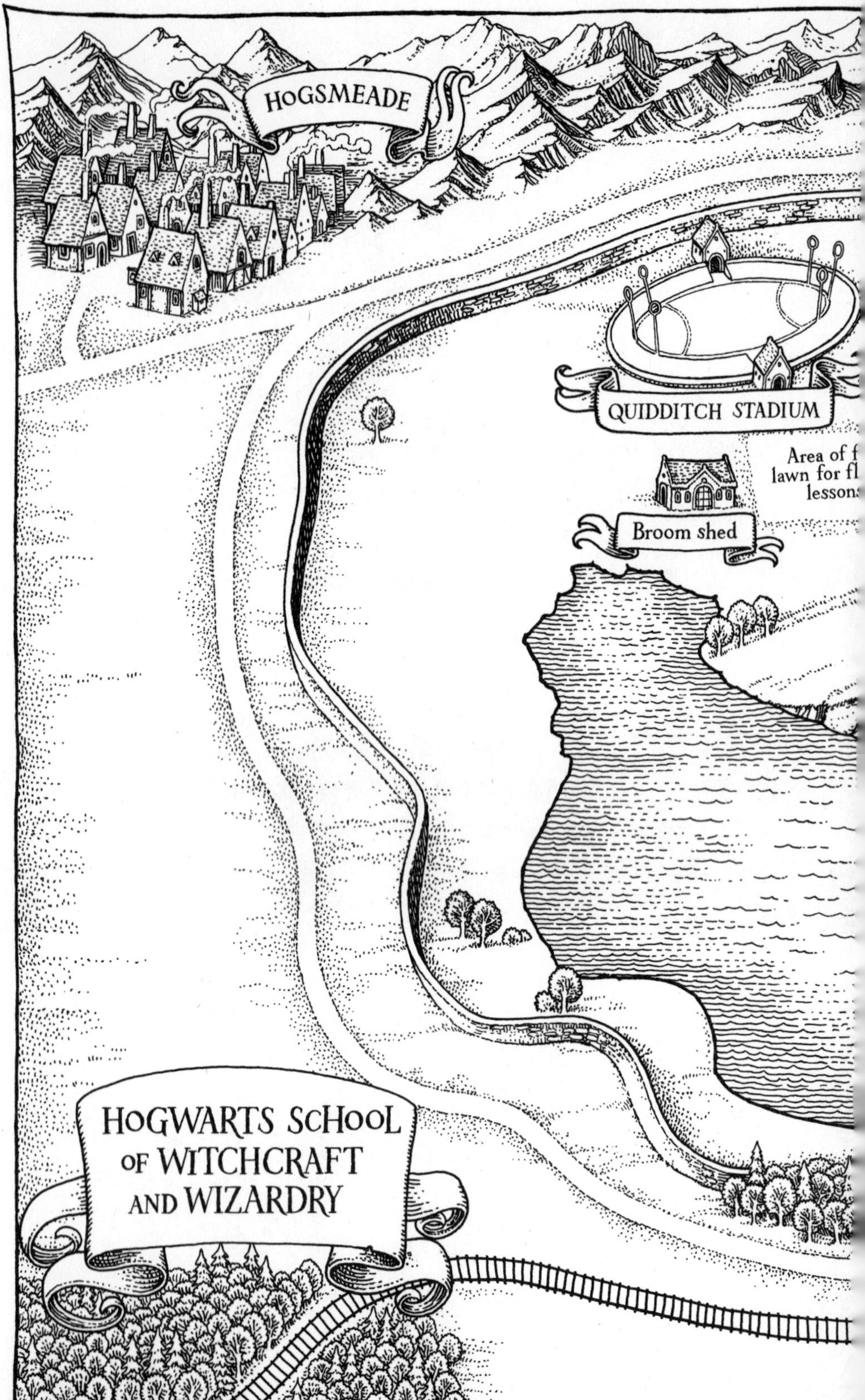
HOGSMEADE
QUIDDITCH STADIUM
Area of f
lawn for fl
lessons
Broom shed
HOGWARTS SCHOOL
OF WITCHCRAFT
AND WIZARDRY

HAGRID'S HUT
FORBIDDEN FOREST
WHOMPING WILLOW
GREENHOUSES
HOGWARTS CASTLE
HOGSMEADE STATION

CONTENTS

目　录

CHAPTER ONE

The Other Minister

It was nearing midnight and the Prime Minister was sitting alone in his office, reading a long memo that was slipping through his brain without leaving the slightest trace of meaning behind. He was waiting for a call from the president of a far-distant country, and between wondering when the wretched man would telephone, and trying to suppress unpleasant memories of what had been a very long, tiring and difficult week, there was not much space in his head for anything else. The more he attempted to focus on the print on the page before him, the more clearly the Prime Minister could see the gloating face of one of his political opponents. This particular opponent had appeared on the news that very day, not only to enumerate all the terrible things that had happened in the last week (as though anyone needed reminding) but also to explain why each and every one of them was the government's fault.

The Prime Minister's pulse quickened at the very thought of these accusations, for they were neither fair nor true. How on earth was his government supposed to have stopped that bridge collapsing? It was outrageous for anybody to suggest that they were not spending enough on bridges. The bridge was less than ten years old, and the best experts were at a loss to explain why it had snapped cleanly in two, sending a dozen cars into the watery depths of the river below. And how dared anyone suggest that it was lack of policemen that had resulted in those two very nasty and well-publicised murders? Or that the government should have somehow foreseen the freak hurricane in the West Country that had caused so much damage to both people and property? And was it his fault that one of *his* Junior Ministers, Herbert Chorley, had chosen this week to act so peculiarly that he was now going to be spending a lot more time with his family?

第 1 章

另类部长

差不多快到午夜了，首相独自坐在办公室里，读着一份长长的备忘录，但是他脑子里一片空白，根本不明白那上面写的是什么意思。他在等一个遥远国家的总统打来电话。他一方面怀疑那个倒霉的家伙到底会不会来电话，另一方面克制着不去回忆这漫长而累人的一周里许多令人不快的事情，所以脑子里便没有多少空间想别的了。他越是想集中精力阅读面前这张纸上的文字，越是清清楚楚地看见他的一个政敌幸灾乐祸的脸。这位政敌那天出现在新闻里，不仅一一列举了上个星期发生的所有可怕的事故（就好像有谁还需要提醒似的），而且还头头是道地分析了每一起事故都是由于政府的过失造成的。

首相一想到这些指责，脉搏就加快了跳动，因为它们很不公正，也不符合事实。他的政府怎么可能阻止那座桥倒塌呢？有人竟然提出政府在桥梁建筑方面投资不够，这真让人忍无可忍。那座桥建成还不到十年，最出色的专家也无法解释它怎么会突然整整齐齐地断成两截，十几辆汽车栽进了下面深深的河水里。另外，有人竟然提出是警方力量不足，才导致了那两起传得沸沸扬扬的恶性谋杀案的发生，还说政府应该预见到英格兰西南部诸郡那场给人们的生命和财产造成巨大损失的古怪飓风。还有，他的一位助理部长赫伯特·乔莱偏偏在这个星期表现怪异，说是要跟家人多待一些时间，这难道也是他的过错吗？

'A grim mood has gripped the country,' the opponent had concluded, barely concealing his own broad grin.

And unfortunately, this was perfectly true. The Prime Minister felt it himself; people really did seem more miserable than usual. Even the weather was dismal; all this chilly mist in the middle of July … it wasn't right, it wasn't normal …

He turned over the second page of the memo, saw how much longer it went on, and gave it up as a bad job. Stretching his arms above his head he looked around his office mournfully. It was a handsome room, with a fine marble fireplace facing the long sash windows, firmly closed against the unseasonable chill. With a slight shiver, the Prime Minister got up and moved over to the windows, looking out at the thin mist that was pressing itself against the glass. It was then, as he stood with his back to the room, that he heard a soft cough behind him.

He froze, nose-to-nose with his own scared-looking reflection in the dark glass. He knew that cough. He had heard it before. He turned, very slowly, to face the empty room.

'Hello?' he said, trying to sound braver than he felt.

For a brief moment he allowed himself the impossible hope that nobody would answer him. However, a voice responded at once, a crisp, decisive voice that sounded as though it were reading a prepared statement. It was coming – as the Prime Minister had known at the first cough – from the froglike little man wearing a long silver wig who was depicted in a small and dirty oil-painting in the far corner of the room.

'To the Prime Minister of Muggles. Urgent we meet. Kindly respond immediately. Sincerely, Fudge.' The man in the painting looked enquiringly at the Prime Minister.

'Er,' said the Prime Minister, 'listen … it's not a very good time for me … I'm waiting for a telephone call, you see … from the president of –'

'That can be rearranged,' said the portrait at once. The Prime Minister's heart sank. He had been afraid of that.

'But I really was rather hoping to speak –'

'We shall arrange for the president to forget to call. He will telephone tomorrow night instead,' said the little man. 'Kindly respond immediately to Mr Fudge.'

“全国上下一片恐慌。”那位反对派最后这么总结道，几乎毫不掩饰脸上得意的笑容。

不幸的是，事实的确如此。首相自己也感觉到了。人们确实显得比平常更加惶恐不安，就连天气也不如人意，还是七月中旬，就已弥漫着寒冷的雾气……这很不对头，很不正常……

他翻到备忘录的第二页，发现后面的内容还很长，知道不可能把它看完，便索性放弃了。他把两只胳膊伸过头顶，郁闷地打量着他的办公室。这是一个很气派的房间，漂亮的大理石壁炉对着长长的框格窗，窗户关得很严实，挡住了外面不合季节的寒雾。首相微微打了个寒战，站起来走到窗户前，望着外面紧贴窗玻璃的薄薄的雾气。正当他背对房间站在那儿的时候，听见身后传来一声轻轻的咳嗽。

他僵住了，面前黑黑的窗玻璃里是他自己那张惊恐的脸。他熟悉这咳嗽声。他以前曾经听见过。他缓缓地转过身，面对着空荡荡的房间。

“喂？”他说，努力使自己的声音显得勇敢一些。

那一瞬间，他明知道不可能，但心里还是隐约希望没有人会答应他。然而，立刻有个声音做了回答，这个声音清脆、果断，好像在念一篇准备好的发言稿。首相听见第一声咳嗽时就知道，这声音来自那个戴着长长的银色假发、长得像青蛙一般的小个子男人，他是房间那头墙角里一幅肮脏的小油画上的人物。

“致麻瓜首相。要求紧急会面。请立刻答复。忠实的，福吉。”油画里的男人询问地望着首相。

“嗯，”首相说，“听着……这个时间对我不合适……我在等一个电话……是一位总统的——”

“那可以重新安排。”肖像不假思索地说。首相的心往下一沉。他担心的就是这个。

“但是我确实希望跟他通话——”

“我们会让总统忘记打电话的事情。他会在明天晚上再打来电话。”小个子男人说，“请立即答复福吉先生。”

'I … oh … very well,' said the Prime Minister weakly. 'Yes, I'll see Fudge.'

He hurried back to his desk, straightening his tie as he went. He had barely resumed his seat, and arranged his face into what he hoped was a relaxed and unfazed expression, when bright green flames burst into life in the empty grate beneath his marble mantelpiece. He watched, trying not to betray a flicker of surprise or alarm, as a portly man appeared within the flames, spinning as fast as a top. Seconds later, he had climbed out on to a rather fine antique rug, brushing ash from the sleeves of his long pinstriped cloak, a lime-green bowler hat in his hand.

'Ah … Prime Minister,' said Cornelius Fudge, striding forwards with his hand outstretched. 'Good to see you again.'

The Prime Minister could not honestly return this compliment, so said nothing at all. He was not remotely pleased to see Fudge, whose occasional appearances, apart from being downright alarming in themselves, generally meant that he was about to hear some very bad news. Furthermore, Fudge was looking distinctly careworn. He was thinner, balder and greyer, and his face had a crumpled look. The Prime Minister had seen that kind of look in politicians before, and it never boded well.

'How can I help you?' he said, shaking Fudge's hand very briefly and gesturing towards the hardest of the chairs in front of the desk.

'Difficult to know where to begin,' muttered Fudge, pulling up the chair, sitting down and placing his green bowler upon his knees. 'What a week, what a week …'

'Had a bad one too, have you?' asked the Prime Minister stiffly, hoping to convey by this that he had quite enough on his plate already without any extra helpings from Fudge.

'Yes, of course,' said Fudge, rubbing his eyes wearily and looking morosely at the Prime Minister. 'I've been having the same week you have, Prime Minister. The Brockdale bridge … the Bones and Vance murders … not to mention the ruckus in the West Country …'

'You – er – your – I mean to say, some of your people were – were involved in those – those things, were they?'

Fudge fixed the Prime Minister with a rather stern look.

'Of course they were,' he said. 'Surely you've realised what's going on?'

“我……噢……好吧，”首相无可奈何地说，“行，我就见见福吉。”

他匆匆走向办公桌，一边正了正领带。他刚刚坐定，把面部表情调整得如他希望的那样轻松、镇定自若，就见大理石壁炉下面空空的炉栅里突然冒出了鲜绿色的火苗。首相竭力掩饰住内心的惊讶和恐慌，眼睁睁地看着一个大胖子出现在火焰中间，像陀螺一样飞快地转个不停。几秒钟后，大胖子跨过炉栅，手里拿着一顶黄绿色的圆顶高帽，站到一方古色古香的精美地毯上，掸了掸他那件细条子斗篷袖子上的炉灰。

“呵……首相，”康奈利·福吉说着，大步走了过来，伸出一只手，“很高兴又跟你见面了。”

首相从心底里不愿回答这句客套话，便什么也没说。他一点儿也不愿意见到福吉，福吉以前的几次露面，除了令人特别惊慌外，一般还意味着又要听到一些特别糟糕的消息。况且，福吉这次明显忧心忡忡。他比以前瘦了，脸色更加晦暗，脑袋也秃得更厉害了，脸看上去没精打采的。首相曾在政客们脸上看见过这种神情，一般来说，这不是一个好征兆。

“我能帮你做点什么吗？”首相问，匆匆握了一下福吉的手，示意他坐到桌子前一把最硬的椅子上。

“真不知道从哪儿说起，”福吉嘟囔道，拉过椅子坐下，把那顶绿色的圆顶高帽放在膝盖上，“这个星期真够呛，真够呛啊……”

“你这个星期也过得不顺心吗？”首相板着脸问，他想让对方明白，他自己需要操心的事情已经够多的了，不想再替福吉分担什么。

“是啊，那还用说。”福吉说着疲倦地揉揉眼睛，愁闷地看着首相，“这个星期我跟你的遭遇差不多，首相。布罗克代尔桥……博恩斯和万斯的命案……更别提西南部诸郡的那场动乱……”

“你们——嗯——你们的——我是说，你们的一些人跟——跟这些事件有关，是吗？”

福吉非常严厉地瞪着首相。

“当然是这样。”他说，“你肯定明白是怎么回事吧？”

'I ...' hesitated the Prime Minister.

It was precisely this sort of behaviour that made him dislike Fudge's visits so much. He was, after all, the Prime Minister, and did not appreciate being made to feel like an ignorant schoolboy. But of course, it had been like this from his very first meeting with Fudge on his very first evening as Prime Minister. He remembered it as though it were yesterday and knew it would haunt him until his dying day.

He had been standing alone in this very office, savouring the triumph that was his after so many years of dreaming and scheming, when he had heard a cough behind him, just like tonight, and turned to find that ugly little portrait talking to him, announcing that the Minister for Magic was about to arrive and introduce himself.

Naturally, he had thought that the long campaign and the strain of the election had caused him to go mad. He had been utterly terrified to find a portrait talking to him, though this had been nothing to how he had felt when a self-proclaimed wizard had bounced out of the fireplace and shaken his hand. He had remained speechless throughout Fudge's kindly explanation that there were witches and wizards still living in secret all over the world, and his reassurances that he was not to bother his head about them as the Ministry of Magic took responsibility for the whole wizarding community and prevented the non-magical population from getting wind of them. It was, said Fudge, a difficult job that encompassed everything from regulations on responsible use of broomsticks to keeping the dragon population under control (the Prime Minister remembered clutching the desk for support at this point). Fudge had then patted the shoulder of the still-dumbstruck Prime Minister in a fatherly sort of way.

'Not to worry,' he had said, 'it's odds on you'll never see me again. I'll only bother you if there's something really serious going on our end, something that's likely to affect the Muggles – the non-magical population, I should say. Otherwise it's live and let live. And I must say, you're taking it a lot better than your predecessor. *He* tried to throw me out of the window, thought I was a hoax planned by the opposition.'

At this, the Prime Minister had found his voice at last.

'You're – you're *not* a hoax, then?'

It had been his last, desperate hope.

"我……"首相迟疑着。

正是这种状况，使他不太喜欢福吉的来访。他毕竟是堂堂的首相，不愿意有人让他感觉自己是个什么都不懂的小学生。可是，自他当上首相的第一个晚上与福吉的第一次见面起，情况就是这样。他还清楚地记得当时的情景，就好像是昨天刚发生的事情，他知道他至死也忘不了那段记忆。

当时他独自站在这间办公室里，品味着经历了那么多年的梦想和精心谋划之后，终于获得成功的喜悦，突然，他听见身后传来一声咳嗽，就像今晚一样，他转身一看，是那幅丑陋的小肖像在跟他说话，通报说魔法部部长要来拜访他。

自然地，他以为是长期的竞选活动和选举的压力导致他的精神有点失常。他发现一幅肖像在跟他说话时确实惊恐极了，这还不算，后来又有一个自称是巫师的人从壁炉里跳了出来，跟他握手，他更是吓得不知所措。首相一言不发，福吉友好地解释说如今仍有巫师秘密地生活在世界各地，还安慰他说这些事用不着他来操心，因为魔法部有责任管理整个巫师界，不让非巫师人群知道他们的存在。福吉说，这是一件相当艰巨的工作，简直无所不包，从规定如何认真负责地使用飞天扫帚，到控制和管辖所有的火龙（首相记得自己听到这里时，不由得紧紧抓住了桌子，以免摔倒）。福吉说完之后，还像慈父一样拍了拍仍然瞠目结舌的首相的肩膀。

"不用担心，"他说，"你多半不会再见到我了。只有在我们那边出了严重的麻烦，有可能影响到麻瓜，就是那些非巫师人群的时候，我才会来打扰你。除此之外，你就顺其自然好了。对了，我还得说一句，你接受这件事的态度比你那位前任强多了。他以为我是他的政敌派来的一个骗子，要把我扔出窗外呢。"

这时，首相终于找到机会能说话了。

"这么说，你——不是骗子？"

这是他仅存的一点渺茫的希望。

'No,' said Fudge gently. 'No, I'm afraid I'm not. Look.'

And he had turned the Prime Minister's teacup into a gerbil.

'But,' said the Prime Minister breathlessly, watching his teacup chewing on the corner of his next speech, 'but why – why has nobody told me –?'

'The Minister for Magic only reveals him or herself to the Muggle Prime Minister of the day,' said Fudge, poking his wand back inside his jacket. 'We find it the best way to maintain secrecy.'

'But then,' bleated the Prime Minister, 'why hasn't a former Prime Minister warned me –?'

At this, Fudge had actually laughed.

'My dear Prime Minister, are *you* ever going to tell anybody?'

Still chortling, Fudge had thrown some powder into the fireplace, stepped into the emerald flames and vanished with a whooshing sound. The Prime Minister had stood there, quite motionless, and realised that he would never, as long as he lived, dare mention this encounter to a living soul, for who in the wide world would believe him?

The shock had taken a little while to wear off. For a time he had tried to convince himself that Fudge had indeed been a hallucination brought on by lack of sleep during his gruelling election campaign. In a vain attempt to rid himself of all reminders of this uncomfortable encounter, he had given the gerbil to his delighted niece and instructed his Private Secretary to take down the portrait of the ugly little man who had announced Fudge's arrival. To the Prime Minister's dismay, however, the portrait had proved impossible to remove. When several carpenters, a builder or two, an art historian and the Chancellor of the Exchequer had all tried unsuccessfully to prise it from the wall, the Prime Minister had abandoned the attempt and simply resolved to hope that the thing remained motionless and silent for the rest of his term in office. Occasionally he could have sworn he saw out of the corner of his eye the occupant of the painting yawning, or else scratching his nose; even, once or twice, simply walking out of his frame and leaving nothing but a stretch of muddy-brown canvas behind. However, he had trained himself not to look at the picture very much, and always to tell himself firmly that his eyes were playing tricks on him when anything like this happened.

Then, three years ago, on a night very like tonight, the Prime Minister

“不是，”福吉温和地说，“对不起，我不是。你看。”

他一挥魔杖，就把首相的茶杯变成了一只沙鼠。

“可是，”首相注视着他的茶杯在啃他的下一次演讲稿，上气不接下气地说，“可是，为什么——为什么没有人告诉过我——？”

“魔法部部长只在执政的麻瓜首相面前暴露自己的身份。”福吉说着把魔杖重新插进了衣服里面，“我们认为这样最有利于保持隐蔽。”

“可是，”首相用颤抖的声音说，“为什么没有一位前任首相提醒过我？”

听了这话，福吉竟然笑出声来。

“我亲爱的首相，难道你会去跟别人说吗？”

福吉仍然呵呵地笑着，往壁炉里扔了一些粉末，然后跨进翠绿色的火苗，呼的一声就消失了。首相一动不动地怔在那里，他知道，只要他还活着，是绝对不敢跟任何人提起这场会面的。在这大千世界里，有谁会相信他呢？

过了一段时间，他那颗受了惊吓的心才慢慢平静下来。他曾经试图说服自己，那个什么福吉只是一个幻觉，是因为竞选活动弄得他心力交瘁，睡眠不足，才出现了这样的幻觉。为了摆脱所有会让他想起这场不愉快会面的东西，他把那只沙鼠送给了欢天喜地的侄女，还吩咐他的私人秘书把那个通报福吉来访的小个子丑八怪的肖像取下来。可令他大为沮丧的是，那幅肖像竟然怎么也弄不走。他们动用了几位木匠、一两个建筑工人、一位艺术史专家，还有财政大臣，费了九牛二虎之力想把它从墙上撬下来，都没有成功。最后首相不再尝试了，只是一门心思地希望那玩意儿在他任期之内一直保持静止和沉默。偶尔，他可以肯定他用余光瞥见肖像里的人在打哈欠或挠鼻子，有一两次甚至走出了相框，只留下空空的一片土灰色帆布。不过，首相训练自己不要经常去看那幅肖像，每当出现这类蹊跷的事情时，他总是坚决地告诉自己是他的眼睛出现了错觉。

后来，也就是三年前，在一个像今天这样的夜晚，首相一个人待

had been alone in his office when the portrait had once again announced the imminent arrival of Fudge, who had burst out of the fireplace, sopping wet and in a state of considerable panic. Before the Prime Minister could ask why he was dripping all over the Axminster, Fudge had started ranting about a prison the Prime Minister had never heard of, a man named 'Serious' Black, something that sounded like Hogwarts and a boy called Harry Potter, none of which made the remotest sense to the Prime Minister.

'... I've just come from Azkaban,' Fudge had panted, tipping a large amount of water out of the rim of his bowler hat into his pocket. 'Middle of the North Sea, you know, nasty flight ... the Dementors are in uproar –' he shuddered '– they've never had a breakout before. Anyway, I had to come to you, Prime Minister. Black's a known Muggle killer and may be planning to rejoin You-Know-Who ... but of course, you don't even know who You-Know-Who is!' He had gazed hopelessly at the Prime Minister for a moment, then said, 'Well, sit down, sit down, I'd better fill you in ... have a whisky ...'

The Prime Minister had rather resented being told to sit down in his own office, let alone offered his own whisky, but he sat nevertheless. Fudge had pulled out his wand, conjured two large glasses full of amber liquid out of thin air, pushed one of them into the Prime Minister's hand and drawn up a chair.

Fudge had talked for over an hour. At one point, he had refused to say a certain name aloud, and wrote it instead on a piece of parchment, which he had thrust into the Prime Minister's whisky-free hand. When at last Fudge had stood up to leave, the Prime Minister had stood up too.

'So you think that ...' he had squinted down at the name in his left hand, 'Lord Vol–'

'*He Who Must Not Be Named!*' snarled Fudge.

'I'm sorry ... you think that He Who Must Not Be Named is still alive, then?'

'Well, Dumbledore says he is,' said Fudge, as he had fastened his pinstriped cloak under his chin, 'but we've never found him. If you ask me, he's not dangerous unless he's got support, so it's Black we ought to be worrying about. You'll put out that warning, then? Excellent. Well, I hope we don't see each other again, Prime Minister! Goodnight.'

But they had seen each other again. Less than a year later a harassed-looking Fudge had appeared out of thin air in the Cabinet Room to inform

在办公室里，那幅肖像又通报福吉即将来访，紧接着福吉就从壁炉里蹿了出来，浑身湿得像只落汤鸡，一副惊慌失措的样子。首相还没来得及问他为什么把水都滴在了阿克斯明斯特绒头地毯上，福吉就气冲冲地唠叨开了，说的是一座首相从来没听说过的监狱，一个被称作“小灰狼”布莱克的男人，一个听着像是霍格沃茨的什么东西，还有一个名叫哈利·波特的男孩，首相听得云里雾里，根本不知道他在说些什么。

“……我刚从阿兹卡班过来。”福吉一边喘着粗气说，一边把圆顶高帽帽檐里的一大堆水倒进了他的口袋，“在北海中央，你知道的，这一路可真够呛……摄魂怪躁动不安——”他打了个寒战，“——他们以前从来没有遇到过越狱事件。总之，我必须上你这儿来一趟，首相。布莱克是个著名的麻瓜杀手，而且很可能准备回到神秘人那边……当然啦，你连神秘人是谁都不知道！”他无奈地望了首相片刻，说道，“唉，坐下，坐下吧，我最好跟你详细说说……来一杯威士忌吧……”

对方明明是在首相的办公室，却反客为主地吩咐他坐下，还请他喝他自己的威士忌。首相本来是很恼火的，但他还是坐下了。福吉抽出魔杖，凭空变出了两只大玻璃杯，里面满是琥珀色的液体，他把其中一杯推到首相手里，然后又拖过来一把椅子。

福吉说了一个多小时。说到某个地方时，他竟不肯把一个名字大声说出来，只写在一张羊皮纸上，塞进了首相那只不拿威士忌的手里。最后，福吉起身准备离开了，首相也站了起来。

“这么说，你认为……”他眯起眼睛看了看左手里的那个名字，“伏地——”

“那个连名字都不能提的人！”福吉咆哮着说。

“对不起……你认为那个连名字都不能提的人还活着，是吗？”

“是啊，邓布利多是这么说的，”福吉说着把细条纹的斗篷在下巴底下系紧，“可是我们一直没有找到他。依我看，他只有得到支持才会构成危险，所以我们要担心的是布莱克。你会把那个警告公布出去吧？太好了。行了，我希望我们不会再见面了，首相！晚安。”

可是他们后来还是又见面了。不到一年，心烦意乱的福吉在内阁

the Prime Minister that there had been a spot of bother at the Kwidditch (or that was what it had sounded like) World Cup and that several Muggles had been 'involved', but that the Prime Minister was not to worry, the fact that You-Know-Who's Mark had been seen again meant nothing; Fudge was sure it was an isolated incident and the Muggle Liaison Office was dealing with all memory modifications as they spoke.

'Oh, and I almost forgot,' Fudge had added. 'We're importing three foreign dragons and a sphinx for the Triwizard Tournament, quite routine, but the Department for the Regulation and Control of Magical Creatures tells me that it's down in the rulebook that we have to notify you if we're bringing highly dangerous creatures into the country.'

'I – what – *dragons*?' spluttered the Prime Minister.

'Yes, three,' said Fudge. 'And a sphinx. Well, good day to you.'

The Prime Minister had hoped beyond hope that dragons and sphinxes would be the worst of it, but no. Less than two years later, Fudge had erupted out of the fire yet again, this time with the news that there had been a mass breakout from Azkaban.

'A *mass* breakout?' the Prime Minister had repeated hoarsely.

'No need to worry, no need to worry!' Fudge had shouted, already with one foot in the flames. 'We'll have them rounded up in no time – just thought you ought to know!'

And before the Prime Minister had been able to shout, 'Now, wait just one moment!' Fudge had vanished in a shower of green sparks.

Whatever the press and the opposition might say, the Prime Minister was not a foolish man. It had not escaped his notice that, despite Fudge's assurances at their first meeting, they were now seeing rather a lot of each other, nor that Fudge was becoming more flustered with each visit. Little though he liked to think about the Minister for Magic (or, as he always called Fudge in his head, the *Other* Minister), the Prime Minister could not help but fear that the next time Fudge appeared it would be with graver news still. The sight, therefore, of Fudge stepping out of the fire once more, looking dishevelled and fretful and sternly surprised that the Prime Minister did not know exactly why he was there, was about the worst thing that had happened in the course of this extremely gloomy week.

会议室里突然凭空出现，告诉首相说“鬼地奇”（至少听上去是这几个字）世界杯赛上出了乱子，有几个麻瓜被“牵扯”了进去，不过首相不用担心，虽然神秘人的标记又出现了，但那说明不了什么问题。福吉相信这只是一个孤立事件，而且就在他们说话的当儿，麻瓜联络办公室正忙着进行修改记忆的工作呢。

“哦，我差点忘记了，”福吉又说道，“为了举办三强争霸赛，我们要从国外进口三条火龙和一头斯芬克斯，这是惯例，不过神奇动物管理控制司的人告诉我，按照规定，如果我们把特别危险的动物带进这个国家，都需要向你通报一声。”

“我——什么——火龙？”首相结结巴巴地问。

“是啊，三条，”福吉说，“还有一头斯芬克斯。好了，祝你顺心。”

首相侥幸地希望不会再出现比火龙和斯芬克斯更可怕的东西了，然而他错了。不到两年，福吉又一次从火里冒了出来，这回带来的消息是：阿兹卡班发生了集体越狱。

“集体越狱？”首相用沙哑的声音重复道。

“不用担心，不用担心！”福吉大声说，一只脚已经跨进了火焰，“我们很快就会把他们一网打尽的——只是觉得应该让你知道而已！”

还没等首相喊一声“喂，等一等！”福吉已经消失在一片绿色的火苗里了。

不管媒体和反对派们怎么说，首相并不是一个愚蠢的人。他注意到，虽说他们第一次见面时福吉向他拍胸脯保证过，但实际上他们现在经常见面，而且每次见面福吉都显得更加心神不宁。首相不太愿意想到那位魔法部部长（他心里总是管福吉叫*另类部长*），但他还是忍不住担心福吉下一次出现时，肯定会带来更糟糕的消息。因此，当看见福吉又一次从火里跨出来时，他觉得这是这个倒霉的星期里发生的最糟糕的一件事了。福吉衣冠不整，神情烦躁，而且似乎对首相竟然不明白他为什么来访感到很生气，很吃惊。

'How should I know what's going on in the – er – wizarding community?' snapped the Prime Minister now. 'I have a country to run and quite enough concerns at the moment without –'

'We have the same concerns,' Fudge interrupted. 'The Brockdale bridge didn't wear out. That wasn't really a hurricane. Those murders were not the work of Muggles. And Herbert Chorley's family would be safer without him. We are currently making arrangements to have him transferred to St Mungo's Hospital for Magical Maladies and Injuries. The move should be effected tonight.'

'What do you … I'm afraid I … *what*?' blustered the Prime Minister.

Fudge took a great, deep breath and said, 'Prime Minister, I am very sorry to have to tell you that he's back. He Who Must Not Be Named is back.'

'Back? When you say "back" … he's alive? I mean –'

The Prime Minister groped in his memory for the details of that horrible conversation of three years previously, when Fudge had told him about the wizard who was feared above all others, the wizard who had committed a thousand terrible crimes before his mysterious disappearance fifteen years earlier.

'Yes, alive,' said Fudge. 'That is – I don't know – is a man alive if he can't be killed? I don't really understand it, and Dumbledore won't explain properly – but anyway, he's certainly got a body and is walking and talking and killing, so I suppose, for the purposes of our discussion, yes, he's alive.'

The Prime Minister did not know what to say to this, but a persistent habit of wishing to appear well-informed on any subject that came up made him cast around for any details he could remember of their previous conversations.

'Is Serious Black with – er – He Who Must Not Be Named?'

'Black? Black?' said Fudge distractedly, turning his bowler rapidly in his fingers. 'Sirius Black, you mean? Merlin's beard, no. Black's dead. Turns out we were – er – mistaken about Black. He was innocent after all. And he wasn't in league with He Who Must Not Be Named either. I mean,' he added defensively, spinning the bowler hat still faster, 'all the evidence pointed – we had more than fifty eye-witnesses – but anyway, as I say, he's dead. Murdered, as a matter of fact. On Ministry of Magic premises. There's going to be an

“我怎么会知道——嗯——巫师界发生的事情呢？”首相这时候生硬地说，“我要管理一个国家，目前需要操心的事情已经够多的了——”

“我们操心的事情是一样的。”福吉打断他的话说，“布罗克代尔桥并不是年久失修；那股风实际上并不是飓风；那几起谋杀案也不是麻瓜所为。还有，如果赫伯特·乔莱走了，他的家人反而会更安全。我们目前正安排把他转到圣芒戈魔法伤病医院。今天晚上就可以办妥。”

“你说什么……对不起我……什么？”首相激动地咆哮起来。

福吉深深地吸了一口气，说道：“首相，我不得不非常遗憾地告诉你，他回来了。那个连名字都不能提的人回来了。”

“回来了？你说他‘回来了’……他还活着？我的意思是——”

首相在记忆中搜索着三年前那段可怕对话的具体内容，当时福吉跟他谈到了那位最令人谈之色变的巫师，那位十五年前犯下无数滔天大罪之后神秘失踪的巫师。

“是啊，还活着，”福吉说，“算是活着吧——我也说不清——一个不能被杀死的人还算活着吗？我搞不明白是怎么回事，邓布利多又不肯好好解释——可是不管怎么说，他肯定有了一具躯体，可以走路、说话，可以杀人了，所以我想，就我们所谈的话题来说，他确实是活着的。”

首相听了这话，竟一时不知道该说什么好，但他有一个根深蒂固的习惯，不管谈论什么话题，他都要显示自己无所不知，因此他在记忆中苦苦搜寻他们前几次谈话的内容。

“小灰狼布莱克跟——嗯——跟那个连名字都不能提的人在一起吗？”

“布莱克？布莱克？”福吉心烦意乱地说，一边用手指飞快地转动着他的圆顶高帽，“你是说小天狼星布莱克吧？梅林的胡子啊，没有。布莱克死了。后来才发现，我们——嗯——我们在布莱克的事情上搞错了。他竟然是无辜的，也没有跟那个连名字都不能提的人勾结在一起。我是说，”他接着又分辩道，圆顶高帽在手里转得更快了，“所有的证据都显示——有五十多位目击证人——可是，唉，正像我刚才说的，他死了。实际上是被杀害的。就在魔法部办公的地方。这件事肯定还

inquiry, actually …'

To his great surprise, the Prime Minister felt a fleeting stab of pity for Fudge at this point. It was, however, eclipsed almost immediately by a glow of smugness at the thought that, deficient though he himself might be in the area of materialising out of fireplaces, there had never been a murder in any of the government departments under *his* charge … not yet, anyway …

While the Prime Minister surreptitiously touched the wood of his desk, Fudge continued, 'But Black's by-the-by now. The point is, we're at war, Prime Minister, and steps must be taken.'

'At war?' repeated the Prime Minister nervously. 'Surely that's a little bit of an overstatement?'

'He Who Must Not Be Named has now been joined by those of his followers who broke out of Azkaban in January,' said Fudge, speaking more and more rapidly, and twirling his bowler so fast that it was a lime-green blur. 'Since they have moved into the open, they have been wreaking havoc. The Brockdale bridge – he did it, Prime Minister, he threatened a mass Muggle killing unless I stood aside for him and –'

'Good grief, so it's *your* fault those people were killed and I'm having to answer questions about rusted rigging and corroded expansion joints and I don't know what else!' said the Prime Minister furiously.

'*My* fault!' said Fudge, colouring up. 'Are you saying you would have caved in to blackmail like that?'

'Maybe not,' said the Prime Minister, standing up and striding about the room, 'but I would have put all my efforts into catching the blackmailer before he committed any such atrocity!'

'Do you really think I wasn't already making every effort?' demanded Fudge heatedly. 'Every Auror in the Ministry was – and is – trying to find him and round up his followers, but we happen to be talking about one of the most powerful wizards of all time, a wizard who has eluded capture for almost three decades!'

'So I suppose you're going to tell me he caused the hurricane in the West Country, too?' said the Prime Minister, his temper rising with every pace he took. It was infuriating to discover the reason for all these terrible disasters and not to be able to tell the public; almost worse than it being the government's fault after all.

要调查的……”

听到这里，首相突然对福吉产生了恻隐之心，这使他自己也大为吃惊。不过，他的同情转瞬即逝，立刻就被一种扬扬自得的心情所取代。他想到，他虽说不具备从壁炉里显形的本领，但是在他所管辖的政府部门里，还从来没出过命案呢……至少现在还没有……

首相偷偷地敲了一下木头桌子，福吉继续说道："不过布莱克的事情已经过去了。现在的问题是，我们正处于战争之中，首相，必须采取一些措施。"

"战争之中？"首相不安地重复了一遍，"这肯定有些夸大其词吧。"

"那个连名字都不能提的人的一些追随者，一月份从阿兹卡班越狱逃出来之后，又投奔到他那儿去了。"福吉的语速越来越快，圆顶高帽转得像飞一样，变成了一片模糊的黄绿色。"自从他们公开亮相以来，已经造成了很大的破坏。布罗克代尔桥——就是他给弄塌的，首相，他威胁说，除非我不插手，不然他就要大批屠杀麻瓜——"

"天哪，那些人被害原来都是你的责任，而我却被逼着回答那些关于设备生锈、伸缩接头腐烂等等莫名其妙的问题！"首相气愤地说。

"我的责任！"福吉涨红了脸，说道，"难道你是说，你会屈服于那样的威胁吗？"

"也许不会，"首相说着站了起来，迈着大步在房间里走来走去，"但是我会想尽办法抓住那个威胁我的人，不让他犯下这样残暴的罪行！"

"你以为我就没有做出种种努力吗？"福吉激动地问，"魔法部的每一位傲罗都在想方设法地寻找他，围捕他的追随者，直到今天！可是我们眼下谈论的，碰巧是有史以来最厉害的一位巫师，他将近三十年来一直逍遥法外！"

"我想，你接着还会告诉我，西南部的那场飓风也是他造成的吧？"首相问。他每走一步，心里的怒火就增长一分。他发现了所有那些可怕灾难的原因，却又不能告诉公众，这简直太令人生气了，如果真是政府的过失反倒还好一些。

'That was no hurricane,' said Fudge miserably.

'Excuse me!' barked the Prime Minister, now positively stamping up and down. 'Trees uprooted, roofs ripped off, lampposts bent, horrible injuries –'

'It was the Death Eaters,' said Fudge. 'He Who Must Not Be Named's followers. And … and we suspect giant involvement.'

The Prime Minister stopped in his tracks as though he had hit an invisible wall.

'*What* involvement?'

Fudge grimaced. 'He used giants last time, when he wanted to go for the grand effect. The Office of Misinformation has been working round the clock, we've had teams of Obliviators out trying to modify the memories of all the Muggles who saw what really happened, we've got most of the Department for the Regulation and Control of Magical Creatures running around Somerset, but we can't find the giant – it's been a disaster.'

'You don't say!' said the Prime Minister furiously.

'I won't deny that morale is pretty low at the Ministry,' said Fudge. 'What with all that, and then losing Amelia Bones.'

'Losing who?'

'Amelia Bones. Head of the Department of Magical Law Enforcement. We think He Who Must Not Be Named may have murdered her in person, because she was a very gifted witch and – and all the evidence was that she put up a real fight.'

Fudge cleared his throat and, with an effort, it seemed, stopped spinning his bowler hat.

'But that murder was in the newspapers,' said the Prime Minister, momentarily diverted from his anger. '*Our* newspapers. Amelia Bones … it just said she was a middle-aged woman who lived alone. It was a – a nasty killing, wasn't it? It's had rather a lot of publicity. The police are baffled, you see.'

Fudge sighed. 'Well, of course they are. Killed in a room that was locked from the inside, wasn't she? We, on the other hand, know exactly who did it, not that that gets us any further towards catching him. And then there was Emmeline Vance, maybe you didn't hear about that one –'

'Oh yes I did!' said the Prime Minister. 'It happened just round the corner

“根本就没有什么飓风。”福吉苦恼地说。

“你说什么？”首相吼道，他已经忍不住在跺脚了，“大树连根拔起，屋顶被掀翻，路标变成了弯的，大批人员伤亡——”

“这都是食死徒干的，”福吉说，“就是那个连名字都不能提的人的追随者。另外……我们还怀疑巨人也参与了。”

首相猛地停住脚步，仿佛撞上了一堵看不见的墙。

“什么也参与了？”

福吉做了个苦脸。“上次他就利用了巨人，想把声势造得很大。现在，错误信息办公室的人们正在加班加点地工作，我们还派出了好几批记忆注销员，修改所有那些亲眼看见了事情经过的麻瓜们的记忆，神奇动物管理控制司的大多数工作人员都被派到萨默塞特去了，他们在那里四处搜寻，但没能找到巨人——真是一场灾难。”

“这不可能！”首相气呼呼地说。

“我不否认，部里现在人心惶惶，士气消沉。”福吉说，“这还不算，后来我们又失去了阿米莉亚·博恩斯。”

“失去了谁？”

“阿米莉亚·博恩斯。魔法法律执行司的司长。我们认为是那个连名字都不能提的人亲手杀害了她，因为她是一个很有天分的女巫——而且所有的迹象都表明她曾经奋力反抗过。”

福吉清了清嗓子，然后，像是费了很大的劲，才停止了旋转他的圆顶高帽。

“可是报纸上报道了那起命案，”首相暂时忘记了他的愤怒，说道，“我们的报纸。阿米莉亚·博恩斯……报上说她是一位独居的中年妇女，这是一起——一起恶性谋杀案，是吗？这件事已经传得沸沸扬扬。警察完全不知道从何入手。”

福吉叹了口气。“唉，那是自然的。她是在一个从里面反锁的房间里被杀害的，是不是？我们倒完全清楚是谁干的，但这也不能帮助我们抓住那家伙。还有爱米琳·万斯，这件事你也许没有听说——”

“我当然听说了！”首相说，“实际上，它就发生在离这儿不远的

from here, as a matter of fact. The papers had a field day with it: *Breakdown of law and order in the Prime Minister's back yard* –'

'And as if all that wasn't enough,' said Fudge, barely listening to the Prime Minister, 'we've got Dementors swarming all over the place, attacking people left right and centre ...'

Once upon a happier time this sentence would have been unintelligible to the Prime Minister, but he was wiser now.

'I thought Dementors guard the prisoners in Azkaban?' he said cautiously.

'They did,' said Fudge wearily. 'But not any more. They've deserted the prison and joined He Who Must Not Be Named. I won't pretend that wasn't a blow.'

'But,' said the Prime Minister, with a sense of dawning horror, 'didn't you tell me they're the creatures that drain hope and happiness out of people?'

'That's right. And they're breeding. That's what's causing all this mist.'

The Prime Minister sank, weak-kneed, into the nearest chair. The idea of invisible creatures swooping through the towns and countryside, spreading despair and hopelessness in his voters, made him feel quite faint.

'Now see here, Fudge – you've got to do something! It's your responsibility as Minister for Magic!'

'My dear Prime Minister, you can't honestly think I'm still Minister for Magic after all this? I was sacked three days ago! The whole wizarding community has been screaming for my resignation for a fortnight. I've never known them so united in my whole term of office!' said Fudge, with a brave attempt at a smile.

The Prime Minister was momentarily lost for words. Despite his indignation at the position into which he had been placed, he still rather felt for the shrunken-looking man sitting opposite him.

'I'm very sorry,' he said finally. 'If there's anything I can do?'

'It's very kind of you, Prime Minister, but there is nothing. I was sent here tonight to bring you up-to-date on recent events and to introduce you to my successor. I rather thought he'd be here by now, but of course he's very busy at the moment, with so much going on.'

Fudge looked round at the portrait of the ugly little man wearing the long curly silver wig, who was digging in his ear with the point of a quill.

Catching Fudge's eye the portrait said, 'He'll be here in a moment, he's

地方。报纸拿这一点大做文章：在首相的后院以身试法——”

“就好像这些还不够糟糕似的，”福吉几乎没听首相说话，只顾自己说道，“现在摄魂怪到处都是，随时向人发起进攻……”

在以前无忧无虑的日子里，首相会觉得这句话难以理解，但是现在他已经知道了许多事情。

“我记得，摄魂怪是看守阿兹卡班犯人的吧？”他谨慎地问。

“以前是这样，”福吉疲倦地说，“现在不是了。他们离开了监狱，投靠了那个连名字都不能提的人。我必须承认这真是祸从天降。”

“可是，”首相说，他心里渐渐产生了一种恐惧，“你不是告诉过我，它们这种生物是专门吸走人们的希望和快乐的吗？”

“没错。而且它们还在不断繁衍，所以形成了这些迷雾。”

首相双膝一软，跌坐在离他最近的一把椅子上。想到这些无形的生物在城市和乡村飞来飞去，在他的选民中散布悲观绝望的情绪，他就感到自己快要晕倒了。

“听我说，福吉——你必须采取措施！这是你作为魔法部部长的责任！”

“我亲爱的首相啊，发生这么多事情之后，你真的认为我还能当魔法部部长吗？我三天前就下台了！整个巫师界两个星期来一直叫嚷着要我辞职。我在任这么多年，还从没见过他们这么团结一致！”福吉说着勉强地笑了一下。

首相一时说不出话来。他对自己被置于这样一种境地感到愤慨，同时又对坐在对面的这个看上去萎缩了的男人心生同情。

“非常遗憾。”最后他说道，“我能帮你做些什么吗？”

“谢谢你的好意，首相，没有什么了。我今晚被派来向你通报最新事态发展，并把你介绍给我的继任者。我本来以为他现在应该到了。当然啦，目前发生了这么多事，把他忙得够呛。”

福吉扭头看了看肖像里那个戴着拳曲的银色长假发、长相丑陋的小个子男人，他正在用羽毛笔的笔尖掏耳朵。

肖像里的男人发现福吉在看他，便说道：“他马上就来。他正在给

just finishing a letter to Dumbledore.'

'I wish him luck,' said Fudge, sounding bitter for the first time. 'I've been writing to Dumbledore twice a day for the past fortnight, but he won't budge. If he'd just been prepared to persuade the boy, I might still be … well, maybe Scrimgeour will have more success.'

Fudge subsided into what was clearly an aggrieved silence, but it was broken almost immediately by the portrait, which suddenly spoke in its crisp, official voice.

'To the Prime Minister of Muggles. Requesting a meeting. Urgent. Kindly respond immediately. Rufus Scrimgeour, Minister for Magic.'

'Yes, yes, fine,' said the Prime Minister distractedly, and he barely flinched as the flames in the grate turned emerald-green again, rose up and revealed a second spinning wizard in their heart, disgorging him moments later on to the antique rug. Fudge got to his feet, and after a moment's hesitation the Prime Minister did the same, watching the new arrival straighten up, dust down his long black robes and look around.

The Prime Minister's first, foolish thought was that Rufus Scrimgeour looked rather like an old lion. There were streaks of grey in his mane of tawny hair and his bushy eyebrows; he had keen yellowish eyes behind a pair of wire-rimmed spectacles and a certain rangy, loping grace even though he walked with a slight limp. There was an immediate impression of shrewdness and toughness; the Prime Minister thought he understood why the wizarding community preferred Scrimgeour to Fudge as a leader in these dangerous times.

'How do you do?' said the Prime Minister politely, holding out his hand.

Scrimgeour grasped it briefly, his eyes scanning the room, then pulled out a wand from under his robes.

'Fudge told you everything?' he asked, striding over to the door and tapping the keyhole with his wand. The Prime Minister heard the lock click.

'Er – yes,' said the Prime Minister. 'And if you don't mind, I'd rather that door remained unlocked.'

'I'd rather not be interrupted,' said Scrimgeour shortly, 'or watched,' he added, pointing his wand at the windows so that the curtains swept across them. 'Right, well, I'm a busy man, so let's get down to business. First of all, we need to discuss your security.'

邓布利多写信，很快就写完了。”

“我祝他好运。”福吉说，语气第一次显得有些尖刻，“在过去的两个星期里，我每天给邓布利多写两封信，但他就是不肯改变主意。如果他愿意说服那个男孩，我恐怕还能……唉，说不定斯克林杰会比我顺利。”

福吉显然很委屈地陷入了沉默，可是，肖像里的那个男人立刻打破他的沉默，突然用打着官腔的清脆声音说话了。

“致麻瓜首相。请求会面。事情紧急。请立即答复。魔法部部长鲁弗斯·斯克林杰。”

“行，行，可以。”首相心绪烦乱地说，炉栅里的火苗又一次变成了翠绿色，火焰中间出现了第二位滴溜溜旋转的巫师。他转了一会儿，走到了古色古香的地毯上。首相看着这情景，没有表露出害怕的样子。福吉站起身，首相迟疑了一下，也站了起来，注视着那个新来的人。他正直起身子，掸掉黑色长袍上的炉灰，向左右张望着。

首相一下子冒出一个荒唐的念头，觉得鲁弗斯·斯克林杰活像一头老狮子。他茶褐色的头发和浓密的眉毛里夹杂着缕缕灰色，金丝边眼镜后面是一双锐利的黄眼睛，尽管腿有点瘸，但走起路来却有一种大步流星的潇洒，使人立刻感觉到他是一个敏锐、强硬的家伙。首相认为自己很能理解在这危急时期，巫师界为什么希望斯克林杰而不是福吉当他们的首领。

“你好。”首相彬彬有礼地说，向他伸出了手。

斯克林杰草草地握了一下首相的手，眼睛在屋里扫来扫去，然后从长袍里抽出一根魔杖。

“福吉把事情都告诉你了？”他一边问一边大步走到门口，用魔杖敲了敲锁眼。首相听见门锁咔嗒一响。

“嗯——是这样。”首相说，“如果你不介意的话，我希望不要锁门。”

“我不愿意被人打搅。”斯克林杰不耐烦地说，“或被人监视。”他又加了一句，同时用魔杖指了指窗户，窗帘便都拉上了。“好了，我是个大忙人，我们就开门见山吧。首先，我们需要讨论一下你的安全问题。”

The Prime Minister drew himself up to his fullest height and replied, 'I am perfectly happy with the security I've already got, thank you very –'

'Well, we're not,' Scrimgeour cut in. 'It'll be a poor lookout for the Muggles if their Prime Minister gets put under the Imperius Curse. The new secretary in your outer office –'

'I'm not getting rid of Kingsley Shacklebolt, if that's what you're suggesting!' said the Prime Minister hotly. 'He's highly efficient, gets through twice the work the rest of them –'

'That's because he's a wizard,' said Scrimgeour, without a flicker of a smile. 'A highly trained Auror, who has been assigned to you for your protection.'

'Now, wait a moment!' declared the Prime Minister. 'You can't just put your people into my office, I decide who works for me –'

'I thought you were happy with Shacklebolt?' said Scrimgeour coldly.

'I am – that's to say, I was –'

'Then there's no problem, is there?' said Scrimgeour.

'I … well, as long as Shacklebolt's work continues to be … er … excellent,' said the Prime Minister lamely, but Scrimgeour barely seemed to hear him.

'Now, about Herbert Chorley – your Junior Minister,' he continued. 'The one who has been entertaining the public by impersonating a duck.'

'What about him?' asked the Prime Minister.

'He has clearly reacted to a poorly performed Imperius Curse,' said Scrimgeour. 'It's addled his brains, but he could still be dangerous.'

'He's only quacking!' said the Prime Minister weakly. 'Surely a bit of a rest … maybe go easy on the drink …'

'A team of Healers from St Mungo's Hospital for Magical Maladies and Injuries is examining him as we speak. So far he has attempted to strangle three of them,' said Scrimgeour. 'I think it best that we remove him from Muggle society for a while.'

'I … well … he'll be all right, won't he?' said the Prime Minister anxiously. Scrimgeour merely shrugged, already moving back towards the fireplace.

'Well, that's really all I had to say. I will keep you posted of developments, Prime Minister – or, at least, I shall probably be too busy to come personally, in which case I shall send Fudge here. He has consented to stay on in an

首相尽量把腰板挺得直直的，回答道："我对现有的安全措施很满意，非常感谢——"

"可是，我们不满意。"斯克林杰打断了他的话，"如果首相大人中了夺魂咒，麻瓜们可就要遭殃了。你办公室外间那位新来的秘书——"

"我绝不会把金斯莱·沙克尔赶走的，如果这就是你的建议的话！"首相激动地说，"他效率极高，做的工作是其他人的两倍——"

"那是因为他是个巫师，"斯克林杰说，脸上不带丝毫笑容，"一位训练有素的傲罗，专门派来保护你的。"

"喂，慢着！"首相大喊起来，"你不能随便把你们的人安插到我的办公室来，谁为我工作由我来决定——"

"我想你对沙克尔很满意吧？"斯克林杰冷冷地说。

"是的——我是说，以前是——"

"那就没有什么问题了，是吗？"斯克林杰问。

"我……是啊，只要沙克尔的工作一直那么……嗯……那么出色。"首相软弱无力地说，可是斯克林杰似乎根本没有听见。

"还有，关于赫伯特·乔莱——你的助理部长，"他继续说道，"就是那个模仿鸭子、逗得公众乐不可支的人。"

"他怎么啦？"首相问。

"这显然是他中了一个蹩脚的夺魂咒之后的反应。"斯克林杰说，"他的脑子被弄糊涂了，但并不排除他会有危险。"

"他只是学了几声鸭子叫！"首相无力地辩解道，"多休息休息……少喝点酒……肯定就会……"

"就在我们说话的工夫，圣芒戈魔法伤病医院的一支医疗队正在给他做检查。到现在为止，他已经试图掐死他们中间的三个人了。"斯克林杰说，"我认为我们最好暂时把他从麻瓜社会转移出去。"

"我……那么……他会好起来吗？"首相担忧地问。斯克林杰只是耸了耸肩膀，已经回身朝壁炉走去。

"好了，我要说的就这么多。我会把事态的发展及时告诉你的，首相——或者，我也许很忙，抽不出时间亲自过来，那样我就派福吉上

advisory capacity.'

Fudge attempted to smile, but was unsuccessful; he merely looked as though he had toothache. Scrimgeour was already rummaging in his pocket for the mysterious powder that turned the fire green. The Prime Minister gazed hopelessly at the pair of them for a moment, then the words he had fought to suppress all evening burst from him at last.

'But for heaven's sake – you're *wizards*! You can do *magic*! Surely you can sort out – well – *anything*!'

Scrimgeour turned slowly on the spot and exchanged an incredulous look with Fudge, who really did manage a smile this time as he said kindly, 'The trouble is, the other side can do magic too, Prime Minister.'

And with that, the two wizards stepped one after the other into the bright green fire and vanished.

这儿来。他已经同意以顾问的身份留下来了。"

福吉想挤出一个笑容，但没有成功，那样子倒像是患了牙痛。斯克林杰已经在口袋里翻找那种使火苗变绿的神秘粉末了。首相不抱希望地凝视了他们俩片刻，然后，他整个晚上一直忍住没说的一句话终于脱口而出。

"可是，看在老天的分儿上——你们是*巫师*！你们会施*魔法*！你们肯定能够解决——是啊——*解决任何问题的*！"

斯克林杰在原地慢慢转过身，与福吉交换了一个疑惑的目光。福吉这次总算露出了笑容，和颜悦色地说："问题是，对方也会施魔法呀，首相大人。"

说完，两位巫师先后跨入鲜绿色的火苗，消失不见了。

CHAPTER TWO

Spinner's End

Many miles away the chilly mist that had pressed against the Prime Minister's windows drifted over a dirty river that wound between overgrown, rubbish-strewn banks. An immense chimney, relic of a disused mill, reared up, shadowy and ominous. There was no sound apart from the whisper of the black water and no sign of life apart from a scrawny fox that had slunk down the bank to nose hopefully at some old fish-and-chip wrappings in the tall grass.

But then, with a very faint *pop*, a slim hooded figure appeared out of thin air on the edge of the river. The fox froze, wary eyes fixed upon this strange new phenomenon. The figure seemed to take its bearings for a few moments, then set off with light, quick strides, its long cloak rustling over the grass.

With a second and louder *pop*, another hooded figure materialised.

'Wait!'

The harsh cry startled the fox, now crouching almost flat in the undergrowth. It leapt from its hiding place and up the bank. There was a flash of green light, a yelp, and the fox fell back to the ground, dead.

The second figure turned over the animal with its toe.

'Just a fox,' said a woman's voice dismissively from under the hood. 'I thought perhaps an Auror – Cissy, wait!'

But her quarry, who had paused and looked back at the flash of light, was already scrambling up the bank the fox had just fallen down.

'Cissy – Narcissa – listen to me –'

The second woman caught the first and seized her arm, but the other wrenched it away.

第2章

蜘蛛尾巷

许多英里之外，曾经在首相的窗户外游荡的寒冷雾气，此刻正在一条肮脏的河流上飘浮。这条河蜿蜒曲折，两岸杂草蔓生，垃圾成堆。一根巨大的烟囱，是一个废弃的工厂留下的遗物，高高地耸立着，阴森森的，透着不祥。四下里没有声音，只有黑黢黢的河水在呜咽，也没有任何生命的迹象，只有一只精瘦的狐狸偷偷溜下河岸，满怀希望地嗅着深深的杂草丛中几张炸鱼和炸薯条的旧包装纸。

这时，随着噗的一声轻响，河边凭空出现了一个戴着兜帽的细长身影。狐狸定住了，一双警觉的眼睛盯着这个新出现的奇怪身影。那身影似乎在弄清自己的方位，过了片刻，便迈着轻快的大步往前走去，长长的斗篷拂过草地沙沙作响。

又是噗的一声，比刚才那声更响，又一个戴兜帽的身影显形了。

“等等！”

狐狸此刻几乎是趴在低矮的灌木丛里，听到这声沙哑的喊叫，更是吓坏了。它嗖地从藏身的地方蹿出来，往岸上跑去。一道绿光，一声尖叫，狐狸跌倒在地上，死了。

第二个身影用脚尖踢了踢狐狸，把它翻了过来。

“原来只是一只狐狸，”兜帽下传出一个女人不屑的声音，“我还以为是傲罗呢——西茜，等一等！”

可是，被她追赶的那个人刚才只是停下来看了看那道闪光，此时正往狐狸刚才摔下来的河岸上爬去。

“西茜——纳西莎——你听我说——”

第二个女人赶上第一个女人，抓住她的胳膊，但被她挣脱了。

'Go back, Bella!'

'You must listen to me!'

'I've listened already. I've made my decision. Leave me alone!'

The woman called Narcissa gained the top of the bank, where a line of old railings separated the river from a narrow cobbled street. The other woman, Bella, followed at once. Side by side they stood looking across the road at the rows and rows of dilapidated brick houses, their windows dull and blind in the darkness.

'He lives here?' asked Bella in a voice of contempt. '*Here*? In this Muggle dunghill? We must be the first of our kind ever to set foot –'

But Narcissa was not listening; she had slipped through a gap in the rusty railings and was already hurrying across the road.

'Cissy, *wait*!'

Bella followed, her cloak streaming behind, and saw Narcissa darting through an alley between the houses into a second, almost identical street. Some of the street lamps were broken; the two women were running between patches of light and deep darkness. The pursuer caught up with her prey just as she turned another corner, this time succeeding in catching hold of her arm and swinging her round so that they faced each other.

'Cissy, you must not do this, you can't trust him –'

'The Dark Lord trusts him, doesn't he?'

'The Dark Lord is … I believe … mistaken,' Bella panted, and her eyes gleamed momentarily under her hood as she looked around to check that they were indeed alone. 'In any case, we were told not to speak of the plan to anyone. This is a betrayal of the Dark Lord's –'

'Let go, Bella!' snarled Narcissa and she drew a wand from beneath her cloak, holding it threateningly in the other's face. Bella merely laughed.

'Cissy, your own sister? You wouldn't –'

'There is nothing I wouldn't do any more!' Narcissa breathed, a note of hysteria in her voice, and as she brought down the wand like a knife, there was another flash of light. Bella let go of her sister's arm as though burned.

'*Narcissa!*'

“回去，贝拉！”

“你必须听我说！”

“我已经听过了。我的决心已定，你别来管我！”

那个叫纳西莎的女人爬到了河岸上，一道旧栏杆把河流和一条窄窄的卵石巷隔开了。另一个女人，贝拉，立刻跟了上来。她们并排站在那里，望着小巷那边一排排破旧的砖房，房子上的窗户在夜色中显得黑洞洞的，毫无生气。

“他就住在这儿？”贝拉用轻蔑的口气问，“这儿？这麻瓜的垃圾堆里？我们的人以前肯定没有光顾过——”

可是纳西莎并没有听。她已经从锈迹斑斑的栏杆的一处豁口钻了过去，正匆匆地穿过小巷。

“西茜，等一等！”

贝拉跟了过去，她的斗篷在身后飘摆。她看见纳西莎飞快地穿过房屋之间的一条小巷，拐进另一条几乎一模一样的街道。有几盏路灯已经坏了，两个奔跑的女人时而被灯光照亮，时而被黑暗笼罩。就在前面的女人拐过另一个街角时，后面的那个追上了她，这次总算一把抓住了她的胳膊，把她拽得转过身来，两个人面对面站住了。

“西茜，你千万不能这么做，你不能相信他——”

“连黑魔王都相信他，不是吗？”

“黑魔王准是……我相信……准是弄错了。”贝拉气喘吁吁地说。她左右看看是不是有人，两只眼睛在兜帽下一闪一闪的。“不管怎么说，我们不能把计划透露给任何人。那意味着出卖了黑魔王的——”

“放开我，贝拉！”纳西莎吼道，从斗篷里面抽出一根魔杖，威胁地举在对方面前。贝拉只是笑了笑。

“西茜，对你亲姐姐这样？你不会——”

“现在没有什么事情是我做不出来的！”纳西莎压低声音说，语气里透着一丝歇斯底里，她把魔杖像刀似的往下一砍，又是一道闪光，贝拉像是被火烧着了一样，顿时松开了妹妹的胳膊。

“纳西莎！”

But Narcissa had rushed ahead. Rubbing her hand, her pursuer followed again, keeping her distance now, as they moved deeper into the deserted labyrinth of brick houses. At last Narcissa hurried up a street called Spinner's End, over which the towering mill chimney seemed to hover like a giant admonitory finger. Her footsteps echoed on the cobbles as she passed boarded and broken windows, until she reached the very last house, where a dim light glimmered through the curtains in a downstairs room.

She had knocked on the door before Bella, cursing under her breath, had caught up. Together they stood waiting, panting slightly, breathing in the smell of the dirty river that was carried to them on the night breeze. After a few seconds, they heard movement behind the door and it opened a crack. A sliver of a man could be seen looking out at them, a man with long black hair parted in curtains around a sallow face and black eyes.

Narcissa threw back her hood. She was so pale that she seemed to shine in the darkness; the long blonde hair streaming down her back gave her the look of a drowned person.

'Narcissa!' said the man, opening the door a little wider, so that the light fell upon her and her sister too. 'What a pleasant surprise!'

'Severus,' she said in a strained whisper. 'May I speak to you? It's urgent.'

'But of course.'

He stood back to allow her to pass him into the house. Her still-hooded sister followed without invitation.

'Snape,' she said curtly as she passed him.

'Bellatrix,' he replied, his thin mouth curling into a slightly mocking smile as he closed the door with a snap behind them.

They had stepped directly into a tiny sitting room, which had the feeling of a dark padded cell. The walls were completely covered in books, most of them bound in old black or brown leather; a threadbare sofa, an old armchair and a rickety table stood grouped together in a pool of dim light cast by a candle-filled lamp hung from the ceiling. The place had an air of neglect, as though it were not usually inhabited.

Snape gestured Narcissa to the sofa. She threw off her cloak, cast it aside and sat down, staring at her white and trembling hands clasped in her lap. Bellatrix lowered her hood more slowly. Dark as her sister was fair, with

可是纳西莎已经往前冲去。贝拉揉了揉手，再次跟了上去，不过现在她跟纳西莎保持着一段距离，两人就这样走进了那些迷宫般的废砖房的更深处。最后，纳西莎快步走上一条名叫蜘蛛尾巷的街道，那根高高的工厂烟囱耸立在天空，就像一根举起来表示警告的巨大手指。她走过一扇扇用木板钉着的破旧的窗户，踏在鹅卵石上的脚步发出阵阵回音。她来到最后一幢房子前，楼下一个房间的窗帘缝里透出昏暗的灯光。

当贝拉骂骂咧咧地赶上来时，纳西莎已经敲响了门。她们一起站在门外等着，微微喘着粗气，嗅着被晚风吹过来的那条污水河的气味。过了几秒钟，她们听见门后面有了动静，接着门被打开了一条缝，一个男人朝她们张望，乌黑的长发像帘子一样披在两边，中间是一张灰黄色的脸和一双乌黑的眼睛。

纳西莎把兜帽掀到脑后。她的脸色十分苍白，在夜色中仿佛泛着白光，一头金色的长发披散在背后，使她看上去像一个溺水而死的人。

"纳西莎！"男人说着把门缝开得大了些，灯光不仅照到了纳西莎，也照到了她的姐姐。"真是令人又惊又喜！"

"西弗勒斯，"纳西莎紧张地小声说，"我可以跟你谈谈吗？事情很紧急。"

"当然。"

他退后一步，把她让进了屋里。她那仍然戴着兜帽的姐姐也跟了进来，尽管没有受到邀请。

"斯内普。"经过他身边时，她简单地招呼了一声。

"贝拉特里克斯。"斯内普回道，薄薄的嘴唇扭曲成一个略带讥讽的微笑，在她们身后咔嗒一声关上了门。

她们直接走进了一间小小的客厅，这里给人的感觉像是一间昏暗的软壁牢房。几面墙都是书，其中大部分是古旧的黑色或褐色的皮封面；一盏点着蜡烛的灯从天花板上挂下来，投下一道昏暗的光圈，光圈里挤挤挨挨地放着一张磨损起毛的沙发、一把旧扶手椅和一张摇摇晃晃的桌子。这地方有一种荒凉冷清的气息，似乎平常没有人居住。

斯内普示意纳西莎坐在沙发上。纳西莎脱掉斗篷扔到一边，坐了下来，眼睛盯着自己交叉在膝盖上的苍白颤抖的双手。贝拉特里克斯

heavily lidded eyes and a strong jaw, she did not take her gaze from Snape as she moved to stand behind Narcissa.

'So, what can I do for you?' Snape asked, settling himself in the armchair opposite the two sisters.

'We … we are alone, aren't we?' Narcissa asked quietly.

'Yes, of course. Well, Wormtail's here, but we're not counting vermin, are we?'

He pointed his wand at the wall of books behind him and, with a bang, a hidden door flew open, revealing a narrow staircase upon which a small man stood frozen.

'As you have clearly realised, Wormtail, we have guests,' said Snape lazily.

The man crept hunchbacked down the last few steps and moved into the room. He had small, watery eyes, a pointed nose and wore an unpleasant simper. His left hand was caressing his right, which looked as though it were encased in a bright silver glove.

'Narcissa!' he said, in a squeaky voice, 'and Bellatrix! How charming –'

'Wormtail will get us drinks, if you'd like them,' said Snape. 'And then he will return to his bedroom.'

Wormtail winced as though Snape had thrown something at him.

'I am not your servant!' he squeaked, avoiding Snape's eye.

'Really? I was under the impression that the Dark Lord placed you here to assist me.'

'To assist, yes – but not to make you drinks and – and clean your house!'

'I had no idea, Wormtail, that you were craving more dangerous assignments,' said Snape silkily. 'This can be easily arranged: I shall speak to the Dark Lord –'

'I can speak to him myself if I want to!'

'Of course you can,' said Snape, sneering. 'But in the meantime, bring us drinks. Some of the elf-made wine will do.'

Wormtail hesitated for a moment, looking as though he might argue, but then turned and headed through a second hidden door. They heard banging, and a clinking of glasses. Within seconds he was back, bearing a dusty bottle and three glasses upon a tray. He dropped these on the rickety table and scurried from their presence, slamming the book-covered door behind him.

慢慢地放下兜帽。她妹妹白得惊人，她的皮肤却很黑，厚厚的眼皮，宽宽的下巴。她走过去站在纳西莎身后，目光一刻也没有离开斯内普。

“那么，我能为你做什么呢？”斯内普在姐妹俩对面的扶手椅上坐了下来，问道。

“这里……这里没有别人吧？”纳西莎轻声问。

“当然没有。噢，对了，虫尾巴在这里，不过我们不把害虫计算在内，是不是？”

他用魔杖一指身后那面书墙，砰的一声，一扇暗门打开了，露出一道窄窄的楼梯，一个小个子男人呆若木鸡地站在上面。

“想必你已经很清楚，虫尾巴，我们来客人了。”斯内普懒洋洋地说。

那男人弓着腰走下最后几级楼梯，来到房间里。他长着一双水汪汪的小眼睛，尖鼻子，脸上堆着不自然的假笑。他用左手抚摸着右手，右手看上去像是戴着一只银亮的白手套。

“纳西莎！”他用吱吱的声音说，“贝拉特里克斯！多么迷人——”

“如果你们愿意的话，虫尾巴会给我们端来饮料，”斯内普说，“然后他就会回到他自己的卧室去。”

虫尾巴闪身一躲，好像斯内普朝他扔出了什么东西。

“我不是你的仆人！”他躲闪着斯内普的目光，用吱吱的声音说。

“是吗？我以为黑魔王把你安排在这里是为了帮助我的。”

“帮助，没错——但不是给你端饮料，也不是——给你打扫房间！”

“虫尾巴，没想到你还渴望得到更危险的任务。”斯内普用油滑的腔调说，“这很容易办到：我去跟黑魔王说——”

“如果我愿意，我自己会跟他说的！”

“你当然可以。”斯内普讥笑着说，“至于眼下嘛，你还是给我们端饮料吧。来一点儿小精灵酿的葡萄酒就行。”

虫尾巴迟疑了片刻，似乎还想争辩一番，但还是转过身，从另一道暗门出去了。她们听见了砰砰的声音，还听见了玻璃杯叮当的碰撞声。几秒钟后他回来了，用托盘端着一个脏兮兮的酒瓶和三个玻璃杯。他把托盘放在那张摇摇晃晃的桌子上，立刻三步并作两步地离开了，重重地关上了那扇被书隐藏的门。

Snape poured out three glasses of blood-red wine and handed two of them to the sisters. Narcissa murmured a word of thanks, whilst Bellatrix said nothing, but continued to glower at Snape. This did not seem to discompose him; on the contrary, he looked rather amused.

'The Dark Lord,' he said, raising his glass and draining it.

The sisters copied him. Snape refilled their glasses.

As Narcissa took her second drink she said in a rush, 'Severus, I'm sorry to come here like this, but I had to see you. I think you are the only one who can help me –'

Snape held up a hand to stop her, then pointed his wand again at the concealed staircase door. There was a loud bang and a squeal, followed by the sound of Wormtail scurrying back up the stairs.

'My apologies,' said Snape. 'He has lately taken to listening at doors, I don't know what he means by it … you were saying, Narcissa?'

She took a great, shuddering breath and started again.

'Severus, I know I ought not to be here, I have been told to say nothing to anyone, but –'

'Then you ought to hold your tongue!' snarled Bellatrix. 'Particularly in present company!'

' "Present company"?' repeated Snape sardonically. 'And what am I to understand by that, Bellatrix?'

'That I don't trust you, Snape, as you very well know!'

Narcissa let out a noise that might have been a dry sob and covered her face with her hands. Snape set his glass down upon the table and sat back again, his hands upon the arms of his chair, smiling into Bellatrix's glowering face.

'Narcissa, I think we ought to hear what Bellatrix is bursting to say; it will save tedious interruptions. Well, continue, Bellatrix,' said Snape. 'Why is it that you do not trust me?'

'A hundred reasons!' she said loudly, striding out from behind the sofa to slam her glass upon the table. 'Where to start! Where were you when the Dark Lord fell? Why did you never make any attempt to find him when he vanished? What have you been doing all these years that you've lived in Dumbledore's pocket? Why did you stop the Dark Lord procuring the

斯内普倒出三杯血红色的葡萄酒，递了两杯给姐妹俩。纳西莎嘟哝了一句“谢谢”，贝拉特里克斯什么也没说，继续狠狠地瞪着斯内普。但这似乎并没有让斯内普感到局促不安，他好像觉得这挺好笑。

“为了黑魔王。”他说着举起杯子，一饮而尽。

姐妹俩也举起杯子一口喝干了。斯内普又把她们的杯子斟满。

纳西莎接过第二杯酒，一口气说开了：“西弗勒斯，真对不起，这个样子来打扰你，可是我必须来见你。我想，只有你一个人能帮助我——”

斯内普举起一只手制止了她，然后再次用魔杖一指那道楼梯暗门。只听砰的一声巨响和一声尖叫，接着便是虫尾巴慌忙逃上楼去的声音。

“抱歉，”斯内普说，“他最近养成了爱偷听的毛病，真不明白他这么做是什么意思……你刚才说到哪儿了，纳西莎？”

纳西莎颤抖着深深吸了口气，又开始说了起来。

“西弗勒斯，我知道我不该来这儿，我被告知，对什么人也不能说，可是——”

“那你就应该管住你的舌头！”贝拉特里克斯吼道，“特别是当着眼前这个人！”

“‘眼前这个人’？”斯内普讥讽地重复道，“这话我该作何理解，贝拉特里克斯？”

“就是我不相信你，斯内普，其实你心里很明白！”

纳西莎发出了一点声音，像是无泪的抽泣，然后用手捂住了脸。斯内普把杯子放在桌上，身体往椅背上一靠，两只手搭在椅子的扶手上，笑眯眯地看着贝拉特里克斯那张怒气冲冲的脸。

“纳西莎，我认为我们最好听听贝拉特里克斯迫不及待地想说些什么，免得她没完没了地打搅我们。好了，你接着说吧，贝拉特里克斯，”斯内普说，“你为什么不相信我？”

“有一百个理由！”贝拉特里克斯一边大声说着一边从沙发后面大步走了过来，把杯子重重地放在桌子上。“从哪儿说起呢？黑魔王失势时，你在哪儿？他消失后，你为什么不做任何努力去寻找他？这些年来，

Philosopher's Stone? Why did you not return at once when the Dark Lord was reborn? Where were you a few weeks ago, when we battled to retrieve the prophecy for the Dark Lord? and why, Snape, is Harry Potter still alive, when you have had him at your mercy for five years?'

She paused, her chest rising and falling rapidly, the colour high in her cheeks. Behind her Narcissa sat motionless, her face still hidden in her hands.

Snape smiled.

'Before I answer you – oh, yes, Bellatrix, I am going to answer! You can carry my words back to the others who whisper behind my back, and carry false tales of my treachery to the Dark Lord! Before I answer you, I say, let me ask a question in turn. Do you really think that the Dark Lord has not asked me each and every one of those questions? And do you really think that, had I not been able to give satisfactory answers, I would be sitting here talking to you?'

She hesitated.

'I know he believes you, but –'

'You think he is mistaken? Or that I have somehow hoodwinked him? Fooled the Dark Lord, the greatest wizard, the most accomplished Legilimens the world has ever seen?'

Bellatrix said nothing, but looked, for the first time, a little discomfited. Snape did not press the point. He picked up his drink again, sipped it, and continued, 'You ask where I was when the Dark Lord fell. I was where he had ordered me to be, at Hogwarts School of Witchcraft and Wizardry, because he wished me to spy upon Albus Dumbledore. You know, I presume, that it was on the Dark Lord's orders that I took up the post?'

She nodded almost imperceptibly and then opened her mouth, but Snape forestalled her.

'You ask why I did not attempt to find him when he vanished. For the same reason that Avery, Yaxley, the Carrows, Greyback, Lucius,' he inclined his head slightly to Narcissa, 'and many others did not attempt to find him. I believed him finished. I am not proud of it, I was wrong, but there it is … if he had not forgiven we who lost faith at that time, he would have very few followers left.'

'He'd have me!' said Bellatrix passionately. 'I, who spent many years in

你在邓布利多手下苟且偷生，究竟做了些什么？你为什么阻止黑魔王得到魔法石？黑魔王复活后，你为什么没有立刻回来？几个星期前，我们奋勇战斗，为黑魔王夺取预言球时，你又在哪儿？还有，斯内普，哈利·波特为什么还活着？他有五年时间随你任意处置！”

她停了下来，胸脯剧烈地起伏着，面颊涨得通红。在她身后，纳西莎一动不动地坐着，脸仍然埋在双手里。

斯内普笑了。

“在我回答你之前——噢，没错，贝拉特里克斯，我是要回答你的！你可以把我的话转告那些在背后议论我的人，可以把关于我叛变的不实之词汇报给黑魔王！但在我回答你之前，先让我问你一个问题。你真的认为黑魔王没有问过我这每一个问题吗？你真的认为，如果我没有给出令人满意的答案，我还能坐在这儿跟你说话吗？”

贝拉特里克斯迟疑着。

“我知道他相信你，但——”

“你认为他弄错了？或者我竟然骗过了他？竟然捉弄了黑魔王——人类有史以来最伟大的巫师，世界上最有成就的摄神取念高手？”

贝拉特里克斯没有说话，但她的神情第一次显得有点困惑。斯内普没有抓住不放。他重新端起杯子，喝了一小口，继续说道：“你刚才问，黑魔王失势时，我在哪儿。我在他命令我去的地方，在霍格沃茨魔法学校，因为他希望我在那儿暗中监视阿不思·邓布利多。我猜你肯定知道，我是听从黑魔王的吩咐才接受那个教职的吧？”

贝拉特里克斯几乎不易察觉地点了点头，张开嘴想说话，但斯内普抢先阻止了她。

“你还问，当他消失后，我为什么没有努力去寻找他。我没有去寻找他的原因，跟埃弗利、亚克斯利、卡罗兄妹、格雷伯克、卢修斯，”他朝纳西莎微微偏了偏脑袋，“以及其他许多人一样。我以为他完蛋了。我并不为此感到自豪，我做错了，但情况就是这样……如果他不能原谅我们在那个时候失去信心，他的追随者就所剩无几了。”

“他还有我！”贝拉特里克斯激动地说，“为了他，我在阿兹卡班

Azkaban for him!'

'Yes, indeed, most admirable,' said Snape in a bored voice. 'Of course, you weren't a lot of use to him in prison, but the gesture was undoubtedly fine –'

'Gesture!' she shrieked; in her fury she looked slightly mad. 'While I endured the Dementors, you remained at Hogwarts, comfortably playing Dumbledore's pet!'

'Not quite,' said Snape calmly. 'He wouldn't give me the Defence Against the Dark Arts job, you know. Seemed to think it might, ah, bring about a relapse … tempt me into my old ways.'

'This was your sacrifice for the Dark Lord, not to teach your favourite subject?' she jeered. 'Why did you stay there all that time, Snape? Still spying on Dumbledore for a master you believed dead?'

'Hardly,' said Snape, 'although the Dark Lord is pleased that I never deserted my post: I had sixteen years of information on Dumbledore to give him when he returned, a rather more useful welcome-back present than endless reminiscences of how unpleasant Azkaban is …'

'But you stayed –'

'Yes, Bellatrix, I stayed,' said Snape, betraying a hint of impatience for the first time. 'I had a comfortable job that I preferred to a stint in Azkaban. They were rounding up the Death Eaters, you know. Dumbledore's protection kept me out of jail, it was most convenient and I used it. I repeat: the Dark Lord does not complain that I stayed, so I do not see why you do.

'I think you next wanted to know,' he pressed on, a little more loudly, for Bellatrix showed every sign of interrupting, 'why I stood between the Dark Lord and the Philosopher's Stone. That is easily answered. He did not know whether he could trust me. He thought, like you, that I had turned from faithful Death Eater to Dumbledore's stooge. He was in a pitiable condition, very weak, sharing the body of a mediocre wizard. He did not dare reveal himself to a former ally if that ally might turn him over to Dumbledore or the Ministry. I deeply regret that he did not trust me. He would have returned to power three years sooner. As it was, I saw only greedy and unworthy Quirrell attempting to steal the Stone and, I admit, I did all I could to thwart him.'

蹲了许多年！”

“是啊，是啊，精神可嘉。”斯内普用干巴巴的声音说，“当然啦，你在监狱里待着，对他并没有多大用处，但这种姿态无疑是很好的——”

“姿态！”贝拉特里克斯尖叫起来，盛怒之下的她，看上去有点疯狂，“我忍受摄魂怪的折磨时，你却躲在霍格沃茨，舒舒服服地扮演邓布利多的宠儿！”

“并不尽然，”斯内普心平气和地说，“他不肯把黑魔法防御术的教职给我，你知道的。他似乎认为那会使我重新堕落……引诱我重走过去的老路。”

“那就是你为黑魔王所做的牺牲？不能教你最喜欢的科目？”她讥笑道，“你为什么一直待在那儿，斯内普？仍然在暗中监视邓布利多，为了一个你相信已经死去的主人？”

“也许不是，”斯内普说，“不过黑魔王很高兴我没有放弃教职：他回来时，我可以向他提供关于邓布利多十六年来的情报，比起没完没了地回忆阿兹卡班的悲惨境况来，这可是一件更有价值的见面礼……”

“可是你留下来了——”

“是的，贝拉特里克斯，我留下来了。”斯内普说，第一次流露出不耐烦，“我有一份舒适的工作，何苦到阿兹卡班去坐牢呢？你知道，他们当时在围捕食死徒。邓布利多的保护使我免受牢狱之苦，这么便利的条件，我不用白不用。我再重复一遍：黑魔王都没有埋怨我留下来，我不明白你凭什么说三道四。

“我想，接下来你想知道的是，”他步步紧逼，并稍微提高了嗓音，因为贝拉特里克斯明显表示出要打断他的话，“我为什么阻止黑魔王得到魔法石。这个问题很容易回答。他不知道可不可以相信我。他和你一样，以为我已经从一个忠实的食死徒变成了邓布利多的走狗。他当时的处境很可怜，非常虚弱，跟一个平庸的巫师共用一具身体。他不敢把自己暴露给一个昔日的支持者，万一那个支持者向邓布利多或魔法部告发他呢？他没有相信我，我感到非常遗憾。不然，他可以早三年东山再起的。当时，我看见的只是贪婪、无能的奇洛想要偷取魔法石，我承认，我尽我的力量阻止了他。”

Bellatrix's mouth twisted as though she had taken an unpleasant dose of medicine.

'But you didn't return when he came back, you didn't fly back to him at once when you felt the Dark Mark burn –'

'Correct. I returned two hours later. I returned on Dumbledore's orders.'

'On Dumbledore's –?' she began, in tones of outrage.

'Think!' said Snape, impatient again. 'Think! By waiting two hours, just two hours, I ensured that I could remain at Hogwarts as a spy! By allowing Dumbledore to think that I was only returning to the Dark Lord's side because I was ordered to, I have been able to pass information on Dumbledore and the Order of the Phoenix ever since! Consider, Bellatrix: the Dark Mark had been growing stronger for months, I knew he must be about to return, all the Death Eaters knew! I had plenty of time to think about what I wanted to do, to plan my next move, to escape like Karkaroff, didn't I?

'The Dark Lord's initial displeasure at my lateness vanished entirely, I assure you, when I explained that I remained faithful, although Dumbledore thought I was his man. Yes, the Dark Lord thought that I had left him for ever, but he was wrong.'

'But what use have you been?' sneered Bellatrix. 'What useful information have we had from you?'

'My information has been conveyed directly to the Dark Lord,' said Snape. 'If he chooses not to share it with you –'

'He shares everything with me!' said Bellatrix, firing up at once. 'He calls me his most loyal, his most faithful –'

'Does he?' said Snape, his voice delicately inflected to suggest his disbelief. 'Does he *still*, after the fiasco at the Ministry?'

'That was not my fault!' said Bellatrix, flushing. 'The Dark Lord has, in the past, entrusted me with his most precious – if Lucius hadn't –'

'Don't you dare – don't you *dare* blame my husband!' said Narcissa, in a low and deadly voice, looking up at her sister.

'There is no point apportioning blame,' said Snape smoothly. 'What is done is done.'

贝拉特里克斯的嘴唇嚅动着，似乎吞下了一剂特别难喝的药。

“可是当他复出时，你没有立刻回来，当你感觉到黑魔标记在烧灼时，也没有火速赶到他身边——”

“不错。我是两个小时之后才回去的。我是听从邓布利多的吩咐回去的。”

“听从邓布利多的——”贝拉特里克斯怒不可遏地说。

“想想吧！”斯内普又一次显出了不耐烦，“想想吧！就等了那么两个小时，短短的两个小时，我保证了我可以继续留在霍格沃茨做密探！我让邓布利多以为，我回到黑魔王身边是听从他的吩咐才这么做的，这样我就能源源不断地汇报邓布利多和凤凰社的情报！你仔细想想，贝拉特里克斯：在那几个月里，黑魔标记越来越清晰，我就知道他肯定要复出，所有的食死徒都知道！我有足够的时间考虑我何去何从，计划我下一步该做什么，比如像卡卡洛夫那样逃之夭夭，不是吗？

“我向黑魔王解释说，我一直对他忠心耿耿，尽管邓布利多以为我是他的人。听了我的解释，黑魔王因为我晚去而产生的不满就消失得无影无踪了。是的，黑魔王本以为我永远离开了他，但是他错了。”

“但是你起过什么作用呢？”贝拉特里克斯讥讽地问，“我们从你那儿得到过什么有用的情报呢？”

“我的情报是直接传给黑魔王的，”斯内普说，“既然他没有把它们告诉你——”

“他什么都会告诉我的！”贝拉特里克斯立刻火冒三丈，“他说我是他最忠诚、最可靠的——”

“是吗？”斯内普说，微微变了声调，表示不相信，“在遭遇了魔法部的那场失败之后，他仍然这么说吗？”

“那不是我的错！”贝拉特里克斯红着脸说，“过去，黑魔王把他最宝贵的东西都托我保管——如果不是卢修斯——”

“你怎么敢——你怎么敢说是我丈夫的错！”纳西莎用低沉的、恶狠狠的声音说，抬头望着她姐姐。

“追究是谁的过错已经没有用了，”斯内普不动声色地说，“事情已经发生了。”

'But not by you!' said Bellatrix furiously. 'No, you were once again absent while the rest of us ran dangers, were you not, Snape?'

'My orders were to remain behind,' said Snape. 'Perhaps you disagree with the Dark Lord, perhaps you think that Dumbledore would not have noticed if I had joined forces with the Death Eaters to fight the Order of the Phoenix? And – forgive me – you speak of dangers … you were facing six teenagers, were you not?'

'They were joined, as you very well know, by half of the Order before long!' snarled Bellatrix. 'And, while we are on the subject of the Order, you still claim you cannot reveal the whereabouts of their Headquarters, don't you?'

'I am not the Secret Keeper, I cannot speak the name of the place. You understand how the enchantment works, I think? The Dark Lord is satisfied with the information I have passed him on the Order. It led, as perhaps you have guessed, to the recent capture and murder of Emmeline Vance, and it certainly helped dispose of Sirius Black, though I give you full credit for finishing him off.'

He inclined his head and toasted her. Her expression did not soften.

'You are avoiding my last question, Snape. Harry Potter. You could have killed him at any point in the past five years. You have not done it. Why?'

'Have you discussed this matter with the Dark Lord?' asked Snape.

'He … lately, we … I am asking *you*, Snape!'

'If I had murdered Harry Potter, the Dark Lord could not have used his blood to regenerate, making him invincible –'

'You claim you foresaw his use of the boy!' she jeered.

'I do not claim it; I had no idea of his plans; I have already confessed that I thought the Dark Lord dead. I am merely trying to explain why the Dark Lord is not sorry that Potter survived, at least until a year ago …'

'But why did you keep him alive?'

'Have you not understood me? It was only Dumbledore's protection that was keeping me out of Azkaban! Do you disagree that murdering his favourite student might have turned him against me? But there was more to it than that. I should remind you that when Potter first arrived at Hogwarts there were still many stories circulating about him, rumours that he himself

“但你什么都没参与！”贝拉特里克斯气愤地说，“是啊，我们其他人都在冒着危险，出生入死，你却又一次不在场，是不是，斯内普？”

“我得到的命令是留在后方。”斯内普说，“莫非你不赞同黑魔王的想法，莫非你以为，如果我加入食死徒的阵营，跟凤凰社作战，邓布利多会毫无察觉？还有——请原谅——你说冒着危险……实际上你面对的只是六个十几岁的孩子，不是吗？”

“你明明知道，很快半个凤凰社的人都加入进来了！”贝拉特里克斯怒吼道，“还有，既然说到了凤凰社，你仍然声称你不能透露他们的总部在什么地方，是不是？”

“我不是保密人，不能说出那个地方的名字。我想，你应该明白那个魔法是怎么起作用的吧？黑魔王对我传递给他的凤凰社的情报很满意。你大概也猜到了，我的情报导致了爱米琳·万斯最近的被捕和被杀，无疑还帮助解决了小天狼星布莱克，不过，结果他性命的功劳还是非你莫属。”

斯内普偏偏脑袋，举杯向她致意。她的表情没有丝毫缓和。

“你在回避我的最后一个问题，斯内普。哈利·波特。在过去的五年里，你随时都能把他置于死地。你却没有动手，为什么？”

“你跟黑魔王讨论过这个问题吗？”斯内普问。

“他……最近，我们……我问的是你，斯内普！”

“如果我杀死了哈利·波特，黑魔王就不能用他的血获得新生，使自己变得不可战胜——”

“你敢说你当时就预见到他要利用那个男孩？”贝拉特里克斯讽刺道。

“我没有这么说。我对他的计划一无所知。我刚才已经坦言，我以为黑魔王已经死了。我只是想解释为什么黑魔王看到波特还活着并不感到遗憾，至少直到一年之前……”

“可是你为什么让他活着呢？”

“你没有明白我的意思吗？多亏邓布利多的保护，我才没有被关进阿兹卡班！你以为我杀害了他的得意门生，他不会和我反目成仇吗？不过事情比这复杂得多。我不妨提醒你，当波特刚进入霍格沃茨时，

was a great Dark wizard, which was how he had survived the Dark Lord's attack. Indeed, many of the Dark Lord's old followers thought Potter might be a standard around which we could all rally once more. I was curious, I admit it, and not at all inclined to murder him the moment he set foot in the castle.

'Of course, it became apparent to me very quickly that he had no extraordinary talent at all. He has fought his way out of a number of tight corners by a simple combination of sheer luck and more talented friends. He is mediocre to the last degree, though as obnoxious and self-satisfied as was his father before him. I have done my utmost to have him thrown out of Hogwarts, where I believe he scarcely belongs, but kill him, or allow him to be killed in front of me? I would have been a fool to risk it, with Dumbledore close at hand.'

'And through all this we are supposed to believe Dumbledore has never suspected you?' asked Bellatrix. 'He has no idea of your true allegiance, he trusts you implicitly still?'

'I have played my part well,' said Snape. 'And you overlook Dumbledore's greatest weakness: he has to believe the best of people. I spun him a tale of deepest remorse when I joined his staff, fresh from my Death Eater days, and he embraced me with open arms – though, as I say, never allowing me nearer the Dark Arts than he could help. Dumbledore has been a great wizard – oh yes, he has' (for Bellatrix had made a scathing noise) 'the Dark Lord acknowledges it. I am pleased to say, however, that Dumbledore is growing old. The duel with the Dark Lord last month shook him. He has since sustained a serious injury because his reactions are slower than they once were. But through all these years, he has never stopped trusting Severus Snape, and therein lies my great value to the Dark Lord.'

Bellatrix still looked unhappy, though she appeared unsure how best to attack Snape next. Taking advantage of her silence, Snape turned to her sister.

'Now … you came to ask me for help, Narcissa?'

Narcissa looked up at him, her face eloquent with despair.

'Yes, Severus. I – I think you are the only one who can help me, I have nowhere else to turn. Lucius is in jail and …'

She closed her eyes and two large tears seeped from beneath her eyelids.

'The Dark Lord has forbidden me to speak of it,' Narcissa continued, her

仍然流传着许多关于他的谣言，说他本人就是一名了不起的黑巫师，所以才能从黑魔王的袭击中死里逃生。确实，黑魔王昔日的许多追随者都认为波特可能成为一面旗帜，我们可以在他周围再一次团结起来。我承认，在他踏进城堡时，我很好奇，根本没有想到要去谋害他。

“当然，我很快就发现，他根本就没有什么超常的天赋。他只是靠了运气，靠了比他更有天赋的朋友才勉强摆脱了许多困境。他平庸到了极点，却跟他的父亲一样自鸣得意，惹人讨厌。我用尽各种办法想把他赶出霍格沃茨，我觉得他根本就不配进来，至于杀死他，或让他在我面前丧命，只有傻瓜才会冒这种风险，因为邓布利多就在近旁。”

“就凭你说的这些，我们就应该相信邓布利多从来没有怀疑过你？”贝拉特里克斯问，“他不知道你实际上为谁效忠？他仍然毫无保留地相信你？”

“我的角色扮演得很出色。”斯内普说，“你忽视了邓布利多的一个最大的弱点：他总是把别人往好处想。我刚离开食死徒、加入他的教师队伍时，编造了一番追悔莫及的谎言说给他听，之后他就张开双臂欢迎了我——不过，我说过，他尽可能不让我接近黑魔法。邓布利多曾经是一位伟大的巫师——没错，不可否认，”（因为贝拉特里克斯轻蔑地哼了一声）“黑魔王也承认这一点。可是，说来让我高兴的是，邓布利多已经老了。上个月跟黑魔王的那场较量让他大伤元气。他受了重伤，因为他的反应比以前慢了。但是这么多年来，他从来没有停止过对西弗勒斯·斯内普的信任，这就使我对黑魔王具有很大的价值。”

贝拉特里克斯仍然显得很不高兴，但似乎拿不准接下来该怎么攻击斯内普才最有效果。斯内普趁她沉默不语，转向了她的妹妹。

“好了……纳西莎，你是来请求我的帮助的？”

纳西莎抬头看着他，满脸绝望的神情。

“是的，西弗勒斯。我——我想，也只有你能够帮助我了，我现在是走投无路了。卢修斯在监狱里，而且……”

她闭上眼睛，两颗大大的泪珠从眼皮下渗了出来。

“黑魔王不许我说这件事，”纳西莎继续说，眼睛仍然闭着，“他不

eyes still closed. 'He wishes none to know of the plan. It is … very secret. But –'

'If he has forbidden it, you ought not to speak,' said Snape at once. 'The Dark Lord's word is law.'

Narcissa gasped as though he had doused her with cold water. Bellatrix looked satisfied for the first time since she had entered the house.

'There!' she said triumphantly to her sister. 'Even Snape says so: you were told not to talk, so hold your silence!'

But Snape had got to his feet and strode to the small window, peered through the curtains at the deserted street, then closed them again with a jerk. He turned round to face Narcissa, frowning.

'It so happens that I know of the plan,' he said in a low voice. 'I am one of the few the Dark Lord has told. Nevertheless, had I not been in on the secret, Narcissa, you would have been guilty of great treachery to the Dark Lord.'

'I thought you must know about it!' said Narcissa, breathing more freely. 'He trusts you so, Severus …'

'You know about the plan?' said Bellatrix, her fleeting expression of satisfaction replaced by a look of outrage. '*You* know?'

'Certainly,' said Snape. 'But what help do you require, Narcissa? If you are imagining I can persuade the Dark Lord to change his mind, I am afraid there is no hope, none at all.'

'Severus,' she whispered, tears sliding down her pale cheeks. 'My son … my only son …'

'Draco should be proud,' said Bellatrix indifferently. 'The Dark Lord is granting him a great honour. And I will say this for Draco: he isn't shrinking away from his duty, he seems glad of a chance to prove himself, excited at the prospect –'

Narcissa began to cry in earnest, gazing beseechingly all the while at Snape.

'That's because he is sixteen and has no idea what lies in store! Why, Severus? Why my son? It is too dangerous! This is vengeance for Lucius's mistake, I know it!'

Snape said nothing. He looked away from the sight of her tears as though they were indecent, but he could not pretend not to hear her.

希望任何人知道那个计划。那是……非常机密的。可是——"

"既然他不许你说，你就不应该说。"斯内普立刻说道，"黑魔王的话就是法律。"

纳西莎倒抽了一口冷气，好像被他兜头浇了一瓢冷水。贝拉特里克斯自从踏进这幢房子之后，脸上第一次露出满意的神情。

"怎么样！"她得意地对她妹妹说，"就连斯内普也这么说：既然不许你说，你就保持沉默吧！"

可是斯内普已经站起身，大步走到那扇小窗户前，透过窗帘朝荒凉的街道上望了望,然后猛地重新拉上了窗帘。他转过身面对着纳西莎，眉头皱了起来。

"我碰巧知道那个计划。"他压低声音说，"黑魔王把计划透露给了很少几个人，我是其中之一。不过，如果我不知道这个秘密，纳西莎，你就会犯下严重背叛黑魔王的大罪。"

"我就猜到你肯定是知道的！"纳西莎说，呼吸自如多了，"他这么信任你，西弗勒斯……"

"你知道那个计划？"贝拉特里克斯说，刚才满意的表情迅速换成了满脸怒气，"你会知道？"

"当然。"斯内普说，"可是你需要什么帮助呢，纳西莎？如果你幻想我能说服黑魔王改变主意,那恐怕是没有希望的,一点儿希望也没有。"

"西弗勒斯，"纳西莎说，眼泪顺着她苍白的面颊滚落下来，"我的儿子……我唯一的儿子……"

"德拉科应该感到骄傲，"贝拉特里克斯冷漠地说，"黑魔王给了他极高的荣誉。而且我要替德拉科说一句：他面对责任没有退缩，他似乎很高兴能有机会证明自己的能力，他对即将发生的事情非常兴奋——"

纳西莎伤心地哭了起来，乞求地盯着斯内普。

"那是因为他才十六岁，根本不知道等待他的是什么！为什么，斯内普？为什么是我的儿子？太危险了！这是为了报复卢修斯的失误，我知道！"

斯内普什么也没说。他避开了纳西莎的目光，不去看她的眼泪，似乎觉得那是不雅观的，但他不能假装没有听见她的话。

'That's why he's chosen Draco, isn't it?' she persisted. 'To punish Lucius?'

'If Draco succeeds,' said Snape, still looking away from her, 'he will be honoured above all others.'

'But he won't succeed!' sobbed Narcissa. 'How can he, when the Dark Lord himself –?'

Bellatrix gasped; Narcissa seemed to lose her nerve.

'I only meant … that nobody has yet succeeded … Severus … please … you are, you have always been, Draco's favourite teacher … you are Lucius's old friend … I beg you … you are the Dark Lord's favourite, his most trusted advisor … will you speak to him, persuade him –?'

'The Dark Lord will not be persuaded, and I am not stupid enough to attempt it,' said Snape flatly. 'I cannot pretend that the Dark Lord is not angry with Lucius. Lucius was supposed to be in charge. He got himself captured, along with how many others, and failed to retrieve the prophecy into the bargain. Yes, the Dark Lord is angry, Narcissa, very angry indeed.'

'Then I am right, he has chosen Draco in revenge!' choked Narcissa. 'He does not mean him to succeed, he wants him to be killed trying!'

When Snape said nothing, Narcissa seemed to lose what little self-restraint she still possessed. Standing up, she staggered to Snape and seized the front of his robes. Her face close to his, her tears falling on to his chest, she gasped, 'You could do it. You could do it instead of Draco, Severus. You would succeed, of course you would, and he would reward you beyond all of us –'

Snape caught hold of her wrists and removed her clutching hands. Looking down into her tear-stained face, he said slowly, 'He intends me to do it in the end, I think. But he is determined that Draco should try first. You see, in the unlikely event that Draco succeeds, I shall be able to remain at Hogwarts a little longer, fulfilling my useful role as spy.'

'In other words, it doesn't matter to him if Draco is killed!'

'The Dark Lord is very angry,' repeated Snape quietly. 'He failed to hear the prophecy. You know as well as I do, Narcissa, that he does not forgive easily.'

“所以他才选中了德拉科，是不是？”纳西莎逼问道，“就为了惩罚卢修斯，是不是？”

“如果德拉科成功了，”斯内普说，眼睛仍然望着别处，“他就能获得比其他所有人都更高的荣誉。”

“可是他不会成功的！”纳西莎哭着说，“他怎么可能呢，就连黑魔王自己——”

贝拉特里克斯倒抽了一口冷气，纳西莎似乎顿时失去了勇气。

“我的意思是……既然没有一个人成功过……西弗勒斯……求求你……你一直是，现在也是德拉科最喜欢的老师……你是卢修斯的老朋友……我求求你……你是黑魔王最得意的亲信，最信任的顾问……你能不能跟他谈谈，说服他——”

“黑魔王是不可能被说服的，我不会愚蠢到去做这种尝试。”斯内普干巴巴地说，“我不能假装说黑魔王没有生卢修斯的气。当时卢修斯本应是行动的负责人，结果他自己被抓住了，还搭上了那么多人，而且预言球也没能取回来。是的，黑魔王很生气，纳西莎，确实非常生气。”

“看来我说得没错，他是为了报复才选中德拉科的！”纳西莎哽咽着说，“他根本就不想让他成功，只想让他去送命！”

看到斯内普没有说话，纳西莎似乎失去了最后的一点自制。她站了起来，踉踉跄跄地走向斯内普，抓住他长袍的前襟，把脸靠近了他的脸，眼泪滚落到他的胸前。她喘着气说：“你能办到的。德拉科办不到，你能办到，西弗勒斯。你会成功的，你肯定会成功的，他给你的奖赏会超过我们所有的人——”

斯内普抓住她的手腕，扳开她紧紧攥住他长袍的手。他低头望着她泪痕斑斑的脸，慢慢说道：“我想，他打算最后再派我去办。但他决定先让德拉科试一试。你知道，万一德拉科成功了，我就能够在霍格沃茨多待一阵子，把我作为一个密探的有用角色扮演到最后。”

“换句话说，他根本就不在乎德拉科是否会送命！”

“黑魔王非常生气。”斯内普轻轻地又说了一遍，“他没能听到预言。你和我一样清楚，纳西莎，他是不会轻易原谅人的。”

She crumpled, falling at his feet, sobbing and moaning on the floor.

'My only son … my only son …'

'You should be proud!' said Bellatrix ruthlessly. 'If I had sons, I would be glad to give them up to the service of the Dark Lord!'

Narcissa gave a little scream of despair and clutched at her long blonde hair. Snape stooped, seized her by the arms, lifted her up and steered her back on to the sofa. He then poured her more wine and forced the glass into her hand.

'Narcissa, that's enough. Drink this. Listen to me.'

She quietened a little; slopping wine down herself, she took a shaky sip.

'It might be possible … for me to help Draco.'

She sat up, her face paper-white, her eyes huge.

'Severus – oh, Severus – you would help him? Would you look after him, see he comes to no harm?'

'I can try.'

She flung away her glass; it skidded across the table as she slid off the sofa into a kneeling position at Snape's feet, seized his hand in both of hers and pressed her lips to it.

'If you are there to protect him … Severus, will you swear it? Will you make the Unbreakable Vow?'

'The Unbreakable Vow?' Snape's expression was blank, unreadable: Bellatrix, however, let out a cackle of triumphant laughter.

'Aren't you listening, Narcissa? Oh, he'll *try*, I'm sure … the usual empty words, the usual slithering out of action … oh, on the Dark Lord's orders, of course!'

Snape did not look at Bellatrix. His black eyes were fixed upon Narcissa's tear-filled blue ones as she continued to clutch his hand.

'Certainly, Narcissa, I shall make the Unbreakable Vow,' he said quietly. 'Perhaps your sister will consent to be our Bonder.'

Bellatrix's mouth fell open. Snape lowered himself so that he was kneeling opposite Narcissa. Beneath Bellatrix's astonished gaze, they grasped right hands.

'You will need your wand, Bellatrix,' said Snape coldly.

纳西莎瘫倒在他脚下，在地板上抽泣、呻吟。

“我唯一的儿子……我唯一的儿子啊……”

“你应该感到骄傲！”贝拉特里克斯冷酷地说，“如果我有儿子，我巴不得牺牲他们去为黑魔王效忠呢！”

纳西莎绝望地叫了一声，揪着自己金色的长发。斯内普弯下腰，抓住她的手臂把她扶了起来，让她重新在沙发上坐好。然后他又给她倒了一些红酒，把杯子硬塞进她的手里。

“纳西莎，行了。把这个喝了，听我说。”

她略微平静了一点儿，颤抖着喝了一小口酒，有一些洒到了身上。

“也许我有可能……帮助德拉科。”

她腾地坐直了身子，脸白得像纸一样，眼睛睁得滚圆。

“西弗勒斯——哦，西弗勒斯——你愿意帮助他？你愿意照顾他，保证他安然无恙？”

“我可以试一试。”

她一扬手扔掉了杯子，杯子滑到了桌子的那头。她从沙发上出溜下去，跪在斯内普的脚边，用两只手抓着他的手，把嘴唇贴了上去。

“如果你会在那里保护他……西弗勒斯，你能保证吗？你能立一个牢不可破的誓言吗？”

“牢不可破的誓言？”斯内普脸上的表情变得不可捉摸了，贝拉特里克斯发出一串得意的笑声。

“你没听明白吗，纳西莎？哦，他会试一试的，我相信……又是那套空话，又是那样临阵脱逃……噢，当然啦，都是听从了黑魔王的吩咐！”

斯内普没有看贝拉特里克斯。他乌黑的眼睛紧紧盯着纳西莎那双沾满泪水的蓝眼睛，纳西莎继续攥着他的手。

“当然，纳西莎，我可以立一个牢不可破的誓言，”他轻声说，“也许你姐姐同意做我们的见证人。”

贝拉特里克斯吃惊地张大了嘴巴。西弗勒斯矮下身子，跪在了纳西莎的对面。在贝拉特里克斯惊愕的目光下，他们互相握住了对方的右手。

“你需要拿着魔杖，贝拉特里克斯。”斯内普冷冷地说。

She drew it, still looking astonished.

'And you will need to move a little closer,' he said.

She stepped forwards so that she stood over them, and placed the tip of her wand on their linked hands.

Narcissa spoke.

'Will you, Severus, watch over my son Draco as he attempts to fulfil the Dark Lord's wishes?'

'I will,' said Snape.

A thin tongue of brilliant flame issued from the wand and wound its way around their hands like a red-hot wire.

'And will you, to the best of your ability, protect him from harm?'

'I will,' said Snape.

A second tongue of flame shot from the wand and interlinked with the first, making a fine, glowing chain.

'And, should it prove necessary … if it seems Draco will fail …' whispered Narcissa (Snape's hand twitched within hers, but he did not draw away), 'will you carry out the deed that the Dark Lord has ordered Draco to perform?'

There was a moment's silence. Bellatrix watched, her wand upon their clasped hands, her eyes wide.

'I will,' said Snape.

Bellatrix's astounded face glowed red in the blaze of a third tongue of flame, which shot from the wand, twisted with the others and bound itself thickly around their clasped hands, like a rope, like a fiery snake.

她抽出魔杖，脸上仍是一副吃惊的样子。

“你需要再靠近一点儿。”他说。

她走上前，站在两人身边，把魔杖头点在他们相握的两只手上。

纳西莎说话了。

“西弗勒斯，在我儿子德拉科试图完成黑魔王的意愿时，你愿意照看他吗？”

“我愿意。”斯内普说。

一道细细的、耀眼的火舌从魔杖里喷了出来，就像一根又红又热的金属丝，缠绕在他们相握的两只手上。

“你愿意尽你最大的能力，保护他不受伤害吗？”

“我愿意。”斯内普说。

第二道火舌从魔杖里喷了出来，与第一道缠绕在一起，构成一根细细的、闪着红光的链条。

“还有，如果必要的话……如果德拉科眼看就要失败……”纳西莎低声说（斯内普的手在她的手里抖动，但他没有把手抽出来），“你愿意把黑魔王吩咐德拉科完成的事情进行到底吗？”

片刻的沉默。贝拉特里克斯注视着他们，她的魔杖悬在他们紧攥的两只手上，她的眼睛瞪得大大的。

“我愿意。”斯内普说。

贝拉特里克斯震惊的脸被第三道火舌的光映得通红，火舌从魔杖里喷出，与前面那两道交织在一起，紧密地缠绕在他们相握的两只手周围，像一根绳索，像一条喷火的蛇。

CHAPTER THREE

Will and Won't

Harry Potter was snoring loudly. He had been sitting in a chair beside his bedroom window for the best part of four hours, staring out at the darkening street, and had finally fallen asleep with one side of his face pressed against the cold windowpane, his glasses askew and his mouth wide open. The misty fug his breath had left on the window sparkled in the orange glare of the street lamp outside, and the artificial light drained his face of all colour so that he looked ghostly beneath his shock of untidy black hair.

The room was strewn with various possessions and a good smattering of rubbish. Owl feathers, apple cores and sweet wrappers littered the floor, a number of spellbooks lay higgledy-piggledy among the tangled robes on his bed, and a mess of newspapers sat in a puddle of light on his desk. The headline of one blared:

HARRY POTTER: THE CHOSEN ONE?

Rumours continue to fly about the mysterious recent disturbance at the Ministry of Magic, during which He Who Must Not Be Named was sighted once more.

'We're not allowed to talk about it, don't ask me anything,' said one agitated Obliviator, who refused to give his name as he left the Ministry last night.

Nevertheless, highly placed sources within the Ministry have confirmed that the disturbance centred on the fabled Hall of Prophecy.

Though Ministry spokeswizards have hitherto refused even to confirm the existence of such a place, a growing number of the wizarding community believe that the Death Eaters now serving

第3章

要与不要

哈利·波特响亮地打着鼾。他在卧室窗前的一把椅子上坐了将近四个小时，一直望着外面渐渐暗下来的街道，后来便睡着了。他的一侧面颊贴在冰凉的窗玻璃上，眼镜歪在一边，嘴巴张得大大的。他呼在窗户上的一团雾气被外面橙黄色的路灯照得闪闪发亮，在这种人造的灯光下，他的脸上毫无血色，乌黑的头发乱蓬蓬的，看上去有点儿像个幽灵。

房间里零零散散地放着各种东西，还扔着许多垃圾。地板上散落着猫头鹰的羽毛、苹果核和糖纸，床上几本魔法书乱七八糟地跟袍子摊在一起，桌上的台灯下放着一堆报纸。其中一张的标题非常醒目：

哈利·波特：救世之星?

人们继续纷纷议论魔法部最近发生的那场神秘骚乱，其间那个连名字也不能提的人再次现身。

“我们不许谈论这件事，什么也别问我。”一位不愿意透露姓名的神情焦虑的记忆注销员昨晚在离开魔法部时说。

然而，据魔法部高层人士证实，那场骚乱的中心是在传说中的预言厅。

尽管到目前为止魔法部发言人仍然不肯证实有这样一个地方存在，但巫师界越来越多的人相信，那些因侵害和盗窃行为在阿

> sentences in Azkaban for trespass and attempted theft were attempting to steal a prophecy. The nature of that prophecy is unknown, although speculation is rife that it concerns Harry Potter, the only person ever known to have survived the Killing Curse, and who is also known to have been at the Ministry on the night in question. Some are going so far as to call Potter the 'Chosen One', believing that the prophecy names him as the only one who will be able to rid us of He Who Must Not Be Named.
>
> The current whereabouts of the prophecy, if it exists, are unknown, although (cont. page 2, column 5)

A second newspaper lay beside the first. This one bore the headline:

SCRIMGEOUR SUCCEEDS FUDGE

Most of this front page was taken up with a large black-and-white picture of a man with a lionlike mane of thick hair and a rather ravaged face. The picture was moving – the man was waving at the ceiling.

> Rufus Scrimgeour, previously Head of the Auror Office in the Department of Magical Law Enforcement, has succeeded Cornelius Fudge as Minister for Magic. The appointment has largely been greeted with enthusiasm by the wizarding community, though rumours of a rift between the new Minister and Albus Dumbledore, newly reinstated Chief Warlock of the Wizengamot, surfaced within hours of Scrimgeour taking office.
>
> Scrimgeour's representatives admitted that he had met with Dumbledore at once upon taking possession of the top job, but refused to comment on the topics under discussion. Albus Dumbledore is known to (cont. page 3, column 2)

To the left of this paper sat another, which had been folded so that a story bearing the title MINISTRY GUARANTEES STUDENTS' SAFETY was visible.

兹卡班服刑的食死徒们当时试图窃取一个预言球。那个预言球的内容不明，不过人们纷纷猜测与哈利·波特有关，他是人们所知的唯一从杀戮咒中生还之人，而且已知事发那天夜里他也在魔法部。有人甚至称波特为“救世之星”，他们相信，那个预言指出只有波特才能使我们摆脱那个连名字也不能提的人。

那个预言球即使真的存在，目前也下落不明，不过（下转第2版，第5栏）

第二张报纸放在第一张旁边，上面的标题是：

斯克林杰接替福吉

头版的大部分版面都被一个男人的大幅黑白照片占据，他有着一头狮子毛般浓密的头发和一张疤痕累累的脸。照片是活动的——那人正朝天花板挥着手。

魔法法律执行司的前任傲罗办公室主任鲁弗斯·斯克林杰接替康奈利·福吉出任魔法部部长。这一任命得到巫师界广泛而热烈的欢迎，不过新部长斯克林杰就任几个小时后，就有传言说他与刚刚恢复原职的威森加摩首席巫师阿不思·邓布利多关系不和。

斯克林杰的代表承认，部长就任最高职务后即与邓布利多会面，但他拒绝透露他们所商谈的话题。据知阿不思·邓布利多（下转第3版，第2栏）

在这张报纸的左边，还有另外一张叠起来的报纸，上面一篇标题为**魔法部保证学生安全**的文章正好露在外面。

Newly appointed Minister for Magic, Rufus Scrimgeour, spoke today of the tough new measures taken by his Ministry to ensure the safety of students returning to Hogwarts School of Witchcraft and Wizardry this autumn.

'For obvious reasons, the Ministry will not be going into detail about its stringent new security plans,' said the Minister, although an insider confirmed that measures include defensive spells and charms, a complex array of counter-curses and a small task force of Aurors dedicated solely to the protection of Hogwarts School.

Most seem reassured by the new Minister's tough stand on student safety. Said Mrs Augusta Longbottom, 'My grandson Neville – a good friend of Harry Potter's, incidentally, who fought the Death Eaters alongside him at the Ministry in June and –

But the rest of this story was obscured by the large birdcage standing on top of it. Inside it was a magnificent snowy owl. Her amber eyes surveyed the room imperiously, her head swivelling occasionally to gaze at her snoring master. Once or twice she clicked her beak impatiently, but Harry was too deeply asleep to hear her.

A large trunk stood in the very middle of the room. Its lid was open: it looked expectant; yet it was almost empty but for a residue of old underwear, sweets, empty ink bottles and broken quills that coated the very bottom. Nearby, on the floor, lay a purple leaflet emblazoned with the words:

Issued on Behalf of the Ministry of Magic
PROTECTING YOUR HOME AND FAMILY AGAINST DARK FORCES

The wizarding community is currently under threat from an organisation calling itself the Death Eaters. Observing the following simple security guidelines will help protect you, your family and your home from attack.

新任魔法部部长鲁弗斯·斯克林杰今天发表讲话说，魔法部采取了一些新的强硬措施，确保霍格沃茨魔法学校的学生于今秋安全返校。

“出于显而易见的原因，魔法部不会透露其严密的最新安全计划的具体内容。”部长说。不过一位内部人士证实，这些措施包括一些防御魔法和咒语、一系列破解咒和一支专门派去保护霍格沃茨学校的傲罗小分队。

新任部长坚决保证学生安全的立场似乎使大多数人消除了疑虑。奥古斯塔·隆巴顿夫人说：“我的孙子纳威——他碰巧是哈利·波特的一个好朋友，六月份曾在部里与哈利一起并肩抗击食死徒，而且……”

这篇报道的其他内容都被一个放在上面的大鸟笼遮住了。鸟笼里关着一只气派非凡的雪白色猫头鹰。它那双琥珀色的眼睛威严地扫视着屋子，脑袋不时地转动一下，望望正在酣睡的主人。有一两次它还不耐烦地磕磕嘴巴，发出咔嗒咔嗒的声音，可是哈利睡得太沉了，根本听不见。

屋子中间放着一个大箱子，盖子开着，似乎在期待着被填满，但里面几乎是空的，只有箱底稀稀落落地扔着一些旧内衣、糖果、空墨水瓶和破羽毛笔。箱子旁边的地板上有一本紫色的小册子，上面印着醒目的文字：

魔法部授权出版

保护你和你的家人
不受黑魔法侵害

目前巫师界受到一个自称食死徒的组织的威胁。遵守下列简单的安全准则将有助于保护您自己、您的家人和您的住宅免遭袭击。

1. You are advised not to leave the house alone.
2. Particular care should be taken during the hours of darkness. Wherever possible, arrange to complete journeys before night has fallen.
3. Review the security arrangements around your house, making sure that all family members are aware of emergency measures such as Shield and Disillusionment Charms and, in the case of under-age family members, Side-Along-Apparition.
4. Agree security questions with close friends and family so as to detect Death Eaters masquerading as others by use of Polyjuice Potion (see page 2).
5. Should you feel that a family member, colleague, friend or neighbour is acting in a strange manner, contact the Magical Law Enforcement Squad at once. They may have been put under the Imperius Curse (see page 4).
6. Should the Dark Mark appear over any dwelling place or other building, DO NOT ENTER, but contact the Auror Office immediately.
7. Unconfirmed sightings suggest that the Death Eaters *may* now be using Inferi (see page 10). Any sighting of an Inferius, or encounter with same, should be reported to the Ministry IMMEDIATELY.

Harry grunted in his sleep and his face slid down the window an inch or so, making his glasses still more lopsided, but he did not wake up. An alarm clock, repaired by Harry several years ago, ticked loudly on the sill, showing one minute to eleven. Beside it, held in place by Harry's relaxed hand, was a piece of parchment covered in thin, slanting writing. Harry had read this letter so often since its arrival three days ago that, although it had been delivered in a tightly furled scroll, it now lay quite flat.

Dear Harry,

If it is convenient to you, I shall call at number four, Privet Drive this coming Friday at eleven p.m. to escort you to The Burrow, where you have been invited to spend the remainder of your school holidays.

1. 不要独自离家。

2. 夜晚需要格外小心。外出尽可能在天黑前赶回。

3. 检查住宅周围的安全防备，确保全家人都知道一些紧急措施，如使用铁甲咒、幻身咒等，家中未成年的孩子则需学会随从显形。

4. 与亲朋好友商定安全暗号，以识破食死徒利用复方汤剂假冒他人（见第2页）。

5. 若察觉某位家庭成员、同事、朋友或邻居行为异常，请立即与魔法法律执行队联系。他们可能已被施了夺魂咒（见第4页）。

6. 如果黑魔标记出现在任何住宅或建筑物上，**千万不要进入**，立即与傲罗办公室联系。

7. 未经证实的目击消息说，食死徒现在可能使用阴尸（见第10页）。若看见或遭遇阴尸，请**即时**向魔法部报告。

哈利在睡梦中哼了哼，脸颊顺着窗户往下滑了一两寸，眼镜歪得更厉害了，但是他没有醒。哈利几年前修好的一只闹钟在窗台上嘀嗒嘀嗒地走着，时间是十一点差一分。闹钟旁边，哈利松开的手里有一张羊皮纸，上面用细长的、歪向一边的笔迹写着一些字。这封信三天前被送来后，哈利经常拿出来看，刚送来时羊皮纸卷得紧紧的，现在已经平平展展了。

亲爱的哈利：

如果你方便的话，我将在本星期五夜里十一点到女贞路4号来接你去陋居，他们邀请你在那里度过暑假剩余的日子。

If you are agreeable, I should also be glad of your assistance in a matter to which I hope to attend on the way to The Burrow. I shall explain this more fully when I see you.

Kindly send your answer by return of this owl. Hoping to see you this Friday,

I am, yours most sincerely,

Albus Dumbledore

Though he already knew it by heart, Harry had been stealing glances at this missive every few minutes since seven o'clock that evening, when he had first taken up his position beside his bedroom window, which had a reasonable view of both ends of Privet Drive. He knew it was pointless to keep rereading Dumbledore's words; Harry had sent back his 'yes' with the delivering owl, as requested, and all he could do now was wait: either Dumbledore was going to come, or he was not.

But Harry had not packed. It just seemed too good to be true that he was going to be rescued from the Dursleys after a mere fortnight of their company. He could not shrug off the feeling that something was going to go wrong – his reply to Dumbledore's letter might have gone astray; Dumbledore could be prevented from collecting him; the letter might turn out not to be from Dumbledore at all, but a trick or joke or trap. Harry had not been able to face packing and then being let down and having to unpack again. The only gesture he had made to the possibility of a journey was to shut his snowy owl, Hedwig, safely in her cage.

The minute hand on the alarm clock reached the number twelve, and at that precise moment, the street lamp outside the window went out.

Harry awoke as though the sudden darkness was an alarm. Hastily straightening his glasses and unsticking his cheek from the glass, he pressed his nose against the window instead and squinted down at the pavement. A tall figure in a long, billowing cloak was walking up the garden path.

Harry jumped up as though he had received an electric shock, knocked over his chair, and started snatching anything and everything within reach from the floor and throwing it into the trunk. Even as he lobbed a set of robes, two spellbooks and a packet of crisps across the room, the doorbell rang.

Downstairs in the living room his Uncle Vernon shouted, 'Who the blazes is calling at this time of night?'

另外，我在去陋居的路上要办一件事，若能得到你的协助我将非常高兴。详情见面时谈。

请将回信托这只猫头鹰捎回。星期五见。

你最忠实的

阿不思·邓布利多

信的内容哈利已经记得滚瓜烂熟，但自从晚上七点坐在卧室的窗户旁（这里能清楚地看见女贞路的两个路口）之后，他还是每过几分钟就忍不住偷偷再朝它瞥上几眼。他知道没有必要反复地看邓布利多的信。哈利已经按照要求，把他肯定的回答让那只送信的猫头鹰捎了回去。他眼下能做的只有等待：不管邓布利多来还是不来。

可是哈利没有收拾行李。刚在德思礼家住了两个星期就要被解救出去，这件事太美妙了，不像是真的。他怎么也摆脱不了心头的焦虑，总觉得会有什么地方出差错——他给邓布利多的回信送到别处去了，邓布利多被耽搁了，不能来接他了，或者那封信根本不是邓布利多写来的，而是一个玩笑、恶作剧或陷阱。如果高高兴兴地收拾好行李，到头来大失所望，还要把东西一件件地从箱子里再拿出来，哈利肯定会受不了的。对于可能到来的旅行，他唯一的准备就是把他那只雪白的猫头鹰海德薇牢牢地关在笼子里。

闹钟的分针指向了十二，几乎就在同时，窗外的路灯突然灭了。

这突如其来的黑暗像闹铃一样惊醒了哈利。他赶紧扶正了眼镜，把贴在玻璃上的面颊移开，而把鼻子贴在了窗户上，眯起眼睛看着下面的人行道。一个身穿飘逸长斗篷的高高的身影正顺着花园小路走来。

哈利像遭到电击一样腾地跳了起来，带翻了椅子。他开始把地板上够得着的东西胡乱地全部抓起来扔进箱子。他刚把一套长袍、两本魔法书和一包薯片从房间那头扔过来，门铃就响了。

楼下的客厅里传来弗农姨父的喊声：“真见鬼，这么晚了谁在叫门？”

Harry froze with a brass telescope in one hand and a pair of trainers in the other. He had completely forgotten to warn the Dursleys that Dumbledore might be coming. Feeling both panicky and close to laughter, he clambered over the trunk and wrenched open his bedroom door in time to hear a deep voice say, 'Good evening. You must be Mr Dursley. I daresay Harry has told you I would be coming for him?'

Harry ran down the stairs two at a time, coming to an abrupt halt several steps from the bottom, as long experience had taught him to remain out of arm's reach of his uncle whenever possible. There in the doorway stood a tall, thin man with waist-length silver hair and beard. Half-moon spectacles were perched on his crooked nose and he was wearing a long black travelling cloak and a pointed hat. Vernon Dursley, whose moustache was quite as bushy as Dumbledore's, though black, and who was wearing a puce dressing-gown, was staring at the visitor as though he could not believe his tiny eyes.

'Judging by your look of stunned disbelief, Harry did *not* warn you that I was coming,' said Dumbledore pleasantly. 'However, let us assume that you have invited me warmly into your house. It is unwise to linger overlong on doorsteps in these troubled times.'

He stepped smartly over the threshold and closed the front door behind him.

'It is a long time since my last visit,' said Dumbledore, peering down his crooked nose at Uncle Vernon. 'I must say, your agapanthuses are flourishing.'

Vernon Dursley said nothing at all. Harry did not doubt that speech would return to him, and soon – the vein pulsing in his uncle's temple was reaching danger point – but something about Dumbledore seemed to have robbed him temporarily of breath. It might have been the blatant wizardishness of his appearance, but it might, too, have been that even Uncle Vernon could sense that here was a man whom it would be very difficult to bully.

'Ah, good evening, Harry,' said Dumbledore, looking up at him through his half-moon glasses with a most satisfied expression. 'Excellent, excellent.'

These words seemed to rouse Uncle Vernon. It was clear that as far as he was concerned, any man who could look at Harry and say 'excellent' was a man with whom he could never see eye to eye.

'I don't mean to be rude –' he began, in a tone that threatened rudeness in every syllable.

哈利僵在了那里，一手拿着黄铜望远镜，一手拎着一双运动鞋。他完全忘记了告诉德思礼一家邓布利多可能会来。他觉得又紧张又好笑，赶紧从箱子上翻过去，拧开卧室的门，正好听见一个低沉的声音说："晚上好。想必你就是德思礼先生吧？我相信哈利一定对你说过我要来接他，是不是？"

哈利一步两级地冲下楼梯，在离楼底还有几级时猛地刹住脚步，长期以来的经验告诉他，任何时候都要尽量与姨父保持距离，别让姨父的手臂够着他。门口站着一个瘦高个子的男人，银白色的头发和胡子一直垂到腰际。他那歪歪扭扭的鼻子上架着一副半月形的眼镜，身上是一件黑色的旅行斗篷，头戴一顶尖帽子。弗农·德思礼的胡子差不多跟邓布利多的一样浓密，不过是黑色的，他身穿一件紫褐色的便袍，正呆呆地盯着来人，似乎不敢相信他那双小眼睛看到的一切。

"从你这么惊讶、不敢相信的神情看，哈利没有告诉你我要来。"邓布利多愉快地说，"不过，让我们假定你已经热情地邀请我进入你的家门了吧。如今时局动荡，在门口逗留时间过长是不明智的。"

他敏捷地跨过门槛，关上了身后的大门。

"我上次来过以后，已经有很长时间了。"邓布利多的目光从歪扭的鼻子上望着弗农姨父，"必须承认，你的百子莲开得很茂盛。"

弗农·德思礼没有吭声。哈利相信他很快就会缓过劲儿来说话的——姨父太阳穴上的血管跳得都快爆炸了——但是邓布利多身上的某种东西似乎使他一时喘不过气来。也许是邓布利多所显露的惹人注目的巫师气质，也许只是因为就连弗农姨父也能感觉到，他很难在这个男人面前耀武扬威。

"啊，晚上好，哈利，"邓布利多从半月形眼镜片的后面望着哈利，脸上带着十分满意的表情，"太好了，太好了。"

这句话似乎唤醒了弗农姨父。显然对他来说，任何一个能够看着哈利说"太好了"的人，他都不可能与之达成共识。

"我不是故意失礼——"他说，每一个音节都透着无礼。

'– yet, sadly, accidental rudeness occurs alarmingly often,' Dumbledore finished the sentence gravely. 'Best to say nothing at all, my dear man. Ah, and this must be Petunia.'

The kitchen door had opened, and there stood Harry's aunt, wearing rubber gloves and a housecoat over her nightdress, clearly halfway through her usual pre-bedtime wipe-down of all the kitchen surfaces. Her rather horsy face registered nothing but shock.

'Albus Dumbledore,' said Dumbledore, when Uncle Vernon failed to effect an introduction. 'We have corresponded, of course.' Harry thought this an odd way of reminding Aunt Petunia that he had once sent her an exploding letter, but Aunt Petunia did not challenge the term. 'And this must be your son Dudley?'

Dudley had that moment peered round the living-room door. His large, blond head rising out of the stripy collar of his pyjamas looked oddly disembodied, his mouth gaping in astonishment and fear. Dumbledore waited a moment or two, apparently to see whether any of the Dursleys were going to say anything, but as the silence stretched on he smiled.

'Shall we assume that you have invited me into your sitting room?'

Dudley scrambled out of the way as Dumbledore passed him. Harry, still clutching the telescope and trainers, jumped the last few stairs and followed Dumbledore, who had settled himself in the armchair nearest the fire and was taking in the surroundings with an expression of benign interest. He looked quite extraordinarily out of place.

'Aren't – aren't we leaving, sir?' Harry asked anxiously.

'Yes, indeed we are, but there are a few matters we need to discuss first,' said Dumbledore. 'And I would prefer not to do so in the open. We shall trespass upon your aunt and uncle's hospitality only a little longer.'

'You will, will you?'

Vernon Dursley had entered the room, Petunia at his shoulder and Dudley skulking behind them both.

'Yes,' said Dumbledore simply, 'I shall.'

He drew his wand so rapidly that Harry barely saw it; with a casual flick, the sofa zoomed forwards and knocked the knees out from under all three of the Dursleys so that they collapsed upon it in a heap. Another flick of the

“——然而，很遗憾，我们还是经常会碰到意外的失礼。”邓布利多严肃地接过他的话头，“最好什么也别说啦，亲爱的伙计。啊，这位肯定是佩妮。”

厨房的门开了，哈利的姨妈站在那里，戴着橡胶手套，睡衣上套着一件家常便服，显然她正像往常一样要在睡觉前把整个厨房的表面都擦一遍。她那长长的马脸上满是惊恐。

“我是阿不思·邓布利多。”邓布利多看到弗农没有给他作介绍，便说道，“当然啦，我们通过信。”哈利觉得，用这种方式提醒佩妮邓布利多曾经给她寄过一封吼叫信，听着有点好笑，但是佩妮姨妈并没有对这种说法表示异议。“这一定是你们的儿子达力吧？”

达力正从客厅门口探出头，他那个黄头发的大脑袋戳在条纹睡衣的领口外，看上去好像不是长在他身体上似的。因为吃惊和害怕，他把嘴巴张得大大的。邓布利多等了片刻，似乎想听听德思礼一家有什么话要说，看到他们继续沉默着，他便笑了。

“我们能不能假设，你们已经邀请我进入你们家的客厅了？”

邓布利多经过达力身边时，达力慌忙闪到一边。哈利跳下最后几级楼梯，跟着邓布利多进了客厅，手里仍然抓着望远镜和运动鞋。邓布利多在最靠近壁炉的扶手椅上坐了下来，带着善意的兴趣打量房间里的一切。他看上去与周围的环境完全不协调。

“我们——我们不是要走吗，先生？”哈利焦急地问。

“走，当然要走，不过有几件事需要先商量一下。”邓布利多说，“这些事我认为我们最好不要在外面谈论，所以只好多打扰你的姨妈和姨父一会儿了。”

“什么，什么？”

弗农姨父也进了客厅，佩妮站在他身边，达力战战兢兢地躲在他们俩后面。

“没错，”邓布利多简短地说，“是这样。”

他忽地拔出魔杖，快得哈利都没看清。魔杖轻轻一挥，沙发嗖地冲了过去，撞在德思礼家三个人的膝盖上。他们一下子没有站住脚，

wand and the sofa zoomed back to its original position.

'We may as well be comfortable,' said Dumbledore pleasantly.

As he replaced his wand in his pocket, Harry saw that his hand was blackened and shrivelled; it looked as though his flesh had been burned away.

'Sir – what happened to your –?'

'Later, Harry,' said Dumbledore. 'Please sit down.'

Harry took the remaining armchair, choosing not to look at the Dursleys, who seemed stunned into silence.

'I would assume that you were going to offer me refreshment,' Dumbledore said to Uncle Vernon, 'but the evidence so far suggests that that would be optimistic to the point of foolishness.'

A third twitch of the wand and a dusty bottle and five glasses appeared in midair. The bottle tipped and poured a generous measure of honey-coloured liquid into each of the glasses, which then floated to each person in the room.

'Madam Rosmerta's finest, oak-matured mead,' said Dumbledore, raising his glass to Harry, who caught hold of his own and sipped. He had never tasted anything like it before, but enjoyed it immensely. The Dursleys, after quick, scared looks at each other, tried to ignore their glasses completely, a difficult feat, as they were nudging them gently on the sides of their heads. Harry could not suppress a suspicion that Dumbledore was rather enjoying himself.

'Well, Harry,' said Dumbledore, turning towards him, 'a difficulty has arisen which I hope you will be able to solve for us. By us, I mean the Order of the Phoenix. But first of all I must tell you that Sirius's will was discovered a week ago and that he left you everything he owned.'

Over on the sofa, Uncle Vernon's head turned, but Harry did not look at him, nor could he think of anything to say except, 'Oh. Right.'

'This is, in the main, fairly straightforward,' Dumbledore went on. 'You add a reasonable amount of gold to your account at Gringotts and you inherit all of Sirius's personal possessions. The slightly problematic part of the legacy –'

'His godfather's dead?' said Uncle Vernon loudly from the sofa. Dumbledore and Harry both turned to look at him. The glass of mead was now knocking quite insistently on the side of Vernon's head; he attempted to

全都栽倒在沙发上，滚作一团。魔杖又是轻轻一挥，沙发又嗖地回到了原处。

“我们也可以舒服一些。”邓布利多愉快地说。

他把魔杖重新放回口袋，这时哈利看见他的那只手既干枯又焦黑，好像上面的肉都被烧干了。

“先生——这是怎么搞的？”

“以后再说，哈利，”邓布利多说，“坐下吧。”

哈利在另外那把扶手椅上坐了下来，尽量不去看德思礼一家，他们似乎被吓得说不出话来了。

“我本来以为你们会让我喝点儿什么，”邓布利多对弗农姨父说，“现在看来，这种期望是乐观到了可笑的程度。”

魔杖第三次轻轻一挥，空中出现了一个脏兮兮的酒瓶和五个玻璃杯。瓶子自动侧过来给每个杯子里倒满了蜜黄色的液体，然后杯子分别飘向房间里的每个人。

“罗斯默塔女士最好的橡木催熟的蜂蜜酒。”邓布利多说着朝哈利举了举杯，哈利抓住他自己的那一杯酒喝了一小口。他以前从没尝过这种东西，感觉非常喜欢。德思礼一家惊慌失措地迅速对视了一下，然后便拼命躲避他们的杯子。这可不太容易，因为杯子不停地轻轻撞着他们的脑袋提醒他们。哈利忍不住怀疑邓布利多是不是在故意搞恶作剧。

“好了，哈利，”邓布利多转向他说，“现在有一个难题，我希望你能帮我们解决。我说的‘我们’是指凤凰社。不过，我首先要告诉你，一个星期前发现了小天狼星的遗嘱，他把他所有的一切都留给了你。”

沙发上的弗农姨父转过头，但是哈利没有看他，也想不出该说什么话，只回了一句：“噢，好。”

“基本上比较简单，”邓布利多继续说道，“你在古灵阁的账户上又多了一大笔金子，你还继承了小天狼星所有的个人财物。遗产中有点问题的部分是——”

“他的教父死了？”弗农姨父在沙发上大声问。邓布利多和哈利都扭头看着他。那杯蜂蜜酒这会儿已经在不依不饶地敲着弗农的脑袋，

beat it away. 'He's dead? His godfather?'

'Yes,' said Dumbledore. He did not ask Harry why he had not confided in the Dursleys. 'Our problem,' he continued to Harry, as if there had been no interruption, 'is that Sirius also left you number twelve, Grimmauld Place.'

'He's been left a house?' said Uncle Vernon greedily, his small eyes narrowing, but nobody answered him.

'You can keep using it as Headquarters,' said Harry. 'I don't care. You can have it, I don't really want it.' Harry never wanted to set foot in number twelve, Grimmauld Place again if he could help it. He thought he would be haunted for ever by the memory of Sirius prowling its dark musty rooms alone, imprisoned within the place he had wanted so desperately to leave.

'That is generous,' said Dumbledore. 'We have, however, vacated the building temporarily.'

'Why?'

'Well,' said Dumbledore, ignoring the mutterings of Uncle Vernon, who was now being rapped smartly over the head by the persistent glass of mead, 'Black family tradition decreed that the house was handed down the direct line, to the next male with the name of Black. Sirius was the very last of the line as his younger brother, Regulus, predeceased him and both were childless. While his will makes it perfectly plain that he wants you to have the house, it is nevertheless possible that some spell or enchantment has been set upon the place to ensure that it cannot be owned by anyone other than a pure-blood.'

A vivid image of the shrieking, spitting portrait of Sirius's mother that hung in the hall of number twelve, Grimmauld Place flashed into Harry's mind. 'I bet there has,' he said.

'Quite,' said Dumbledore. 'And if such an enchantment exists, then the ownership of the house is most likely to pass to the eldest of Sirius's living relatives, which would mean his cousin, Bellatrix Lestrange.'

Without realising what he was doing, Harry sprang to his feet; the telescope and trainers in his lap rolled across the floor. Bellatrix Lestrange, Sirius's killer, inherit his house?

'No,' he said.

'Well, obviously we would prefer that she didn't get it, either,' said

他则拼命想把它赶走。“他死了？他的教父？”

“是的。”邓布利多说。他没有问哈利为什么没把这件事告诉德思礼一家。“现在的问题是，”他继续对哈利说，就好像没被打断似的，“小天狼星还把格里莫广场12号也留给了你。”

“给他留下了一幢房子？”弗农姨父贪婪地说，一双小眼睛眯了起来，但是没有人理睬他。

“你们可以继续用它做总部。”哈利说，“我不在乎。你们可以用它，我其实并不需要。”只要可能，哈利再也不想跨进格里莫广场12号。他觉得自己一辈子都忘不了小天狼星曾经在那些昏暗发霉的房间里独自徘徊，被囚禁在那个他日夜渴望离开的地方。

“那太慷慨了。”邓布利多说，“不过，我们暂时撤出了那幢房子。”

“为什么？”

“是这样，”邓布利多没有理会弗农姨父的嘟囔，继续往下说——此时弗农姨父的脑袋被那杯蜂蜜酒敲得当当直响，“布莱克家族的传统规定，房子在父子间世代相传，要传给下一个姓布莱克的男性。小天狼星是他们家族里最后一位传人，他的弟弟雷古勒斯死在他之前，而他们俩都没有孩子。虽然他的遗嘱里说得很清楚，要把房子留给你，但那地方可能被施过一些魔法或咒语，以确保不让任何一个非纯血统的人占据它。”

哈利脑海里闪过一个画面：格里莫广场12号大厅里那幅小天狼星的母亲尖叫、怒骂的肖像。“肯定是那样。”他说。

“是啊，”邓布利多说，“如果存在这种魔咒，那么，这幢房子的所有权很可能就要属于布莱克家族现存的年纪最长的人，也就是小天狼星的堂姐，贝拉特里克斯·莱斯特兰奇了。”

哈利还没意识到自己在做什么，就一下子跳了起来，腿上的望远镜和运动鞋都滚到了地上。贝拉特里克斯·莱斯特兰奇，杀死小天狼星的凶手，继承他的房子？

“不！”他说。

“是啊，我们肯定也不希望她得到房子。”邓布利多平静地说，“情

Dumbledore calmly. 'The situation is fraught with complications. We do not know whether the enchantments we ourselves have placed upon it, for example, making it unplottable, will hold now that ownership has passed from Sirius's hands. It might be that Bellatrix will arrive on the doorstep at any moment. Naturally we had to move out until such time as we have clarified the position.'

'But how are you going to find out if I'm allowed to own it?'

'Fortunately,' said Dumbledore, 'there is a simple test.'

He placed his empty glass on a small table beside his chair, but before he could do anything else, Uncle Vernon shouted, '*Will you get these ruddy things off us?*'

Harry looked round; all three of the Dursleys were cowering with their arms over their heads as their glasses bounced up and down on their skulls, the contents flying everywhere.

'Oh, I'm so sorry,' said Dumbledore politely, and he raised his wand again. All three glasses vanished. 'But it would have been better manners to drink it, you know.'

It looked as though Uncle Vernon was bursting with any number of unpleasant retorts, but he merely shrank back into the cushions with Aunt Petunia and Dudley and said nothing, keeping his small piggy eyes on Dumbledore's wand.

'You see,' Dumbledore said, turning back to Harry and again speaking as though Uncle Vernon had not uttered, 'if you have indeed inherited the house, you have also inherited –'

He flicked his wand for a fifth time. There was a loud *crack* and a house-elf appeared, with a snout for a nose, giant bat's ears and enormous bloodshot eyes, crouching on the Dursleys' shagpile carpet and covered in grimy rags. Aunt Petunia let out a hair-raising shriek: nothing this filthy had entered her house in living memory; Dudley drew his large bare pink feet off the floor and sat with them raised almost above his head, as though he thought the creature might run up his pyjama trousers, and Uncle Vernon bellowed, 'What the *hell* is that?'

'Kreacher,' finished Dumbledore.

'Kreacher won't, Kreacher won't, Kreacher won't!' croaked the house-elf, quite as loudly as Uncle Vernon, stamping his long gnarled feet and pulling his ears. 'Kreacher belongs to Miss Bellatrix, oh, yes, Kreacher belongs to

况相当复杂。房子的所有权不归小天狼星了，我们就不知道我们原来给它施的一些魔法，比如让它无法在地图上标绘等等，现在还管不管用。贝拉特里克斯随时都会出现在门口。所以我们只好先搬出去，等情况弄清楚了再说。”

“但是怎么能弄清我是不是可以拥有它呢？”

“幸好，”邓布利多说，“有一种简单的测试办法。”

他把空杯子放在椅子边的小桌子上，没等他再做什么，弗农姨父喊道：“你能把这些该死的东西从我们这儿弄走吗？”

哈利扭头一看，德思礼家的三个人都用胳膊护着脑袋，因为他们的杯子正跳上跳下地撞着他们的脑壳，里面的酒洒得到处都是。

“哦，对不起。”邓布利多不失礼貌地说，又把魔杖举了起来。三个玻璃杯一下子就消失了。“可是你知道，把它喝掉才更有风度。”

弗农姨父似乎忍不住想说几句难听的话作为反击，但他只是跟佩妮姨妈和达力一起缩进沙发垫子里，一声不吭，一双小小的猪眼睛紧盯着邓布利多的魔杖。

“你看，”邓布利多说着又转向哈利，就当弗农姨父根本没开口似的继续说道，“如果你确实继承了那幢房子，你便同时会继承——”

他第五次挥动魔杖。随着一记很响的爆裂声，一个家养小精灵出现了，他鼻子向上突起，长着一对大大的蝙蝠状耳朵和一双铜铃般的、充血的眼睛。他身上穿着脏兮兮的破衣服，蹲在德思礼家的长绒地毯上。佩妮姨妈发出一声令人汗毛直竖的尖叫：从她记事起，她家里从没进来过这么肮脏的东西。达力赶紧把他那双粉红色的大光脚丫从地板上抬起来，差不多举过了头顶，似乎害怕那怪物会顺着他睡衣的裤腿爬上去。弗农姨父吼道：“那是个什么玩意儿？”

“克利切。”邓布利多接着自己刚才的话说。

“克利切不要，克利切不要，克利切不要！”家养小精灵哑着嗓子说，声音几乎跟弗农姨父的一样高，一边还跺着一双长长的、皱巴巴的脚，揪着他那对大耳朵，“克利切属于贝拉特里克斯小姐，噢，没错，克利切属于布莱克家的人，克利切想要新的女主人，克利切不要归那个波

the Blacks, Kreacher wants his new mistress, Kreacher won't go to the Potter brat, Kreacher won't, won't, won't –'

'As you can see, Harry,' said Dumbledore loudly, over Kreacher's continued croaks of 'won't, won't, won't', 'Kreacher is showing a certain reluctance to pass into your ownership.'

'I don't care,' said Harry again, looking with disgust at the writhing, stamping house-elf. 'I don't want him.'

'*Won't, won't, won't, won't* –'

'You would prefer him to pass into the ownership of Bellatrix Lestrange? Bearing in mind that he has lived at the Headquarters of the Order of the Phoenix for the past year?'

'*Won't, won't, won't, won't* –'

Harry stared at Dumbledore. He knew that Kreacher could not be permitted to go and live with Bellatrix Lestrange, but the idea of owning him, of having responsibility for the creature that had betrayed Sirius, was repugnant.

'Give him an order,' said Dumbledore. 'If he has passed into your ownership, he will have to obey. If not, then we shall have to think of some other means of keeping him from his rightful mistress.'

'*Won't, won't, won't, WON'T!*'

Kreacher's voice had risen to a scream. Harry could think of nothing to say, except, 'Kreacher, shut up!'

It looked for a moment as though Kreacher was going to choke. He grabbed his throat, his mouth still working furiously, his eyes bulging. After a few seconds of frantic gulping, he threw himself face forwards on to the carpet (Aunt Petunia whimpered) and beat the floor with his hands and feet, giving himself over to a violent, but entirely silent, tantrum.

'Well, that simplifies matters,' said Dumbledore cheerfully. 'It seems that Sirius knew what he was doing. You are the rightful owner of number twelve, Grimmauld Place, and of Kreacher.'

'Do I – do I have to keep him with me?' Harry asked, aghast, as Kreacher thrashed around at his feet.

'Not if you don't want to,' said Dumbledore. 'If I might make a suggestion, you could send him to Hogwarts to work in the kitchen there. In that way, the other house-elves could keep an eye on him.'

特小子，克利切不要，不要，不要——”

“你也看出来了，哈利，”邓布利多提高了音量，盖过了克利切不停歇的“不要，不要，不要”的嘶喊，“克利切不愿意归你所有。”

“我不在乎，”哈利厌恶地看着那个不断扭动、跺着脚的家养小精灵，又把话说了一遍，“我不想要他。”

“不要，不要，不要，不要——”

“那么你情愿让他落到贝拉特里克斯·莱斯特兰奇手里啰？你别忘了，他去年可一直住在凤凰社的总部啊！”

“不要，不要，不要，不要——”

哈利呆呆地望着邓布利多。他知道绝不能让克利切跟贝拉特里克斯·莱斯特兰奇生活在一起，但是想到克利切归他所有，想到他要对这个曾经背叛过小天狼星的家伙负责，他感到一阵厌恶。

“给他下个命令吧。”邓布利多说，“如果他现在属于你了，他就不得不服从。如果你不要他，我们就必须想出别的办法不让他跟他法定的女主人在一起。”

“不要，不要，不要，**不要！**”

克利切简直是在声嘶力竭地尖叫了。哈利想不出什么可说，就喊了一句：“克利切，闭嘴！”

顿时，克利切好像被呛住了。他掐住自己的喉咙，嘴巴还在愤怒地动个不停，眼睛向外突起。他大口大口地喘息了几秒钟，突然向前扑倒在地毯上（佩妮姨妈抽抽搭搭地哭了起来），双手和双脚使劲敲打着地板，发起了一通来势凶猛但绝对无声的脾气。

“好，这样事情就简单了，”邓布利多高兴地说，“看来小天狼星头脑很清楚。你是格里莫广场12号以及克利切的合法主人了。”

“我——我必须把他带在身边吗？”哈利惊恐地问，克利切在他脚边剧烈地扭动着。

“如果你不愿意，就不用。”邓布利多说，“我不妨提一个建议，你可以把他派到霍格沃茨，让他在厨房里干活。那样，别的家养小精灵还可以监视他。”

'Yeah,' said Harry in relief, 'yeah, I'll do that. Er – Kreacher – I want you to go to Hogwarts and work in the kitchens there with the other house-elves.'

Kreacher, who was now lying flat on his back with his arms and legs in the air, gave Harry one upside-down look of deepest loathing and, with another loud *crack*, vanished.

'Good,' said Dumbledore. 'There is also the matter of the Hippogriff, Buckbeak. Hagrid has been looking after him since Sirius died, but Buckbeak is yours now, so if you would prefer to make different arrangements –'

'No,' said Harry at once, 'he can stay with Hagrid. I think Buckbeak would prefer that.'

'Hagrid will be delighted,' said Dumbledore, smiling. 'He was thrilled to see Buckbeak again. Incidentally, we have decided, in the interests of Buckbeak's safety, to rechristen him Witherwings for the time being, though I doubt that the Ministry would ever guess he is the Hippogriff they once sentenced to death. Now, Harry, is your trunk packed?'

'Erm ...'

'Doubtful that I would turn up?' Dumbledore suggested shrewdly.

'I'll just go and – er – finish off,' said Harry hastily, hurrying to pick up his fallen telescope and trainers.

It took him a little over ten minutes to track down everything he needed; at last he had managed to extract his Invisibility Cloak from under the bed, screwed the top back on his jar of Colour-Change Ink and forced the lid of his trunk shut on his cauldron. Then, heaving his trunk in one hand and holding Hedwig's cage in the other, he made his way back downstairs.

He was disappointed to discover that Dumbledore was not waiting in the hall, which meant that he had to return to the living room.

Nobody was talking. Dumbledore was humming quietly, apparently quite at his ease, but the atmosphere was thicker than cold custard and Harry did not dare look at the Dursleys as he said, 'Professor – I'm ready now.'

'Good,' said Dumbledore. 'Just one last thing, then.' And he turned to speak to the Dursleys once more. 'As you will no doubt be aware, Harry comes of age in a year's time –'

'No,' said Aunt Petunia, speaking for the first time since Dumbledore's arrival.

“好，”哈利松了口气说，“好，就这么办。嗯——克利切——我要你到霍格沃茨去，在那里的厨房里跟别的家养小精灵一起干活。”

克利切此刻平躺在地上，四脚朝天，翻着眼睛充满怨恨地朝上看了哈利一眼。然后，又是一记很响的爆裂声，他消失了。

“很好。”邓布利多说，“还有一件事，关于鹰头马身有翼兽巴克比克。自从小天狼星死后，一直是海格在照料它，但巴克比克现在属于你了，所以，如果你愿意另作安排——”

“不，”哈利立刻说道，“就让它跟海格在一起吧。我想巴克比克也愿意那样。”

“海格会很高兴的。”邓布利多微笑着说，“顺便说一句，为了巴克比克的安全，我们决定暂时给它改名叫蔫翼，其实我不相信魔法部会猜到它就是曾经被判处死刑的那头鹰头马身有翼兽。好，哈利，你的箱子收拾好了吗？”

“嗯……”

“不相信我真的会来？”邓布利多尖锐地指出。

“我这就去——嗯——把它收拾好。”哈利赶紧说道，一边匆匆捡起掉在地上的望远镜和运动鞋。

他花了十多分钟才把他需要的每件东西都找齐了。最后他总算从床底下抽出了他的隐形衣，拧上那瓶变色墨水的盖子，又把箱子盖使劲压在坩埚上盖好。然后，他一手拎着箱子，一手提着海德薇的笼子，下楼来了。

他失望地发现，邓布利多并没有在门厅里等着，这就意味着他不得不再回客厅。

没有一个人说话。邓布利多轻声哼着小曲儿，一副自得其乐的样子，但是屋里的空气比冰冻的牛奶蛋糊还要凝固。哈利不敢看德思礼一家，只是说道：“教授——我准备好了。”

“很好。”邓布利多说，“还有最后一件事，”他又一次转过身对德思礼一家说，“你们无疑也意识到了，哈利再过一年就成年了——”

“不。”佩妮姨妈说，这是她在邓布利多到来后第一次开口说话。

'I'm sorry?' said Dumbledore politely.

'No, he doesn't. He's a month younger than Dudley, and Dudders doesn't turn eighteen until the year after next.'

'Ah,' said Dumbledore pleasantly, 'but in the wizarding world, we come of age at seventeen.'

Uncle Vernon muttered 'preposterous', but Dumbledore ignored him.

'Now, as you already know, the wizard called Lord Voldemort has returned to this country. The wizarding community is currently in a state of open warfare. Harry, whom Lord Voldemort has already attempted to kill on a number of occasions, is in even greater danger now than the day when I left him upon your doorstep fifteen years ago, with a letter explaining about his parents' murder and expressing the hope that you would care for him as though he were your own.'

Dumbledore paused, and although his voice remained light and calm, and he gave no obvious sign of anger, Harry felt a kind of chill emanating from him and noticed that the Dursleys drew very slightly closer together.

'You did not do as I asked. You have never treated Harry as a son. He has known nothing but neglect and often cruelty at your hands. The best that can be said is that he has at least escaped the appalling damage you have inflicted upon the unfortunate boy sitting between you.'

Both Aunt Petunia and Uncle Vernon looked around instinctively, as though expecting to see someone other than Dudley squeezed between them.

'Us – mistreat Dudders? What d'you –?' began Uncle Vernon furiously, but Dumbledore raised his finger for silence, a silence which fell as though he had struck Uncle Vernon dumb.

'The magic I evoked fifteen years ago means that Harry has powerful protection while he can still call this house home. However miserable he has been here, however unwelcome, however badly treated, you have at least, grudgingly, allowed him houseroom. This magic will cease to operate the moment that Harry turns seventeen; in other words, the moment he becomes a man. I ask only this: that you allow Harry to return, once more, to this house, before his seventeenth birthday, which will ensure that the protection continues until that time.'

None of the Dursleys said anything. Dudley was frowning slightly, as though he was still trying to work out when he had ever been mistreated.

“对不起，你说什么？”邓布利多礼貌地问。

“不，他还没有成年。他比达力小一个月，达力要到后年才满十八岁呢。”

“啊，”邓布利多愉快地说，“可是在巫师界，满十七岁就成年了。”

弗农姨父嘟囔了一句“荒唐”，但邓布利多没有理他。

“你们已经知道，如今，那个名叫伏地魔的巫师又回到了这个国家。巫师界目前正处于一种公开交战的状态。伏地魔已经多次试图杀害哈利，现在哈利的处境，比十五年前我把他放在你们家台阶上时更加危险。当时我留下一封信，解释说他的父母已被杀害，希望你们会像对待自己的孩子一样照顾他。”

邓布利多停住了，尽管他的声音还是那么轻松、平静，脸上也没有表现出丝毫的怒容，但哈利感觉到他身上散发出一股寒意。他注意到德思礼一家互相挤缩得更紧了。

“你们没有按我说的去做。你们从来不把哈利当成自己的儿子。他在你们手里，得到的只是忽视和经常性的虐待。不幸中的万幸，他至少逃脱了你们对坐在你们中间那个倒霉男孩造成的可怕伤害。”

佩妮姨妈和弗农姨父都本能地转过目光，似乎以为会看见挤坐在他们中间的不是达力，而是别的什么人。

“我们——虐待达力？你这是——？”弗农姨父气愤地说，可是邓布利多举起一只手示意安静，屋里立刻静了下来，仿佛他一下子把弗农姨父变成了哑巴。

“我十五年前施的那个魔法，意味着在哈利仍然可以把这里当家期间，会得到强有力的保护。他在这里不管过得多么可怜，多么不受欢迎，多么遭人虐待，你们至少还很不情愿地给了他一个容身之处。当哈利年满十七岁，也就是说，当他成为一个男人时，这个魔法就会失效。我只要求一点：你们在哈利十七岁生日前允许他再一次回到这个家，这将保证那种保护力量持续到那个时候。”

德思礼一家谁也没有吭声。达力微微皱着眉头，似乎还在琢磨他到底受到了什么虐待。弗农姨父看上去像是喉咙里卡了什么东西。佩

Uncle Vernon looked as though he had something stuck in his throat; Aunt Petunia, however, was oddly flushed.

'Well, Harry … time for us to be off,' said Dumbledore at last, standing up and straightening his long black cloak. 'Until we meet again,' he said to the Dursleys, who looked as though that moment could wait for ever as far as they were concerned, and after doffing his hat, he swept from the room.

'Bye,' said Harry hastily to the Dursleys, and followed Dumbledore, who paused beside Harry's trunk, upon which Hedwig's cage was perched.

'We do not want to be encumbered by these just now,' he said, pulling out his wand again. 'I shall send them to The Burrow to await us there. However, I would like you to bring your Invisibility Cloak … just in case.'

Harry extracted his Cloak from his trunk with some difficulty, trying not to show Dumbledore the mess within. When he had stuffed it into an inside pocket of his jacket, Dumbledore waved his wand and the trunk, cage and Hedwig vanished. Dumbledore then waved his wand again and the front door opened on to cool, misty darkness.

'And now, Harry, let us step out into the night and pursue that flighty temptress, adventure.'

妮姨妈呢，却莫名其妙地涨红了脸。

“好了,哈利……我们该出发了。”邓布利多最后说道。他站了起来，整了整长长的黑斗篷。“下次再见。”他对德思礼一家说，而从他们的表情看,他们希望永远不要再见才好。然后,邓布利多脱帽致意了一下，快步走出了房间。

“再见。”哈利匆匆向德思礼一家道了个别，便也跟了出来。邓布利多在哈利的箱子旁停住脚步，箱子上还放着海德薇的鸟笼子。

“现在我们可不想带着它们碍事，”他说着又抽出了魔杖，“我把它们送到陋居，让它们在那儿等着我们吧。不过，我希望你把隐形衣带上……以防万一。”

哈利费了一些力气才把隐形衣从箱子里抽出来，因为他不想让邓布利多看到箱子里有多乱。他把隐形衣塞进夹克衫里面的口袋，邓布利多一挥魔杖，箱子、笼子和海德薇便一下子全消失了。然后，邓布利多又挥了一下魔杖，大门便朝着寒冷的、雾蒙蒙的夜色敞开了。

“好了，哈利，让我们走进黑夜，去追逐那个轻浮而诱人的妖妇——冒险吧。”

CHAPTER FOUR

Horace Slughorn

Despite the fact that he had spent every waking moment of the past few days hoping desperately that Dumbledore would indeed come to fetch him, Harry felt distinctly awkward as they set off down Privet Drive together. He had never had a proper conversation with his headmaster outside Hogwarts before; there was usually a desk between them. The memory of their last face-to-face encounter kept intruding, too, and it rather heightened Harry's sense of embarrassment; he had shouted a lot on that occasion, not to mention doing his best to smash several of Dumbledore's most prized possessions.

Dumbledore, however, seemed completely relaxed.

'Keep your wand at the ready, Harry,' he said brightly.

'But I thought I'm not allowed to use magic outside school, sir?'

'If there is an attack,' said Dumbledore, 'I give you permission to use any counter-jinx or -curse that might occur to you. However, I do not think you need worry about being attacked tonight.'

'Why not, sir?'

'You are with me,' said Dumbledore simply. 'This will do, Harry.'

He came to an abrupt halt at the end of Privet Drive.

'You have not, of course, passed your Apparition test?' he said.

'No,' said Harry. 'I thought you had to be seventeen?'

'You do,' said Dumbledore. 'So you will need to hold on to my arm very tightly. My left, if you don't mind – as you have noticed, my wand arm is a little fragile at the moment.'

Harry gripped Dumbledore's proffered forearm.

'Very good,' said Dumbledore. 'Well, here we go.'

第 4 章

霍拉斯·斯拉格霍恩

在过去的日子里，哈利只要醒着，就无时无刻不在热切地盼望邓布利多真的会来接他，可是，当两人一同出发，走在女贞路上时，他却觉得非常别扭。以前，他从来没有在霍格沃茨之外跟校长正经交谈过，他们中间一般都隔着一张桌子。他忍不住想起两人最后一次见面的情形，这更增加了他的尴尬。那次见面时，他不仅大吵大嚷，而且还不顾一切地打碎了邓布利多几件最宝贵的东西。

邓布利多却显得非常轻松。

"把魔杖准备好，哈利。"他语调轻快地说。

"可是，我在校外好像不能使用魔法吧，先生？"

"如果遇到袭击，"邓布利多说，"我允许你使用你能想到的任何魔法和咒语去反击。不过，我认为你今晚用不着担心遭到袭击。"

"为什么呢，先生？"

"因为你和我在一起，"邓布利多简单地说，"这就没事了，哈利。"

他在女贞路的路口突然停住了脚步。

"你肯定还没有通过幻影显形的考试吧？"他问。

"没有，"哈利回答说，"我记得好像要年满十七岁才行。"

"是啊，"邓布利多说，"那么你就需要紧紧抓住我的胳膊。是我的左胳膊，如果你不介意的话——你肯定注意到了，我拿魔杖的胳膊目前有点不得劲儿。"

哈利抓住了邓布利多伸过来的前臂。

"很好。"邓布利多说，"好了，我们出发。"

Harry felt Dumbledore's arm twist away from him and redoubled his grip: the next thing he knew, everything went black; he was being pressed very hard from all directions; he could not breathe, there were iron bands tightening around his chest; his eyeballs were being forced back into his head; his eardrums were being pushed deeper into his skull, and then –

He gulped great lungfuls of cold night air and opened his streaming eyes. He felt as though he had just been forced through a very tight rubber tube. It was a few seconds before he realised that Privet Drive had vanished. He and Dumbledore were now standing in what appeared to be a deserted village square, in the centre of which stood an old war memorial and a few benches. His comprehension catching up with his senses, Harry realised that he had just Apparated for the first time in his life.

'Are you all right?' asked Dumbledore, looking down at him solicitously. 'The sensation does take some getting used to.'

'I'm fine,' said Harry, rubbing his ears, which felt as though they had left Privet Drive rather reluctantly. 'But I think I might prefer brooms.'

Dumbledore smiled, drew his travelling cloak a little more tightly around his neck and said, 'This way.'

He set off at a brisk pace, past an empty inn and a few houses. According to a clock on a nearby church, it was almost midnight.

'So tell me, Harry,' said Dumbledore. 'Your scar … has it been hurting at all?'

Harry raised a hand unconsciously to his forehead and rubbed the lightning-shaped mark.

'No,' he said, 'and I've been wondering about that. I thought it would be burning all the time now Voldemort's getting so powerful again.'

He glanced up at Dumbledore and saw that he was wearing a satisfied expression.

'I, on the other hand, thought otherwise,' said Dumbledore. 'Lord Voldemort has finally realised the dangerous access to his thoughts and feelings you have been enjoying. It appears that he is now employing Occlumency against you.'

'Well, I'm not complaining,' said Harry, who missed neither the disturbing dreams nor the startling flashes of insight into Voldemort's mind.

They turned a corner, passing a telephone box and a bus shelter. Harry looked sideways at Dumbledore again.

哈利觉得邓布利多的胳膊好像要从他手里挣脱，便赶紧抓得更牢，随即他发现周围变得一片漆黑。他受到来自各个方向的强烈挤压，根本透不过气来，胸口像是被几道铁箍紧紧勒着。他的眼球被挤回了脑袋里，耳膜被压进了头颅深处，接着——

他大口大口地吸着夜晚寒冷的空气，睁开流泪的双眼。他觉得自己刚才似乎是从一根非常狭窄的橡皮管子里挤了出来。几秒钟后他才缓过神来，发现女贞路已经消失。他和邓布利多现在站着的这个地方，像是某个被遗弃的村落的广场，中间竖着一座古老的战争纪念碑，还摆着几条长凳。哈利回过神来，意识到自己刚才经历了生平第一次幻影显形。

"你没事吧？"邓布利多低头关切地看着他问道，"这种感觉需要慢慢适应。"

"我挺好的，"哈利揉着耳朵说，觉得他的耳朵似乎是很不情愿地离开了女贞路，"但我好像更喜欢骑着扫帚飞行。"

邓布利多笑了，他用旅行斗篷紧紧裹住脖子，说道："这边走。"

他迈着轻快的脚步走着，经过一家空荡荡的小酒馆和几所房屋。从附近一座教堂的钟上看，时间已经差不多是午夜了。

"那么你告诉我，哈利，"邓布利多说，"你的伤疤……它还在疼吗？"

哈利下意识地把手伸到额头上，摸了摸那道闪电形的伤疤。

"没有，"他说，"我也一直在纳闷呢。现在伏地魔卷土重来，我还以为伤疤会一直火辣辣地疼呢。"

他抬眼看了看邓布利多，发现他脸上露出一种满意的神情。

"我的想法跟你不同。"邓布利多说，"伏地魔终于意识到你一直能够进入他的思想和情感，他觉得这很危险。看来，他现在对你使用大脑封闭术了。"

"那好，我巴不得这样呢。"哈利说，他并不怀念那些折磨人的噩梦，也不怀念那些突然洞悉伏地魔心理活动的可怕经历。

他们拐过街角，经过一个电话亭和一个公共汽车候车亭。哈利又偏头看了看邓布利多。

'Professor?'

'Harry?'

'Er – where exactly are we?'

'This, Harry, is the charming village of Budleigh Babberton.'

'And what are we doing here?'

'Ah, yes, of course, I haven't told you,' said Dumbledore. 'Well, I have lost count of the number of times I have said this in recent years, but we are, once again, one member of staff short. We are here to persuade an old colleague of mine to come out of retirement and return to Hogwarts.'

'How can I help with that, sir?'

'Oh, I think we'll find a use for you,' said Dumbledore vaguely. 'Left here, Harry.'

They proceeded up a steep, narrow street lined with houses. All the windows were dark. The odd chill that had lain over Privet Drive for two weeks persisted here, too. Thinking of Dementors, Harry cast a look over his shoulder and grasped his wand reassuringly in his pocket.

'Professor, why couldn't we just Apparate directly into your old colleague's house?'

'Because it would be quite as rude as kicking down the front door,' said Dumbledore. 'Courtesy dictates that we offer fellow wizards the opportunity of denying us entry. In any case, most wizarding dwellings are magically protected from unwanted Apparators. At Hogwarts, for instance –'

'– you can't Apparate anywhere inside the buildings or grounds,' said Harry quickly. 'Hermione Granger told me.'

'And she is quite right. We turn left again.'

The church clock chimed midnight behind them. Harry wondered why Dumbledore did not consider it rude to call on his old colleague so late, but now that conversation had been established, he had more pressing questions to ask.

'Sir, I saw in the *Daily Prophet* that Fudge has been sacked …'

'Correct,' said Dumbledore, now turning up a steep side-street. 'He has been replaced, as I am sure you also saw, by Rufus Scrimgeour, who used to be Head of the Auror Office.'

'Is he … do you think he's good?' asked Harry.

“教授？”

“哈利？”

“嗯——我们到底在哪儿呢？”

“这儿就是迷人的巴德莱·巴伯顿村庄，哈利。”

“我们到这儿来做什么呢？”

“啊，对了，我还没有告诉你。”邓布利多说，“唉，我都记不清最近几年这件事我说过多少遍了，可是没办法，现在我们又缺一名教师。我们是来劝说我的一名退休的同事重新出来工作，回到霍格沃茨的。”

“我能帮上什么忙呢，先生？”

“噢，我想我们会让你派上用场的。”邓布利多含糊地说，“向左转，哈利。”

他们走上了一条陡直、狭窄的街道，两边是一排排住房，所有的窗户都黑漆漆的。笼罩了女贞路两个星期的寒气在这里也滞留不去。哈利想到了摄魂怪，转过头朝后看了看，用手抓住口袋里的魔杖给自己壮胆。

“教授，我们为什么不能直接幻影显形到你的老同事家里呢？”

“因为那就像踢开别人家的大门一样无礼。”邓布利多说，“礼貌要求我们向别的巫师提供拒绝我们的机会。再者，大多数巫师住宅都有魔法抵御不受欢迎的幻影显形者。比如，在霍格沃茨——”

“——在城堡和场地上都不可以幻影显形。”哈利抢着说，“赫敏·格兰杰告诉我的。”

“她说得不错。我们再往左拐。”

在他们身后，教堂响起了午夜的钟声。哈利心里纳闷：邓布利多怎么不认为这么晚去拜访老同事是失礼呢？但现在谈话已经展开，他还有更加迫切的问题要问。

“先生，我在《预言家日报》上看到，福吉已经下台了……”

“不错，”邓布利多说着拐上了另一条陡直的小街，“我相信你已经看到了，接替他的是鲁弗斯·斯克林杰，他以前是傲罗办公室主任。”

“他……你认为他这个人怎么样？”哈利问。

'An interesting question,' said Dumbledore. 'He is able, certainly. A more decisive and forceful personality than Cornelius.'

'Yes, but I meant –'

'I know what you meant. Rufus is a man of action and, having fought Dark wizards for most of his working life, does not underestimate Lord Voldemort.'

Harry waited, but Dumbledore did not say anything about the disagreement with Scrimgeour that the *Daily Prophet* had reported, and he did not have the nerve to pursue the subject, so he changed it.

'And … sir … I saw about Madam Bones.'

'Yes,' said Dumbledore quietly. 'A terrible loss. She was a great witch. Just up here, I think – ouch.'

He had pointed with his injured hand.

'Professor, what happened to your –?'

'I have no time to explain now,' said Dumbledore. 'It is a thrilling tale, I wish to do it justice.'

He smiled at Harry, who understood that he was not being snubbed, and that he had permission to keep asking questions.

'Sir – I got a Ministry of Magic leaflet by owl, about security measures we should all take against the Death Eaters …'

'Yes, I received one myself,' said Dumbledore, still smiling. 'Did you find it useful?'

'Not really.'

'No, I thought not. You have not asked me, for instance, what is my favourite flavour of jam, to check that I am indeed Professor Dumbledore, and not an impostor.'

'I didn't …' Harry began, not entirely sure whether he was being reprimanded or not.

'For future reference, Harry, it is raspberry … although of course, if I were a Death Eater, I would have been sure to research my own jam-preferences before impersonating myself.'

'Er … right,' said Harry. 'Well, on that leaflet, it said something about Inferi. What exactly are they? The leaflet wasn't very clear.'

“这是个有趣的问题。”邓布利多说，“他很有能力，这是不用说的。比康奈利更果断，更有魄力。”

“是啊，不过我指的是——”

“我知道你指的是什么。鲁弗斯是个雷厉风行的人，他参加工作后的大部分精力都致力于对付黑巫师，所以不会低估伏地魔的力量。”

哈利等待着，但邓布利多只字不提《预言家日报》报道的他跟斯克林杰的不和，哈利也不敢追问，便改变了话题。

“还有……先生……我看到了博恩斯女士的事。”

“是啊，”邓布利多轻声说，“一个惨重的损失。她是一个了不起的巫师。我想就在那上边——哎哟！”

他用来指路的是那只受伤的手。

“教授，你这是怎么弄的？”

“现在没有时间解释了。”邓布利多说，“这是一个惊心动魄的故事，我希望能够展开来描述。”

他微笑地看着哈利，哈利明白自己没有受到斥责，还可以继续再提问题。

“先生——我收到猫头鹰送来的一份魔法部的小册子，讲的是对付食死徒的安全措施……”

“是啊，我也收到一份。”邓布利多仍然笑眯眯地说，“你觉得有用吗？”

“不太有用。”

“是啊，我也认为没用。比如，你并没有问我最喜欢哪一种果酱，以此来检验我确实就是邓布利多教授，而不是一个冒牌货。”

“我没有……”哈利没有说完，他不能肯定自己是不是受到了批评。

“为了将来用得着，我不妨告诉你，哈利，我最喜欢的是覆盆子果酱……不过，当然啦，如果我是个食死徒，我肯定会把我喜欢什么果酱弄清楚了再去冒充我自己的。”

“嗯……是这样。”哈利说，“对了，小册子上还提到了阴尸。它们到底是什么呢？小册子上说得不太清楚。”

'They are corpses,' said Dumbledore calmly. 'Dead bodies that have been bewitched to do a Dark wizard's bidding. Inferi have not been seen for a long time, however, not since Voldemort was last powerful … he killed enough people to make an army of them, of course. This is the place, Harry, just here …'

They were nearing a small, neat stone house set in its own garden. Harry was too busy digesting the horrible idea of Inferi to have much attention left for anything else, but as they reached the front gate Dumbledore stopped dead and Harry walked into him.

'Oh dear. Oh dear, dear, dear.'

Harry followed his gaze up the carefully tended front path and felt his heart sink. The front door was hanging off its hinges.

Dumbledore glanced up and down the street. It seemed quite deserted.

'Wand out and follow me, Harry,' he said quietly.

He opened the gate and walked swiftly and silently up the garden path, Harry at his heels, then pushed the front door very slowly, his wand raised and at the ready.

'*Lumos.*'

Dumbledore's wand-tip ignited, casting its light up a narrow hallway. To the left, another door stood open. Holding his illuminated wand aloft, Dumbledore walked into the sitting room with Harry right behind him.

A scene of total devastation met their eyes. A grandfather clock lay splintered at their feet, its face cracked, its pendulum lying a little further away like a dropped sword. A piano was on its side, its keys strewn across the floor. The wreckage of a fallen chandelier glittered nearby. Cushions lay deflated, feathers oozing from slashes in their sides; fragments of glass and china lay like powder over everything. Dumbledore raised his wand even higher, so that its light was thrown upon the walls, where something darkly red and glutinous was spattered over the wallpaper. Harry's small intake of breath made Dumbledore look round.

'Not pretty, is it,' he said heavily. 'Yes, something horrible has happened here.'

Dumbledore moved carefully into the middle of the room, scrutinising the wreckage at his feet. Harry followed, gazing around, half scared of what he

“它们是死尸，”邓布利多平静地说，“是被施了巫术、为黑巫师效劳的死尸。不过，阴尸已经有很长时间没人见过，自从伏地魔上次失势之后就绝迹了……不用说，伏地魔当时杀了许多人，制造了大批阴尸。我们到了，哈利，就是这儿……”

他们走近一幢坐落在花园里的整洁的石头小房子。哈利一门心思只顾琢磨关于阴尸的可怕说法，没留心周围的事情。走到大门前，邓布利多突然停住脚步，哈利猝不及防，撞到了他身上。

“噢，天哪。噢，天哪，天哪，天哪。”

哈利顺着邓布利多的目光，朝精心养护的小路那边望去，心顿时往下一沉。前门的铰链开了，门歪歪斜斜地悬着。

邓布利多望了望街道两边，似乎一个人也没有。

“哈利，拔出魔杖，跟我来。”他小声说。

他推开院门，悄没声儿地快步走上花园的小路，哈利紧随其后。然后邓布利多慢慢推开前门，手里举着魔杖，随时准备出击。

“荧光闪烁。”

邓布利多的魔杖顶端亮了，映照出一道狭窄的门廊。左边又有一扇敞开的门。邓布利多高高地举着发亮的魔杖，走进那间客厅，哈利紧紧跟在后面。

眼前一片狼藉，一座老爷钟摔碎在他们脚边，钟面裂了，钟摆躺在稍远一点的地方，像一把被遗弃的宝剑。一架钢琴翻倒在地上，琴键散落在四处。近旁还有一盏被摔散的枝形吊灯的碎片在闪闪发光。垫子乱七八糟地扔得到处都是，已经变瘪了，羽毛从裂口处钻了出来。碎玻璃和碎瓷片像粉末一样洒了一地。邓布利多把魔杖举得更高一些，照亮了墙壁，墙纸上溅了许多暗红色的黏糊糊的东西。哈利小声抽了口气，邓布利多听见了，四下里看了看。

“不太好看，是不是？”他沉重地说，“是啊，这儿发生了一起恐怖事件。”

邓布利多小心地走到屋子中间，仔细观察脚边的破碎残片。哈利跟了过去，打量着四周，隐隐地担心会看见什么可怕的东西藏在残破

might see hidden behind the wreck of the piano or the overturned sofa, but there was no sign of a body.

'Maybe there was a fight and – and they dragged him off, Professor?' Harry suggested, trying not to imagine how badly wounded a man would have to be to leave those stains spattered halfway up the walls.

'I don't think so,' said Dumbledore quietly, peering behind an over-stuffed armchair lying on its side.

'You mean he's –?'

'Still here somewhere? Yes.'

And without warning, Dumbledore swooped, plunging the tip of his wand into the seat of the overstuffed armchair, which yelled, 'Ouch!'

'Good evening, Horace,' said Dumbledore, straightening up again.

Harry's jaw dropped. Where a split second before there had been an armchair, there now crouched an enormously fat, bald old man who was massaging his lower belly and squinting up at Dumbledore with an aggrieved and watery eye.

'There was no need to stick the wand in that hard,' he said gruffly, clambering to his feet. 'It hurt.'

The wand-light sparkled on his shiny pate, his prominent eyes, his enormous, silver walrus-like moustache, and the highly polished buttons on the maroon velvet jacket he was wearing over a pair of lilac silk pyjamas. The top of his head barely reached Dumbledore's chin.

'What gave it away?' he grunted as he staggered to his feet, still rubbing his lower belly. He seemed remarkably unabashed for a man who had just been discovered pretending to be an armchair.

'My dear Horace,' said Dumbledore, looking amused, 'if the Death Eaters really had come to call, the Dark Mark would have been set over the house.'

The wizard clapped a pudgy hand to his vast forehead.

'The Dark Mark,' he muttered. 'Knew there was something … ah well. Wouldn't have had time, anyway. I'd only just put the finishing touches to my upholstery when you entered the room.'

He heaved a great sigh that made the ends of his moustache flutter.

'Would you like my assistance clearing up?' asked Dumbledore politely.

的钢琴或翻倒的沙发后面，但他并没有看见尸体的影子。

“也许有过一场搏斗，后来——后来他们把他拖走了，是吗，教授？”哈利猜测道，尽量不去想象一个人受了多么严重的伤，才会在墙上那么高的地方溅上那些血迹。

“我不认为是这样。”邓布利多平静地说，一边朝翻倒在地的一把鼓鼓囊囊的扶手椅后面看了看。

“你是说他——？”

“仍然在这里？没错。”

说时迟那时快，邓布利多突然出手，把魔杖尖扎进了鼓鼓囊囊的扶手椅的椅垫，椅子发出一声惨叫：“哎哟！”

“晚上好，霍拉斯。”邓布利多说着重新站直了身子。

哈利吃惊地张大了嘴巴。刚才还是一把扶手椅，眨眼之间却变成了一个秃顶的胖老头儿蹲在那里。他揉着小肚子，眯起一只痛苦的、泪汪汪的眼睛看着邓布利多。

“你没必要用魔杖扎得那么狠嘛。”他气呼呼地说，费劲地爬了起来，“疼死我了。”

魔杖的光照着他那明晃晃的秃头、鼓起的双眼、海象般的银白色胡须，还照着他淡紫色丝绸睡衣外面那件褐紫色天鹅绒夹克上的亮闪闪的纽扣。他的头顶只及邓布利多的下巴。

“是怎么露馅儿的？”他粗声粗气地问，一边踉踉跄跄地站起来，仍然揉着小肚子。看来他的脸皮厚得惊人，要知道他刚刚可是装成一把扶手椅被人识破的。

“我亲爱的霍拉斯，”邓布利多似乎觉得很可笑，说道，“如果食死徒真的来过，肯定会在房子上空留下黑魔标记的。”

巫师用胖乎乎的手拍了一下宽大的前额。

“黑魔标记。”他嘟囔道，“我就觉着还缺点儿什么……啊，对啦。不过，也来不及了。我刚把椅套调整好，你们就进屋了。”

他重重地叹了一口气，两根胡子尖都被吹得翘了起来。

“要我帮你收拾吗？”邓布利多彬彬有礼地问。

'Please,' said the other.

They stood back to back, the tall thin wizard and the short round one, and waved their wands in one identical sweeping motion.

The furniture flew back to its original place; ornaments reformed in midair; feathers zoomed into their cushions; torn books repaired themselves as they landed upon their shelves; oil lanterns soared on to side tables and reignited; a vast collection of splintered silver picture frames flew glittering across the room and alighted, whole and untarnished, upon a desk; rips, cracks and holes healed everywhere; and the walls wiped themselves clean.

'What kind of blood was that, incidentally?' asked Dumbledore loudly over the chiming of the newly unsmashed grandfather clock.

'On the walls? Dragon,' shouted the wizard called Horace as, with a deafening grinding and tinkling, the chandelier screwed itself back into the ceiling.

There was a final *plunk* from the piano, and silence.

'Yes, dragon,' repeated the wizard conversationally. 'My last bottle, and prices are sky-high at the moment. Still, it might be reusable.'

He stumped over to a small crystal bottle standing on top of a sideboard and held it up to the light, examining the thick liquid within.

'Hm. Bit dusty.'

He set the bottle back on the sideboard and sighed. It was then that his gaze fell upon Harry.

'Oho,' he said, his large round eyes flying to Harry's forehead and the lightning-shaped scar it bore. '*Oho*!'

'This,' said Dumbledore, moving forwards to make the introduction, 'is Harry Potter. Harry, this is an old friend and colleague of mine, Horace Slughorn.'

Slughorn turned on Dumbledore, his expression shrewd.

'So that's how you thought you'd persuade me, is it? Well, the answer's no, Albus.'

He pushed past Harry, his face turned resolutely away with the air of a man trying to resist temptation.

'I suppose we can have a drink, at least?' asked Dumbledore. 'For old times' sake?'

“请吧。”那人说。

他们背对背站着，一个又高又瘦，一个又矮又胖，步调一致地挥舞着魔杖。

家具一件件跳回原来的位置，装饰品在半空中恢复了原形，羽毛重新钻回了软垫里，破损的图书自动修复，整整齐齐地排列在书架上。油灯飞到墙边的小桌上，重新点亮了。一大堆碎裂的银色相框闪闪烁烁地飞到了房间那头，落在一张写字台上，重又变得光亮如新。房间各处破损、撕裂、豁开的地方都恢复如初。墙上的污迹也自动擦干净了。

“顺便问一句，那是什么血呀？”邓布利多问道，声音盖过了刚修好的老爷钟的钟摆声。

“墙上的？是火龙血。”这位名叫霍拉斯的巫师大声喊着回答，那盏枝形吊灯自动跳回天花板上，吱吱嘎嘎、叮叮当当的声音震耳欲聋。

随着钢琴最后发出咣啷一响，房间里总算安静下来。

“是啊，火龙血，”巫师谈兴很浓地说，“我的最后一瓶，目前价格贵得惊人。不过，也许还能用。”

他迈着沉重的脚步走到餐具柜前，拿起柜顶上的一只小水晶瓶，对着光线仔细看了看里面黏稠的液体。

“嗯，有点儿脏了。”

他把小瓶重新放到餐具柜上，叹了一口气。这时，他的目光才落在哈利的身上。

“嗬，”他说，圆圆的大眼睛立刻望向哈利的额头，以及额头上那道闪电形的伤疤，“嗬！”

“这位，”邓布利多走上前去做介绍，“是哈利·波特。哈利，这是我的一位老朋友、老同事，叫霍拉斯·斯拉格霍恩。”

斯拉格霍恩转向邓布利多，脸上一副机敏的表情。

“你以为靠这个就能说服我，是吗？我告诉你，阿不思，答案是不行！”

他推开哈利走了过去，并且坚决地把脸转向一边，像在抵御什么诱惑似的。

“我想，至少我们可以喝一杯吧？”邓布利多问，“为了过去的时光？”

Slughorn hesitated.

'All right then, one drink,' he said ungraciously.

Dumbledore smiled at Harry and directed him towards a chair not unlike the one that Slughorn had so recently impersonated, which stood right beside the newly burning fire and a brightly glowing oil lamp. Harry took the seat with the distinct impression that Dumbledore, for some reason, wanted to keep him as visible as possible. Certainly when Slughorn, who had been busy with decanters and glasses, turned to face the room again, his eyes fell immediately upon Harry.

'Humph,' he said, looking away quickly as though frightened of hurting his eyes. 'Here –' He gave a drink to Dumbledore, who had sat down without invitation, thrust the tray at Harry and then sank into the cushions of the repaired sofa and a disgruntled silence. His legs were so short that they did not touch the floor.

'Well, how have you been keeping, Horace?' Dumbledore asked.

'Not so well,' said Slughorn at once. 'Weak chest. Wheezy. Rheumatism too. Can't move like I used to. Well, that's to be expected. Old age. Fatigue.'

'And yet you must have moved fairly quickly to prepare such a welcome for us at such short notice,' said Dumbledore. 'You can't have had more than three minutes' warning?'

Slughorn said, half irritably, half proudly, 'Two. Didn't hear my Intruder Charm go off, I was taking a bath. Still,' he added sternly, seeming to pull himself back together again, 'the fact remains that I'm an old man, Albus. A tired old man who's earned the right to a quiet life and a few creature comforts.'

He certainly had those, thought Harry, looking around the room. It was stuffy and cluttered, yet nobody could say it was uncomfortable; there were soft chairs and footstools, drinks and books, boxes of chocolates and plump cushions. If Harry had not known who lived there, he would have guessed at a rich, fussy old lady.

'You're not yet as old as I am, Horace,' said Dumbledore.

'Well, maybe you ought to think about retirement yourself,' said Slughorn bluntly. His pale gooseberry eyes had found Dumbledore's injured hand. 'Reactions not what they were, I see.'

斯拉格霍恩迟疑着。

“好吧，就喝一杯。”他态度生硬地说。

邓布利多朝哈利笑了笑，领着他走向一把椅子。这把椅子很像斯拉格霍恩刚才冒充过的那把，椅子旁边是刚刚燃起的炉火和一盏明亮的油灯。哈利在椅子上坐了下来，他有一种感觉，似乎邓布利多出于某种原因，尽量把他安排在显眼的地方。果然，斯拉格霍恩对付完那些瓶子和杯子，重新转过脸来时，他的目光一下子就落在了哈利身上。

“哼。”他赶紧移开目光，好像害怕眼睛会受伤似的，“给——”他递了一杯给已经自己坐下来的邓布利多，又把托盘朝哈利面前一推，然后便坐进那张刚刚修复的沙发上的一堆软垫里，板着脸陷入了沉默。他的腿因为太短，够不着地面。

“怎么样，霍拉斯，近来你身子骨还好吧？”邓布利多问。

“不太好，”斯拉格霍恩立刻说道，“透不过气来。哮喘，还有风湿，腿脚不像以前那么灵便了。唉，这也是意料中的。人老了，不中用了。”

“不过，你在这么短的时间里准备了这么一个欢迎现场，动作肯定够敏捷的。”邓布利多说，“你得到警报的时间不会超过三分钟吧？”

斯拉格霍恩半是恼怒半是得意地说：“两分钟。我在洗澡，没听见我的入侵咒警报响了。不过，”他似乎重新镇静下来，板着脸说道，“事实不可否认，我是个老头子啦，阿不思。一个疲惫的老头子，有权过一种清静的生活，得到一些物质享受。”

他无疑不缺乏物质享受，哈利看了看房间里的摆设，想道。房间里又挤又乱，但没有人会说它不舒适。这里有软椅、垫脚凳、饮料和书籍，还有一盒盒巧克力和一堆鼓鼓囊囊的靠垫。如果哈利不知道是谁住在这里，准会猜想是一位挑剔讲究又上了年纪的贵妇人。

“你的年龄还没我大呢，霍拉斯。”邓布利多说。

“是啊，也许你自己也该考虑退休了。”斯拉格霍恩直话直说。他那双浅绿色的眼睛盯住了邓布利多受伤的手，“看得出来，反应不如过去那么敏捷了。”

'You're quite right,' said Dumbledore serenely, shaking back his sleeve to reveal the tips of those burned and blackened fingers; the sight of them made the back of Harry's neck prickle unpleasantly. 'I am undoubtedly slower than I was. But on the other hand …'

He shrugged and spread his hands wide, as though to say that age had its compensations, and Harry noticed a ring on his uninjured hand that he had never seen Dumbledore wear before: it was large, rather clumsily made of what looked like gold, and was set with a heavy black stone that had cracked down the middle. Slughorn's eyes lingered for a moment on the ring, too, and Harry saw a tiny frown momentarily crease his wide forehead.

'So, all these precautions against intruders, Horace … are they for the Death Eaters' benefit, or mine?' asked Dumbledore.

'What would the Death Eaters want with a poor broken-down old buffer like me?' demanded Slughorn.

'I imagine that they would want you to turn your considerable talents to coercion, torture and murder,' said Dumbledore. 'Are you really telling me that they haven't come recruiting yet?'

Slughorn eyed Dumbledore balefully for a moment, then muttered, 'I haven't given them the chance. I've been on the move for a year. Never stay in one place more than a week. Move from Muggle house to Muggle house – the owners of this place are on holiday in the Canary Islands. It's been very pleasant, I'll be sorry to leave. It's quite easy once you know how, one simple Freezing Charm on these absurd burglar alarms they use instead of Sneakoscopes and make sure the neighbours don't spot you bringing in the piano.'

'Ingenious,' said Dumbledore. 'But it sounds a rather tiring existence for a broken-down old buffer in search of a quiet life. Now, if you were to return to Hogwarts –'

'If you're going to tell me my life would be more peaceful at that pestilential school, you can save your breath, Albus! I might have been in hiding, but some funny rumours have reached me since Dolores Umbridge left! If that's how you treat teachers these days –'

'Professor Umbridge ran afoul of our centaur herd,' said Dumbledore. 'I think you, Horace, would have known better than to stride into the forest and call a horde of angry centaurs "filthy half-breeds".'

“你说得对，”邓布利多平静地说，把袖子往上抖了抖，露出了烧焦变黑的手指的指尖。哈利看了，觉得脖子后面一阵异样的刺痛。“我显然是比过去迟钝了。可是另一方面……”

他耸耸肩膀，摊开了两只手，似乎想说年老也有年老的好处。这时哈利注意到邓布利多那只没有受伤的手上戴着一枚戒指，是他以前从没见过的。戒指很大，像是金子做的，工艺粗糙，上面嵌着一块沉甸甸的、中间有裂纹的黑石头。斯拉格霍恩的目光也在戒指上停留了片刻，哈利看见有一瞬间他微微蹙起眉头，宽脑门上出现了几道皱纹。

“那么，霍拉斯，所有这些抵挡入侵者的安全措施……它们是针对食死徒的，还是针对我的呢？”邓布利多问。

“食死徒要我这把不中用的老骨头有什么用？”斯拉格霍恩反问道。

“我想，他们想把你的聪明才智用于镇压、酷刑和谋杀。”邓布利多说，“你敢说他们没有来拉你入伙吗？”

斯拉格霍恩恶狠狠地瞪了邓布利多片刻，然后低声说：“我没有给他们机会。一年来，我一直行踪不定。待在一个地方从来不超过一个星期。从一处麻瓜住宅搬到另一处麻瓜住宅——这幢房子的主人正在加那利群岛度假呢。我在这儿住得很舒服，真舍不得离开。一旦找到窍门就很容易啦，麻瓜们不用窥镜，而用那些可笑的防盗警报器，你只要在上面施一个冰冻咒，还有，搬钢琴进来时别让邻居们看见就行了。”

“真巧妙。”邓布利多说，“不过，对于一个想过清静日子的不中用的老家伙来说，这种生活不是太累人了吗？想一想，如果你回到霍格沃茨——”

“如果你想告诉我在那所讨厌的学校里我会生活得更平静，阿不思，你不妨省省力气，别再往下说了！不错，我是在到处东躲西藏，但自从多洛雷斯 · 乌姆里奇离开后，我也听说了一些离奇的传言！如果你们现在就是这样对待教师的——”

“乌姆里奇教授跟我们的那些马人发生了冲突。”邓布利多说，“我想，霍拉斯，你肯定不会大摇大摆地走进禁林，管一群愤怒的马人叫‘肮脏的杂种’吧？”

'That's what she did, did she?' said Slughorn. 'Idiotic woman. Never liked her.'

Harry chuckled and both Dumbledore and Slughorn looked round at him.

'Sorry,' Harry said hastily. 'It's just – I didn't like her, either.'

Dumbledore stood up rather suddenly.

'Are you leaving?' asked Slughorn at once, looking hopeful.

'No, I was wondering whether I might use your bathroom,' said Dumbledore.

'Oh,' said Slughorn, clearly disappointed. 'Second on the left down the hall.'

Dumbledore crossed the room. Once the door had closed behind him there was silence. After a few moments Slughorn got to his feet, but seemed uncertain what to do with himself. He shot a furtive look at Harry, then strode to the fire and turned his back on it, warming his wide behind.

'Don't think I don't know why he's brought you,' he said abruptly.

Harry merely looked at Slughorn. Slughorn's watery eyes slid over Harry's scar, this time taking in the rest of his face.

'You look very like your father.'

'Yeah, I've been told,' said Harry.

'Except for your eyes. You've got –'

'My mother's eyes, yeah.' Harry had heard it so often he found it a bit wearing.

'Humph. Yes, well. You shouldn't have favourites as a teacher, of course, but she was one of mine. Your mother,' Slughorn added, in answer to Harry's questioning look. 'Lily Evans. One of the brightest I ever taught. Vivacious, you know. Charming girl. I used to tell her she ought to have been in my house. Very cheeky answers I used to get back, too.'

'Which was your house?'

'I was Head of Slytherin,' said Slughorn. 'Oh, now,' he went on quickly, seeing the expression on Harry's face and wagging a stubby finger at him, 'don't go holding that against me! You'll be Gryffindor like her, I suppose? Yes, it usually goes in families. Not always, though. Ever heard of Sirius Black? You must have done – been in the papers for the last couple of years –

"她竟然做出这种事情？"斯拉格霍恩说，"真是个傻婆娘，我一向讨厌她。"

哈利轻轻地笑出了声，邓布利多和斯拉格霍恩都扭过头来看着他。

"对不起，"哈利赶紧说道，"只是——我也不喜欢她。"

邓布利多突然站了起来。

"你要走了吗？"斯拉格霍恩立刻满脸期待地问。

"不，我只想问一下我能不能用用你的卫生间。"邓布利多说。

"噢。"斯拉格霍恩显然很失望，说道，"顺着门厅，左边第二个门就是。"

邓布利多向房间那头走去。门在他身后关上后，房间里静下来。过了片刻，斯拉格霍恩站起身，但似乎拿不定主意要做什么。他偷偷瞥了一眼哈利，然后大步走到壁炉前，转身背对炉火，烘烤自己肥大的屁股。

"别以为我不知道他为什么把你带来。"他突然说道。

哈利只是看着斯拉格霍恩。斯拉格霍恩那双泪汪汪的眼睛瞟向了哈利的伤疤，而且这次把他的整张脸都看清楚了。

"你长得很像你父亲。"

"是的，别人也这么说。"哈利说。

"只是眼睛不像。你的眼睛——"

"像我母亲，是的。"这话哈利听了无数遍，都觉得有点腻烦了。

"哼。是啊。当然啦，作为一名教师，是不应该偏爱学生的，但我就是偏爱她。你的母亲，"斯拉格霍恩看到哈利疑问的目光，补充说道，"莉莉 · 伊万斯，是我教过的最聪明的学生之一。活泼可爱。一个迷人的姑娘。我经常对她说，她应该在我的学院才对。我经常得到她很不客气的回答。"

"你在哪个学院？"

"我当时是斯莱特林的院长。"斯拉格霍恩说。"哦，得了，"他看到哈利脸上的表情，立刻朝他晃着一根短粗的手指说道，"别因为这个就对我有敌意！我想，你一定像她一样，是格兰芬多的吧？是啊，一般都是世代相传。不过也有例外。听说过小天狼星布莱克吗？你肯定

died a few weeks ago –'

It was as though an invisible hand had twisted Harry's intestines and held them tight.

'Well, anyway, he was a big pal of your father's at school. The whole Black family had been in my house, but Sirius ended up in Gryffindor! Shame – he was a talented boy. I got his brother Regulus when he came along, but I'd have liked the set.'

He sounded like an enthusiastic collector who had been outbid at auction. Apparently lost in memories, he gazed at the opposite wall, turning idly on the spot to ensure an even heat on his backside.

'Your mother was Muggle-born, of course. Couldn't believe it when I found out. Thought she must have been pure-blood, she was so good.'

'One of my best friends is Muggle-born,' said Harry, 'and she's the best in our year.'

'Funny how that sometimes happens, isn't it?' said Slughorn.

'Not really,' said Harry coldly.

Slughorn looked down at him in surprise.

'You mustn't think I'm prejudiced!' he said. 'No, no, no! Haven't I just said your mother was one of my all-time favourite students? And there was Dirk Cresswell in the year after her, too – now Head of the Goblin Liaison Office, of course – another Muggle-born, a very gifted student, and still gives me excellent inside information on the goings-on at Gringotts!'

He bounced up and down a little, smiling in a self-satisfied way, and pointed at the many glittering photograph frames on the dresser, each peopled with tiny moving occupants.

'All ex-students, all signed. You'll notice Barnabas Cuffe, editor of the *Daily Prophet*, he's always interested to hear my take on the day's news. And Ambrosius Flume, of Honeydukes – a hamper every birthday, and all because I was able to give him an introduction to Ciceron Harkiss, who gave him his first job! and at the back – you'll see her if you just crane your neck – that's Gwenog Jones, who of course captains the Holyhead Harpies … people are always astonished to hear I'm on first-name terms with the Harpies, and free tickets whenever I want them!'

听说过——前两年报上经常出现的——几个星期前死了——”

似乎有一双无形的手紧紧揪住了哈利的五脏六腑。

“是啊，想当年，他可是你父亲在学校的好朋友。布莱克家的人都在我的学院，没想到小天狼星却到了格兰芬多！真可惜——他是个很有天分的男孩。他弟弟雷古勒斯一来我就把他弄到手了，但要是兄弟俩都在我那儿就好了。”

他说话的口气，就像一位热心的收藏家在拍卖中输给了对手。他显然陷入了回忆，眼睛望着对面的墙壁，身子懒洋洋地原地转动，好让整个后背均匀受热。

“当然啦，你母亲是麻瓜出身。我发现这一点时简直不敢相信。我本来以为，她那么优秀，肯定是纯血统的。”

“我有一个最好的朋友也是麻瓜出身，”哈利说，“她是全年级最优秀的学生。”

“有时候就会出现这种事，真奇怪，是不是？”斯拉格霍恩说。

“不奇怪。”哈利冷冷地说。

斯拉格霍恩吃惊地低头看着他。

“你可别以为我有偏见！”他说，“不，不，不！我不是刚说过，你母亲是我这辈子最喜欢的学生之一吗？还有比她低一级的德克 · 克莱斯韦——现在是妖精联络处的主任——也是麻瓜出身，一个资质很高的学生，现在仍然经常向我透露古灵阁里宝贵的内部消息！”

他脸上带着得意的笑容，往上跳了跳，指着柜子上那许多闪闪发亮的相框，每个相框里都有活动的小人儿。

“这都是我以前的学生，都是签名照片。你会看见巴拿巴斯 · 古费，《预言家日报》的编辑，他总是很有兴趣听我对时局发表见解。还有蜂蜜公爵糖果店的安布罗修 · 弗鲁姆——每年我过生日时，他都要送我一个礼品篮，因为当年是我把他介绍给了西塞隆 · 哈基斯，使他得到了他的第一份工作！还有后面——你伸长脖子就能看见——是格韦诺格 · 琼斯，霍利黑德哈比队的队长……人们经常奇怪我为什么跟哈比队队员的交情那么好，只要我愿意，就能搞到不花钱的球票！”

This thought seemed to cheer him up enormously.

'And all these people know where to find you, to send you stuff?' asked Harry, who could not help wondering why the Death Eaters had not yet tracked down Slughorn if hampers of sweets, Quidditch tickets and visitors craving his advice and opinions could find him.

The smile slid from Slughorn's face as quickly as the blood from his walls.

'Of course not,' he said, looking down at Harry. 'I have been out of touch with everybody for a year.'

Harry had the impression that the words shocked Slughorn himself; he looked quite unsettled for a moment. Then he shrugged.

'Still … the prudent wizard keeps his head down in such times. All very well for Dumbledore to talk, but taking up a post at Hogwarts just now would be tantamount to declaring my public allegiance to the Order of the Phoenix! And while I'm sure they're very admirable and brave and all the rest of it, I don't personally fancy the mortality rate –'

'You don't have to join the Order to teach at Hogwarts,' said Harry, who could not quite keep a note of derision out of his voice: it was hard to sympathise with Slughorn's cosseted existence when he remembered Sirius, crouching in a cave and living on rats. 'Most of the teachers aren't in it and none of them has ever been killed – well, unless you count Quirrell, and he got what he deserved seeing as he was working with Voldemort.'

Harry had been sure Slughorn would be one of those wizards who could not bear to hear Voldemort's name spoken aloud, and was not disappointed: Slughorn gave a shudder and a squawk of protest, which Harry ignored.

'I reckon the staff are safer than most people while Dumbledore's headmaster; he's supposed to be the only one Voldemort ever feared, isn't he?' Harry went on.

Slughorn gazed into space for a moment or two: he seemed to be thinking over Harry's words.

'Well, yes, it is true that He Who Must Not Be Named has never sought a fight with Dumbledore,' he muttered grudgingly. 'And I suppose one could argue that as I have not joined the Death Eaters, He Who Must Not Be Named can hardly count me a friend … in which case, I might well be safer a little closer to Albus … I cannot pretend that Amelia Bones's death did not

说到这里，他似乎情绪大振。

“这些人都知道在哪儿能找到你，能把东西送给你吗？”哈利问，他忍不住怀疑，既然装满糖果的礼品篮、魁地奇球票，以及征询他的观点和忠告的那些人都能找到斯拉格霍恩，食死徒怎么会追查不到他的下落呢？

斯拉格霍恩的笑容突然从脸上滑落下来，就像刚才墙上的血迹一样。

“当然不能，”他低头看着哈利说，“我已经一年没有跟任何人联系了。”

哈利感觉到斯拉格霍恩被自己的话吓了一跳。一时间，他显得有点不安，接着耸了耸肩。

“不过……这年头，谨慎的巫师都尽量不抛头露面。邓布利多说得也有道理，但这个时候到霍格沃茨任职，就等于公开宣布我是拥护凤凰社的！尽管我相信他们勇敢无畏，令人钦佩，但是我个人不太喜欢那种死亡率——”

“你到霍格沃茨来教书，不一定要加入凤凰社啊。”哈利说，口气里忍不住透着一点嘲笑。想到小天狼星躲在山洞里，靠吃老鼠活命，他很难同情斯拉格霍恩这种养尊处优的生活。“大多数教师都不是凤凰社的成员，而且没有一个人被害——当然啦，除非你把奇洛算上，但那是他活该，因为他是替伏地魔卖命的。”

哈利知道斯拉格霍恩肯定会像其他巫师一样，听到他大声说出伏地魔的名字就吓得不行。果然不出所料，斯拉格霍恩打了个寒战，尖叫一声以示抗议，但哈利没有理会。

“我认为，只要邓布利多担任校长，学校的教工就会比大多数人都安全。据说，伏地魔只害怕他一个人，是不是？”哈利继续说。

斯拉格霍恩出了一会儿神，似乎在仔细考虑哈利的话。

“唉，是啊，那个连名字都不能提的人确实从来没敢跟邓布利多较量过。”他满不情愿地嘟囔道，“我想，既然我没有加入食死徒，那个连名字都不能提的人就不可能把我当成朋友……那样的话，我待在阿不思身边恐怕会更安全些……我不能假装阿米莉亚·博恩斯的死对我

shake me … if she, with all her Ministry contacts and protection …'

Dumbledore re-entered the room and Slughorn jumped as though he had forgotten he was in the house.

'Oh, there you are, Albus,' he said. 'You've been a very long time. Upset stomach?'

'No, I was merely reading the Muggle magazines,' said Dumbledore. 'I do love knitting patterns. Well, Harry, we have trespassed upon Horace's hospitality quite long enough; I think it is time for us to leave.'

Not at all reluctant to obey, Harry jumped to his feet. Slughorn seemed taken aback.

'You're leaving?'

'Yes, indeed. I think I know a lost cause when I see one.'

'Lost …?'

Slughorn seemed agitated. He twiddled his fat thumbs and fidgeted as he watched Dumbledore fastening his travelling cloak and Harry zipping up his jacket.

'Well, I'm sorry you don't want the job, Horace,' said Dumbledore, raising his uninjured hand in a farewell salute. 'Hogwarts would have been glad to see you back again. Our greatly increased security not-withstanding, you will always be welcome to visit, should you wish to.'

'Yes … well … very gracious … as I say …'

'Goodbye, then.'

'Bye,' said Harry.

They were at the front door when there was a shout from behind them.

'All right, all right, I'll do it!'

Dumbledore turned to see Slughorn standing breathless in the doorway to the sitting room.

'You will come out of retirement?'

'Yes, yes,' said Slughorn impatiently. 'I must be mad, but yes.'

'Wonderful,' said Dumbledore, beaming. 'Then, Horace, we shall see you on the first of September.'

'Yes, I daresay you will,' grunted Slughorn.

毫无触动……她在部里有那么多熟人，那么多保护，都……”

邓布利多重新走进了屋里，斯拉格霍恩吓了一跳，他似乎忘记了邓布利多还没离开这幢房子。

“哦，你回来了，阿不思，”他说，“你去的时间可不短啊，闹肚子了？”

“没有，我只是翻了翻那些麻瓜杂志。”邓布利多说，“我很喜欢毛衣编织图案。好了，哈利，我们已经叨扰霍拉斯很长时间了，我认为我们应该告辞了。”

哈利欣然从命，立刻站了起来。斯拉格霍恩似乎吃了一惊。

“你们要走了？”

“是啊。我想，我能看得出来败局已定。”

“败局……？”

斯拉格霍恩显得很不安。他摆弄着两根胖胖的大拇指，焦虑地看着邓布利多裹紧旅行斗篷，哈利拉上他的夹克衫拉链。

“唉，我很遗憾你不肯接受这份工作，霍拉斯，”邓布利多说着举起那只没有受伤的手，做了个告别的姿势，“如果你能回来，霍格沃茨会很高兴的。尽管我们大大加强了安全防范措施，但只要你愿意，随时欢迎你过来看看。”

“好……唉……太客气了……我说过……”

“那就再见了。”

“再见。”哈利说。

他们刚走到前门，就听见身后传来一声喊叫。

“好吧，好吧，我干！”

邓布利多一转身，看见斯拉格霍恩气喘吁吁地站在客厅门口。

“你愿意重新出来工作？”

“是啊，是啊，”斯拉格霍恩不耐烦地说，“我肯定是疯了，但是没错，我愿意。”

“太好了。”邓布利多顿时喜形于色，“那么，霍拉斯，我们九月一日见。”

“好吧，没问题。”斯拉格霍恩嘟囔道。

As they set off down the garden path, Slughorn's voice floated after them.

'I'll want a pay rise, Dumbledore!'

Dumbledore chuckled. The garden gate swung shut behind them and they set off back down the hill through the dark and the swirling mist.

'Well done, Harry,' said Dumbledore.

'I didn't do anything,' said Harry in surprise.

'Oh yes you did. You showed Horace exactly how much he stands to gain by returning to Hogwarts. Did you like him?'

'Er …'

Harry wasn't sure whether he liked Slughorn or not. He supposed he had been pleasant in his way, but he had also seemed vain and, whatever he said to the contrary, much too surprised that a Muggle-born should make a good witch.

'Horace,' said Dumbledore, relieving Harry of the responsibility to say any of this, 'likes his comfort. He also likes the company of the famous, the successful and the powerful. He enjoys the feeling that he influences these people. He has never wanted to occupy the throne himself; he prefers the back seat – more room to spread out, you see. He used to handpick favourites at Hogwarts, sometimes for their ambition or their brains, sometimes for their charm or their talent, and he had an uncanny knack for choosing those who would go on to become outstanding in their various fields. Horace formed a kind of club of his favourites with himself at the centre, making introductions, forging useful contacts between members, and always reaping some kind of benefit in return, whether a free box of his favourite crystallised pineapple or the chance to recommend the next junior member of the Goblin Liaison Office.'

Harry had a sudden and vivid mental image of a great swollen spider, spinning a web around him, twitching a thread here and there to bring its large and juicy flies a little closer.

'I tell you all this,' Dumbledore continued, 'not to turn you against Horace – or, as we must now call him, Professor Slughorn – but to put you on your guard. He will undoubtedly try to collect you, Harry. You would be the jewel of his collection: the Boy Who Lived … or, as they call you these days, the Chosen One.'

他们走在花园的小径上时，身后又传来了斯拉格霍恩的声音。

“我会要求涨工资的，邓布利多！”

邓布利多轻声笑了。花园的门在他们身后自动关上，他们穿过黑压压的、袅袅绕绕的迷雾，朝山下走去。

“干得不错，哈利。”邓布利多说。

“我什么也没做呀。”哈利吃惊地说。

“噢，你做了。你让霍拉斯看到了他回霍格沃茨能得到多少好处。你喜欢他吗？”

“嗯……”

哈利不能肯定自己是不是喜欢斯拉格霍恩。他觉得斯拉格霍恩在某些方面还是挺讨人喜欢的，但似乎有些虚荣。还有，虽然他嘴上说的是另一套，但他对于一个麻瓜出身的人竟能成为出色的女巫，表露出了太多的惊讶。

“霍拉斯喜欢物质享受，”邓布利多接着说道，哈利就用不着把他这些心里想法说出来了，“还喜欢结交著名的、成功的、有权有势的人物。他喜欢那种别人受他影响的感觉。他自己从来不想掌管大权，而更喜欢屈居幕后——那样天地更宽，更加游刃有余。他在霍格沃茨时，总愿意挑选自己最喜欢的学生，有时是因为他们的抱负或智慧，有时是因为他们的魅力或天赋，而且他有一种很不寻常的本领，总能挑选到日后会在各行各业出人头地的人。霍拉斯以自己为核心搞了一个俱乐部，由他的得意门生组成。他让他们之间互相认识，建立有用的联系，最后总能获得某种好处，或是免费得到一箱他最喜欢的菠萝蜜饯，或是有机会向妖精联络处推荐一名办事员。”

哈利脑海里立刻出现了一只胖鼓鼓的大蜘蛛，它这里吐一根丝，那里吐一根丝，在身体周围结了一张网，把美味多汁的大苍蝇引到自己身边。

“我告诉你这些，”邓布利多继续说，“不是叫你对霍拉斯——我们现在必须称他为斯拉格霍恩教授了——产生反感，而是希望你保持警惕。他肯定会来拉拢你的，哈利。你会成为他收藏品中的瑰宝：大难不死的男孩……或者，用他们最近对你的称呼，‘救世之星’。”

At these words, a chill that had nothing to do with the surrounding mist stole over Harry. He was reminded of words he had heard a few weeks ago, words that had a horrible and particular meaning to him:

Neither can live while the other survives …

Dumbledore had stopped walking, level with the church they had passed earlier.

'This will do, Harry. If you will grasp my arm.'

Braced this time, Harry was ready for the Apparition, but still found it unpleasant. When the pressure disappeared and he found himself able to breathe again, he was standing in a country lane beside Dumbledore and looking ahead to the crooked silhouette of his second favourite building in the world: The Burrow. In spite of the feeling of dread that had just swept through him, his spirits could not help but lift at the sight of it. Ron was in there … and so was Mrs Weasley, who could cook better than anyone he knew …

'If you don't mind, Harry,' said Dumbledore, as they passed through the gate, 'I'd like a few words with you before we part. In private. Perhaps in here?'

Dumbledore pointed towards a run-down stone outhouse where the Weasleys kept their broomsticks. A little puzzled, Harry followed Dumbledore through the creaking door into a space a little smaller than the average cupboard. Dumbledore illuminated the tip of his wand, so that it glowed like a torch, and smiled down at Harry.

'I hope you will forgive me for mentioning it, Harry, but I am pleased and a little proud at how well you seem to be coping after everything that happened at the Ministry. Permit me to say that I think Sirius would have been proud of you.'

Harry swallowed; his voice seemed to have deserted him. He did not think he could stand to discuss Sirius. It had been painful enough to hear Uncle Vernon say 'His godfather's dead?'; even worse to hear Sirius's name thrown out casually by Slughorn.

'It was cruel,' said Dumbledore softly, 'that you and Sirius had such a short time together. A brutal ending to what should have been a long and happy relationship.'

听了这些话，哈利身上起了一丝寒意，这寒意与周围的浓雾没有关系。他想起了几个星期前听到的那句话，那句对他有着可怕而特殊含义的话：

两个人不能都活着……

邓布利多已经停下脚步，站在与他们先前经过的那座教堂平行的地方。

“行了，哈利。你只要抓紧我的胳膊。”

这次，哈利对幻影显形有了心理准备，但仍然觉得很不舒服。当压力消失，他发现自己又能顺畅地呼吸时，他已和邓布利多并肩站在一条乡村小路上，面前那个歪歪斜斜的剪影，正是他在这个世界上第二喜欢的地方：陋居。尽管刚才有一丝恐惧侵入他的内心，但一看到陋居，他的情绪就不由得欢快起来。这里有罗恩……还有韦斯莱夫人，她做的饭菜，比他认识的任何人做的都好吃……

“如果你不反对，哈利，”他们穿过大门时，邓布利多说，“分手前我想跟你说几句话。不想让别人听见。也许就在那里？”

邓布利多指着房子外面一间破败的小石屋，那是韦斯莱一家放扫帚的地方。哈利有些困惑地跟着邓布利多走进嘎吱作响的小门，来到一个比普通储物间还要小上一点儿的地方。邓布利多点亮魔杖，让它像火把一样照明，然后他微笑地看着哈利。

“哈利，希望你能原谅我提起这个话题，但是在部里发生了那些事情之后，你似乎一直应对得不错，对此我很高兴，还有点儿自豪。请允许我说一句，我认为小天狼星也会为你感到自豪的。”

哈利咽了口唾沫，他的声音好像弃他而去了。他认为自己无法忍受谈论小天狼星。听到弗农姨父说“他的教父死了？”就已经使他很痛苦了，后来听斯拉格霍恩那么轻描淡写地吐出小天狼星的名字，更让他感到伤心。

“这很残酷，”邓布利多温和地说，“你和小天狼星只在一起待了那么短的时间。你们本来应该一起共度许多快乐时光，这种结局真让人难受。”

Harry nodded, his eyes fixed resolutely on the spider now climbing Dumbledore's hat. He could tell that Dumbledore understood, that he might even suspect that until his letter arrived Harry had spent nearly all his time at the Dursleys' lying on his bed, refusing meals and staring at the misted window, full of the chill emptiness that he had come to associate with Dementors.

'It's just hard,' Harry said finally, in a low voice, 'to realise he won't write to me again.'

His eyes burned suddenly and he blinked. He felt stupid for admitting it, but the fact that he had had someone outside Hogwarts who cared what happened to him, almost like a parent, had been one of the best things about discovering his godfather … and now the post owls would never bring him that comfort again …

'Sirius represented much to you that you had never known before,' said Dumbledore gently. 'Naturally, the loss is devastating …'

'But while I was at the Dursleys',' interrupted Harry, his voice growing stronger, 'I realised I can't shut myself away or – or crack up. Sirius wouldn't have wanted that, would he? And anyway, life's too short … look at Madam Bones, look at Emmeline Vance … it could be me next, couldn't it? But if it is,' he said fiercely, now looking straight into Dumbledore's blue eyes, gleaming in the wand-light, 'I'll make sure I take as many Death Eaters with me as I can, and Voldemort too if I can manage it.'

'Spoken both like your mother and father's son and Sirius's true godson!' said Dumbledore, with an approving pat on Harry's back. 'I take my hat off to you – or I would, if I were not afraid of showering you in spiders.

'And now, Harry, on a closely related subject … I gather that you have been taking the *Daily Prophet* over the last two weeks?'

'Yes,' said Harry, and his heart beat a little faster.

'Then you will have seen that there have been not so much leaks, as floods, concerning your adventure in the Hall of Prophecy?'

'Yes,' said Harry again. 'And now everyone knows that I'm the one –'

'No, they do not,' interrupted Dumbledore. 'There are only two people in the whole world who know the full contents of the prophecy made about you and Lord Voldemort, and they are both standing in this smelly, spidery broom shed. It is true, however, that many have guessed, correctly, that

哈利点了点头，眼睛固执地盯着一只正往邓布利多帽子上爬的蜘蛛。他可以感觉到邓布利多是理解他的，邓布利多甚至可能猜到，哈利在收到那封信之前，几乎从早到晚都躺在德思礼家的床上，不吃不喝，盯着水汽模糊的窗户，内心充满了如同摄魂怪留下的那种空洞和寒意。

"很难相信，"哈利终于低声说道，"他再也不会给我写信了。"

他的眼睛突然火辣辣的，赶紧眨了眨眼。他不好意思承认，实际上，找到教父之后给他带来的最美好的一件事情，就是知道有一个人在霍格沃茨校外像父母一样时刻关心着他……如今，送信的猫头鹰再也不会带给他那种慰藉了……

"对你来说，小天狼星代表着许多你以前从不知道的东西。"邓布利多温和地说，"失去他肯定令你感到无比痛苦……"

"可是我在德思礼家的时候，"哈利打断了他的话，声音变得有力了，"我知道我不能把自己封闭起来，也不能——不能自暴自弃。小天狼星肯定不愿意这样，是吗？生命太短暂了……看看博恩斯女士，看看爱米琳 · 万斯……下一个可能就是我，对不对？如果真的轮到我，"他直视着邓布利多那双在魔杖的亮光下闪烁的蓝眼睛，激动地说，"我一定要尽量多消灭几个食死徒，如果可能的话，就跟伏地魔同归于尽。"

"说得好，不愧是你父母的儿子、小天狼星的教子！"邓布利多说着赞许地拍了拍哈利的后背，"我要脱帽向你表示敬意——我很想这么做，但我担心会弄得你满身都是蜘蛛。

"另外，哈利，还有一个与此密切相关的话题……我想，最近两个星期你一直都在订阅《预言家日报》吧？"

"是的。"哈利说，心脏突然跳得更快了。

"那你就会看到，你在预言厅的那场经历像洪水一样泄漏出去了，是吗？"

"是啊，"哈利又说道，"现在大家都知道我是——"

"不，他们不知道，"邓布利多打断了他的话，"世界上只有两个人知道那个关于你和伏地魔的预言的完整内容，而这两个人眼下都站在这间臭烘烘的、爬满蜘蛛的扫帚棚里。不过，确实有许多人猜到了伏

Voldemort sent his Death Eaters to steal a prophecy, and that the prophecy concerned you.

'Now, I think I am correct in saying that you have not told anybody that you know what the prophecy said?'

'No,' said Harry.

'A wise decision, on the whole,' said Dumbledore. 'Although I think you ought to relax it in favour of your friends, Mr Ronald Weasley and Miss Hermione Granger. Yes,' he continued, when Harry looked startled, 'I think they ought to know. You do them a disservice by not confiding something this important to them.'

'I didn't want –'

'– to worry or frighten them?' said Dumbledore, surveying Harry over the top of his half-moon spectacles. 'Or perhaps, to confess that you yourself are worried and frightened? You need your friends, Harry. As you so rightly said, Sirius would not have wanted you to shut yourself away.'

Harry said nothing, but Dumbledore did not seem to require an answer. He continued, 'On a different, though related, subject, it is my wish that you take private lessons with me this year.'

'Private – with you?' said Harry, surprised out of his preoccupied silence.

'Yes. I think it is time that I took a greater hand in your education.'

'What will you be teaching me, sir?'

'Oh, a little of this, a little of that,' said Dumbledore airily.

Harry waited hopefully, but Dumbledore did not elaborate, so he asked something else that had been bothering him slightly.

'If I'm having lessons with you, I won't have to do Occlumency lessons with Snape, will I?'

'*Professor* Snape, Harry – and no, you will not.'

'Good,' said Harry in relief, 'because they were a –'

He stopped, careful not to say what he really thought.

'I think the word "fiasco" would be a good one here,' said Dumbledore, nodding.

Harry laughed.

'Well, that means I won't see much of Professor Snape from now on,' he said, 'because he won't let me carry on Potions unless I get "Outstanding" in my O.W.L., which I know I haven't.'

地魔曾派他的食死徒去盗取一个预言球，而那个预言跟你有关。

“那么，我可不可以断言，你没有告诉任何人你知道预言的内容呢？”

“没有。”哈利说。

“总的来说，这么做是明智的，”邓布利多说，“不过我认为你不妨在你的朋友罗恩·韦斯莱先生和赫敏·格兰杰小姐面前松松口。是啊，”看到哈利惊愕的神色，他又说道，“我认为可以让他们知道。你把这么重要的事情瞒着他们，会伤害他们的感情的。”

“我不想——”

“——让他们担惊受怕？”邓布利多从他的半月形眼镜片上方打量着哈利，说道，“或者，不想坦白你自己的担心和恐惧？哈利，你需要朋友。你刚才说得对，小天狼星肯定不愿意你把自己封闭起来。”

哈利什么也没说，但邓布利多似乎并不需要他做出回答。他接着说道：“再谈另外一个与此有关的话题，我希望这学期给你单独上课。”

“单独上课——跟你？”哈利太惊讶了，从沉思中突然回过神来。

“是的。我想，现在我应该更多地管管你的教育了。”

“你会教我什么呢，先生？”

“噢，教一点这个，教一点那个呗。”邓布利多轻描淡写地说。

哈利还等着往下听，但邓布利多不再多说了，于是哈利就问了一件一直困扰着他的事情。

“如果我跟你上课，就用不着跟斯内普学习大脑封闭术了，是吗？”

“是斯内普教授，哈利——是的，用不着了。”

“太好了，”哈利如释重负，“那些课简直就是——”

他停住了，强忍着没把心里的想法说出来。

“我认为‘彻底失败’这个词用在这里很合适。”邓布利多点点头说。

哈利笑了起来。

“啊，那就意味着我从此不大见得到斯内普教授了，”他说，“除非我 O.W.L. 得了‘优秀’，不然他是不会让我选修魔药学的，但我知道我肯定拿不到‘优秀’。”

'Don't count your owls before they are delivered,' said Dumbledore gravely. 'Which, now I think of it, ought to be some time later today. Now, two more things, Harry, before we part.

'Firstly, I wish you to keep your Invisibility Cloak with you at all times from this moment onwards. Even within Hogwarts itself. Just in case, you understand me?'

Harry nodded.

'And lastly, while you stay here, The Burrow has been given the highest security the Ministry of Magic can provide. These measures have caused a certain amount of inconvenience to Arthur and Molly – all their post, for instance, is being searched at the Ministry, before being sent on. They do not mind in the slightest, for their only concern is your safety. However, it would be poor repayment if you risked your neck while staying with them.'

'I understand,' said Harry quickly.

'Very well, then,' said Dumbledore, pushing open the broom-shed door and stepping out into the yard. 'I see a light in the kitchen. Let us not deprive Molly any longer of the chance to deplore how thin you are.'

“信没送到之前，先别忙着数猫头鹰。”邓布利多沉着脸说，“估计成绩在今天什么时候就能送到了。好了，哈利，分手之前，还有两件事。

“第一，我希望从此以后，你把你的隐形衣时刻带在身上，即使是在霍格沃茨校内。以防万一，明白吗？”

哈利点点头。

“最后，你住在这里时，陋居得到了魔法部所能提供的最严密的安全保护。这些措施给亚瑟和莫丽带来了一定程度的不便——比如，他们所有的邮件都要经部里审查后才能送达。但他们丝毫不介意，一心只牵挂着你的安全。可是，如果你跟他们住在一起时冒险胡来，可就太对不起他们了。”

“我明白。”哈利赶紧说道。

“那就好，”邓布利多说完，推开了扫帚棚的门，走到外面的院子里，“我看见厨房里亮着灯。我们就让莫丽赶紧有机会哀叹你瘦成什么样了吧。”

CHAPTER FIVE

An Excess of Phlegm

Harry and Dumbledore approached the back door of The Burrow, which was surrounded by the familiar litter of old wellington boots and rusty cauldrons; Harry could hear the soft clucking of sleepy chickens coming from a distant shed. Dumbledore knocked three times and Harry saw sudden movement behind the kitchen window.

'Who's there?' said a nervous voice that he recognised as Mrs Weasley's. 'Declare yourself!'

'It is I, Dumbledore, bringing Harry.'

The door opened at once. There stood Mrs Weasley, short, plump and wearing an old green dressing-gown.

'Harry, dear! Gracious, Albus, you gave me a fright, you said not to expect you before morning!'

'We were lucky,' said Dumbledore, ushering Harry over the threshold. 'Slughorn proved much more persuadable than I had expected. Harry's doing, of course. Ah, hello, Nymphadora!'

Harry looked around and saw that Mrs Weasley was not alone, despite the lateness of the hour. A young witch with a pale, heart-shaped face and mousy-brown hair was sitting at the table clutching a large mug between her hands.

'Hello, Professor,' she said. 'Wotcher, Harry.'

'Hi, Tonks.'

Harry thought she looked drawn, even ill, and there was something forced in her smile. Certainly her appearance was less colourful than usual without her customary shade of bubblegum-pink hair.

第 5 章

黏痰过多

哈利和邓布利多朝陋居的后门走去，那里仍然像以前一样乱糟糟地堆放着许多旧靴子和生锈的坩埚。哈利听见远处棚子里传来鸡睡着时发出的轻轻咕咕声。邓布利多在门上敲了三下，哈利看见厨房的窗户后面突然有了动静。

“是谁？”一个声音紧张地问，哈利听出是韦斯莱夫人，“报上尊姓大名！”

“是我，邓布利多，带着哈利。”

门立刻就开了。门口站着韦斯莱夫人，矮矮胖胖的，身上穿着一件旧的绿色睡袍。

“哈利，亲爱的！天哪，阿不思，你吓了我一跳，你说过你们明天早晨才会来的！”

“我们运气不坏，”邓布利多把哈利让进屋，说道，“斯拉格霍恩很容易就说通了，根本不像我原来想的那么困难。当然啦，这都是哈利的功劳。啊，你好，尼法朵拉！”

哈利环顾一下周围，才发现尽管时间已经很晚了，韦斯莱夫人却并不是独自一人。一个年轻的女巫正坐在桌旁，两只手里捧着一个大茶杯。她心形的面孔显得有些苍白，头发是灰褐色的。

“你好，教授。”她说，“你好哇，哈利。”

“你好，唐克斯。”

哈利觉得她神情憔悴，甚至有些病态，笑容里也带着一些勉强的成分。她的头发不再是平常那种泡泡糖般的粉红色，这无疑使她的模样少了几分生气。

'I'd better be off,' she said quickly, standing up and pulling her cloak around her shoulders. 'Thanks for the tea and sympathy, Molly.'

'Please don't leave on my account,' said Dumbledore courteously. 'I cannot stay, I have urgent matters to discuss with Rufus Scrimgeour.'

'No, no, I need to get going,' said Tonks, not meeting Dumbledore's eyes. ''Night –'

'Dear, why not come to dinner at the weekend, Remus and Mad-Eye are coming –?'

'No, really, Molly … thanks anyway … goodnight, everyone.'

Tonks hurried past Dumbledore and Harry into the yard; a few paces beyond the doorstep, she turned on the spot and vanished into thin air. Harry noticed that Mrs Weasley looked troubled.

'Well, I shall see you at Hogwarts, Harry,' said Dumbledore. 'Take care of yourself. Molly, your servant.'

He made Mrs Weasley a bow and followed Tonks, vanishing at precisely the same spot. Mrs Weasley closed the door on the empty yard and then steered Harry by the shoulders into the full glow of the lantern on the table to examine his appearance.

'You're like Ron,' she sighed, looking him up and down. 'Both of you look as though you've had Stretching Jinxes put on you. I swear Ron's grown four inches since I last bought him school robes. Are you hungry, Harry?'

'Yeah, I am,' said Harry, suddenly realising just how hungry he was.

'Sit down, dear, I'll knock something up.'

As Harry sat down a furry ginger cat with a squashed face jumped on to his knees and settled there, purring.

'So Hermione's here?' he asked happily as he tickled Crookshanks behind the ear.

'Oh yes, she arrived the day before yesterday,' said Mrs Weasley, rapping a large iron pot with her wand: it bounced on to the stove with a loud clang and began to bubble at once. 'Everyone's in bed, of course, we didn't expect you for hours. Here you are –'

She tapped the pot again; it rose into the air, flew towards Harry and tipped over; Mrs Weasley slid a bowl neatly beneath it just in time to catch the stream of thick, steaming onion soup.

“我得走了。”她仓促地说，起身用斗篷裹住肩膀，“谢谢你的茶，谢谢你的安慰，莫丽。”

“请别因为我的缘故而离开。”邓布利多谦恭有礼地说，“我不能久待，我还有要紧的事情去跟鲁弗斯·斯克林杰商量呢。”

“不是，不是，我确实要走了。”唐克斯躲避着邓布利多的目光说，“晚安……”

“亲爱的，周末来吃晚饭吧，莱姆斯和疯眼汉都来——”

“不了，莫丽，真的不了……非常感谢……祝你们大家晚安。”

唐克斯匆匆地从邓布利多和哈利身边走进院子，下了台阶后走了几步，原地转了个身，便一下子消失了。哈利注意到韦斯莱夫人显得很烦恼。

“好了，我们在霍格沃茨再见，哈利，”邓布利多说，“好好照顾自己。莫丽，有事尽管吩咐。”

他朝韦斯莱夫人鞠了一躬，紧跟在唐克斯后面，就在同一个地方消失了。院子里没了人，韦斯莱夫人关上门，扶着哈利的肩膀，把他领到桌上那盏灯的灯光下，仔细端详他的模样。

“你跟罗恩一样，”她上上下下地打量着哈利，说道，“你们俩都好像中了伸展咒似的。我敢说，自从我上次给罗恩买校袍到现在，他长了整整四英寸。你饿了吗，哈利？”

“是啊，饿了。”哈利这才发现他确实饿坏了。

“坐下吧，亲爱的。我这就给你做点儿吃的。”

哈利刚坐下，一只扁平脸、毛茸茸的姜黄色的猫就跳上了他的膝头，趴在他腿上呼噜呼噜地叫着。

“赫敏也在这儿？”他挠着克鲁克山的耳朵根，高兴地问。

“是啊，她是前天来的。”韦斯莱夫人说着用魔杖敲了敲一只大铁锅。铁锅咣当一声跳到炉子上，立刻开始翻滚冒泡。“当然啦，这会儿大家都睡觉了，我们以为你过几个小时才会来呢。给——”

她又敲了敲铁锅。铁锅升到空中，朝哈利飞来，然后歪向一边，韦斯莱夫人赶紧把一个碗塞在下面，正好接住了铁锅倒出来的浓浓的、热气腾腾的洋葱汤。

'Bread, dear?'

'Thanks, Mrs Weasley.'

She waved her wand over her shoulder; a loaf of bread and a knife soared gracefully on to the table. As the loaf sliced itself and the soup pot dropped back on to the stove, Mrs Weasley sat down opposite him.

'So you persuaded Horace Slughorn to take the job?'

Harry nodded, his mouth so full of hot soup that he could not speak.

'He taught Arthur and me,' said Mrs Weasley. 'He was at Hogwarts for ages, started around the same time as Dumbledore, I think. Did you like him?'

His mouth now full of bread, Harry shrugged and gave a noncommittal jerk of the head.

'I know what you mean,' said Mrs Weasley, nodding wisely. 'Of course he can be charming when he wants to be, but Arthur's never liked him much. The Ministry's littered with Slughorn's old favourites, he was always good at giving leg-ups, but he never had much time for Arthur – didn't seem to think he was enough of a high-flier. Well, that just shows you, even Slughorn makes mistakes. I don't know whether Ron's told you in any of his letters – it's only just happened – but Arthur's been promoted!'

It could not have been clearer that Mrs Weasley had been bursting to say this. Harry swallowed a large amount of very hot soup and thought he could feel his throat blistering.

'That's great!' he gasped.

'You are sweet,' beamed Mrs Weasley, possibly taking his watering eyes for emotion at the news. 'Yes, Rufus Scrimgeour has set up several new offices in response to the present situation, and Arthur's heading the Office for the Detection and Confiscation of Counterfeit Defensive Spells and Protective Objects. It's a big job, he's got ten people reporting to him now!'

'What exactly –?'

'Well, you see, in all the panic about You-Know-Who, odd things have been cropping up for sale everywhere, things that are supposed to guard against You-Know-Who and the Death Eaters. You can imagine the kind of thing – so-called protective potions that are really gravy with a bit of Bubotuber pus added, or instructions for defensive jinxes that actually make

“要面包吗，亲爱的？”

“谢谢，韦斯莱夫人。”

她把魔杖朝肩膀后面一挥，一块面包和一把刀子就优雅地飞到了桌上。面包自动切成了片，汤锅又飞回去落在炉子上。韦斯莱夫人在哈利对面坐了下来。

“这么说，是你说服霍拉斯·斯拉格霍恩接受了那份工作？”

哈利点了点头，他嘴里满是热汤，说不出话来。

“他以前教过亚瑟和我。”韦斯莱夫人说，“他在霍格沃茨待了很多年，我想，他和邓布利多是差不多同时间进校的。你喜欢他吗？”

哈利嘴里又塞满了面包，只好耸耸肩膀，不置可否地甩了一下脑袋。

“我明白你的意思。”韦斯莱夫人心领神会地点点头，“不错，如果他愿意，是可以使自己变得很有魅力的，但亚瑟从来就不太喜欢他。魔法部里有许多他过去的得意门生，他总是愿意给学生提供帮助，但从来不肯在亚瑟身上多花时间——他似乎认为亚瑟没有什么抱负。嘿，这就证明就连斯拉格霍恩也会看走了眼。不知道罗恩是不是已经写信告诉你了——这还是最近的事呢——亚瑟升职了！”

显然，韦斯莱夫人一直迫不及待地要说这件事。哈利赶紧吞下一大口滚烫的热汤，觉得喉咙都被烫出了泡。

“太棒了！”他喘着气说。

“你真可爱。”韦斯莱夫人笑眯眯地说，她大概以为哈利眼泪汪汪是因为听了喜讯激动的，“是啊，为了对目前的局势做出反应，鲁弗斯·斯克林杰又新设了几个部门，亚瑟现在主管‘伪劣防御咒及防护用品侦查收缴办公室’。这个工作很重要，现在手下有十个人呢！”

“那究竟是——”

“噢，是这样，神秘人搞得大家人心惶惶，到处都有人弄一些稀奇古怪的东西出来卖钱，说是能够抵御神秘人和食死徒。你能想象那类玩意儿——所谓的防身药剂，实际上就是肉汤里加一点儿巴波块茎脓水，还有防御咒的操作指南，实际上只会让你掉了耳朵……唉，一般来说，做这些坏事的只是蒙顿格斯·弗莱奇那样的人，他们一辈子没

your ears fall off … well, in the main the perpetrators are just people like Mundungus Fletcher, who've never done an honest day's work in their lives and are taking advantage of how frightened everybody is, but every now and then something really nasty turns up. The other day Arthur confiscated a box of cursed Sneakoscopes that were almost certainly planted by a Death Eater. So you see, it's a very important job, and I tell him it's just silly to miss dealing with spark-plugs and toasters and all the rest of that Muggle rubbish.'

Mrs Weasley ended her speech with a stern look, as if it had been Harry suggesting that it was natural to miss spark-plugs.

'Is Mr Weasley still at work?' Harry asked.

'Yes, he is. As a matter of fact, he's a tiny bit late … he said he'd be back around midnight …'

She turned to look at a large clock that was perched awkwardly on top of a pile of sheets in the washing basket at the end of the table. Harry recognised it at once: it had nine hands, each inscribed with the name of a family member, and usually hung on the Weasleys' sitting-room wall, though its current position suggested that Mrs Weasley had taken to carrying it around the house with her. Every single one of its nine hands was now pointing at *mortal peril.*

'It's been like that for a while now,' said Mrs Weasley, in an unconvincingly casual voice, 'ever since You-Know-Who came back into the open. I suppose everybody's in mortal peril now … I don't think it can be just our family … but I don't know anyone else who's got a clock like this, so I can't check. Oh!'

With a sudden exclamation she pointed at the clock's face. Mr Weasley's hand had switched to *travelling.*

'He's coming!'

And sure enough, a moment later there was a knock on the back door. Mrs Weasley jumped up and hurried to it; with one hand on the doorknob and her face pressed against the wood she called softly, 'Arthur, is that you?'

'Yes,' came Mr Weasley's weary voice. 'But I would say that even if I were a Death Eater, dear. Ask the question!'

'Oh, honestly …'

'Molly!'

'All right, all right … what is your dearest ambition?'

有一天干正经工作的，现在利用人们的恐惧心理趁火打劫。可是偶尔也会碰到真正的恶性事件。那天，亚瑟收缴了一箱施了魔咒的窥镜，几乎可以肯定是某个食死徒安置在那里的。所以你看，这是一项很重要的工作，我跟他说，现在再惦记着火花塞、烤面包机以及麻瓜们的其他破烂，就显得太可笑了。”韦斯莱夫人说到最后，眼神变得严厉起来，似乎是哈利提出应该惦记火花塞的。

“韦斯莱先生还在上班吗？”哈利问。

“是啊。说实在的，有点儿晚了……他说大概午夜前后回来的……”

她扭头去看那个大钟，大钟放在桌边洗衣篮里的一大堆床单上，显得很不协调。哈利一眼就认了出来：它有九根指针，每根针上都刻着家里一位成员的名字，平常总是挂在韦斯莱家客厅的墙上。它现在放在这里，可见韦斯莱夫人在家里走到哪儿就把它带到哪儿。眼下，那九根针都指着生命危险。

“它这个样子有一段时间了，”韦斯莱夫人装出一种轻描淡写的口气说，但装得不像，“自从神秘人公开复出以后，它就是这样。我想现在每个人都处于生命危险中……不可能只是我们家里的人……但我不知道谁家还有这样的钟，所以没法核实。哦！”

她突然尖叫一声，指着钟面。韦斯莱先生的那根指针突然跳到了在路上。

“他回来了！”

果然，片刻之后，后门传来了敲门声。韦斯莱夫人一跃而起，匆匆过去开门。她用手握住球形把手，把脸贴在木门上，轻轻喊道：“亚瑟，是你吗？”

“是，”门外传来韦斯莱先生疲惫的声音，“但假如我是一个食死徒，也会这么说的，亲爱的。快问问题！”

“哦，说实在的……”

“莫丽！”

“好吧，好吧……你最大的抱负是什么？”

'To find out how aeroplanes stay up.'

Mrs Weasley nodded and turned the doorknob, but apparently Mr Weasley was holding tight to it on the other side, because the door remained firmly shut.

'Molly! I've got to ask you your question first!'

'Arthur, really, this is just silly …'

'What do you like me to call you when we're alone together?'

Even by the dim light of the lantern Harry could tell that Mrs Weasley had turned bright red; he himself felt suddenly warm around the ears and neck, and hastily gulped soup, clattering his spoon as loudly as he could against the bowl.

'Mollywobbles,' whispered a mortified Mrs Weasley into the crack at the edge of the door.

'Correct,' said Mr Weasley. 'Now you can let me in.'

Mrs Weasley opened the door to reveal her husband, a thin, balding, red-haired wizard wearing horn-rimmed spectacles and a long and dusty travelling cloak.

'I still don't see why we have to go through that every time you come home,' said Mrs Weasley, still pink in the face as she helped her husband out of his cloak. 'I mean, a Death Eater might have forced the answer out of you before impersonating you!'

'I know, dear, but it's Ministry procedure and I have to set an example. Something smells good – onion soup?'

Mr Weasley turned hopefully in the direction of the table.

'Harry! We didn't expect you until morning!'

They shook hands and Mr Weasley dropped into the chair beside Harry as Mrs Weasley set a bowl of soup in front of him, too.

'Thanks, Molly. It's been a tough night. Some idiot's started selling Metamorph-Medals. Just sling them around your neck and you'll be able to change your appearance at will. A hundred thousand disguises, all for ten Galleons!'

'And what really happens when you put them on?'

'Mostly you just turn a fairly unpleasant orange colour, but a couple of people have also sprouted tentacle-like warts all over their bodies. As if St

“弄清飞机怎么能待在天上。”

韦斯莱夫人点点头，转动把手想把门打开，但显然韦斯莱先生在外面紧紧地攥住门把手，门仍然纹丝不动。

“莫丽！我先要问问你那个问题！”

“亚瑟，说真的，这太荒唐了……”

“我们独自在一起时，你喜欢我叫你什么？”

即使就着昏暗的桌灯，哈利也能看出韦斯莱夫人的脸一下子涨得通红。他自己也觉得耳朵和脖子都在发烧，赶紧大口喝汤，尽量把勺子在碗里碰得叮当作响。

“莫丽小颤颤。”韦斯莱夫人不好意思地对着门边的那道裂缝小声说。

“正确，”韦斯莱先生说，“现在你可以让我进来了。”

韦斯莱夫人打开门，她丈夫出现了，一位谢顶、红发的瘦巫师，戴着一副角质架眼镜，身穿一件灰扑扑的旅行斗篷。

“我还是不明白，为什么你每次回家都要来这么一套。”韦斯莱夫人说着帮丈夫脱下斗篷，她的脸仍然微微泛红，“我的意思是，食死徒会先逼你说出答案，然后再冒充你的！”

“我知道，亲爱的，但这是魔法部规定的，我必须做出表率。什么东西这么好闻——洋葱汤？”

韦斯莱先生眼巴巴地朝桌子上望了过来。

“哈利！我们还以为你明天早晨才能到呢！”

他们握了握手，韦斯莱先生坐到哈利旁边的椅子上，韦斯莱夫人在他面前也放了一碗热汤。

“谢谢，莫丽。今天晚上真够呛。一个白痴居然卖起了变形勋章。说是只要把它挂在脖子上，就能随心所欲地改变相貌。千万张面孔，变化无穷，只卖十个加隆！”

“那么实际上戴了以后会怎么样呢？”

“一般来说只会将面孔变成一种难看的橘黄色，不过也有两个人全身长出了触角般的肉瘤。就好像圣芒戈魔法伤病医院还不够忙乱

Mungo's didn't have enough to do already!'

'It sounds like the sort of thing Fred and George would find funny,' said Mrs Weasley hesitantly. 'Are you sure –?'

'Of course I am!' said Mr Weasley. 'The boys wouldn't do anything like that now, not when people are desperate for protection!'

'So is that why you're late, Metamorph-Medals?'

'No, we got wind of a nasty Backfiring Jinx down in Elephant and Castle, but luckily the Magical Law Enforcement Squad had sorted it out by the time we got there …'

Harry stifled a yawn behind his hand.

'Bed,' said an undeceived Mrs Weasley at once. 'I've got Fred and George's room all ready for you, you'll have it to yourself.'

'Why, where are they?'

'Oh, they're in Diagon Alley, sleeping in the little flat over their joke shop as they're so busy,' said Mrs Weasley. 'I must say, I didn't approve at first, but they do seem to have a bit of a flair for business! Come on, dear, your trunk's already up there.'

' 'Night, Mr Weasley,' said Harry, pushing back his chair. Crookshanks leapt lightly from his lap and slunk out of the room.

'G'night, Harry,' said Mr Weasley.

Harry saw Mrs Weasley glance at the clock in the washing basket as they left the kitchen. All the hands were, once again, at *mortal peril.*

Fred and George's bedroom was on the second floor. Mrs Weasley pointed her wand at a lamp on the bedside table and it ignited at once, bathing the room in a pleasant golden glow. Though a large vase of flowers had been placed on a desk in front of the small window, their perfume could not disguise the lingering smell of what Harry thought was gunpowder. A considerable amount of floor space was devoted to a vast number of unmarked, sealed cardboard boxes, amongst which stood Harry's school trunk. The room looked as though it was being used as a temporary warehouse.

Hedwig hooted happily at Harry from her perch on top of a large wardrobe, then took off through the window; Harry knew she had been waiting to see him before going hunting. Harry bade Mrs Weasley good-

似的！”

“这类玩意儿，倒像是弗雷德和乔治感兴趣的东西。”韦斯莱夫人迟疑地说，“你能肯定不是——”

“当然能肯定！”韦斯莱先生说，“那两个小子现在不会做出那种东西的，现在人们都在不顾一切地寻求保护！”

“所以你才回来得这么晚，就为了变形勋章？”

“不是，我们得到情报，说象堡那儿有人施了一个危险的回火咒，幸好我们赶到那儿的时候，魔法法律执行队已经把事情解决了……”

哈利用手捂住了一个哈欠。

“睡去吧。”心明眼亮的韦斯莱夫人立刻说道，“我已经把弗雷德和乔治的房间给你准备好了，你一个人住在里面！”

“为什么，他们俩呢？”

“噢，在对角巷呢，现在生意这么忙，他们就睡在笑话店楼上的小套房里。”韦斯莱夫人说，“我不得不说，我起先并不赞成，但他们似乎确实有点儿生意头脑！来吧，亲爱的，你的箱子已经搬上去了。”

“晚安，韦斯莱先生。”哈利说着推开椅子站了起来。克鲁克山敏捷地从他腿上跳下去，溜出了房间。

“晚安，哈利。”韦斯莱先生说。

离开厨房时，哈利看见韦斯莱夫人扫了一眼放在洗衣篮里的大钟。所有的指针又全部指向了生命危险。

弗雷德和乔治的卧室在三楼。韦斯莱夫人用魔杖指了指床头柜上的一盏台灯，它立刻就亮了，给房间里洒下一片温馨柔和的光。那扇小窗户前面的桌上放着一大瓶鲜花，但它们的香味并不能掩盖残留在房间里的气味——哈利认为是火药味。地板上一大片地方都堆放着许多没有标名的密封的硬纸箱，哈利上学用的箱子也在其中。这个房间看上去像一个临时仓库。

海德薇在一个大衣柜顶上朝哈利高兴地叫了几声，然后便振翅飞出了窗外，哈利知道它一直在等着见他一面之后才去觅食。哈利向韦斯莱夫人道了晚安，换好睡衣上了一张床。枕套里有个硬东西，他把

night, put on pyjamas and got into one of the beds. There was something hard in the pillowcase. He groped inside it and pulled out a sticky purple and orange sweet, which he recognised as a Puking Pastille. Smiling to himself, he rolled over and was instantly asleep.

Seconds later, or so it seemed to Harry, he was woken by what sounded like cannon-fire as the door burst open. Sitting bolt upright, he heard the rasp of the curtains being pulled back: the dazzling sunlight seemed to poke him hard in both eyes. Shielding them with one hand, he groped hopelessly for his glasses with the other.

'Wuzzgoinon?'

'We didn't know you were here already!' said a loud and excited voice, and he received a sharp blow to the top of the head.

'Ron, don't hit him!' said a girl's voice reproachfully.

Harry's hand found his glasses and he shoved them on, though the light was so bright he could hardly see anyway. A long, looming shadow quivered in front of him for a moment; he blinked and Ron Weasley came into focus, grinning down at him.

'All right?'

'Never been better,' said Harry, rubbing the top of his head and slumping back on to his pillows. 'You?'

'Not bad,' said Ron, pulling over a cardboard box and sitting on it. 'When did you get here? Mum's only just told us!'

'About one o'clock this morning.'

'Were the Muggles all right? Did they treat you OK?'

'Same as usual,' said Harry, as Hermione perched herself on the edge of his bed. 'They didn't talk to me much, but I like it better that way. How're you, Hermione?'

'Oh, I'm fine,' said Hermione, who was scrutinising Harry as though he was sickening for something.

He thought he knew what was behind this and, as he had no wish to discuss Sirius's death or any other miserable subject at the moment, he said, 'What's the time? Have I missed breakfast?'

'Don't worry about that, Mum's bringing you up a tray; she reckons you look underfed,' said Ron, rolling his eyes. 'So, what's been going on?'

手伸进去一摸，掏出来一块黏糊糊的、一半紫色一半橘黄色的糖，他认出来了，是吐吐糖。他暗暗笑了笑，翻了个身，立刻睡着了。

几秒钟后，至少哈利感觉是这样，他被一声炮火般的巨响惊醒，房门被突然撞开了。他腾地坐直身子，听见了窗帘被拉开的刺耳声音：明晃晃的阳光刺得他两眼生疼。他用一只手挡住眼睛，用另一只手慌乱地摸索他的眼镜。

“怎么回事？”

“我们不知道你已经来了！”一个声音激动地大声说，接着哈利的头顶上狠狠地挨了一巴掌。

“罗恩，别打他！”一个女孩子的声音责备道。

哈利总算摸到了眼镜，赶紧戴上，不过光线太强烈了，他还是什么都看不见。一个模模糊糊的长长的影子在他面前晃了一会儿，他眨了眨眼睛，才看清是罗恩·韦斯莱，正笑眯眯地低头看着他呢。

“你好吗？”

“从来没这么好过。”哈利说完揉了揉头顶，重新跌回到枕头上，“你呢？”

“还行，”罗恩说着拖过一个硬纸箱，坐在上面，“你什么时候来的？妈妈刚告诉我们！”

“大概夜里一点钟吧。”

“那些麻瓜们怎么样？他们待你还好吧？”

“跟平常一样，”哈利说，赫敏在他床沿坐了下来，“不怎么跟我说话，我倒情愿这样。你怎么样，赫敏？”

“噢，我挺好的。”赫敏说，她一直在仔细地端详哈利，就好像他有什么不对劲的地方似的。

哈利知道赫敏心里在想什么，但他眼下不想谈论小天狼星的死，不想谈论任何令人难过的话题，于是他说：“什么时间了？你们已经吃过早饭了吧？”

“不用担心，妈妈会给你端上来的。她认为你看上去营养不够。”罗恩说着翻了个白眼，“好了，快说吧，到底发生了什么事？”

'Nothing much, I've just been stuck at my aunt and uncle's, haven't I?'

'Come off it!' said Ron. 'You've been off with Dumbledore!'

'It wasn't that exciting. He just wanted me to help him persuade this old teacher to come out of retirement. His name's Horace Slughorn.'

'Oh,' said Ron, looking disappointed. 'We thought –'

Hermione flashed a warning look at Ron and Ron changed tack at top speed.

'– we thought it'd be something like that.'

'You did?' said Harry, amused.

'Yeah … yeah, now Umbridge has left, obviously we need a new Defence Against the Dark Arts teacher, don't we? So, er, what's he like?'

'He looks a bit like a walrus and he used to be Head of Slytherin,' said Harry. 'Something wrong, Hermione?'

She was watching him as though expecting strange symptoms to manifest themselves at any moment. She rearranged her features hastily in an unconvincing smile.

'No, of course not! So, um, did Slughorn seem like he'll be a good teacher?'

'Dunno,' said Harry. 'He can't be worse than Umbridge, can he?'

'I know someone who's worse than Umbridge,' said a voice from the doorway. Ron's younger sister slouched into the room, looking irritable. 'Hi, Harry.'

'What's up with you?' Ron asked.

'It's *her*,' said Ginny, plonking herself down on Harry's bed. 'She's driving me mad.'

'What's she done now?' asked Hermione sympathetically.

'It's the way she talks to me – you'd think I was about three!'

'I know,' said Hermione, dropping her voice. 'She's so full of herself.'

Harry was astonished to hear Hermione talking about Mrs Weasley like this and could not blame Ron for saying angrily, 'Can't you two lay off her for five seconds?'

'Oh, that's right, defend her,' snapped Ginny. 'We all know you can't get enough of her.'

This seemed an odd comment to make about Ron's mother; starting to feel that he was missing something, Harry said, 'Who are you –?'

“没发生什么呀，我一直闷在我姨妈姨父家里，不是吗？”

“得了吧！”罗恩说，“你跟邓布利多一起出去了！”

“那也没什么刺激的。他只是让我帮他说服那个退休的老教师重新出来工作。那人名叫霍拉斯·斯拉格霍恩。”

“噢，”罗恩显出一副失望的样子，“我们还以为——”

赫敏警告地瞪了罗恩一眼，罗恩赶紧换了一种说法。

“——我们就猜到会是这种事情。”

“是吗？”哈利觉得怪好玩的。

“是啊……是啊，现在乌姆里奇走了，我们的黑魔法防御术显然需要一位新老师，对不对？那么，嗯，他长得什么样儿？”

“他长得有点儿像海象，以前当过斯莱特林学院的院长。”哈利说，“有什么不对吗，赫敏？”

赫敏注视着他，似乎担心他随时会显露出某种奇怪的症状。这时她赶紧调整一下面部表情，露出一个不自然的微笑。

“没有，绝对没有！那么，嗯，斯拉格霍恩看上去会是个好老师吗？”

“不知道，”哈利说，“总不会比乌姆里奇还糟糕吧？”

“我知道有一个人比乌姆里奇还糟糕。”门口传来一个声音。罗恩的妹妹没精打采地走进房间，一脸气呼呼的样子。“你好，哈利。”

“你这是怎么了？”罗恩问。

“是她，”金妮说着一屁股坐在哈利的床上，“她简直要把我逼疯了。”

“她这次又怎么啦？”赫敏同情地问。

“她对我说话的那种方式——好像把我当成了三岁的孩子！”

“我知道，”赫敏压低了声音说，“她心里只想着她自己。”

哈利听见赫敏这么谈论韦斯莱夫人，感到非常吃惊，所以也就怪不得罗恩生气地说：“你们俩能不能有五秒钟不要谈她？”

“嗬，行啊，你护着她。”金妮不客气地回嘴说，“我们都知道你怎么也看不够她。”

这么说罗恩的妈妈可有点儿莫名其妙，哈利这才发觉是自己听岔了，便问道：“你们说的是——”

But his question was answered before he could finish it. The bedroom door flew open again and Harry instinctively yanked the bedcovers up to his chin so hard that Hermione and Ginny slid off the bed on to the floor.

A young woman was standing in the doorway, a woman of such breathtaking beauty that the room seemed to have become strangely airless. She was tall and willowy with long blonde hair and appeared to emanate a faint, silvery glow. To complete this vision of perfection, she was carrying a heavily laden breakfast tray.

' 'Arry,' she said in a throaty voice. 'Eet 'as been too long!'

As she swept over the threshold towards him, Mrs Weasley was revealed, bobbing along in her wake, looking rather cross.

'There was no need to bring up the tray, I was just about to do it myself!'

'Eet was no trouble,' said Fleur Delacour, setting the tray across Harry's knees and then swooping to kiss him on each cheek: he felt the places where her mouth had touched him burn. 'I 'ave been longing to see 'im. You remember my seester, Gabrielle? She never stops talking about 'Arry Potter. She will be delighted to see you again.'

'Oh … is she here too?' Harry croaked.

'No, no, silly boy,' said Fleur with a tinkling laugh, 'I mean next summer, when we – but do you not know?'

Her great blue eyes widened and she looked reproachfully at Mrs Weasley, who said, 'We hadn't got around to telling him yet.'

Fleur turned back to Harry, swinging her silvery sheet of hair so that it whipped Mrs Weasley across the face.

'Bill and I are going to be married!'

'Oh,' said Harry blankly. He could not help noticing how Mrs Weasley, Hermione and Ginny were all determinedly avoiding each other's gaze. 'Wow. Er – congratulations!'

She swooped down upon him and kissed him again.

'Bill is very busy at ze moment, working very 'ard, and I only work part-time at Gringotts for my Eenglish, so he brought me 'ere for a few days to get to know 'is family properly. I was so pleased to 'ear you would be coming – zere isn't much to do 'ere, unless you like cooking and chickens! Well – enjoy your breakfast, 'Arry!'

他的问题还没有问出来就得到了答案。卧室的门又一次被猛地推开了，哈利本能地拽过床罩盖到下巴。他使的劲儿太大了，赫敏和金妮都从床上滑到了地板上。

一个年轻女子站在门口，她真是美艳惊人，房间里顿时让人透不过气来。她身材修长苗条，披着一头金黄色的秀发，周身似乎散发出淡淡的银光。而且，她手里还用托盘端着一顿丰盛的早餐，使得整个画面更加完美。

“阿利，”她用沙哑的喉音说，“好久没见了！”

她轻快地跨过门槛朝哈利走来，这才露出了紧跟在她身后的韦斯莱夫人，她的神情显得很恼怒。

“用不着你把托盘端上来，我正想自己端呢！”

“没关系，”芙蓉·德拉库尔说着把托盘放在哈利膝头，俯身在他的两边腮帮子上各亲了一下。哈利觉得被她嘴唇触到的地方火辣辣地发烧。“我一直盼着见到你。还记得我妹妹加布丽吗？她一刻不停地谈着阿利·波特。她再次见到你肯定会很高兴的。”

“噢……她也在这儿吗？”哈利哑着嗓子问。

“不，不，傻孩子，”芙蓉发出一串银铃般的笑声，“我是说明年夏天，我们——难道你还不知道吗？”

她那双大大的蓝眼睛睁得更大了，责怪地看着韦斯莱夫人，韦斯莱夫人说：“我们还没有抽出空儿来告诉他呢。”

芙蓉转向哈利，一甩瀑布般的金色秀发，发梢扫在韦斯莱夫人的脸上。

“比尔和我要结婚啦！”

“噢！”哈利茫然地说。他不由得注意到韦斯莱夫人、赫敏和金妮都故意躲避着彼此的目光。“哇，嗯——祝贺你们！”

芙蓉又俯身亲了亲他。

“眼下比尔很忙，工作很辛苦，我只在古灵阁做兼职，为了补习我的英语，所以他就把我带到这儿来住几天，多了解了解他的家人。听说你要来，可把我高兴坏了——在这里没有多少事情可做，除非喜欢烧菜，喜欢鸡！好了——美美地吃你的早餐吧，阿利！”

With these words she turned gracefully and seemed to float out of the room, closing the door quietly behind her.

Mrs Weasley made a noise that sounded like 'tchah!'

'Mum hates her,' said Ginny quietly.

'I do not hate her!' said Mrs Weasley in a cross whisper. 'I just think they've hurried into this engagement, that's all!'

'They've known each other a year,' said Ron, who looked oddly groggy and was staring at the closed door.

'Well, that's not very long! I know why it's happened, of course. It's all this uncertainty with You-Know-Who coming back, people think they might be dead tomorrow, so they're rushing all sorts of decisions they'd normally take time over. It was the same last time he was powerful, people eloping left right and centre –'

'Including you and Dad,' said Ginny slyly.

'Yes, well, your father and I were made for each other, what was the point in waiting?' said Mrs Weasley. 'Whereas Bill and Fleur … well … what have they really got in common? He's a hard-working, down-to-earth sort of person, whereas she's –'

'A cow,' said Ginny, nodding. 'But Bill's not that down-to-earth. He's a curse-breaker, isn't he, he likes a bit of adventure, a bit of glamour … I expect that's why he's gone for Phlegm.'

'Stop calling her that, Ginny,' said Mrs Weasley sharply, as Harry and Hermione laughed. 'Well, I'd better get on … eat your eggs while they're warm, Harry.'

Looking careworn, she left the room. Ron still seemed slightly punch-drunk; he was shaking his head experimentally like a dog trying to rid its ears of water.

'Don't you get used to her if she's staying in the same house?' Harry asked.

'Well, you do,' said Ron, 'but if she jumps out at you unexpectedly, like then …'

'It's pathetic,' said Hermione furiously, striding away from Ron as far as she could go and turning to face him with her arms folded once she had reached the wall.

'You don't really want her around for ever?' Ginny asked Ron incredulously. When he merely shrugged, she said, 'Well, Mum's going to put a stop to it if

说完，她优雅地一转身，一阵风似的飘出了房间，轻轻关上了房门。

韦斯莱夫人发出一个声音，听着好像是“去！”

“妈妈讨厌她。”金妮小声说。

“我没有讨厌她！”韦斯莱夫人气恼地压低声音说，“我只是认为他们的订婚太仓促了，仅此而已！”

“他们已经认识一年了。”罗恩说，他脸上神情恍惚，呆呆地望着关上的房门。

“是啊，那并没有多长时间！当然啦，我也明白为什么会这样。都是因为神秘人回来了，大家人心惶惶，都有一种朝不保夕的感觉，所以，本来需要时间好好考虑的事情，全都匆匆忙忙就做了决定。上次神秘人得势的时候就是这样，到处都有人私奔——”

“包括你和爸爸。”金妮调皮地说。

“是啊，没错，但你们的父亲和我是天生的一对，还需要等什么呢？”韦斯莱夫人说，“可是比尔和芙蓉……唉……他们到底有什么共同之处呢？比尔是一个勤勤恳恳、脚踏实地的人，芙蓉却——”

“是一个懒婆娘，”金妮点点头抢着说道，“不过，比尔并不是那么脚踏实地。他是个解咒员，对吗？他喜欢来点儿冒险，来点儿精彩……所以他才会喜欢黏痰。”

“不许那么叫她，金妮。”韦斯莱夫人严厉地说，而哈利和赫敏都笑出了声，“好了，我得赶紧……快把鸡蛋趁热吃了吧，哈利。”

她说完便离开了房间，看上去忧心忡忡。罗恩仍然显得有点儿神情恍惚，他试探性地晃了晃脑袋，像一条狗想甩掉耳朵上的水珠。

“她跟你住在同一幢房子里，你还没有习惯她吗？”哈利问。

“唉，习惯是习惯了，”罗恩说，“可是如果她在你没防备的时候突然跳出来，就像刚才那样……”

“活该！”赫敏气呼呼地说。她大步离开了罗恩，一直走到房间那头的墙边，转身抱起双臂瞪着他。

“你不会真的希望她在这里永远住下去吧？”金妮不敢相信地问罗恩。看到罗恩只是耸了耸肩，她又说：“嘿，妈妈会想办法阻止这件事的，

she can, I bet you anything.'

'How's she going to manage that?' asked Harry.

'She keeps trying to get Tonks round for dinner. I think she's hoping Bill will fall for Tonks instead. I hope he does, I'd much rather have her in the family.'

'Yeah, that'll work,' said Ron sarcastically. 'Listen, no bloke in his right mind's going to fancy Tonks when Fleur's around. I mean, Tonks is OK-looking when she isn't doing stupid things to her hair and her nose, but –'

'She's a damn sight nicer than *Phlegm*,' said Ginny.

'And she's more intelligent, she's an Auror!' said Hermione from the corner.

'Fleur's not stupid, she was good enough to enter the Triwizard Tournament,' said Harry.

'Not you as well!' said Hermione bitterly.

'I suppose you like the way Phlegm says "'Arry", do you?' asked Ginny scornfully.

'No,' said Harry, wishing he hadn't spoken, 'I was just saying, Phlegm – I mean, Fleur –'

'I'd much rather have Tonks in the family,' said Ginny. 'At least she's a laugh.'

'She hasn't been much of a laugh lately,' said Ron. 'Every time I've seen her she's looked more like Moaning Myrtle.'

'That's not fair,' snapped Hermione. 'She still hasn't got over what happened … you know … I mean, he was her cousin!'

Harry's heart sank. They had arrived at Sirius. He picked up a fork and began shovelling scrambled eggs into his mouth, hoping to deflect any invitation to join in this part of the conversation.

'Tonks and Sirius barely knew each other!' said Ron. 'Sirius was in Azkaban half her life and before that their families never met –'

'That's not the point,' said Hermione. 'She thinks it was her fault he died!'

'How does she work that one out?' asked Harry, in spite of himself.

'Well, she was fighting Bellatrix Lestrange, wasn't she? I think she feels that if only she had finished her off, Bellatrix couldn't have killed Sirius.'

信不信由你。”

“她怎么可能办到呢？”哈利问。

“她三天两头请唐克斯来吃饭。我想她是希望比尔能爱上唐克斯。我也巴不得这样，我情愿让唐克斯成为我们家的一员。”

“是啊，想得真妙。”罗恩讽刺道，“听着，只要有芙蓉在，没有哪个头脑正常的人会喜欢唐克斯。我是说，如果唐克斯不把她的头发和鼻子搞得一团糟的话，她的样子还不算难看，可是——”

“她比黏痰好看多了。”金妮说。

“而且她更有智慧，她是个傲罗！”赫敏从墙角那儿说道。

“芙蓉也不傻，她很优秀，还参加了三强争霸赛呢。”哈利说。

“想不到你也这样！”赫敏尖刻地说。

“我想,你大概是喜欢黏痰叫你‘阿利’时的那副腔调吧,是不是？”金妮轻蔑地问。

“不是，”哈利后悔自己不该说话，“我只是说，黏痰——我是说芙蓉——”

“我宁愿让唐克斯上我们家来。”金妮说，“她至少还能逗人开心。”

“她最近不大逗人开心了。”罗恩说，“我每次看见她，她都显得更像哭泣的桃金娘了。”

“这么说不公平。”赫敏厉声说道，“她仍然没有从那件事情中缓过来……你知道的……我是说，他毕竟是她的亲戚啊！”

哈利的心往下一沉。他们终于谈到小天狼星了。他拿起叉子，狼吞虎咽地吃起了炒鸡蛋，希望别人不再邀请他加入这部分谈话。

“唐克斯和小天狼星根本就算不上认识！”罗恩说，“在唐克斯出生后的一半时间里，小天狼星都待在阿兹卡班，而且在那之前他们两家从没碰过面——”

“关键不在这里,”赫敏说,“唐克斯认为小天狼星的死都是她的责任。”

“她怎么会得出那样的结论呢？”哈利忍不住问道。

“唉，当时是她在对付贝拉特里克斯·莱斯特兰奇，对吧？她大概以为，如果她能把贝拉特里克斯干掉，那女人就不会杀死小天狼星了。”

'That's stupid,' said Ron.

'It's survivor's guilt,' said Hermione. 'I know Lupin's tried to talk her round, but she's still really down. She's actually having trouble with her Metamorphosing!'

'With her –?'

'She can't change her appearance like she used to,' explained Hermione. 'I think her powers must have been affected by shock, or something.'

'I didn't know that could happen,' said Harry.

'Nor did I,' said Hermione, 'but I suppose if you're really depressed …'

The door opened again and Mrs Weasley popped her head in.

'Ginny,' she whispered, 'come downstairs and help me with the lunch.'

'I'm talking to this lot!' said Ginny, outraged.

'Now!' said Mrs Weasley, and withdrew.

'She only wants me there so she doesn't have to be alone with Phlegm!' said Ginny crossly. She swung her long red hair around in a very good imitation of Fleur and pranced across the room with her arms held aloft like a ballerina.

'You lot had better come down quickly too,' she said as she left.

Harry took advantage of the temporary silence to eat more breakfast. Hermione was peering into Fred and George's boxes, though every now and then she cast sideways looks at Harry. Ron, who was now helping himself to Harry's toast, was still gazing dreamily at the door.

'What's this?' Hermione asked eventually, holding up what looked like a small telescope.

'Dunno,' said Ron, 'but if Fred and George've left it here, it's probably not ready for the joke shop yet, so be careful.'

'Your mum said the shop's going well,' said Harry. 'Said Fred and George have got a real flair for business.'

'That's an understatement,' said Ron. 'They're raking in the Galleons! I can't wait to see the place. We haven't been to Diagon Alley yet, because Mum says Dad's got to be there for extra security and he's been really busy at work, but it sounds excellent.'

'And what about Percy?' asked Harry; the third-eldest Weasley brother had fallen out with the rest of the family. 'Is he talking to your mum and dad again?'

“那太荒唐了。”罗恩说。

“这就是幸存者的内疚心理。”赫敏说，“我知道卢平想把她开导过来，但她仍然情绪低落。她现在甚至不能得心应手地搞她的易容术了！”

“她的什么？”

“她不能像过去那样改变她的容貌了，”赫敏解释道，“大概因为受了惊吓什么的，使她的法术打了折扣。”

“没想到还会有这种事情。”哈利说。

“我也没想到，”赫敏说，“但我猜想，如果你的心情非常糟糕……”

门又被推开了，韦斯莱夫人探进头来。

“金妮，”她小声说，“下楼来帮我做午饭。”

“我在跟大伙儿说话呢！”金妮生气地说。

“快来！”韦斯莱夫人说完就关门走了。

“她只是不想跟黏痰单独待在一起，才叫我下去的！”金妮恼火地说。她把长长的红头发往后一甩，那样子活脱脱一个芙蓉，然后像芭蕾舞演员那样悬着两个手臂，翩翩然地飘出了房间。

“你们大家最好也赶紧下来。”她临出门时又说了一句。

哈利利用这短暂的沉默，加紧吃他的早餐。赫敏在查看弗雷德和乔治的那些箱子，偶尔也朝哈利这边瞥上几眼。罗恩一边吃着哈利的面包，一边仍然神思恍惚地盯着房门。

“这是什么？”赫敏最后举起一个小望远镜似的东西，问道。

“不知道，”罗恩说，“不过既然弗雷德和乔治把它留在这儿，它恐怕还不能拿到笑话店里去卖，你可得小心点儿。”

“你妈妈说小店生意不错，”哈利说，“还说弗雷德和乔治挺有生意头脑的。”

“这么说太轻描淡写了。”罗恩说，“他们现在是大把地捞钱啊！我真想赶紧去那个地方看看。我们还没去对角巷呢，妈妈说为了安全起见，爸爸也得一起去，可现在爸爸工作忙得要命。不过他们那里听起来真棒！”

“珀西怎么样了？”哈利问，韦斯莱家的这位三儿子同家人闹翻了，“他跟你爸爸妈妈说话了吗？”

'Nope,' said Ron.

'But he knows your dad was right all along now about Voldemort being back –'

'Dumbledore says people find it far easier to forgive others for being wrong than being right,' said Hermione. 'I heard him telling your mum, Ron.'

'Sounds like the sort of mental thing Dumbledore would say,' said Ron.

'He's going to be giving me private lessons this year,' said Harry conversationally.

Ron choked on his bit of toast and Hermione gasped.

'You kept that quiet!' said Ron.

'I only just remembered,' said Harry honestly. 'He told me last night in your broom shed.'

'Blimey … private lessons with Dumbledore!' said Ron, looking impressed. 'I wonder why he's …?'

His voice tailed away. Harry saw him and Hermione exchange looks. Harry laid down his knife and fork, his heart beating rather fast considering that all he was doing was sitting in bed. Dumbledore had said to do it … why not now? He fixed his eyes on his fork, which was gleaming in the sunlight streaming on to his lap, and said, 'I don't know exactly why he's going to be giving me lessons, but I think it must be because of the prophecy.'

Neither Ron nor Hermione spoke. Harry had the impression that both had frozen. He continued, still speaking to his fork, 'You know, the one they were trying to steal at the Ministry.'

'Nobody knows what it said, though,' said Hermione quickly. 'It got smashed.'

'Although the *Prophet* says –' began Ron, but Hermione said, 'Shh!'

'The *Prophet's* got it right,' said Harry, looking up at them both with a great effort: Hermione seemed frightened and Ron amazed. 'That glass ball that smashed wasn't the only record of the prophecy. I heard the whole thing in Dumbledore's office, he was the one the prophecy was made to, so he could tell me. From what it said,' Harry took a deep breath, 'it looks like I'm the one who's got to finish off Voldemort … at least, it said neither of us could live while the other survives.'

The three of them gazed at each other in silence for a moment. Then

“没有。”罗恩说。

“可是他现在知道，你爸爸关于伏地魔会回来的说法是对的——”

“邓布利多说，人们容易原谅别人的错误，却很难原谅别人的正确。”赫敏说，“我听见他跟你妈妈说的，罗恩。”

“这一听就是邓布利多那种神神叨叨的话。”罗恩说。

“他今年要给我单独上课呢。”哈利引出了话题。

罗恩被嘴里的面包噎住了，赫敏吃惊地倒抽了一口气。

“你跟我们保密！”罗恩说。

“我刚想起来。”哈利如实地说，“他昨晚在你们家的扫帚棚里告诉我的。”

“天哪……邓布利多给你单独上课！”罗恩一副肃然起敬的样子，说道，“不知道他为什么……？”

罗恩的声音低了下去。哈利看见他和赫敏交换了一下目光。哈利放下刀叉，他的心跳加快，而他现在只是坐在床上，什么也没做。邓布利多说过可以告诉他们……为什么不是现在呢？他眼睛盯着叉子，阳光洒在他腿上，照得叉子闪闪发亮，他说：“我不知道他到底为什么要给我上课，但我想肯定是因为那个预言球。”

罗恩和赫敏都没有说话。哈利感觉到他们俩都呆住了。他眼睛盯着叉子继续说：“你们知道，就是他们想从魔法部偷走的那个。”

“可是谁也不知道那上面写着什么。”赫敏立刻说道，“它被打碎了。”

“不过《预言家日报》说——”罗恩话没说完，赫敏就制止了他，“嘘！”

“《预言家日报》说得没错，”哈利说着费力地抬起头望着他们俩：赫敏看上去很惊慌，罗恩则是一副惊愕的样子，“那个打碎的玻璃球并不是预言的唯一记录。我在邓布利多的办公室听说了事情的来龙去脉，那个预言就是说给他听的，所以他能够告诉我。从那个预言来看，”哈利深深地吸了口气，“似乎我就是那个要干掉伏地魔的人……至少，它说我们俩不可能同时活着。”

三个人面面相觑了一会儿。突然，砰的一声巨响，赫敏消失在一

there was a loud bang and Hermione vanished behind a puff of black smoke.

'Hermione!' shouted Harry and Ron; the breakfast tray slid to the floor with a crash.

Hermione emerged, coughing, out of the smoke, clutching the telescope and sporting a brilliantly purple black eye.

'I squeezed it and it – it punched me!' she gasped.

And sure enough, they now saw a tiny fist on a long spring protruding from the end of the telescope.

'Don't worry,' said Ron, who was plainly trying not to laugh, 'Mum'll fix that, she's good at healing minor injuries –'

'Oh, well, never mind that now!' said Hermione hastily. 'Harry, oh, Harry …' She sat down on the edge of his bed again.

'We wondered, after we got back from the Ministry … obviously, we didn't want to say anything to you, but from what Lucius Malfoy said about the prophecy, how it was about you and Voldemort, well, we thought it might be something like this … oh, Harry …' She stared at him, then whispered, 'Are you scared?'

'Not as much as I was,' said Harry. 'When I first heard it, I was … but now, it seems as though I always knew I'd have to face him in the end …'

'When we heard Dumbledore was collecting you in person, we thought he might be telling you something, or showing you something, to do with the prophecy,' said Ron eagerly. 'And we were kind of right, weren't we? He wouldn't be giving you lessons if he thought you were a goner, wouldn't waste his time – he must think you've got a chance!'

'That's true,' said Hermione. 'I wonder what he'll teach you, Harry? Really advanced defensive magic, probably … powerful counter-curses … anti-jinxes …'

Harry did not really listen. A warmth was spreading through him that had nothing to do with the sunlight; a tight obstruction in his chest seemed to be dissolving. He knew that Ron and Hermione were more shocked than they were letting on, but the mere fact that they were still there on either side of him, speaking bracing words of comfort, not shrinking from him as though he were contaminated or dangerous, was worth more than he could ever tell them.

大团黑烟后面。

“赫敏！”哈利和罗恩同时喊起来，早餐托盘哐啷一声滑到了地板上。

赫敏从黑烟里出现，不停地咳嗽着，手里仍抓着那个望远镜，一只眼睛变成了乌眼青。

“我一挤，它就——它就给了我一下！”她喘着气说。

果然，他们这才看见望远镜的顶端伸出一根长长的弹簧，上面有一只小小的拳头。

“别担心，”罗恩说，他显然在拼命忍住笑，“妈妈会给你治好的，她治疗小伤小痛最拿手了——”

“噢，没关系，现在先不管它！”赫敏赶紧说道，“哈利，哦，哈利……”

她又在哈利的床边坐了下来。

“从魔法部回来以后，我们心里就在嘀咕……当然啦，我们什么都不想跟你说，但听了卢修斯·马尔福说的关于那个预言，以及关于你和伏地魔的话之后，唉，我们就已经猜到可能会是这样……哦，哈利……”她望着他，又低声问道，“你害怕吗？”

“不像当时那么害怕了。”哈利说，“我第一次听见时，确实……不过现在，我觉得好像早就知道我最后要跟他面对面地较量的……”

“当我们听说邓布利多要亲自去接你时，我们就猜想他大概会跟你说一些或给你看一些跟预言有关的东西，”罗恩急急地说道，“我们没有猜错吧？如果他认为你注定要完蛋，他就不会给你上课，不会浪费他的时间了——他肯定认为你还是有希望取胜的！”

“对，”赫敏说，“不知道他会教你什么，哈利？大概是绝顶高深的防御魔法……特别厉害的破解咒……反恶咒……”

哈利并没有认真地听。他感到全身暖融融的，而且这暖意跟阳光毫无关系，堵在他胸口的那块东西似乎正在渐渐融化。他知道罗恩和赫敏并没有把内心的恐惧都显露出来，但看到他们仍然和他站在一起，说着安慰和鼓励的话，而没有把他当成异类或危险分子，远远地躲开，他觉得这价值是他无法用语言向他们表达的。

'… and evasive enchantments generally,' concluded Hermione. 'Well, at least you know one lesson you'll be having this year, that's one more than Ron and me. I wonder when our O.W.L. results will come?'

'Can't be long now, it's been a month,' said Ron.

'Hang on,' said Harry, as another part of the previous night's conversation came back to him. 'I think Dumbledore said our O.W.L. results would be arriving today!'

'Today?' shrieked Hermione. '*Today?* But why didn't you – oh my God – you should have said –'

She leapt to her feet.

'I'm going to see whether any owls have come …'

But when Harry arrived downstairs ten minutes later, fully dressed and carrying his empty breakfast tray, it was to find Hermione sitting at the kitchen table in great agitation, while Mrs Weasley tried to lessen her resemblance to half a panda.

'It just won't budge,' Mrs Weasley was saying anxiously, standing over Hermione with her wand in her hand and a copy of *The Healer's Helpmate* open at 'Bruises, Cuts and Abrasions'. 'This has always worked before, I just can't understand it.'

'It'll be Fred and George's idea of a funny joke, making sure it can't come off,' said Ginny.

'But it's got to come off!' squeaked Hermione. 'I can't go around looking like this for ever!'

'You won't, dear, we'll find an antidote, don't worry,' said Mrs Weasley soothingly.

'Bill told me 'ow Fred and George are very amusing!' said Fleur, smiling serenely.

'Yes, I can hardly breathe for laughing,' snapped Hermione.

She jumped up and started walking round and round the kitchen, twisting her fingers together.

'Mrs Weasley, you're quite, quite sure no owls have arrived this morning?'

'Yes, dear, I'd have noticed,' said Mrs Weasley patiently. 'But it's barely nine, there's still plenty of time …'

'I know I messed up Ancient Runes,' muttered Hermione feverishly, 'I definitely made at least one serious mistranslation. And the Defence Against

“……还有其他闪避类魔法。”赫敏终于说完了，“好了，你至少知道今年要上的一门课了，比罗恩和我都多一门。不知道我们的O.W.L.成绩什么时候寄来？”

“不会太久，已经有一个月了。”罗恩说。

“等一等，”哈利突然想起昨晚的另一段对话，说道，“邓布利多好像说我们的O.W.L.成绩今天就能寄到！”

“今天？”赫敏惊叫起来，“今天？那你为什么不早——哦，天哪——你应该早点告诉——”

她腾地跳了起来。

“我去看看有没有猫头鹰飞来……”

可是，十分钟后，当哈利穿戴整齐，端着空托盘下楼时，却发现赫敏焦虑不安地坐在厨房的桌子旁，韦斯莱夫人正在试着给她治疗，使她的那只眼睛看上去不再那么像熊猫眼。

“它就是不肯让步，”韦斯莱夫人发愁地说，她站在赫敏面前，一手拿着魔杖，一手拿着一本《疗伤手册》，翻到“碰伤、割伤和擦伤”那部分，“以前总是挺管用的，我真闹不明白。”

“这就是弗雷德和乔治想出来的恶作剧点子，确保它不会褪色。”金妮说。

“它怎么能不褪色呢！”赫敏尖叫起来，“我不能走到哪里都永远是这副样子呀！”

“不会的，亲爱的，我们会找到解药的，别担心。”韦斯莱夫人安慰她。

“比尔告诉过我，弗雷德和乔治非常风趣！”芙蓉优雅地微笑着说。

“是啊，我笑得都喘不过气来了。”赫敏没好气地说。

她一跃而起，在厨房里一圈一圈地踱步，手指绞在一起。

“韦斯莱夫人，你绝对能够肯定，今天早晨没有猫头鹰飞来吗？”

“是的，亲爱的，如果有我会注意到的。”韦斯莱夫人耐心地说，“现在还不到九点呢，仍然有许多时间……”

“我知道我的古代如尼文考砸了，”赫敏心烦意乱地嘟囔道，“肯定至少有一处完全译错。还有黑魔法防御术的实践课，我也考得一塌糊涂。

the Dark Arts practical was no good at all. I thought Transfiguration went all right at the time, but looking back –'

'Hermione, will you shut up, you're not the only one who's nervous!' barked Ron. 'And when you've got your ten "Outstanding" O.W.L.s ...'

'Don't, don't, don't!' said Hermione, flapping her hands hysterically. 'I know I've failed everything!'

'What happens if we fail?' Harry asked the room at large, but it was again Hermione who answered.

'We discuss our options with our Head of House, I asked Professor McGonagall at the end of last term.'

Harry's stomach squirmed. He wished he had eaten less breakfast.

'At Beauxbatons,' said Fleur complacently, 'we 'ad a different way of doing things. I think eet was better. We sat our examinations after six years of study, not five, and then –'

Fleur's words were drowned in a scream. Hermione was pointing through the kitchen window. Three black specks were clearly visible in the sky, growing larger all the time.

'They're definitely owls,' said Ron hoarsely, jumping up to join Hermione at the window.

'And there are three of them,' said Harry, hastening to her other side.

'One for each of us,' said Hermione in a terrified whisper. 'Oh no ... oh no ... oh no ...'

She gripped both Harry and Ron tightly around the elbows.

The owls were flying directly at The Burrow, three handsome tawnies, each of which, it became clear as they flew lower over the path leading up to the house, was carrying a large square envelope.

'Oh *no*!' squealed Hermione.

Mrs Weasley squeezed past them and opened the kitchen window. One, two, three, the owls soared through it and landed on the table in a neat line. All three of them lifted their right legs.

Harry moved forwards. The letter addressed to him was tied to the leg of the owl in the middle. He untied it with fumbling fingers. To his left, Ron was trying to detach his own results; to his right, Hermione's hands were shaking so much she was making her whole owl tremble.

我当时觉得变形术考得还可以，但现在回想一下——”

“赫敏,你能不能闭嘴,又不是只有你一个人感到紧张！”罗恩吼道，“等你拿到十个 O.W.L.‘优秀’……”

“不，不，不要说了！”赫敏歇斯底里地拍打着双手说，“我知道我每门都不及格！”

“如果不及格怎么办呢？”哈利问大家，但又是赫敏抢着回答。

“去跟院长商量我们选修哪些课，我上学期结束时问过麦格教授。”

哈利的胃里开始翻腾，他后悔不该吃那么多早饭。

“在我们布斯巴顿，”芙蓉只顾得意地说，“情况完全不一样，我认为那样更好。我们不是五年级就考试，而是学满六年再考，然后——”

芙蓉的话被一声尖叫吞没了。赫敏指着厨房的窗户外。天空中出现了三个清清楚楚的小黑点，而且越来越大。

“肯定是猫头鹰。”罗恩哑着嗓子说，跳过去和赫敏一起站在窗口。

“一共有三只。”哈利说着也奔过去站在赫敏的另一边。

“我们每人一只，”赫敏惊慌地小声说，“哦，不……哦，不……哦，不……”

她紧紧地抓住哈利和罗恩的胳膊肘。

猫头鹰径直朝陋居飞来，是三只漂亮的棕褐色猫头鹰，当它们降低高度，在通向陋居的那条小路上空飞过时，他们看清了每只猫头鹰都抓着一个方方的大信封。

“哦，不！”赫敏尖叫道。

韦斯莱夫人挤过他们身边，打开厨房的窗户。一只、两只、三只猫头鹰从窗口飞了进来，落在桌子上，整整齐齐地站成一排，步调一致地抬起了右腿。

哈利凑上前去。中间的那只猫头鹰腿上绑的信封上写着他的名字。他用不听使唤的手指把信取下来。在他左边，罗恩也在手忙脚乱地解下他的考试成绩；在他右边，赫敏的手抖得太厉害了，弄得她那只猫头鹰也跟着全身发抖。

Nobody in the kitchen spoke. At last, Harry managed to detach the envelope. He slit it open quickly and unfolded the parchment inside.

ORDINARY WIZARDING LEVEL RESULTS

Pass Grades:	**Fail Grades:**
Outstanding (O)	Poor (P)
Exceeds Expectations (E)	Dreadful (D)
Acceptable (A)	Troll (T)

HARRY JAMES POTTER HAS ACHIEVED:

Astronomy:	A
Care of Magical Creatures:	E
Charms:	E
Defence Against the Dark Arts:	O
Divination:	P
Herbology:	E
History of Magic:	D
Potions:	E
Transfiguration:	E

Harry read the parchment through several times, his breathing becoming easier with each reading. It was all right: he had always known that he would fail Divination, and he had had no chance of passing History of Magic, given that he had collapsed halfway through the examination, but he had passed everything else! He ran his finger down the grades … he had passed well in Transfiguration and Herbology, he had even Exceeded Expectations at Potions! And best of all, he had achieved 'Outstanding' in Defence Against the Dark Arts!

He looked round. Hermione had her back to him and her head bent, but Ron was looking delighted.

'Only failed Divination and History of Magic, and who cares about them?' he said happily to Harry. 'Here – swap –'

Harry glanced down Ron's grades: there were no 'Outstandings' there …

'Knew you'd be top in Defence Against the Dark Arts,' said Ron,

厨房里谁也没有说话。最后，哈利终于把信解了下来。他赶紧撕开信封，展开里面的羊皮纸。

普通巫师等级考试成绩

合格成绩：优秀（O）	不合格成绩：差（P）
良好（E）	很差（D）
及格（A）	极差（T）

哈利·詹姆·波特成绩如下：

天文学：	A
保护神奇动物：	E
魔咒学：	E
黑魔法防御术：	O
占卜学：	P
草药学：	E
魔法史：	D
魔药学：	E
变形术：	E

哈利拿着羊皮纸反复看了几遍，呼吸越来越自如了。还好，他早就知道占卜课不会及格，而魔法史考试进行到一半他昏倒了，肯定没有希望通过，其他几门功课居然都过关了！他的手指在成绩单上滑过……变形术和草药学成绩不错，就连魔药学也得了个“良好”！最棒的是，他的黑魔法防御术竟然拿到了“优秀”！

他扭头看去，赫敏背对着他，低着脑袋，罗恩倒是满脸喜色。

“只有占卜课和魔法史没及格，谁在乎那些玩意儿？”他高兴地对哈利说，“给——交换——”

哈利低头看了一眼罗恩的成绩单：没有一个“优秀”……

“我就知道你会在黑魔法防御术上拔尖，”罗恩捶了一下哈利的肩

punching Harry on the shoulder. 'We've done all right, haven't we?'

'Well done!' said Mrs Weasley proudly, ruffling Ron's hair. 'Seven O.W.L.s, that's more than Fred and George got together!'

'Hermione?' said Ginny tentatively, for Hermione still hadn't turned round. 'How did you do?'

'I – not bad,' said Hermione in a small voice.

'Oh, come off it,' said Ron, striding over to her and whipping her results out of her hand. 'Yep – nine "Outstandings" and one "Exceeds Expectations" in Defence Against the Dark Arts.' He looked down at her, half amused, half exasperated. 'You're actually disappointed, aren't you?'

Hermione shook her head, but Harry laughed.

'Well, we're N.E.W.T. students now!' grinned Ron. 'Mum, are there any more sausages?'

Harry looked back down at his results. They were as good as he could have hoped for. He felt just one tiny twinge of regret ... this was the end of his ambition to become an Auror. He had not secured the required Potions grade. He had known all along that he wouldn't, but he still felt a sinking in his stomach as he looked again at that small black 'E'.

It was odd, really, seeing that it had been a Death Eater in disguise who had first told Harry he would make a good Auror, but somehow the idea had taken hold of him, and he couldn't really think of anything else he would like to be. Moreover, it had seemed the right destiny for him since he had heard the prophecy a month ago ... *neither can live while the other survives* ... wouldn't he be living up to the prophecy, and giving himself the best chance of survival, if he joined those highly trained wizards whose job it was to find and kill Voldemort?

膀，说道，“我们都干得不错，是不是？”

“不错！”韦斯莱夫人骄傲地说，揉了揉罗恩的头发，“O.W.L.过了七门，比弗雷德和乔治加在一起还多！”

“赫敏？”金妮试探地叫道，因为赫敏仍然没有转过身来，“你成绩怎么样？”

“我……还好。”赫敏小声说。

“哦，得了吧，”罗恩三步并作两步走到她跟前，一把从她手里抢过成绩单，“嘿——九个‘优秀’，一个‘良好’——是黑魔法防御术。”他半是好笑半是恼火地低头看着她，“你竟然还觉得失望，是吗？”

赫敏摇了摇头，哈利笑了起来。

“太好了，我们现在是N.E.W.T.生了！”罗恩笑着说，“妈妈，还有香肠吗？”

哈利又低头看着他的成绩单。他考得不错，比预想的好得多。他只是感到有一点小小的遗憾……他想要成为一名傲罗的理想破灭了。他的魔药学成绩没有达到要求。他早就知道会是这样，但此刻再一次看着那个黑色的小字母“E”，他仍然感到心里沉甸甸的。

说来奇怪，最初告诉哈利他会成为一名出色的傲罗的，是一个伪装的食死徒。但不知怎的，这个想法在哈利心里生了根，他想象不出除此之外他还愿意做什么。而且，自从一个月前听了那个预言之后，这似乎已是他注定的命运……*两个人不能都活着*……如果他加入那支训练有素、以追捕和消灭伏地魔为己任的巫师队伍，他岂不是就能实践那个预言，同时给自己一个最大的生存机会吗？

CHAPTER SIX

Draco's Detour

Harry remained within the confines of The Burrow's garden over the next few weeks. He spent most of his days playing two-a-side Quidditch in the Weasleys' orchard (he and Hermione against Ron and Ginny; Hermione was dreadful and Ginny good, so they were reasonably well-matched) and his evenings eating triple helpings of everything Mrs Weasley put in front of him.

It would have been a happy, peaceful holiday had it not been for the stories of disappearances, odd accidents, even of deaths now appearing almost daily in the *Prophet*. Sometimes Bill and Mr Weasley brought home news before it even reached the paper. To Mrs Weasley's displeasure, Harry's sixteenth birthday celebrations were marred by grisly tidings brought to the party by Remus Lupin, who was looking gaunt and grim, his brown hair streaked liberally with grey, his clothes more ragged and patched than ever.

'There have been another couple of Dementor attacks,' he announced, as Mrs Weasley passed him a large slice of birthday cake. 'And they've found Igor Karkaroff's body in a shack up north. The Dark Mark had been set over it – well, frankly, I'm surprised he stayed alive for even a year after deserting the Death Eaters; Sirius's brother Regulus only managed a few days as far as I can remember.'

'Yes, well,' said Mrs Weasley, frowning, 'perhaps we should talk about something diff–'

'Did you hear about Florean Fortescue, Remus?' asked Bill, who was being plied with wine by Fleur. 'The man who ran –'

'– the ice-cream place in Diagon Alley?' Harry interrupted, with an unpleasant, hollow sensation in the pit of his stomach. 'He used to give me

第6章

德拉科兜圈子

接下来的几个星期，哈利一直没有离开过陋居花园的范围。他大部分时间都在韦斯莱家的果园里玩两人对两人的魁地奇（他和赫敏对罗恩和金妮。赫敏打得很糟糕，金妮倒是球技不凡，所以这样搭配正合适）。到了晚上，韦斯莱夫人端到他面前的每样东西，他都要吃三份。

如果不是《预言家日报》几乎每天都要报道有人失踪甚至死亡，以及其他一些稀奇古怪的事件，这个暑假本来可以过得很开心、很平静。有时候，比尔和韦斯莱先生会带回来一些还没来得及登报的消息。哈利十六岁生日的庆祝会，因为莱姆斯·卢平带来的一些恐怖消息而黯然失色，韦斯莱夫人大感不快。卢平看上去消瘦、憔悴，表情严峻，棕褐色的头发里夹杂着大量白发，衣服比以前还要破烂，补丁更多。

“又发生了两起摄魂怪袭击事件，”他宣布道，这时韦斯莱夫人正递给他一大块生日蛋糕，“他们在北方的一个小木屋里发现了伊戈尔·卡卡洛夫的尸体。黑魔标记悬在上空——唉，坦白地说，他离开食死徒后居然还能活够一年，倒真让我吃惊。我记得，小天狼星的弟弟雷古勒斯只活了几天就死了。”

“是啊，”韦斯莱夫人皱着眉头说，“好了，也许我们应该谈点儿别的——”

“福洛林·福斯科的事你听说了吗，莱姆斯？”问话的是比尔，芙蓉正给他一杯接一杯地斟酒，“就是那个——”

“——在对角巷开冰淇淋店的？”哈利插嘴道，心里有一种很不舒

free ice creams. What's happened to him?'

'Dragged off, by the look of his place.'

'Why?' asked Ron, while Mrs Weasley pointedly glared at Bill.

'Who knows? He must've upset them somehow. He was a good man, Florean.'

'Talking of Diagon Alley,' said Mr Weasley, 'looks like Ollivander's gone too.'

'The wand-maker?' said Ginny, looking startled.

'That's the one. Shop's empty. No sign of a struggle. No one knows whether he left voluntarily or was kidnapped.'

'But wands – what'll people do for wands?'

'They'll make do with other makers,' said Lupin. 'But Ollivander was the best, and if the other side have got him it's not so good for us.'

The day after this rather gloomy birthday tea, their letters and book lists arrived from Hogwarts. Harry's included a surprise: he had been made Quidditch captain.

'That gives you equal status with prefects!' cried Hermione happily. 'You can use our special bathroom now, and everything!'

'Wow, I remember when Charlie wore one of these,' said Ron, examining the badge with glee. 'Harry, this is so cool, you're my captain – if you let me back on the team, I suppose, ha ha ...'

'Well, I don't suppose we can put off a trip to Diagon Alley much longer now you've got these,' sighed Mrs Weasley, looking down Ron's book list. 'We'll go on Saturday as long as your father doesn't have to go into work again. I'm not going there without him.'

'Mum, d'you honestly think You-Know-Who's going to be hiding behind a bookshelf in Flourish and Blotts?' sniggered Ron.

'Fortescue and Ollivander went on holiday, did they?' said Mrs Weasley, firing up at once. 'If you think security's a laughing matter you can stay behind and I'll get your things myself –'

'No, I wanna come, I want to see Fred and George's shop!' said Ron hastily.

'Then you just buck up your ideas, young man, before I decide you're too immature to come with us!' said Mrs Weasley angrily, snatching up her

服的空落落的感觉，“以前他经常给我吃免费的冰淇淋。他怎么啦？”

“从小店里的情况看，他被劫走了。”

“为什么？”罗恩问，韦斯莱夫人则严厉地瞪着比尔。

“谁知道呢？他准是不知怎么得罪了他们。这个福洛林，他可是个好人啊。”

“说到对角巷，”韦斯莱先生说，“好像奥利凡德也不见了。”

“就是那个做魔杖的？”金妮显得很吃惊。

“就是他。店里空无一人。没有搏斗的痕迹。谁也不知道他是自己离开了，还是被绑架了。”

“可是魔杖呢——人们要买魔杖怎么办呢？”

“只好去找别的魔杖制造商了。”卢平说，“可是奥利凡德是最优秀的，如果另一派把他弄去，对我们可就非常不利了。”

在这相当沉闷的生日茶会的第二天，霍格沃茨给他们寄来了信和书单。哈利的信封里还装着一个喜讯：他被选为魁地奇球队的队长。

“这样你的地位就跟级长一样了！”赫敏高兴地大声说，“现在你也可以用我们的专用盥洗室了，还有其他所有的东西！”

“哇，我记得查理戴过这玩意儿。”罗恩喜滋滋地端详着那枚徽章，说道，“哈利，真是太酷了，你是我的队长了——如果你能让我归队的话，我想，哈哈……”

“我说，你们已经收到了这些，”韦斯莱夫人低头看着罗恩的书单，叹着气说，“我们不能再拖延了，必须抓紧时间去对角巷。只要你们的父亲不加班，我们就星期六去。没有他陪着，我可不去那儿。”

“妈妈，你真的以为神秘人会藏在丽痕书店的一排书架后面吗？”罗恩坏笑着说。

“福斯科和奥利凡德是去度假了，是吗？”韦斯莱夫人立刻就火了，抢白道，“如果你认为安全问题是一场儿戏，你可以留在家里，我去替你们买东西——”

“不行，我要去，我还想看看弗雷德和乔治的店呢！”罗恩赶紧说道。

“那你就赶紧提高认识，年轻人，免得我觉得你太不成熟，不能跟

clock, all nine hands of which were still pointing at *mortal peril*, and balancing it on top of a pile of just-laundered towels. 'And that goes for returning to Hogwarts, as well!'

Ron turned to stare incredulously at Harry as his mother hoisted the laundry basket and the teetering clock into her arms and stormed out of the room.

'Blimey … you can't even make a joke round here any more …'

But Ron was careful not to be flippant about Voldemort over the next few days. Saturday dawned without any more outbursts from Mrs Weasley, though she seemed very tense at breakfast. Bill, who would be staying at home with Fleur (much to Hermione and Ginny's pleasure), passed a full money bag across the table to Harry.

'Where's mine?' demanded Ron at once, his eyes wide.

'That's already Harry's, idiot,' said Bill. 'I got it out of your vault for you, Harry, because it's taking about five hours for the public to get to their gold at the moment, the goblins have tightened security so much. Two days ago Arkie Philpott had a Probity Probe stuck up his … well, trust me, this way's easier.'

'Thanks, Bill,' said Harry, pocketing his gold.

''E is always so thoughtful,' purred Fleur adoringly, stroking Bill's nose. Ginny mimed vomiting into her cereal behind Fleur. Harry choked over his cornflakes and Ron thumped him on the back.

It was an overcast, murky day. One of the special Ministry of Magic cars, in which Harry had ridden once before, was awaiting them in the front yard when they emerged from the house pulling on their cloaks.

'It's good Dad can get us these again,' said Ron appreciatively, stretching luxuriously as the car moved smoothly away from The Burrow, Bill and Fleur waving from the kitchen window. He, Harry, Hermione and Ginny were all sitting in roomy comfort in the wide back seat.

'Don't get used to it, it's only because of Harry,' said Mr Weasley over his shoulder. He and Mrs Weasley were in front with the Ministry driver; the front passenger seat had obligingly stretched into what resembled a two-seater sofa. 'He's been given top-grade security status. And we'll be joining up with additional security at the Leaky Cauldron, too.'

我们一起去！”韦斯莱夫人生气地说着，一把抓起她的大钟，放在刚刚洗干净的一堆毛巾上，钟上的九根针仍然都指着生命危险，“回霍格沃茨上学的事也是这样！”

罗恩转身不敢相信地瞪着哈利，他妈妈拎起洗衣篮，气冲冲地走出了房间，大钟在篮子上面摇晃着。

“天哪……在这个家里连玩笑也不能开了……”

不过，在后来的几天里，罗恩变得很小心，再也不敢随便乱说伏地魔的事了。一直到星期六早晨，韦斯莱夫人没有再发火，但吃早饭时她显得非常紧张。比尔留在家里陪芙蓉（这使赫敏和金妮大感庆幸），他隔着桌子递给哈利一只满满的钱袋。

“我的呢？”罗恩立刻问道，眼睛睁得大大的。

“这都是哈利的，你这傻瓜。”比尔说，“哈利，我替你从保险库里取出来的，目前小妖精们加强了保安，戒备森严，普通人取钱要花大约五个小时。两天前，阿基·菲尔坡特被人把一根诚实探测器插在他的……唉，信不信由你，这样子更方便些。”

“谢谢你，比尔。”哈利说着把钱装进了口袋。

“他总是这么体贴周到。”芙蓉含情脉脉地低语，一边抚摸着比尔的鼻子。她身后的金妮对着碗里的麦片做呕吐状。哈利被玉米片呛住了，罗恩使劲拍着他的后背。

这是一个昏暗的、阴云密布的日子。当他们裹着斗篷从房子里出来时，魔法部的一辆专用汽车已经在前院等着了，这辆汽车哈利曾经坐过一次。

“幸好爸爸又能给我们派车。”罗恩美滋滋地说着，舒舒服服地伸展了一下四肢。汽车轻快地驶离了陋居，比尔和芙蓉在厨房窗口朝他们挥手。罗恩、哈利、赫敏和金妮都坐在宽敞、舒适的后座上。

“你可别坐习惯了，这只是为了哈利。”韦斯莱先生扭头说。他和韦斯莱夫人以及魔法部的司机坐在前面。司机旁边的乘客座位很体贴地变宽了，像一张双人沙发。“他现在享受一级安全保卫。到了破釜酒吧，还要给我们加强保安呢。”

Harry said nothing; he did not much fancy doing his shopping while surrounded by a battalion of Aurors. He had stowed his Invisibility Cloak in his backpack and felt that, if that was good enough for Dumbledore, it ought to be good enough for the Ministry, though now he came to think of it, he was not sure the Ministry knew about his Cloak.

'Here you are, then,' said the driver a surprisingly short while later, speaking for the first time as he slowed in Charing Cross Road and stopped outside the Leaky Cauldron. 'I'm to wait for you, any idea how long you'll be?'

'A couple of hours, I expect,' said Mr Weasley. 'Ah, good, he's here!'

Harry imitated Mr Weasley and peered through the window; his heart leapt. There were no Aurors waiting outside the inn, but instead the gigantic, black-bearded form of Rubeus Hagrid, the Hogwarts gamekeeper, wearing a long beaverskin coat, beaming at the sight of Harry's face and oblivious to the startled stares of passing Muggles.

'Harry!' he boomed, sweeping Harry into a bone-crushing hug the moment Harry had stepped out of the car. 'Buckbeak – Witherwings, I mean – yeh should see him, Harry, he's so happy ter be back in the open air –'

'Glad he's pleased,' said Harry, grinning as he massaged his ribs. 'We didn't know "security" meant you!'

'I know, jus' like old times, innit? See, the Ministry wanted ter send a bunch o' Aurors, but Dumbledore said I'd do,' said Hagrid proudly, throwing out his chest and tucking his thumbs into his pockets. 'Let's get goin', then – after yeh, Molly, Arthur –'

The Leaky Cauldron was, for the first time in Harry's memory, completely empty. Only Tom the landlord, wizened and toothless, remained of the old crowd. He looked up hopefully as they entered, but before he could speak, Hagrid said importantly, 'Jus' passin' through today, Tom, sure yeh understand. Hogwarts business, yeh know.'

Tom nodded gloomily and returned to wiping glasses; Harry, Hermione, Hagrid and the Weasleys walked through the bar and out into the chilly little courtyard at the back where the dustbins stood. Hagrid raised his pink umbrella and rapped a certain brick in the wall, which opened at once to form an archway on to a winding cobbled street. They stepped through the

哈利什么也没说。他可不愿意买东西时周围有一大批傲罗跟着。他已经把隐形衣塞在了背包里。他曾想，既然邓布利多不反对，魔法部应该也不会反对，不过现在仔细想来，他不能肯定魔法部是不是知道他有一件隐形衣。

“你们到了。”没过一会儿司机就说，这是他说的第一句话。他放慢速度驶进了查令十字街，在破釜酒吧外面停了下来。“我等你们回来，知道需要多长时间吗？”

“大概两个小时吧。”韦斯莱先生说，“啊，太好了，他已经来了！”

哈利也像韦斯莱先生那样透过车窗朝外望去。他的心顿时欢跳起来。酒吧外面并没有什么傲罗在等着，而是站着大块头、黑胡子的鲁伯·海格，霍格沃茨的猎场看守，他穿着一件长长的海狸皮大衣，一看见哈利的面孔就露出了喜悦的笑容，毫不理会过路的麻瓜们惊异的目光。

“哈利！”他粗声大气地说，哈利刚一下车，海格就使劲把他搂进怀里，把他的骨头都要挤碎了，“巴克比克——我是说蔫翼——你真应该看看它，哈利，它回到露天可高兴了——”

“它高兴就好，”哈利一边揉着肋骨，一边笑着说，“没想到‘保安’指的就是你呀！”

“我知道，就像过去一样，是不？你看，魔法部本来想派一批傲罗来的，但邓布利多说我来就行了。”海格得意地说，他挺起胸膛，把两个大拇指插进了口袋里，“好了，我们进去吧——你们先请，莫丽，亚瑟——”

在哈利的记忆里，破釜酒吧第一次显得这么冷清，空无一人。过去那些热闹的人群不见了，只剩下满脸皱纹、牙齿掉光了的店主汤姆。他们一进去，汤姆满怀希望地抬起头，可是没等他开口，海格就郑重其事地说：“今天只是路过，汤姆，你肯定明白。是霍格沃茨的公事，你知道的。”

汤姆闷闷不乐地点点头，继续擦他的玻璃杯。哈利、赫敏、海格和韦斯莱家的人穿过酒吧，来到后面放垃圾箱的阴冷的小院子里。海

entrance and paused, looking around.

Diagon Alley had changed. The colourful, glittering window displays of spellbooks, potion ingredients and cauldrons were lost to view, hidden behind the large Ministry of Magic posters that had been pasted over them. Most of these sombre purple posters carried blown-up versions of the security advice on the Ministry pamphlets that had been sent out over the summer, but others bore moving black-and-white photographs of Death Eaters known to be on the loose. Bellatrix Lestrange was sneering from the front of the nearest apothecary. A few windows were boarded up, including those of Florean Fortescue's Ice-Cream Parlour. On the other hand, a number of shabby-looking stalls had sprung up along the street. The nearest one, which had been erected outside Flourish and Blotts under a striped, stained awning, had a cardboard sign pinned to its front:

AMULETS:

EFFECTIVE AGAINST WEREWOLVES, DEMENTORS AND INFERI

A seedy-looking little wizard was rattling armfuls of silver symbols on chains at passers-by.

'One for your little girl, madam?' he called at Mrs Weasley as they passed, leering at Ginny. 'Protect her pretty neck?'

'If I were on duty …' said Mr Weasley, glaring angrily at the amulet seller.

'Yes, but don't go arresting anyone now, dear, we're in a hurry,' said Mrs Weasley, nervously consulting a list. 'I think we'd better do Madam Malkin's first, Hermione wants new dress robes and Ron's showing much too much ankle in his school robes, and you must need new ones too, Harry, you've grown so much – come on, everyone –'

'Molly, it doesn't make sense for all of us to go to Madam Malkin's,' said Mr Weasley. 'Why don't those three go with Hagrid, and we can go to

格举起手里的粉红色雨伞，敲了敲墙上的一块砖，那里立刻出现了一个门洞，通向一条蜿蜒曲折的卵石小路。他们跨过门洞，停下来四下张望。

对角巷完全变了样儿。橱窗里原先陈列着咒语书、魔药原料和坩埚，五光十色的，如今都看不见了，而是被魔法部张贴的大幅通告遮得严严实实。这些令人生畏的紫色通告，大部分都是魔法部暑期散发的那些小册子上的安全忠告的放大版，还有一些通告上印着被通缉的食死徒的黑白活动照片。贝拉特里克斯·莱斯特兰奇在近旁那家药店门口狰狞地冷笑着。有几扇窗户被木板钉死了，包括福洛林·福斯科冰淇淋店。而另一方面，街道两边突然冒出了许多破破烂烂的小摊子。离他们最近的一个摊子就搭在丽痕书店外污迹斑斑的条纹雨棚下面，摊前钉着一块硬纸板招牌：

护身符：有效抵御狼人、摄魂怪和阴尸

一个邋里邋遢的小个子巫师向路人兜售一大串带链子的银质吉祥物，把它们抖得哗哗直响。

"夫人，买一个给你的小姑娘吧？"他们经过时，他朝韦斯莱夫人喊道，同时色眯眯地看了一眼金妮，"保护她那漂亮的脖子？"

"如果我在值勤……"韦斯莱先生说，怒气冲冲地瞪着那个卖护身符的人。

"是啊，但你现在就别到处去抓人啦，亲爱的，我们时间很紧。"韦斯莱夫人说着焦急地看了看一份清单，"我想最好先去摩金夫人长袍专卖店，赫敏需要一件新礼服长袍，罗恩的校服短了，脚腕子露出一大截，还有，哈利，你肯定也需要买新衣服了，你长得太快——好，大家快走吧——"

"莫丽，没有必要大家都去摩金夫人长袍专卖店。"韦斯莱先生说，"不如让他们三个跟着海格去，我们可以到丽痕书店去把大家的课本都

Flourish and Blotts and get everyone's school books?'

'I don't know,' said Mrs Weasley anxiously, clearly torn between a desire to finish the shopping quickly and the wish to stick together in a pack. 'Hagrid, do you think –?'

'Don' fret, they'll be fine with me, Molly,' said Hagrid soothingly, waving an airy hand the size of a dustbin lid. Mrs Weasley did not look entirely convinced, but allowed the separation, scurrying off towards Flourish and Blotts with her husband and Ginny while Harry, Ron, Hermione and Hagrid set off for Madam Malkin's.

Harry noticed that many of the people who passed them had the same harried, anxious look as Mrs Weasley, and that nobody was stopping to talk any more; the shoppers stayed together in their own tightly knit groups, moving intently about their business. Nobody seemed to be shopping alone.

'Migh' be a bit of a squeeze in there with all o' us,' said Hagrid, stopping outside Madam Malkin's and bending down to peer through the window. 'I'll stand guard outside, all righ'?'

So Harry, Ron and Hermione entered the little shop together. It appeared, at first glance, to be empty, but no sooner had the door swung shut behind them than they heard a familiar voice issuing from behind a rack of dress robes in spangled green and blue.

'... not a child, in case you haven't noticed, Mother. I am perfectly capable of doing my shopping *alone*.'

There was a clucking noise and a voice Harry recognised as that of Madam Malkin said, 'Now, dear, your mother's quite right, none of us is supposed to go wandering around on our own any more, it's nothing to do with being a child –'

'Watch where you're sticking that pin, will you!'

A teenage boy with a pale, pointed face and white-blond hair appeared from behind the rack wearing a handsome set of dark green robes that glittered with pins around the hem and the edges of the sleeves. He strode to the mirror and examined himself; it was a few moments before he noticed Harry, Ron and Hermione reflected over his shoulder. His light grey eyes narrowed.

'If you're wondering what the smell is, Mother, a Mudblood just walked in,' said Draco Malfoy.

买齐，好吗？”

“我不知道怎么办才好，”韦斯莱夫人烦恼地说，显然，她既希望赶紧买完东西，又希望大家不要分开，真是左右为难，“海格，你觉得——？”

“别担心，他们跟着我不会有问题的，莫丽。”海格安慰道，一边潇洒地挥了挥他那垃圾桶盖般大的手掌。韦斯莱夫人似乎并不完全放心，但还是让大家分开了，她跟着丈夫和金妮一起匆匆奔向丽痕书店，而哈利、罗恩、赫敏和海格则去了摩金夫人长袍专卖店。

哈利注意到，许多路人的脸上都带着和韦斯莱夫人一样烦恼焦虑的神情，不再有人停下来说话。买东西的人都三五成群地贴在一起，直奔他们要买的东西，似乎没有一个人单独购物。

“如果我们都进去，可能会有点儿挤。”海格说，他在摩金夫人长袍专卖店外面停下脚步，俯身朝窗户里看了看，“我在外面站岗，好吗？”

于是，哈利、罗恩和赫敏一起走进小店。第一眼看去，店里好像空无一人，可是门刚在他们身后关上，就听见一排绿色和蓝色的礼服长袍后面传来一个熟悉的声音。

“……不是个小孩子了，你也许没有注意到，妈妈。我完全有能力独自出来买东西。”

接着是一阵大惊小怪的发作，然后一个人说话了，哈利听出是摩金夫人的声音：“是啊，亲爱的，你妈妈说得对，现在我们谁也不应该单独出来闲逛，这跟小孩子不小孩子没有关系——”

“你那根针往哪儿戳？留点儿神！”

一个脸色苍白、头发淡金的尖脸少年从挂衣架后面出现了，他穿着一套漂亮的墨绿色长袍，贴边和袖口都别着闪闪发亮的别针。他大步走到镜子前，仔细端详自己。片刻之后，他才从镜子里注意到哈利、罗恩和赫敏就站在他身后。他眯起了淡灰色的眼睛。

“妈妈，如果你不明白这是一股什么怪味儿，我可以告诉你，这里刚进来了一个泥巴种。”德拉科·马尔福说。

'I don't think there's any need for language like that!' said Madam Malkin, scurrying out from behind the clothes rack holding a tape measure and a wand. 'And I don't want wands drawn in my shop, either!' she added hastily, for a glance towards the door had shown her Harry and Ron both standing there with their wands out and pointing at Malfoy.

Hermione, who was standing slightly behind them, whispered, 'No, don't, honestly, it's not worth it ...'

'Yeah, like you'd dare do magic out of school,' sneered Malfoy. 'Who blacked your eye, Granger? I want to send them flowers.'

'That's quite enough!' said Madam Malkin sharply, looking over her shoulder for support. 'Madam – please –'

Narcissa Malfoy strolled out from behind the clothes rack.

'Put those away,' she said coldly to Harry and Ron. 'If you attack my son again, I shall ensure that it is the last thing you ever do.'

'Really?' said Harry, taking a step forwards and gazing into the smoothly arrogant face that, for all its pallor, still resembled her sister's. He was as tall as she was now. 'Going to get a few Death Eater pals to do us in, are you?'

Madam Malkin squealed and clutched at her heart.

'Really, you shouldn't accuse – dangerous thing to say – wands away, please!'

But Harry did not lower his wand. Narcissa Malfoy smiled unpleasantly.

'I see that being Dumbledore's favourite has given you a false sense of security, Harry Potter. But Dumbledore won't always be there to protect you.'

Harry looked mockingly all around the shop.

'Wow ... look at that ... he's not here now! So why not have a go? They might be able to find you a double cell in Azkaban with your loser of a husband!'

Malfoy made an angry movement towards Harry, but stumbled over his overlong robe. Ron laughed loudly.

'Don't you dare talk to my mother like that, Potter!' Malfoy snarled.

'It's all right, Draco,' said Narcissa, restraining him with her thin white fingers upon his shoulder. 'I expect Potter will be reunited with dear Sirius before I am reunited with Lucius.'

“我认为没有必要这样说话！”摩金夫人说着从挂衣架后面匆匆走了出来，手里拿着皮尺和一根魔杖。“而且，我也不希望在我的店里把魔杖抽出来！”她朝门口扫了一眼，看见哈利和罗恩都拔出魔杖指着马尔福，便赶紧加了一句。

赫敏站在他们后面一点的地方，低声说：“别，别这么做，说实在的，不值得……”

“是啊，就好像你们敢在校外施魔法似的。”马尔福讥笑道，“是谁把你的眼睛打青了，格兰杰？我要给那些人献花。”

“够了！”摩金夫人厉声说，扭头寻求支持，“夫人——请你——”

纳西莎·马尔福慢慢地从挂衣架后面走了出来。

“把它们收起来，”她冷冷地对哈利和罗恩说，“如果再敢对我的儿子动手，我就让你们永远动弹不得。”

“是吗？”哈利说着跨前一步，盯着那张自得、傲慢的脸，那张脸尽管皮肤白皙，却跟她姐姐的脸仍有相似之处。现在哈利个头已和她一样高了。“想找几个食死徒哥们儿把我们干掉，是吗？”

摩金夫人尖叫一声，一把揪住了胸口。

“说真的，你不应该这样指责——说这种话很危险——请你快把魔杖收起来！”

但哈利没有放下魔杖。纳西莎·马尔福脸上露出难看的笑容。

“看得出来，你做了邓布利多的得意门生，就误以为自己安全了，哈利·波特。可是邓布利多不会总在你身边保护你的。”

哈利假装打量了一下小店。

“哇……你瞧……他眼下不在这里！那你为什么不试一试呢？说不定他们会给你在阿兹卡班找一个双人牢房，跟你那失败的丈夫关在一起呢！”

马尔福气愤地朝哈利逼了过来，却被他那过长的袍子绊了一下。罗恩大声笑了起来。

“你竟敢对我妈妈这么说话，波特！”马尔福恶狠狠地吼道。

“没关系，德拉科，”纳西莎用苍白纤细的手指按住他的肩膀，阻止了他，“我想，不等我去跟卢修斯团聚，波特就去跟亲爱的小天狼星团聚了。”

Harry raised his wand higher.

'Harry, no!' moaned Hermione, grabbing his arm and attempting to push it down by his side. 'Think … you mustn't … you'll be in such trouble …'

Madam Malkin dithered for a moment on the spot, then seemed to decide to act as though nothing was happening in the hope that it wouldn't. She bent towards Malfoy, who was still glaring at Harry.

'I think this left sleeve could come up a little bit more, dear, let me just –'

'Ouch!' bellowed Malfoy, slapping her hand away. 'Watch where you're putting your pins, woman! Mother – I don't think I want these any more –'

He pulled the robes over his head and threw them on to the floor at Madam Malkin's feet.

'You're right, Draco,' said Narcissa, with a contemptuous glance at Hermione, 'now I know the kind of scum that shops here … we'll do better at Twilfitt and Tatting's.'

And with that, the pair of them strode out of the shop, Malfoy taking care to bang as hard as he could into Ron on the way out.

'Well, *really*!' said Madam Malkin, snatching up the fallen robes and moving the tip of her wand over them like a vacuum cleaner, so that it removed the dust.

She was distracted all through the fitting of Ron and Harry's new robes, tried to sell Hermione wizard's dress robes instead of witch's, and when she finally bowed them out of the shop it was with an air of being glad to see the back of them.

'Got ev'rything?' asked Hagrid brightly when they reappeared at his side.

'Just about,' said Harry. 'Did you see the Malfoys?'

'Yeah,' said Hagrid, unconcerned. 'Bu' they wouldn' dare make trouble in the middle o' Diagon Alley, Harry, don' worry abou' them.'

Harry, Ron and Hermione exchanged looks, but before they could disabuse Hagrid of this comfortable notion Mr and Mrs Weasley and Ginny appeared, all clutching heavy packages of books.

'Everyone all right?' said Mrs Weasley. 'Got your robes? Right then, we can pop in at the apothecary and Eeylops on the way to Fred and George's – stick close, now …'

Neither Harry nor Ron bought any ingredients at the apothecary, seeing

哈利把魔杖举得更高了。

“哈利，别！”赫敏低声说，一把抓住他的胳膊，使劲往下压，“考虑一下……千万不能……你会闯大祸的……”

摩金夫人在原地踌躇了一会儿，然后似乎打算假装什么事也没发生，并希望什么事也别发生。她朝仍然瞪着哈利的马尔福弯下腰去。

“我觉得左边这只袖子可以再往上收一点儿，亲爱的，让我——”

“哎哟！”马尔福大叫一声，啪地把她的手打开了，“仔细点儿，看你的针往哪儿扎，蠢婆子！妈妈——这件衣服我不要了——”

他从头上把长袍扯下来，扔在摩金夫人脚下。

“你说得对，德拉科，”纳西莎说，轻蔑地扫了一眼赫敏，“现在我知道是哪些社会渣滓在这里买衣服了……我们到脱凡成衣店能买到更好的。”

说完，他们俩就大步走出了小店，马尔福出门前故意狠狠地撞了一下罗恩。

“唉，*真够呛！*”摩金夫人说着抓起扔在地上的长袍，用魔杖尖在上面一扫，灰尘就像被吸尘器吸走一样消失了。

她给罗恩和哈利裁剪新袍子时一直心不在焉，甚至还要把男巫的礼服长袍卖给赫敏。最后，当她鞠躬把他们送出小店时，似乎满心庆幸他们终于离开了。

“东西都买齐了？”海格看到他们出来，高兴地问。

“差不多吧。”哈利说，“你看见马尔福和他妈妈了吗？”

“看见了。”海格不太介意地说，“不过在对角巷里，他们是不敢轻举妄动的，哈利，不用担心他们。”

哈利、罗恩和赫敏交换了一下目光，他们还没来得及消除海格的错误想法，韦斯莱夫妇和金妮就出现了，每个人怀里都抱着一大包书。

“大伙儿都没事吧？”韦斯莱夫人说，“袍子买到了？好吧，我们在去弗雷德和乔治的小店的路上，顺便去一趟药店和咿啦猫头鹰商店——走吧，跟紧一点儿……”

哈利和罗恩知道他们不再上魔药课了，便没有在药店里买任何原

that they were no longer studying Potions, but both bought large boxes of owl nuts for Hedwig and Pigwidgeon at Eeylops Owl Emporium. Then, with Mrs Weasley checking her watch every minute or so, they headed further along the street in search of Weasleys' Wizard Wheezes, the joke shop run by Fred and George.

'We really haven't got too long,' Mrs Weasley said. 'So we'll just have a quick look around and then back to the car. We must be close, that's number ninety-two … ninety-four …'

'*Whoa*,' said Ron, stopping in his tracks.

Set against the dull, poster-muffled shop fronts around them, Fred and George's windows hit the eye like a firework display. Casual passers-by were looking back over their shoulders at the windows, and a few rather stunned-looking people had actually come to a halt, transfixed. The left-hand window was dazzlingly full of an assortment of goods that revolved, popped, flashed, bounced and shrieked; Harry's eyes began to water just looking at it. The right-hand window was covered with a gigantic poster, purple like those of the Ministry, but emblazoned with flashing yellow letters:

Why Are You Worrying About You-Know-Who?
You SHOULD Be Worrying About
U-NO-POO –
the Constipation Sensation
That's GRIPPING the Nation!

Harry started to laugh. He heard a weak sort of moan beside him and looked round to see Mrs Weasley gazing, dumbfounded, at the poster. Her lips moved, silently mouthing the name, 'U-No-Poo.'

'They'll be murdered in their beds!' she whispered.

'No they won't!' said Ron, who like Harry was laughing. 'This is brilliant!'

And he and Harry led the way into the shop. It was packed with customers; Harry could not get near the shelves. He stared around, looking up at the boxes piled to the ceiling: here were the Skiving Snackboxes that the twins had perfected during their last, unfinished year at Hogwarts; Harry noticed that the Nosebleed Nougat was most popular, with only one battered

料，但两人都在咿啦猫头鹰商店里给海德薇和小猪买了大盒的猫头鹰坚果。然后，他们在街上继续往前走，寻找弗雷德和乔治开的笑话商店——韦斯莱魔法把戏坊，韦斯莱夫人每隔一分钟就要看一次表。

“我们真的不能待很久，”韦斯莱夫人说，“只是抓紧时间在店里看看，然后就回到车上。大家必须跟紧一点儿，这是九十二号……九十四号……”

“哇！”罗恩猛地停住脚步，惊呼道。

周围店铺的门脸都暗淡无光，被通告埋没了，而弗雷德和乔治的橱窗像烟火展览一样吸引着人们的眼球。普通的行人都忍不住扭头看着那橱窗，还有几个人显得特别震惊，竟然停下脚步，一副痴迷的样子。左边的橱窗里五光十色，摆着各种各样旋转、抽动、闪烁、跳跃和尖叫的商品，哈利看着看着，眼泪就涌了出来。右边的橱窗上蒙着一张巨幅海报，和魔法部的那些通告一样也是紫色的，但上面印着耀眼的黄色大字：

你为什么担心神秘人？

你**应该**关心

便秘仁——

便秘的感觉折磨着国人！

哈利笑了起来。他听见身边传来一声无力的呻吟，转脸一看，韦斯莱夫人正目瞪口呆地看着那张海报。她的嘴唇无声地嚅动着，默念那几个字：**便秘仁**。

“他们会在床上被人谋杀的！”她小声说。

“不会的！”罗恩说，他和哈利一样笑出了声，“这简直太精彩了！”

他和哈利领头走进了小店。里面全是顾客，哈利简直挤不到货架前面。他左右看看，只见纸箱子一直堆到了天花板上：是双胞胎在霍格沃茨肄业前的最后一年完善过后的速效逃课糖。哈利注意到最受欢迎的是鼻血牛轧糖，货架上只剩下最后被压扁了的一盒。另外还有好

box left on the shelf. There were bins full of trick wands, the cheapest merely turning into rubber chickens or pairs of pants when waved; the most expensive beating the unwary user around the head and neck; boxes of quills, which came in Self-Inking, Spell-Checking and Smart-Answer varieties. A space cleared in the crowd and Harry pushed his way towards the counter, where a gaggle of delighted ten-year-olds was watching a tiny little wooden man slowly ascending the steps to a real set of gallows, both perched on a box that read: *Reusable Hangman – Spell It Or He'll Swing!*

'"Patented Daydream Charms ..."'

Hermione had managed to squeeze through to a large display near the counter and was reading the information on the back of a box bearing a highly coloured picture of a handsome youth and a swooning girl who were standing on the deck of a pirate ship.

'"*One simple incantation and you will enter a top-quality, highly realistic thirty-minute daydream, easy to fit into the average school lesson and virtually undetectable (side-effects include vacant expression and minor drooling). Not for sale to under-sixteens.*" You know,' said Hermione, looking up at Harry, 'that really is extraordinary magic!'

'For that, Hermione,' said a voice behind them, 'you can have one for free.'

A beaming Fred stood before them, wearing a set of magenta robes that clashed magnificently with his flaming hair.

'How are you, Harry?' They shook hands. 'And what's happened to your eye, Hermione?'

'Your punching telescope,' she said ruefully.

'Oh, blimey, I forgot about those,' said Fred. 'Here –'

He pulled a tub out of his pocket and handed it to her; she unscrewed it gingerly to reveal a thick yellow paste.

'Just dab it on, that bruise'll be gone within the hour,' said Fred. 'We had to find a decent bruise-remover, we're testing most of our products on ourselves.'

Hermione looked nervous. 'It is *safe*, isn't it?'

'Course it is,' said Fred bracingly. 'Come on, Harry, I'll give you a tour.'

Harry left Hermione dabbing her black eye with paste and followed Fred

几箱戏法魔杖，其中最便宜的一挥就能变成橡皮鸡或内裤，而最贵的那种，如果使用者没有防备，脖子和脑袋就会挨上一顿打。还有一盒盒的羽毛笔，包括自动加墨、拼写检查、机智抢答等品种。这时，人群稍微松动了点儿，哈利朝柜台挤去，一群十来岁的孩子兴奋地注视着一个木头小人慢慢地登上台阶，爬向一套逼真的绞索架，这两样东西都在一个箱子顶上，箱子上写着：可反复使用的刽子手游戏——拼不出就吊死他！

“专利产品：白日梦咒……”

赫敏好不容易挤到柜台旁边一个大的陈列柜前，正在阅读一只箱子背面的说明文字。那箱子上印着一幅色彩鲜艳的图画：一位英俊青年和一个如痴如醉的姑娘一起站在海盗船的甲板上。

“只要念一个咒语，你就能进入一场高质量的、绝顶逼真的三十分钟白日梦，适用于普通学校上课，操作简单，绝对令人难以察觉（副作用包括表情呆滞和轻微流口水）。不向十六岁以下少年出售。嘿，你看，”赫敏抬头看着哈利说，“这种魔法可真奇特！”

“既然你这么说了，赫敏，”一个声音在他们后面说，“你可以免费拿走一个。”

笑容满面的弗雷德站在他们面前，身上穿着一套品红色的长袍，跟他红色的头发配在一起对比鲜明，十分耀眼。

“你好吗，哈利？”他们握了握手，“赫敏，你的眼睛怎么啦？”

“都怪你的打拳望远镜。”赫敏懊恼地说。

“哦，天哪，我都把它们给忘了。”弗雷德说，“给——”

他从口袋里掏出一个小瓶子递给赫敏，赫敏小心地拧开盖子，里面是一种黏稠的黄色膏体。

“把它涂上，一小时内青肿就消了。”弗雷德说，“我们必须找到一种有效的青肿消除剂，大多数产品我们都在自己身上试验的。”

赫敏显得有点儿顾虑：“它安全吗？”

“那还用说。”弗雷德宽慰她道，“哈利，走吧，我带你到处转转。”

赫敏在那儿往黑眼圈上抹药膏，哈利跟着弗雷德朝小店后面走去，

towards the back of the shop, where he saw a stand of card and rope tricks.

'Muggle magic tricks!' said Fred happily, pointing them out. 'For freaks like Dad, you know, who love Muggle stuff. It's not a big earner, but we do fairly steady business, they're great novelties … oh, here's George …'

Fred's twin shook Harry's hand energetically.

'Giving him the tour? Come through to the back, Harry, that's where we're making the real money – *pocket anything, you, and you'll pay in more than Galleons*!' he added warningly to a small boy who hastily whipped his hand out of the tub labelled: Edible Dark Marks – They'll Make Anyone Sick!

George pushed back a curtain beside the Muggle tricks and Harry saw a darker, less crowded room. The packaging on the products lining these shelves was more subdued.

'We've just developed this more serious line,' said Fred. 'Funny how it happened …'

'You wouldn't believe how many people, even people who work at the Ministry, can't do a decent Shield Charm,' said George. 'Course, they didn't have you teaching them, Harry.'

'That's right … well, we thought Shield Hats were a bit of a laugh. You know, challenge your mate to jinx you while wearing it and watch his face when the jinx just bounces off. But the Ministry bought five hundred for all its support staff! And we're still getting massive orders!'

'So we've expanded into a range of Shield Cloaks, Shield Gloves …'

'… I mean, they wouldn't help much against the Unforgivable Curses, but for minor to moderate hexes or jinxes …'

'And then we thought we'd get into the whole area of Defence Against the Dark Arts, because it's such a money-spinner,' continued George enthusiastically. 'This is cool. Look, Instant Darkness Powder, we're importing it from Peru. Handy if you want to make a quick escape.'

'And our Decoy Detonators are just walking off the shelves, look,' said Fred, pointing at a number of weird-looking black hooter-type objects that were indeed attempting to scurry out of sight. 'You just drop one surreptitiously and it'll run off and make a nice loud noise out of sight, giving you a diversion if you need one.'

他看见那里有一个摊子上摆着纸牌和绳索戏法。

“麻瓜的魔术！”弗雷德高兴地把它们一一指给他看，“专门卖给我爸爸那种喜欢麻瓜东西的怪人，你知道的。赚得不多，但细水长流，都是非常新奇的玩意儿……哦，乔治来了……”

弗雷德的孪生兄弟热情地跟哈利握手。

“带他到处转转？到后面来吧，哈利，那才是我们真正赚大钱的地方——如果谁敢偷东西，到时候要付出的就不只是加隆了！”他突然对一个小男孩发出警告，那男孩赶紧把手从标着可食用黑魔标记——谁吃谁恶心！的塑料瓶上缩了回去。

乔治掀开麻瓜魔术用品旁边的帘子，哈利看见了一个更加黑暗、但没有那么拥挤的房间，排在架子上的产品包装都显得比较低调。

“我们刚研制出这些更加严肃的产品。”弗雷德说，“说起来真有趣……”

“你简直不能相信有那么多人，甚至在魔法部工作的人，都念不出一个像样的铁甲咒。”乔治说，“当然啦，他们没有碰到你这么好的老师，哈利。”

“没错……嘿，我们本来以为防咒帽只是一种搞笑的玩意儿。你知道的，就是你戴着这种帽子叫你的同伴给你施恶咒，然后你就可以欣赏恶咒反弹出去时他脸上的表情。没想到魔法部给他们所有的工作人员买了五百顶！现在我们还不断接到大额订单呢！”

“所以我们又接着开发了一系列防咒斗篷、防咒手套……”

“……我的意思是，它们对不可饶恕咒没有多大作用，但对付一些小魔法、小恶咒什么的……”

“我们打算全面进入黑魔法防御术的领域，因为那简直就是摇钱树啊。”乔治兴奋地往下说，“太酷了。你看，隐身烟幕弹，秘鲁进口。如果你想快速脱身，用起来是很方便的。”

“还有我们的诱饵炸弹，快卖得脱销了，看，”弗雷德指着一大堆怪模怪样、黑色喇叭似的玩意儿，它们看起来就像是随时准备逃之夭夭，“你只要偷偷扔一个出去，它就会快速逃窜，闹出很响的动静，在你需要的时候转移别人的注意力。”

'Handy,' said Harry, impressed.

'Here,' said George, catching a couple and throwing them to Harry.

A young witch with short blonde hair poked her head round the curtain; Harry saw that she too was wearing magenta staff robes.

'There's a customer out here looking for a joke cauldron, Mr Weasley and Mr Weasley,' she said.

Harry found it very odd to hear Fred and George called 'Mr Weasley', but they took it in their stride.

'Right you are, Verity, I'm coming,' said George promptly. 'Harry, you help yourself to anything you want, all right? No charge.'

'I can't do that!' said Harry, who had already pulled out his money bag to pay for the Decoy Detonators.

'You don't pay here,' said Fred firmly, waving away Harry's gold.

'But –'

'You gave us our start-up loan, we haven't forgotten,' said George sternly. 'Take whatever you like, and just remember to tell people where you got it, if they ask.'

George swept off through the curtain to help with the customers and Fred led Harry back into the main part of the shop to find Hermione and Ginny still poring over the Patented Daydream Charms.

'Haven't you girls found our special WonderWitch products yet?' asked Fred. 'Follow me, ladies …'

Near the window was an array of violently pink products around which a cluster of excited girls was giggling enthusiastically. Hermione and Ginny both hung back, looking wary.

'There you go,' said Fred proudly. 'Best range of love potions you'll find anywhere.'

Ginny raised an eyebrow sceptically. 'Do they work?'

'Certainly they work, for up to twenty-four hours at a time depending on the weight of the boy in question –'

'– and the attractiveness of the girl,' said George, reappearing suddenly at their side. 'But we're not selling them to our sister,' he added, becoming suddenly stern, 'not when she's already got about five boys on the go from what we've –'

“真方便。”哈利赞叹道。

“给。”乔治说着抓起两个扔给了哈利。

一个金色短发的年轻女巫从帘子后面探进头来，哈利看见她也穿着品红色的店袍。

“外面有一位顾客想要笑话坩埚，韦斯莱先生和韦斯莱先生。”她说。

哈利听见弗雷德和乔治被称为“韦斯莱先生”，觉得非常滑稽，但他们倒是从容地接受了这个称呼。

“好吧，维丽蒂，我这就来。”乔治立刻说道，“哈利，你想要什么就随便拿，好吗？不用付钱。”

“那怎么行！”哈利说，他已经掏出钱袋，准备为诱饵炸弹付款了。

“这里不用你花钱。”弗雷德坚决地说，挥手挡开了哈利的金币。

“可是——”

“我们的启动资金是你借给我们的，这我们可没有忘记。”乔治严肃地说，“你喜欢什么就拿去，如果别人问起来，别忘了告诉他们是从这儿弄到的。”

乔治穿过帘子，帮顾客挑选商品去了，弗雷德领着哈利回到前面的店里，发现赫敏和金妮仍然若有所思地盯着那个白日梦咒的专利产品。

“你们这两个小丫头还没有找到我们特制的‘神奇女巫’产品吗？”弗雷德问，“跟我来吧，姑娘们……”

在靠近窗口的地方放着一排耀眼的粉红色商品，旁边围了一群兴奋的女孩子，叽叽喳喳地笑个不停。赫敏和金妮都迟疑着不肯上前，显得很警觉。

“去看看吧，”弗雷德得意地说道，“最高级的迷情剂，别处是找不到的。”

金妮怀疑地扬起一道眉毛：“管用吗？”

“那还用说，每次效果可以长达二十四个小时，这取决于那个男孩的体重——”

“——和那个女孩的迷人程度。”乔治突然又出现在他们身边，说道，“但我们可不能把它卖给我们的亲妹妹，”他补充道，表情突然变得严肃了，“尤其是她现在已经走马灯似的跟五个男孩搞得挺热乎，这是我们从——”

'Whatever you've heard from Ron is a big fat lie,' said Ginny calmly, leaning forwards to take a small pink pot off the shelf. 'What's this?'

'Guaranteed Ten-Second Pimple Vanisher,' said Fred. 'Excellent on everything from boils to blackheads, but don't change the subject. Are you or are you not currently going out with a boy called Dean Thomas?'

'Yes, I am,' said Ginny. 'And last time I looked, he was definitely one boy, not five. What are those?'

She was pointing at a number of round balls of fluff in shades of pink and purple, all rolling around the bottom of a cage and emitting high-pitched squeaks.

'Pygmy Puffs,' said George. 'Miniature puffskeins, we can't breed them fast enough. So what about Michael Corner?'

'I dumped him, he was a bad loser,' said Ginny, putting a finger through the bars of the cage and watching the Pygmy Puffs crowd around it. 'They're really cute!'

'They're fairly cuddly, yes,' conceded Fred. 'But you're moving through boyfriends a bit fast, aren't you?'

Ginny turned to look at him, her hands on her hips. There was such a Mrs Weasley-ish glare on her face that Harry was surprised Fred didn't recoil.

'It's none of your business. And I'll thank *you*,' she added angrily to Ron, who had just appeared at George's elbow, laden with merchandise, 'not to tell tales about me to these two!'

'That's three Galleons, nine Sickles and a Knut,' said Fred, examining the many boxes in Ron's arms. 'Cough up.'

'I'm your brother!'

'And that's our stuff you're nicking. Three Galleons, nine Sickles. I'll knock off the Knut.'

'But I haven't got three Galleons, nine Sickles!'

'You'd better put it all back then, and mind you put it on the right shelves.'

Ron dropped several boxes, swore and made a rude hand gesture at Fred that was unfortunately spotted by Mrs Weasley, who had chosen that moment to appear.

'If I see you do that again I'll jinx your fingers together,' she said sharply.

“这是你们从罗恩那儿听来的胡编乱造的鬼话。”金妮平静地说，探身从架子上拿了一个粉红色的小罐子，“这是什么？”

“十秒消除脓包特效灵，”弗雷德说，“对疖子和黑头粉刺什么的都有奇效，但是你别改换话题呀。你目前是不是正跟一个名叫迪安·托马斯的男孩谈恋爱？”

“对，没错，”金妮说，“但我上次见他时，他毫无疑问只是一个男孩，而不是五个。那些是什么？”

她指着一大堆深深浅浅的粉红色和紫色的绒毛小球，小球在一只笼子的底部滚来滚去，发出刺耳的尖叫。

“侏儒蒲，”乔治说，“微型蒲绒绒，我们没法让它们很快地繁殖。那么，迈克尔·科纳又是怎么回事？”

“我把他甩了，他是个输不起的人。”金妮说着把一根手指伸进笼子，看着那些侏儒蒲全都围拢过来，“它们好可爱啊！”

“是啊，确实怪招人喜爱的。”弗雷德勉强承认道，“可是你的男朋友换得有点儿太勤了吧？”

金妮转身盯着他，两只手叉在后腰上。她脸上怒气冲冲的表情像极了韦斯莱夫人，哈利很吃惊弗雷德竟然没有退缩。

“我的事用不着你管。还有，”这时候，罗恩怀里抱着一堆商品突然出现在乔治身旁，金妮恼火地冲着罗恩喊，“劳驾你别在他们两个面前造我的谣！”

“一共三个加隆、九个西可、一个纳特，”弗雷德仔细看了看罗恩怀里大大小小的盒子，说道，“付钱吧。”

“我是你们的亲弟弟！”

“你拿的是我们的东西。三加隆九西可，那个纳特给你免了。”

“可是我没有三加隆九西可！”

“那你最好把东西放回去，记住别放错了架子。”

罗恩扔掉几个盒子，嘴里骂骂咧咧，朝弗雷德做了一个粗鲁的手势，不巧的是，却被偏偏这个时候出现的韦斯莱夫人看见了。

“如果我再看见你这么做，我就念个恶咒把你的手指都粘在一起。”她严厉地说。

'Mum, can I have a Pygmy Puff?' said Ginny at once.

'A what?' said Mrs Weasley warily.

'Look, they're so sweet …'

Mrs Weasley moved aside to look at the Pygmy Puffs, and Harry, Ron and Hermione momentarily had an unimpeded view out of the window. Draco Malfoy was hurrying up the street alone. As he passed Weasleys' Wizard Wheezes, he glanced over his shoulder. Seconds later, he moved beyond the scope of the window and they lost sight of him.

'Wonder where his mummy is?' said Harry, frowning.

'Given her the slip by the looks of it,' said Ron.

'Why, though?' said Hermione.

Harry said nothing; he was thinking too hard. Narcissa Malfoy would not have let her precious son out of her sight willingly; Malfoy must have made a real effort to free himself from her clutches. Harry, knowing and loathing Malfoy, was sure the reason could not be innocent.

He glanced around. Mrs Weasley and Ginny were bending over the Pygmy Puffs. Mr Weasley was delightedly examining a pack of Muggle marked playing cards. Fred and George were both helping customers. On the other side of the glass, Hagrid was standing with his back to them, looking up and down the street.

'Get under here, quick,' said Harry, pulling his Invisibility Cloak out of his bag.

'Oh – I don't know, Harry,' said Hermione, looking uncertainly towards Mrs Weasley.

'Come *on*!' said Ron.

She hesitated for a second longer, then ducked under the Cloak with Harry and Ron. Nobody noticed them vanish; they were all too interested in Fred and George's products. Harry, Ron and Hermione squeezed their way out of the door as quickly as they could, but by the time they gained the street, Malfoy had disappeared just as successfully as they had.

'He was going in that direction,' murmured Harry as quietly as possible, so that the humming Hagrid would not hear them. 'C'mon.'

They scurried along, peering left and right, through shop windows and doors, until Hermione pointed ahead.

"妈妈，我可以买一只侏儒蒲吗？"金妮立即抢着问。

"一只什么？"韦斯莱夫人警惕地说。

"看，它们多可爱啊……"

韦斯莱夫人走过去看侏儒蒲了，哈利、罗恩和赫敏正好可以清楚地看到窗户外面的情况。只见德拉科·马尔福一个人匆匆地走在街上。他经过韦斯莱魔法把戏坊时，还扭头看了一眼。几秒钟后，他就走过窗户。他们看不见他了。

"不知道他妈妈上哪儿去了。"哈利皱着眉头说。

"看样子他把他妈妈给甩掉了。"罗恩说。

"可是为什么呢？"赫敏问。

哈利什么也没说。他正在紧张地思考。纳西莎·马尔福自己肯定不愿意让宝贝儿子离开她的视线。马尔福准是下了一番功夫才摆脱了她的控制。哈利非常了解和讨厌马尔福，他知道这里头肯定不会有什么好事。

他扭头看了看，韦斯莱夫人和金妮正俯身看着那些侏儒蒲。韦斯莱先生欣喜地琢磨着一副麻瓜扑克牌。弗雷德和乔治都忙着接待顾客。在玻璃窗外，海格背对他们站着，监视着街上的情况。

"快，快钻进来。"哈利从包里掏出他的隐形衣，说道。

"哦——这好吗，哈利？"赫敏迟疑地朝韦斯莱夫人那边望了望，问道。

"快点儿！"罗恩说。

赫敏又犹豫了一秒钟，然后和哈利、罗恩一起钻到了隐形衣下面。谁也没有注意到他们的消失，大家都被弗雷德和乔治的商品吸引住了。哈利、罗恩和赫敏尽快挤出小店，可是等他们来到街上，马尔福早已像他们一样成功地消失了。

"他是往那个方向去了。"哈利尽量压低声音说话，以免让哼着小曲儿的海格听见，"快走。"

他们加快脚步往前赶去，一边留意街道两旁的橱窗和店门，最后赫敏突然用手指着前面。

'That's him, isn't it?' she whispered. 'Turning left?'

'Big surprise,' whispered Ron.

For Malfoy had glanced round, then slid into Knockturn Alley and out of sight.

'Quick, or we'll lose him,' said Harry, speeding up.

'Our feet'll be seen!' said Hermione anxiously, as the Cloak flapped a little around their ankles; it was much more difficult hiding all three of them under it nowadays.

'It doesn't matter,' said Harry impatiently, 'just hurry!'

But Knockturn Alley, the side street devoted to the Dark Arts, looked completely deserted. They peered into windows as they passed, but none of the shops seemed to have any customers at all. Harry supposed it was a bit of a giveaway in these dangerous and suspicious times to buy Dark artefacts – or at least, to be seen buying them.

Hermione gave his arm a hard pinch.

'Ouch!'

'Shh! Look! He's in there!' she breathed in Harry's ear.

They had drawn level with the only shop in Knockturn Alley that Harry had ever visited: Borgin and Burkes, which sold a wide variety of sinister objects. There in the midst of the cases full of skulls and old bottles stood Draco Malfoy with his back to them, just visible beyond the very same large black cabinet in which Harry had once hidden to avoid Malfoy and his father. Judging by the movements of Malfoy's hands he was talking animatedly. The proprietor of the shop, Mr Borgin, an oily-haired, stooping man, stood facing Malfoy. He was wearing a curious expression of mingled resentment and fear.

'If only we could hear what they're saying!' said Hermione.

'We can!' said Ron excitedly. 'Hang on – damn –'

He dropped a couple more of the boxes he was still clutching as he fumbled with the largest.

'Extendable Ears, look!'

'Fantastic!' said Hermione, as Ron unravelled the long, flesh-coloured strings and began to feed them towards the bottom of the door. 'Oh, I hope the door isn't Imperturbable –'

'No!' said Ron gleefully. 'Listen!'

“他在那儿，是不是？”她低声说，“往左拐了？”

“真让人吃惊。”罗恩轻声道。

只见马尔福左右张望了一下，闪身钻进翻倒巷不见了。

“快，别把目标给丢了。”哈利说着，加快了脚步。

“我们的脚会被人看见的！”赫敏担心地说，因为隐形衣的下摆在他们脚脖子周围掀动。如今，他们三个藏在它下面比以前困难多了。

“没关系，”哈利不耐烦地说，“快走！”

可是，翻倒巷——这条与黑魔法密切相关的小街上空无一人。他们一边走一边朝窗户里张望，似乎每家店铺都没有顾客。哈利猜想，在这段危险而多疑的时期购买——尤其被人看见购买黑魔法制品，是会暴露身份的。

赫敏使劲拧了一下他的胳膊。

“哎哟！”

“嘘——快看！他在那里面！”她贴着哈利的耳朵低声道。

现在他们身边的这家商店，是哈利在翻倒巷光顾过的唯一一家店铺：博金－博克黑魔法商店，专门出售各种各样凶险不祥的东西。果然，在那些装满骷髅和旧瓶子的箱子中间，马尔福背对他们站着，就站在那个黑色大柜子的后面。当年哈利为了回避马尔福和他的父亲，曾经在那个大柜子里躲过。从马尔福的手势看，他正在兴致勃勃地说话。店主博金先生是一个头发油亮、身材佝偻的人，此刻就站在马尔福面前。他脸上的表情很古怪，夹杂着怨恨和恐惧。

“要是我们能听见他们在说什么就好了！”赫敏说。

“可以呀！”罗恩兴奋地说，“等等——该死——”

他在那只最大的盒子里摸索，结果手里仍然拿着的两只盒子掉在了地上。

“伸缩耳，看！”

“太棒了！”赫敏说，罗恩解开长长的、肉色的细绳，开始把它们塞到门缝下面，“哦，希望这扇门没有被施了抗扰——”

“没有！”罗恩欢喜地说，“听！”

They put their heads together and listened intently to the ends of the strings, through which Malfoy's voice could be heard loud and clear, as though a radio had been turned on.

'… you know how to fix it?'

'Possibly,' said Borgin, in a tone that suggested he was unwilling to commit himself. 'I'll need to see it, though. Why don't you bring it into the shop?'

'I can't,' said Malfoy. 'It's got to stay put. I just need you to tell me how to do it.'

Harry saw Borgin lick his lips nervously.

'Well, without seeing it, I must say it will be a very difficult job, perhaps impossible. I couldn't guarantee anything.'

'No?' said Malfoy and Harry knew, just by his tone, that Malfoy was sneering. 'Perhaps this will make you more confident.'

He moved towards Borgin and was blocked from view by the cabinet. Harry, Ron and Hermione shuffled sideways to try and keep him in sight, but all they could see was Borgin, looking very frightened.

'Tell anyone,' said Malfoy, 'and there will be retribution. You know Fenrir Greyback? He's a family friend, he'll be dropping in from time to time to make sure you're giving the problem your full attention.'

'There will be no need for –'

'I'll decide that,' said Malfoy. 'Well, I'd better be off. And don't forget to keep *that* one safe, I'll need it.'

'Perhaps you'd like to take it now?'

'No, of course I wouldn't, you stupid little man, how would I look carrying that down the street? Just don't sell it.'

'Of course not … sir.'

Borgin made a bow as deep as the one Harry had once seen him give Lucius Malfoy.

'Not a word to anyone, Borgin, and that includes my mother, understand?'

'Naturally, naturally,' murmured Borgin, bowing again.

Next moment, the bell over the door tinkled loudly as Malfoy stalked out of the shop looking very pleased with himself. He passed so close to Harry,

他们把脑袋凑在一起，贴在细绳的绳头上专心地听着，马尔福的声音响亮、清晰地传了出来，就好像打开了一台收音机。

“……你知道怎么把它修好吗？”

“可能吧，”博金说，从他的口气上听，他似乎不愿意明确表态，“不过我需要先看一看。你为什么不把它拿到店里来呢？”

“我不能，”马尔福说，“它必须留在原处。你只需要告诉我怎么修就行了。”

哈利看见博金紧张地舔了舔嘴唇。

“唉，我没有亲眼看见它，恐怕很难说得清，可能根本就没办法。我什么也不能保证。”

“不能？”马尔福说，哈利听他的口气就知道他在讥笑，“也许这会让你更有信心。”

他逼近博金，大柜子挡住了他的身体。哈利、罗恩和赫敏赶紧挪到旁边，不让他从视线中消失，可是他们只能看见博金，他神色非常惊恐。

“要敢告诉别人，”马尔福说，“叫你吃不了兜着走。你知道芬里尔·格雷伯克吧？他是我们家的朋友，他会时常过来看看你是不是在专心解决这个问题。”

“没有必要——”

“这由我来决定。”马尔福说，“好了，我得走了。别忘了替我好好保管那东西，我会用得着的。”

“你不想现在就拿走吗？”

“不，当然不想，你这个愚蠢的矮子，我拿着它走在街上像什么话？你别把它卖掉就是了。”

“当然不会……先生。”

博金深深地鞠了一躬，哈利曾经看见他对卢修斯·马尔福也是这样鞠躬。

“不许对任何人说，博金，包括我妈妈，明白吗？”

“当然，当然。”博金喃喃地说，又鞠了一躬。

接着，店门上的铃铛响了起来，马尔福大步走出小店，一副志得

Ron and Hermione that they felt the Cloak flutter around their knees again. Inside the shop, Borgin remained frozen; his unctuous smile had vanished; he looked worried.

'What was that about?' whispered Ron, reeling in the Extendable Ears.

'Dunno,' said Harry, thinking hard. 'He wants something mended … and he wants to reserve something in there … could you see what he pointed at when he said "that one"?'

'No, he was behind that cabinet –'

'You two stay here,' whispered Hermione.

'What are you –?'

But Hermione had already ducked out from under the Cloak. She checked her hair in the reflection in the glass, then marched into the shop, setting the bell tinkling again. Ron hastily fed the Extendable Ears back under the door and passed one of the strings to Harry.

'Hello, horrible morning, isn't it?' Hermione said brightly to Borgin, who did not answer, but cast her a suspicious look. Humming cheerily, Hermione strolled through the jumble of objects on display.

'Is this necklace for sale?' she asked, pausing beside a glass-fronted case.

'If you've got one and a half thousand Galleons,' said Borgin coldly.

'Oh – er – no, I haven't got quite that much,' said Hermione, walking on. 'And … what about this lovely – um – skull?'

'Sixteen Galleons.'

'So it's for sale, then? It isn't being … kept for anyone?'

Borgin squinted at her. Harry had the nasty feeling he knew exactly what Hermione was up to. Apparently Hermione felt she had been rumbled, too, because she suddenly threw caution to the winds.

'The thing is, that – er – boy who was in here just now, Draco Malfoy, well, he's a friend of mine, and I want to get him a birthday present, but if he's already reserved anything I obviously don't want to get him the same thing, so … um …'

It was a pretty lame story in Harry's opinion, and apparently Borgin thought so too.

'Out,' he said sharply. 'Get out!'

Hermione did not wait to be asked twice, but hurried to the door with

意满的样子。他贴着哈利、罗恩和赫敏走了过去，他们感觉到隐形衣又在扑打他们的膝盖。店里，博金仍然僵在那里，脸上虚假的笑容消失了，神情显得很忧虑。

“这到底是怎么回事？”罗恩小声问，一边把伸缩耳的细绳收了回来。

“不知道。”哈利努力思索着说，“他有个东西要修理……还有个东西希望店里替他留着……他说‘那东西’时，你们看见他指的是什么了吗？”

“没有，他被那个柜子挡住了——”

“你们俩待着别动。”赫敏小声说。

“你想干什么——”

可是赫敏已经从隐形衣下面钻了出去。她对着玻璃照了照她的头发，然后迈着大步走进店里，铃铛又一次叮叮当当地响了起来。罗恩赶紧把伸缩耳又塞到门缝下面，把一根细绳递给了哈利。

“你好，天气真糟糕，是不是？”赫敏愉快地对博金说，博金怀疑地瞥了她一眼，没有回答。赫敏欢快地哼着歌儿，在店里陈列的乱七八糟的商品间溜达。

“这条项链卖吗？”她在一个玻璃柜前停下脚步，问道。

“如果你掏一千五百个加隆，就卖。”博金冷冷地说。

“噢——嗯——不，我可没有那么多钱。”赫敏说着，继续往前走去，“那么……这只可爱的——嗯——骷髅呢？”

“十六个加隆。”

“那么它是可以卖的？不是……不是给什么人留着的？”

博金眯起眼睛看着她。哈利有一种不妙的感觉，博金很清楚赫敏想干什么。看来赫敏也发觉自己被识破了，她突然豁了出去。

“事情是这样的——嗯——刚才进来的那个男孩，德拉科·马尔福，他是我的一个朋友，我想送给他一件生日礼物，但如果他已经预订了什么东西，我当然不想再给他买一件同样的，所以……嗯……”

哈利觉得，这个故事编得太蹩脚了，博金显然也是这么认为。

“出去。”他厉声吼道，“滚出去！”

赫敏没等他说第二遍，就匆匆逃了出来，博金一直追到了门口。

Borgin at her heels. As the bell tinkled again, Borgin slammed the door behind her and put up the *Closed* sign.

'Ah well,' said Ron, throwing the cloak back over Hermione. 'Worth a try, but you were a bit obvious –'

'Well, next time you can show me how it's done, Master of Mystery!' she snapped.

Ron and Hermione bickered all the way back to Weasleys' Wizard Wheezes, where they were forced to stop so that they could dodge undetected around a very anxious-looking Mrs Weasley and Hagrid, who had clearly noticed their absence. Once in the shop, Harry whipped off the Invisibility Cloak, hid it in his bag, and joined in with the other two when they insisted, in answer to Mrs Weasley's accusations, that they had been in the back room all along, and that she could not have looked properly.

铃铛又是一阵乱响，博金在她身后砰的一声关上门，挂出了停业的牌子。

“不错，”罗恩说着把隐形衣重新罩在赫敏身上，“值得一试，不过你做得也太明显了——”

“好，下次你来做给我看看，神秘大师！”她回敬道。

在返回的路上，罗恩和赫敏一直在打嘴仗，不过到了韦斯莱魔法把戏坊，他们就不得不住嘴了，这样才能神不知鬼不觉地躲过惊慌失措的韦斯莱夫人和海格，这两人显然已经发现他们失踪了。一到店里，哈利就脱下隐形衣，把它藏进包里，然后，面对韦斯莱夫人的责问，他和两个伙伴一口咬定他们一直待在后面的小屋里，她只是没有认真去找。

CHAPTER SEVEN

The Slug Club

Harry spent a lot of the last week of the holidays pondering the meaning of Malfoy's behaviour in Knockturn Alley. What disturbed him most was the satisfied look on Malfoy's face as he had left the shop. Nothing that made Malfoy look that happy could be good news. To his slight annoyance, however, neither Ron nor Hermione seemed quite as curious about Malfoy's activities as he was; or at least, they seemed to get bored of discussing it after a few days.

'Yes, I've already agreed it was fishy, Harry,' said Hermione a little impatiently. She was sitting on the window-sill in Fred and George's room with her feet up on one of the cardboard boxes and had only grudgingly looked up from her new copy of *Advanced Rune Translation*. 'But haven't we agreed there could be a lot of explanations?'

'Maybe he's broken his Hand of Glory,' said Ron vaguely, as he attempted to straighten his broomstick's bent tail twigs. 'Remember that shrivelled-up arm Malfoy had?'

'But what about when he said "Don't forget to keep *that* one safe"?' asked Harry for the umpteenth time. 'That sounded to me like Borgin's got another one of the broken objects, and Malfoy wants both.'

'You reckon?' said Ron, now trying to scrape some dirt off his broom handle.

'Yeah, I do,' said Harry. When neither Ron nor Hermione answered, he said, 'Malfoy's father's in Azkaban. Don't you think Malfoy'd like revenge?'

Ron looked up, blinking.

'Malfoy, revenge? What can he do about it?'

'That's my point, I don't know!' said Harry, frustrated. 'But he's up to something and I think we should take it seriously. His father's a Death Eater and –'

第 7 章

鼻涕虫俱乐部

暑假的最后一个星期，哈利许多时候都在思考马尔福在翻倒巷的所作所为。最让他感到不安的是马尔福离开商店时脸上那副得意的表情。能让马尔福显得那么高兴的准不是什么好事。然而，令他感到有些恼怒的是，罗恩和赫敏对于马尔福的行为似乎都不像他这么好奇。至少，他们几天后就厌倦了，不愿意再谈这件事。

"是啊，哈利，我已经承认这有点可疑。"赫敏有点不耐烦地说。她坐在弗雷德和乔治房间的窗台上，两只脚踏着一个硬纸箱，满不情愿地从她那本新书《高级如尼文翻译》上抬起目光。"但我们不是一致认为这件事可以有许多种解释吗？"

"也许他打坏了他的光荣之手。"罗恩一边用力把他扫帚上的弯树枝扳直，一边含混地嘟囔说，"还记得马尔福的那只干枯的手吗？"

"可是他说'别忘了把那东西替我保管好'，这又是什么意思呢？"这个问题哈利已经问了无数遍，"在我看来，好像那个打坏的东西博金还有一件，马尔福两件都想要。"

"你是这么想的？"罗恩说着擦去扫帚把上的灰尘。

"是啊。"哈利说。看到罗恩和赫敏都没有回答，他又说："马尔福的父亲在阿兹卡班。你们说，马尔福会不会想要报仇？"

罗恩抬起头，眨巴眨巴眼睛。

"马尔福，报仇？他能做什么呢？"

"这就是问题，我不知道！"哈利泄气地说，"可是他肯定有什么打算，我认为我们应该认真对待。他父亲是个食死徒，而且——"

Harry broke off, his eyes fixed on the window behind Hermione, his mouth open. A startling thought had just occurred to him.

'Harry?' said Hermione in an anxious voice. 'What's wrong?'

'Your scar's not hurting again, is it?' asked Ron nervously.

'He's a Death Eater,' said Harry slowly. 'He's replaced his father as a Death Eater!'

There was a silence, then Ron erupted in laughter.

'*Malfoy?* He's sixteen, Harry! You think You-Know-Who would let *Malfoy* join?'

'It seems very unlikely, Harry,' said Hermione, in a repressive sort of voice. 'What makes you think –?'

'In Madam Malkin's. She didn't touch him, but he yelled and jerked his arm away from her when she went to roll up his sleeve. It was his left arm. He's been branded with the Dark Mark.'

Ron and Hermione looked at each other.

'Well …' said Ron, sounding thoroughly unconvinced.

'I think he just wanted to get out of there, Harry,' said Hermione.

'He showed Borgin something we couldn't see,' Harry pressed on stubbornly. 'Something that seriously scared Borgin. It was the Mark, I know it – he was showing Borgin who he was dealing with, you saw how seriously Borgin took him!'

Ron and Hermione exchanged another look.

'I'm not sure, Harry …'

'Yeah, I still don't reckon You-Know-Who would let Malfoy join …'

Annoyed, but absolutely convinced he was right, Harry snatched up a pile of filthy Quidditch robes and left the room; Mrs Weasley had been urging them for days not to leave their washing and packing until the last moment. On the landing he bumped into Ginny, who was returning to her room carrying a pile of freshly laundered clothes.

'I wouldn't go in the kitchen just now,' she warned him. 'There's a lot of Phlegm around.'

'I'll be careful not to slip in it,' smiled Harry.

Sure enough, when he entered the kitchen it was to find Fleur sitting at the kitchen table, in full flow about plans for her wedding to Bill, while Mrs Weasley kept watch over a pile of self-peeling sprouts, looking bad-tempered.

哈利顿住话头，眼睛盯着赫敏身后的窗户，嘴巴张得大大的。他脑子里灵光一现，闪出一个可怕的念头。

“哈利？”赫敏用担心的口气说，“你怎么啦？”

“不是你的伤疤又疼了吧？”罗恩也紧张地问。

“他是个食死徒。”哈利慢慢地说，“他顶替他父亲，也做了食死徒！”

一阵沉默之后，罗恩哈哈大笑起来。

“马尔福？他才十六岁啊，哈利！你认为神秘人会让马尔福加入？”

“确实不太可能，哈利，”赫敏捺着性子说，“你怎么会认为——”

“在摩金夫人长袍专卖店里。摩金夫人去给他卷袖子时，根本就没有碰到他，他就尖叫起来，猛地把胳膊抽了回去。那是他的左胳膊。他被烙上了黑魔标记。”

罗恩和赫敏互相看了看。

“这个……”罗恩的口气是完全不相信。

“我认为他当时只是想离开那儿，哈利。”赫敏说。

“他给博金看了什么东西，我们没有看见，”哈利固执地往下说道，“那东西把博金吓得够呛。我知道那准是黑魔标记——他让博金看清楚是在跟谁打交道，你们看见博金拿他多当回事啊！”

罗恩和赫敏又交换了一下目光。

“我说不准，哈利……”

“是啊，我仍然认为神秘人不会让马尔福加入……”

哈利很懊恼，但坚信自己是对的。他抓起一堆脏乎乎的魁地奇球袍，离开了房间。这些天，韦斯莱夫人一直在催他们抓紧时间洗衣服和收拾行李，免得临时抱佛脚。在楼梯平台上，他碰见了金妮。金妮正要返回自己的房间，怀里抱着一堆刚洗干净的衣服。

“换了我，现在可不去厨房，”她提醒哈利，“那里有一大堆黏痰。”

“我会小心别踩着它滑倒的。”哈利微笑着说。

果然，他一走进厨房，就看见芙蓉坐在桌子旁，滔滔不绝地筹划她跟比尔的婚礼。韦斯莱夫人守着一堆正在自动削皮的甘蓝，脸上一副没好气的样子。

'… Bill and I 'ave almost decided on only two bridesmaids, Ginny and Gabrielle will look very sweet togezzer. I am theenking of dressing zem in pale gold – pink would of course be 'orrible with Ginny's 'air –'

'Ah, Harry!' said Mrs Weasley loudly, cutting across Fleur's monologue. 'Good, I wanted to explain about the security arrangements for the journey to Hogwarts tomorrow. We've got Ministry cars again, and there will be Aurors waiting at the station –'

'Is Tonks going to be there?' asked Harry, handing over his Quidditch things.

'No, I don't think so, she's been stationed somewhere else from what Arthur said.'

'She 'as let 'erself go, zat Tonks,' mused Fleur, examining her own stunning reflection in the back of a teaspoon. 'A big mistake, if you ask –'

'Yes, *thank* you,' said Mrs Weasley tartly, cutting across Fleur again. 'You'd better get on, Harry, I want the trunks ready tonight, if possible, so we don't have the usual last-minute scramble.'

And in fact, their departure the following morning was smoother than usual. The Ministry cars glided up to the front of The Burrow to find them waiting: trunks packed, Hermione's cat, Crookshanks, safely enclosed in his travelling basket, and Hedwig, Ron's owl Pigwidgeon, and Ginny's new purple Pygmy Puff, Arnold, in cages.

'Au revoir, 'Arry,' said Fleur throatily, kissing him goodbye. Ron hurried forwards, looking hopeful, but Ginny stuck out her foot and Ron fell, sprawling in the dust at Fleur's feet. Furious, red-faced and dirt-spattered, he hurried into the car without saying goodbye.

There was no cheerful Hagrid waiting for them at King's Cross Station. Instead, two grim-faced, bearded Aurors in dark Muggle suits moved forwards the moment the cars stopped and, flanking the party, marched them into the station without speaking.

'Quick, quick, through the barrier,' said Mrs Weasley, who seemed a little flustered by this austere efficiency. 'Harry had better go first, with –'

She looked enquiringly at one of the Aurors, who nodded briefly, seized Harry's upper arm and attempted to steer him towards the barrier between platforms nine and ten.

"……比尔和我差不多已经决定只请两个伴娘，金妮和加布丽站在一起会显得非常可爱。我打算让她们穿淡金色的衣服——粉红色配着金妮的头发肯定很难看——"

"啊，哈利！"韦斯莱夫人大声说，打断了芙蓉的长篇独白，"太好了，我正要跟你说说明天去霍格沃茨一路上的安全措施呢。我们又借到了魔法部的汽车，到时候将有傲罗在车站等着——"

"唐克斯也在吗？"哈利把魁地奇球袍递了过去，问道。

"不，大概不会，听亚瑟说，她被安排在别的地方了。"

"那个唐克斯，她现在变得不修边幅了。"芙蓉若有所思地说，一边对着一把茶匙的背面照了照她美丽的脸蛋，"要我说，这可是个很大的错误——"

"是啊，多谢你啦。"韦斯莱夫人尖刻地说，又一次打断了芙蓉的话，"你最好抓紧时间继续收拾吧，哈利。如果可能的话，我希望今晚就把箱子整理好，省得像往常那样临走时乱成一团。"

确实，第二天早晨他们出发时比往常顺利多了。魔法部的汽车开到陋居门前时，他们都已经等在那里了：箱子收拾好了，赫敏的猫克鲁克山安安稳稳地待在它的旅行篮里，海德薇、罗恩的猫头鹰小猪，以及金妮新买的紫色侏儒蒲阿囡，都好好儿地在笼子里关着呢。

"再见，阿利。"芙蓉用沙哑的喉音说，并亲了一下哈利。罗恩赶紧上前，一脸期待的神情，可是金妮伸出一只脚，把罗恩绊了一跤，使他摔在芙蓉脚边的泥土里。罗恩气得满脸通红，身上沾满了灰尘，连声"再见"也没说，就匆匆钻进了车里。

在国王十字车站等待他们的，不是满脸喜色的海格。汽车刚一停下，就有两个身穿黑色麻瓜西装、神色严峻的大胡子傲罗走上前来，一言不发，左右掩护着他们走进了车站。

"快，快，快穿过挡墙，"韦斯莱夫人说，这戒备森严的阵势似乎使她也有点紧张慌乱，"最好让哈利先走，和——"

她征询地看着一位傲罗，那人微微点了点头，一把抓住哈利的胳膊，领着他朝第 9 和第 10 站台之间的挡墙走去。

'I can walk, thanks,' said Harry irritably, jerking his arm out of the Auror's grip. He pushed his trolley directly at the solid barrier, ignoring his silent companion, and found himself, a second later, standing on platform nine and three-quarters, where the scarlet Hogwarts Express stood belching steam over the crowd.

Hermione and the Weasleys joined him within seconds. Without waiting to consult his grim-faced Auror, Harry motioned to Ron and Hermione to follow him up the platform, looking for an empty compartment.

'We can't, Harry,' said Hermione, looking apologetic. 'Ron and I've got to go to the prefect carriage first and then patrol the corridors for a bit.'

'Oh yeah, I forgot,' said Harry.

'You'd better get straight on the train, all of you, you've only got a few minutes to go,' said Mrs Weasley, consulting her watch. 'Well, have a lovely term, Ron ...'

'Mr Weasley, can I have a quick word?' said Harry, making up his mind on the spur of the moment.

'Of course,' said Mr Weasley, who looked slightly surprised, but followed Harry out of earshot of the others nevertheless.

Harry had thought it through carefully and come to the conclusion that, if he were to tell anyone, Mr Weasley would be the right person; firstly, because he worked at the Ministry and was therefore in the best position to make further investigations, and secondly, because he thought that there was not too much risk of Mr Weasley exploding with anger.

He could see Mrs Weasley and the grim-faced Auror casting the pair of them suspicious looks as they moved away.

'When we were in Diagon Alley –' Harry began, but Mr Weasley forestalled him with a grimace.

'Am I about to discover where you, Ron and Hermione disappeared to while you were supposed to be in the back room of Fred and George's shop?'

'How did you –?'

'Harry, please. You're talking to the man who raised Fred and George.'

'Er ... yeah, all right, we weren't in the back room.'

“我自己能走，谢谢。”哈利恼火地说，将胳膊从傲罗手里挣脱出来。他推着手推车朝坚固的挡墙直冲过去，毫不理会那位沉默的陪同。一秒钟后，他就发现自己站在了$9\frac{3}{4}$站台上，深红色的霍格沃茨特快列车喷出的蒸汽飘荡在人群上空。

几秒钟后，赫敏和韦斯莱一家也过来了。哈利没有征求那位脸色阴沉的傲罗的意见，就示意罗恩和赫敏跟他一起顺着站台往前走，寻找没有人的空包厢。

“我们不能一起走，哈利，”赫敏满脸歉意地说，“我和罗恩先要去级长车厢，然后还要在走廊里巡视。”

“噢，对了，我忘记了。”哈利说。

“你们最好都赶紧上车，只剩下几分钟时间了。”韦斯莱夫人看了看表，说道，“好了，祝你这学期过得愉快，罗恩……”

“韦斯莱先生，我可以和你说两句话吗？”哈利一时冲动，做了一个决定。

“没问题。”韦斯莱先生说，他显得有点儿意外，但还是跟着哈利走到别人听不见他们说话的地方。

哈利反复考虑之后，得出了这样的结论：如果他想告诉某个人，韦斯莱先生是最合适的人选。首先，他在魔法部工作，这个位置最有利于展开调查；第二，哈利认为韦斯莱先生不太可能一下子火冒三丈。

他们俩走向一边时，他看见韦斯莱夫人和那个脸色阴沉的傲罗朝他们投来怀疑的目光。

“我们在对角巷的时候——”哈利开始说道，但韦斯莱先生做了个鬼脸，阻止了他。

“你是准备告诉我，你和罗恩、赫敏到底去哪儿了吗？你们还假装说是在弗雷德和乔治商店后面的小屋里。”

“你怎么——”

“哈利，别跟我兜圈子了。你知道你在跟谁说话吗？是我把弗雷德和乔治带大的。”

“嗯……是啊，没错，我们确实没在后面的小屋里。”

'Very well, then, let's hear the worst.'

'Well, we followed Draco Malfoy. We used my Invisibility Cloak.'

'Did you have any particular reason for doing so, or was it a mere whim?'

'Because I thought Malfoy was up to something,' said Harry, disregarding Mr Weasley's look of mingled exasperation and amusement. 'He'd given his mother the slip and I wanted to know why.'

'Of course you did,' said Mr Weasley, sounding resigned. 'Well? Did you find out why?'

'He went into Borgin and Burkes,' said Harry, 'and started bullying the bloke in there, Borgin, to help him fix something. And he said he wanted Borgin to keep something else for him. He made it sound like it was the same kind of thing that needed fixing. Like they were a pair. And ...'

Harry took a deep breath.

'There's something else. We saw Malfoy jump about a mile when Madam Malkin tried to touch his left arm. I think he's been branded with the Dark Mark. I think he's replaced his father as a Death Eater.'

Mr Weasley looked taken aback. After a moment he said, 'Harry, I doubt whether You-Know-Who would allow a sixteen-year-old –'

'Does anyone really know what You-Know-Who would or wouldn't do?' asked Harry angrily. 'Mr Weasley, I'm sorry, but isn't it worth investigating? If Malfoy wants something fixing, and he needs to threaten Borgin to get it done, it's probably something Dark or dangerous, isn't it?'

'I doubt it, to be honest, Harry,' said Mr Weasley slowly. 'You see, when Lucius Malfoy was arrested, we raided his house. We took away everything that might have been dangerous.'

'I think you missed something,' said Harry stubbornly.

'Well, maybe,' said Mr Weasley, but Harry could tell that Mr Weasley was humouring him.

There was a whistle behind them; nearly everyone had boarded the train and the doors were closing.

'You'd better hurry,' said Mr Weasley, as Mrs Weasley cried, 'Harry, quickly!'

"很好，那么，让我们听听最糟糕的吧。"

"是这样，我们跟踪了德拉科・马尔福。我们披了我的隐形衣。"

"你们这么做，有什么特别的理由吗？还是一时心血来潮？"

"因为我怀疑马尔福在搞什么阴谋。"哈利没有理会韦斯莱先生脸上流露出的恼火的、觉得他可笑的神情，接着说道，"他把他妈妈甩掉了，我想弄清是为什么。"

"你想得没错。"韦斯莱先生用迁就的口吻说，"后来呢？你弄清原因了吗？"

"他进了博金－博克商店，"哈利说，"开始恶狠狠地命令店里的那个家伙——博金帮他修理什么东西。然后，他还说希望博金替他留着另外一件东西。听他的意思，这跟那件需要修理的是同样的东西。好像是一对。后来……"

哈利深深吸了口气。

"还有别的呢。当摩金夫人想去碰马尔福的左胳膊时，他一下子跳出了八丈远。我认为他被烙上了黑魔标记。我认为他顶替他父亲当了食死徒。"

韦斯莱先生似乎吃了一惊。他顿了顿，说道："哈利，我不相信神秘人会让一个十六岁的——"

"有谁真的知道神秘人会做什么、不会做什么呢？"哈利生气地问，"韦斯莱先生，原谅我的冒昧，但这件事不值得调查吗？如果马尔福有一件东西要修理，而且需要威胁博金替他修理，那东西很可能与黑魔法有关，是危险的，对不对？"

"说实在的，我不能肯定，哈利，"韦斯莱先生慢慢地说，"你知道，卢修斯・马尔福被捕后，我们搜查了他家，把可能有危险的东西都抄走了。"

"我想你们大概漏掉了什么。"哈利固执地说。

"是啊，也说不定。"韦斯莱先生说，但哈利可以感觉到韦斯莱先生是在敷衍他。

身后传来了口哨声。差不多每个人都上了火车，车门正在关上。

"你得赶紧了。"韦斯莱先生说，这时韦斯莱夫人喊道："哈利，快点儿！"

He hurried forwards and Mr and Mrs Weasley helped him load his trunk on to the train.

'Now, dear, you're coming to us for Christmas, it's all fixed with Dumbledore, so we'll see you quite soon,' said Mrs Weasley through the window, as Harry slammed the door shut behind him and the train began to move. 'You make sure you look after yourself and –'

The train was gathering speed.

'– be good and –'

She was jogging to keep up now.

'– stay safe!'

Harry waved until the train had turned a corner and Mr and Mrs Weasley were lost from view, then turned to see where the others had got to. He supposed Ron and Hermione were cloistered in the prefect carriage, but Ginny was a little way along the corridor, chatting to some friends. He made his way towards her, dragging his trunk.

People stared shamelessly as he approached. They even pressed their faces against the windows of their compartments to get a look at him. He had expected an upswing in the amount of gaping and gawping he would have to endure this term after all the 'Chosen One' rumours in the *Daily Prophet*, but he did not enjoy the sensation of standing in a very bright spotlight. He tapped Ginny on the shoulder.

'Fancy trying to find a compartment?'

'I can't, Harry, I said I'd meet Dean,' said Ginny brightly. 'See you later.'

'Right,' said Harry. He felt a strange twinge of annoyance as she walked away, her long red hair dancing behind her. He had become so used to her presence over the summer that he had almost forgotten that Ginny did not hang around with him, Ron and Hermione while at school. Then he blinked and looked around: he was surrounded by mesmerised girls.

'Hi, Harry!' said a familiar voice from behind him.

'Neville!' said Harry in relief, turning to see a round-faced boy struggling towards him.

'Hello, Harry,' said a girl with long hair and large, misty eyes, who was just behind Neville.

'Luna, hi, how are you?'

哈利飞快地冲过去，韦斯莱夫妇帮他把箱子搬上了火车。

“好了，亲爱的，你来跟我们一起过圣诞节，已经跟邓布利多谈好了，所以我们很快就会再见面的。”韦斯莱夫人隔着车窗说，这时哈利重重地关上车门，火车开动了，“一定要好好照顾自己——”

火车在加速。

“——要乖乖的——”

她跟着火车小跑。

“——别出危险！”

哈利不停地挥手，直到火车拐了个弯，再也看不见韦斯莱夫妇了，然后他转过身，想看看别人都去了哪里。他猜想罗恩和赫敏肯定都被关在级长包厢里，幸好金妮就在那边的走廊上，正在跟几个朋友说话。他便拖着箱子朝她走去。

在他走近时，人们毫不掩饰地盯着他看。有人为了看他一眼，甚至把脸贴在了包厢的玻璃上。他早就知道，在《预言家日报》登了那些关于“救世之星”的谣言之后，这学期他肯定要忍受人们对他变本加厉的瞪视和围观，他实在不喜欢这种站在耀眼的聚光灯下的感觉。他拍了拍金妮的肩膀。

“想去找一间包厢吗？”

“我不能，哈利，我说好了要等迪安的。”金妮欢快地说，“待会儿见。”

“好吧。”哈利说。他看着金妮转身离去，长长的红发在身后飘动，哈利心里产生了一种异样的惆怅。暑假里他已经习惯了跟金妮朝夕相处，几乎忘记了她在学校里是不跟他和罗恩、赫敏为伍的。然后，他眨眨眼睛，看了看四周：围在他身边的都是一些为他痴迷的女孩子。

“嘿，哈利！”身后传来一个熟悉的声音。

“纳威！”哈利松了口气，转身看见一个圆圆脸的男孩费力地朝这边挤来。

“你好，哈利。”纳威身后一个长发姑娘说，她的一双大眼睛看上去雾蒙蒙的。

“卢娜，你好，怎么样？”

'Very well, thank you,' said Luna. She was clutching a magazine to her chest; large letters on the front announced that there was a pair of free Spectrespecs inside.

'*The Quibbler* still going strong, then?' asked Harry, who felt a certain fondness for the magazine, having given it an exclusive interview the previous year.

'Oh yes, circulation's well up,' said Luna happily.

'Let's find seats,' said Harry, and the three of them set off along the train through hordes of silently staring students. At last they found an empty compartment and Harry hurried inside gratefully.

'They're even staring at *us*,' said Neville, indicating himself and Luna, 'because we're with you!'

'They're staring at you because you were at the Ministry, too,' said Harry, as he hoisted his trunk into the luggage rack. 'Our little adventure there was all over the *Daily Prophet*, you must've seen it.'

'Yes, I thought Gran would be angry about all the publicity,' said Neville, 'but she was really pleased. Says I'm starting to live up to my dad at long last. She bought me a new wand, look!'

He pulled it out and showed it to Harry.

'Cherry and unicorn hair,' he said proudly. 'We think it was one of the last Ollivander ever sold, he vanished next day – oi, come back here, Trevor!'

And he dived under the seat to retrieve his toad as it made one of its frequent bids for freedom.

'Are we still doing DA meetings this year, Harry?' asked Luna, who was detaching a pair of psychedelic spectacles from the middle of *The Quibbler*.

'No point now we've got rid of Umbridge, is there?' said Harry, sitting down. Neville bumped his head against the seat as he emerged from under it. He looked most disappointed.

'I liked the DA! I learned loads with you!'

'I enjoyed the meetings, too,' said Luna serenely. 'It was like having friends.'

This was one of those uncomfortable things Luna often said and which made Harry feel a squirming mixture of pity and embarrassment. Before he could respond, however, there was a disturbance outside their compartment

"挺好的，谢谢。"卢娜说。她把一本杂志按在胸口，封面上醒目的大字宣布里面有一副免费赠送的防妖眼镜。

"《唱唱反调》仍然办得很红火吧？"哈利问，他对这份杂志抱有一定的好感，因为前一年接受过它的独家采访。

"是啊，发行量稳步上升。"卢娜高兴地说。

"我们去找座位吧。"哈利说，于是三个人一起挤过那些默默地盯着他们的学生，顺着过道往前走。最后终于找到了一间空包厢，哈利如释重负，赶紧钻了进去。

"他们甚至还盯着我们看呢，"纳威说，指的是卢娜和他自己，"就因为我们和你在一起！"

"他们盯着你们看，是因为你们当时也在魔法部。"哈利说着把箱子举起来塞进了行李架，"我们那场小小的奇遇都上了《预言家日报》，你们肯定看见了。"

"是啊，我本来以为这样张扬出去，奶奶肯定会生气的，"纳威说，"没想到她很高兴，说我终于不愧是我父亲的儿子了。她还给我买了一根新魔杖呢，看！"

他抽出魔杖，递给了哈利。

"樱桃木，独角兽的毛，"他得意地说，"我们认为这是奥利凡德卖出的最后一批魔杖之一，他第二天就失踪了——喂，快回来，莱福！"

他钻到座位底下去抓他的蟾蜍，这东西经常逃出去寻求自由。

"我们今年还搞 D.A. 集会吗，哈利？"卢娜问，她正在把一副色彩艳丽的眼镜从《唱唱反调》中间拆下来。

"现在已经摆脱了乌姆里奇，就没必要再搞了，是不是？"哈利说着坐了下来。纳威从座位底下钻出来时，脑袋被重重地撞了一下。他显得失望极了。

"我喜欢 D.A. 集会！我跟你在一起学到了许多东西！"

"我也很喜欢那些聚会，"卢娜平静地说，"就像自己有了朋友一样。"

卢娜经常说一些这种令人不舒服的话，使哈利不由得产生既同情、又尴尬的复杂感情。然而，他还没来得及回答，包厢外面就起了一阵

door; a group of fourth-year girls was whispering and giggling together on the other side of the glass.

'You ask him!'

'No, you!'

'I'll do it!'

And one of them, a bold-looking girl with large dark eyes, a prominent chin and long black hair, pushed her way through the door.

'Hi, Harry, I'm Romilda, Romilda Vane,' she said loudly and confidently. 'Why don't you join us in our compartment? You don't have to sit with *them*,' she added in a stage whisper, indicating Neville's bottom, which was sticking out from under the seat again as he groped around for Trevor, and Luna, who was now wearing her free Spectrespecs, which gave her the look of a demented, multicoloured owl.

'They're friends of mine,' said Harry coldly.

'Oh,' said the girl, looking very surprised. 'Oh. OK.'

And she withdrew, sliding the door closed behind her.

'People expect you to have cooler friends than us,' said Luna, once again displaying her knack for embarrassing honesty.

'You are cool,' said Harry shortly. 'None of them was at the Ministry. They didn't fight with me.'

'That's a very nice thing to say,' beamed Luna, and she pushed her Spectrespecs further up her nose and settled down to read *The Quibbler*.

'We didn't face *him*, though,' said Neville, emerging from under the seat with fluff and dust in his hair and a resigned-looking Trevor in his hand. 'You did. You should hear my gran talk about you. "*That Harry Potter's got more backbone than the whole Ministry of Magic put together!* " She'd give anything to have you as a grandson …'

Harry laughed uncomfortably and changed the subject to O.W.L. results as soon as he could. While Neville recited his grades and wondered aloud whether he would be allowed to take a Transfiguration N.E.W.T. with only an 'Acceptable', Harry watched him without really listening.

Neville's childhood had been blighted by Voldemort just as much as Harry's had, but Neville had no idea how close he had come to having Harry's destiny. The prophecy could have referred to either of them, yet, for

骚动。一群四年级女生在玻璃外窃窃私语，叽叽嘎嘎地傻笑。

“你去问他！”

“不，你去！”

“还是我去吧！”

其中一个看着很大胆的姑娘推门走了进来，她长着黑黑的大眼睛、突出的下巴和一头乌黑的长发。

“你好，哈利，我是罗米达，罗米达·万尼。”她自信地大声说，“你为什么不坐到我们包厢里去呢？你犯不着跟他们坐在一起。”她压低声音说，却又故意让别人听见，并指了指纳威再次钻到座位底下去抓莱福时露在外面的屁股，还有卢娜，她现在已经戴上了那副免费赠送的眼镜，看上去就像一只五颜六色、精神错乱的猫头鹰。

“他们是我的朋友。”哈利冷冷地说。

“噢，”那姑娘显得非常吃惊，说道，“噢，好吧。”

然后她退了出去，关上了身后的滑门。

“人们认为你应该有比我们更带劲的朋友。”卢娜说，又一次显示了她哪壶不开提哪壶的特长。

“你们就很带劲啊，”哈利简短地说，“当时她们谁也没在部里。她们没有跟我一起战斗。”

“这话说得真中听。”卢娜顿时眉开眼笑，把防妖眼镜往鼻梁上推了推，埋头读起了《唱唱反调》。

“不过我们并没有面对他，”纳威说着从座位底下钻了出来，头发上沾着绒毛和灰尘，手里捧着那只显得老实多了的莱福，“面对他的是你。你真该听听我奶奶是怎么说你的。‘那个哈利·波特比整个魔法部的人加在一起还有骨气！’要是你能当她的孙子，她拿什么去换都愿意……”

哈利尴尬地笑了笑，赶紧把话题引到了 O.W.L. 考试成绩上。纳威把他的成绩报了一遍，然后说出了内心的忧虑：他的变形术只得了“及格”，不知道能不能选修 N.E.W.T. 课程。哈利似听非听地看着他。

和哈利一样，纳威的童年也被伏地魔摧残了，但是纳威不知道他差一点儿就遭到了哈利的命运。预言原来指的是他们两个人中间的任

his own inscrutable reasons, Voldemort had chosen to believe that Harry was the one meant.

Had Voldemort chosen Neville, it would be Neville sitting opposite Harry bearing the lightning-shaped scar and the weight of the prophecy … or would it? Would Neville's mother have died to save him, as Lily had died for Harry? Surely she would … but what if she had been unable to stand between her son and Voldemort? Would there, then, have been no 'Chosen One' at all? An empty seat where Neville now sat and a scarless Harry who would have been kissed goodbye by his own mother, not Ron's?

'You all right, Harry? You look funny,' said Neville.

Harry started.

'Sorry – I –'

'Wrackspurt got you?' asked Luna sympathetically, peering at Harry through her enormous coloured spectacles.

'I – what?'

'A Wrackspurt … they're invisible, they float in through your ears and make your brain go fuzzy,' she said. 'I thought I felt one zooming around in here.'

She flapped her hands at thin air, as though beating off large invisible moths. Harry and Neville caught each other's eye and hastily began to talk of Quidditch.

The weather beyond the train windows was as patchy as it had been all summer; they passed through stretches of the chilling mist, then out into weak, clear sunlight. It was during one of the clear spells, when the sun was visible almost directly overhead, that Ron and Hermione entered the compartment at last.

'Wish the lunch trolley would hurry up, I'm starving,' said Ron longingly, slumping into the seat beside Harry and rubbing his stomach. 'Hi, Neville, hi, Luna. Guess what?' he added, turning to Harry. 'Malfoy's not doing prefect duty. He's just sitting in his compartment with the other Slytherins, we saw him when we passed.'

Harry sat up straight, interested. It was not like Malfoy to pass up the chance to demonstrate his power as prefect, which he had happily abused all the previous year.

何一个，然而，出于一些不可理解的原因，伏地魔愿意相信它指的是哈利。

如果伏地魔选择了纳威，那么，头上带着闪电形伤疤、承受着那个预言的重负的，就会是坐在哈利对面的纳威……是不是？纳威的母亲会不会为了救他而死，就像莉莉为了救哈利而死一样？肯定会的……可是，如果她不能阻挡伏地魔毒害她的儿子呢？那么，是不是就根本不会有“救世之星”了呢？那样的话，纳威现在坐的位子上就会空无一人，而刚才吻别哈利的就会是哈利自己的母亲，而不是罗恩的母亲了。是不是？

“你没事吧，哈利？你看上去挺怪的。”纳威说。

哈利突然惊醒。

“对不起——我——”

“被骚扰虻缠住了？”卢娜同情地问，一边从那副彩色的大眼镜后面看着哈利。

“我——你说什么？”

“骚扰虻……它们是隐形的，会飘到你耳朵里，把你的脑子搞乱。”她说，“我刚才好像觉得有一只在这里嗡嗡地飞。”

她两只手拍打着空气，好像在赶走看不见的大飞蛾。哈利和纳威对视了一下，赶紧聊起了魁地奇。

车窗外的天气忽晴忽阴，整个夏天都是这样。刚驶过寒冷的迷雾，就见到了晴朗而微弱的阳光，等到窗外的阳光几乎当空高照时，罗恩和赫敏总算走进了包厢。

“真希望送餐的车子赶紧过来，我饿坏了。”罗恩眼巴巴地说，一屁股坐在哈利旁边，揉着他的肚子，“你好，纳威，你好，卢娜。你们猜怎么着？”他接着转向哈利说，“马尔福作为级长竟然没去值勤。他只是跟斯莱特林的另外几个同学一起坐在包厢里，我们经过时看见的。”

哈利腾地坐直身子，一下子就来了兴致。错过炫耀级长权威的好机会，这可不像是马尔福的做派，他上学年可是一直耀武扬威的。

'What did he do when he saw you?'

'The usual,' said Ron indifferently, demonstrating a rude hand gesture. 'Not like him, though, is it? Well – *that* is –' he did the hand gesture again, 'but why isn't he out there bullying first-years?'

'Dunno,' said Harry, but his mind was racing. Didn't this look as though Malfoy had more important things on his mind than bullying younger students?

'Maybe he preferred the Inquisitorial Squad,' said Hermione. 'Maybe being a prefect seems a bit tame after that.'

'I don't think so,' said Harry, 'I think he's –'

But before he could expound on his theory, the compartment door slid open again and a breathless third-year girl stepped inside.

'I'm supposed to deliver these to Neville Longbottom and Harry P-Potter,' she faltered, as her eyes met Harry's and she turned scarlet. She was holding out two scrolls of parchment tied with violet ribbon. Perplexed, Harry and Neville took the scroll addressed to each of them and the girl stumbled back out of the compartment.

'What is it?' Ron demanded, as Harry unrolled his.

'An invitation,' said Harry.

> *Harry,*
>
> *I would be delighted if you would join me for a bite of lunch in compartment C.*
>
> *Sincerely, Professor H.E.F. Slughorn*

'Who's Professor Slughorn?' asked Neville, looking perplexedly at his own invitation.

'New teacher,' said Harry. 'Well, I suppose we'll have to go, won't we?'

'But what does he want me for?' asked Neville nervously, as though he were expecting detention.

'No idea,' said Harry, which was not entirely true, though he had no proof yet that his hunch was correct. 'Listen,' he added, seized by a sudden brainwave, 'let's go under the Invisibility Cloak, then we might get a good look at Malfoy on the way, see what he's up to.'

“他看见你们时是什么反应？”

“跟平常一样。”罗恩漫不经心地说，比画了一个粗鲁的手势，“这可有点反常，是不是？不过——这点倒像他——”他又做了一遍那个手势，“可是他为什么不出来欺负一年级学生了呢？”

“不知道。”哈利嘴上虽然这么说，脑子里却在飞快地转着。这是不是意味着马尔福心里装着比欺负小同学更重要的事情呢？

“也许他更喜欢调查行动组，”赫敏说，“也许在那之后当级长就显得乏味了。”

“我认为不是这样，”哈利说，“我认为——”

没等他说明自己的观点，包厢的门又被拉开，一个气喘吁吁的三年级女生走了进来。

“我来把这些送给纳威·隆巴顿和哈利·波——波特。”她结结巴巴地说，目光刚与哈利的对上，立刻羞得满脸通红。她递过来两卷扎着紫色绸带的羊皮纸。哈利和纳威疑惑地接过写着他们各自姓名的纸卷，那女生就跌跌撞撞地跑出了包厢。

“什么东西？”罗恩看着哈利打开纸卷，问道。

“一封请柬。”哈利说。

哈利：

如果你能在C号包厢与我共进午餐，我将非常高兴。

你忠实的

H.E.F.斯拉格霍恩教授

“斯拉格霍恩教授是谁？”纳威一头雾水地看着他那份请柬，问道。

“新老师。”哈利说，“看来我们肯定得去了，是不是？”

“可是他为什么叫我去呢？”纳威不安地问，好像他会被弄去关禁闭似的。

“不清楚。”哈利说，这并不完全属实，但他还不能证明自己的预感是对的。“听我说，”他脑子里突然想到一个好办法，说道，“我们穿着隐形衣去，路上能仔细观察一下马尔福，看他想做什么。”

This idea, however, came to nothing: the corridors, which were packed with people on the lookout for the lunch trolley, were impossible to negotiate while wearing the Cloak. Harry stowed it regretfully back in his bag, reflecting that it would have been nice to wear it just to avoid all the staring, which seemed to have increased in intensity even since he had last walked down the train. Every now and then students would hurtle out of their compartments to get a better look at him. The exception was Cho Chang, who darted into her compartment when she saw Harry coming. as Harry passed the window he saw her deep in determined conversation with her friend Marietta, who was wearing a very thick layer of make-up that did not entirely obscure the odd formation of pimples still etched across her face. Smirking slightly, Harry pushed on.

When they reached compartment C, they saw at once that they were not Slughorn's only invitees, although judging by the enthusiasm of Slughorn's welcome, Harry was the most warmly anticipated.

'Harry, m'boy!' said Slughorn, jumping up at the sight of him so that his great velvet-covered belly seemed to fill all the remaining space in the compartment. His shiny bald head and great silver moustache gleamed as brightly in the sunlight as the golden buttons on his waistcoat. 'Good to see you, good to see you! And you must be Mr Longbottom!'

Neville nodded, looking scared. At a gesture from Slughorn, they sat down opposite each other in the only two empty seats, which were nearest the door. Harry glanced around at their fellow guests. He recognised a Slytherin from their year, a tall black boy with high cheekbones and long, slanting eyes; there were also two seventh-year boys Harry did not know and, squashed in the corner beside Slughorn and looking as though she was not entirely sure how she had got there, Ginny.

'Now, do you know everyone?' Slughorn asked Harry and Neville. 'Blaise Zabini is in your year, of course –'

Zabini did not make any sign of recognition or greeting, and nor did Harry or Neville: Gryffindor and Slytherin students loathed each other on principle.

'This is Cormac McLaggen, perhaps you've come across each other –? No?'

McLaggen, a large, wire-haired youth, raised a hand and Harry and

然而，这个办法没有成功。走廊上挤满了等待送餐的人，穿着隐形衣根本没法通过。哈利遗憾地把隐形衣塞进了包里，心想：穿着它躲避人们瞪视的目光倒是个好办法，自从上学期下了火车之后，这种瞪视变得更让他难以招架了。有时同学们还从包厢里匆匆跑出来，就为了好好看他一眼。只有秋·张例外，她一看见哈利过来，就一头钻进了自己的包厢。哈利经过她的窗口时，看见她正煞有介事地跟她的朋友玛丽埃塔聊得起劲。玛丽埃塔化了很浓的妆，但并没有完全遮住那些深深刻在脸上的奇怪的疹子。哈利暗暗笑了笑，继续往前走。

当他们赶到C号包厢时，才发现斯拉格霍恩邀请的不止他们两个，不过从斯拉格霍恩热烈欢迎的程度看，哈利是他最盼望见到的。

“哈利，我的孩子！”斯拉格霍恩一看见哈利就跳了起来，穿着天鹅绒衣服的大肚子几乎把包厢里剩余的空间都填满了。他那明晃晃的光头、那一大把银白色的胡子，都和他马甲上的金纽扣一样，在阳光下闪着耀眼的光芒。“见到你太好了，见到你太好了！那么，你一定是隆巴顿先生吧！”

纳威点点头，似乎被吓坏了。斯拉格霍恩做了个手势，他们俩就在最靠近门口的仅有的两个空座位上面对面坐了下来。哈利扫了一圈其他被邀请的人。他认出了与他同一年级的一位斯莱特林学生，那是个高个子的黑人男孩，高高的颧骨，长长的眼睛，眼角有些上挑。还有两个哈利不认识的七年级男生，而那个被挤在斯拉格霍恩身边的角落里、一脸茫然、不知道自己为何会在这里的，竟然是金妮！

“好了，这些人你们都认识吧？”斯拉格霍恩问哈利和纳威，“布雷司·沙比尼跟你们同一个年级，你们肯定认识——”

沙比尼既没有表示出认识，也没有打招呼，哈利和纳威这边也毫无反应：一般来说，格兰芬多和斯莱特林的同学都是互相仇视的。

“这位是考迈克·麦克拉根，也许你们以前见过——？没有？”

麦克拉根是一位头发粗硬的大块头小伙子，他举起一只手，哈利

Neville nodded back at him.

'– and this is Marcus Belby, I don't know whether –?'

Belby, who was thin and nervous-looking, gave a strained smile.

'– and *this* charming young lady tells me she knows you!' Slughorn finished.

Ginny grimaced at Harry and Neville from behind Slughorn's back.

'Well now, this is most pleasant,' said Slughorn cosily. 'A chance to get to know you all a little better. Here, take a napkin. I've packed my own lunch, the trolley, as I remember it, is heavy on Liquorice Wands, and a poor old man's digestive system isn't quite up to such things … pheasant, Belby?'

Belby started, and accepted what looked like half a cold pheasant.

'I was just telling young Marcus here that I had the pleasure of teaching his Uncle Damocles,' Slughorn told Harry and Neville, now passing around a basket of rolls. 'Outstanding wizard, outstanding, and his Order of Merlin most well-deserved. Do you see much of your uncle, Marcus?'

Unfortunately, Belby had just taken a large mouthful of pheasant; in his haste to answer Slughorn he swallowed too fast, turned purple and began to choke.

'*Anapneo*,' said Slughorn calmly, pointing his wand at Belby, whose airway seemed to clear at once.

'Not … not much of him, no,' gasped Belby, his eyes streaming.

'Well, of course, I daresay he's busy,' said Slughorn, looking questioningly at Belby. 'I doubt he invented the Wolfsbane Potion without considerable hard work!'

'I suppose …' said Belby, who seemed afraid to take another bite of pheasant until he was sure that Slughorn had finished with him. 'Er … he and my dad don't get on very well, you see, so I don't really know much about …'

His voice tailed away as Slughorn gave him a cold smile and turned to McLaggen instead.

'Now, *you*, Cormac,' said Slughorn, 'I happen to know you see a lot of your Uncle Tiberius, because he has a rather splendid picture of the two of you hunting Nogtails in, I think, Norfolk?'

和纳威也朝他点了点头。

"——这位是马科斯·贝尔比，不知道你们是不是——"

贝尔比身材消瘦，神色紧张，他不自然地微笑了一下。

"——这位迷人的年轻女士告诉我，她认识你们！"斯拉格霍恩终于说完了。

金妮在斯拉格霍恩身后朝哈利和纳威做了个鬼脸。

"好了，真令人愉快，"斯拉格霍恩满意地说，"一个更多地了解你们大家的机会。给，拿一张餐巾。我的午饭是自己带的，我记得送餐车上的饭菜总是有太重的甘草魔杖的味儿，一个可怜的上了年纪的人，他的消化系统受不了这些东西……来点儿野鸡肉吧，贝尔比？"

贝尔比吃了一惊，随即接受了像是半只冷野鸡似的东西。

"我刚才正在对这位年轻的马科斯说，我当年有幸教过他的叔叔达摩克利斯，"斯拉格霍恩一边传着一篮面包卷一边对哈利和纳威说，"很出色的巫师，非常出色，他的梅林勋章绝对受之无愧。你经常看见你叔叔吗，马科斯？"

不幸的是，马科斯刚吃了一大口野鸡肉，他急于回答斯拉格霍恩的问题，咽得太快，脸一下子转成了猪肝色，呛得说不出话来。

"安咳消。"斯拉格霍恩用魔杖指着贝尔比，平静地说，贝尔比的气管似乎一下子就通畅了。

"不……不怎么见到他。"贝尔比喘着气说，眼泪都呛出来了。

"是啊，当然，我敢说他一定很忙。"斯拉格霍恩询问地看着贝尔比说道，"我想他准是下了不少功夫才发明了狼毒药剂吧？"

"我想是吧……"贝尔比说，在确信斯拉格霍恩对他的审问结束之前，他似乎不敢再吃野鸡肉了，"嗯……是这样，他和我爸爸关系不太好，所以我实际上不太清楚……"

他的声音低了下去，因为斯拉格霍恩朝他冷笑了一声，转向了麦克拉根。

"你呢，考迈克，"斯拉格霍恩说，"我碰巧知道，你是经常见到你的叔叔提贝卢斯的，因为他那儿有一张你们俩在……让我想想，在诺福克捕猎矮猪怪的精彩照片，是不是？"

'Oh, yeah, that was fun, that was,' said McLaggen. 'We went with Bertie Higgs and Rufus Scrimgeour – this was before he became Minister, obviously –'

'Ah, you know Bertie and Rufus, too?' beamed Slughorn, now offering around a small tray of pies; somehow, Belby was missed out. 'Now tell me …'

It was as Harry had suspected. Everyone here seemed to have been invited because they were connected to somebody well-known or influential – everyone except Ginny. Zabini, who was interrogated after McLaggen, turned out to have a famously beautiful witch for a mother (from what Harry could make out, she had been married seven times, each of her husbands dying mysteriously and leaving her mounds of gold). It was Neville's turn next: this was a very uncomfortable ten minutes, for Neville's parents, well-known Aurors, had been tortured into insanity by Bellatrix Lestrange and a couple of Death Eater cronies. At the end of Neville's interview, Harry had the impression that Slughorn was reserving judgement on Neville, yet to see whether he had any of his parents' flair.

'And now,' said Slughorn, shifting massively in his seat with the air of a compère introducing his star act. 'Harry Potter! *Where* to begin? I feel I barely scratched the surface when we met over the summer!'

He contemplated Harry for a moment as though he were a particularly large and succulent piece of pheasant, then said, 'The "Chosen One", they're calling you now!'

Harry said nothing. Belby, McLaggen and Zabini were all staring at him.

'Of course,' said Slughorn, watching Harry closely, 'there have been rumours for years … I remember when – well – after that *terrible* night – Lily – James – and you survived – and the word was that you must have powers beyond the ordinary –'

Zabini gave a tiny little cough that was clearly supposed to indicate amused scepticism. An angry voice burst out from behind Slughorn.

'Yeah, Zabini, because *you're* so talented … at posing …'

'Oh dear!' chuckled Slughorn comfortably, looking round at Ginny who was glaring at Zabini around Slughorn's great belly. 'You want to be careful, Blaise! I saw this young lady perform the most marvellous Bat-Bogey Hex as I was passing her carriage! I wouldn't cross her!'

“噢，是啊，那可好玩了，”麦克拉根说，“跟我们一起去的还有贝蒂·希格斯和鲁弗斯·斯克林杰——当然啦，那是在他当部长之前——”

“啊，你还认识贝蒂和鲁弗斯？”斯拉格霍恩顿时笑逐颜开，端起一小盘馅饼分给大家，不知怎的偏偏漏掉了贝尔比，“那你跟我说说……”

正如哈利早就怀疑的，这儿的每个人似乎都是因为跟某个有影响的大人物沾亲带故才受到邀请的——只有金妮除外。在麦克拉根之后接受审问的是沙比尼，没想到他母亲竟是一位大名鼎鼎的漂亮女巫（从哈利得出的结论看，她一共结过七次婚，每一位丈夫都死得很蹊跷，并给她留下了一大笔遗产）。接着轮到纳威：这真是非常令人不快的十分钟，因为纳威的父母都是著名的傲罗，被贝拉特里克斯·莱斯特兰奇和两个食死徒同党折磨致疯。对纳威的访谈结束时，哈利得到这么一个印象，似乎斯拉格霍恩对于纳威是否继承了父母的禀赋还存有疑虑。

“现在，”斯拉格霍恩说，他气派地在座位上挪动了一下，像主持人隆重推出一位大明星一样，“哈利·波特！从哪儿说起呢？我觉得，我们暑假的那次见面，我只是触及了一点皮毛！”

他沉思地端详着哈利，似乎哈利是一大块美味多汁的野鸡肉，然后他说：“‘救世之星’，他们现在这么称呼你了！”

哈利一声不吭。贝尔比、麦克拉根和沙比尼都盯着他。

“当然，”斯拉格霍恩仔细看着哈利说，“多少年来一直谣言不断……我记得当年——是啊……在那个可怕的夜晚之后——莉莉——詹姆——你死里逃生——有人说你肯定拥有超常的力量——”

沙比尼轻轻地咳嗽一声，显然为了表示他对此感到怀疑和可笑。斯拉格霍恩身后突然传出一个怒气冲冲的声音。

“是啊，沙比尼，因为你太有天赋了……在装腔作势方面……”

“哦，天哪！”斯拉格霍恩快慰地轻轻笑了笑，扭头看着金妮——金妮正隔着斯拉格霍恩的大肚皮朝沙比尼怒目而视，“你可得小心点儿哟，布雷司！我经过这位年轻女士的包厢时，看见她施了一个绝顶精彩的蝙蝠精咒！我可不敢惹她！”

Zabini merely looked contemptuous.

'Anyway,' said Slughorn, turning back to Harry. '*Such* rumours this summer. Of course, one doesn't know what to believe, the *Prophet* has been known to print inaccuracies, make mistakes – but there seems little doubt, given the number of witnesses, that there was *quite* a disturbance at the Ministry and that you were there in the thick of it all!'

Harry, who could not see any way out of this without flatly lying, nodded but still said nothing. Slughorn beamed at him.

'So modest, so modest, no wonder Dumbledore is so fond – you *were* there, then? But the rest of the stories – so sensational, of course, one doesn't know quite what to believe – this fabled prophecy, for instance –'

'We never heard a prophecy,' said Neville, turning geranium-pink as he said it.

'That's right,' said Ginny staunchly. 'Neville and I were both there too, and all this "Chosen One" rubbish is just the *Prophet* making things up as usual.'

'You were both there too, were you?' said Slughorn with great interest, looking from Ginny to Neville, but both of them sat clamlike before his encouraging smile. 'Yes … well … it is true that the *Prophet* often exaggerates, of course …' Slughorn continued, sounding a little disappointed. 'I remember dear Gwenog telling me – Gwenog Jones, I mean, of course, captain of the Holyhead Harpies –'

He meandered off into a long-winded reminiscence, but Harry had the distinct impression that Slughorn had not finished with him, and that he had not been convinced by Neville and Ginny.

The afternoon wore on with more anecdotes about illustrious wizards Slughorn had taught, all of whom had been delighted to join what he called the 'Slug Club' at Hogwarts. Harry could not wait to leave, but couldn't see how to do so politely. Finally the train emerged from yet another long misty stretch into a red sunset, and Slughorn looked around, blinking in the twilight.

'Good gracious, it's getting dark already! I didn't notice that they'd lit the lamps! You'd better go and change into your robes, all of you. McLaggen, you must drop by and borrow that book on Nogtails. Harry, Blaise – any time

沙比尼只是一副轻蔑的表情。

“总之，”斯拉格霍恩重新转向哈利，说道，“今年夏天真是谣言四起。当然啦，谁也不知道应该相信什么，大家都清楚《预言家日报》经常登一些错误消息，以讹传讹——不过既然有这么多证人，似乎不应该再有什么怀疑，魔法部确实发生了一场骚乱，而你就在战斗最激烈的地方！”

除了撒谎，哈利看不出还有什么办法可以脱身，于是便点点头，但还是什么也没说。斯拉格霍恩笑眯眯地看着他。

“多么谦虚，多么谦虚啊，怪不得邓布利多这么喜欢——如此说来，你确实在场？可是其他那些报道——哎呀，太精彩，太刺激了，弄得人简直不知道该相信什么——比如，那个传说中的预言球——”

“我们从来没听说过什么预言球。”纳威说，脸涨得通红。

“对，”金妮毫不含糊地说，“当时我和纳威也在场，所有那些‘救世之星’的鬼话，像往常一样都是《预言家日报》胡编乱造出来的。”

“你们俩也在场，是吗？”斯拉格霍恩饶有兴趣地问，看看金妮，又看看纳威，但他们俩面对他鼓励的微笑都守口如瓶。“是啊……是啊……不错，《预言家日报》确实经常夸大其词……”斯拉格霍恩继续说道，口气显得有点儿失望，“我记得亲爱的格韦诺格告诉过我——当然啦，我指的是格韦诺格·琼斯，霍利黑德哈比队的队长——”

他漫无边际地岔开话题，啰里啰唆地回忆起了往事，但是哈利有一种直觉，斯拉格霍恩不会就此放过他的，而且也并没有相信纳威和金妮的话。

整个下午，斯拉格霍恩又讲了许多他当年教过的杰出巫师的趣闻逸事，他们在霍格沃茨时都欣然加入了一个他称为鼻涕虫俱乐部的组织。哈利巴不得赶紧离开，却又不知道怎样脱身才不失礼。最后，火车驶过一段长长的浓雾地区，进入红彤彤的晚霞里，斯拉格霍恩环顾一下四周，在暮色中眨了眨眼睛。

“哎哟，天都快黑了！我没注意他们把灯都点上了！你们最好赶紧回去换上校袍吧。麦克拉根，你有空一定要过来借那本关于矮猪怪的书。

you're passing. Same goes for you, miss,' he twinkled at Ginny. 'Well, off you go, off you go!'

As he pushed past Harry into the darkening corridor, Zabini shot him a filthy look that Harry returned with interest. He, Ginny and Neville followed Zabini back along the train.

'I'm glad that's over,' muttered Neville. 'Strange man, isn't he?'

'Yeah, he is a bit,' said Harry, his eyes on Zabini. 'How come you ended up in there, Ginny?'

'He saw me hex Zacharias Smith,' said Ginny, 'you remember that idiot from Hufflepuff who was in the DA? He kept on and on asking about what happened at the Ministry and in the end he annoyed me so much I hexed him – when Slughorn came in I thought I was going to get detention, but he just thought it was a really good hex and invited me to lunch! Mad, eh?'

'Better reason for inviting someone than because their mother's famous,' said Harry, scowling at the back of Zabini's head, 'or because their uncle –'

But he broke off. An idea had just occurred to him, a reckless but potentially wonderful idea ... in a minute's time, Zabini was going to re-enter the Slytherin sixth-year compartment and Malfoy would be sitting there, thinking himself unheard by anybody except fellow Slytherins ... if Harry could only enter, unseen, behind him, what might he not see or hear? True, there was little of the journey left – Hogsmeade Station had to be less than half an hour away, judging by the wildness of the scenery flashing by the windows – but nobody else seemed prepared to take Harry's suspicions seriously, so it was down to him to prove them.

'I'll see you two later,' said Harry under his breath, pulling out his Invisibility Cloak and flinging it over himself.

'But what're you – ?' asked Neville.

'Later!' whispered Harry, darting after Zabini as quietly as possible, though the rattling of the train made such caution almost pointless.

The corridors were almost completely empty now. Nearly everyone had returned to their carriages to change into their school robes and pack up their possessions. Though he was as close as he could get to Zabini without touching him, Harry was not quick enough to slip into the compartment when Zabini opened the door. Zabini was already sliding it shut when Harry

哈利，布雷司——欢迎你们随时过来。你也一样，小姐。”他朝金妮眨眨眼睛，“好了，你们走吧，快走吧！”

沙比尼从哈利身边挤到昏暗的过道上时，恶狠狠地瞪了哈利一眼，而哈利则更狠地瞪着他。哈利、金妮和纳威都跟着沙比尼顺着过道往回走。

“谢天谢地，总算结束了。”纳威轻声说，“真是个怪人，是吧？”

“是啊，有点儿，”哈利说，眼睛仍然盯着沙比尼，“你怎么也跑到那儿去了，金妮？”

“他看见我给扎卡赖斯·史密斯施恶咒来着。”金妮说，“你还记得那个参加D.A.集会的赫奇帕奇的傻瓜吗？他不停地缠着我问部里发生的事情，弄得我不胜其烦，就给他施了个恶咒——斯拉格霍恩进来时，我还以为他要关我的禁闭呢，没想到他倒觉得那个恶咒施得非常漂亮，并邀请我去吃午饭！真怪，是吧？”

“因为这个而受到邀请，总比因为他们的母亲有名，”哈利瞪着沙比尼的后脑勺说，“或因为他们的叔叔——”

他突然顿住了。一个主意在他脑海里闪现，一个不顾后果但说不定很绝妙的主意……再过一分钟，沙比尼就要回到斯莱特林六年级学生的包厢了，马尔福肯定会坐在那里，以为只有他的斯莱特林同学才能听见他的话……如果哈利跟在沙比尼后面，神不知鬼不觉地混进去，他还有什么看不到、听不到的呢？不错，火车很快就要到站了——从窗外闪过的荒凉景色来看，距霍格莫德车站还有不到半小时——可是，既然谁也不把哈利的怀疑当真，他就只好自己去取证了。

“我待会儿再来找你们俩。”哈利压低声音说了一句，便抽出他的隐形衣，披在身上。

“可是你想干什么——”纳威问。

“待会儿见！”哈利低声说了一句，便快步朝沙比尼追去，尽量不发出一点儿声响，其实火车正在哐啷哐啷地行驶，他没有必要这么谨慎。

现在过道里几乎空无一人。差不多每个人都回到包厢里去换校袍、收拾行李了。哈利在不碰到沙比尼的前提下，尽量与他贴得很近，但是沙比尼把包厢的门拉开后，哈利溜进去的速度还是不够快。沙比尼

hastily stuck out his foot to prevent it closing.

'What's wrong with this thing?' said Zabini angrily as he smashed the sliding door repeatedly into Harry's foot.

Harry seized the door and pushed it open, hard; Zabini, still clinging on to the handle, toppled over sideways into Gregory Goyle's lap and, in the ensuing ruckus, Harry darted into the compartment, leapt on to Zabini's temporarily empty seat and hoisted himself up into the luggage rack. It was fortunate that Goyle and Zabini were snarling at each other, drawing all eyes on to them, for Harry was quite sure his feet and ankles had been revealed as the Cloak had flapped around them; indeed, for one horrible moment he thought he saw Malfoy's eyes follow his trainer as it whipped upwards out of sight; but then Goyle slammed the door shut and flung Zabini off him, Zabini collapsed into his own seat looking ruffled, Vincent Crabbe returned to his comic and Malfoy, sniggering, lay back down across two seats with his head in Pansy Parkinson's lap. Harry lay curled uncomfortably under the Cloak to ensure that every inch of him remained hidden, and watched Pansy stroke the sleek blond hair off Malfoy's forehead, smirking as she did so, as though anyone would have loved to have been in her place. The lanterns swinging from the carriage ceiling cast a bright light over the scene: Harry could read every word of Crabbe's comic directly below him.

'So, Zabini,' said Malfoy, 'what did Slughorn want?'

'Just trying to make up to well-connected people,' said Zabini, who was still glowering at Goyle. 'Not that he managed to find many.'

This information did not seem to please Malfoy.

'Who else had he invited?' he demanded.

'McLaggen from Gryffindor,' said Zabini.

'Oh yeah, his uncle's big in the Ministry,' said Malfoy.

'– someone else called Belby, from Ravenclaw –'

'Not him, he's a prat!' said Pansy.

'– and Longbottom, Potter and that Weasley girl,' finished Zabini.

Malfoy sat up very suddenly, knocking Pansy's hand aside.

'He invited *Longbottom*?'

'Well, I assume so, as Longbottom was there,' said Zabini indifferently.

眼看就要把门关上了，哈利赶紧伸出一只脚挡住。

“这玩意儿出什么毛病了？”沙比尼恼火地说，把滑门一次次地撞在哈利脚上。

哈利抓住门，使劲把它推开，仍然攥着门把手的沙比尼被甩到一边，摔在格雷戈里·高尔的大腿上。趁着混乱，哈利冲进包厢，纵身跳上沙比尼暂时空着的座位，一个引体向上，爬上了行李架。幸亏高尔和沙比尼两个人正互相咆哮，把大家的目光都吸引了过去。哈利知道刚才隐形衣掀了起来，他的脚和脚脖子肯定都露在外面了。确实，在那可怕的一瞬间，他似乎看见马尔福的目光追着他的运动鞋，看着它往上一提然后消失。这时，高尔重重地关上门，把沙比尼从他身上甩了下去。沙比尼跌坐在自己的座位上，一副气急败坏的样子。文森特·克拉布继续看他的漫画书，马尔福轻笑了几声，重新横躺在两个座位上，脑袋枕着潘西·帕金森的大腿。哈利很不舒服地蜷缩在隐形衣里，确保浑身上下都被藏得严严实实。他注视着潘西一边把马尔福脑门上柔顺的金发轻轻撩开，一边得意地傻笑着，就好像谁都眼巴巴地想得到她这个位置似的。天花板上的灯笼左右摇晃，照亮了包厢里的一切。哈利可以清清楚楚地看见下面克拉布那本漫画书上的每一个字。

“怎么样，沙比尼，”马尔福说，“斯拉格霍恩想干什么？”

“只是想巴结巴结跟显贵人物沾亲带故的人，”沙比尼仍然怒气冲冲地瞪着高尔，“不过他没能找到多少。”

这个情报似乎使马尔福不太高兴。

“他还邀请了谁？”他问。

“格兰芬多的麦克拉根。”沙比尼说。

“噢，对了，他叔叔是部里的大官。”马尔福说。

“——还有一个叫贝尔比的，是拉文克劳的——”

“别提他了，他是个草包！”潘西说。

“——还有隆巴顿、波特和韦斯莱家的那个姑娘。”沙比尼汇报完毕。

马尔福腾地坐了起来，把潘西的手打到一边。

“他还邀请了隆巴顿？”

“对，我想是吧，因为隆巴顿也去了。”沙比尼不太介意地说。

'What's Longbottom got to interest Slughorn?'

Zabini shrugged.

'Potter, precious Potter, obviously he wanted a look at the *Chosen One*,' sneered Malfoy, 'but that Weasley girl! What's so special about *her*?'

'A lot of boys like her,' said Pansy, watching Malfoy out of the corner of her eyes for his reaction. 'Even you think she's good-looking, don't you, Blaise, and we all know how hard you are to please!'

'I wouldn't touch a filthy little blood traitor like her whatever she looked like,' said Zabini coldly, and Pansy looked pleased. Malfoy sank back across her lap and allowed her to resume the stroking of his hair.

'Well, I pity Slughorn's taste. Maybe he's going a bit senile. Shame, my father always said he was a good wizard in his day. My father used to be a bit of a favourite of his. Slughorn probably hasn't heard I'm on the train, or –'

'I wouldn't bank on an invitation,' said Zabini. 'He asked me about Nott's father when I first arrived. They used to be old friends, apparently, but when he heard he'd been caught at the Ministry he didn't look happy, and Nott didn't get an invitation, did he? I don't think Slughorn's interested in Death Eaters.'

Malfoy looked angry, but forced out a singularly humourless laugh.

'Well, who cares what he's interested in? What is he, when you come down to it? Just some stupid teacher.' Malfoy yawned ostentatiously. 'I mean, I might not even be at Hogwarts next year, what's it matter to me if some fat old has-been likes me or not?'

'What do you mean, you might not be at Hogwarts next year?' said Pansy indignantly, ceasing grooming Malfoy at once.

'Well, you never know,' said Malfoy with the ghost of a smirk. 'I might have – er – moved on to bigger and better things.'

Crouched in the luggage rack under his Cloak, Harry's heart began to race. What would Ron and Hermione say about this? Crabbe and Goyle were gawping at Malfoy; apparently they had had no inkling of any plans to move on to bigger and better things. Even Zabini had allowed a look of curiosity to mar his haughty features. Pansy resumed the slow stroking of Malfoy's hair, looking dumb-founded.

"隆巴顿有什么地方让斯拉格霍恩感兴趣呢？"

沙比尼耸了耸肩。

"波特，稀罕的波特，他显然是想亲眼看看*救世之星*，"马尔福讥笑道，"可是韦斯莱家的那个姑娘！她有什么不寻常的？"

"许多男孩喜欢她。"潘西一边说一边用眼角注视着马尔福的反应，"就连你也觉得她挺漂亮，是不是，布雷司？而我们都知道你的眼光有多挑剔！"

"我才不会去碰她那样一个肮脏的小败类呢，不管她长得什么样儿。"沙比尼冷冷地说，潘西顿时喜形于色。马尔福重新倒在她的大腿上，让她继续给他梳理头发。

"唉，我真为斯拉格霍恩的品位感到遗憾。大概他有点儿老糊涂了。可惜啊，我父亲总说他是当时一位很出色的巫师。我父亲曾经在他面前挺得宠的。斯拉格霍恩大概没听说我在车上，不然——"

"我认为你不太可能受到邀请。"沙比尼说，"我刚到时，他向我打听诺特的父亲，看来他们曾经是老朋友。他听说诺特的父亲被部里逮捕了，他的脸色就沉了下去，结果诺特就没被邀请，不是吗？我认为斯拉格霍恩对食死徒不感兴趣。"

马尔福显得很生气，但勉强挤出一声干巴巴的怪笑。

"哼，谁在乎他对什么感兴趣？再说了，他又算个什么东西？不过是个愚蠢的教书匠。"马尔福夸张地打了个哈欠，"我的意思是，没准我明年就不在霍格沃茨了，某个过了气的老胖子喜欢不喜欢我，对我又有什么关系？"

"你说什么，没准你明年就不在霍格沃茨了？"潘西气哼哼地问，立刻停止了给马尔福梳理头发。

"是啊，说不准，"马尔福带着一丝得意的笑容说道，"也许我高升了，要去做——嗯——更重要更精彩的事情。"

哈利裹着隐形衣蜷缩在行李架上，心突然跳得飞快。罗恩和赫敏听了这话会怎么说呢？克拉布和高尔傻乎乎地瞪着马尔福，显然，他们对于他要去做更重要更精彩的事情的计划一无所知。就连沙比尼高傲的脸上也露出了一丝好奇。潘西带着一副目瞪口呆的神情，又开始慢慢地梳理马尔福的头发。

'Do you mean – *Him*?'

Malfoy shrugged.

'Mother wants me to complete my education, but personally, I don't see it as that important these days. I mean, think about it … when the Dark Lord takes over, is he going to care how many O.W.L.s or N.E.W.T.s anyone's got? Of course he isn't … it'll be all about the kind of service he received, the level of devotion he was shown.'

'And you think *you'll* be able to do something for him?' asked Zabini scathingly. 'Sixteen years old and not even fully qualified yet?'

'I've just said, haven't I? Maybe he doesn't care if I'm qualified. Maybe the job he wants me to do isn't something that you need to be qualified for,' said Malfoy quietly.

Crabbe and Goyle were both sitting with their mouths open like gargoyles. Pansy was gazing down at Malfoy as though she had never seen anything so awe-inspiring.

'I can see Hogwarts,' said Malfoy, clearly relishing the effect he had created as he pointed out of the blackened window. 'We'd better get our robes on.'

Harry was so busy staring at Malfoy he did not notice Goyle reaching up for his trunk; as he swung it down, it hit Harry hard on the side of the head. He let out an involuntary gasp of pain and Malfoy looked up at the luggage rack, frowning.

Harry was not afraid of Malfoy, but he still did not much like the idea of being discovered hiding under his Invisibility Cloak by a group of unfriendly Slytherins. Eyes still watering and head still throbbing, he drew his wand, careful not to disarrange the Cloak, and waited, breath held. To his relief, Malfoy seemed to decide that he had imagined the noise; he pulled on his robes like the others, locked his trunk and, as the train slowed to a jerky crawl, fastened a thick new travelling cloak round his neck.

Harry could see the corridors filling up again and hoped that Hermione and Ron would take his things out on to the platform for him; he was stuck where he was until the compartment had quite emptied. At last, with a final lurch, the train came to a complete halt. Goyle threw the door open and muscled his way out into a crowd of second-years, punching them aside; Crabbe and Zabini followed.

“你指的是——他？”

马尔福耸了耸肩。

“妈妈希望我完成学业，但我个人认为，如今这已经没有那么重要了。想想吧……黑魔王得势之后，他还会在乎谁通过了几门 O.W.L. 或 N.E.W.T. 吗？当然不会……他只关心别人怎么为他效劳，怎么向他表示赤胆忠心。”

“你认为你能为他做事？”沙比尼尖刻地问，“你才十六岁，还没有取得正式的资格呢。”

“我刚才不是说了吗？也许他不在乎我是不是有资格。也许他想让我做的那份工作，是不需要多少资格的。”马尔福轻声说。

克拉布和高尔呆呆地坐在那里，嘴巴张得老大，活像两尊滴水嘴石兽。潘西低头凝视着马尔福，似乎从没见过这么令人敬畏的东西。

“我看见霍格沃茨了。”马尔福显然很满意他制造的这种效果，指着漆黑的窗外说道，“我们最好赶紧换上校袍吧。”

哈利只顾盯着马尔福，没有注意到高尔站起来取他的箱子。高尔把箱子抽下去时，箱子重重地撞在哈利的脑袋上，痛得他忍不住吸了一口凉气。马尔福抬头看看行李架，皱起了眉头。

哈利倒不害怕马尔福，但觉得让一群不友好的斯莱特林发现他藏在隐形衣里，总归不是一件什么好事。眼睛仍然在流泪，脑袋仍然一跳一跳地疼，但他抽出魔杖，同时小心不把隐形衣弄乱，然后屏住呼吸，等待着。令他感到宽慰的是，马尔福似乎认定刚才听到的声音只是他的幻觉，他像别人一样套上校袍，锁好箱子。当火车减慢速度，缓缓向前滑动时，他将一件崭新的厚旅行斗篷在脖子周围裹紧。

哈利可以看见过道里又挤满了人，他希望赫敏和罗恩能替他把行李搬到站台上。他被困在这里，要等包厢空了以后才能出去。终于，随着最后的哐当一声响，火车完全停住了。高尔忽地把门拉开，使劲挤到一群二年级学生中间，拳打脚踢地把他们推到一边。克拉布和沙比尼也跟了过去。

'You go on,' Malfoy told Pansy, who was waiting for him with her hand held out as though hoping he would hold it. 'I just want to check something.'

Pansy left. Now Harry and Malfoy were alone in the compartment. People were filing past, descending on to the dark platform. Malfoy moved over to the compartment door and let down the blinds, so that people in the corridor beyond could not peer in. He then bent down over his trunk and opened it again.

Harry peered down over the edge of the luggage rack, his heart pumping a little faster. What had Malfoy wanted to hide from Pansy? Was he about to see the mysterious broken object it was so important to mend?

'*Petrificus Totalus!*'

Without warning, Malfoy pointed his wand at Harry, who was instantly paralysed. As though in slow motion, he toppled out of the luggage rack and fell, with an agonising, floor-shaking crash, at Malfoy's feet, the Invisibility Cloak trapped beneath him, his whole body revealed with his legs still curled absurdly into the cramped kneeling position. He couldn't move a muscle; he could only gaze up at Malfoy, who smiled broadly.

'I thought so,' he said jubilantly. 'I heard Goyle's trunk hit you. And I thought I saw something white flash through the air after Zabini came back …' His eyes lingered for a moment upon Harry's trainers. 'That was you blocking the door when Zabini came back in, I suppose?'

He considered Harry for a moment.

'You didn't hear anything I care about, Potter. But while I've got you here …'

And he stamped, hard, on Harry's face. Harry felt his nose break; blood spurted everywhere.

'That's from my father. Now, let's see …'

Malfoy dragged the Cloak out from under Harry's immobilised body and threw it over him.

'I don't reckon they'll find you till the train's back in London,' he said quietly. 'See you around, Potter … or not.'

And taking care to tread on Harry's fingers, Malfoy left the compartment.

“你先走，”马尔福对潘西说，潘西伸着手等他，似乎希望他能牵住她的手，“我还要查看一件东西。”

潘西走了。现在车厢里只剩下哈利和马尔福两个人。人们鱼贯而过，下车来到漆黑的站台上。马尔福走到包厢门口，放下帘子，这样外面过道里的人就不能朝里面窥视了。然后他弯下腰，把箱子又打开了。

哈利从行李架的边缘探头往下看着，心跳得更快了。马尔福有什么东西瞒着潘西呢？他是不是就要看见那件坏掉的、需要修理的神秘东西了？

“统统石化！”

说时迟那时快，马尔福用魔杖一指哈利，哈利立刻就僵住了。就像慢镜头一样，他从行李架上往下一歪，重重地、无比痛苦地倒在马尔福的脚边，隐形衣被压在身下，他的身体暴露无遗，两条腿仍然可笑地蜷缩着，是一种僵硬的跪着的姿势。他完全动弹不得，只能抬眼望着马尔福。马尔福得意地笑了。

“我就猜到是这样。”他开心地说，“我听见高尔的箱子撞到了你。而且，沙比尼回来后，我好像看见有个白色的东西一闪而过……”他的目光在哈利的运动鞋上停留了一下，“我猜，沙比尼进来时，就是你把门挡住了吧？”

他仔细端详了哈利片刻。

“你并没有听到什么值得我在意的东西，波特。不过既然我抓住了你……”

他照着哈利的脸狠狠跺了一脚。哈利觉得鼻子断了，鲜血溅得到处都是。

“这一脚是为了我父亲。现在，让我瞧瞧……”

马尔福把隐形衣从哈利一动不动的身体底下抽了出来，罩在哈利身上。

“我想，他们要等火车返回伦敦时才会发现你。”他轻声说，“再见，波特……也许再也见不到了。”

马尔福故意踩着哈利的手离开了包厢。

CHAPTER EIGHT

Snape Victorious

Harry could not move a muscle. He lay there beneath the Invisibility Cloak feeling the blood from his nose flow, hot and wet, over his face, listening to the voices and footsteps in the corridor beyond. His immediate thought was that someone, surely, would check the compartments before the train departed again? But at once came the dispiriting realisation that even if somebody looked into the compartment, he would be neither seen nor heard. His best hope was that somebody else would walk in and step on him.

Harry had never hated Malfoy more than as he lay there, like an absurd turtle on its back, blood dripping sickeningly into his open mouth. What a stupid situation to have landed himself in … and now the last few footsteps were dying away; everyone was shuffling along the dark platform outside; he could hear the scraping of trunks and the loud babble of talk.

Ron and Hermione would think that he had left the train without them. Once they arrived at Hogwarts and took their places in the Great Hall, looked up and down the Gryffindor table a few times and finally realised that he was not there, he, no doubt, would be halfway back to London.

He tried to make a sound, even a grunt, but it was impossible. Then he remembered that some wizards, like Dumbledore, could perform spells without speaking, so he tried to Summon his wand, which had fallen out of his hand, by saying the words '*Accio wand!*' over and over again in his head, but nothing happened.

He thought he could hear the rustling of the trees that surrounded the lake, and the far-off hoot of an owl, but no hint of a search being made, or even (he despised himself slightly for hoping it) panicked voices wondering where Harry Potter had gone. A feeling of hopelessness spread through him

第 8 章

斯内普如愿以偿

哈利全身一点也动弹不得。他躺在隐形衣下，感觉到热乎乎的鲜血从鼻子里流出来，糊在脸上。他听着外面过道里的脚步声和说话声，先是想道：在火车再次出发之前，肯定会有人来检查每一个包厢吧？可是，紧接着他又万分沮丧地意识到，即使有人往包厢里看一眼，也不会看见他或听见他的声音。他只能希望有人会走进来，踩在他身上。

哈利躺在那里，像一只可笑的四脚朝天的乌龟，鼻血直接淌进了张开的嘴巴里，令他感到恶心，他从来没有像此刻这样恨透了马尔福。他现在的处境多么狼狈啊……这时，最后一阵脚步声也消失了，大家拖着疲倦的脚步走在外面漆黑的站台上，他可以听见箱子拖在地上的声音和同学们大声的说话声。

罗恩和赫敏肯定以为他撇下他们自己下车了。等他们到了霍格沃茨，在大礼堂里坐下来，朝格兰芬多的桌子扫视几遍之后，才会发现他不在那儿，而那个时候，他已经在返回伦敦的半路上了。

他拼命想发出点儿声音，哪怕是一声嘟囔，可是怎么也发不出来。接着他想起有些巫师，比如邓布利多，可以不出声地念咒语，他便试着在心里一遍遍地默念“魔杖飞来！魔杖飞来！”想把从他手里掉落的魔杖召唤回来。然而，什么反应也没有。

他仿佛听见了湖边树叶的沙沙声和远处一只猫头鹰的叫声，但是并没有人来检查包厢，甚至（他有点看不起自己居然存有这种希望）没有人惊慌地询问哈利·波特怎么不见了。他想象着夜骐拉的车队慢

as he imagined the convoy of Thestral-drawn carriages trundling up to the school and the muffled yells of laughter issuing from whichever carriage Malfoy was riding in, where he would be recounting his attack on Harry to his fellow Slytherins.

The train lurched, causing Harry to roll over on to his side. Now he was staring at the dusty underside of the seats instead of the ceiling. The floor began to vibrate as the engine roared into life. The Express was leaving and nobody knew he was still on it …

Then he felt his Invisibility Cloak fly off him and a voice overhead said, 'Wotcher, Harry.'

There was a flash of red light and Harry's body unfroze; he was able to push himself into a more dignified sitting position, hastily wipe the blood off his bruised face with the back of his hand and raise his head to look up at Tonks, who was holding the Invisibility Cloak she had just pulled away.

'We'd better get out of here, quickly,' she said, as the train windows became obscured with steam and the train began to move out of the station. 'Come on, we'll jump.'

Harry hurried after her into the corridor. Tonks pulled open the train door and leapt on to the platform, which seemed to be sliding underneath them as the train gathered momentum. Harry followed her, staggered a little on landing, then straightened up in time to see the gleaming scarlet steam engine pick up speed, round the corner and disappear from view.

The cold night air was soothing on his throbbing nose. Tonks was looking at him; he felt angry and embarrassed that he had been discovered in such a ridiculous position. Silently, she handed him back the Invisibility Cloak.

'Who did it?'

'Draco Malfoy,' said Harry bitterly. 'Thanks for … well …'

'No problem,' said Tonks, without smiling. From what Harry could see in the darkness, she was as mousy-haired and miserable-looking as she had been when he had met her at The Burrow. 'I can fix your nose if you stand still.'

Harry did not think much of this idea; he had been intending to visit Madam Pomfrey, the matron, in whom he had a little more confidence when it came to Healing spells, but it seemed rude to say this, so he stayed stock-still and closed his eyes.

慢朝学校移动，某辆马车里隐约地传来马尔福的大笑，他肯定在跟那些斯莱特林的同学们讲述他是怎么教训哈利·波特的……想到这儿，一种绝望的情绪在哈利心头蔓延开来。

火车猛地动了一下，震得哈利翻滚过去，侧身躺着。现在他不再瞪着天花板，而是面对着满是灰尘的座位下面。发动机启动了，地板微微震颤。特快列车正在驶离站台，而没有一个人知道哈利还在车上……

突然，他感觉到隐形衣被掀开了，头顶上一个声音说道："你好哇，哈利。"

一道红光闪过，哈利的身体解咒了。他坐起来，尽量使自己显得体面一些，并赶紧用手背把鲜血从受伤的脸上擦去，抬头看着唐克斯。唐克斯手里拿着她刚才揭开的隐形衣。

"我们最好赶紧离开这儿。"她说，这时车窗已被蒸汽罩住，变得模模糊糊，火车开始驶离站台，"快，我们跳车。"

哈利匆匆跟着她来到过道里。唐克斯拉开车门，纵身跳到了站台上。随着火车加速，下面的站台似乎在向后滑动。哈利跟着她跳了下去，落地时差点儿摔倒。他直起身子，正好看见耀眼的深红色蒸汽机车加快了速度，拐过一个弯道，消失了。

夜晚凉飕飕的空气扑面而来，使哈利突突跳痛的鼻子感到很舒服。唐克斯正看着他。他觉得又恼火又尴尬，居然在这种狼狈的状况下被人发现。唐克斯默默地把隐形衣递给了他。

"谁干的？"

"德拉科·马尔福，"哈利恨恨地说，"谢谢你……嗯……"

"没什么。"唐克斯面无笑容地说。哈利就着夜色看去，发现唐克斯和他上次在陋居看见时一样，灰褐色的头发，面容憔悴。"你站着别动，我把你的鼻子治好。"

哈利不太赞成这个主意。他本来打算去找校医庞弗雷女士的，在用咒语疗伤方面，哈利对她更有信心一些。但是这么说似乎不太礼貌，所以哈利一动不动地站住，闭上了眼睛。

'*Episkey*,' said Tonks.

Harry's nose felt very hot, and then very cold. He raised a hand and felt it gingerly. It seemed to be mended.

'Thanks a lot!'

'You'd better put that Cloak back on, and we can walk up to the school,' said Tonks, still unsmiling. As Harry swung the Cloak back over himself she waved her wand; an immense silvery four-legged creature erupted from it and streaked off into the darkness.

'Was that a Patronus?' asked Harry, who had seen Dumbledore send messages like this.

'Yes, I'm sending word to the castle that I've got you, or they'll worry. Come on, we'd better not dawdle.'

They set off towards the lane that led to the school.

'How did you find me?'

'I noticed you hadn't left the train and I knew you had that Cloak. I thought you might be hiding for some reason. When I saw the blinds were drawn down on that compartment I thought I'd check.'

'But what are you doing here, anyway?' Harry asked.

'I'm stationed in Hogsmeade now, to give the school extra protection,' said Tonks.

'Is it just you who's stationed up here, or –?'

'No, Proudfoot, Savage and Dawlish are here too.'

'Dawlish, that Auror Dumbledore attacked last year?'

'That's right.'

They trudged up the dark, deserted lane, following the freshly made carriage tracks. Harry looked sideways at Tonks under his Cloak. Last year she had been inquisitive (to the point of being a little annoying at times), she had laughed easily, she had made jokes. Now she seemed older and much more serious and purposeful. Was this all the effect of what had happened at the Ministry? He reflected uncomfortably that Hermione would have suggested he say something consoling about Sirius to her, that it hadn't been her fault at all, but he couldn't bring himself to do it. He was far from blaming her for Sirius's death; it was no more her fault than anyone else's (and much less than his), but he did not like talking about Sirius if he could avoid

“愈合如初！”唐克斯说。

哈利感到鼻子一下子变得火辣辣，接着又变得冰凉凉。他抬起手小心地摸了摸。鼻子似乎已经愈合了。

“太感谢了！”

“你最好把隐形衣披上，我们可以步行去学校。”唐克斯说，脸上还是毫无笑容。

哈利把隐形衣重新披在身上时，唐克斯挥了一下魔杖。一头巨大的银白色四脚动物从魔杖里冒出来，飞快地跑进了夜色中。

“那是守护神吗？”哈利问，他曾经看见邓布利多用这种方式传递消息。

“对，我通知学校我已经找到你了，免得他们着急。走吧，最好别再耽搁了。”

他们朝那条通向学校的小路走去。

“你是怎么找到我的？”

“我注意到你没有下车，而且知道你有隐形衣。我就猜到你不知为什么藏了起来。后来我看见那个包厢拉着帘子，觉得应该进去检查一下。”

“可是，你在这里做什么呢？”哈利问。

“我目前守在霍格莫德，给学校增加一些保护。”唐克斯说。

“守在这里的只有你一个人，还是——？”

“不，普劳特、塞维奇和德力士也都在这里。”

“德力士，就是邓布利多上次击倒的那个傲罗吗？”

“是的。”

他们顺着马车刚轧出的车辙，艰难地走在漆黑荒凉的小路上。哈利从隐形衣下侧脸看着唐克斯。去年，她是那么爱打听别人的事情（有时甚至有点惹人讨厌），那么爱笑，那么爱讲笑话。现在她好像一下子老了好几岁，显得严肃和刚毅多了。难道这都是部里发生的那件事带来的后果吗？哈利不安地想到，赫敏肯定会建议他对唐克斯说一些安慰的话，说小天狼星的死根本不能怪她，但是，他没有勇气这么说。

it. And so they tramped on through the cold night in silence, Tonks's long cloak whispering on the ground behind them.

Having always travelled there by carriage, Harry had never before appreciated just how far Hogwarts was from Hogsmeade Station. With great relief he finally saw the tall pillars on either side of the gates, each topped with a winged boar. He was cold, he was hungry, and he was quite keen to leave this new, gloomy Tonks behind. But when he put out a hand to push open the gates, he found them chained shut.

'*Alohomora!* ' he said confidently, pointing his wand at the padlock, but nothing happened.

'That won't work on these,' said Tonks. 'Dumbledore bewitched them himself.'

Harry looked around.

'I could climb a wall,' he suggested.

'No, you couldn't,' said Tonks flatly. 'Anti-intruder jinxes on all of them. Security's been tightened a hundredfold this summer.'

'Well then,' said Harry, starting to feel annoyed at her lack of helpfulness, 'I suppose I'll just have to sleep out here and wait for morning.'

'Someone's coming down for you,' said Tonks. 'Look.'

A lantern was bobbing at the distant foot of the castle. Harry was so pleased to see it he felt he could even endure Filch's wheezy criticisms of his tardiness and rants about how his timekeeping would improve with the regular application of thumbscrews. It was not until the glowing yellow light was ten feet away from them, and Harry had pulled off his Invisibility Cloak so that he could be seen, that he recognised, with a rush of pure loathing, the uplit hooked nose and long, black, greasy hair of Severus Snape.

'Well, well, well,' sneered Snape, taking out his wand and tapping the padlock once, so that the chains snaked backwards and the gates creaked open. 'Nice of you to turn up, Potter, although you have evidently decided that the wearing of school robes would detract from your appearance.'

'I couldn't change, I didn't have my –' Harry began, but Snape cut across him.

'There is no need to wait, Nymphadora. Potter is quite – ah – safe in my hands.'

他丝毫不认为小天狼星的死是唐克斯的过错，她的责任不比任何人大（远没有哈利的大），但是他实在不愿意谈到小天狼星，能回避就尽量回避。于是，他们默默地走在寒冷的夜色中，唐克斯的斗篷拖在身后的地上，发出沙沙的声响。

哈利以前都是坐的马车，从不知道霍格沃茨离霍格莫德车站有多远。当他终于看见学校大门两边高高的、顶上装饰着带翼野猪的石柱时，总算松了口气。他又冷又饿，而且巴不得赶紧离开这位令人感到陌生的、脸色阴沉的唐克斯。可是当他伸手推大门时，发现大门用链条锁住了。

“阿拉霍洞开！”他用魔杖指着门锁，很有把握地喊道，可是大门毫无反应。

“这个对它不会管用的。”唐克斯说，“邓布利多亲自给它施了魔法。”

哈利转过脸来。

“我可以翻墙进去。”他提议道。

“不行，绝对不行，”唐克斯面无表情地说，“墙上都施了反侵入咒。今年夏天，安全措施加强了一百倍。”

“那好，”哈利对她这样袖手旁观感到有点生气，说道，“我想我只能睡在外面，等明天早上再说了。”

“有人来接你了。”唐克斯说，“看。”

远处城堡脚下出现了一盏摇摇晃晃的提灯。哈利高兴极了，觉得甚至能够忍受费尔奇呼哧带喘地批评他迟到，并叫嚷着说如果定期给他动点儿酷刑，他的时间观念就会增强了。闪亮的橙黄色灯光离他只有不到十步远了，哈利脱掉隐形衣好让来人看见他，这时他才认出了斯内普那个被灯光从下面照亮的鹰钩鼻和那一头乌黑油腻的长头发，他顿时产生了一种强烈的厌恶感。

“很好，很好，很好，”斯内普讥笑道，一边抽出魔杖，在锁上敲了一下，链条便像蛇一样缩了回去，大门吱吱嘎嘎地开了，“你总算露面了，波特，不过你似乎认为穿上校袍会有损你的容颜。”

“我没法换衣服，我的箱子——”哈利话没说完，就被斯内普打断了。

“没必要再等了，尼法朵拉。波特在我手里非常——嗯——安全。”

'I meant Hagrid to get the message,' said Tonks, frowning.

'Hagrid was late for the start-of-term feast, just like Potter here, so I took it instead. And incidentally,' said Snape, standing back to allow Harry to pass him, 'I was interested to see your new Patronus.'

He shut the gates in her face with a loud clang and tapped the chains with his wand again, so that they slithered, clinking, back into place.

'I think you were better off with the old one,' said Snape, the malice in his voice unmistakeable. 'The new one looks weak.'

As Snape swung the lantern about Harry saw, fleetingly, a look of shock and anger on Tonks's face. Then she was covered in darkness once more.

'Goodnight,' Harry called to her over his shoulder, as he began the walk up to the school with Snape. 'Thanks for … everything.'

'See you, Harry.'

Snape did not speak for a minute or so. Harry felt as though his body was generating waves of hatred so powerful that it seemed incredible that Snape could not feel them burning him. He had loathed Snape from their first encounter, but Snape had placed himself for ever and irrevocably beyond the possibility of Harry's forgiveness by his attitude towards Sirius. Whatever Dumbledore said, Harry had had time to think over the summer, and had concluded that Snape's snide remarks to Sirius about remaining safely hidden while the rest of the Order of the Phoenix were fighting Voldemort had probably been a powerful factor in Sirius rushing off to the Ministry the night that he had died. Harry clung to this notion, because it enabled him to blame Snape, which felt satisfying, and also because he knew that if anyone was not sorry that Sirius was dead, it was the man now striding next to him in the darkness.

'Fifty points from Gryffindor for lateness, I think,' said Snape. 'And, let me see, another twenty for your Muggle attire. You know, I don't believe any house has ever been in negative figures this early in the term – we haven't even started pudding. You might have set a record, Potter.'

The fury and hatred bubbling inside Harry seemed to blaze white-hot, but he would rather have been immobilised all the way back to London than tell Snape why he was late.

“我本来是把消息告诉海格的。”唐克斯皱着眉头说。

“海格像波特一样，没能准时参加开学宴会，所以我就代收了。顺便说一句，”斯内普退后一步，让哈利过去，“我对你的新守护神很感兴趣。”

他当着唐克斯的面哐当一声关上大门，又用魔杖敲了敲链条，随着一阵金属的碰撞声，链条又像蛇一样窜回了原处。

“我认为还是原来的那个更好，”斯内普说，声音里毫无疑问透着恶意，“新的这个看上去没什么力气。”

斯内普把提灯一晃，哈利看见唐克斯脸上闪过一丝震惊和愤怒，但紧接着她就又被黑暗笼罩了。

“晚安，”哈利跟斯内普一起朝学校走去时，扭头对唐克斯喊道，“谢谢……谢谢你做的一切。”

“再见，哈利。”

斯内普一时间没有说话。哈利觉得自己身体里释放出非常强烈的仇恨，他简直不敢相信斯内普竟然感觉不到这些仇恨在烧灼着他。从他们第一次见面起，哈利就讨厌斯内普，而斯内普对待小天狼星的态度，又使哈利永远也不可能原谅他。不管邓布利多怎么说，哈利在暑假里反复思忖之后得出了这样的结论：斯内普不怀好意地讥讽小天狼星，说凤凰社的其他成员都在跟伏地魔战斗，而他却躲在安全的地方，后来正是斯内普的这番话促使小天狼星在那天夜里冲进魔法部，丢掉了性命。哈利抱着这种想法不放，这样就可以把责任怪罪到斯内普身上，使自己感到解恨，而且他知道，如果有谁对小天狼星的死无动于衷，那就是此刻在黑暗中走在他身边的这个男人。

“因为迟到，格兰芬多扣掉五十分。”斯内普说，“还有，让我想想，因为你穿着麻瓜衣服，再扣掉二十分。我想，还没有哪个学院在学期刚刚开始——布丁还没有端上来——就被扣了分数呢。你大概是创纪录了，波特。”

哈利内心的愤怒和仇恨简直达到了白热化，他宁愿全身僵硬地返回伦敦，也不愿告诉斯内普他迟到的原因。

'I suppose you wanted to make an entrance, did you?' Snape continued. 'And with no flying car available you decided that bursting into the Great Hall halfway through the feast ought to create a dramatic effect.'

Still Harry remained silent, though he thought his chest might explode. He knew that Snape had come to fetch him for this, for the few minutes when he could needle and torment Harry without anyone else listening.

They reached the castle steps at last and as the great oaken front doors swung open on to the vast flagged Entrance Hall, a burst of talk and laughter and of tinkling plates and glasses greeted them through the doors standing open into the Great Hall. Harry wondered whether he could slip his Invisibility Cloak back on, thereby gaining his seat at the long Gryffindor table (which, inconveniently, was the furthest from the Entrance Hall) without being noticed.

As though he had read Harry's mind, however, Snape said, 'No Cloak. You can walk in so that everyone sees you, which is what you wanted, I'm sure.'

Harry turned on the spot and marched straight through the open doors: anything to get away from Snape. The Great Hall, with its four long house tables and its staff table set at the top of the room, was decorated as usual with floating candles that made the plates below glitter and glow. It was all a shimmering blur to Harry, however, who walked so fast that he was passing the Hufflepuff table before people really started to stare, and by the time they were standing up to get a good look at him, he had spotted Ron and Hermione, sped along the benches towards them and forced his way in between them.

'Where've you – blimey, what've you done to your face?' said Ron, goggling at him along with everyone else in the vicinity.

'Why, what's wrong with it?' said Harry, grabbing a spoon and squinting at his distorted reflection.

'You're covered in blood!' said Hermione. 'Come here –'

She raised her wand, said, '*Tergeo!*' and siphoned off the dried blood.

'Thanks,' said Harry, feeling his now clean face. 'How's my nose looking?'

'Normal,' said Hermione anxiously. 'Why shouldn't it? Harry, what happened, we've been terrified!'

'I'll tell you later,' said Harry curtly. He was very conscious that Ginny,

“我猜你是想来一个登场亮相吧？”斯内普继续说道，“你弄不到会飞的汽车，就以为在宴会进行到一半时冲进礼堂也会产生戏剧性的效果。”

哈利仍然保持沉默，尽管他觉得肺都要气炸了。他知道斯内普来接他就是为了这个，可以有几分钟时间激怒和折磨哈利，而不会被任何人听见。

他们终于来到了城堡的台阶上，当那两扇橡木大门打开，露出里面铺着石板的宽大门厅时，一阵阵欢声笑语和杯盘碰撞的声音通过礼堂敞开的门，传到了他们的耳朵里。哈利心想，不知道他能不能偷偷披上隐形衣，神不知鬼不觉地溜到格兰芬多的长桌旁坐下。很不方便的是，格兰芬多的桌子在礼堂的最里头。

然而，斯内普似乎猜到了哈利的心思，他说：“不许穿隐形衣。你就这样走进去，让大家都看看你，我相信这正是你想要的效果。”

哈利原地转了个身，大步穿过敞开的大门：只要能离开斯内普就行。礼堂里有四张学院餐桌，顶头还有一张教工餐桌，空中像往常一样装饰着许多飘浮的蜡烛，照得下面的盘子闪闪发亮。然而，所有这些在哈利眼里只是亮晃晃的模糊一片。他走得飞快，当人们开始盯着他看时，他正在穿过赫奇帕奇餐桌，而当人们站起来打量他时，他已经看见了罗恩和赫敏。他快步从一条条长凳旁奔过，挤到他们俩中间坐了下来。

“你去哪儿了——天哪，你的脸怎么了？”罗恩说，他和近旁的每个人都睁大了眼睛瞪着哈利。

“怎么啦，有什么不对吗？”哈利说着抓起一把汤勺，眯起眼睛打量映在上面的那张变形的脸。

“你满脸都是血！”赫敏说，“来——”

她举起魔杖，念道：“*旋风扫净！*”那些干硬的血痂就被吸走了。

“谢谢。”哈利摸着干干净净的脸说，“我的鼻子看上去怎么样？”

“很正常。”赫敏担忧地说，“你的鼻子会有什么问题？哈利，出什么事了，真把我们吓坏了！”

“待会儿再告诉你们。”哈利简短地说了一句。他警觉地发现金妮、

Neville, Dean and Seamus were listening in; even Nearly Headless Nick, the Gryffindor ghost, had come floating along the bench to eavesdrop.

'But –' said Hermione.

'Not now, Hermione,' said Harry, in a darkly significant voice. He hoped very much that they would all assume he had been involved in something heroic, preferably involving a couple of Death Eaters and a Dementor. Of course, Malfoy would spread the story as far and wide as he could, but there was always a chance it wouldn't reach too many Gryffindor ears.

He reached across Ron for a couple of chicken legs and a handful of chips, but before he could take them they vanished, to be replaced with puddings.

'You missed the Sorting, anyway,' said Hermione, as Ron dived for a large chocolate gateau.

'Hat say anything interesting?' asked Harry, taking a piece of treacle tart.

'More of the same, really … advising us all to unite in the face of our enemies, you know.'

'Dumbledore mentioned Voldemort at all?'

'Not yet, but he always saves his proper speech for after the feast, doesn't he? It can't be long now.'

'Snape said Hagrid was late for the feast –'

'You've seen Snape? How come?' said Ron between frenzied mouthfuls of gateau.

'Bumped into him,' said Harry evasively.

'Hagrid was only a few minutes late,' said Hermione. 'Look, he's waving at you, Harry.'

Harry looked up at the staff table and grinned at Hagrid, who was indeed waving at him. Hagrid had never quite managed to comport himself with the dignity of Professor McGonagall, Head of Gryffindor House, the top of whose head came up to somewhere between Hagrid's elbow and shoulder as they were sitting side by side, and who was looking disapproving at this enthusiastic greeting. Harry was surprised to see the Divination teacher, Professor Trelawney, sitting on Hagrid's other side; she rarely left her tower room and he had never seen her at the start-of-term feast before. She looked as odd as ever, glittering with beads and trailing shawls, her eyes magnified

纳威、迪安和西莫都在听着，就连格兰芬多的鬼魂——差点没头的尼克也顺着长凳飘过来想偷听。

“可是——”赫敏说。

“先不说了吧，赫敏。”哈利用一种神秘的、意味深长的口吻说。他真希望他们都以为他去做了一件很勇敢的事，最好是面对两个食死徒和一个摄魂怪。当然啦，马尔福肯定会逢人便讲这个故事，但可能不会传到太多的格兰芬多同学的耳朵里。

他隔着罗恩去拿两根鸡腿和一把炸薯条，可是没等拿到手，它们就消失了，取而代之的是甜点心。

“你错过了分院仪式。”赫敏说，罗恩伸手去够一大块巧克力蛋糕。

“帽子说了什么有趣的话没有？”哈利一边问一边拿过一块蜂蜜馅饼。

“跟以前大同小异……建议我们团结起来，共同面对我们的敌人，你知道的。”

“邓布利多提到伏地魔了吗？”

“还没有，不过他总是在宴会结束后才正式讲话，对吧？快了。”

“斯内普说海格也没准时参加宴会……”

“你看见斯内普了？怎么会呢？”罗恩狼吞虎咽地吃着蛋糕，问道。

“正好碰到他了。”哈利含糊其词地说。

“海格只迟到了几分钟。”赫敏说，“看，哈利，他正冲你招手呢。”

哈利朝教工餐桌望去，海格果然在冲他招手，他便也朝海格笑了笑。海格和威严的麦格教授总是显得很不协调，麦格教授是格兰芬多的院长，他们坐在一起时她的头顶只齐到海格的臂肘和肩膀之间。此刻，她看见海格这样热情洋溢地打招呼，露出了不赞同的神情。哈利惊讶地看到，坐在海格另一边的竟然是占卜课老师特里劳尼教授。她平常很少离开她塔楼上的房间，哈利以前从没在开学宴会上看见过她。她的模样还像以前一样古怪，身上戴着闪闪发亮的珠子，裹着长长的披肩，一双眼睛被眼镜片放大了许多倍。哈利以前一直把她看成骗子，没想到在上学期快要结束时，竟得知是她说出了那个预言，导致伏地魔杀

to enormous size by her spectacles. Having always considered her a bit of a fraud, Harry had been shocked to discover at the end of the previous term that it had been she who had made the prediction that caused Lord Voldemort to kill Harry's parents and attack Harry himself. The knowledge had made him even less eager to find himself in her company, but thankfully, this year he would be dropping Divination. Her great beacon-like eyes swivelled in his direction; he hastily looked away towards the Slytherin table. Draco Malfoy was miming the shattering of a nose to raucous laughter and applause. Harry dropped his gaze to his treacle tart, his insides burning again. What he would not give to fight Malfoy one on one …

'So what did Professor Slughorn want?' Hermione asked.

'To know what really happened at the Ministry,' said Harry.

'Him and everyone else here,' sniffed Hermione. 'People were interrogating us about it on the train, weren't they, Ron?'

'Yeah,' said Ron. 'All wanting to know if you really are the Chosen One –'

'There has been much talk on that very subject even amongst the ghosts,' interrupted Nearly Headless Nick, inclining his barely connected head towards Harry so that it wobbled dangerously on its ruff. 'I am considered something of a Potter authority; it is widely known that we are friendly. I have assured the spirit community that I will not pester you for information, however. "Harry Potter knows that he can confide in me with complete confidence," I told them. "I would rather die than betray his trust."'

'That's not saying much, seeing as you're already dead,' Ron observed.

'Once again, you show all the sensitivity of a blunt axe,' said Nearly Headless Nick in affronted tones, and he rose into the air and glided back towards the far end of the Gryffindor table just as Dumbledore got to his feet at the staff table. The talk and laughter echoing around the Hall died away almost instantly.

'The very best of evenings to you!' he said, smiling broadly, his arms opened wide as though to embrace the whole room.

'What happened to his hand?' gasped Hermione.

She was not the only one who had noticed. Dumbledore's right hand was as blackened and dead-looking as it had been on the night he had come to fetch Harry from the Dursleys'. Whispers swept the room; Dumbledore, interpreting them correctly, merely smiled and shook his purple and gold

死了哈利的父母并对哈利本人下了毒手。知道这件事后，哈利更不愿意跟她待在一起了，幸好，他这学年不再选修占卜课。她那双大得吓人的、灯泡般的眼睛朝他这边望了过来，哈利赶紧把目光转向斯莱特林的桌子。德拉科·马尔福正在表演他怎么砸烂了一个鼻子，博得了一阵刺耳的笑声和掌声。哈利垂下眼睛望着那块蜂蜜馅饼，心里又是怒火燃烧。他真恨不得跟马尔福面对面地干上一仗……

“那么斯拉格霍恩教授想要什么？”赫敏问。

“想要知道部里到底发生了什么事。”哈利说。

“不光他，这里的每个人都想知道。”赫敏轻蔑地说，“火车上总有人审问我们，是吧，罗恩？”

“没错，”罗恩说，“大家都想知道你是不是真的就是‘救世之星’——”

“就连幽灵们对这个话题也有很多议论。”差点没头的尼克插进来说道，他那颗仅连着一点皮的脑袋朝哈利偏了过来，在轮状皱领上危险地摇晃着，“我差不多被看成是波特权威，大家都知道我们的关系很好。不过，我向幽灵们保证，我不会缠着波特打听情况的。‘哈利·波特知道可以绝对信任我，他对我推心置腹。’我告诉他们说，‘我宁死也不会背叛他的信任。’”

“那不能说明什么问题，因为你已经死了。”罗恩尖锐地指出。

“又来了，你总是像钝斧头一样迟钝而伤人。”差点没头的尼克用受冒犯的语气说完，便升到空中，朝格兰芬多餐桌的那头飘去。就在这时，邓布利多在教工餐桌后面站了起来，回荡在礼堂里的说笑声几乎立刻就平静下来。

“祝大家晚上好！”他慈祥地微笑着说，一边张开双臂，似乎要拥抱整个礼堂。

“他的手怎么啦？”赫敏惊愕地问。

注意到这点的不只是她一个人。邓布利多的右手仍然像那晚他到德思礼家接走哈利时一样，焦黑干枯，毫无生机。礼堂里一片窃窃私语。邓布利多知道大家在议论什么，他只是笑了笑，抖抖紫色和金色相间

sleeve over his injury.

'Nothing to worry about,' he said airily. 'Now … to our new students, welcome; to our old students, welcome back! Another year full of magical education awaits you …'

'His hand was like that when I saw him over the summer,' Harry whispered to Hermione. 'I thought he'd have cured it by now, though … or Madam Pomfrey would've done.'

'It looks as if it's died,' said Hermione, with a nauseated expression. 'But there are some injuries you can't cure … old curses … and there are poisons without antidotes …'

'… and Mr Filch, our caretaker, has asked me to say that there is a blanket ban on any joke items bought at the shop called Weasleys' Wizard Wheezes.

'Those wishing to play for their house Quidditch teams should give their names to their Heads of House as usual. We are also looking for new Quidditch commentators, who should do likewise.

'We are pleased to welcome a new member of staff this year. Professor Slughorn,' Slughorn stood up, his bald head gleaming in the candlelight, his big waistcoated belly casting the table below into shadow, 'is a former colleague of mine who has agreed to resume his old post of Potions master.'

'Potions?'

'*Potions?*'

The word echoed all over the Hall as people wondered whether they had heard right.

'Potions?' said Ron and Hermione together, turning to stare at Harry. 'But you said –'

'Professor Snape, meanwhile,' said Dumbledore, raising his voice so that it carried over all the muttering, 'will be taking over the position of Defence Against the Dark Arts teacher.'

'No!' said Harry, so loudly that many heads turned in his direction. He did not care; he was staring up at the staff table, incensed. How could Snape be given the Defence Against the Dark Arts job after all this time? Hadn't it been widely known for years that Dumbledore did not trust him to do it?

'But, Harry, you said that Slughorn was going to be teaching Defence Against the Dark Arts!' said Hermione.

的衣袖，遮住了那只受伤的手。

“不用担心。”他轻描淡写地说，“好了……新同学们，欢迎入学；老同学们，欢迎回校！等待你们的是新一学年的魔法教育……”

“我暑假里看见他时，他的手就是这样。”哈利小声对赫敏说，“我本来以为他早就治好了……或者庞弗雷女士给他治好了。”

“那只手看上去像是死了。”赫敏脸上带着难受的表情说，“有些伤永远治不好……古老的咒语……还有一些魔药是没有解药的……”

“……管理员费尔奇让我告诉大家，今年绝对禁止学生携带从韦斯莱魔法把戏坊购买的任何笑话商品。

“想要参加学院魁地奇球队的同学，像往常一样把名字报给院长。我们还在物色新的魁地奇比赛解说员，有意者也到院长那儿报名。

“今年，我们很高兴地迎来了一位新教师。斯拉格霍恩教授，”斯拉格霍恩站了起来，那颗光秃秃的脑袋在烛光下闪闪发亮，穿着马甲的大肚子在桌上投下一大片阴影，“他是我以前的一位同事，同意重操旧职，担任魔药课教师。”

“魔药课？”

“魔药课？”

这个词在整个礼堂里回荡，大家都怀疑自己是不是听错了。

“魔药课？”罗恩和赫敏异口同声地说，同时都偏过脑袋瞪着哈利，“可是你原来说——”

“与此同时，斯内普教授，”邓布利多提高声音盖过了人们的议论，“将担任黑魔法防御术课的教师。”

“不！”哈利的声音太响了，许多脑袋都朝他这边转了过来。但他不管，只是愤怒地瞪着教工餐桌。怎么到头来还是把黑魔法防御术的教职给了斯内普呢？这么多年来大家不是都知道，邓布利多不相信他能胜任这份工作吗？

“可是，哈利，你说过斯拉格霍恩要教黑魔法防御术的！”赫敏说。

'I thought he was!' said Harry, racking his brains to remember when Dumbledore had told him this, but now that he came to think of it, he was unable to recall Dumbledore ever telling him what Slughorn would be teaching.

Snape, who was sitting on Dumbledore's right, did not stand up at the mention of his name, merely raised a hand in lazy acknowledgement of the applause from the Slytherin table, yet Harry was sure he could detect a look of triumph on the features he loathed so much.

'Well, there's one good thing,' he said savagely. 'Snape'll be gone by the end of the year.'

'What do you mean?' asked Ron.

'That job's jinxed. No one's lasted more than a year … Quirrell actually died doing it. Personally, I'm going to keep my fingers crossed for another death …'

'Harry!' said Hermione, shocked and reproachful.

'He might just go back to teaching Potions at the end of the year,' said Ron reasonably. 'That Slughorn bloke might not want to stay long-term, Moody didn't.'

Dumbledore cleared his throat. Harry, Ron and Hermione were not the only ones who had been talking; the whole Hall had erupted in a buzz of conversation at the news that Snape had finally achieved his heart's desire. Seemingly oblivious to the sensational nature of the news he had just imparted, Dumbledore said nothing more about staff appointments, but waited a few seconds to ensure that the silence was absolute before continuing.

'Now, as everybody in this Hall knows, Lord Voldemort and his followers are once more at large and gaining in strength.'

The silence seemed to tauten and strain as Dumbledore spoke. Harry glanced at Malfoy. Malfoy was not looking at Dumbledore, but making his fork hover in midair with his wand, as though he found the Headmaster's words unworthy of his attention.

'I cannot emphasise strongly enough how dangerous the present situation is, and how much care each of us at Hogwarts must take to ensure that we remain safe. The castle's magical fortifications have been strengthened over the summer, we are protected in new and more powerful ways, but we must still guard scrupulously against carelessness on the part of any student or member

“我以为是他！”哈利说。他拼命回忆邓布利多什么时候告诉过他，然而现在仔细想来，他根本记不起邓布利多跟他说过斯拉格霍恩要教哪门课程。

斯内普坐在邓布利多的右侧，他听见邓布利多提到自己的名字时并没有起身，只是懒洋洋地抬了抬一只手，表示听见了斯莱特林餐桌上的喝彩声，可是哈利清清楚楚地看见，那张他恨之入骨的脸上透着一丝得意的喜色。

“也好，这件事有一点好处，”哈利咬牙切齿地说，“斯内普不到一年就会滚蛋。”

“你这是什么意思？”罗恩问。

“那份工作是被施了恶咒的。没有一个人能超过一年……奇洛连命都搭进去了。我个人衷心希望再发生一桩命案……”

“哈利！”赫敏惊恐地责备道。

“到了期末，他大概又回去教他的魔药课了。”罗恩理智地说，“那个叫斯拉格霍恩的家伙大概不愿意长期待在这儿，穆迪就是这样。”

邓布利多清了清嗓子。在下面说话的不只哈利、罗恩和赫敏，听到斯内普终于如愿以偿的消息，整个礼堂里的人都在议论纷纷。邓布利多似乎没有意识到他刚才公布的消息有多么轰动，他不再说教师职务的事，而是等了几秒钟，确保大家完全安静下来后才继续说话。

“这座礼堂里的每个人都知道，伏地魔和他的随从再次兴风作浪，并且势力在不断壮大。”

邓布利多说话时，礼堂里一片紧张的揪心的沉默。哈利扫了一眼马尔福。马尔福没有看着邓布利多，而是用魔杖把他的叉子悬在半空，仿佛他觉得校长的话根本不值得一听。

“我需要格外强调的是，目前局势非常危险，我们霍格沃茨的每一个人都需要万分谨慎才能保证大家的安全。城堡的魔法防御工事在暑假期间被加强了，我们得到了新的更有效的保护，但是每一位师生仍然必须时刻提高警惕，丝毫不能掉以轻心。因此，我要求你们必须严格遵守老师制定的每一条安全规定，不管那些条条框框可能有多么

of staff. I urge you, therefore, to abide by any security restrictions that your teachers might impose upon you, however irksome you might find them – in particular, the rule that you are not to be out of bed after hours. I implore you, should you notice anything strange or suspicious within or outside the castle, to report it to a member of staff immediately. I trust you to conduct yourselves, always, with the utmost regard for your own and each other's safety.'

Dumbledore's blue eyes swept over the students before he smiled once more.

'But now, your beds await, as warm and comfortable as you could possibly wish, and I know that your top priority is to be well-rested for your lessons tomorrow. Let us therefore say goodnight. Pip pip!'

With the usual deafening scraping noise, the benches were moved back and the hundreds of students began to file out of the Great Hall towards their dormitories. Harry, who was in no hurry at all to leave with the gawping crowd, nor to get near enough to Malfoy to allow him to retell the story of the nose-stamping, lagged behind, pretending to retie the lace on his trainer, allowing most of the Gryffindors to draw ahead of him. Hermione had darted ahead to fulfil her prefect's duty of shepherding the first-years, but Ron remained with Harry.

'What really happened to your nose?' he asked, once they were at the very back of the throng pressing out of the Hall, and out of earshot of anyone else.

Harry told him. It was a mark of the strength of their friendship that Ron did not laugh.

'I saw Malfoy miming something to do with a nose,' he said darkly.

'Yeah, well, never mind that,' said Harry bitterly. 'Listen to what he was saying before he found out I was there …'

Harry had expected Ron to be stunned by Malfoy's boasts. With what Harry considered pure pigheadedness, however, Ron was unimpressed.

'Come on, Harry, he was just showing off for Parkinson … what kind of mission would You-Know-Who have given him?'

'How d'you know Voldemort doesn't need someone at Hogwarts? It wouldn't be the first –'

'I wish yeh'd stop sayin' tha' name, Harry,' said a reproachful voice behind them. Harry looked over his shoulder to see Hagrid shaking his head.

烦人——特别要遵守熄灯后不得起床外出的规定。我恳请你们，不管在校内还是校外，只要发现任何异常或可疑的情况，都要立刻向教工汇报。我相信，你们为了自己和他人的安全，一定会约束自己的行为。”

邓布利多的蓝眼睛扫过所有的学生，然后脸上又露出了微笑。

“好了，你们的床铺在等待你们，像你们期望的那样温暖和舒适，我知道你们的当务之急是好好休息，准备明天上课。所以，让我们道一声‘晚安’吧。再会！”

像往常一样，一条条长凳被推到身后，发出刺耳的摩擦声，几百名学生开始鱼贯离开大礼堂，朝宿舍走去。哈利并不急着离开，他不愿意跟那些瞪大眼睛盯着他看的同学挤在一起，也不愿意挨近马尔福，让他有机会把踩鼻子的故事再讲一遍，所以他就假装系鞋带，故意落在后面，让大多数格兰芬多同学都走到他前面去了。赫敏早已跑去履行她级长的职责，去照顾那些一年级新生了，只有罗恩留下来陪着哈利。

“你的鼻子到底是怎么了？”等他们确保那些挤出礼堂的人群已经远远离开，不会再听见他们说话时，罗恩问道。

哈利把事情告诉了他。罗恩没有笑,这显示了他们的友谊多么牢固。

“我看见马尔福在那里表演对付一只鼻子什么的。”他愤愤不平地说。

“是啊，好了，不去管它了。”哈利气恼地说，“你听听他在发现我之前说的那些话吧……”

哈利本来以为罗恩听了马尔福那些吹牛的话会感到很震惊。可是罗恩竟然无动于衷，哈利觉得他简直变成榆木脑袋了。

“得了，哈利，他只是在帕金森面前炫耀自己……神秘人会派给他什么任务呢？”

“你怎么知道伏地魔不需要在霍格沃茨安插一个什么人呢？这可不是第一次——”

“我希望你别再说那个名字了，哈利。”他们身后响起了一个责备的声音。哈利扭头一看，海格正在那里摇头。

'Dumbledore uses that name,' said Harry stubbornly.

'Yeah, well, tha's Dumbledore, innit?' said Hagrid mysteriously. 'So how come yeh were late, Harry? I was worried.'

'Got held up on the train,' said Harry. 'Why were *you* late?'

'I was with Grawp,' said Hagrid happily. 'Los' track o' the time. He's got a new home up in the mountains now, Dumbledore fixed it – nice big cave. He's much happier than he was in the Forest. We were havin' a good chat.'

'Really?' said Harry, taking care not to catch Ron's eye; the last time he had met Hagrid's half-brother, a vicious giant with a talent for ripping up trees by the roots, his vocabulary had comprised five words, two of which he was unable to pronounce properly.

'Oh yeah, he's really come on,' said Hagrid proudly. 'Yeh'll be amazed. I'm thinkin' o' trainin' him up as me assistant.'

Ron snorted loudly, but managed to pass it off as a violent sneeze. They were now standing beside the oak front doors.

'Anyway, I'll see yeh tomorrow, firs' lesson's straight after lunch. Come early an' yeh can say hello ter Buck– I mean, Witherwings!'

Raising an arm in cheery farewell, he headed out of the front doors into the darkness.

Harry and Ron looked at each other. Harry could tell that Ron was experiencing the same sinking feeling as himself.

'You're not taking Care of Magical Creatures, are you?'

Ron shook his head.

'And you're not either, are you?'

Harry shook his head, too.

'And Hermione,' said Ron, 'she's not, is she?'

Harry shook his head again. Exactly what Hagrid would say when he realised his three favourite students had given up his subject, he did not like to think.

“邓布利多就直呼其名。”哈利固执地说。

“没错，但那是邓布利多呀，对不？”海格神秘兮兮地说，“你怎么会迟到的，哈利？我真担心哪。”

“在车上耽搁了。”哈利说，“你为什么迟到？”

“我跟格洛普在一起，”海格高兴地说，“忘记了时间。现在，他在山里有了一个新家，邓布利多安排的——是一个漂亮的大山洞。他比待在禁林里的时候开心多了。我们好好地聊了一会儿。”

“真的？”哈利说，尽量不去看罗恩的眼睛。上次他看见海格同母异父的弟弟——那个专会把大树连根拔起的凶狠的巨人时，他的词汇量只有五个，其中两个的发音还不准。

“是啊，他进步可大了。”海格骄傲地说，“你会感到吃惊的。我在考虑把他培养成我的助手。”

罗恩很响地哼了一声，不过总算及时把它变成了一个响亮的喷嚏。这时他们已经站在橡木大门旁了。

“好了，我们明天见，午饭后的第一节课，早点过来，可以跟巴克——我是说蔫翼打个招呼！”

海格喜滋滋地举起一只胳膊和他们告别，然后便出了大门，融进了夜色中。

哈利和罗恩面面相觑。哈利看得出来，罗恩的心情跟他一样沮丧。

“你不准备选保护神奇动物课了，是吗？”

罗恩摇了摇头。

“你也不选了，是吗？”

哈利也摇了摇头。

“赫敏呢？”罗恩说，“她也不选了？”

哈利又摇了摇头。当海格发现他最喜欢的三个学生都不再上他的课时，他会说什么呢？对此哈利不愿意去想。

CHAPTER NINE

The Half-Blood Prince

Harry and Ron met Hermione in the common room before breakfast next morning. Hoping for some support for his theory, Harry lost no time in telling Hermione what he had overheard Malfoy saying on the Hogwarts Express.

'But he was obviously showing off for Parkinson, wasn't he?' interjected Ron quickly, before Hermione could say anything.

'Well,' she said uncertainly, 'I don't know … it would be like Malfoy to make himself seem more important than he is … but that's a big lie to tell …'

'Exactly,' said Harry, but he could not press the point, because so many people were trying to listen in to his conversation, not to mention staring at him and whispering behind their hands.

'It's rude to point,' Ron snapped at a particularly minuscule first-year as they joined the queue to climb out of the portrait hole. The boy, who had been muttering something about Harry behind his hand to his friend, promptly turned scarlet and toppled out of the hole in alarm. Ron sniggered. 'I love being a sixth-year. *And* we're going to be getting free time this year. Whole periods when we can just sit up here and relax.'

'We're going to need that time for studying, Ron!' said Hermione, as they set off down the corridor.

'Yeah, but not today,' said Ron, 'today's going to be a real doss, I reckon.'

'Hold it!' said Hermione, throwing out an arm and halting a passing fourth-year, who was attempting to push past her with a lime-green disc clutched tightly in his hand. 'Fanged Frisbees are banned, hand it over,' she told him sternly. The scowling boy handed over the snarling Frisbee, ducked under Hermione's arm and took off after his friends. Ron waited for him to

第 9 章

混血王子

第二天早上吃早饭前，哈利、罗恩和赫敏在公共休息室里碰面了。哈利希望有人支持他的想法，便立刻把他在霍格沃茨特快列车上偷听到的马尔福的话告诉了赫敏。

“他显然是在帕金森面前吹牛，是不是？”没等赫敏开口，罗恩就抢着说道。

“嗯，”赫敏迟疑地说，“我也说不清……也许马尔福是故意虚张声势，想显示自己很了不起……不过编出这样的谎话也太……”

“是啊。”哈利说，可是他没法进一步说明他的观点，因为许多同学不仅好奇地盯着他看，用手捂着嘴窃窃私语，而且还侧着耳朵听他说话。

“指指点点不礼貌！”他们排队通过肖像洞口时，罗恩冲一个特别矮小的一年级男生厉声喝道。那男生正在用手挡着嘴巴跟朋友嘀咕关于哈利的什么话，被罗恩这么一喝，顿时脸涨得通红，惊慌失措地从洞口跌了出去。罗恩得意地笑出了声。

“我真喜欢上六年级。而且今年我们会有许多自由时间，可以整节课整节课地坐在这里，什么也不干。”

“我们需要用那些时间来学习，罗恩！”赫敏说，这时他们正顺着走廊往前走。

“知道啦，但不是今天。”罗恩说，“我猜今天会相当轻松。”

“站住！”赫敏说着一把拦住一个四年级学生，那学生手里紧紧抓着一个深绿色的圆盘，正想从她身边挤过去。“狼牙飞碟是违禁物，快交出来。”赫敏严厉地对他说。那个愁眉苦脸的男生交出了咆哮的飞碟，

vanish, then tugged the Frisbee from Hermione's grip.

'Excellent, I've always wanted one of these.'

Hermione's remonstration was drowned by a loud giggle; Lavender Brown had apparently found Ron's remark highly amusing. She continued to laugh as she passed them, glancing back at Ron over her shoulder. Ron looked rather pleased with himself.

The ceiling of the Great Hall was serenely blue and streaked with frail, wispy clouds, just like the squares of sky visible through the high mullioned windows. While they tucked into porridge and eggs and bacon, Harry and Ron told Hermione about their embarrassing conversation with Hagrid the previous evening.

'But he can't really think we'd continue Care of Magical Creatures!' she said, looking distressed. 'I mean, when has any of us expressed … you know … any enthusiasm?'

'That's it, though, innit?' said Ron, swallowing an entire fried egg whole. 'We were the ones who made the most effort in classes because we like Hagrid. But he thinks we liked the stupid *subject*. D'you reckon anyone's going to go on to N.E.W.T.?'

Neither Harry nor Hermione answered; there was no need. They knew perfectly well that nobody in their year would want to continue Care of Magical Creatures. They avoided Hagrid's eye and returned his cheery wave only half-heartedly when he left the staff table ten minutes later.

After they had eaten, they remained in their places, awaiting Professor McGonagall's descent from the staff table. The distribution of timetables was more complicated than usual this year, for Professor McGonagall needed first to confirm that everybody had achieved the necessary O.W.L. grades to continue with their chosen N.E.W.T.s.

Hermione was immediately cleared to continue with Charms, Defence Against the Dark Arts, Transfiguration, Herbology, Arithmancy, Ancient Runes and Potions, and shot off to a first-period Ancient Runes class without further ado. Neville took a little longer to sort out; his round face was anxious as Professor McGonagall looked down his application and then consulted his O.W.L. results.

'Herbology, fine,' she said. 'Professor Sprout will be delighted to see you

一猫腰从赫敏胳膊底下钻过，追他的朋友们去了。罗恩等他走远了，把飞碟从赫敏手里夺了过来。

“太棒了，我早就想要一个这样的东西。”

赫敏的抗议被一阵响亮的咯咯笑声淹没了。拉文德·布朗似乎觉得罗恩的话特别好玩，她从他们身边经过时也一直笑着，还扭头朝罗恩看了几眼。罗恩显得非常得意。

大礼堂的天花板瓦蓝瓦蓝的，飘着几缕淡淡的浮云，就像高高的、装着竖框的窗户外面的天空一样。哈利和罗恩一边大口喝粥，吃着鸡蛋和熏咸肉，一边把前一天晚上跟海格的那段尴尬的对话告诉了赫敏。

“他不可能真的以为我们还会去上保护神奇动物课吧！”赫敏显得很苦恼，说道，“我是说，其实我们谁也没有表示出……你们知道的……表示出任何热情呀。”

“是这么回事。对吧？”罗恩说着把一个煎鸡蛋囫囵吞了下去，“我们因为喜欢海格，所以在他的课上是最用功的。可他还以为我们喜欢那门愚蠢的功课。你们说有谁会去上他的提高班呢？”

哈利和赫敏都没有回答。这个问题无须回答。他们知道得很清楚，他们年级没有一个人想上保护神奇动物课。十分钟后，当海格离开教工餐桌，兴高采烈地跟他们挥手打招呼时，他们躲避着他的目光，应付地朝他挥了挥手。

吃过早饭，他们仍然坐在座位上，等麦格教授从教工餐桌下来。这学期发放课程表的工作比往常复杂，麦格教授要先确保每个学生的O.W.L.成绩达到要求，才能让他继续学习他所选择的N.E.W.T.提高班课程。

赫敏的课程立刻就确定下来了，她要继续学习魔咒学、黑魔法防御术、变形术、草药学、算术占卜、古代如尼文和魔药学。她没再耽搁，立刻赶去上第一节古代如尼文课了。纳威的情况多费了一些周折。麦格教授低头看着他的申请，核对他的O.W.L.成绩，纳威圆圆的脸上满是焦虑。

“草药学，很好，”麦格教授说，“O.W.L.成绩是‘优秀’，斯普劳

back with an "Outstanding" O.W.L. and you qualify for Defence Against the Dark Arts with "Exceeds Expectations". But the problem is Transfiguration. I'm sorry, Longbottom, but an "Acceptable" really isn't good enough to continue to N.E.W.T. level, I just don't think you'd be able to cope with the coursework.'

Neville hung his head. Professor McGonagall peered at him through her square spectacles.

'Why do you want to continue with Transfiguration, anyway? I've never had the impression that you particularly enjoyed it.'

Neville looked miserable and muttered something about 'my grandmother wants'.

'Humph,' snorted Professor McGonagall. 'It's high time your grandmother learned to be proud of the grandson she's got, rather than the one she thinks she ought to have – particularly after what happened at the Ministry.'

Neville turned very pink and blinked confusedly; Professor McGonagall had never paid him a compliment before.

'I'm sorry, Longbottom, but I cannot let you into my N.E.W.T. class. I see that you have an "Exceeds Expectations" in Charms, however – why not try for a N.E.W.T. in Charms?'

'My grandmother thinks Charms is a soft option,' mumbled Neville.

'Take Charms,' said Professor McGonagall, 'and I shall drop Augusta a line reminding her that just because she failed *her* Charms O.W.L., the subject is not necessarily worthless.' Smiling slightly at the look of delighted incredulity on Neville's face, Professor McGonagall tapped a blank timetable with the tip of her wand and handed it, now carrying details of his new classes, to Neville.

Professor McGonagall turned next to Parvati Patil, whose first question was whether Firenze, the handsome centaur, was still teaching Divination.

'He and Professor Trelawney are dividing classes between them this year,' said Professor McGonagall, a hint of disapproval in her voice; it was common knowledge that she despised the subject of Divination. 'The sixth year is being taken by Professor Trelawney.'

Parvati set off for Divination five minutes later looking slightly crestfallen.

'So, Potter, Potter …' said Professor McGonagall, consulting her notes as she turned to Harry. 'Charms, Defence Against the Dark Arts, Herbology, Transfiguration … all fine. I must say, I was pleased with your Transfiguration mark, Potter, very pleased. Now, why haven't you applied to continue with

特教授肯定很高兴看到你回去。黑魔法防御术的成绩是‘良好’，也有资格继续选修。问题是变形课。对不起，隆巴顿，‘及格’的成绩不够好，不能进修变形课的N.E.W.T.课程，我担心你可能会完成不了课程作业。”

纳威垂下脑袋。麦格教授透过方形眼镜片望着他。

“你为什么要继续学习变形课呢？我觉得你好像不是特别喜欢它。”

纳威显得很难过，嘴里嘟囔了一句什么，像是“我奶奶要我学的”。

“噢，”麦格教授哼着鼻子说，“你奶奶真的该学着为她的孙子感到骄傲，而不是总认为她的孙子应该更优秀了——特别是在魔法部的那件事之后。”

纳威的脸变得绯红，眼睛困惑地眨巴着。麦格教授以前从来没有表扬过他。

“对不起，隆巴顿，我不能让你进入我的提高班。不过，我看到你的魔咒课成绩是‘良好’——你为什么不申请魔咒课的提高班呢？”

“我奶奶认为选魔咒课是图省事。”纳威嘟囔道。

“选魔咒课吧。”麦格教授说，“我要给奥古斯塔写封信提醒她，不能因为她的魔咒课O.W.L.考试不及格，就认为这门课不值得一学。”看到纳威脸上不敢相信的欣喜表情，麦格教授微微一笑，用魔杖尖敲了敲一张空白课程表，然后递给了纳威，那上面已经详细填好了他这学期要上的课程。

接着，麦格教授转向了帕瓦蒂·佩蒂尔。佩蒂尔的第一个问题是，那个帅气的马人费伦泽今年还教不教占卜课。

“他和特里劳尼教授今年共同承担占卜课。”麦格教授的语气里透着一丝不快，大家都知道她一向看不起占卜课，“给六年级上占卜课的是特里劳尼教授。”

五分钟后，帕瓦蒂有些垂头丧气地去上占卜课了。

“下面，波特。波特……”麦格教授一边查看她的笔记，一边转向哈利，“魔咒学，黑魔法防御术，草药学，变形术……都可以。我得说一句，我对你变形术的成绩很满意，波特，非常满意。可是，你为什

Potions? I thought it was your ambition to become an Auror?'

'It was, but you told me I had to get an "Outstanding" in my O.W.L., Professor.'

'And so you did when Professor Snape was teaching the subject. Professor Slughorn, however, is perfectly happy to accept N.E.W.T. students with "Exceeds Expectations" at O.W.L. Do you wish to proceed with Potions?'

'Yes,' said Harry, 'but I didn't buy the books or any ingredients or anything –'

'I'm sure Professor Slughorn will be able to lend you some,' said Professor McGonagall. 'Very well, Potter, here is your timetable. Oh, by the way – twenty hopefuls have already put down their names for the Gryffindor Quidditch team. I shall pass the list to you in due course and you can fix up trials at your leisure.'

A few minutes later, Ron was cleared to do the same subjects as Harry, and the two of them left the table together.

'Look,' said Ron delightedly, gazing at his timetable, 'we've got a free period now … and a free period after break … and after lunch … *excellent*!'

They returned to the common room, which was empty apart from half a dozen seventh-years including Katie Bell, the only remaining member of the original Gryffindor Quidditch team that Harry had joined in his first year.

'I thought you'd get that, well done,' she called over, pointing at the Captain's badge on Harry's chest. 'Tell me when you call trials!'

'Don't be stupid,' said Harry, 'you don't need to try out, I've watched you play for five years …'

'You mustn't start off like that,' she said warningly. 'For all you know, there's someone much better than me out there. Good teams have been ruined before now because captains just kept playing the old faces, or letting in their friends …'

Ron looked a little uncomfortable and began playing with the Fanged Frisbee Hermione had taken from the fourth-year. It zoomed around the common room, snarling and attempting to take bites of the tapestry. Crookshanks's yellow eyes followed it and he hissed when it came too close.

An hour later they reluctantly left the sunlit common room for the Defence Against the Dark Arts classroom four floors below. Hermione was already queuing outside, carrying an armful of heavy books and looking put-upon.

么不申请继续学习魔药课呢？我记得你的理想是将来当一名傲罗！”

“是的，可是你告诉过我，我的魔药课 O.W.L. 成绩必须达到‘优秀’才行，教授。”

“斯内普教授教这门课的时候是这样。斯拉格霍恩教授很愿意接受 O.W.L. 成绩‘良好’的学生进入提高班。你愿意继续学习魔药课吗？”

“愿意。”哈利说，“但是我没买课本和原料什么的……”

“我相信斯拉格霍恩教授可以借给你一些。”麦格教授说，“很好，波特，这是你的课程表。对了，顺便说一句——已经有二十位同学报名参加魁地奇球队了。到时候我把名单给你，你抽空安排一下选拔。”

几分钟后，罗恩的课程表也排好了，他要上的课跟哈利一样，他们俩一起离开了餐桌。

“看，”罗恩看着他的课程表高兴地说，“我们现在没有课……课间休息以后也没有课……吃过午饭还是没有课……太棒了！”

他们回到了公共休息室，里面只有六七个七年级的学生，凯蒂·贝尔也在，她是哈利一年级时加入的那支格兰芬多球队里仅剩的一名队员。

“我就猜到你会得到它的，真不错。”她指着哈利胸前的队长徽章，大声对他说道，“进行选拔时告诉我一声！”

“别说傻话了，”哈利说，“你用不着参加选拔，我看你打球已经有五年了……”

“你可别一开始就这么没原则。”她警告说，“你们都知道有些人球技比我好得多。以前有一些很不错的球队，就因为队长总让熟面孔打球，让自己的朋友入队，结果把好好的球队给毁了……”

罗恩有点不自在了，低头玩起了赫敏从四年级学生那里没收来的狼牙飞碟。飞碟在公共休息室里飞来飞去，咆哮着去咬墙上的挂毯。克鲁克山的黄眼睛紧盯着它，每次看到它飞得太近，便发出嘶嘶的叫声。

一个小时后，他们满不情愿地离开了洒满阳光的公共休息室，下了四层楼去上黑魔法防御术课。赫敏已经排在教室外面了，怀里抱着一大堆沉甸甸的书，一副受了虐待的样子。

'We got so much homework for Runes,' she said anxiously, when Harry and Ron joined her. 'A fifteen-inch essay, two translations and I've got to read these by Wednesday!'

'Shame,' yawned Ron.

'You wait,' she said resentfully. 'I bet Snape gives us loads.'

The classroom door opened as she spoke and Snape stepped into the corridor, his sallow face framed as ever by two curtains of greasy black hair. Silence fell over the queue immediately.

'Inside,' he said.

Harry looked around as they entered. Snape had imposed his personality upon the room already; it was gloomier than usual as curtains had been drawn over the windows, and was lit by candlelight. New pictures adorned the walls, many of them showing people who appeared to be in pain, sporting grisly injuries or strangely contorted body parts. Nobody spoke as they settled down, looking around at the shadowy, gruesome pictures.

'I have not asked you to take out your books,' said Snape, closing the door and moving to face the class from behind his desk; Hermione hastily dropped her copy of *Confronting the Faceless* back into her bag and stowed it under her chair. 'I wish to speak to you and I want your fullest attention.'

His black eyes roved over their upturned faces, lingering for a fraction of a second longer on Harry's than anyone else's.

'You have had five teachers in this subject so far, I believe.'

You believe … like you haven't watched them all come and go, Snape, hoping you'd be next, thought Harry scathingly.

'Naturally, these teachers will all have had their own methods and priorities. Given this confusion I am surprised so many of you scraped an O.W.L. in this subject. I shall be even more surprised if all of you manage to keep up with the N.E.W.T. work, which will be much more advanced.'

Snape set off around the edge of the room, speaking now in a lower voice; the class craned their necks to keep him in view.

'The Dark Arts,' said Snape, 'are many, varied, ever-changing and eternal. Fighting them is like fighting a many-headed monster, which, each time a

“如尼文课的作业一大堆，”她焦虑地说，这时哈利和罗恩跟她一起排进了队伍里，“一篇十五英寸长的文章，两篇翻译，还要在星期三之前读完这么多书！”

“真倒霉。”罗恩打了个哈欠说。

“你等着吧，”赫敏愤愤地说，“我敢说斯内普也会给我们布置一大堆作业。”

就在她说话的当儿，教室的门开了，斯内普来到了走廊里。他和以前一样，油腻腻的黑发从两边分下来，框住了那张蜡黄色的脸。队伍里立刻沉默下来。

“进来。”他说。

走进教室时，哈利四下里看了看。斯内普已经在这间教室里烙上了他自己的性格特征。窗帘拉得紧紧的，只有蜡烛发出微光，光线比平常更加昏暗。墙上贴了一些以前没有的图画，许多画面上都是遭受痛苦的人、狰狞的伤口和离奇扭曲的身体局部。同学们坐下后，谁也没有说话，都扭头望着墙上这些阴森恐怖的图画。

“我还没有叫你们把书拿出来。”斯内普说着关上教室的门，走到讲台后面朝着全班同学。赫敏赶紧把她那本《对抗无脸妖怪》扔回书包，塞到了椅子下面。“我有话要对你们说，希望你们的注意力高度集中。”

他那双黑眼睛扫过一张张仰起的面孔，在哈利脸上停留的时间比别人略长一些。

“迄今为止，你们的这门课程想必已经换过五位老师了。”

*想必……就好像你斯内普没有看见他们一个个来了又走，并希望下一个就是你自己一样。*哈利尖刻地想。

“不用说，这些老师都有他们自己的教学方式和教学重点。在这种混乱的状况下，我很吃惊你们竟然有这么多人勉强通过了这门课的O.W.L.考试。如果你们都能跟上提高班的课程，我将会更加吃惊，因为它的内容要高深得多。”

斯内普走下讲台，绕着教室走来走去，说话的声音放低了。为了能看见他，同学们一个个伸长了脖子。

neck is severed, sprouts a head even fiercer and cleverer than before. You are fighting that which is unfixed, mutating, indestructible.'

Harry stared at Snape. It was surely one thing to respect the Dark Arts as a dangerous enemy, another to speak of them, as Snape was doing, with a loving caress in his voice?

'Your defences,' said Snape, a little louder, 'must therefore be as flexible and inventive as the Arts you seek to undo. These pictures,' he indicated a few of them as he swept past, 'give a fair representation of what happens to those who suffer, for instance, the Cruciatus Curse' (he waved a hand towards a witch who was clearly shrieking in agony) 'feel the Dementor's Kiss' (a wizard lying huddled and blank-eyed slumped against a wall) 'or provoke the aggression of the Inferius' (a bloody mass upon the ground).

'Has an Inferius been seen, then?' said Parvati Patil in a high-pitched voice. 'Is it definite, is he using them?'

'The Dark Lord has used Inferi in the past,' said Snape, 'which means you would be well-advised to assume he might use them again. Now …'

He set off again around the other side of the classroom towards his desk, and again, the class watched him as he walked, his dark robes billowing behind him.

'… you are, I believe, complete novices in the use of non-verbal spells. What is the advantage of a non-verbal spell?'

Hermione's hand shot into the air. Snape took his time looking around at everybody else, making sure he had no choice, before saying curtly, 'Very well – Miss Granger?'

'Your adversary has no warning about what kind of magic you're about to perform,' said Hermione, 'which gives you a split-second advantage.'

'An answer copied almost word for word from *The Standard Book of Spells, Grade 6*,' said Snape dismissively (over in the corner, Malfoy sniggered), 'but correct in essentials. Yes, those who progress to using magic without shouting incantations gain an element of surprise in their spell-casting. Not all wizards can do this, of course; it is a question of concentration and mind power which some,' his gaze lingered maliciously upon Harry once more, 'lack.'

Harry knew Snape was thinking of their disastrous Occlumency lessons of the previous year. He refused to drop his gaze, but glowered at Snape until

“黑魔法，”斯内普说，“五花八门，种类繁多，变化多端，永无止境。与它们搏斗，就像与一只多头怪兽搏斗，刚砍掉一个脑袋，立刻又冒出一个新的脑袋，比原先那个更凶狠、更狡猾。你们要面对的是一种变幻莫测、不可毁灭的东西。”

哈利盯着斯内普。把黑魔法当成危险的敌人来重视是一码事，而像斯内普这样，用喜爱和景仰的口吻谈论它们，就显然是另一码事了。

“因此，你们的防御，”斯内普稍稍提高了音量说，“也必须像你们需要对付的黑魔法一样灵活多变，富有创新。这些图画，”他一边走一边顺手指指其中几幅，“生动表现了那些受害者的情形，比如，中了钻心咒，”（他挥手指向一个显然在痛苦惨叫的女巫）“感受到摄魂怪的亲吻，”（一个男巫蜷缩在墙角，两眼失神）“或遭到阴尸的侵害。”（地上一片血肉模糊）

“那么，人们真的看见过阴尸吗？”帕瓦蒂·佩蒂尔用尖细的声音问，“他是不是真的在利用阴尸？”

“黑魔王过去用过阴尸，”斯内普说，“这意味着我们应当假设他还会再次使用它们。好了……”

他又绕到教室的另一边，朝讲台走去，黑色的长袍在身后摆动，全班同学的目光又一次追随着他。

“……我想，你们对于无声咒的使用还很陌生。无声咒有什么好处？”

赫敏立刻举起了手。斯内普不慌不忙地扫视了一下全班同学，看到没有别的选择，才生硬地说：“很好——格兰杰小姐？”

“对手不知道你打算施什么魔法，”赫敏说，“这样你就占有一刹那间的优势。”

“这个回答几乎是从《标准咒语，六级》上原封不动抄来的，”斯内普轻蔑地说（马尔福在墙角发出讥笑），“不过基本正确。是的，施魔法时不把咒语大声念出来，可以达到一种出其不意的效果。当然啦，不是所有的巫师都能做到这点。这需要很强的注意力和意志力，而有些人，”他的目光又一次恶意地停留在哈利脸上，“是没有的。”

哈利知道，斯内普想起了上学期那几节糟糕透顶的大脑封闭术课。

Snape looked away.

'You will now divide,' Snape went on, 'into pairs. One partner will attempt to jinx the other *without speaking*. The other will attempt to repel the jinx *in equal silence*. Carry on.'

Although Snape did not know it, Harry had taught at least half the class (everyone who had been a member of the DA) how to perform a Shield Charm the previous year. None of them had ever cast the Charm without speaking, however. A reasonable amount of cheating ensued; many people were merely whispering the incantation instead of saying it aloud. Typically, ten minutes into the lesson Hermione managed to repel Neville's muttered Jelly-Legs Jinx without uttering a single word, a feat that would surely have earned her twenty points for Gryffindor from any reasonable teacher, thought Harry bitterly, but which Snape ignored. He swept between them as they practised, looking just as much like an overgrown bat as ever, lingering to watch Harry and Ron struggling with the task.

Ron, who was supposed to be jinxing Harry, was purple in the face, his lips tightly compressed to save himself from the temptation of muttering the incantation. Harry had his wand raised, waiting on tenterhooks to repel a jinx that seemed unlikely ever to come.

'Pathetic, Weasley,' said Snape, after a while. 'Here – let me show you –'

He turned his wand on Harry so fast that Harry reacted instinctively; all thought of non-verbal spells forgotten he yelled, '*Protego!*'

His Shield Charm was so strong Snape was knocked off-balance and hit a desk. The whole class had looked round and now watched as Snape righted himself, scowling.

'Do you remember me telling you we are practising non-verbal spells, Potter?'

'Yes,' said Harry stiffly.

'Yes *sir*.'

'There's no need to call me "sir", Professor.'

The words had escaped him before he knew what he was saying. Several people gasped, including Hermione. Behind Snape, however, Ron, Dean and Seamus grinned appreciatively.

哈利怒视着斯内普，不肯垂下眼睛，最后是斯内普移开了目光。

“现在你们分成两个人一组，”斯内普继续说道，“一个试着给另一个施恶咒，但不许念出声来。另一个试着击退那个恶咒，同样也不许出声。开始吧。”

斯内普不知道，上学期哈利教过班上至少半数同学（那些曾是D.A.成员的同学）怎样施铁甲咒。但他们谁也没有不出声地念过这个咒语。可想而知，接下来便是大量的作弊。许多同学在小声念咒，只是不把声音放大而已。不出所料，课上到十分钟的时候，赫敏一个字也没说就成功击退了纳威小声念出的软腿咒。哈利怨恨地想，这么了不起的成绩，换了任何一位通情达理的老师，都会给格兰芬多加二十分的，可是斯内普只当没看见。同学们练习时，他和以前一样，拖着长袍在他们中间巡视，如同一只巨大的蝙蝠，并故意停下来注视哈利和罗恩艰难地练习。

罗恩要给哈利施恶咒，脸憋得红红的，嘴巴闭得紧紧的，生怕自己挡不住诱惑轻声念出咒语。哈利举着魔杖，提心吊胆地等着击退一个看来永远不会发过来的咒语。

“真差劲，韦斯莱。”斯内普看了一会儿，说道，“来——让我做给你看——”

说时迟那时快，他突然把魔杖转向哈利，哈利本能地做出反应，把无声咒的事忘得一干二净，大喊一声：“盔甲护身！”

他的铁甲咒力量太大了，斯内普被击得失去平衡，撞在一张桌子上。全班同学都转过头来，看着斯内普挣扎着站稳脚跟，满脸怒容。

“你还记得我告诉过你，我们是在练习无声咒吗，波特？”

“记得。”哈利生硬地说。

“记得，先生。”

“用不着叫我‘先生’，教授。”

没等他反应过来，这句话已脱口而出。几个同学吃惊地抽了一口冷气，包括赫敏。然而在斯内普身后，罗恩、迪安和西莫的脸上露出了赞赏的笑容。

'Detention, Saturday night, my office,' said Snape. 'I do not take cheek from anyone, Potter … not even the *Chosen One*.'

'That was brilliant, Harry!' chortled Ron, once they were safely on their way to break a short while later.

'You really shouldn't have said it,' said Hermione, frowning at Ron. 'What made you?'

'He tried to jinx me, in case you didn't notice!' fumed Harry. 'I had enough of that during those Occlumency lessons! Why doesn't he use another guinea pig for a change? What's Dumbledore playing at, anyway, letting him teach Defence? Did you hear him talking about the Dark Arts? He loves them! All that *unfixed, indestructible* stuff –'

'Well,' said Hermione, 'I thought he sounded a bit like you.'

'Like *me*?'

'Yes, when you were telling us what it's like to face Voldemort. You said it wasn't just memorising a bunch of spells, you said it was just you and your brains and your guts – well, wasn't that what Snape was saying? That it really comes down to being brave and quick-thinking?'

Harry was so disarmed that she had thought his words as well worth memorising as *The Standard Book of Spells* that he did not argue.

'Harry! Hey, Harry!'

Harry looked round; Jack Sloper, one of the Beaters on the previous year's Gryffindor Quidditch team, was hurrying towards him holding a roll of parchment.

'For you,' panted Sloper. 'Listen, I heard you're the new captain. When're you holding trials?'

'I'm not sure yet,' said Harry, thinking privately that Sloper would be very lucky to get back on the team. 'I'll let you know.'

'Oh, right. I was hoping it'd be this weekend –'

But Harry was not listening; he had just recognised the thin, slanting writing on the parchment. Leaving Sloper in mid-sentence, he hurried away with Ron and Hermione, unrolling the parchment as he went.

“关禁闭，星期六晚上，在我的办公室。”斯内普说，“我不允许任何人对我无礼，波特……即便是*救世之星*。”

“太漂亮了，哈利！”片刻之后，他们出来课间休息时，罗恩开心地咯咯笑着说。

“你真不应该那么说的。”赫敏说，皱着眉头看了一眼罗恩，“你当时是怎么了？”

“他想给我施恶咒，你大概没有注意到！”哈利气冲冲地说，“我在那些大脑封闭术课上已经受够了这一套！他为什么不另外找个人给他当试验品？邓布利多葫芦里卖的什么药，竟然让他来教防御术？你有没有听见他谈黑魔法时的那种口气？他喜欢它们！所有那些*变幻莫测、不可毁灭的东西*——”

“是啊，”赫敏说，“我觉得他的口气有点儿像你。”

“像*我*？”

“是啊，你告诉我们面对伏地魔的感觉时就是这么说的。你说，光靠背熟一大堆咒语是不行的，还需要你整个人、你的头脑和你的勇气——嘿，这不就是斯内普说的吗？他不是说这涉及勇敢和思维敏捷吗？”

哈利没料到赫敏居然认为他的话像《标准咒语》一样值得牢记在心，他顿时消了怒气，没有再说什么。

“哈利！嘿，哈利！”

哈利扭头一看，杰克·斯劳珀——上学期格兰芬多魁地奇球队的一名击球手——匆匆朝他奔来，手里拿着一卷羊皮纸。

“给你的。”斯劳珀气喘吁吁地说，“嘿，我听说你当上了队长。什么时候搞选拔？”

“还没定下来呢，”哈利说，他私下里认为斯劳珀重回球队除非吉星高照，“到时候我会通知你的。”

“噢，好吧。我本来希望会在这个周末——”

可是哈利已经不再听他说了，他认出了羊皮纸上细长、歪斜的字体。没等斯劳珀把话说完，他就和罗恩、赫敏匆匆走开了，边走边展开了羊皮纸。

Dear Harry,

I would like to start our private lessons this Saturday. Kindly come along to my office at eight p.m. I hope you are enjoying your first day back at school.

Yours sincerely,

Albus Dumbledore

P.S. I enjoy Acid Pops.

'He enjoys Acid Pops?' said Ron, who had read the message over Harry's shoulder and was looking perplexed.

'It's the password to get past the gargoyle outside his study,' said Harry in a low voice. 'Ha! Snape's not going to be pleased … I won't be able to do his detention!'

He, Ron and Hermione spent the whole of break speculating on what Dumbledore would teach Harry. Ron thought it most likely to be spectacular jinxes and hexes of the type the Death Eaters would not know. Hermione said such things were illegal, and thought it much more likely that Dumbledore wanted to teach Harry advanced defensive magic. After break, she went off to Arithmancy while Harry and Ron returned to the common room, where they grudgingly started Snape's homework. This turned out to be so complex that they still had not finished when Hermione joined them for their after-lunch free period (though she considerably speeded up the process). They had only just finished when the bell rang for the afternoon's double Potions and they beat the familiar path down to the dungeon classroom that had, for so long, been Snape's.

When they arrived in the corridor they saw that there were only a dozen people progressing to N.E.W.T. level. Crabbe and Goyle had evidently failed to achieve the required O.W.L. grade, but four Slytherins had made it through, including Malfoy. Four Ravenclaws were there, and one Hufflepuff, Ernie Macmillan, whom Harry liked despite his rather pompous manner.

'Harry,' Ernie said portentously, holding out his hand as Harry approached, 'didn't get a chance to speak in Defence Against the Dark Arts this morning. Good lesson, I thought, but Shield Charms are old hat, of course, for us old DA lags … and how are you, Ron – Hermione?'

亲爱的哈利：

我打算本周六就开始给你单独上课。请在晚上八点到我的办公室来。希望你开学第一天过得很愉快。

你忠实的

阿不思·邓布利多

又及：我喜欢酸味爆爆糖。

“他喜欢酸味爆爆糖？”罗恩说，他隔着哈利的肩头把短信看了一遍，一脸的迷惑不解。

“这是通过他办公室外面那只滴水嘴石兽的口令。”哈利压低声音说，“哈！斯内普肯定会不高兴……我不能去他那儿关禁闭了！”

整个课间休息时，哈利、罗恩和赫敏都在猜测邓布利多会教哈利什么。罗恩认为很可能是食死徒不知道的一些厉害的咒语和魔法。赫敏说这些东西是不合法的，她认为邓布利多更有可能教哈利一些高深的魔法防御术。课间休息结束后，她去上算术占卜课了，哈利和罗恩回到公共休息室，满不情愿地开始做斯内普布置的家庭作业。作业太难了，在吃完午饭后的休息时间里，赫敏也来做作业了，他们的作业还没有做完（不过赫敏一来，速度就快得多了）。刚刚做完，下午两节魔药课的铃声就响了。他们顺着熟悉的路赶往地下教室，那里很长时间以来一直是斯内普专用的。

他们来到教室外面的走廊里，看见只有十二个同学来上提高班。显然，克拉布和高尔的O.W.L.成绩没有达到要求，但是有四个斯莱特林学生通过了考试，其中就有马尔福。另外还有四个拉文克劳学生和一个赫奇帕奇学生——厄尼·麦克米兰，他为人有些自负傲慢，但是哈利很喜欢他。

“哈利，”厄尼看见哈利走近，便伸出一只手，端着架子说，“上午的黑魔法防御术课上没有机会跟你说话。课上得不错，不过对于我们这些D.A.老成员来说，铁甲咒已经是老掉牙了……你们怎么样，罗恩——赫敏？”

Before they could say more than 'fine', the dungeon door opened and Slughorn's belly preceded him out of the door. As they filed into the room, his great walrus moustache curved above his beaming mouth and he greeted Harry and Zabini with particular enthusiasm.

The dungeon was, most unusually, already full of vapours and odd smells. Harry, Ron and Hermione sniffed interestedly as they passed large, bubbling cauldrons. The four Slytherins took a table together, as did the four Ravenclaws. This left Harry, Ron and Hermione to share a table with Ernie. They chose the one nearest a gold-coloured cauldron that was emitting one of the most seductive scents Harry had ever inhaled: somehow it reminded him simultaneously of treacle tart, the woody smell of a broomstick handle and something flowery he thought he might have smelled at The Burrow. He found that he was breathing very slowly and deeply and that the potion's fumes seemed to be filling him up like drink. A great contentment stole over him; he grinned across at Ron, who grinned lazily back.

'Now then, now then, now then,' said Slughorn, whose massive outline was quivering through the many shimmering vapours. 'Scales out, everyone, and potion kits, and don't forget your copies of *Advanced Potion-Making* ...'

'Sir?' said Harry, raising his hand.

'Harry, m'boy?'

'I haven't got a book or scales or anything – nor's Ron – we didn't realise we'd be able to do the N.E.W.T., you see –'

'Ah yes, Professor McGonagall did mention ... not to worry, my dear boy, not to worry at all. You can use ingredients from the store cupboard today, and I'm sure we can lend you some scales, and we've got a small stock of old books here, they'll do until you can write to Flourish and Blotts ...'

Slughorn strode over to a corner cupboard and after a moment's foraging emerged with two very battered-looking copies of *Advanced Potion-Making* by Libatius Borage, which he gave to Harry and Ron along with two sets of tarnished scales.

'Now then,' said Slughorn, returning to the front of the class and inflating his already bulging chest, so that the buttons on his waistcoat threatened to burst off, 'I've prepared a few potions for you to have a look at, just out of interest, you know. These are the kind of thing you ought to be able to make

他们只来得及说了一句“还好”，地下教室的门就打开了，斯拉格霍恩人还没露面，那个大肚子已经先挺了出来。同学们鱼贯走进教室，他的海象胡子在笑弯弯的嘴巴上拳曲着，他招呼哈利和沙比尼时显得格外热情。

与往常不同的是，地下教室里已经弥漫着蒸气，充满了各种古怪的气味。哈利、罗恩和赫敏走过一口口冒泡的大坩埚，饶有兴趣地闻着。四个斯莱特林学生坐一张桌子，四个拉文克劳学生也是一样。这么一来，哈利、罗恩和赫敏就只好跟厄尼坐在一起了。他们挑了张离一口金色坩埚最近的桌子，坩埚里散发出阵阵香气。哈利从没有闻过这么诱人的气味：这使他想到了蜂蜜馅饼，想到了飞天扫帚的木头味儿，还想到了一股准是在陋居闻到过的花香味儿。他发现自己正缓缓地、深深地往里吸气，药剂的气味像酒精一样充盈在他体内，一种巨大的满足感慢慢向他袭来。他咧嘴朝罗恩笑着，罗恩也在懒洋洋地望着他笑。

“好了，好了，好了。”斯拉格霍恩说。隔着许多热腾腾的蒸气望去，他那大块头的身形显得飘飘忽忽。“各位同学，请拿出天平、配药箱，还有，别忘了拿出你们的《高级魔药制作》课本……”

“先生？”哈利举起手说。

“怎么啦，哈利，我的孩子？”

“我没有书，没有天平，什么也没有——罗恩也是——因为我们没想到还能上提高班——”

“啊，对了，麦格教授提到过这事……别担心，孩子，一点儿也不用担心。你们今天可以先用储藏柜里的原料，天平也可以借给你们，这里还有一些旧课本，你们先用着，然后你们可以写信给丽痕书店……”

斯拉格霍恩大步走到墙角的一个储藏柜前，在里面摸索了一会儿，拿出两本破破烂烂的利巴修·波拉奇所著的《高级魔药制作》和两套暗淡褪色的天平，一起递给了哈利和罗恩。

“好了，”斯拉格霍恩说着回到教室前面，把已经很鼓的胸膛又往前挺了挺，马甲上的纽扣眼看就要绷掉了，“我准备了几种药剂让你们开开眼界，当然啦，这么做只是出于兴趣。等你们完成了提高班的课程，

after completing your N.E.W.T.s. You ought to have heard of 'em, even if you haven't made 'em yet. Anyone tell me what this one is?'

He indicated the cauldron nearest the Slytherin table. Harry raised himself slightly in his seat and saw what looked like plain water boiling away inside it.

Hermione's well-practised hand hit the air before anybody else's; Slughorn pointed at her.

'It's Veritaserum, a colourless, odourless potion that forces the drinker to tell the truth,' said Hermione.

'Very good, very good!' said Slughorn happily. 'Now,' he continued, pointing at the cauldron nearest the Ravenclaw table, 'this one here is pretty well-known … featured in a few Ministry leaflets lately, too … who can –?'

Hermione's hand was fastest once more.

'It's Polyjuice Potion, sir,' she said.

Harry, too, had recognised the slow-bubbling, mudlike substance in the second cauldron, but did not resent Hermione getting the credit for answering the question; she, after all, was the one who had succeeded in making it, back in their second year.

'Excellent, excellent! Now, this one here … yes, my dear?' said Slughorn, now looking slightly bemused as Hermione's hand punched the air again.

'It's Amortentia!'

'It is indeed. It seems almost foolish to ask,' said Slughorn, who was looking mightily impressed, 'but I assume you know what it does?'

'It's the most powerful love potion in the world!' said Hermione.

'Quite right! You recognised it, I suppose, by its distinctive mother-of-pearl sheen?'

'And the steam rising in characteristic spirals,' said Hermione enthusiastically, 'and it's supposed to smell differently to each of us, according to what attracts us, and I can smell freshly mown grass and new parchment and –'

But she turned slightly pink and did not complete the sentence.

'May I ask your name, my dear?' said Slughorn, ignoring Hermione's embarrassment.

'Hermione Granger, sir.'

就应该能做出这样的东西了。你们虽然没有亲手做过，但肯定听说过。谁能告诉我这一种是什么？”

他指着最靠近斯莱特林桌子的那口坩埚。哈利从座位上微微欠起身，看见那里面像是一锅清水在翻滚。

赫敏那只久经锻炼的手抢先举了起来。斯拉格霍恩指了指她。

“是吐真剂，一种无色无味的药剂，能使喝它的人被迫说出实话。”赫敏说。

“很好，很好！”斯拉格霍恩高兴地说。“现在，”他指着最靠近拉文克劳桌子的那口坩埚，继续说道，“这种比较出名……最近部里发的几本小册子上也重点介绍过……谁能……？”

赫敏的手又一次抢先举了起来。

“是复方汤剂，先生。”她说。

哈利也认出了第二口坩埚里慢慢泛着气泡的泥浆般的东西，但他并不怪赫敏抢先回答了这个问题。毕竟，在他们二年级时，是赫敏成功地熬制出了这种药剂。

“太好了，太好了！还有这里的这种……你说，亲爱的？”斯拉格霍恩说，他看见赫敏又一次举起了手，显得有点儿惊异。

“是痴心水！”

“一点儿不错。似乎根本用不着问，”斯拉格霍恩这时露出了由衷的佩服，说道，“我想你肯定知道它是做什么用的？”

“它是世界上最有效的迷情剂！”赫敏说。

“非常正确！我想，你是通过它特有的珍珠母的光泽认出来的吧？”

“还有它特有的呈螺旋形上升的蒸气。”赫敏兴趣盎然地说，“而且，它的气味因人而异，根据各人最喜欢什么。我可以闻到刚修剪过的草地，崭新的羊皮纸，还有——”

她突然绯红了脸，不再往下说了。

“亲爱的，可以把你的名字告诉我吗？”斯拉格霍恩问道，似乎没注意到赫敏的不好意思。

“赫敏·格兰杰，先生。”

'Granger? Granger? Can you possibly be related to Hector Dagworth-Granger, who founded the Most Extraordinary Society of Potioneers?'

'No, I don't think so, sir. I'm Muggle-born, you see.'

Harry saw Malfoy lean close to Nott and whisper something; both of them sniggered, but Slughorn showed no dismay; on the contrary, he beamed and looked from Hermione to Harry, who was sitting next to her.

'Oho! "*One of my best friends is Muggle-born and she's the best in our year!* " I'm assuming this is the very friend of whom you spoke, Harry?'

'Yes, sir,' said Harry.

'Well, well, take twenty well-earned points for Gryffindor, Miss Granger,' said Slughorn genially.

Malfoy looked rather as he had done the time Hermione had punched him in the face. Hermione turned to Harry with a radiant expression and whispered, 'Did you really tell him I'm the best in the year? Oh, Harry!'

'Well, what's so impressive about that?' whispered Ron, who for some reason looked annoyed. 'You *are* the best in the year – I'd've told him so if he'd asked me!'

Hermione smiled but made a 'shush'ing gesture, so that they could hear what Slughorn was saying. Ron looked slightly disgruntled.

'Amortentia doesn't really create *love*, of course. It is impossible to manufacture or imitate love. No, this will simply cause a powerful infatuation or obsession. It is probably the most dangerous and powerful potion in this room – oh yes,' he said, nodding gravely at Malfoy and Nott, both of whom were smirking sceptically. 'When you have seen as much of life as I have, you will not underestimate the power of obsessive love …

'And now,' said Slughorn, 'it is time for us to start work.'

'Sir, you haven't told us what's in this one,' said Ernie Macmillan, pointing at a small black cauldron standing on Slughorn's desk. The potion within was splashing about merrily; it was the colour of molten gold, and large drops were leaping like goldfish above the surface, though not a particle had spilled.

'Oho,' said Slughorn again. Harry was sure that Slughorn had not forgotten the potion at all, but had waited to be asked for dramatic effect. 'Yes. That. Well, *that* one, ladies and gentlemen, is a most curious little potion

“格兰杰？格兰杰？你是不是跟非凡药剂师协会的创办人赫克托·达格沃斯－格兰杰有亲戚关系？”

“不，应该不是，先生。我是麻瓜出身。”

哈利看见马尔福凑近诺特低声嘀咕了几句什么，两人偷偷地笑了起来。可是斯拉格霍恩倒没有表示出失望的样子。相反，他满脸笑容，看看赫敏，又看看坐在她身边的哈利。

“嗬，对了！‘我有一个最好的朋友也是麻瓜出身，她是全年级最优秀的！’我敢断定，这就是你说的那位朋友吧，哈利？”

“是的，先生。”哈利说。

“很好，很好，给格兰芬多的格兰杰小姐加上当之无愧的二十分。”斯拉格霍恩亲切地说。

马尔福脸上的表情就跟上次赫敏迎面给他一拳时差不多。赫敏喜滋滋地转向哈利，小声说：“你真的对他说过我是全年级最优秀的？哦，哈利！”

“得了，这有什么了不起的？”罗恩小声说，不知为什么显得有些恼怒，“你本来就是全年级最优秀的嘛——如果他问我，我也会这么说的！”

赫敏笑了，但又做了个“嘘”的手势，以便他们能听见斯拉格霍恩说话。罗恩看上去有点不高兴。

“当然啦，痴心水并不能真的创造爱情。爱情是不可能制造或仿造的。不，这种药剂只会导致强烈的痴迷或迷恋。这大概是这间教室里最危险最厉害的一种药剂了——对，没错，”他朝马尔福和诺特严肃地点了点头，他们俩正在那里怀疑地坏笑，“等你们的人生阅历像我这么丰富之后，就不会低估中了魔的痴情有多大的威力了……”

“现在，”斯拉格霍恩接着说，“我们应该开始上课了。”

“先生，你还没有告诉我们这里面是什么呢。”厄尼·麦克米兰指着斯拉格霍恩讲台上的一口黑色小坩埚说。小坩埚里面的药剂欢快地飞溅着，颜色如同熔化了的金子，表面跳跃着的大滴大滴液体，像一条条金鱼，但没有一滴洒到外面。

“嗬！”斯拉格霍恩又来了这么一声。哈利相信斯拉格霍恩根本没有忘记那种药剂，他只是等着别人来问，以制造一种戏剧性的效果。“对

called Felix Felicis. I take it,' he turned, smiling, to look at Hermione, who had let out an audible gasp, 'that you know what Felix Felicis does, Miss Granger?'

'It's liquid luck,' said Hermione excitedly. 'It makes you lucky!'

The whole class seemed to sit up a little straighter. Now all Harry could see of Malfoy was the back of his sleek blond head, because he was at last giving Slughorn his full and undivided attention.

'Quite right, take another ten points for Gryffindor. Yes, it's a funny little potion, Felix Felicis,' said Slughorn. 'Desperately tricky to make, and disastrous to get wrong. However, if brewed correctly, as this has been, you will find that all your endeavours tend to succeed … at least until the effects wear off.'

'Why don't people drink it all the time, sir?' said Terry Boot eagerly.

'Because if taken in excess, it causes giddiness, recklessness and dangerous overconfidence,' said Slughorn. 'Too much of a good thing, you know … highly toxic in large quantities. But taken sparingly, and very occasionally …'

'Have you ever taken it, sir?' asked Michael corner with great interest.

'Twice in my life,' said Slughorn. 'Once when I was twenty-four, once when I was fifty-seven. Two tablespoonfuls taken with breakfast. Two perfect days.'

He gazed dreamily into the distance. Whether he was play-acting or not, thought Harry, the effect was good.

'And that,' said Slughorn, apparently coming back to earth, 'is what I shall be offering as a prize in this lesson.'

There was a silence in which every bubble and gurgle of the surrounding potions seemed magnified tenfold.

'One tiny bottle of Felix Felicis,' said Slughorn, taking a minuscule glass bottle with a cork in it out of his pocket and showing it to them all. 'Enough for twelve hours' luck. From dawn till dusk, you will be lucky in everything you attempt.

'Now, I must give you warning that Felix Felicis is a banned substance in organised competitions … sporting events, for instance, examinations or elections. So the winner is to use it on an ordinary day only … and watch how that ordinary day becomes extraordinary!

了，那种还没说呢。女士们先生们，那玩意儿是一种最为奇特的小魔药，叫福灵剂。我想，”他笑眯眯地转过身来，看着发出一声惊叫的赫敏，“你肯定知道福灵剂有什么作用吧，格兰杰小姐？”

“它是幸运药水，”赫敏兴奋地说，“会给你带来好运！”

全班同学似乎顿时挺直了腰板。哈利只能看见马尔福油光水滑的金色头发后脑勺，因为马尔福终于全神贯注地听斯拉格霍恩讲课了。

“非常正确，给格兰芬多再加十分。是的，这是一种奇特的小魔药——福灵剂，”斯拉格霍恩说，“熬制起来非常复杂，一旦弄错，后果不堪设想。不过，如果熬制得法，就像这坩埚里的一样，你会发现你不管做什么都能成功……至少在药效消失之前。”

“那为什么人们不整天喝它呢，先生？”泰瑞·布特急切地问。

“因为，如果过量服用，就会导致眩晕、鲁莽和危险的狂妄自大。”斯拉格霍恩说，“你们知道，好东西多了也有害……剂量太大，便有很强的毒性。不过偶尔谨慎地、有节制地服用一点儿……”

“你服用过吗，先生？”迈克尔·科纳兴趣很浓地问。

“我这辈子服用过两次，”斯拉格霍恩说，“一次是二十四岁，一次是五十七岁。早饭时服用了两勺，那两天过得真是完美啊。”

他神情恍惚地凝望着远处。哈利觉得，不管他是不是在演戏，效果都是很诱人的。

“这个嘛，”斯拉格霍恩似乎回到了现实中，说道，“我将作为这节课的奖品。”

教室里一片寂静，周围那些药剂的每一个冒泡声、沸腾声似乎都放大了十倍。

“小小一瓶福灵剂，”斯拉格霍恩从口袋里掏出一个塞着木塞的小玻璃瓶，举给全班同学看，“可以带来十二个小时的好运。从天亮到天黑，不管做什么都会吉星高照。

“不过，我必须提醒你们，福灵剂在有组织的比赛中是禁止使用的……比如体育竞赛、考试或竞选。因此，拿到奖品的人，只能在平常日子里使用……然后等着看那个平常日子会变得怎样不同寻常！

'So,' said Slughorn, suddenly brisk, 'how are you to win my fabulous prize? Well, by turning to page ten of *Advanced Potion-Making*. We have a little over an hour left to us, which should be time for you to make a decent attempt at the Draught of Living Death. I know it is more complex than anything you have attempted before, and I do not expect a perfect potion from anybody. The person who does best, however, will win little Felix here. Off you go!'

There was a scraping as everyone drew their cauldrons towards them, and some loud clunks as people began adding weights to their scales, but nobody spoke. The concentration within the room was almost tangible. Harry saw Malfoy riffling feverishly through his copy of *Advanced Potion-Making*. It could not have been clearer that Malfoy really wanted that lucky day. Harry bent swiftly over the tattered book Slughorn had lent him.

To his annoyance he saw that the previous owner had scribbled all over the pages, so that the margins were as black as the printed portions. Bending low to decipher the ingredients (even here, the previous owner had made annotations and crossed things out) Harry hurried off towards the store cupboard to find what he needed. As he dashed back to his cauldron, he saw Malfoy cutting up valerian roots as fast as he could.

Everyone kept glancing around at what the rest of the class was doing; this was both an advantage and a disadvantage of Potions, that it was hard to keep your work private. Within ten minutes, the whole place was full of bluish steam. Hermione, of course, seemed to have progressed furthest. Her potion already resembled the 'smooth, black-currant-coloured liquid' mentioned as the ideal halfway stage.

Having finished chopping his roots, Harry bent low over his book again. It was really very irritating, having to try and decipher the directions under all the stupid scribbles of the previous owner, who for some reason had taken issue with the order to cut up the Sopophorous Bean and had written in the alternative instruction:

> *Crush with flat side of silver dagger,*
> *releases juice better than cutting.*

'Sir, I think you knew my grandfather, Abraxas Malfoy?'

“那么，”斯拉格霍恩说，突然变得精神振奋起来，“怎么才能赢得我这份奇妙的奖品呢？好，请把《高级魔药制作》翻到第十页。还有一个多小时，你们就用这段时间好好地熬制一份生死水。我知道，这比你们以前做过的任何东西都复杂，我也不指望有人熬出十全十美的汤剂。不过，做得最好的那位同学会赢得这小瓶福灵剂。好了，开始吧！”

只听得一片刺耳的擦刮声，大家都把坩埚拉到了自己面前，然后是咣当咣当把砝码放在天平上的声音，但是没有一个人说话，同学们高度集中的注意力简直触手可及。哈利看见马尔福在疯狂地翻他那本《高级魔药制作》。马尔福显然很想得到那幸运的一天，这是再清楚不过了。哈利赶紧低头看斯拉格霍恩借给他的那本破破烂烂的课本。

令他恼火的是，他发现课本以前的主人在书上到处乱写，弄得每一页的空白处也跟印着字的地方一样黑乎乎的。哈利一边低头辨认药剂成分（以前那位主人对这部分内容也做了许多注解，还划掉了几种成分），一边匆匆奔向储藏柜，寻找他需要的东西。当他冲回自己的坩埚时，看见马尔福正在飞快地切着缬草根。

每个人都不停地张望其他同学在做什么，这既是魔药课上的一个优点，也是一个缺点，你很难不让别人看见你做的事情。不到十分钟，整个教室里已弥漫着淡蓝色的蒸汽。当然，进展最快的似乎还是赫敏。她的药剂已经很接近那种“调匀的黑加仑色的液体”，书上说这正是药剂熬到一半时的理想状态。

哈利切完草根，又低头去看课本。真是太让人恼火了，他必须费力地从课本的前主人胡乱涂写的文字中辨认操作指南。那位老兄不知为什么，不同意书上说的要把瞌睡豆切成片，而是另外写了一条说明：

用银短刀的侧面挤压，

比切片更容易出汁。

“先生，我想你一定认识我爷爷阿布拉克萨斯·马尔福吧？”

Harry looked up; Slughorn was just passing the Slytherin table.

'Yes,' said Slughorn, without looking at Malfoy, 'I was sorry to hear he had died, although of course it wasn't unexpected, dragon pox at his age …'

And he walked away. Harry bent back over his cauldron, smirking. He could tell that Malfoy had expected to be treated like Harry or Zabini; perhaps even hoped for some preferential treatment of the type he had learned to expect from Snape. It looked as though Malfoy would have to rely on nothing but talent to win the bottle of Felix Felicis.

The Sopophorous Bean was proving very difficult to cut up. Harry turned to Hermione.

'Can I borrow your silver knife?'

She nodded impatiently, not taking her eyes off her potion, which was still deep purple, though according to the book ought to be turning a light shade of lilac by now.

Harry crushed his bean with the flat side of the dagger. To his astonishment, it immediately exuded so much juice he was amazed the shrivelled bean could have held it all. Hastily scooping it all into the cauldron he saw, to his surprise, that the potion immediately turned exactly the shade of lilac described by the textbook.

His annoyance with the previous owner vanishing on the spot, Harry now squinted at the next line of instructions. According to the book, he had to stir counter-clockwise until the potion turned clear as water. According to the addition the previous owner had made, however, he ought to add a clockwise stir after every seventh counter-clockwise stir. Could the old owner be right twice?

Harry stirred counter-clockwise, held his breath, and stirred once clockwise. The effect was immediate. The potion turned palest pink.

'How are you doing that?' demanded Hermione, who was red-faced and whose hair was growing bushier and bushier in the fumes from her cauldron; her potion was still resolutely purple.

'Add a clockwise stir –'

'No, no, the book says counter-clockwise!' she snapped.

Harry shrugged and continued what he was doing. Seven stirs counter-clockwise, one clockwise, pause … seven stirs counter-clockwise, one stir clockwise …

Across the table, Ron was cursing fluently under his breath; his potion

哈利抬头一看，斯拉格霍恩正走过斯莱特林的桌子。

“认识，”斯拉格霍恩看也没看马尔福，说道，“听说他死了，我很难过，不过这也是意料之中的事，那么大岁数还患了龙痘疮……”

说着他就走开了。哈利幸灾乐祸地暗笑着，又埋头对付他的坩埚。他看得出来，马尔福希望像哈利或沙比尼那样得到斯拉格霍恩的另眼相看，甚至还希望得到当年斯内普对他的那种优待。不过眼下看来，马尔福要想赢得那瓶福灵剂只能靠自己的聪明才智了。

哈利发现瞌睡豆很难切。他转向了赫敏。

“我能借你的银刀子用用吗？”

赫敏不耐烦地点了点头，眼睛一刻也没有离开她的药剂。书上说，药剂现在应该变成一种淡丁香紫色了，可她的埚里还是深紫色的。

哈利用短刀的侧面挤压瞌睡豆。真没想到，豆子立刻渗出了大量的汁液，哈利简直不敢相信这颗干瘪瘪的豆子里竟有这么多水分。他赶紧把汁液全部放进坩埚，药剂马上变成了书上所说的那种淡丁香紫色，他真是惊讶极了。

哈利对先前那位主人的恼怒立刻烟消云散，他眯起眼睛读下一条说明。课本上说，必须逆时针搅拌，直到药剂变得像水一样清。可根据先前那位主人所加的笔记，应该逆时针搅拌七下之后再顺时针搅拌一下。那位老兄会两次都说对吗？

哈利屏住呼吸，逆时针搅拌了七下，又顺时针搅拌了一下。效果立竿见影，药剂立刻变成了淡淡的粉红色。

“你是怎么做到的？”赫敏问，她的坩埚里冒出的热气熏得她满脸通红，头发也越来越乱了。她的药剂还是紫色的，丝毫不肯改变。

“再顺时针搅拌一下——”

“不行，不行，书上说的是逆时针！”她武断地说。

哈利耸了耸肩，继续忙他自己的药剂。逆时针搅拌七下，顺时针搅拌一下，停一停，再逆时针搅拌七下，顺时针搅拌一下……

桌子那边的罗恩一直在低声骂个不停，他的药剂看上去就像是稀

looked like liquid liquorice. Harry glanced around. As far as he could see, no one else's potion had turned as pale as his. He felt elated, something that had certainly never happened before in this dungeon.

'And time's … up!' called Slughorn. 'Stop stirring, please!'

Slughorn moved slowly between the tables, peering into cauldrons. He made no comment, but occasionally gave the potions a stir, or a sniff. At last he reached the table where Harry, Ron, Hermione and Ernie were sitting. He smiled ruefully at the tarlike substance in Ron's cauldron. He passed over Ernie's navy concoction. Hermione's potion he gave an approving nod. Then he saw Harry's, and a look of incredulous delight spread over his face.

'The clear winner!' he cried to the dungeon. 'Excellent, excellent, Harry! Good Lord, it's clear you've inherited your mother's talent, she was a dab hand at Potions, Lily was! Here you are, then, here you are – one bottle of Felix Felicis, as promised, and use it well!'

Harry slipped the tiny bottle of golden liquid into his inner pocket, feeling an odd combination of delight at the furious looks on the Slytherins' faces, and guilt at the disappointed expression on Hermione's. Ron looked simply dumbfounded.

'How did you do that?' he whispered to Harry as they left the dungeon.

'Got lucky, I suppose,' said Harry, because Malfoy was within earshot.

Once they were securely ensconced at the Gryffindor table for dinner, however, he felt safe enough to tell them. Hermione's face became stonier with every word he uttered.

'I s'pose you think I cheated?' he finished, aggravated by her expression.

'Well, it wasn't exactly your own work, was it?' she said stiffly.

'He only followed different instructions to ours,' said Ron. 'Could've been a catastrophe, couldn't it? But he took a risk and it paid off.' He heaved a sigh. 'Slughorn could've handed me that book, but no, I get the one no one's ever written in. *Puked on*, by the look of page fifty-two, but –'

'Hang on,' said a voice close by Harry's left ear and he caught a sudden waft of that flowery smell he had picked up in Slughorn's dungeon. He looked round and saw that Ginny had joined them. 'Did I hear right? You've been taking orders from something someone wrote in a book, Harry?'

薄的甘草糖。哈利的目光在教室里扫了一圈，没有看见哪个同学的药剂像他的一样变成那么浅的颜色。他觉得精神大振，这可是这间地下教室以前从没有过的事情。

“好，时间……到！”斯拉格霍恩大声说道，“请停止搅拌！”

斯拉格霍恩在桌子之间慢慢走动，轮流检查每一口坩埚。他没作任何评论，只是偶尔搅拌一下，或凑上去闻一闻。最后，他走到了哈利、罗恩、赫敏和厄尼的桌子旁。他朝罗恩埚里那堆柏油似的东西苦笑了一下，又从厄尼熬出的那埚蓝色混合物旁走过去。看到赫敏的药剂，他赞许地点了点头。可是当他看见哈利坩埚里的东西时，脸上露出了难以置信的喜悦神色。

“无可争议的优胜者！”他对地下教室的全班同学大声说，“出色，太出色了，哈利！天哪，你显然继承了你母亲的天赋，莉莉当年在魔药课上就是如此心灵手巧！给，拿去吧——我说话算数，给你一瓶福灵剂，好好利用！”

哈利把那一小瓶金色液体塞进了袍子里面的口袋，心情十分复杂，几个斯莱特林学生脸上气恼的表情让他看了心花怒放，而赫敏失望的神情又让他感到内疚。罗恩则完全是一副目瞪口呆的样子。

“你是怎么做到的？”他们离开地下教室时，他问哈利。

“大概是运气好吧。”哈利说，因为马尔福就在旁边，能听见他的话。

他们在格兰芬多餐桌旁坐定，准备吃午饭时，他觉得比较安全了，才把实话告诉了他们。赫敏听着他的叙述，脸色越来越阴沉。

“你大概以为我是作弊了吧？”哈利被她脸上的表情弄得很恼火，讲完后便问了她一句。

“是啊，你并不是自己独立完成的，是不是？”她生硬地说。

“他只是按照和我们不同的方法操作，”罗恩说，“也可能会闯大祸的，是不是？他冒险了，所以得到了补偿。”他叹了口气，“斯拉格霍恩本来可能把那本书递给我的，可是，唉，没有谁在我的课本上写过字。从五十二页的情形来看，好像有人在上面吐过，但是——”

“等等。”哈利左耳边一个声音说道，他又闻到了他在斯拉格霍恩课堂里闻到的那种花香味儿。他扭头看见金妮也加入了他们的谈话。“我没有听错吧，哈利？你在按照别人写在一本书里的指令做事？”

She looked alarmed and angry. Harry knew what was on her mind at once.

'It's nothing,' he said reassuringly, lowering his voice. 'It's not like, you know, Riddle's diary. It's just an old textbook someone's scribbled in.'

'But you're doing what it says?'

'I just tried a few of the tips written in the margins, honestly, Ginny, there's nothing funny –'

'Ginny's got a point,' said Hermione, perking up at once. 'We ought to check that there's nothing odd about it. I mean, all these funny instructions, who knows?'

'Hey!' said Harry indignantly, as she pulled his copy of *Advanced Potion-Making* out of his bag and raised her wand.

'*Specialis revelio!*' she said, rapping it smartly on the front cover.

Nothing whatsoever happened. The book simply lay there, looking old and dirty and dog-eared.

'Finished?' said Harry irritably. 'Or d'you want to wait and see if it does a few back flips?'

'It seems all right,' said Hermione, still staring at the book suspiciously. 'I mean, it really does seem to be … just a textbook.'

'Good. Then I'll have it back,' said Harry, snatching it off the table, but it slipped from his hand and landed open on the floor.

Nobody else was looking. Harry bent low to retrieve the book and, as he did so, he saw something scribbled along the bottom of the back cover in the same small, cramped handwriting as the instructions that had won him his bottle of Felix Felicis, now safely hidden inside a pair of socks in his trunk upstairs.

This Book is the Property of the Half-Blood Prince

她显得惊慌而气愤。哈利立刻猜到她脑子里在想什么了。

“这没什么，”他压低声音宽慰她道，“你知道，这不像里德尔的日记，只是一本被人涂写过的旧课本。”

“可是你照那上面写的做了？”

“说实在的，金妮，我只是试了试书上空白处写的几点小窍门，没有什么反常的——”

“金妮说得有道理，”赫敏一下子来了精神，说道，“我们应该检查一下它有没有什么不对劲儿。我是说，所有那些古怪的说明，谁知道是怎么回事？”

“喂！”哈利气愤地抗议道，赫敏一把抽出哈利书包里的那本《高级魔药制作》，举起了魔杖。

“原形立现！”她干脆利落地敲了敲封面，念道。

什么动静也没有。课本还是课本，破旧，肮脏，书角都卷起来了。

“完了吗？”哈利恼火地问，“你还想等着看它会不会来几个后滚翻？”

“看来没问题，”赫敏仍然怀疑地盯着课本，说道，“我是说，它看上去确实……只是一本课本。”

“很好，那我就把它拿回来了。”哈利说着把课本从桌上夺了过去，可是课本从他手里滑落，掉在地上摊开了。

谁也没有注意。哈利弯下腰正要把书捡起来，突然看见封底的下端写着什么东西，还是那种小小的、密密麻麻的笔迹，跟那些帮他赢得福灵剂的说明一样，而那瓶福灵剂，现在已安安稳稳地藏在楼上他箱子里的一双袜子里了。

本书属于混血王子

CHAPTER TEN

The House of Gaunt

For the rest of the week's Potions lessons Harry continued to follow the Half-Blood Prince's instructions wherever they deviated from Libatius Borage's, with the result that by their fourth lesson Slughorn was raving about Harry's abilities, saying that he had rarely taught anyone so talented. Neither Ron nor Hermione was delighted by this. although Harry had offered to share his book with both of them, Ron had more difficulty deciphering the handwriting than Harry did, and could not keep asking Harry to read aloud or it might look suspicious. Hermione, meanwhile, was resolutely ploughing on with what she called the 'official' instructions, but becoming increasingly bad-tempered as they yielded poorer results than the Prince's.

Harry wondered vaguely who the Half-Blood Prince had been. Although the amount of homework they had been given prevented him from reading the whole of his copy of *Advanced Potion-Making*, he had skimmed through it sufficiently to see that there was barely a page on which the Prince had not made additional notes, not all of them concerned with potion-making. Here and there were directions for what looked like spells that the Prince had made up himself.

'Or herself,' said Hermione irritably, overhearing Harry pointing some of these out to Ron in the common room on Saturday evening. 'It might have been a girl. I think the handwriting looks more like a girl's than a boy's.'

'The Half-Blood *Prince*, he was called,' Harry said. 'How many girls have been princes?'

Hermione seemed to have no answer to this. She merely scowled and twitched her essay on 'The Principles of Rematerialisation' away from Ron, who was trying to read it upside-down.

Harry looked at his watch and hurriedly put the old copy of *Advanced*

第 10 章

冈特老宅

这星期后来几节魔药课上，每次混血王子对利巴修·波拉奇的课本提出异议，哈利就按混血王子的建议去做，结果在第四节魔药课上，斯拉格霍恩就对哈利的能力赞不绝口，说他很少教过这么有天分的学生。罗恩和赫敏对此都不太高兴。尽管哈利提出把他的书拿出来与他俩共享，但罗恩不能像哈利那么熟练地辨认那些字迹，又不能总是叫哈利念出声来给他听，免得惹人怀疑。赫敏呢，她毫不动摇地按照她所说的“正式”指南去操作，结果熬制出的魔药远不如按照王子的那些说明操作的令人满意，所以她的脾气越来越坏。

哈利暗暗猜测这位混血王子到底是什么人。由于家庭作业太多，他还没能把那本《高级魔药制作》仔细研读一遍，但已经从头到尾大致翻了翻，发现王子几乎在每一页上都添加了笔记，而且那些笔记并不都与魔药制作有关。有一些说明看上去像王子自己编的咒语。

“说不定那是个女人呢，”星期六的晚上，赫敏在公共休息室里听哈利把那些咒语说给罗恩听的时候，不耐烦地说，“也可能是个女生。我觉得那笔迹不像男生的，更像女生的。”

“他叫‘混血王子’。”哈利说，“有多少女生管自己叫王子？”

赫敏似乎无言以对。她只是皱起眉头，一把抽走了她写的那篇题为《幽灵显形的原理》的文章，罗恩正倒着偷看呢。

哈利看了看表，急忙把他那本《高级魔药制作》旧课本塞进了

Potion-Making back into his bag.

'It's five to eight, I'd better go, I'll be late for Dumbledore.'

'Ooooh!' gasped Hermione, looking up at once. 'Good luck! We'll wait up, we want to hear what he teaches you!'

'Hope it goes OK,' said Ron, and the pair of them watched Harry leave through the portrait hole.

Harry proceeded through deserted corridors, though he had to step hastily behind a statue when Professor Trelawney appeared round a corner, muttering to herself as she shuffled a pack of dirty-looking playing cards, reading them as she walked.

'Two of spades: conflict,' she murmured, as she passed the place where Harry crouched, hidden. 'Seven of spades: an ill omen. Ten of spades: violence. Knave of spades: a dark young man, possibly troubled, one who dislikes the questioner –'

She stopped dead, right on the other side of Harry's statue.

'Well, that can't be right,' she said, annoyed, and Harry heard her reshuffling vigorously as she set off again, leaving nothing but a whiff of cooking sherry behind her. Harry waited until he was quite sure she had gone, then hurried off again until he reached the spot in the seventh-floor corridor where a single gargoyle stood against the wall.

'Acid Pops,' said Harry. The gargoyle leapt aside; the wall behind it slid apart, and a moving spiral stone staircase was revealed, on to which Harry stepped, so that he was carried in smooth circles up to the door with the brass knocker that led to Dumbledore's office.

Harry knocked.

'Come in,' said Dumbledore's voice.

'Good evening, sir,' said Harry, walking into the Headmaster's office.

'Ah, good evening, Harry. Sit down,' said Dumbledore, smiling. 'I hope you've had an enjoyable first week back at school?'

'Yes thanks, sir,' said Harry.

'You must have been busy, a detention under your belt already!'

'Er …' began Harry awkwardly, but Dumbledore did not look too stern.

'I have arranged with Professor Snape that you will do your detention next Saturday instead.'

书包。

“八点差五分了，我得赶紧走，到邓布利多那儿要迟到了。”

“哟！”赫敏吃了一惊，立刻抬起头来，“祝你好运！我们会一直等你回来。想听听他会教你什么。”

“希望一切顺利。”罗恩说，他们俩目送哈利从肖像洞口离开。

哈利快步穿过空无一人的走廊，突然，他看见特里劳尼教授转过拐角，手里洗着一副脏兮兮的扑克牌，一边读着牌上的点数，一边自言自语，哈利赶紧闪身躲到一座雕像后面。

“黑桃2：冲突；”她走过哈利躲藏的地方时，嘴里念念有词地说，“黑桃7：凶兆；黑桃10：暴力；黑桃杰克：一个阴沉的年轻人，很可能心烦意乱，不愿意别人审问他——”

她停住脚，就站在哈利藏身的那座雕像的另一边。

“唉，这肯定不对。”她烦恼地说，哈利听见她一边起劲地重新洗牌，一边又往前走去，只在身后留下一股雪利料酒的气味。哈利直到相信她已经走远，才赶紧拔腿离开雕像，一口气走到八楼走廊里有尊单独的滴水嘴石兽的地方。

“酸味爆爆糖。”哈利说。石兽跳到一旁，它身后的墙壁裂成两半，露出后面的一道活动的螺旋形楼梯。哈利跨了上去，随着楼梯一圈圈地旋转，越升越高，最后来到了那扇带有黄铜门环的邓布利多办公室门前。

哈利敲了敲门。

“请进。”是邓布利多的声音。

“晚上好，先生。”哈利说着走进了校长办公室。

“啊，晚上好，哈利。坐下吧，”邓布利多笑眯眯地说，“我想，开学第一个星期你过得很愉快吧？”

“是的，先生，谢谢。”哈利说。

“你一定很忙啊，已经吃了一个禁闭了！”

“嗯……”哈利不知道该说什么，不过邓布利多的表情并不是很严厉。

“我已经跟斯内普教授说好了，你下个星期六再去关禁闭。”

'Right,' said Harry, who had more pressing matters on his mind than Snape's detention, and now looked around surreptitiously for some indication of what Dumbledore was planning to do with him that evening. The circular office looked just as it always did: the delicate silver instruments stood on spindle-legged tables, puffing smoke and whirring; portraits of previous headmasters and headmistresses dozed in their frames; and Dumbledore's magnificent phoenix, Fawkes, stood on his perch behind the door, watching Harry with bright interest. It did not even look as though Dumbledore had cleared a space for duelling practice.

'So, Harry,' said Dumbledore, in a businesslike voice. 'You have been wondering, I am sure, what I have planned for you during these – for want of a better word – lessons?'

'Yes, sir.'

'Well, I have decided that it is time, now that you know what prompted Lord Voldemort to try and kill you fifteen years ago, for you to be given certain information.'

There was a pause.

'You said, at the end of last term, you were going to tell me everything,' said Harry. It was hard to keep a note of accusation from his voice. 'Sir,' he added.

'And so I did,' said Dumbledore placidly. 'I told you everything I know. From this point forth, we shall be leaving the firm foundation of fact and journeying together through the murky marshes of memory into thickets of wildest guesswork. From hereon in, Harry, I may be as woefully wrong as Humphrey Belcher, who believed the time was ripe for a cheese cauldron.'

'But you think you're right?' said Harry.

'Naturally I do, but as I have already proven to you, I make mistakes like the next man. In fact, being – forgive me – rather cleverer than most men, my mistakes tend to be correspondingly huger.'

'Sir,' said Harry tentatively, 'does what you're going to tell me have anything to do with the prophecy? Will it help me … survive?'

'It has a very great deal to do with the prophecy,' said Dumbledore, as casually as if Harry had asked him about the next day's weather, 'and I certainly hope that it will help you to survive.'

Dumbledore got to his feet and walked around the desk, past Harry, who

“好的。”哈利说，他脑子里装着更要紧的事情，顾不上去想斯内普的禁闭。他偷偷打量着四周，想猜出邓布利多今晚叫他来做什么。这间圆形办公室看上去和往常一样：细长腿的桌子上摆着许多精致的银器，它们旋转着，喷出一小股一小股的烟雾。那些男男女女老校长们的肖像都在各自的相框里打着瞌睡。邓布利多那只气派非凡的凤凰福克斯站在门后的栖枝上，兴趣盎然地注视着哈利。看样子，邓布利多并没有腾出一个地方来练习格斗。

“我想，哈利，”邓布利多用一本正经的口吻说，“你肯定在纳闷，我打算怎么给你——没有更好的说法——上课？”

“是的，先生。”

“是这样，既然你已经知道十五年前是什么促使伏地魔对你下毒手的，我认为现在应该让你了解一些情况了。”

片刻的停顿。

“上学期结束时，你就说要把一切都告诉我的。”哈利说。他很难消除自己话里的一点儿责怪口气。“先生。”他又补了一句。

“我是那么做了。”邓布利多心平气和地说，“我把我所知道的一切都告诉了你。从现在起，我们就要离开坚实的事实基础，共同穿越昏暗模糊的记忆沼泽，进入错综复杂的大胆猜测了。在这一点上，哈利，我可能会像汉弗莱·贝尔切一样犯下可悲的错误，他竟然相信可以用干酪做坩埚。”

“但你认为你是对的？”哈利说。

“我自然这样以为，但是，正如我已经向你证实的，我也像普通人一样会犯错误。事实上，由于我——请原谅——由于我比大多数人聪明得多，我的错误也就相应地更加严重。”

“先生，”哈利试探地说，“你要跟我说的事情，是不是跟那个预言有关？是不是为了帮助我……活下来？”

“跟那个预言很有关系。”邓布利多说，语气是那样随便，就好像哈利是在问他明天天气如何，“我当然希望它能帮助你活下来。”

邓布利多站起来，绕过桌子，从哈利旁边走过去。哈利在椅子上

turned eagerly in his seat to watch Dumbledore bending over the cabinet beside the door. When Dumbledore straightened up, he was holding a familiar shallow stone basin etched with odd markings around its rim. He placed the Pensieve on the desk in front of Harry.

'You look worried.'

Harry had indeed been eyeing the Pensieve with some apprehension. His previous experiences with the odd device that stored and revealed thoughts and memories, though highly instructive, had also been uncomfortable. The last time he had disturbed its contents, he had seen much more than he would have wished. But Dumbledore was smiling.

'This time, you enter the Pensieve with me … and, even more unusually, with permission.'

'Where are we going, sir?'

'For a trip down Bob Ogden's memory lane,' said Dumbledore, pulling from his pocket a crystal bottle containing a swirling silvery-white substance.

'Who was Bob Ogden?'

'He was employed by the Department of Magical Law Enforcement,' said Dumbledore. 'He died some time ago, but not before I had tracked him down and persuaded him to confide these recollections to me. We are about to accompany him on a visit he made in the course of his duties. If you will stand, Harry …'

But Dumbledore was having difficulty pulling out the stopper of the crystal bottle: his injured hand seemed stiff and painful.

'Shall – shall I, sir?'

'No matter, Harry –'

Dumbledore pointed his wand at the bottle and the cork flew out.

'Sir – how did you injure your hand?' Harry asked again, looking at the blackened fingers with a mixture of revulsion and pity.

'Now is not the moment for that story, Harry. Not yet. We have an appointment with Bob Ogden.'

Dumbledore tipped the silvery contents of the bottle into the Pensieve, where they swirled and shimmered, neither liquid nor gas.

'After you,' said Dumbledore, gesturing towards the bowl.

热切地转过身，注视着邓布利多在门旁的那个柜子前俯下身去。邓布利多直起腰时，手里端着一个哈利熟悉的浅底石盆，盆口刻着一圈古怪的符箓。他把冥想盆放在哈利面前的桌上。

“你看上去很担心。”

确实，哈利是以担忧害怕的目光打量冥想盆的。对于这个储藏和展现思想和记忆的古怪器物，他以前有过的几次经历虽然颇有启发性，但是都很不舒服。比如，他上次擅自闯进去时，看到了许多他不愿意看到的东西。不过，邓布利多脸上带着微笑。

“这一次，你跟我一起进入冥想盆……而且，更不同寻常的是，你是获得准许的。”

“我们去哪儿呢，先生？”

“到鲍勃·奥格登的记忆小路上走一走。”邓布利多说着从口袋里掏出一个水晶瓶，里面盛着一种旋转飘浮的银白色物质。

“鲍勃·奥格登是谁？”

“他当年在魔法法律执行司工作。”邓布利多说，“死了有一些日子了。不过在他死之前，我想方设法找到了他，说服他把这些记忆告诉了我。现在，我们要陪他一起到他执行任务时去过的一个地方。哈利，你站起来……”

可是邓布利多拔不出水晶瓶的木塞子：他那只受伤的手似乎很疼，不听使唤。

“我——我来好吗，先生？”

“没关系，哈利——”

邓布利多用魔杖指了指瓶子，塞子立刻跳了出来。

“先生——你的手是怎么受伤的？”哈利既嫌恶又同情地看着那些焦黑的手指，又问了一遍。

“现在不是说这件事的时候，哈利。还不到时候。我们跟鲍勃·奥格登有个约会呢。”

邓布利多把瓶子里的银色物质倒进了冥想盆，它们在盆里慢慢地旋转起来，发出淡淡的微光，既不像液体，也不像气体。

“你先进去。”邓布利多指了指冥想盆，说道。

Harry bent forwards, took a deep breath, and plunged his face into the silvery substance. He felt his feet leave the office floor; he was falling, falling, through whirling darkness and then, quite suddenly, he was blinking in dazzling sunlight. Before his eyes had adjusted, Dumbledore landed beside him.

They were standing in a country lane bordered by high, tangled hedgerows, beneath a summer sky as bright and blue as a forget-me-not. Some ten feet in front of them stood a short, plump man wearing enormously thick glasses that reduced his eyes to molelike specks. He was reading a wooden signpost that was sticking out of the brambles on the left-hand side of the road. Harry knew this must be Ogden; he was the only person in sight, and he was also wearing the strange assortment of clothes so often chosen by inexperienced wizards trying to look like Muggles: in this case, a frock-coat and spats over a striped one-piece bathing costume. Before Harry had time to do more than register his bizarre appearance, however, Ogden had set off at a brisk walk down the lane.

Dumbledore and Harry followed. As they passed the wooden sign, Harry looked up at its two arms. The one pointing back the way they had come read: *Great Hangleton, 5 miles*. The arm pointing after Ogden said: 'Little Hangleton, 1 mile'.

They walked a short way with nothing to see but the hedgerows, the wide blue sky overhead and the swishing, frock-coated figure ahead, then the lane curved to the left and fell away, sloping steeply down a hillside, so that they had a sudden, unexpected view of a whole valley laid out in front of them. Harry could see a village, undoubtedly Little Hangleton, nestled between two steep hills, its church and grave-yard clearly visible. Across the valley, set on the opposite hillside, was a handsome manor house surrounded by a wide expanse of velvety green lawn.

Ogden had broken into a reluctant trot due to the steep downward slope. Dumbledore lengthened his stride and Harry hurried to keep up. He thought Little Hangleton must be their final destination and wondered, as he had done on the night they had found Slughorn, why they had to approach it from such a distance. He soon discovered that he was mistaken in thinking that they were going to the village, however. The lane curved to the right, and when they rounded the corner, it was to see the very edge of Ogden's frock-coat vanishing through a gap in the hedge.

哈利往前探着身子，深深吸了一口气，一头扎进了银色的物质中。他感觉双脚离开了办公室的地面。他穿过不断旋转的黑暗，往下坠落，坠落，突然，强烈的阳光刺得他闭上了眼睛。没等他的眼睛适应过来，邓布利多在他旁边降落了。

他们站在一条乡间小路上，两边都是高高的、枝叶纠结的灌木树篱，头顶上是夏日的天空，像勿忘我花一样清澈、湛蓝。在他们前面大约十步远的地方，站着一个矮矮胖胖的男人，戴着一副镜片特别厚的眼镜，两只眼睛被缩成了两个小点，像鼹鼠的眼睛一样。他在阅读从小路左边的荆棘丛里伸出来的一根木头路标。哈利知道这一定就是奥格登了，因为四下里看不见别人，而且他跟那些想打扮成麻瓜模样却又经验不足的巫师一样，穿着一身古里古怪的衣服：一件带条纹的连体泳衣外面披了一件礼服大衣，脚上还套着鞋罩。哈利刚打量完他古怪的模样，奥格登就顺着小路快步走去。

邓布利多和哈利跟了上去。经过那根木头路标时，哈利抬头看了看它的两个指示箭头。指着他们来路的那个写着：大汉格顿，5 英里。指着奥格登所去方向的那个写着：小汉格顿，1 英里。

他们走了一会儿，周围看不见别的，只有两边高高的灌木树篱、头顶上湛蓝辽阔的夏日天空和前面那个穿着礼服大衣、沙沙行走的身影。接着，小路向左一拐，顺着山坡陡直而下，于是他们突然意外地发现一座山谷，一览无遗地呈现在面前。哈利看见了一个村庄，那无疑便是小汉格顿了，坐落在两座陡峭的山坡之间，教堂和墓地都清晰可见。山谷对面的山坡上，有一座非常气派的大宅子，周围是大片绿茵茵的草地。

下坡的路太陡，奥格登不由自主地小跑起来。邓布利多把步子迈得更大，哈利也加快脚步跟在后面。他以为小汉格顿肯定是他们最终的目的地，所以就像他们去找斯拉格霍恩的那天夜里一样，心里纳闷为什么要从这么远的距离走过去。很快他就发现自己弄错了，他们并不是要去那个村庄。小路往右一拐，等转过那个弯道，只见奥格登礼服大衣的衣摆一闪，他在篱笆的一个豁口处不见了。

Dumbledore and Harry followed him on to a narrow dirt track bordered by higher and wilder hedgerows than those they had left behind. The path was crooked, rocky and potholed, sloping downhill like the last one, and it seemed to be heading for a patch of dark trees a little below them. Sure enough, the track soon opened up at the copse, and Dumbledore and Harry came to a halt behind Ogden, who had stopped and drawn his wand.

Despite the cloudless sky, the old trees ahead cast deep, dark, cool shadows and it was a few seconds before Harry's eyes discerned the building half-hidden amongst the tangle of trunks. It seemed to him a very strange location to choose for a house, or else an odd decision to leave the trees growing nearby, blocking all light and the view of the valley below. He wondered whether it was inhabited; its walls were mossy and so many tiles had fallen off the roof that the rafters were visible in places. Nettles grew all around it, their tips reaching the windows, which were tiny and thick with grime. Just as he had concluded that nobody could possibly live there, however, one of the windows was thrown open with a clatter and a thin trickle of steam or smoke issued from it, as though somebody was cooking.

Ogden moved forwards quietly and, it seemed to Harry, rather cautiously. As the dark shadows of the trees slid over him, he stopped again, staring at the front door, to which somebody had nailed a dead snake.

Then there was a rustle and a crack and a man in rags dropped from the nearest tree, landing on his feet right in front of Ogden, who leapt backwards so fast that he stood on the tails of his frock-coat and stumbled.

'*You're not welcome.*'

The man standing before them had thick hair so matted with dirt it could have been any colour. Several of his teeth were missing. His eyes were small and dark and stared in opposite directions. He might have looked comical, but he did not; the effect was frightening, and Harry could not blame Ogden for backing away several more paces before he spoke.

'Er – good morning. I'm from the Ministry of Magic –'

'*You're not welcome.*'

'Er – I'm sorry – I don't understand you,' said Ogden nervously.

Harry thought Ogden was being extremely dim; the stranger was making himself very clear in Harry's opinion, particularly as he was brandishing a

邓布利多和哈利跟着他来到一条狭窄的土路上，两边的灌木树篱比刚才他们经过的那些更加高大茂密。土路弯弯曲曲，坑坑洼洼，布满乱石，像刚才那条小路一样陡直向下，似乎通向下面一小片漆黑的树林。果然，没走多远，土路就接上了那片矮树林，奥格登停下脚步，拔出魔杖，邓布利多和哈利也在他身后停了下来。

尽管天空晴朗无云，但前面那些古树投下了凉飕飕的黑暗浓密的阴影，过了几秒钟，哈利的眼睛才看见一座房子在盘根错节的树丛中半隐半现。他觉得挑这个地方造房子真有些奇怪，或者说，让那些大树长在房子旁边真是个古怪的决定，树木挡住了所有的光线，也挡住了下面的山谷。他不知道这地方是不是有人居住：墙上布满苔藓，房顶上的许多瓦片都掉了，这里那里露出了里面的椽木。房子周围长着茂密的荨麻，高高的一直齐到窗口，那些窗户非常小，积满了厚厚的陈年污垢。哈利正要断定这里不会有人住，突然，咔嗒一声，一扇窗户打开了，从里面冒出一股细细的蒸汽或青烟，似乎有人正在烧饭。

奥格登悄悄地向前走去，哈利觉得他的动作非常谨慎。黑乎乎的树影从他身上掠过，他又停下了脚步，两眼直直地望着房子的前门，什么人把一条死蛇钉在了门上。

就在这时，一阵沙沙声响起，紧接着又是咔嚓一声，一个穿着破衣烂衫的男人从近旁一棵树上跳了下来，恰好落在奥格登的面前。奥格登赶紧后退，结果踩在自己大衣的后摆上，差点儿摔倒。

“你不受欢迎。”

站在他们面前的这个男人，浓密的头发里缠结着厚厚的污垢，已经辨不出原来的颜色。他嘴里掉了几颗牙，一双黑溜溜的小眼睛瞪着两个相反的方向。他本来应该看上去挺滑稽，然而事实上不是这样。他的模样很吓人，哈利心想，难怪奥格登又往后退了几步才开口说话。

“呃——上午好。我是魔法部——”

“你不受欢迎。”

“呃——对不起——我听不懂你的话。”奥格登不安地说。

哈利认为奥格登真是迟钝到了极点。在哈利看来，陌生人已经把他的意思表达得很清楚了，特别是他一只手挥着魔杖，另一只手握着

wand in one hand and a short and rather bloody knife in the other.

'You understand him, I'm sure, Harry?' said Dumbledore quietly.

'Yes, of course,' said Harry, slightly nonplussed. 'Why can't Ogden –?'

But as his eyes found the dead snake on the door again, he suddenly understood.

'He's speaking Parseltongue?'

'Very good,' said Dumbledore, nodding and smiling.

The man in rags was now advancing on Ogden, knife in one hand, wand in the other.

'Now, look –' Ogden began, but too late: there was a bang, and Ogden was on the ground, clutching his nose, while a nasty yellowish goo squirted from between his fingers.

'Morfin!' said a loud voice.

An elderly man had come hurrying out of the cottage, banging the door behind him so that the dead snake swung pathetically. This man was shorter than the first, and oddly proportioned; his shoulders were very broad and his arms overlong, which, with his bright brown eyes, short scrubby hair and wrinkled face, gave him the look of a powerful, aged monkey. He came to a halt beside the man with the knife, who was now cackling with laughter at the sight of Ogden on the ground.

'Ministry, is it?' said the older man, looking down at Ogden.

'Correct!' said Ogden angrily, dabbing his face. 'And you, I take it, are Mr Gaunt?'

''S right,' said Gaunt. 'Got you in the face, did he?'

'Yes, he did!' snapped Ogden.

'Should've made your presence known, shouldn't you?' said Gaunt aggressively. 'This is private property. Can't just walk in here and not expect my son to defend himself.'

'Defend himself against what, man?' said Ogden, clambering back to his feet.

'Busybodies. Intruders. Muggles and filth.'

Ogden pointed his wand at his own nose, which was still issuing large amounts of what looked like yellow pus, and the flow stopped at once. Mr Gaunt spoke out of the corner of his mouth to Morfin.

一把看上去血淋淋的短刀。

“我想，你肯定能听得懂他的话吧，哈利？”邓布利多轻声问道。

“是啊，那还用说。”哈利有点不解地说，“为什么奥格登听不——”

接着，他的眼睛又看到门上的那条死蛇，他突然明白了。

“他说的是蛇佬腔？”

“很好。”邓布利多点点头，微笑着说。

这时，那个穿着破衣烂衫的人一手握刀，一手挥着魔杖，一步步朝奥格登逼近。

“喂，你别——”奥格登刚想说话，可已经迟了：砰的一声巨响，奥格登倒在地上，用手捂着鼻子，一股令人恶心的黄兮兮、黏糊糊的东西从他指缝间涌了出来。

“莫芬！”一个声音大喊道。

一位上了年纪的男人从木房子里匆匆跑了出来，重重地带上身后的门，那条死蛇可怜巴巴地左右摇摆着。这个男人比刚才那个略矮一些，身材怪模怪样的，长得不成比例：肩膀太宽，手臂过长，再加上一双亮晶晶的褐色眼睛、一头又短又硬的头发和一张皱巴巴的面孔，看上去活像一只凶猛的老猴子。他走过去站在那个拿刀的男人旁边，拿刀的男人看到奥格登倒在地上，开心得嘎嘎大笑起来。

“部里来的，嗯？”年长一些的男人低头看着奥格登，问道。

“正是！”奥格登一边擦着脸一边生气地说，“我想，你就是冈特先生吧？”

“没错。”冈特说，“他打中了你的脸，是吗？”

“是的！”奥格登没好气地说。

“你来这里应该先通知我们，是不是？”冈特盛气凌人地说，“这是私人领地。你这么大摇大摆地走进来，我儿子能不采取防卫行动吗？”

“他有什么要防卫的？”奥格登挣扎着爬起来，说道。

“爱管闲事的人。闯私宅的强盗。麻瓜和垃圾。”

奥格登的鼻子仍在大量流出黄脓状的东西，他用魔杖指了自己一下，它们立刻就止住了。冈特先生撇着嘴对莫芬说：

'Get in the house. Don't argue.'

This time, ready for it, Harry recognised Parseltongue; even while he could understand what was being said, he distinguished the weird hissing noise that was all Ogden could hear. Morfin seemed to be on the point of disagreeing, but when his father cast him a threatening look he changed his mind, lumbering away to the cottage with an odd rolling gait and slamming the front door behind him, so that the snake swung sadly again.

'It's your son I'm here to see, Mr Gaunt,' said Ogden, as he mopped the last of the pus from the front of his coat. 'That was Morfin, wasn't it?'

'Ar, that was Morfin,' said the old man indifferently. 'Are you pure-blood?' he asked, suddenly aggressive.

'That's neither here nor there,' said Ogden coldly, and Harry felt his respect for Ogden rise.

Apparently Gaunt felt rather differently. He squinted into Ogden's face and muttered, in what was clearly supposed to be an offensive tone, 'Now I come to think about it, I've seen noses like yours down in the village.'

'I don't doubt it, if your son's been let loose on them,' said Ogden. 'Perhaps we could continue this discussion inside?'

'Inside?'

'Yes, Mr Gaunt. I've already told you. I'm here about Morfin. We sent an owl –'

'I've no use for owls,' said Gaunt. 'I don't open letters.'

'Then you can hardly complain that you get no warning of visitors,' said Ogden tartly. 'I am here following a serious breach of wizarding law which occurred here in the early hours of this morning –'

'All right, all right, all right!' bellowed Gaunt. 'Come in the bleeding house, then, and much good it'll do you!'

The house seemed to contain three tiny rooms. Two doors led off the main room, which served as kitchen and living room combined. Morfin was sitting in a filthy armchair beside the smoking fire, twisting a live adder between his thick fingers and crooning softly at it in Parseltongue:

'Hissy hissy, little snakey,
Slither on the floor,

“进屋去。不许废话。”

这次哈利有了思想准备，听出了他的蛇佬腔。他听懂了话的意思，同时也分辨出奥格登所能听见的那种奇怪的咝咝声。莫芬似乎还想辩解几句，但他父亲朝他狠狠地瞪了一眼，他便改变了主意，迈着古怪的、摇摇晃晃的脚步，慢吞吞地朝木房子走去，进去后又重重地关上门，那条蛇再次可怜巴巴地摇摆起来。

“我来是想见见你的儿子，冈特先生，”奥格登说，一边擦去衣襟上的最后一点黄脓，“刚才那就是莫芬吧？”

“啊，那就是莫芬。”老人漫不经心地说，“你是纯血统吗？”他问，态度突然变得咄咄逼人。

“这与今天的谈话无关。”奥格登冷冷地说，哈利顿时对他肃然起敬。

但冈特显然不以为然。他眯起眼睛盯着奥格登的脸，用一种显然是故意冒犯的口吻嘟囔道：“现在我仔细想想，确实在村子里见过你这样的鼻子。”

“对此我毫不怀疑，因为你儿子这样随意地攻击别人。”奥格登说，“也许我们可以进屋去谈？”

“进屋？”

“是的，冈特先生。我已经告诉过你。我是为了莫芬的事来的。我们派了一只猫头鹰——”

“猫头鹰对我没有用。”冈特说，“我从来不看信。”

“那你就不能抱怨说不知道有人要来了。”奥格登尖刻地说，“我来这里，是为了处理今天凌晨这里发生的一件严重违反巫师法律的事情——”

“好吧，好吧，好吧！”冈特吼道，“就到该死的房子里去吧，那样你会舒服得多！”

这座房子似乎共有三间小屋，中间的大屋兼作厨房和客厅，另有两扇门通向别的屋子。莫芬坐在黑烟滚滚的火炉旁的一把肮脏的扶手椅上，粗大的手指间摆弄着一条活的小毒蛇，嘴里轻轻地用蛇佬腔哼唱着：

咝咝，咝咝，蛇宝宝，
快快在地上爬过来，

You be good to Morfin
Or he'll nail you to the door.'

There was a scuffling noise in the corner beside the open window and Harry realised that there was somebody else in the room, a girl whose ragged grey dress was the exact colour of the dirty stone wall behind her. She was standing beside a steaming pot on a grimy black stove, and was fiddling around with the shelf of squalid-looking pots and pans above it. Her hair was lank and dull and she had a plain, pale, rather heavy face. Her eyes, like her brother's, stared in opposite directions. She looked a little cleaner than the two men, but Harry thought he had never seen a more defeated-looking person.

'M'daughter, Merope,' said Gaunt grudgingly, as Ogden looked enquiringly towards her.

'Good morning,' said Ogden.

She did not answer, but with a frightened glance at her father turned her back on the room and continued shifting the pots on the shelf behind her.

'Well, Mr Gaunt,' said Ogden, 'to get straight to the point, we have reason to believe that your son Morfin performed magic in front of a Muggle late last night.'

There was a deafening *clang*. Merope had dropped one of the pots.

'*Pick it up!*' Gaunt bellowed at her. 'That's it, grub on the floor like some filthy Muggle, what's your wand for, you useless sack of muck?'

'Mr Gaunt, please!' said Ogden in a shocked voice, as Merope, who had already picked up the pot, flushed blotchily scarlet, lost her grip on the pot again, drew her wand shakily from her pocket, pointed it at the pot and muttered a hasty, inaudible spell that caused the pot to shoot across the floor away from her, hit the opposite wall and crack in two.

Morfin let out a mad cackle of laughter. Gaunt screamed, 'Mend it, you pointless lump, mend it!'

Merope stumbled across the room, but before she had time to raise her wand, Ogden had lifted his own and said firmly, '*Reparo*.' The pot mended itself instantly.

你要对莫芬特别好，
不然就把你钉在大门外。

那扇敞开的窗户旁的墙角里传来慢吞吞的脚步声，哈利这才发现屋里还有另一个人，是一个姑娘，身上穿的那件破破烂烂的灰色衣裙简直跟她身后肮脏的石墙一个颜色。她站在积满烟灰的炉子上一口冒着热气的炖锅旁，正在炉子上方搁架上的一堆肮脏的盆盆罐罐里寻找什么。她平直的头发毫无光泽，脸色苍白，相貌平平，神情显得很愁闷。她的眼睛和她哥哥的一样，朝两个相反的方向瞪着。她看上去比那两个男人干净一些，但哈利觉得从没见过比她更没精打采的人。

“我女儿，梅洛普。”冈特看见奥格登询问地望着那姑娘，便满不情愿地介绍道。

“上午好。”奥格登说。

姑娘没有回答，惊慌地看了父亲一眼，就赶紧背转身，继续摆弄搁架上的那些盆盆罐罐。

“好吧，冈特先生，”奥格登说，“我们开门见山地说吧，我们有理由相信你的儿子莫芬昨天深夜在一个麻瓜面前施了魔法。”

咣当一声，震耳欲聋。梅洛普把一只罐子碰掉在地上。

“捡起来！”冈特朝她吼道，“怎么，像一个肮脏的麻瓜那样趴到地上去找？你的魔杖是干什么用的，你这个废物草包？”

“冈特先生，请不要这样！”奥格登用惊愕的口气说，这时梅洛普已经把罐子捡了起来，可突然之间，她的脸涨得红一块白一块的。她手一松，罐子又掉在了地上。她战战兢兢地从口袋里掏出魔杖，指着罐子，慌里慌张地轻声念了一句什么咒语，罐子噌地从她脚下贴着地面飞了出去，撞在对面的墙上，裂成了两半。

莫芬发出一阵疯狂的嘎嘎大笑。冈特尖声大叫起来：“修好它，你这个没用的傻大个儿，修好它！”

梅洛普跌跌撞撞地走到屋子那头，但没等她举起魔杖，奥格登已经用自己的魔杖指了过去，沉着地说了一句：“恢复如初！”罐子立刻自动修好了。

Gaunt looked for a moment as though he was going to shout at Ogden, but seemed to think better of it: instead he jeered at his daughter, 'Lucky the nice man from the Ministry's here, isn't it? Perhaps he'll take you off my hands, perhaps he doesn't mind dirty Squibs …'

Without looking at anybody or thanking Ogden, Merope picked up the pot and returned it, hands trembling, to its shelf. She then stood quite still, her back against the wall between the filthy window and the stove, as though she wished for nothing more than to sink into the stone and vanish.

'Mr Gaunt,' Ogden began again, 'as I've said: the reason for my visit –'

'I heard you the first time!' snapped Gaunt. 'And so what? Morfin gave a Muggle a bit of what was coming to him – what about it, then?'

'Morfin has broken wizarding law,' said Ogden sternly.

'*Morfin has broken wizarding law.*' Gaunt imitated Ogden's voice, making it pompous and singsong. Morfin cackled again. 'He taught a filthy Muggle a lesson, that's illegal now, is it?'

'Yes,' said Ogden. 'I'm afraid it is.'

He pulled from an inside pocket a small scroll of parchment and unrolled it.

'What's that, then, his sentence?' said Gaunt, his voice rising angrily.

'It is a summons to the Ministry for a hearing –'

'Summons! *Summons*? Who do you think you are, summoning my son anywhere?'

'I'm Head of the Magical Law Enforcement Squad,' said Ogden.

'And you think we're scum, do you?' screamed Gaunt, advancing on Ogden now, with a dirty yellow-nailed finger pointing at his chest. 'Scum who'll come running when the Ministry tells 'em to? Do you know who you're talking to, you filthy little Mudblood, do you?'

'I was under the impression that I was speaking to Mr Gaunt,' said Ogden, looking wary, but standing his ground.

'That's right!' roared Gaunt. For a moment, Harry thought Gaunt was making an obscene hand gesture, but then realised that he was showing Ogden the ugly, black-stoned ring he was wearing on his middle finger, waving it before Ogden's eyes. 'See this? See this? Know what it is? Know where it came from? Centuries it's been in our family, that's how far back we

有那么一会儿，冈特似乎想冲奥格登嚷嚷一通，但又似乎改变了主意。他讥笑着对女儿说："幸好有魔法部的这位大好人在这儿，是不是？说不定他会把你从我手里弄走，说不定他不讨厌龌龊的哑炮……"

梅洛普对谁也没看一眼，也没对奥格登道声感谢，只是捡起罐子，用颤抖的双手把它重新放到搁板上。然后，她一动不动地站在那里，后背贴在肮脏的窗户和炉子之间的墙壁上，似乎一心只希望自己能陷进石墙里，彻底消失。

"冈特先生，"奥格登先生又开口道，"正如我刚才说的，我此行的原因是——"

"我第一次就听明白了！"冈特怒气冲冲地说，"那又怎么样？莫芬随手教训了一个麻瓜——那又怎么样呢？"

"莫芬违反了巫师法。"奥格登严肃地说。

"莫芬违反了巫师法。"冈特模仿着奥格登的声音，并故意拖腔拖调，透着一股子傲慢。莫芬又嘎嘎大笑起来。"他给了一个肮脏的麻瓜一点颜色瞧瞧，怎么，如今这也算非法的了？"

"对，"奥格登说，"恐怕是这样。"

他从大衣内侧的口袋里掏出一小卷羊皮纸，展了开来。

"这是什么，给他的判决？"冈特气愤地提高了嗓门。

"传唤他到魔法部接受审讯——"

"传唤！传唤？你以为你是谁呀，竟敢传唤我的儿子？"

"我是魔法法律执行队的队长。"奥格登说。

"你以为我们是下三烂吗？"冈特尖叫着说，一边逼近奥格登，一边用指甲发黄的脏手指戳着他的胸口，"魔法部一声召唤，我们就得颠儿颠儿地跑去？你知道你在跟谁说话吗，你这个龌龊的小泥巴种，嗯？"

"我记得我好像是在跟冈特先生说话。"奥格登显得很警惕，但毫不退缩。

"没错！"冈特吼道。哈利一时以为冈特是在做一个下流的手势，接着才发现，冈特是在给奥格登看他中指上戴的那枚丑陋的黑宝石戒指。他把戒指在奥格登面前晃来晃去。"看见这个了吗？看见这个了吗？知道这是什么吗？知道这是从哪儿来的吗？它在我们家传了好几个世

go, and pure-blood all the way! Know how much I've been offered for this, with the Peverell coat of arms engraved on the stone?'

'I've really no idea,' said Ogden, blinking as the ring sailed within an inch of his nose, 'and it's quite beside the point, Mr Gaunt. Your son has committed –'

With a howl of rage, Gaunt ran towards his daughter. For a split second, Harry thought he was going to throttle her as his hand flew to her throat; next moment, he was dragging her towards Ogden by a gold chain around her neck.

'See this?' he bellowed at Ogden, shaking a heavy gold locket at him, while Merope spluttered and gasped for breath.

'I see it, I see it!' said Ogden hastily.

'*Slytherin's!* ' yelled Gaunt. 'Salazar Slytherin's! We're his last living descendants, what do you say to that, eh?'

'Mr Gaunt, your daughter!' said Ogden in alarm, but Gaunt had already released Merope; she staggered away from him, back to her corner, massaging her neck and gulping for air.

'So!' said Gaunt triumphantly, as though he had just proved a complicated point beyond all possible dispute. 'Don't you go talking to us as if we're dirt on your shoes! Generations of pure-bloods, wizards all – more than *you* can say, I don't doubt!'

And he spat on the floor at Ogden's feet. Morfin cackled again. Merope, huddled beside the window, her head bowed and her face hidden by her lank hair, said nothing.

'Mr Gaunt,' said Ogden doggedly, 'I am afraid that neither your ancestors nor mine have anything to do with the matter in hand. I am here because of Morfin, Morfin and the Muggle he accosted late last night. Our information,' he glanced down at his scroll of parchment, 'is that Morfin performed a jinx or hex on the said Muggle, causing him to erupt in highly painful hives.'

Morfin giggled.

'*Be quiet, boy,*' snarled Gaunt in Parseltongue, and Morfin fell silent again.

'And so what if he did, then?' Gaunt said defiantly to Ogden. 'I expect you've wiped the Muggle's filthy face clean for him, and his memory to boot –'

纪了，我们家族的历史就有这么久，而且一直是纯血统！知道有人想出多大的价钱把它从我手里买走吗？宝石上刻着佩弗利尔的饰章呢！”

“我确实不知道，”奥格登说，那戒指在他鼻子前一英寸的地方晃过，他眨了眨眼睛，“而且它跟这件事没有关系，冈特先生。你儿子犯了——”

冈特愤怒地大吼一声，冲向他的女儿，一只手直伸向女儿的喉咙。一时间，哈利还以为他要把女儿掐死。接着，冈特拽着女儿脖子上的一条金链子，把她拉到了奥格登面前。

“看见这个了吗？”他朝奥格登咆哮道，一边冲他摇晃着金链子上的一个沉甸甸的金挂坠盒，梅洛普憋得连连咳嗽，连气都喘不过来了。

“我看见了，我看见了！”奥格登急忙说。

“斯莱特林的！”冈特嚷道，“萨拉查·斯莱特林的！我们是他最后一支活着的传人，对此你有什么话说，嗯？”

“冈特先生，你的女儿！”奥格登惊慌地说，但冈特已经把梅洛普放开了。梅洛普跌跌撞撞地离开了他，回到原来那个角落里，一边揉着脖子，一边使劲地喘着气。

“怎么样！”冈特得意地说，似乎他刚把一个复杂的问题证明得清清楚楚，不会再有任何争议，“所以别用那副口气跟我们说话，别把我们当成你鞋底上的泥巴！我们祖祖辈辈都是纯血统，都是巫师——我相信，你没有这些可炫耀吧！”

他朝奥格登脚下吐了一口唾沫，莫芬又嘎嘎大笑起来。梅洛普蜷缩在窗户边，垂着脑袋，一声不吭，直直的头发遮住了她的面庞。

“冈特先生，”奥格登固执地说，“恐怕无论你我的祖先都跟眼下这件事情毫无关系。我到这里来是为了莫芬，还有昨天深夜他招惹的那个麻瓜。我们得到情报，”他低头看了看那卷羊皮纸，“说莫芬对那个麻瓜念了一个恶咒，或施了一个魔法，使他全身长出了剧痛无比的荨麻疹。”

莫芬咯咯地笑了。

“闭嘴，小子！”冈特用蛇佬腔喝道，莫芬立刻不吭声了。

“就算他这么做了，那又怎么样？”冈特挑衅地对奥格登说，“我想，你们一定替那个麻瓜把肮脏的脸擦干净了，还把他的记忆——”

'That's hardly the point, is it, Mr Gaunt?' said Ogden. 'This was an unprovoked attack on a defenceless –'

'Ar, I had you marked out as a Muggle-lover the moment I saw you,' sneered Gaunt and he spat on the floor again.

'This discussion is getting us nowhere,' said Ogden firmly. 'It is clear from your son's attitude that he feels no remorse for his actions.' He glanced down at his scroll of parchment again. 'Morfin will attend a hearing on the fourteenth of September to answer the charges of using magic in front of a Muggle and causing harm and distress to that same Mugg–'

Ogden broke off. The jingling, clopping sounds of horses and loud, laughing voices were drifting in through the open window. Apparently the winding lane to the village passed very close to the copse where the house stood. Gaunt froze, listening, his eyes wide. Morfin hissed and turned his face towards the sounds, his expression hungry. Merope raised her head. Her face, Harry saw, was starkly white.

'My God, what an eyesore!' rang out a girl's voice, as clearly audible through the open window as if she had stood in the room beside them. 'Couldn't your father have that hovel cleared away, Tom?'

'It's not ours,' said a young man's voice. 'Everything on the other side of the valley belongs to us, but that cottage belongs to an old tramp called Gaunt and his children. The son's quite mad, you should hear some of the stories they tell in the village –'

The girl laughed. The jingling, clopping noises were growing louder and louder. Morfin made to get out of his armchair.

'*Keep your seat,*' said his father warningly, in Parseltongue.

'Tom,' said the girl's voice again, now so close they were clearly right beside the house, 'I might be wrong – but has somebody nailed a snake to that door?'

'Good Lord, you're right!' said the man's voice. 'That'll be the son, I told you he's not right in the head. Don't look at it, Cecilia, darling.'

The jingling and clopping sounds were now growing fainter again.

'"*Darling*",' whispered Morfin in Parseltongue, looking at his sister. '"*Darling*", *he called her. So he wouldn't have you anyway.*'

“问题不在这里，对吗，冈特先生？”奥格登说，“这是一起无缘无故袭击一个毫无防御能力的——”

“哈，刚才我一看见你，就知道你是一个喜欢麻瓜的人。”冈特讥笑着说，又往地上吐了一口唾沫。

“这种谈话不会有任何结果。”奥格登义正词严地说，“从你儿子的态度来看，他显然对他的所作所为没有一丝懊悔。”他又扫了一眼那卷羊皮纸，“莫芬将于九月十四日接受审讯，对他在一位麻瓜面前使用魔法、并给那位麻瓜造成伤害和痛苦的指控做出答辩——”

奥格登突然停住了。丁零的铃铛声、嘚嘚的马蹄声，还有响亮的说笑声，从敞开的窗户外面飘了进来。显然，通向村庄的那条羊肠小道离这座房子所在的矮树林非常近。冈特愣住了，他侧耳倾听，眼睛瞪得大大的。莫芬的嘴里咝咝作响，他转眼望着声音传来的地方，一脸贪婪的表情。梅洛普抬起头。哈利看到她的脸色白得吓人。

“天哪，多么煞风景的东西！”一个姑娘清脆的声音从敞开的窗口飘了进来，他们听得清清楚楚，好像她就站在屋子里，站在他们身边似的，“汤姆，你父亲就不能把那间小破棚子拆掉吗？”

“那不是我们的。”一个年轻人的声音说道，“山谷另一边的东西都属于我们家，但那座小木屋属于一个名叫冈特的老流浪汉和他的孩子们。那儿子疯疯癫癫的，你真该听听村里人是怎么议论他的——”

姑娘笑了起来。丁零的铃铛声、嘚嘚的马蹄声越来越响。莫芬想从扶手椅上跳起来。

“坐好了别动！”他父亲用蛇佬腔警告他。

“汤姆，”姑娘的声音又响了起来，现在离得更近了，显然他们就在房子旁边，“我不会看错吧——难道有人在那扇门上钉了一条蛇？”

“天啊，你没有看错！”那个男人的声音说，“肯定是那儿子干的，我对你说过他脑子不大正常。别看它了，塞西利娅，亲爱的。”

丁零的铃铛声、嘚嘚的马蹄声又渐渐地远去了。

“‘亲爱的’，”莫芬望着他妹妹，用蛇佬腔小声说道，“他管她叫‘亲爱的’，看来他是不会要你了。”

Merope was so white Harry felt sure she was going to faint.

'*What's that?*' said Gaunt sharply, also in Parseltongue, looking from his son to his daughter. '*What did you say, Morfin?*'

'*She likes looking at that Muggle,*' said Morfin, a vicious expression on his face as he stared at his sister, who now looked terrified. '*Always in the garden when he passes, peering through the hedge at him, isn't she? And last night –*'

Merope shook her head jerkily, imploringly, but Morfin went on ruthlessly, '*Hanging out of the window waiting for him to ride home, wasn't she?*'

'*Hanging out of the window to look at a Muggle?*' said Gaunt quietly.

All three of the Gaunts seemed to have forgotten Ogden, who was looking both bewildered and irritated at this renewed outbreak of incomprehensible hissing and rasping.

'*Is it true?*' said Gaunt in a deadly voice, advancing a step or two towards the terrified girl. '*My daughter – pure-blooded descendant of Salazar Slytherin – hankering after a filthy, dirt-veined Muggle?*'

Merope shook her head frantically, pressing herself into the wall, apparently unable to speak.

'*But I got him, Father!*' cackled Morfin. '*I got him as he went by, and he didn't look so pretty with hives all over him, did he, Merope?*'

'*You disgusting little Squib, you filthy little blood traitor!*' roared Gaunt, losing control, and his hands closed around his daughter's throat.

Both Harry and Ogden yelled 'No!' at the same time; Ogden raised his wand and cried, '*Relashio!*' Gaunt was thrown backwards, away from his daughter; he tripped over a chair and fell flat on his back. With a roar of rage, Morfin leapt out of his chair and ran at Ogden, brandishing his bloody knife and firing hexes indiscriminately from his wand.

Ogden ran for his life. Dumbledore indicated that they ought to follow and Harry obeyed, Merope's screams echoing in his ears.

Ogden hurtled up the path and erupted on to the main lane, his arms over his head, where he collided with the glossy chestnut horse ridden by a very handsome, dark-haired young man. Both he and the pretty girl riding beside him on a grey horse roared with laughter at the sight of Ogden, who

梅洛普脸色煞白，哈利觉得她肯定要晕倒了。

“怎么回事？”冈特厉声问道，用的也是蛇佬腔，眼睛看看儿子，又看看女儿，“你说什么，莫芬？”

“她喜欢看那个麻瓜，”莫芬说着盯住妹妹，脸上露出恶毒的表情，梅洛普则显得非常惊恐，“每次那个麻瓜经过，她都在花园里隔着篱笆看他，是不是？昨天夜里——”

梅洛普哀求地使劲摇头，但是莫芬毫不留情地说了下去：“她在窗户外面徘徊，等着看那麻瓜骑马回家，是不是？”

“在窗户外面徘徊，等着看一个麻瓜？”冈特小声问。

冈特家的三个人似乎都忘记了奥格登的存在。奥格登面对这新一轮爆发的刺耳而不可理解的咝咝声，显得既迷惑又恼怒。

“这是真的吗？”冈特用阴沉沉的声音问，一边朝那个惊恐万状的姑娘逼近了一两步，“我的女儿——萨拉查·斯莱特林纯血统的后裔——竟然追求一个肮脏的下三烂的麻瓜？”

梅洛普疯狂地摇着头，拼命把身体挤缩在墙角，显然一句话也说不出来。

“可是我教训了那家伙，爸爸！”莫芬嘎嘎地笑着说，“他走过时，我教训了他，他满头满脸的荨麻疹，看上去就没那么漂亮了，是不是，梅洛普？”

“你这个可恶的小哑炮，你这个龌龊的小败类！”冈特吼道，他失去了控制，两只手扼住了女儿的喉咙。

“不！”哈利和奥格登同时叫道。奥格登举起魔杖，喊了一句：“力松劲泄！”冈特被击得连连后退，丢下了女儿。他被椅子绊了一下，仰面摔倒在地。莫芬怒吼一声，从椅子上一跃而起，冲向奥格登，一边挥舞着那把血淋淋的刀子，并从魔杖里射出一大堆乱七八糟的恶咒。

奥格登夺路而逃。邓布利多示意他们也跟上去。哈利跟了出去，梅洛普的尖叫声还在他耳畔回响。

奥格登用手臂护着脑袋，冲上土路，又飞快地拐上主路，撞上了那匹油亮亮的枣红马。骑马的是一位非常英俊的黑头发年轻人，他和身边那位骑一匹灰马的漂亮姑娘看到奥格登的模样，被逗得开怀大笑。

bounced off the horse's flank and set off again, his frock-coat flying, covered from head to foot in dust, running pell-mell up the lane.

'I think that will do, Harry,' said Dumbledore. He took Harry by the elbow and tugged. Next moment, they were both soaring weightlessly through darkness, until they landed squarely on their feet, back in Dumbledore's now twilit office.

'What happened to the girl in the cottage?' said Harry at once, as Dumbledore lit extra lamps with a flick of his wand. 'Merope, or whatever her name was?'

'Oh, she survived,' said Dumbledore, reseating himself behind his desk and indicating that Harry should sit down too. 'Ogden Apparated back to the Ministry and returned with reinforcements within fifteen minutes. Morfin and his father attempted to fight, but both were over-powered, removed from the cottage and subsequently convicted by the Wizengamot. Morfin, who already had a record of Muggle attacks, was sentenced to three years in Azkaban. Marvolo, who had injured several Ministry employees in addition to Ogden, received six months.'

'Marvolo?' Harry repeated wonderingly.

'That's right,' said Dumbledore, smiling in approval. 'I am glad to see you're keeping up.'

'That old man was –?'

'Voldemort's grandfather, yes,' said Dumbledore. 'Marvolo, his son Morfin and his daughter Merope were the last of the Gaunts, a very ancient wizarding family noted for a vein of instability and violence that flourished through the generations due to their habit of marrying their own cousins. Lack of sense coupled with a great liking for grandeur meant that the family gold was squandered several generations before Marvolo was born. He, as you saw, was left in squalor and poverty, with a very nasty temper, a fantastic amount of arrogance and pride, and a couple of family heirlooms that he treasured just as much as his son, and rather more than his daughter.'

'So Merope,' said Harry, leaning forwards in his chair and staring at Dumbledore, 'so Merope was … sir, does that mean she was … *Voldemort's mother?*'

'It does,' said Dumbledore. 'And it so happens that we also had a glimpse of Voldemort's father. I wonder whether you noticed?'

奥格登从枣红马的身上弹了出去，立刻撒腿又跑，顺着小路落荒而逃，他从头到脚都沾满了灰尘，礼服大衣在他身后飘摆着。

“我认为差不多了，哈利。”邓布利多说。他握住哈利的胳膊肘，轻轻一拽。转眼间，他们俩就失重般地在黑暗中越飞越高，最后稳稳地落回到邓布利多的办公室里，这时窗外已经是一片夜色。

“小木屋里的那个姑娘怎么样了？”哈利立刻问道，邓布利多一挥魔杖，又点亮了几盏灯，“就是那个叫梅洛普什么的。”

“噢，她活下来了。”邓布利多说着在桌子后面重新坐定，并示意哈利也坐下来，“奥格登幻影显形到了部里，不到十五分钟后就带着增援回去了。莫芬和他父亲负隅顽抗，但两人都被制服了，被押出了小木屋，后来威森加摩判了他们的罪。莫芬已经有过攻击麻瓜的前科，被判在阿兹卡班服刑三年。马沃罗除了伤害奥格登之外，还伤害了魔法部的另外几名官员，被判六个月有期徒刑。”

“马沃罗？”哈利疑惑地重复道。

“对，”邓布利多说，露出了赞许的微笑，“我很高兴你跟上了我的思路。”

“那个老人就是——？”

“伏地魔的外祖父，是的。”邓布利多说，“马沃罗、他儿子莫芬、女儿梅洛普是冈特家族最后的传人，那是一个非常古老的巫师家族，以不安分和暴力出名，由于他们习惯于近亲结婚，这种性格特点一代比一代更显著。他们缺乏理性，再加上特别喜欢豪华的排场，所以，早在马沃罗之前的好几辈，家族的财产就被挥霍殆尽。你刚才也看到了，马沃罗最后落得穷困潦倒，脾气坏得吓人，却又狂傲、自负得不可理喻，他手里还有两样祖传的遗物，他把它们看得像他儿子一样珍贵，看得比他女儿珍贵得多。”

“那么，梅洛普，”哈利在椅子上探身向前，盯着邓布利多说道，“梅洛普就是……先生，这是不是意味着，她就是……伏地魔的母亲？”

“没错，”邓布利多说，“我们碰巧还看了一眼伏地魔的父亲。不知道你有没有注意？”

'The Muggle Morfin attacked? The man on the horse?'

'Very good indeed,' said Dumbledore, beaming. 'Yes, that was Tom Riddle Senior, the handsome Muggle who used to go riding past the Gaunt cottage and for whom Merope Gaunt cherished a secret, burning passion.'

'And they ended up married?' Harry said in disbelief, unable to imagine two people less likely to fall in love.

'I think you are forgetting,' said Dumbledore, 'that Merope was a witch. I do not believe that her magical powers appeared to their best advantage when she was being terrorised by her father. Once Marvolo and Morfin were safely in Azkaban, once she was alone and free for the first time in her life, then, I am sure, she was able to give full rein to her abilities and to plot her escape from the desperate life she had led for eighteen years.

'Can you not think of any measure Merope could have taken to make Tom Riddle forget his Muggle companion, and fall in love with her instead?'

'The Imperius Curse?' Harry suggested. 'Or a love potion?'

'Very good. Personally, I am inclined to think that she used a love potion. I am sure it would have seemed more romantic to her and I do not think it would have been very difficult, some hot day, when Riddle was riding alone, to persuade him to take a drink of water. In any case, within a few months of the scene we have just witnessed, the village of Little Hangleton enjoyed a tremendous scandal. You can imagine the gossip it caused when the squire's son ran off with the tramp's daughter Merope.

'But the villagers' shock was nothing to Marvolo's. He returned from Azkaban, expecting to find his daughter dutifully awaiting his return with a hot meal ready on his table. Instead, he found a clear inch of dust and her note of farewell, explaining what she had done.

'From all that I have been able to discover, he never mentioned her name or existence from that time forth. The shock of her desertion may have contributed to his early death – or perhaps he had simply never learned to feed himself. Azkaban had greatly weakened Marvolo and he did not live to see Morfin return to the cottage.'

'And Merope? She … she died, didn't she? Wasn't Voldemort brought up in an orphanage?'

“就是莫芬袭击的那个麻瓜？那个骑马的男人？”

“非常正确。”邓布利多笑眯眯地说，“是啊，那就是老汤姆·里德尔，一位相貌英俊的麻瓜，常常骑马经过冈特家的小木屋，梅洛普·冈特痴痴地暗恋着他。”

“他们后来真的结婚了？”哈利不敢相信地问，他想不出有谁比这两人更不可能相爱。

“我认为你大概忘记了，”邓布利多说，“梅洛普是个女巫。我想，当她在父亲的高压恐怖统治下时，她的魔法力量似乎不能完全发挥出来。一旦马沃罗和莫芬都被关进了阿兹卡班，一旦她第一次独自一人，可以随心所欲时，我相信她就可以充分施展她的才能，策划逃离她过了十八年的那种水深火热的生活了。

“你能不能设想一下，梅洛普会采取什么措施，让汤姆·里德尔忘记他那位麻瓜情侣而爱上她呢？”

“夺魂咒？”哈利猜测道，“或者迷情剂？”

“很好。我个人倾向于她使用了迷情剂。我相信她会觉得那样更加浪漫，而且操作起来也不太困难。某个炎热的日子，里德尔独自骑马过来，梅洛普劝他喝了一杯水。总之，在我们刚才目睹的那一幕的几个月后，小汉格顿村爆出了一个惊人的丑闻。你可以想象，当人们听说了乡绅的儿子跟流浪汉的女儿梅洛普一起私奔的消息，会怎样议论纷纷啊。

“可是跟马沃罗感到的震惊相比，村民们的惊讶就不算什么了。马沃罗从阿兹卡班回来时，本以为会看到女儿乖乖地等着他，桌上摆着热气腾腾的饭菜。他没想到屋里的灰尘积了一寸多厚，女儿留了一张诀别的纸条，上面写了她所干的事情。

“从我所能发掘的情况来看，从那以后，他再也没有提起女儿的名字，或谈到过女儿的存在。女儿弃家出走给他带来的震惊，大概是他过早去世的一个原因——或者，他大概一直没有学会怎么弄饭给自己吃。阿兹卡班搞垮了马沃罗的身体，他没有活着看到莫芬回到那座小木屋。”

“那么梅洛普呢？她……她死了，是不是？伏地魔不是在孤儿院长大的吗？”

'Yes, indeed,' said Dumbledore. 'We must do a certain amount of guessing here, although I do not think it is difficult to deduce what happened. You see, within a few months of their runaway marriage, Tom Riddle reappeared at the manor house in Little Hangleton without his wife. The rumour flew around the neighbourhood that he was talking of being "hoodwinked" and "taken in". What he meant, I am sure, is that he had been under an enchantment that had now lifted, though I daresay he did not dare use those precise words for fear of being thought insane. When they heard what he was saying, however, the villagers guessed that Merope had lied to Tom Riddle, pretending that she was going to have his baby, and that he had married her for this reason.'

'But she *did* have his baby.'

'Yes, but not until a year after they were married. Tom Riddle left her while she was still pregnant.'

'What went wrong?' asked Harry. 'Why did the love potion stop working?'

'Again, this is guesswork,' said Dumbledore, 'but I believe that Merope, who was deeply in love with her husband, could not bear to continue enslaving him by magical means. I believe that she made the choice to stop giving him the potion. Perhaps, besotted as she was, she had convinced herself that he would by now have fallen in love with her in return. Perhaps she thought he would stay for the baby's sake. If so, she was wrong on both counts. He left her, never saw her again, and never troubled to discover what became of his son.'

The sky outside was inky black and the lamps in Dumbledore's office seemed to glow more brightly than before.

'I think that will do for tonight, Harry,' said Dumbledore after a moment or two.

'Yes, sir,' said Harry.

He got to his feet, but did not leave.

'Sir … is it important to know all this about Voldemort's past?'

'Very important, I think,' said Dumbledore.

'And it … it's got something to do with the prophecy?'

'It has everything to do with the prophecy.'

'Right,' said Harry, a little confused, but reassured all the same.

He turned to go, then another question occurred to him, and he turned back again.

“是啊，没错，”邓布利多说，“这里我们必须做一些猜测，不过我认为后来发生的事情不难推断。是这样，他们私奔结婚几个月之后，汤姆·里德尔又回到了小汉格顿的大宅子里，但身边并没有带着他的妻子。邻居们纷纷传言，说他一口咬定自己是被‘欺骗’和被‘蒙蔽’了。我想，他的意思一定是说他中了魔法，现在魔法已经解除，但我相信他肯定不敢使用这样的字眼，以免别人把他看成疯子。不过，村民们听了他的话，都猜想是梅洛普对汤姆·里德尔撒了谎，假装说她肚里怀了他的孩子，逼得他只好娶了她。”

“可是她确实生了他的孩子呀。”

“是啊，但那是他们结婚一年之后了。汤姆·里德尔离开她时，她正怀着身孕。”

“出什么事了？”哈利问道，“为什么迷情剂不管用了？”

“这又只能靠猜测了。”邓布利多说，“我认为，梅洛普深深地爱着她的丈夫，不能忍受继续靠魔法手段把他控制在手心里。我想，她做出了一个决定，不再给他服用迷情剂。也许她是由于爱得太痴迷，便相信丈夫也会反过来爱上她。也许她以为丈夫会为了孩子的缘故留下来。如果真是这样，她的这两个打算都落空了。汤姆·里德尔离开了她，从此再也没有见过她，也没有费心去打听他的儿子的下落。”

外面的天空已经墨黑墨黑，邓布利多办公室的灯光似乎比以前更亮了。

“哈利，我看今天晚上就到这儿吧。”片刻之后邓布利多说道。

“好的，先生。”哈利说。

他站了起来，但没有马上离开。

“先生……了解伏地魔过去的这些事情很重要吗？”

“我认为非常重要。”邓布利多说。

“那么……它跟那个预言有关系吗？”

“跟那个预言很有关系。”

“好的。”哈利说，虽然还有些困惑，但心中的疑虑被打消了。

他转身准备离去，突然又想起了另一个问题，便又转回身。

'Sir, am I allowed to tell Ron and Hermione everything you've told me?'

Dumbledore considered him for a moment, then said, 'Yes, I think Mr Weasley and Miss Granger have proved themselves trust-worthy. But, Harry, I am going to ask you to ask them not to repeat any of this to anybody else. It would not be a good idea if word got around how much I know, or suspect, about Lord Voldemort's secrets.'

'No, sir, I'll make sure it's just Ron and Hermione. Goodnight.'

He turned away again, and was almost at the door when he saw it. Sitting on one of the little spindle-legged tables that supported so many frail-looking silver instruments was an ugly gold ring set with a large, cracked black stone.

'Sir,' said Harry, staring at it. 'That ring –'

'Yes?' said Dumbledore.

'You were wearing it when we visited Professor Slughorn that night.'

'So I was,' Dumbledore agreed.

'But isn't it … sir, isn't it the same ring Marvolo Gaunt showed Ogden?'

Dumbledore bowed his head.

'The very same.'

'But how come –? Have you always had it?'

'No, I acquired it very recently,' said Dumbledore. 'A few days before I came to fetch you from your aunt and uncle's, in fact.'

'That would be around the time you injured your hand, then, sir?'

'Around that time, yes, Harry.'

Harry hesitated. Dumbledore was smiling.

'Sir, how exactly –?'

'Too late, Harry! You shall hear the story another time. Goodnight.'

'Goodnight, sir.'

“先生，我可以把你对我说的一切告诉罗恩和赫敏吗？”

邓布利多打量了他一会儿，然后说道：“可以，我认为韦斯莱先生和格兰杰小姐已经证明自己是值得信任的。可是，哈利，我要求你不许他们再把这些事情告诉任何人。如果消息传出去，让人知道我了解或察觉到伏地魔的多少秘密，恐怕就不妙了。”

“不会的，先生，我保证只让罗恩和赫敏两个人知道。晚安。”

他又转身准备离去，快走到门口时，看见了一件东西。在一张放着许多精致银器的细长腿小桌上，有一枚丑陋的金戒指，中间镶着一块有裂纹的大大的黑宝石。

“先生，”哈利瞪着它，问道，“那枚戒指——”

“怎么？”邓布利多说。

“那天晚上我们去拜访斯拉格霍恩教授时，你就戴着它。”

“没错。”邓布利多承认。

“但它不是……先生，它不是马沃罗·冈特给奥格登看的那枚戒指吗？”

邓布利多微微点了点头。

“正是那一枚。”

“可是怎么会——？它一直在你这儿吗？”

“不，我是最近才弄到的，”邓布利多说，“实际上，是在我到你姨妈姨父家去接你的几天之前。”

“你的手就是在那个时候受伤的吗，先生？”

“差不多就在那个时候，没错，哈利。”

哈利迟疑着。邓布利多面带微笑。

“先生，究竟是怎么——？”

“太晚了，哈利！下次再给你讲这个故事吧。晚安。”

“晚安，先生。”

CHAPTER ELEVEN

Hermione's Helping Hand

As Hermione had predicted, the sixth-years' free periods were not the hours of blissful relaxation Ron had anticipated, but times in which to attempt to keep up with the vast amount of homework they were being set. Not only were they studying as though they had exams every day, but the lessons themselves had become more demanding than ever before. Harry barely understood half of what Professor McGonagall said to them these days; even Hermione had had to ask her to repeat instructions once or twice. Incredibly, and to Hermione's increasing resentment, Harry's best subject had suddenly become Potions, thanks to the Half-Blood Prince.

Non-verbal spells were now expected, not only in Defence Against the Dark Arts, but in Charms and Transfiguration too. Harry frequently looked over at his classmates in the common room or at mealtimes to see them purple in the face and straining as though they had overdosed on U-No-Poo; but he knew that they were really struggling to make spells work without saying incantations aloud. It was a relief to get outside into the greenhouses; they were dealing with more dangerous plants than ever in Herbology, but at least they were still allowed to swear loudly if the Venomous Tentacula seized them unexpectedly from behind.

One result of their enormous workload and the frantic hours of practising non-verbal spells was that Harry, Ron and Hermione had so far been unable to find time to go and visit Hagrid. He had stopped coming to meals at the staff table, an ominous sign, and on the few occasions when they had passed him in the corridors or out in the grounds, he had mysteriously failed to notice them or hear their greetings.

'We've got to go and explain,' said Hermione, looking up at Hagrid's huge

第 11 章

赫敏出手相助

正如赫敏所预言的，六年级没有课的那些时间，根本不像罗恩期待的那样可以尽情地放松休息，而是必须用来努力完成老师布置的大量家庭作业。他们像每天都要应付考试似的拼命用功，而且功课本身也比以前难多了。这些日子麦格教授所教的东西，哈利差不多一半都听不懂，就连赫敏也有一两次不得不让麦格教授把讲的内容重复一遍。令人不敢相信的是，哈利最拿手的科目突然变成了魔药学，这多亏了那位混血王子，也使赫敏越来越感到愤愤不平。

现在要求他们使用无声咒了，不仅黑魔法防御术课，而且魔咒课和变形课也这样要求。哈利在公共休息室或者在吃饭的时候，经常看见他的同班同学脸憋得通红，暗暗地运气，像是服用了过量的便秘仁。他知道，他们实际上是在苦苦练习不把咒语念出声来而让魔法生效的本领。只有来到外面的温室里，大家才算松了口气。现在草药课上对付的植物比过去更危险了，但是当毒触手猝不及防地从后面抓住他们时，他们至少可以大声地咒骂。

由于功课繁重，没日没夜地练习无声咒，哈利、罗恩和赫敏一直没有时间去看望海格。海格已经不来教工餐桌吃饭了，这是一个不祥的兆头，有几次他们在走廊里或外面操场上遇到他，他竟然假装没看见他们，也没听见他们跟他打招呼，这真是太奇怪了。

“我们一定要去解释一下。”星期六吃早饭时，赫敏抬头望着教工餐桌上海格的那张空空的大座位，说道。

“今天上午有魁地奇选拔呢！”罗恩说，“而且还要练习弗立维布

empty chair at the staff table the following Saturday at breakfast.

'We've got Quidditch tryouts this morning!' said Ron. '*And* we're supposed to be practising that *Aguamenti* charm for Flitwick! Anyway, explain what? How are we going to tell him we hated his stupid subject?'

'We didn't hate it!' said Hermione.

'Speak for yourself, I haven't forgotten the Skrewts,' said Ron darkly. 'And I'm telling you now, we've had a narrow escape. You didn't hear him going on about his gormless brother – we'd have been teaching Grawp how to tie his shoelaces if we'd stayed.'

'I hate not talking to Hagrid,' said Hermione, looking upset.

'We'll go down after Quidditch,' Harry assured her. He, too, was missing Hagrid, although like Ron he thought that they were better off without Grawp in their lives. 'But trials might take all morning, the number of people who have applied.' He felt slightly nervous at confronting the first hurdle of his captaincy. 'I dunno why the team's this popular all of a sudden.'

'Oh, come on, Harry,' said Hermione, suddenly impatient. 'It's not *Quidditch* that's popular, it's you! You've never been more interesting and, frankly, you've never been more fanciable.'

Ron gagged on a large piece of kipper. Hermione spared him one look of disdain before turning back to Harry.

'Everyone knows you've been telling the truth now, don't they? The whole wizarding world has had to admit that you were right about Voldemort being back and that you really have fought him twice in the last two years and escaped both times. And now they're calling you the "Chosen One" – well, come on, can't you see why people are fascinated by you?'

Harry was finding the Great Hall very hot all of a sudden, even though the ceiling still looked cold and rainy.

'*And* you've been through all that persecution from the Ministry when they were trying to make out you were unstable and a liar. You can still see the marks where that evil woman made you write with your own blood, but you stuck to your story anyway ...'

'You can still see where those brains got hold of me in the Ministry, look,' said Ron, shaking back his sleeves.

'And it doesn't hurt that you've grown about a foot over the summer,

置的清水如泉咒！再说了，有什么可解释的？我们总不能跟他说我们讨厌他那门愚蠢的课吧！”

“我们不讨厌它！”赫敏说。

“那是你自己这么说，我可没忘记那些炸尾螺。”罗恩愁眉苦脸地说，“现在我告诉你吧，我们能逃脱真是够侥幸的。你是没听见他怎么谈他那个傻瓜弟弟——如果我们留下来继续上课，现在可能在教格洛普怎么系鞋带呢。”

“我不愿意跟海格不说话。”赫敏说，显得很难过。

“那我们就等魁地奇选拔结束以后再去。”哈利安慰她道。他也很想念海格，不过他和罗恩一样，觉得最好一辈子别跟格洛普打交道。“有这么多人提出申请，选拔可能要进行一个上午呢。”想到就要面对他当队长后的第一个障碍，他感到有点儿紧张，“不知道为什么球队突然变得这么受欢迎了。”

“哦，得了吧，哈利，”赫敏突然不耐烦起来，说道，“受欢迎的不是魁地奇，而是你！你从来没像现在这样让人感兴趣，坦白地说吧，你从来没像现在这样招人喜欢。”

罗恩被嘴里的一大块腌鱼呛住了。赫敏朝他鄙夷地瞪了一眼，又转向哈利。

“现在大家都知道你说的是实话了，对不对？整个巫师界都不得不承认，你说的伏地魔卷土重来的消息是正确的，而且你在过去两年里真的跟他较量过两次，两次都死里逃生。现在他们管你叫‘救世之星’——怎么样，现在你还不明白人们为什么对你着迷吗？”

哈利突然觉得礼堂里热得难受，尽管天花板看上去仍然阴雨蒙蒙。

“还有啊，你遭受了魔法部对你的那些迫害，他们拼命想把你说成是一个反复无常的人、一个说谎专家。那个恶毒的女人逼你用自己的鲜血写出的印迹，现在还能看得出来，可是你仍然坚持自己的说法……”

“部里那些大脑抓我时留下的痕迹，现在也能看得出来，你看。”罗恩说着把衣袖往上抖了抖。

“还有，你暑假里长高了将近一英尺，这也让人刮目相看。”赫敏

either,' Hermione finished, ignoring Ron.

'I'm tall,' said Ron inconsequentially.

The post owls arrived, swooping down through rain-flecked windows, scattering everyone with droplets of water. Most people were receiving more post than usual; anxious parents were keen to hear from their children and to reassure them, in turn, that all was well at home. Harry had received no mail since the start of term; his only regular correspondent was now dead and although he had hoped that Lupin might write occasionally, he had so far been disappointed. He was very surprised, therefore, to see the snowy-white Hedwig circling amongst all the brown and grey owls. She landed in front of him carrying a large, square package. A moment later, an identical package landed in front of Ron, crushing beneath it his minuscule and exhausted owl, Pigwidgeon.

'Ha!' said Harry, unwrapping the parcel to reveal a new copy of *Advanced Potion-Making*, fresh from Flourish and Blotts.

'Oh good,' said Hermione, delighted. 'Now you can give that graffitied copy back.'

'Are you mad?' said Harry. 'I'm keeping it! Look, I've thought it out –'

He pulled the old copy of *Advanced Potion-Making* out of his bag and tapped the cover with his wand, muttering, '*Diffindo!*' The cover fell off. He did the same thing with the brand new book (Hermione looked scandalised). He then swapped the covers, tapped each and said, '*Reparo!*'

There sat the Prince's copy, disguised as a new book, and there sat the fresh copy from Flourish and Blotts, looking thoroughly second-hand.

'I'll give Slughorn back the new one. He can't complain, it cost nine Galleons.'

Hermione pressed her lips together, looking angry and disapproving, but was distracted by a third owl landing in front of her carrying that day's copy of the *Daily Prophet*. She unfolded it hastily and scanned the front page.

'Anyone we know dead?' asked Ron in a determinedly casual voice; he posed the same question every time Hermione opened her paper.

'No, but there have been more Dementor attacks,' said Hermione. 'And an arrest.'

没有理睬罗恩，兀自把话说下去。

“我个子也高了。”罗恩没头没脑地来了这么一句。

送信的猫头鹰来了，俯冲着穿过溅满雨水的窗户，把雨滴洒在礼堂里每个人的头上和身上。大多数人的邮件都比平常多。忧心忡忡的家长急着想知道自己孩子的消息，并反过来告诉孩子他们在家一切都好。哈利自从开学以来就没有收到过信。唯一一个经常给他写信的人已经死了，他曾暗暗希望卢平偶尔会给他写写信，但这个期盼也落空了。因此，当他在那些褐色和灰色的猫头鹰中看到海德薇雪白的身影时，不禁大感意外。海德薇带着一个四四方方的大包裹落在哈利面前。片刻之后，罗恩面前也掉下来一个一模一样的包裹，他那身材娇小的猫头鹰小猪被压在下面，已经累得喘不过气来了。

“哈！”哈利说着拆开了包裹，露出一本崭新的《高级魔药制作》，是丽痕书店刚刚寄来的。

“哦，太好了，”赫敏高兴地说，“现在你可以把那本被乱涂乱画得一团糟的课本还回去了。”

“你疯了吗？”哈利说，“我要留着它！看，我早就想好了——”

他从书包里抽出那本旧的《高级魔药制作》，用魔杖敲了敲封面，念了一句：“四分五裂！”封面立刻脱落下来。他又对着那本新书如法炮制（赫敏一副震惊的样子）。然后，哈利把两个封面互相交换，再挨个儿敲了敲，说道：“恢复如初！”

于是，王子的那一本被伪装成了新书，而丽痕书店刚寄来的那本新书则显得破破烂烂，完全像个二手货了。

“我把新书还给斯拉格霍恩。他没什么可抱怨的，这花了我九个加隆呢。”

赫敏抿着嘴唇，满脸的愤怒和不满。就在这时，第三只猫头鹰带着当天的《预言家日报》落在她面前，转移了她的注意力。她急忙打开报纸，扫了几眼第一版。

“有我们认识的人死了吗？”罗恩用假装随便的口气问。每次赫敏打开报纸，他都要提出这个问题。

“没有，但是又有摄魂怪袭击的报道，”赫敏说，“还有一个人被捕了。”

'Excellent, who?' said Harry, thinking of Bellatrix Lestrange.

'Stan Shunpike,' said Hermione.

'What?' said Harry, startled.

'"*Stanley Shunpike, conductor on the popular wizarding conveyance the Knight Bus, has been arrested on suspicion of Death Eater activity. Mr Shunpike, 21, was taken into custody late last night after a raid on his Clapham home …*"'

'Stan Shunpike, a Death Eater?' said Harry, remembering the spotty youth he had first met three years before. 'No way!'

'He might have been put under the Imperius Curse,' said Ron reasonably. 'You never can tell.'

'It doesn't look like it,' said Hermione, who was still reading. 'It says here he was arrested after he was overheard talking about the Death Eaters' secret plans in a pub.' She looked up with a troubled expression on her face. 'If he was under the Imperius Curse, he'd hardly stand around gossiping about their plans, would he?'

'It sounds like he was trying to make out he knew more than he did,' said Ron. 'Isn't he the one who claimed he was going to become Minister for Magic when he was trying to chat up those Veela?'

'Yeah, that's him,' said Harry. 'I dunno what they're playing at, taking Stan seriously.'

'They probably want to look as though they're doing something,' said Hermione, frowning. 'People are terrified – you know the Patil twins' parents want them to go home? And Eloise Midgeon has already been withdrawn. Her father picked her up last night.'

'What!' said Ron, goggling at Hermione. 'But Hogwarts is safer than their homes, bound to be! We've got Aurors, and all those extra protective spells, and we've got Dumbledore!'

'I don't think we've got him all the time,' said Hermione very quietly, glancing towards the staff table over the top of the *Prophet*. 'Haven't you noticed? His seat's been empty as often as Hagrid's this past week.'

Harry and Ron looked up at the staff table. The Headmaster's chair was indeed empty. Now Harry came to think of it, he had not seen Dumbledore since their private lesson a week ago.

'I think he's left the school to do something with the Order,' said

“太棒了，谁？”哈利说，心里想到了贝拉特里克斯·莱斯特兰奇。

“斯坦·桑帕克。”赫敏说。

“什么？”哈利大吃一惊。

斯坦·桑帕克，巫师界著名的骑士公共汽车售票员，因涉嫌从事食死徒活动而被捕。桑帕克先生现年二十一岁，傲罗昨夜在突袭搜查其在克拉彭区的住所后将其拘捕……

“斯坦·桑帕克，是个食死徒？”哈利想起了他三年前第一次遇到的那个脸上长着青春痘的小伙子，“不可能！”

“他大概是中了夺魂咒吧，”罗恩合理地分析道，“这可是说不准的事儿。”

“看来不像。”赫敏仍然在看报纸，说道，“这上面说，是有人听见他在一家酒馆里谈论食死徒的秘密计划之后才逮捕他的。”她抬起头，脸上带着苦恼的表情。“如果他中了夺魂咒，就不可能到处跟人议论他们的计划，是不是？”

“看样子他是想炫耀自己知道许多东西，但其实不然。”罗恩说，“当年他想跟那些媚娃套近乎时，不是还吹牛说他就要当魔法部部长了吗？”

“是啊，就是他。”哈利说，“真不明白他们在搞什么名堂，竟然把斯坦的话当真。”

“大概是想让大家看到他们在做事吧。”赫敏皱着眉头说，“现在人心惶惶——你知道吗？佩蒂尔双胞胎的父母要把她们接回家了。爱洛伊丝·米德根已经退学，她父亲昨天晚上来接她的。”

“什么？”罗恩瞪大眼睛看着赫敏说，“可是霍格沃茨比他们家里安全呀，这是毫无疑问的！我们有傲罗，又新增了那么多防护咒，还有邓布利多！”

“我认为他其实并不一直在我们身边。”赫敏压低声音说，她的目光从《预言家日报》上扫了一眼教工餐桌，“你们没有注意到吗？最近

Hermione in a low voice. 'I mean … it's all looking serious, isn't it?'

Harry and Ron did not answer, but Harry knew that they were all thinking the same thing. There had been a horrible incident the day before, when Hannah Abbott had been taken out of Herbology to be told her mother had been found dead. They had not seen Hannah since.

When they left the Gryffindor table five minutes later to head down to the Quidditch pitch, they passed Lavender Brown and Parvati Patil. Remembering what Hermione had said about the Patil twins' parents wanting them to leave Hogwarts, Harry was unsurprised to see that the two best friends were whispering together, looking distressed. What did surprise him was that when Ron drew level with them, Parvati suddenly nudged Lavender, who looked round and gave Ron a wide smile. Ron blinked at her, then returned the smile uncertainly. His walk instantly became something more like a strut. Harry resisted the temptation to laugh, remembering that Ron had refrained from doing so after Malfoy had broken Harry's nose; Hermione, however, looked cold and distant all the way down to the stadium through the cool, misty drizzle, and departed to find a place in the stands without wishing Ron good luck.

As Harry had expected, the trials took most of the morning. Half of Gryffindor house seemed to have turned up, from first-years who were nervously clutching a selection of the dreadful old school brooms, to seventh-years who towered over the rest looking coolly intimidating. The latter included a large, wiry-haired boy Harry recognised immediately from the Hogwarts Express.

'We met on the train, in old Sluggy's compartment,' he said confidently, stepping out of the crowd to shake Harry's hand. 'Cormac McLaggen, Keeper.'

'You didn't try out last year, did you?' asked Harry, taking note of the breadth of McLaggen and thinking that he would probably block all three goalhoops without even moving.

'I was in the hospital wing when they held the trials,' said McLaggen, with something of a swagger. 'Ate a pound of Doxy eggs for a bet.'

这个星期，他的座位经常像海格的一样空着。”

哈利和罗恩抬头看了看教工餐桌。果然，校长的座位上没有人。哈利仔细一想，自从一个星期前邓布利多给他单独上课之后，他就再也没有看见他。

“我想，他离开学校是去做跟凤凰社有关的事情，”赫敏低声说，“我是说……现在形势显得很严峻，是不是？”

哈利和罗恩没有回答，但哈利知道他们脑子里都想到了同一件事。前一天出了一起可怕的事故，汉娜·艾博在草药课上被叫了出去，被告知她母亲遇害身亡。从那之后，他们就再也没有看见汉娜。

五分钟后，当他们离开格兰芬多餐桌，朝魁地奇球场走去时，迎面看见了拉文德·布朗和帕瓦蒂·佩蒂尔。哈利想起了赫敏说过佩蒂尔孪生姐妹的父母想要她们离开霍格沃茨的事，所以，他看到这两个好朋友在那里窃窃私语，神情忧伤，就不感到奇怪了。让他吃惊的是，当罗恩走过她们旁边时，帕瓦蒂突然用胳膊肘捅了捅拉文德，拉文德回过头来，送给罗恩一个灿烂的微笑。罗恩朝她眨巴眨巴眼睛，也迟疑不决地笑了笑。他走路的姿势立刻变得大摇大摆，架子十足起来。哈利看了想笑，但赶紧忍住了，他想起马尔福踩断自己鼻子时，罗恩没有笑话自己。赫敏则显得傲慢、冷漠，她穿过冷飕飕、雾蒙蒙的毛毛细雨，走向球场，然后，也没向罗恩道一声好运，就径自到看台上找座位去了。

正如哈利早就料到的，选拔进行了差不多一个上午。格兰芬多学院从一年级到七年级的半数同学都来了。一年级同学紧张地攥着从学校仓库里挑出的几把破破烂烂的旧扫帚，七年级同学则显得高高大大，鹤立鸡群，气势怪吓人的。七年级同学里有一个头发又粗又硬的大个子，哈利一眼就认出他是霍格沃茨特快列车上的那个男生。

“我们在火车上见过，在老鼻涕虫的包厢里。”他信心十足地说，从人群里走了出来，要跟哈利握手，“考迈克·麦克拉根，守门员。”

“你去年没有参加选拔，是吗？”哈利注意到麦克拉根长得膀大腰圆，心想即使他在那里不动，大概也能把三个球门封堵得严严实实。

“去年他们搞选拔时，我还住在医院里呢。”麦克拉根带着点儿吹牛的口气说，“我跟人打赌，吃了一磅狐媚子蛋。”

'Right,' said Harry. 'Well … if you wait over there …'

He pointed over to the edge of the pitch, close to where Hermione was sitting. He thought he saw a flicker of annoyance pass over McLaggen's face and wondered whether McLaggen expected preferential treatment because they were both 'old Sluggy's' favourites.

Harry decided to start with a basic test, asking all applicants for the team to divide into groups of ten and fly once around the pitch. This was a good decision: the first ten was made up of first-years and it could not have been plainer that they had hardly ever flown before. Only one boy managed to remain airborne for more than a few seconds, and he was so surprised he promptly crashed into one of the goalposts.

The second group comprised ten of the silliest girls Harry had ever encountered, who, when he blew his whistle, merely fell about giggling and clutching each other. Romilda Vane was amongst them. When he told them to leave the pitch they did so quite cheerfully and went to sit in the stands to heckle everyone else.

The third group had a pile-up halfway around the pitch. Most of the fourth group had come without broomsticks. The fifth group were Hufflepuffs.

'If there's anyone else here who's not from Gryffindor,' roared Harry, who was starting to get seriously annoyed, 'leave now, please!'

There was a pause, then a couple of little Ravenclaws went sprinting off the pitch, snorting with laughter.

After two hours, many complaints and several tantrums, one involving a crashed Comet Two Sixty and several broken teeth, Harry had found himself three Chasers: Katie Bell, returned to the team after an excellent trial, a new find called Demelza Robins, who was particularly good at dodging Bludgers, and Ginny Weasley, who had outflown all the competition and scored seventeen goals to boot. Pleased though he was with his choices, Harry had also shouted himself hoarse at the many complainers and was now enduring a similar battle with the rejected Beaters.

'That's my final decision and if you don't get out of the way for the Keepers I'll hex you,' he bellowed.

Neither of his chosen Beaters had the old brilliance of Fred and George,

“噢，”哈利说，“好吧……你就在那儿等着吧……”

他指了指球场边缘靠近赫敏坐的地方。他仿佛看见麦克拉根脸上闪过一丝懊恼的表情，他想，莫非麦克拉根以为他们俩都是老鼻涕虫的宠儿，他就能得到特殊的待遇？

哈利决定先进行一个基本测试，他叫所有申请加入球队的人分成十个人一组，绕着球场飞一圈。这真是一个明智的决定。第一组的十个人全是一年级新生，显然以前几乎就没有飞过。只有一个男孩在空中待了几秒钟，他自己也吃惊得要命，结果很快就撞到了球门柱子上。

第二组是十个女生，哈利从没碰见过这么傻的姑娘，他一吹哨子，她们就叽叽咕咕地笑得直不起腰，互相抱作一团。罗米达·万尼也在她们中间。当哈利叫她们离开球场时，她们高高兴兴地走了，然后坐在看台上七嘴八舌地互相指责。

第三组绕球场飞到一半时摔成了一堆。第四组的大多数人没带扫帚就来了。第五组竟然都是赫奇帕奇的学生。

“这里还有谁不是格兰芬多学院的，”哈利吼道，他心里真的恼火了，“请马上离开！”

停顿片刻后，两个拉文克劳的低年级学生扑哧一声大笑着奔出了球场。

两个小时后，听了满耳朵牢骚，看了好几次他人发脾气，其中一次砸烂了一把彗星 260，还有人打掉了几颗牙齿，哈利终于给自己挑选了三名追球手：凯蒂·贝尔，她表现出色，重新归队；一位名叫德米尔扎·罗宾斯的新秀，她躲避游走球特别敏捷；还有金妮·韦斯莱，她飞得比所有选手都快，并且投中了十七个球。哈利对他选出的这几个人很满意，但因为不停地冲许多发牢骚的人嚷嚷，他的嗓子都哑了，此刻又要对付那些落选的击球手们的抱怨。

“就这么定了，如果不赶快滚开让守门员进来，我就给你们施恶咒。”他吼道。

他挑选的两位击球手都不如弗雷德和乔治那么出类拔萃，但还算让人满意：吉米·珀克斯，一位宽胸膛、矮个子的三年级同学，他大

but he was still reasonably pleased with them: Jimmy Peakes, a short but broad-chested third-year who had managed to raise a lump the size of an egg on the back of Harry's head with a ferociously hit Bludger, and Ritchie Coote, who looked weedy but aimed well. They now joined the spectators in the stands to watch the selection of their last team member.

Harry had deliberately left the trial of the Keepers until last, hoping for an emptier stadium and less pressure on all concerned. Unfortunately, however, all the rejected players and a number of people who had come down to watch after a lengthy breakfast had joined the crowd by now, so that it was larger than ever. As each Keeper flew up to the goalhoops, the crowd roared and jeered in equal measure. Harry glanced over at Ron, who had always had a problem with nerves; Harry had hoped that winning their final match last term might have cured it, but apparently not: Ron was a delicate shade of green.

None of the first five applicants saved more than two goals apiece. To Harry's great disappointment, Cormac McLaggen saved four penalties out of five. On the last one, however, he shot off in completely the wrong direction; the crowd laughed and booed and McLaggen returned to the ground grinding his teeth.

Ron looked ready to pass out as he mounted his Cleansweep Eleven.

'Good luck!' cried a voice from the stands. Harry looked around, expecting to see Hermione, but it was Lavender Brown. He would have quite liked to have hidden his face in his hands, as she did a moment later, but thought that as the Captain he ought to show slightly more grit, and so turned to watch Ron do his trial.

Yet he need not have worried: Ron saved one, two, three, four, five penalties in a row. Delighted, and resisting joining in the cheers of the crowd with difficulty, Harry turned to McLaggen to tell him that, most unfortunately, Ron had beaten him, only to find McLaggen's red face inches from his own. He stepped back hastily.

'His sister didn't really try,' said McLaggen menacingly. There was a vein pulsing in his temple like the one Harry had often admired in Uncle Vernon's. 'She gave him an easy save.'

'Rubbish,' said Harry coldly. 'That was the one he nearly missed.'

力击出的游走球在哈利的后脑勺上撞出了一个鸡蛋大的鼓包；里切·古特，看上去弱不禁风，但瞄得很准。他们俩现在跟观众一起坐在看台上，观看哈利挑选他们的最后一名队员。

哈利故意把守门员的选拔放在最后，希望这时候球场上的人会少一些，这样给参赛选手的压力也会小一些。不幸的是，所有那些落选的球员，还有许多拖拖拉拉刚吃完早饭的人，现在又都加入到观众当中，看台上的人比刚才更多了。每位守门员飞向球门时，观众都爆发出同样热烈的欢呼声和讥笑声。哈利扫了一眼罗恩，罗恩总是有怯场的毛病。哈利本来希望，他们上学期最后一场比赛大获全胜，大概可以治好他这个毛病，然而看来没有。罗恩的脸色微微有些发绿。

前面五位选手都最多只救起了两个球。让哈利大为失望的是，考迈克·麦克拉根竟然一连救起了五个球中的四个。不过，在救最后一个球时，他朝着完全相反的方向扑去。观众们哄堂大笑，给他喝倒彩，麦克拉根咬着牙回到了球场上。

罗恩骑上他那把横扫十一星时，看上去随时都会晕倒。

"祝你好运！"看台上一个声音喊道。哈利扭过头，以为看见的会是赫敏，没想到却是拉文德·布朗。片刻之后，哈利也巴不得能像她那样用两只手把脸捂住，但他觉得自己身为队长，应该表现得更有勇气一些，便转脸注视着罗恩参选。

其实他用不着担心：罗恩一连救起了一个、两个、三个、四个、五个罚球。哈利高兴得心花怒放，他拼命克制自己，没有跟着观众一起欢呼喝彩。他转向麦克拉根，准备告诉他：很不幸，罗恩击败了他。没想到他一扭头，麦克拉根那张通红的脸就在眼前，近在咫尺。哈利赶紧退后几步。

"他妹妹根本就没认真发球。"麦克拉根恶狠狠地说。他太阳穴上的一根血管突突直跳，这景象是哈利经常在弗农姨父身上看到并暗自称奇的。"她给他的球很容易救起来。"

"胡说，"哈利冷冷地说，"就是那个球，他差一点儿就失手了。"

McLaggen took a step nearer Harry, who stood his ground this time.

'Give me another go.'

'No,' said Harry. 'You've had your go. You saved four. Ron saved five. Ron's Keeper, he won it fair and square. Get out of my way.'

He thought for a moment that McLaggen might punch him, but he contented himself with an ugly grimace and stormed away, growling what sounded like threats to thin air.

Harry turned round to find his new team beaming at him.

'Well done,' he croaked. 'You flew really well –'

'You did brilliantly, Ron!'

This time it really was Hermione running towards them from the stands; Harry saw Lavender walking off the pitch, arm in arm with Parvati, a rather grumpy expression on her face. Ron looked extremely pleased with himself and even taller than usual as he grinned around at the team and at Hermione.

After fixing the time of their first full practice for the following Thursday, Harry, Ron and Hermione bade goodbye to the rest of the team and headed off towards Hagrid's. A watery sun was trying to break through the clouds now and it had stopped drizzling at last. Harry felt extremely hungry; he hoped there would be something to eat at Hagrid's.

'I thought I was going to miss that fourth penalty,' Ron was saying happily. 'Tricky shot from Demelza, did you see, had a bit of spin on it –'

'Yes, yes, you were magnificent,' said Hermione, looking amused.

'I was better than that McLaggen anyway,' said Ron in a highly satisfied voice. 'Did you see him lumbering off in the wrong direction on his fifth? Looked like he'd been Confunded …'

To Harry's surprise, Hermione turned a very deep shade of pink at these words. Ron noticed nothing; he was too busy describing each of his other penalties in loving detail.

The great grey Hippogriff, Buckbeak, was tethered in front of Hagrid's cabin. He clicked his razor-sharp beak at their approach and turned his huge head towards them.

'Oh dear,' said Hermione nervously. 'He's still a bit scary, isn't he?'

'Come off it, you've ridden him, haven't you?' said Ron.

麦克拉根朝哈利逼近了一步，哈利这次没有退缩。

“让我再试一次。”

“不行，”哈利说，“你已经试过了。你救起了四个，罗恩救起了五个。罗恩是守门员，他赢得光明正大。你快给我滚开。”

一时间，他以为麦克拉根会出拳揍他，但麦克拉根只是做了一个难看的鬼脸，便嗵嗵嗵地走开了，一边对着空气叫嚷一些威胁的话。

哈利转过脸，发现他的新队员们都在笑眯眯地看着他。

“干得漂亮，”他哑着嗓子说，“你们飞得真不错——”

“你太棒了，罗恩！”

这次真的是赫敏从看台上朝他们跑来了。哈利看见拉文德跟帕瓦蒂手挽着手走出球场，脸上一副气呼呼的样子。罗恩似乎对自己满意极了，他看着队员和赫敏，傻呵呵地直笑，个头显得比平常更高了。

定好第一次全队训练的时间是下个星期四，哈利、罗恩和赫敏便向其他队员说了声再见，朝海格的小屋走去。这时，一轮水汪汪的太阳正拼命从云彩里探出头来，毛毛雨终于停了。哈利觉得饿极了。他希望海格的小屋里能有点吃的东西。

“我还以为第四个球我救不起来呢。”罗恩眉飞色舞地说，“德米尔扎的那个球真刁，你们看见了吗，带着点儿旋转——”

“是啊，是啊，你真出色。”赫敏似乎感到很有趣。

“我反正比那个麦克拉根强。”罗恩用非常得意的口气说，“你看见他救第五个球时，竟然笨头笨脑地扑错了方向吗？就好像中了混淆咒似的……”

听了这话，赫敏的脸色突然变得通红，哈利看了觉得很吃惊。罗恩什么也没注意到，只顾在那里津津乐道地描述他是怎么救起另外几个球的。

巴克比克，那头庞大的灰色鹰头马身有翼兽就拴在海格小屋的门前。它看见他们走近，咔嗒咔嗒地咂了咂刀片般锋利的尖嘴，把大脑袋朝他们转了过来。

“哦，天哪，”赫敏紧张地说，“它仍然有点儿吓人，是不是？”

“得了吧，你还骑过它呢，不是吗？”罗恩说。

Harry stepped forwards and bowed low to the Hippogriff without breaking eye contact or blinking. After a few seconds, Buckbeak sank into a bow too.

'How are you?' Harry asked him in a low voice, moving forwards to stroke the feathery head. 'Missing him? But you're OK here with Hagrid, aren't you?'

'Oi!' said a loud voice.

Hagrid had come striding round the corner of his cabin wearing a large flowery apron and carrying a sack of potatoes. His enormous boarhound, Fang, was at his heels; Fang gave a booming bark and bounded forwards.

'Git away from him! He'll have yer fingers – oh. It's yeh lot.'

Fang was jumping up at Hermione and Ron, attempting to lick their ears. Hagrid stood and looked at them all for a split second, then turned and strode into his cabin, slamming the door behind him.

'Oh dear!' said Hermione, looking stricken.

'Don't worry about it,' said Harry grimly. He walked over to the door and knocked loudly.

'Hagrid! Open up, we want to talk to you!'

There was no sound from within.

'If you don't open the door, we'll blast it open!' Harry said, pulling out his wand.

'Harry!' said Hermione, sounding shocked. 'You can't possibly –'

'Yeah, I can!' said Harry. 'Stand back –'

But before he could say anything else, the door flew open again as Harry had known it would, and there stood Hagrid, glowering down at him and looking, despite the flowery pinny, positively alarming.

'I'm a teacher!' he roared at Harry. 'A teacher, Potter! How dare yeh threaten ter break down my door!'

'I'm sorry, *sir*,' said Harry, emphasising the last word as he stowed his wand inside his robes.

Hagrid looked stunned.

'Since when have *yeh* called me "sir"?'

'Since when have you called me "Potter"?'

'Oh, very clever,' growled Hagrid. 'Very amusin'. That's me outsmarted,

哈利走上前，与鹰头马身有翼兽的目光对视，眼睛一眨不眨地朝它深深地鞠了一躬。过了几秒钟，巴克比克也弯下身去。

“你好吗？”哈利低声问，一边上前轻轻抚摸它那覆盖着羽毛的脑袋，“想他了？但你待在海格这里也蛮开心的，是不是？”

“喂！”一个响亮的声音说。

海格从小屋后面转了过来，系着一条印花的大围裙，拎着一口袋土豆。他那条大猎狗牙牙跟在他脚边。牙牙低吼一声，朝哈利他们扑了过来。

“别去惹它！它会咬掉你的手指——噢，是你们几个。”

牙牙冲着赫敏和罗恩上蹿下跳，想舔他们的耳朵。海格停住脚，看了他们三个一眼，便转身大步走进小屋，重重地把门关上了。

“哦，天哪！”赫敏说，显得难过极了。

“别担心。”哈利板着脸说。他走到小屋前使劲地敲门。

“海格！快开门，我们想跟你谈谈！”

里面没有声音。

“如果你不开门，我们就把门炸开！”哈利说着抽出了魔杖。

“哈利！”赫敏用惊恐的声音说，“你绝不能——”

“怎么不能！”哈利说，“往后站站——”

可是，没等他再说话，小屋的门突然打开了——这是哈利早就料到的，海格站在那里气冲冲地瞪着他，海格虽然系着印花围裙，但那样子还是挺吓人的。

“我是个老师！”他冲哈利吼道，“老师，波特！你怎么敢威胁说要炸坏我的门！”

“对不起，先生。”哈利说，故意把最后两个字咬得很重，一边把魔杖插进了长袍里。

海格似乎惊呆了。

“你从什么时候开始叫我‘先生’了？”

“你从什么时候开始叫我‘波特’了？”

“嗬，够机灵，”海格咆哮着说，“够有趣的。把我给绕进去了，是不？

innit? All righ', come in then, yeh ungrateful little …'

Mumbling darkly, he stood back to let them pass. Hermione scurried in after Harry, looking rather frightened.

'Well?' said Hagrid grumpily, as Harry, Ron and Hermione sat down around his enormous wooden table, Fang laying his head immediately upon Harry's knee and drooling all over his robes. 'What's this? Feelin' sorry for me? Reckon I'm lonely or summat?'

'No,' said Harry at once. 'We wanted to see you.'

'We've missed you!' said Hermione tremulously.

'Missed me, have yeh?' snorted Hagrid. 'Yeah. Righ'.'

He stomped around, brewing up tea in his enormous copper kettle, muttering all the while. Finally he slammed down three bucket-sized mugs of mahogany-brown tea in front of them and a plate of his rock cakes. Harry was hungry enough even for Hagrid's cooking, and took one at once.

'Hagrid,' said Hermione timidly, when he joined them at the table and started peeling his potatoes with a brutality that suggested that each tuber had done him a great personal wrong, 'we really wanted to carry on with Care of Magical Creatures, you know.'

Hagrid gave another great snort. Harry rather thought some bogies landed on the potatoes, and was inwardly thankful that they were not staying for dinner.

'We did!' said Hermione. 'But none of us could fit it into our timetables!'

'Yeah. Righ',' said Hagrid again.

There was a funny squelching sound and they all looked around: Hermione let out a tiny shriek and Ron leapt out of his seat and hurried around the table away from the large barrel standing in the corner that they had only just noticed. It was full of what looked like foot-long maggots; slimy, white and writhing.

'What are they, Hagrid?' asked Harry, trying to sound interested rather than revolted, but putting down his rock cake all the same.

'Jus' giant grubs,' said Hagrid.

'And they grow into …?' said Ron, looking apprehensive.

'They won' grow inter nuthin',' said Hagrid. 'I got 'em ter feed ter Aragog.'

好吧，进来吧，你们这些忘恩负义的……”

他气呼呼地嘟囔着，往后一闪给他们让出了门。赫敏紧跟着哈利进了小屋，显出非常害怕的样子。

“怎么啦？”海格没好气地说，哈利、罗恩和赫敏在他那张大木桌旁坐了下来，牙牙立刻把脑袋搁在哈利膝盖上，口水哩哩啦啦地滴在他的袍子上。“这是怎么啦？觉得我可怜？以为我很孤独什么的？”

“不是，”哈利立刻说道，“我们只是想来看看你。”

“我们很想你！”赫敏战战兢兢地说。

“想我，是吗？”海格轻蔑地哼了一声说，“是啊，没错。”

他跺着脚走来走去，用那把巨大的铜茶壶沏上了茶，嘴里不停地嘟囔着什么。最后，他把三只小桶那么大的茶杯重重地放在他们面前，里面茶水的颜色深得像红木一样，他还端来了一盘他自制的岩皮饼。哈利饿极了，顾不上挑剔海格的烹调手艺，立刻伸手拿了一块。

“海格，”赫敏怯生生地说，这时海格跟他们一起坐在桌子旁，开始削土豆皮，他用的劲儿那么狠，似乎每个土豆都跟他有深仇大恨，“其实，我们真的想继续上保护神奇动物课来着。”

海格的鼻子里又使劲哼了一声。哈利简直怀疑有几块鼻屎落进了土豆里，他暗自庆幸他们不会留下来吃午饭。

“真的！”赫敏说，“可是我们的课程表都排不过来了！”

“是啊，没错！”海格又这么说。

这时，突然传来一种古怪的嘎吱嘎吱的声音，他们都转过头去。赫敏轻轻地尖叫了一声，罗恩忽地从座位上跳起来，绕到桌子那头，躲开他们刚刚注意到的那只放在墙角的大桶。桶里装满了一尺来长的蛆一般的东西，黏糊糊、白生生的，不停地扭动着。

“这是什么呀，海格？”哈利问，尽量使自己的语气听上去是好奇而不是厌恶，但还是赶紧放下了手里的岩皮饼。

“巨蛴螬嘛。”海格说。

“它们长大后会变成……？”罗恩神色惶恐地问。

“不会变成什么。”海格说，“我养它们是为了喂阿拉戈克。”

And without warning, he burst into tears.

'Hagrid!' cried Hermione, leaping up, hurrying around the table the long way to avoid the barrel of maggots, and putting an arm around his shaking shoulders. 'What is it?'

'It's … him …' gulped Hagrid, his beetle-black eyes streaming as he mopped his face with his apron. 'It's … Aragog … I think he's dyin' … he got ill over the summer an' he's not gettin' better … I don' know what I'll do if he … if he … we've bin tergether so long …'

Hermione patted Hagrid's shoulder, looking at a complete loss for anything to say. Harry knew how she felt. He had known Hagrid to present a vicious baby dragon with a teddy bear, seen him croon over giant scorpions with suckers and stings, attempt to reason with his brutal giant of a half-brother, but this was perhaps the most incomprehensible of all his monster fancies: the gigantic talking spider, Aragog, that dwelled deep in the Forbidden Forest and which he and Ron had only narrowly escaped four years previously.

'Is there – is there anything we can do?' Hermione asked, ignoring Ron's frantic grimaces and head-shakings.

'I don' think there is, Hermione,' choked Hagrid, attempting to stem the flood of his tears. 'See, the rest o' the tribe … Aragog's family … they're gettin' a bit funny now he's ill … bit restive …'

'Yeah, I think we saw a bit of that side of them,' said Ron in an undertone.

'… I don' reckon it'd be safe fer anyone but me ter go near the colony at the mo',' Hagrid finished, blowing his nose hard on his apron and looking up. 'But thanks fer offerin', Hermione … it means a lot …'

After that the atmosphere lightened considerably, for although neither Harry nor Ron had shown any inclination to go and feed giant grubs to a murderous, gargantuan spider, Hagrid seemed to take it for granted that they would have liked to have done and became his usual self once more.

'Ar, I always knew yeh'd find it hard ter squeeze me inter yeh timetables,' he said gruffly, pouring them more tea. 'Even if yeh applied fer Time-Turners –'

'We couldn't have done,' said Hermione. 'We smashed the entire stock of Ministry Time-Turners when we were there in the summer. It was in the *Daily Prophet*.'

毫无来由地，他突然哭了起来。

“海格！”赫敏叫了一声，跳起来匆匆绕过桌子——为了避开那桶巨蛴螬，她特意从远的那端绕过去。她用胳膊搂住海格颤抖的肩膀。“怎么啦？”

“是……是他……”海格抽泣着说，泪水从黑亮的小眼睛里流淌下来，他用围裙擦着脸，“是……阿拉戈克……我觉得他快死了……他病了一个夏天，一直不见好……我不知道，如果他……如果他……我该怎么办……我们在一起这么长时间了……”

赫敏拍着海格的肩膀，完全不知道该说什么才好。哈利明白她的感觉。他知道海格曾经把一个玩具熊送给一头凶恶的小火龙，还看见海格给那些长着吸盘和螯刺的大蝎子轻轻地哼歌儿，并试图跟他那个同母异父的弟弟、那个残暴的巨人讲道理，但是，在海格喜欢过的所有这些庞然大物中，要数这个最让人难以理解了：阿拉戈克，一只会说话的巨型蜘蛛，居住在禁林深处，四年前，哈利和罗恩差点儿在它那里送了命。

“我们——我们能做点什么吗？”赫敏没理睬使劲冲他做鬼脸、摇头的罗恩，问道。

“恐怕没办法了，赫敏，”海格抽抽搭搭地说，拼命忍住汹涌而下的泪水，“知道吗，在部落里……在阿拉戈克家族里……他们看到他病了，表现得很奇怪……有点儿不好控制了……”

“没错，我们当时就看出它们有那种倾向。”罗恩低声说。

“……我想，眼下除了我，不管谁走近那片地方都不安全。”海格说完，在围裙上使劲擤了擤鼻子，抬起了头，“不过谢谢你这么说，赫敏……这对我来说太重要了……”

在那之后，气氛就变得轻松多了，尽管哈利和罗恩都没有表示出愿意拿巨蛴螬去喂一只凶狠残暴、体格庞大的蜘蛛，但海格似乎想当然地认为他们有这个意思，于是，他立刻恢复了常态。

“嗬，我早就知道你们会觉得很难把我塞进你们的课程表，”他粗声粗气地说，又给他们倒了些茶，“即使你们用上了时间转换器——”

“我们用不上了。”赫敏说，“夏天我们在魔法部时，把部里库存的时间转换器都砸碎了。《预言家日报》上写着呢。”

'Ar, well then,' said Hagrid. 'There's no way yeh could've done it … I'm sorry I've bin – yeh know – I've jus' bin worried abou' Aragog … an' I did wonder whether, if Professor Grubbly-Plank had bin teachin' yeh –'

At which all three of them stated categorically and untruthfully that Professor Grubbly-Plank, who had substituted for Hagrid a few times, was a dreadful teacher, with the result that by the time Hagrid waved them off the premises at dusk, he looked quite cheerful.

'I'm starving,' said Harry, once the door had closed behind them and they were hurrying through the dark and deserted grounds; he had abandoned the rock cake after an ominous cracking noise from one of his back teeth. 'And I've got that detention with Snape tonight, I haven't got much time for dinner …'

As they came into the castle they spotted Cormac McLaggen entering the Great Hall. It took him two attempts to get through the doors; he ricocheted off the frame on the first attempt. Ron merely guffawed gloatingly and strode off into the Hall after him, but Harry caught Hermione's arm and held her back.

'What?' said Hermione defensively.

'If you ask me,' said Harry quietly, 'McLaggen looks like he *was* Confunded. And he was standing right in front of where you were sitting.'

Hermione blushed.

'Oh, all right then, I did it,' she whispered. 'But you should have heard the way he was talking about Ron and Ginny! Anyway, he's got a nasty temper, you saw how he reacted when he didn't get in – you wouldn't have wanted someone like that on the team.'

'No,' said Harry. 'No, I suppose that's true. But wasn't that dishonest, Hermione? I mean, you're a prefect, aren't you?'

'Oh, be quiet,' she snapped, as he smirked.

'What are you two doing?' demanded Ron, reappearing in the doorway to the Great Hall and looking suspicious.

'Nothing,' said Harry and Hermione together, and they hurried after Ron. The smell of roast beef made Harry's stomach ache with hunger, but they had barely taken three steps towards the Gryffindor table when Professor Slughorn appeared in front of them, blocking their path.

“嗬，所以呀，”海格说，“你们就没有办法了……对不起，我刚才——你们知道——我只是在为阿拉戈克担心……不过我确实有点怀疑，既然格拉普兰教授给你们上过课——”

他们三个听了这话，立刻言不由衷地声讨起了曾给海格代过几次课的格拉普兰教授，一口咬定她是一个特别糟糕的老师。结果，当黄昏降临，海格站在屋外同他们挥手告别时，他显得情绪高昂多了。

“我饿坏了。”小屋的门一关上，哈利便说道。他们匆匆走在昏暗的、空无一人的场地上。刚才他在吃岩皮饼时，一颗后槽牙不祥地嘎巴响了一下，他便赶紧把饼放下了。“我今天晚上还要到斯内普那里去关禁闭呢，没有多少时间吃晚饭了……”

他们进了城堡，正好看见考迈克·麦克拉根走进大礼堂。他走了两次才穿过那道门，第一次撞到门框上弹了回来。罗恩幸灾乐祸地大笑起来，跟在他后面大摇大摆地走进礼堂，哈利一把抓住赫敏的胳膊，把她拉了回来。

“怎么啦？”赫敏警觉地问。

“据我看，”哈利小声说，“麦克拉根像是中了混淆咒，而他当时就在你的座位前面。”

赫敏脸红了。

“噢，好吧，是我干的，”她小声说，“但是你真应该听听他是怎么议论罗恩和金妮的！而且，他脾气坏透了，你看见了他落选后是什么反应——你肯定不希望球队里有这么一个家伙。”

“对，”哈利说，“对，我想确实是这样。但那不是作弊吗，赫敏？我是说，你还是个级长呢，是不是？”

“哦，你小声点儿！”赫敏断喝道，哈利暗暗地笑了。

“你们俩在做什么？”罗恩问，他又回到礼堂的门口，脸上露出怀疑的神色。

“没什么。”哈利和赫敏同时说道，然后便匆匆跟着罗恩走了进去。烤牛排的香味使哈利的肚子饿得更难受了，可是，他们刚朝格兰芬多的餐桌走了两三步，斯拉格霍恩教授就出现在他们面前，挡住了他们的路。

'Harry, Harry, just the man I was hoping to see!' he boomed genially, twiddling the ends of his walrus moustache and puffing out his enormous belly. 'I was hoping to catch you before dinner! What do you say to a spot of supper tonight in my rooms instead? We're having a little party, just a few rising stars. I've got McLaggen coming, and Zabini, the charming Melinda Bobbin – I don't know whether you know her? Her family owns a large chain of apothecaries – and, of course, I hope very much that Miss Granger will favour me by coming, too.'

Slughorn made Hermione a little bow as he finished speaking. It was as though Ron was not present; Slughorn did not so much as look at him.

'I can't come, Professor,' said Harry at once. 'I've got a detention with Professor Snape.'

'Oh dear!' said Slughorn, his face falling comically. 'Dear, dear, I was counting on you, Harry! Well, now, I'll just have to have a word with Severus and explain the situation, I'm sure I'll be able to persuade him to postpone your detention. Yes, I'll see you both later!'

He bustled away out of the Hall.

'He's got no chance of persuading Snape,' said Harry, the moment Slughorn was out of earshot. 'This detention's already been postponed once; Snape did it for Dumbledore, but he won't do it for anyone else.'

'Oh, I wish you could come, I don't want to go on my own!' said Hermione anxiously; Harry knew that she was thinking about McLaggen.

'I doubt you'll be alone, Ginny'll probably be invited,' snapped Ron, who did not seem to have taken kindly to being ignored by Slughorn.

After dinner they made their way back to Gryffindor Tower. The common room was very crowded, as most people had finished dinner by now, but they managed to find a free table and sat down; Ron, who had been in a bad mood ever since the encounter with Slughorn, folded his arms and frowned at the ceiling. Hermione reached out for a copy of the *Evening Prophet*, which somebody had left abandoned on a chair.

'Anything new?' said Harry.

'Not really …' Hermione had opened the newspaper and was scanning the inside pages. 'Oh, look, your dad's in here, Ron – he's all right!' she added quickly, for Ron had looked round in alarm. 'It just says he's been

“哈利，哈利，正是我希望见到的人！”他热情地大声说，鼓着大肚子，手指玩弄着海象胡须尖，“我就希望在吃饭前堵住你！今天晚上到我那里去吃一顿便饭如何？我们有一个小小的晚会，只请了几位冉冉升起的新星。我邀请了麦克拉根、沙比尼，还有迷人的梅林达·波宾——不知道你是不是认识她，她家里开着大型的连锁药店——还有，当然啦，我非常希望格兰杰小姐也能赏光。”

斯拉格霍恩说到最后，朝赫敏微微鞠了一躬，就好像罗恩根本不存在似的，看也没看他一眼。

“我不能来，教授，”哈利赶紧说道，“我要到斯内普教授那里去关禁闭。”

“哦，天哪！”斯拉格霍恩的脸一下子就拉长了，显得很滑稽，“天哪，天哪，我可就指望着你呢，哈利！好吧，我这就去找西弗勒斯谈谈，把情况解释一下，我相信我能说服他推迟你的禁闭。好，待会儿见，你们俩！”

他匆匆忙忙地走出了礼堂。

“他根本就不可能说服斯内普，”哈利等到斯拉格霍恩走得听不见了，便说道，“这个禁闭已经被推迟了一次。斯内普上回是看了邓布利多的面子，他绝不会再为任何人推迟了。”

“哦，我真希望你能来，我一个人可不想去！”赫敏焦虑地说。哈利知道她想起了麦克拉根。

“你恐怕不会一个人去的，金妮大概也受到了邀请。”罗恩没好气地说，斯拉格霍恩对他的忽视似乎令他耿耿于怀。

晚饭后，他们回到格兰芬多塔楼。这时候大部分同学都已经吃过晚饭，公共休息室里非常拥挤，但他们总算找到一张空桌子坐了下来。自从他们跟斯拉格霍恩碰过面后，罗恩就一直闷闷不乐。他抱着双臂，皱着眉头，望着天花板。赫敏伸手拿来别人扔在一把椅子上的一份《预言家晚报》。

“有什么新消息？”哈利问。

“没有什么……”赫敏已经打开报纸，浏览着上面的内容，“噢，罗恩，快看，这里有你爸爸——他没事！”罗恩惊慌地转过头来，赫敏赶

to visit the Malfoys' house. "*This second search of the Death Eater's residence does not seem to have yielded any results. Arthur Weasley of the Office for the Detection and Confiscation of Counterfeit Defensive Spells and Protective Objects said that his team had been acting upon a confidential tip-off.*"'

'Yeah, mine!' said Harry. 'I told him at King's Cross about Malfoy and that thing he was trying to get Borgin to fix! Well, if it's not at their house, he must have brought whatever it is to Hogwarts with him –'

'But how can he have done, Harry?' said Hermione, putting down the newspaper with a surprised look. 'We were all searched when we arrived, weren't we?'

'Were you?' said Harry, taken aback. 'I wasn't!'

'Oh no, of course you weren't, I forgot you were late ... well, Filch ran over all of us with Secrecy Sensors when we got into the Entrance Hall. Any Dark object would have been found, I know for a fact Crabbe had a shrunken head confiscated. So you see, Malfoy can't have brought in anything dangerous!'

Momentarily stymied, Harry watched Ginny Weasley playing with Arnold the Pygmy Puff for a while before seeing a way around this objection.

'Someone's sent it to him by owl, then,' he said. 'His mother or someone.'

'All the owls are being checked, too,' said Hermione. 'Filch told us so when he was jabbing those Secrecy Sensors everywhere he could reach.'

Really stumped this time, Harry found nothing else to say. There did not seem to be any way Malfoy could have brought a dangerous or Dark object into the school. He looked hopefully at Ron, who was sitting with his arms folded, staring over at Lavender Brown.

'Can you think of any way Malfoy –?'

'Oh, drop it, Harry,' said Ron.

'Listen, it's not my fault Slughorn invited Hermione and me to his stupid party, neither of us wanted to go, you know!' said Harry, firing up.

'Well, as I'm not invited to any parties,' said Ron, getting to his feet again, 'I think I'll go to bed.'

He stomped off towards the door to the boys' dormitories, leaving Harry and Hermione staring after him.

紧加了一句，“报上只是说他去了马尔福家。对这位食死徒住所的第二次搜查似乎没有任何收获。伪劣防御咒及防护用品侦查收缴办公室的亚瑟·韦斯莱说，他的小组是在得到某人暗中透露的情报后才采取行动的。”

“对啊，那就是我！”哈利说，“我在国王十字车站跟他说了马尔福的事，还有马尔福想要博金替他修理的那件东西！嗯，既然不在他们家，他肯定把那东西带到了霍格沃茨——”

“他怎么可能办到呢，哈利？”赫敏说着放下报纸，脸上露出一副惊讶的表情，“我们进校时都被检查过的呀。”

“什么？”哈利吃惊地说，“我可没有！”

“噢，对了，你当然没有，我忘记你迟到了……唉，我们进入门厅时，费尔奇用探密器在我们全身上下扫了个遍。凡是黑魔法的物品都会被搜出来的，我就知道克拉布有一个干枯的人头被没收了。所以你看，马尔福不可能把危险的东西带进来！”

哈利暂时无话可说，他注视着金妮·韦斯莱逗弄那只侏儒蒲阿囡，过了一会儿才想出了一句反驳的话。

“有人可以通过猫头鹰把东西寄给他，”他说，“他妈妈或其他什么人。”

“所有的猫头鹰也要受到检查。”赫敏说，“费尔奇用探密器到处乱捅时这么告诉我们的。”

哈利这次败下阵来，彻底无话可说了。看来，马尔福确实没有办法把危险物品或黑魔法物品带进学校。他期待地看了看罗恩，但罗恩抱着双臂坐在那里，看着那边的拉文德·布朗。

“你能想出马尔福用什么办法——？”

“哦，别提这件事了，哈利。”罗恩说。

“听着，斯拉格霍恩邀请赫敏和我去参加他那愚蠢的晚会，这不是我的错，我们俩都不想去，你知道的！”哈利一下子火了，冲口而出。

“好吧，既然没有人邀请我去参加晚会，”罗恩说着站了起来，“我还是上床睡觉吧。”

他嗵嗵嗵地朝男生宿舍的门口走去，哈利和赫敏呆呆地望着他的背影。

'Harry?' said the new Chaser, Demelza Robins, appearing suddenly at his shoulder. 'I've got a message for you.'

'From Professor Slughorn?' asked Harry, sitting up hopefully.

'No … from Professor Snape,' said Demelza. Harry's heart sank. 'He says you're to come to his office at half past eight tonight to do your detention – er – no matter how many party invitations you've received. And he wanted you to know you'll be sorting out rotten Flobberworms from good ones, to use in Potions, and – and he says there's no need to bring protective gloves.'

'Right,' said Harry grimly. 'Thanks a lot, Demelza.'

“哈利？”新任追球手德米尔扎·罗宾斯突然出现在他身边，“我有一个口信带给你。”

“斯拉格霍恩教授的？”哈利满怀希望地坐起身。

“不……是斯内普教授的，”德米尔扎说，哈利的心往下一沉，“他说你今晚八点半必须到他办公室去关禁闭——嗯——不管有多少人邀请你去参加晚会都是白搭。他还叫我通知你，你的任务是把腐烂的弗洛伯毛虫从好的里面挑出来，魔药课上要用——他还说你不用带防护手套。”

“好的，”哈利沉着脸说，“非常感谢，德米尔扎。”

CHAPTER TWELVE

Silver and Opals

Where was Dumbledore, and what was he doing? Harry caught sight of the Headmaster only twice over the next few weeks. He rarely appeared at meals any more, and Harry was sure Hermione was right in thinking that he was leaving the school for days at a time. Had Dumbledore forgotten the lessons he was supposed to be giving Harry? Dumbledore had said that the lessons were leading to something to do with the prophecy; Harry had felt bolstered, comforted, and now he felt slightly abandoned.

Halfway through October came their first trip of the term to Hogsmeade. Harry had wondered whether these trips would still be allowed, given the increasingly tight security measures around the school, but was pleased to know that they were going ahead; it was always good to get out of the castle grounds for a few hours.

Harry woke early on the morning of the trip, which was proving stormy, and whiled away the time until breakfast by reading his copy of *Advanced Potion-Making*. He did not usually lie in bed reading his textbooks; that sort of behaviour, as Ron rightly said, was indecent in anybody except Hermione, who was simply weird that way. Harry felt, however, that the Half-Blood Prince's copy of *Advanced Potion-Making* hardly qualified as a textbook. The more Harry pored over the book, the more he realised how much was in there, not only the handy hints and short cuts on potions that were earning him such a glowing reputation with Slughorn, but also the imaginative little jinxes and hexes scribbled in the margins which Harry was sure, judging by the crossings-out and revisions, that the Prince had invented himself.

Harry had already attempted a few of the Prince's self-invented spells. There had been a hex that caused toenails to grow alarmingly fast (he had

第 12 章

银器和蛋白石

邓布利多去了哪儿？他在做什么？在接下来的几个星期里，哈利只见过校长两次。邓布利多很少在吃饭的时候露面，看来赫敏认为校长一次离开好几天的说法是对的。难道邓布利多忘记了他应该给哈利单独上课吗？邓布利多说过，那些课最终跟那个预言有关。哈利曾经觉得很受鼓舞，心里很踏实，现在却有点儿被遗弃的感觉。

十月中旬，他们第一次去霍格莫德村。由于学校周围的防范措施越来越严密，哈利本来以为不会允许他们去霍格莫德村了。现在知道还是要去，他心里很高兴。离开城堡散散心，哪怕只有几个小时也是愉快的。

去霍格莫德村的那天早晨，外面风雨交加，哈利醒得很早，翻看着那本《高级魔药制作》消磨早饭前的时间。平常他是不躺在床上看课本的，罗恩说得对，除了赫敏，这种行为放在任何人身上都显得不合适，而赫敏那么做无非是她的一种怪癖。不过哈利觉得，混血王子的那本《高级魔药制作》几乎不能算作课本。哈利越仔细研读那本书，越觉得里面内容丰富，不仅有容易操作的提示和快捷方法——正是这些让哈利赢得了斯拉格霍恩的热烈称赞，而且书的空白处还胡乱记着许多很有创意的小恶咒和小魔法，从那些涂涂改改的笔迹看，哈利断定这些都是王子自己发明的。

哈利已经尝试过王子发明的几个咒语。有一个恶咒是让人的趾甲噌噌地疯长（他在走廊上拿克拉布做了试验，效果有趣极了）；还有一

tried this on Crabbe in the corridor, with very entertaining results); a jinx that glued the tongue to the roof of the mouth (which he had twice used, to general applause, on an unsuspecting Argus Filch); and, perhaps most useful of all, *Muffliato*, a spell that filled the ears of anyone nearby with an unidentifiable buzzing, so that lengthy conversations could be held in class without being overheard. The only person who did not find these charms amusing was Hermione, who maintained a rigidly disapproving expression throughout and refused to talk at all if Harry had used the *Muffliato* spell on anyone in the vicinity.

Sitting up in bed, Harry turned the book sideways so as to examine more closely the scribbled instructions for a spell that seemed to have caused the Prince some trouble. There were many crossings-out and alterations, but finally, crammed into a corner of the page, the scribble:

Levicorpus (n-vbl)

While the wind and sleet pounded relentlessly on the windows and Neville snored loudly, Harry stared at the letters in brackets. *N-vbl* … that had to mean non-verbal. Harry rather doubted he would be able to bring off this particular spell; he was still having difficulty with non-verbal spells, something Snape had been quick to comment on in every DADA class. On the other hand, the Prince had proved a much more effective teacher than Snape so far.

Pointing his wand at nothing in particular, he gave it an upward flick and said *Levicorpus!* inside his head.

'Aaaaaaaargh!'

There was a flash of light and the room was full of voices: everyone had woken up as Ron had let out a yell. Harry sent *Advanced Potion-Making* flying in panic; Ron was dangling upside-down in midair as though an invisible hook had hoisted him up by the ankle.

'Sorry!' yelled Harry, as Dean and Seamus roared with laughter and Neville picked himself up from the floor, having fallen out of bed. 'Hang on – I'll let you down –'

He groped for the potion book and riffled through it in a panic, trying to find the right page; at last he located it and deciphered one cramped word underneath the spell: praying that this was the counter-jinx, Harry thought *Liberacorpus!* with all his might.

个咒语是把人的舌头粘在上腭上（他在阿格斯·费尔奇身上用了两次，赢得了大家的热烈喝彩，而费尔奇还蒙在鼓里，毫无察觉）；最有用的要数闭耳塞听咒了，这个咒语能让周围每个人的耳朵里充满一种无法辨别的嗡嗡声，这样，在课堂上就能随心所欲地聊天，不怕被别人听见了。唯一觉得这些魔法不好玩的是赫敏，她始终板着脸，一副不以为然的样子，如果哈利对近旁的什么人施了闭耳塞听咒，她就干脆一句话也不说。

哈利坐在床上，把课本侧过来仔细研读那潦草的笔迹写出的一个咒语，王子似乎在这个咒语上费了不少脑筋。经过无数次的涂涂改改，最后在那一页的角落上挤挤挨挨地写了这么几个字：

倒挂金钟（无声）

狂风裹着雨夹雪，无情地打在窗户上，纳威很响地打着呼噜，哈利盯着括号里的那两个字。*无声*……肯定是指无声咒。哈利不知道自己能不能练成这个特殊的咒语。他对于无声咒仍然不能得心应手，斯内普在黑魔法防御术课上动不动拿这件事说三道四。其实，王子教给哈利的东西比斯内普多得多。

哈利用魔杖随便指着一个地方，轻轻往上一挥，脑子里默念：*倒挂金钟！*

“啊啊啊啊啊！”

一道强光闪过，房间里乱成一团。罗恩发出一声惨叫，把大家都惊醒了。哈利惊慌地扔掉了《高级魔药制作》。罗恩头朝下悬在空中，似有一只无形的钩子钩住他的脚脖子，把他倒挂了起来。

“对不起！”哈利喊道，迪安和西莫放声大笑，纳威刚才摔到了地上，现在正慢慢地爬起来，“等等——我这就把你放下来——”

他摸到那本魔药书，慌乱地翻找刚才那一页。最后总算找到了，他在那个咒语下面辨认出挤成一团的几个字：哈利暗自祈祷这就是破解咒，然后集中意念，在脑子里念道：*金钟落地！*

There was another flash of light and Ron fell in a heap on to his mattress.

'Sorry,' repeated Harry weakly, while Dean and Seamus continued to roar with laughter.

'Tomorrow,' said Ron in a muffled voice, 'I'd rather you set the alarm clock.'

By the time they had got dressed, padding themselves out with several of Mrs Weasley's hand-knitted sweaters and carrying cloaks, scarves and gloves, Ron's shock had subsided and he had decided that Harry's new spell was highly amusing; so amusing, in fact, that he lost no time in regaling Hermione with the story as they sat down for breakfast.

'… and then there was another flash of light and I landed on the bed again!' grinned Ron, helping himself to sausages.

Hermione had not cracked a smile during this anecdote, and now turned an expression of wintry disapproval upon Harry.

'Was this spell, by any chance, another one from that potion book of yours?' she asked.

Harry frowned at her.

'Always jump to the worst conclusion, don't you?'

'Was it?'

'Well … yeah, it was, but so what?'

'So you just decided to try out an unknown, handwritten incantation and see what would happen?'

'Why does it matter if it's handwritten?' said Harry, preferring not to answer the rest of the question.

'Because it's probably not Ministry of Magic-approved,' said Hermione. 'And also,' she added, as Harry and Ron rolled their eyes, 'because I'm starting to think this Prince character was a bit dodgy.'

Both Harry and Ron shouted her down at once.

'It was a laugh!' said Ron, up-ending a ketchup bottle over his sausages. 'Just a laugh, Hermione, that's all!'

'Dangling people upside-down by the ankle?' said Hermione. 'Who puts their time and energy into making up spells like that?'

'Fred and George,' said Ron, shrugging, 'it's their kind of thing. And, er –'

'My dad,' said Harry. He had only just remembered.

又是一道强光闪过，罗恩掉在床上，摔成一堆。

“对不起。”哈利又轻声说了一遍，迪安和西莫还在那里放声大笑。

“我希望你明天还是上闹钟吧。”罗恩声音闷闷地说。

他们穿好衣服，在身上鼓鼓囊囊地套了几件韦斯莱夫人织的毛衣，拿上了斗篷、围巾和手套。罗恩已经从刚才的惊吓中缓过劲来，认为哈利的新咒语非常好玩。实际上，他觉得这个咒语太好玩了，他们刚坐下来吃早饭，他就迫不及待地把这件事讲给赫敏听。

“……然后又闪过一道亮光，我就掉回到床上了！”罗恩笑嘻嘻地说，一边动手给自己拿香肠。

赫敏听着，脸上没有一丝笑容，她板着冷冰冰的脸，不满地转向哈利。

“或许，这个咒语又是你那本魔药书里的吧？”她问。

哈利朝她皱起眉头。

“你总是一下子就得出最坏的结论，是吗？”

“到底是不是？”

“好吧……没错，是又怎么样？”

“你竟然决定拿一个手写的陌生咒语来做试验，看看会发生什么事？”

“手写的又怎么样？”哈利说，故意避重就轻，不回答其他问题。

“因为这可能是魔法部禁止使用的。”赫敏说。“而且，”她看到哈利和罗恩翻了翻眼珠，便又说道，“因为我开始觉得这个叫王子的家伙有点儿不可靠。”

哈利和罗恩同时喊她住口。

“那是闹着玩的！”罗恩把一瓶番茄酱倒过来浇在他的香肠上，说道，“只是闹着玩，赫敏，没什么大不了的！”

“钩住脚脖子把人倒挂起来？”赫敏问，“谁会花时间和精力编出这样的咒语呢？”

“弗雷德和乔治，”罗恩耸了耸肩膀说，“他们就爱搞这类玩意儿。还有，嗯——”

“我爸爸。”哈利说。他是刚刚想起来的。

'What?' said Ron and Hermione together.

'My dad used this spell,' said Harry. 'I – Lupin told me.'

This last part was not true; in fact, Harry had seen his father use the spell on Snape, but he had never told Ron and Hermione about that particular excursion into the Pensieve. Now, however, a wonderful possibility occurred to him. Could the Half-Blood Prince possibly be –?

'Maybe your dad did use it, Harry,' said Hermione, 'but he's not the only one. We've seen a whole bunch of people use it, in case you've forgotten. Dangling people in the air. Making them float along, asleep, helpless.'

Harry stared at her. With a sinking feeling he, too, remembered the behaviour of the Death Eaters at the Quidditch World Cup. Ron came to his aid.

'That was different,' he said robustly. 'They were abusing it. Harry and his dad were just having a laugh. You don't like the Prince, Hermione,' he added, pointing a sausage at her sternly, 'because he's better than you at Potions –'

'It's got nothing to do with that!' said Hermione, her cheeks reddening. 'I just think it's very irresponsible to start performing spells when you don't even know what they're for, and stop talking about "the Prince" as if it's his title, I bet it's just a stupid nickname and it doesn't seem as though he was a very nice person to me!'

'I don't see where you get that from,' said Harry heatedly, 'if he'd been a budding Death Eater he wouldn't have been boasting about being "Half-Blood", would he?'

Even as he said it, Harry remembered that his father had been pure-blood, but he pushed the thought out of his mind; he would worry about that later …

'The Death Eaters can't all be pure-blood, there aren't enough pure-blood wizards left,' said Hermione stubbornly. 'I expect most of them are half-bloods pretending to be pure. It's only Muggle-borns they hate, they'd be quite happy to let you and Ron join up.'

'There is no way they'd let me be a Death Eater!' said Ron indignantly, a bit of sausage flying off the fork he was now brandishing at Hermione and hitting Ernie Macmillan on the head. 'My whole family are blood traitors! That's as bad as Muggle-borns to Death Eaters!'

“什么？”罗恩和赫敏同时说道。

“我爸爸使用过那个咒语。”哈利说，“我——卢平告诉我的。”

最后这句不是实话。实际上，哈利是亲眼看见他父亲给斯内普施了这个魔法，但他一直没有把他在冥想盆里的那段经历告诉罗恩和赫敏。眼下，他突然想起一种很奇妙的可能性。混血王子会不会就是——？

“或许你爸爸使用过它，哈利，”赫敏说，“但使用过它的不止你爸爸一个人。我们看见过一大堆人都在使用它，也许你已经忘记了。把人悬在半空，让他们昏昏沉沉、无能为力地在半空飘浮。”

哈利呆呆地望着她。他也想起了食死徒在魁地奇世界杯赛上的所作所为，不由得心往下一沉。罗恩出来给他解了围。

“那是两码事。”他坚定地说，“他们是在滥用这个魔法。哈利和他爸爸只是闹着玩儿。赫敏，你不喜欢王子，”他严肃地用香肠指着赫敏说道，“是因为他的魔药课学得比你好——”

“跟那个没有半点关系！”赫敏说，面颊一下子变得通红，“我只是认为，还不了解一种魔法是做什么用的就随便拿来使用，这是非常不负责任的。还有，别再一口一个‘王子’，就好像那是他的头衔似的，我敢说那只是一个愚蠢的外号，而且他给我的感觉不像是个正经人！”

“我不知道你这是从哪儿得到的印象。”哈利激动地说，“如果他未来要成为食死徒，就不会口口声声说自己是‘混血’的了，是不是？”

哈利嘴里这么说，心里却想起他父亲是纯血统的，但他把这个念头从脑海里赶走，留待以后再去考虑……

“食死徒不可能都是纯血统的，现在已经没有多少纯血统的巫师了。”赫敏固执地说，“我猜想他们大多数都是混血，却假装自己是纯血统。他们仇恨的只是麻瓜出身的人，他们肯定很愿意让你和罗恩入伙。”

“他们休想让我成为食死徒！”罗恩气愤地说，朝赫敏挥舞手里的叉子，结果叉子上的一小片香肠飞了出去，砸在厄尼·麦克米兰的脑袋上，“我们全家都背叛了自己的血统！在食死徒看来，这跟麻瓜出身一样糟糕！”

'And they'd love to have me,' said Harry sarcastically. 'We'd be best pals if they didn't keep trying to do me in.'

This made Ron laugh; even Hermione gave a grudging smile, and a distraction arrived in the shape of Ginny.

'Hey, Harry, I'm supposed to give you this.'

It was a scroll of parchment with Harry's name written upon it in familiar thin, slanting writing.

'Thanks, Ginny … it's Dumbledore's next lesson!' Harry told Ron and Hermione, pulling open the parchment and quickly reading its contents. 'Monday evening!' He felt suddenly light and happy. 'Want to join us in Hogsmeade, Ginny?' he asked.

'I'm going with Dean – might see you there,' she replied, waving at them as she left.

Filch was standing at the oak front doors as usual, checking off the names of people who had permission to go into Hogsmeade. The process took even longer than normal as Filch was triple-checking everybody with his Secrecy Sensor.

'What does it matter if we're smuggling Dark stuff OUT?' demanded Ron, eyeing the long thin Secrecy Sensor with apprehension. 'Surely you ought to be checking what we bring back IN?'

His cheek earned him a few extra jabs with the Sensor, and he was still wincing as they stepped out into the wind and sleet.

The walk into Hogsmeade was not enjoyable. Harry wrapped his scarf over his lower face; the exposed part soon felt both raw and numb. The road to the village was full of students bent double against the bitter wind. More than once Harry wondered whether they might not have had a better time in the warm common room, and when they finally reached Hogsmeade and saw that Zonko's Joke Shop had been boarded up, Harry took it as confirmation that this trip was not destined to be fun. Ron pointed with a thickly gloved hand towards Honeydukes, which was mercifully open, and Harry and Hermione staggered in his wake into the crowded shop.

“他们倒是很愿意要我。”哈利讥讽地说，“要不是他们总想干掉我，说不定我跟他们还会成为铁哥们儿呢。”

罗恩笑了起来，就连赫敏也勉强露出了笑容，这时金妮出现，转移了他们的注意力。

“喂，哈利，有人让我把这个交给你。”

是一卷羊皮纸，上面是那种熟悉的细细长长、歪向一边的字体，写着哈利的名字。

“谢谢你，金妮……邓布利多又要给我上课了！”哈利又对罗恩和赫敏说，一边展开羊皮纸，飞快地扫了一遍上面的内容，“星期一晚上！”他觉得心情一下子变得轻松、愉快。“你跟我们一起去霍格莫德吗，金妮？”他问。

“我和迪安一起去——也许会在那儿见到你们。”她说完便朝他们挥挥手走了。

费尔奇和往常一样站在橡木大门口，一个个核对获准去霍格莫德村的同学的名字。这个时间比以往更漫长，因为费尔奇用他的探密器在每个人身上反复地测来测去。

“就算我们把黑魔法物品偷带出去又有什么关系？”罗恩忐忑不安地盯着那根细细长长的探密器，问道，“你恐怕应该检查我们带进来的东西吧？”

他出言不逊，结果被探密器额外多戳了几下，当他们走到外面的狂风和雨雪中时，他还疼得龇牙咧嘴呢。

步行去霍格莫德村的一路上很不舒服。哈利用围巾裹住脸的下半部，暴露在外的部分很快就被冻得生疼生疼，后来都发麻了。在通往村口的路上，到处可见弯着腰顶风前进的学生。哈利不止一次地怀疑，待在暖融融的公共休息室里可能会更愉快。当他们终于走到霍格莫德村时，却看见佐科笑话店被木板封死了，哈利认为这更证实了这趟旅行注定是毫无乐趣的。罗恩用戴着厚手套的手指着蜂蜜公爵糖果店，谢天谢地，那里还开着门，哈利和赫敏便跟着罗恩摇摇晃晃地朝那家拥挤的小店走去。

'Thank God,' shivered Ron as they were enveloped by warm, toffee-scented air. 'Let's stay here all afternoon.'

'Harry, m'boy!' said a booming voice from behind them.

'Oh, no,' muttered Harry. The three of them turned to see Professor Slughorn, who was wearing an enormous furry hat and overcoat with matching fur collar, clutching a large bag of crystallised pineapple and occupying at least a quarter of the shop.

'Harry, that's three of my little suppers you've missed now!' said Slughorn, poking him genially in the chest. 'It won't do, m'boy, I'm determined to have you! Miss Granger loves them, don't you?'

'Yes,' said Hermione helplessly, 'they're really –'

'So why don't you come along, Harry?' demanded Slughorn.

'Well, I've had Quidditch practice, Professor,' said Harry, who had indeed been scheduling practices every time Slughorn had sent him a little violet-ribbon-adorned invitation. This strategy meant that Ron was not left out and they usually had a laugh with Ginny imagining Hermione shut up with McLaggen and Zabini.

'Well, I certainly expect you to win your first match after all this hard work!' said Slughorn. 'But a little recreation never hurt anybody. Now, how about Monday night, you can't possibly want to practise in this weather …'

'I can't, Professor, I've got – er – an appointment with Professor Dumbledore that evening.'

'Unlucky again!' cried Slughorn dramatically. 'Ah, well … you can't evade me for ever, Harry!'

And with a regal wave, he waddled out of the shop, taking as little notice of Ron as though he had been a display of Cockroach Cluster.

'I can't believe you've wriggled out of another one,' said Hermione, shaking her head. 'They're not *that* bad, you know … they're even quite fun sometimes …' But then she caught sight of Ron's expression. 'Oh, look – they've got Deluxe Sugar Quills – those would last hours!'

Glad that Hermione had changed the subject, Harry showed much more interest in the new extra-large Sugar Quills than he would normally have done, but Ron continued to look moody and merely shrugged when Hermione asked him where he wanted to go next.

“感谢上帝，”弥漫着乳脂糖香味的温暖气息扑面而来，罗恩瑟瑟发抖地说，“我们就在这里待一个下午吧。”

“哈利，孩子！”他们身后响起一个洪钟般的声音。

“哦，糟糕。”哈利嘟囔道。他们三个一回头，看见了斯拉格霍恩教授，他戴着一顶硕大无比的毛绒帽子，身上是一件带有配套毛绒领子的大衣，手里攥着一大袋菠萝蜜饯，他至少占据了这个小店四分之一的空间。

“哈利，你已经错过我的三次小型晚餐会了！”斯拉格霍恩亲热地捅了捅哈利的胸口，“这可不行，孩子，我是铁了心要你来的！格兰杰小姐很喜欢这些晚会，是不是？”

“是的，”赫敏无奈地说，“它们确实——”

“那你为什么不来呢，哈利？”斯拉格霍恩责问道。

“嗯，我要参加魁地奇训练呢，教授。”哈利说。确实，每次斯拉格霍恩给他送来一张小小的系着紫色绸带的请柬时，他就故意安排球队训练。这个策略能保证不把罗恩一个人撇下。他们还经常和金妮一道想象赫敏与麦克拉根、沙比尼被关在一起的情景，乐得哈哈大笑。

“好啊，训练得这么刻苦，你们的第一场比赛肯定能赢！”斯拉格霍恩说，“不过偶尔来点儿娱乐也没有害处。那么，星期一晚上怎么样？这种天气你们不可能训练的……”

“不行，教授，我——我——我那天晚上跟邓布利多教授约好了。”

“又是不巧！”斯拉格霍恩夸张地大叫了一声，“啊，好吧……你不可能永远躲着我，哈利！”

他架子十足地挥了挥手，大摇大摆地走出了糖果店，几乎没有注意到罗恩，就好像他只是店里陈列的一个蟑螂串。

“真不敢相信，居然又让你躲过了一次。”赫敏摇着头说，“其实并没有那么糟糕……有时候还蛮好玩的……”她突然看见罗恩脸上的表情。“哦，看——他们有高级糖棒羽毛笔——可以吮好几个小时呢！”

哈利庆幸赫敏改变了话题，他假装对这种新的超大型糖棒羽毛笔特别感兴趣，但罗恩还是显得闷闷不乐，当赫敏问他接下来想去哪里时，他只是耸了耸肩膀。

'Let's go to the Three Broomsticks,' said Harry. 'It'll be warm.'

They bundled their scarves back over their faces and left the sweet shop. The bitter wind was like knives on their faces after the sugary warmth of Honeydukes. The street was not very busy; nobody was lingering to chat, just hurrying towards their destinations. The exceptions were two men a little ahead of them, standing just outside the Three Broomsticks. One was very tall and thin; squinting through his rain-washed glasses Harry recognised the barman who worked in the other Hogsmeade pub, the Hog's Head. As Harry, Ron and Hermione drew closer, the barman drew his cloak more tightly around his neck and walked away, leaving the shorter man to fumble with something in his arms. They were barely feet from him when Harry realised who the man was.

'Mundungus!'

The squat, bandy-legged man with long straggly ginger hair jumped and dropped an ancient suitcase, which burst open, releasing what looked like the entire contents of a junk shop window.

'Oh, 'ello, 'Arry,' said Mundungus Fletcher, with a most unconvincing stab at airiness. 'Well, don't let me keep ya.'

And he began scrabbling on the ground to retrieve the contents of his suitcase with every appearance of a man eager to be gone.

'Are you selling this stuff?' asked Harry, watching Mundungus grabbing an assortment of grubby-looking objects from the ground.

'Oh, well, gotta scrape a living,' said Mundungus. 'Gimme that!'

Ron had stooped down and picked up something silver.

'Hang on,' Ron said slowly. 'This looks familiar –'

'Thank you!' said Mundungus, snatching the goblet out of Ron's hand and stuffing it back into the case. 'Well, I'll see you all – OUCH!'

Harry had pinned Mundungus against the wall of the pub by the throat. Holding him fast with one hand, he pulled out his wand.

'Harry!' squealed Hermione.

'You took that from Sirius's house,' said Harry, who was almost nose-to-nose with Mundungus and was breathing in an unpleasant smell of old tobacco and spirits. 'That had the Black family crest on it.'

“我们去三把扫帚吧，”哈利说，“那里肯定暖和。”

他们重新用围巾把脸裹住，离开了糖果店。刚从暖融融、甜丝丝的蜂蜜公爵店里出来，凛冽的寒风刮在他们脸上，像刀子一样。街上比较冷清，没有人停下来闲聊天，大家都在匆匆赶路，直奔自己要去的地方。唯一例外的是他们前面的两个人。他们就站在三把扫帚的外面，其中一个很高很瘦，哈利眯起眼睛，透过被雨水打湿的眼镜认出他是霍格莫德村另一家酒吧——猪头酒吧里的男招待。哈利、罗恩和赫敏走近时，那男招待用斗篷裹紧脖子，转身走开了，只留下那个矮个子在摸索着怀里的什么东西。他们离那男人不到一步远了，哈利突然认出了他。

“蒙顿格斯！”

那个两腿外八字、留着一头乱糟糟的姜黄色长发的矮胖男人吓了一跳，怀里一只古色古香的小提箱掉在地上弹了开来，里面的东西五花八门，像是一家古董店整个橱窗里的物品。

“噢，你好，哈利，”蒙顿格斯·弗莱奇说，装出非常轻快的样子，却装得一点儿也不像，“别让我耽误了你的时间。”

他蹲在地上摸索着捡起箱子里的东西，一副巴不得马上离开的样子。

“你在卖这些东西？”哈利看着蒙顿格斯从地上抓起一堆各式各样、破破烂烂的东西，问道。

“唉，没办法，总得想办法糊口啊。”蒙顿格斯说，“把那个给我！”

罗恩正俯下身捡起一个银器。

“等等，”罗恩慢悠悠地说，“这个看着眼熟——”

“谢谢！”蒙顿格斯说着，一把从罗恩手里夺过那只高脚酒杯，塞进了箱子，“好了，咱们以后再见——哎哟！”

哈利掐住蒙顿格斯的脖子，把他顶在酒吧的外墙上。他一只手紧紧地掐着他，另一只手拔出了魔杖。

“哈利！”赫敏惊叫道。

“这东西你是从小天狼星家里偷出来的，”哈利说，他与蒙顿格斯几乎鼻子碰鼻子，闻到了一股臭烘烘的烟草和烈酒的气味，“上面有布莱克家族的饰章。”

'I – no – what –?' spluttered Mundungus, who was turning slowly purple.

'What did you do, go back the night he died and strip the place?' snarled Harry.

'I – no –'

'Give it to me!'

'Harry, you mustn't!' shrieked Hermione, as Mundungus started to turn blue.

There was a bang and Harry felt his hands fly off Mundungus's throat. Gasping and spluttering, Mundungus seized his fallen case, then – CRACK – he Disapparated.

Harry swore at the top of his voice, spinning on the spot to see where Mundungus had gone.

'COME BACK, YOU THIEVING –!'

'There's no point, Harry.'

Tonks had appeared out of nowhere, her mousy hair wet with sleet.

'Mundungus will probably be in London by now. There's no point yelling.'

'He's nicked Sirius's stuff! Nicked it!'

'Yes, but still,' said Tonks, who seemed perfectly untroubled by this piece of information, 'you should get out of the cold.'

She watched them through the door of the Three Broomsticks. The moment he was inside, Harry burst out, '*He was nicking Sirius's stuff!*'

'I know, Harry, but please don't shout, people are staring,' whispered Hermione. 'Go and sit down, I'll get you a drink.'

Harry was still fuming when Hermione returned to their table a few minutes later holding three bottles of Butterbeer.

'Can't the Order control Mundungus?' Harry demanded of the other two in a furious whisper. 'Can't they at least stop him stealing everything that's not fixed down when he's at Headquarters?'

'Shh!' said Hermione desperately, looking around to make sure nobody was listening; there were a couple of warlocks sitting close by who were staring at Harry with great interest, and Zabini was lolling against a pillar not far away. 'Harry, I'd be annoyed too, I know it's your things he's stealing –'

“我——没有——什么？”蒙顿格斯结结巴巴地说，脸慢慢涨成了猪肝色。

“你干了什么？在他死的那天夜里，你去把那个地方洗劫一空了？”哈利吼道。

“我——没有——”

“把它给我！”

“哈利，你不能！”赫敏尖叫着说，蒙顿格斯的脸已经发青了。

砰的一声巨响，哈利觉得自己双手从蒙顿格斯的脖子上弹开了。蒙顿格斯呼哧呼哧地喘着气，抓起掉在地上的箱子，然后——**啪**——幻影移形了。

哈利扯着嗓子叫骂，原地转着圈儿看蒙顿格斯跑到哪儿去了。

“回来，你这个贼——！”

“没有用了，哈利。”

唐克斯不知从哪儿冒了出来，灰褐色的头发被雨雪淋得湿漉漉的。“蒙顿格斯这会儿大概已经到了伦敦。再嚷嚷也没有用了。”

“他偷了小天狼星的东西！他偷东西！”

“是啊，不过，”唐克斯说，似乎对这个消息完全无动于衷，“你们不应该待在这儿受冻。”

她看着他们进了三把扫帚酒吧的门。哈利一进酒吧就吼了起来：“他在偷小天狼星的东西！”

“我知道，哈利，可是请你别再嚷嚷了，别人都在看你呢。”赫敏小声说，“快去坐下来，我给你端饮料。”

几分钟后，赫敏端着三瓶黄油啤酒回到他们的桌子旁，哈利还在那里气呼呼的。

“社里就不能管管蒙顿格斯吗？”哈利气愤地小声责问他们两个，“他在总部的时候，他们就不能管着他点儿？至少别让他把搬得走的东西都偷光啊！”

“嘘——”赫敏焦急地说，一边看看周围有没有人在偷听。坐在近旁的两个男巫怀着极大的兴趣盯着哈利，沙比尼懒洋洋地靠在不远处的一根柱子上。“哈利，换了我也会很生气的，我知道他偷的是你的东西——”

Harry gagged on his Butterbeer; he had momentarily forgotten that he owned number twelve, Grimmauld Place.

'Yeah, it's my stuff!' he said. 'No wonder he wasn't pleased to see me! Well, I'm going to tell Dumbledore what's going on, he's the only one who scares Mundungus.'

'Good idea,' whispered Hermione, clearly pleased that Harry was calming down. 'Ron, what are you staring at?'

'Nothing,' said Ron, hastily looking away from the bar, but Harry knew he was trying to catch the eye of the curvy and attractive barmaid, Madam Rosmerta, for whom he had long nursed a soft spot.

'I expect "nothing"'s in the back getting more Firewhisky,' said Hermione waspishly.

Ron ignored this jibe, sipping his drink in what he evidently considered to be a dignified silence. Harry was thinking about Sirius, and how he had hated those silver goblets anyway. Hermione drummed her fingers on the table, her eyes flickering between Ron and the bar.

The moment Harry drained the last drops in his bottle she said, 'Shall we call it a day and go back to school, then?'

The other two nodded; it had not been a fun trip and the weather was getting worse the longer they stayed. Once again they drew their cloaks tightly around them, rearranged their scarves, pulled on their gloves; then followed Katie Bell and a friend out of the pub and back up the High Street. Harry's thoughts strayed to Ginny as they trudged up the road to Hogwarts through the frozen slush. They had not met up with her, undoubtedly, thought Harry, because she and Dean were cosily closeted in Madam Puddifoot's teashop, that haunt of happy couples. Scowling, he bowed his head against the swirling sleet and trudged on.

It was a little while before Harry became aware that the voices of Katie Bell and her friend, which were being carried back to him on the wind, had become shriller and louder. Harry squinted at their indistinct figures. The two girls were having an argument about something Katie was holding in her hand.

'It's nothing to do with you, Leanne!' Harry heard Katie say.

哈利被黄油啤酒呛了一口。他一时忘记了他已经是格里莫广场12号的主人。

"对啊，是我的东西！"他说，"怪不得他看见我那么心虚呢！哼，我要把这件事告诉邓布利多，他是蒙顿格斯唯一害怕的人。"

"好主意。"赫敏小声说，她显然很高兴看到哈利终于平静下来，"罗恩，你在盯着什么呢？"

"没什么。"罗恩说着慌忙把目光从吧台那儿挪开了，哈利知道他是想引起那位妩媚动人的老板娘——罗斯默塔女士的注意，罗恩已经暗暗喜欢她好长时间了。

"我想，你的那位'没什么'正在后面拿更多的火焰威士忌吧？"赫敏尖刻地说。

罗恩没理会这句嘲讽的话，一言不发地慢慢喝着黄油啤酒，显然以为自己这副派头很高贵、很深沉。哈利在想着小天狼星，他想起小天狼星当时是多么仇恨那些银质高脚酒杯。赫敏用手指敲着桌子，眼睛忽而望望罗恩，忽而望望吧台。

哈利刚把瓶里的啤酒喝完，赫敏就说："今天就到这里，我们回学校吧？"

另外两个人点了点头。这趟旅行没有什么乐趣，再待下去，天气只会越来越糟糕。于是，他们又一次把斗篷裹得紧紧的，用围巾把脸挡住，戴上手套，跟在凯蒂·贝尔和一位朋友后面出了酒吧，顺着大路往回走。他们踩着路上被冻得硬邦邦的雪泥，步履艰难地朝霍格沃茨的方向走去，哈利没来由地想起了金妮。他们没有碰见她，哈利心想，她肯定和迪安一起舒舒服服地待在帕笛芙夫人的茶馆里呢，那是快乐的情侣们最爱去的地方。哈利皱起双眉，埋头顶着随风飞舞的雨雪，一步步艰难地往前走。

过了一会儿哈利才意识到，被风刮到他耳朵里的凯蒂·贝尔和她朋友的声音变得越来越响、越来越尖厉了。哈利眯起眼睛打量她们模糊的身影。两个女孩正为凯蒂手里的什么东西在争吵。

"这跟你没有关系，利妮！"哈利听见凯蒂说。

They rounded a corner in the lane, sleet coming thick and fast, blurring Harry's glasses. Just as he raised a gloved hand to wipe them, Leanne made to grab hold of the package Katie was holding; Katie tugged it back and the package fell to the ground.

At once, Katie rose into the air, not as Ron had done, suspended comically by the ankle, but gracefully, her arms outstretched, as though she were about to fly. Yet there was something wrong, something eerie … her hair was whipped around her by the fierce wind, but her eyes were closed and her face was quite empty of expression. Harry, Ron, Hermione and Leanne had all halted in their tracks, watching.

Then, six feet above the ground, Katie let out a terrible scream. Her eyes flew open but whatever she could see, or whatever she was feeling, was clearly causing her terrible anguish. She screamed and screamed; Leanne started to scream too, and seized Katie's ankles, trying to tug her back to the ground. Harry, Ron and Hermione rushed forwards to help, but even as they grabbed Katie's legs, she fell on top of them; Harry and Ron managed to catch her but she was writhing so much they could hardly hold her. Instead they lowered her to the ground where she thrashed and screamed, apparently unable to recognise any of them.

Harry looked around; the landscape seemed deserted.

'Stay there!' he shouted at the others over the howling wind. 'I'm going for help!'

He began to sprint towards the school; he had never seen anyone behave as Katie had just done and could not think what had caused it; he hurtled round a bend in the lane and collided with what seemed to be an enormous bear on its hind legs.

'Hagrid!' he panted, disentangling himself from the hedgerow into which he had fallen.

'Harry!' said Hagrid, who had sleet trapped in his eyebrows and beard, and was wearing his great, shaggy beaverskin coat. 'Jus' bin visitin' Grawp, he's comin' on so well yeh wouldn' –'

'Hagrid, someone's hurt back there, or cursed, or something –'

'Wha'?' said Hagrid, bending lower to hear what Harry was saying over the raging wind.

'Someone's been cursed!' bellowed Harry.

他们在小路上拐了一个弯，雨雪下得更密更急了，把哈利的眼镜弄得一片模糊。他用戴着手套的手擦拭着镜片，就在这时，利妮突然伸手去夺凯蒂拿的那包东西。凯蒂使劲往回一拽，东西掉在了地上。

一下子，凯蒂就升到了空中，她不像罗恩那样被可笑地钩住脚脖子倒挂起来，她的姿态非常优雅，双臂平伸，像是要飞起来似的。然而，她身上有一些怪异，有一些不对劲儿的地方……她的头发被猛烈的狂风吹得四下飘舞，但是一双眼睛紧闭着，脸上一点儿表情也没有。哈利、罗恩、赫敏和利妮都停住了脚步，呆呆地看着她。

然后，在离地面六英尺高的地方，凯蒂突然发出一声恐怖的尖叫。她的眼睛猛地睁开了，而她所能看见或感觉到的东西显然给她带来了可怕的痛苦。她一声接一声地尖叫。利妮也跟着叫了起来，她拽住凯蒂的脚脖子，拼命想把她拖回地面。哈利、罗恩和赫敏也冲过去帮忙。就在他们抓住凯蒂的双腿时，她一下子落到他们身上。哈利和罗恩总算把她抱住了，但她扭动得太厉害，他们简直控制不住她。于是，他们就把她放到了地上。她剧烈地扭动着，失声惨叫，显然认不出他们中的任何一个了。

哈利看看周围，四下里一个人也没有。

"你们待在这儿！"他在呼啸的狂风中对另外几个人喊道，"我去叫人来帮忙！"

哈利撒腿朝学校的方向跑去。他以前从没见过有谁像凯蒂这样，想不出究竟是怎么回事。他飞快地拐过一个弯道，却跟一个庞然大物撞了个满怀，那家伙像是一头靠后腿站立的大熊。

"海格！"哈利摔进了一片树篱中，他喘着气，挣扎着钻出来叫道。

"哈利！"海格说，他的眉毛和胡子上都沾着雨雪，身上穿着那件巨大无比、邋里邋遢的海狸皮大衣，"我去看格洛普了，他进步可快了，你都——"

"海格，那边有人受伤了，也许是中了魔咒什么的——"

"什么？"海格俯下身听哈利说话，狂风的声音太响了。

"有人中了魔咒！"哈利扯开嗓子喊道。

'Cursed? Who's bin cursed – not Ron? Hermione?'

'No, it's not them, it's Katie Bell – this way …'

Together they ran back along the lane. It took them no time to find the little group of people around Katie, who was still writhing and screaming on the ground; Ron, Hermione and Leanne were all trying to quieten her.

'Get back!' shouted Hagrid. 'Lemme see her!'

'Something's happened to her!' sobbed Leanne. 'I don't know what –'

Hagrid stared at Katie for a second, then, without a word, bent down, scooped her into his arms and ran off towards the castle with her. Within seconds, Katie's piercing screams had died away and the only sound was the roar of the wind.

Hermione hurried over to Katie's wailing friend and put an arm around her.

'It's Leanne, isn't it?'

The girl nodded.

'Did it just happen all of a sudden, or –?'

'It was when that package tore,' sobbed Leanne, pointing at the now sodden brown-paper package on the ground, which had split open to reveal a greenish glitter. Ron bent down, his hand outstretched, but Harry seized his arm and pulled him back.

'Don't touch it!'

He crouched down. An ornate opal necklace was visible, poking out of the paper.

'I've seen that before,' said Harry, staring at the thing. 'It was on display in Borgin and Burkes ages ago. The label said it was cursed. Katie must have touched it.' He looked up at Leanne, who had started to shake uncontrollably. 'How did Katie get hold of this?'

'Well, that's why we were arguing. She came back from the bathroom in the Three Broomsticks holding it, said it was a surprise for somebody at Hogwarts and she had to deliver it. She looked all funny when she said it … oh no, oh no, I bet she'd been Imperiused, and I didn't realise!'

Leanne shook with renewed sobs. Hermione patted her shoulder gently.

'She didn't say who'd given it to her, Leanne?'

'No … she wouldn't tell me … and I said she was being stupid and not

“中了魔咒？谁中了魔咒——不是罗恩？赫敏？”

“不，不是他们，是凯蒂·贝尔——在这边……”

他们一起顺着小路往回跑，很快就看见那一小群人围在凯蒂身边。凯蒂仍然躺在地上扭动、惨叫，罗恩、赫敏和利妮都在想办法使她安静下来。

“闪开！”海格喊道，“让我看看！”

“她出事了！”利妮哭泣着说，“我不知道是怎么——”

海格盯着凯蒂看了一秒钟，然后一言不发地弯腰把她抱起来，转身就朝城堡的方向跑去。几秒钟后，凯蒂的尖叫声就听不见了，四下里只有狂风的阵阵呼啸。

赫敏匆匆走到凯蒂那位号啕大哭的朋友身边，伸出胳膊搂住了她。

“你是利妮，是吗？”

姑娘点了点头。

“这件事是突然发生的，还是——？”

“那个包裹一撕开就出事了。”利妮抽抽搭搭地说，指着地上那个已经湿透的牛皮纸包。纸包裂开了，里面有什么东西发出绿莹莹的光。罗恩弯下腰伸出手去，哈利一把抓住他的胳膊，把他拉了回来。

“别碰它！”

哈利蹲下身。他看见纸包里露出一条华丽的蛋白石项链。

“我见过它，”哈利注视着那东西说，“它很久以前陈列在博金-博克店里。商标上说它带着魔咒。凯蒂肯定是碰到它了。”他抬头看着利妮，利妮这会儿已经全身抖得无法控制，“凯蒂是怎么弄到这东西的？”

“唉，我们刚才就为这个争吵来着。她从三把扫帚的厕所里出来时，手里就拿着它，说那是送给霍格沃茨什么人的礼物，由她转交。她说话的时候表情很奇怪……哦，糟糕，哦，糟糕，她肯定是中了夺魂咒，我当时没有意识到！”

利妮又哭得浑身发抖。赫敏轻轻拍着她的肩膀。

“她没有说是谁给她的吗，利妮？”

“没有……她不肯告诉我……我说她昏了头，这东西绝不能拿到学

to take it up to school, but she just wouldn't listen and … and then I tried to grab it from her … and – and –' Leanne let out a wail of despair.

'We'd better get up to school,' said Hermione, her arm still around Leanne, 'we'll be able to find out how she is. Come on …'

Harry hesitated for a moment, then pulled his scarf from around his face and, ignoring Ron's gasp, carefully covered the necklace in it and picked it up.

'We'll need to show this to Madam Pomfrey,' he said.

As they followed Hermione and Leanne up the road, Harry was thinking furiously. They had just entered the grounds when he spoke, unable to keep his thoughts to himself any longer.

'Malfoy knows about this necklace. It was in a case at Borgin and Burkes four years ago, I saw him having a good look at it while I was hiding from him and his dad. *This* is what he was buying that day when we followed him! He remembered it and he went back for it!'

'I – I dunno, Harry,' said Ron hesitantly. 'Loads of people go to Borgin and Burkes … and didn't that girl say Katie got it in the girls' bathroom?'

'She said she came back from the bathroom with it, she didn't necessarily get it in the bathroom itself –'

'McGonagall!' said Ron warningly.

Harry looked up. Sure enough, Professor McGonagall was hurrying down the stone steps through swirling sleet to meet them.

'Hagrid says you four saw what happened to Katie Bell – upstairs to my office at once, please! What's that you're holding, Potter?'

'It's the thing she touched,' said Harry.

'Good Lord,' said Professor McGonagall, looking alarmed as she took the necklace from Harry. 'No, no, Filch, they're with me!' she added hastily, as Filch came shuffling eagerly across the Entrance Hall holding his Secrecy Sensor aloft. 'Take this necklace to Professor Snape at once, but be sure not to touch it, keep it wrapped in the scarf!'

Harry and the others followed Professor McGonagall upstairs and into her office. The sleet-spattered windows were rattling in their frames and the room was chilly despite the fire crackling in the grate. Professor McGonagall closed the door and swept round her desk to face Harry, Ron, Hermione and

校去，可她就是不听，后来……后来我想把东西从她手里抢过来……后来——后来——”利妮发出一声绝望的尖叫。

“我们最好赶紧回学校去，”赫敏仍然搂着利妮说，“这样就能弄清她现在怎么样了。走吧……”

哈利迟疑了一会儿，把脸上裹的围巾解了下来，他没有理会罗恩的惊叫，小心翼翼地用围巾裹住那条项链，把它捡了起来。

“我们需要把这个拿给庞弗雷女士看看。”他说。

他们跟着赫敏和利妮往前走，哈利心里苦苦思索着。刚走进学校的场地，他就忍不住把自己的想法说了出来。

“马尔福知道这条项链。它四年前就在博金－博克店的一只匣子里，当时我藏在店里，躲避马尔福和他爸爸，我看见马尔福仔细打量过它。我们跟踪他的那天，他想买的就是*这个东西*！他对它念念不忘，想回去把它买下来！”

“我——我看不见得吧，哈利，”罗恩犹豫不决地说，“去博金－博克店的人多着呢……而且，那女生不是说凯蒂是在女厕所里拿到项链的吗？”

“她说凯蒂从厕所出来时手里拿着项链，并没说是在厕所里拿到的——”

“麦格来了！”罗恩警告说。

哈利抬头一看，果然，麦格教授冒着随风飞旋的雨雪匆匆走下石头台阶来迎他们了。

“海格说你们四个人看见了凯蒂·贝尔出事的经过——请立刻到楼上我的办公室来一趟！你手里拿的什么，波特？”

“就是凯蒂碰的那个东西。”哈利说。

“天哪，”麦格教授说着从哈利手里接过项链，神色显得十分紧张，“不，不，费尔奇，他们是跟我在一起的！”她看见费尔奇举着探密器，兴致勃勃、踢踏踢踏地从门厅走来，便赶紧对他说，“立刻把这条项链拿去给斯内普教授，千万不要碰它，就让它一直包在围巾里！”

哈利和其他几个人跟着麦格教授，上楼走进了她的办公室。溅满雨雪的窗玻璃在窗框里咔咔作响，尽管炉栅里噼噼啪啪地燃着旺火，屋里还是很冷。麦格教授关上门，快步绕到桌子后面，看着哈利、罗恩、

the still-sobbing Leanne.

'Well?' she said sharply. 'What happened?'

Haltingly, and with many pauses while she attempted to control her crying, Leanne told Professor McGonagall how Katie had gone to the bathroom in the Three Broomsticks and returned holding the unmarked package, how Katie had seemed a little odd and how they had argued about the advisability of agreeing to deliver unknown objects, the argument culminating in the tussle over the parcel, which tore open. At this point, Leanne was so overcome there was no getting another word out of her.

'All right,' said Professor McGonagall, not unkindly, 'go up to the hospital wing, please, Leanne, and get Madam Pomfrey to give you something for shock.'

When she had left the room, Professor McGonagall turned back to Harry, Ron and Hermione.

'What happened when Katie touched the necklace?'

'She rose up in the air,' said Harry, before either Ron or Hermione could speak. 'And then began to scream, and collapsed. Professor, can I see Professor Dumbledore, please?'

'The Headmaster is away until Monday, Potter,' said Professor McGonagall, looking surprised.

'Away?' Harry repeated angrily.

'Yes, Potter, away!' said Professor McGonagall tartly. 'But anything you have to say about this horrible business can be said to me, I'm sure!'

For a split second, Harry hesitated. Professor McGonagall did not invite confidences; Dumbledore, though in many ways more intimidating, still seemed less likely to scorn a theory, however wild. This was a life and death matter, though, and no moment to worry about being laughed at.

'I think Draco Malfoy gave Katie that necklace, Professor.'

On one side of him, Ron rubbed his nose in apparent embarrassment; on the other, Hermione shuffled her feet as though quite keen to put a bit of distance between herself and Harry.

'That is a very serious accusation, Potter,' said Professor McGonagall, after a shocked pause. 'Do you have any proof?'

'No,' said Harry, 'but …' and he told her about following Malfoy to Borgin and Burkes and the conversation they had overheard between him and Borgin.

赫敏和仍然哭个不停的利妮。

“说吧，”她严厉地说，“怎么回事？”

利妮结结巴巴地说开了，因为哭得控制不住，中间停顿了好几次。她告诉麦格教授，凯蒂怎么在三把扫帚酒吧去了一趟厕所，回来时怎么显得有点怪怪的，手里拿着那个没有任何标记的包裹；她们俩怎么争吵，因为她认为凯蒂不应该答应转交一件不知名的东西；争吵到最激烈的时候，两人便开始抢夺那个包裹，结果包裹被扯开了。说到这里，利妮情绪完全崩溃了，再也说不出一个字来。

“好了，”麦格教授不失温和地说，“利妮，你到校医院去，让庞弗雷女士给你点儿药压压惊。”

利妮走后，麦格教授转向哈利、罗恩和赫敏。

“凯蒂碰了那条项链后发生了什么？”

“她升到了空中，”哈利抢在罗恩和赫敏前面说，“然后开始尖叫，接着便掉了下来。教授，请问我能见见邓布利多教授吗？”

“校长出去了，要星期一才回来，波特。”麦格教授显得很惊讶，说道。

“出去了？”哈利气恼地重复了一遍。

“是的，波特，出去了！”麦格教授尖刻地说，“但是我认为，关于这件可怕的事情，你有什么要说的都可以跟我说！”

一刹那间，哈利有些犹豫。他好像很难对麦格教授推心置腹。而邓布利多尽管在许多方面令人生畏，却似乎不太可能对某个想法嗤之以鼻，不管这个想法多么荒唐离奇。然而，这是一件生死攸关的事，没有工夫考虑是否会遭到嘲笑了。

“我认为是德拉科·马尔福给了凯蒂那条项链，教授。”

站在他一侧的罗恩尴尬地揉着鼻子；站在他另一侧的赫敏把脚在地上滑来滑去，似乎巴不得跟哈利保持一定的距离。

“这是一个很严重的指控，波特，”麦格教授惊愕地停顿了一下，说道，“你有证据吗？”

“没有，”哈利说，“但是……”他把那天跟踪马尔福到博金-博克店，偷听到他和博金之间的那段对话告诉了麦格教授。

When he had finished speaking, Professor McGonagall looked slightly confused.

'Malfoy took something to Borgin and Burkes for repair?'

'No, Professor, he just wanted Borgin to tell him how to mend something, he didn't have it with him. But that's not the point, the thing is that he bought something at the same time and I think it was that necklace –'

'You saw Malfoy leaving the shop with a similar package?'

'No, Professor, he told Borgin to keep it in the shop for him –'

'But, Harry,' Hermione interrupted, 'Borgin asked him if he wanted to take it with him, and Malfoy said "no" –'

'Because he didn't want to touch it, obviously!' said Harry angrily.

'What he actually said was, "How would I look carrying that down the street?",' said Hermione.

'Well, he would look a bit of a prat carrying a necklace,' interjected Ron.

'Oh, Ron,' said Hermione despairingly, 'it would be all wrapped up, so he wouldn't have to touch it, and quite easy to hide inside a cloak, so nobody would see it! I think whatever he reserved at Borgin and Burkes was noisy or bulky; something he knew would draw attention to him if he carried it down the street – and in any case,' she pressed on loudly, before Harry could interrupt, 'I asked Borgin about the necklace, don't you remember? When I went in to try and find out what Malfoy had asked him to keep, I saw it there. And Borgin just told me the price, he didn't say it was already sold or anything –'

'Well, you were being really obvious, he realised what you were up to within about five seconds, of course he wasn't going to tell you – anyway, Malfoy could've sent off for it since –'

'That's enough!' said Professor McGonagall, as Hermione opened her mouth to retort, looking furious. 'Potter, I appreciate you telling me this, but we cannot point the finger of blame at Mr Malfoy purely because he visited the shop where this necklace might have been purchased. The same is probably true of hundreds of people –'

'– that's what I said –' muttered Ron.

'– and in any case, we have put stringent security measures in place this year, I do not believe that necklace can possibly have entered this school without our knowledge –'

他说完后，麦格教授显得有点儿迷惑。

“马尔福把一件东西拿到博金－博克店去修理？”

“不，教授，他只是要博金告诉他怎么修理一件东西，并没有把它带去。但问题不在这里，问题是他同时还买了一件东西，我认为就是那条项链——”

“你看见马尔福离开商店时拿着那样一个包裹？”

“不，教授，他叫博金替他保存在店里——”

“可是，哈利，”赫敏打断了他的话，“博金问他是不是想把东西拿走，马尔福说‘不’——”

“因为他不想碰那东西，这还用说吗！”哈利生气地说。

“他的原话是：‘我拿着它走在街上像什么话？’”赫敏说。

“是啊，他拿着一条项链确实会显得很傻。”罗恩插嘴说。

“哦，罗恩，”赫敏绝望地说，“项链肯定是包起来的，他用不着碰到它，而且很容易藏在斗篷内侧的口袋里，没有人会看得见！我认为他保存在博金－博克店里的那件东西要么体积很大，要么会发出很响的动静，他知道如果带着那东西在街上走，肯定会引起别人的注意——而且，”她不让哈利有机会打断她，只顾大声地往下说，“我向博金打听过那条项链，记得吗？当时我走进店里，想弄清马尔福要他保存什么，我看见项链还在那儿。博金告诉了我项链的价钱，并没有说已经卖出去了——”

“嘿，你做得太显眼了，他五秒钟内就发现了你想干什么，自然不会告诉你啦——而且，马尔福可以通过邮购的方式——”

“够了！”赫敏刚想张嘴反驳，麦格教授就气呼呼地说道，“波特，感谢你告诉我这些，但我们不能因为马尔福先生光顾过那家可能卖出这条项链的商店，就随随便便地指责他。去过那家商店的可能有好几百人——”

“——我也是这么说的——”罗恩嘟囔道。

“——而且，今年我们加强了严密的安全防范措施，我不相信那条项链会在我们不知道的情况下进入这所学校——”

'– but –'

'– and what is more,' said Professor McGonagall, with an air of awful finality, 'Mr Malfoy was not in Hogsmeade today.'

Harry gaped at her, deflating.

'How do you know, Professor?'

'Because he was doing detention with me. He has now failed to complete his Transfiguration homework twice in a row. So, thank you for telling me your suspicions, Potter,' she said as she marched past them, 'but I need to go up to the hospital wing now to check on Katie Bell. Good day to you all.'

She held open her office door. They had no choice but to file past her without another word.

Harry was angry with the other two for siding with McGonagall; nevertheless, he felt compelled to join in once they started discussing what had happened.

'So who do you reckon Katie was supposed to give the necklace to?' asked Ron, as they climbed the stairs to the common room.

'Goodness only knows,' said Hermione. 'But whoever it was has had a narrow escape. No one could have opened that package without touching the necklace.'

'It could've been meant for loads of people,' said Harry. 'Dumbledore – the Death Eaters would love to get rid of him, he must be one of their top targets. Or Slughorn – Dumbledore reckons Voldemort really wanted him and they can't be pleased that he's sided with Dumbledore. Or –'

'Or you,' said Hermione, looking troubled.

'Couldn't have been,' said Harry, 'or Katie would've just turned round in the lane and given it to me, wouldn't she? I was behind her all the way out of the Three Broomsticks. It would have made much more sense to deliver the parcel outside Hogwarts, what with Filch searching everyone who goes in and out. I wonder why Malfoy told her to take it into the castle?'

'Harry, Malfoy wasn't in Hogsmeade!' said Hermione, actually stamping her foot in frustration.

'He must have used an accomplice, then,' said Harry. 'Crabbe or Goyle – or, come to think of it, another Death Eater, he'll have loads better cronies than Crabbe and Goyle now he's joined up –'

“可是——”

“——还有一点，”麦格教授以一种斩钉截铁的口气说，“马尔福先生今天没有去霍格莫德村。”

哈利呆呆地望着她，顿时泄了气。

“你怎么知道的，教授？”

“因为他在我这里关禁闭呢。他已经接连两次没有完成变形课的作业。好了，波特，感谢你把你的怀疑告诉了我，”她大步从他们身边走过，“但是我现在要去医院看看凯蒂·贝尔。祝你们愉快。”

她打开办公室的门。他们别无选择，只好一言不发地挨个儿从她身边走了出去。

哈利很生罗恩和赫敏的气，因为他们跟麦格站在一边。不过，当他俩开始谈论刚才发生的事情时，他还是不由自主地加入了进去。

“那么，你们认为凯蒂要把那条项链交给谁呢？”他们上楼去公共休息室时，罗恩问道。

“只有天知道了，”赫敏说，“不过，不管那个人是谁，这次都是侥幸逃脱。只要打开那个包裹，就肯定会碰到项链。”

“许多人都有可能。”哈利说，“邓布利多——食死徒巴不得摆脱他呢，他肯定是他们的首选目标；或者斯拉格霍恩——邓布利多认为伏地魔很想把他拉过去，现在他们看到他站到了邓布利多一边，肯定很不高兴；或者——”

“或者是你。”赫敏很焦虑地说。

“不可能，”哈利说，“要是那样的话，凯蒂只要在路上转个身，直接交给我就行了，不是吗？从三把扫帚出来后，我就一直走在她后面。费尔奇对每个进出霍格沃茨的人都要搜查一番，凯蒂在校外把包裹交给我不是要明智得多吗？我不明白马尔福为什么要叫她把项链带进城堡。”

“哈利，马尔福不在霍格莫德村！”赫敏说，她无奈地跺着脚。

“那他肯定还有一个同谋，”哈利说，“克拉布或高尔——对了，说不定是另一个食死徒，现在马尔福肯定有一大堆比克拉布和高尔更像样的哥们儿了，因为他已经加入——”

Ron and Hermione exchanged looks that plainly said 'there's no point arguing with him'.

'Dilligrout,' said Hermione firmly, as they reached the Fat Lady.

The portrait swung open to admit them to the common room. It was quite full and smelled of damp clothing; many people seemed to have returned from Hogsmeade early because of the bad weather. There was no buzz of fear or speculation, however: clearly, the news of Katie's fate had not yet spread.

'It wasn't a very slick attack, really, when you stop and think about it,' said Ron, casually turfing a first-year out of one of the good armchairs by the fire, so that he could sit down. 'The curse didn't even make it into the castle. Not what you'd call foolproof.'

'You're right,' said Hermione, prodding Ron out of the chair with her foot and offering it to the first-year again. 'It wasn't very well-thought-out at all.'

'But since when has Malfoy been one of the world's great thinkers?' asked Harry.

Neither Ron nor Hermione answered him.

罗恩和赫敏交换了一个目光，显然是说“跟他争论没用”。

“杏仁鸡羹！”赫敏果断地说，这时他们已经来到胖夫人跟前。

肖像向前旋开，放他们进了公共休息室。休息室里挤满了人，弥漫着湿衣服的气味。由于天气恶劣，许多人似乎都提早从霍格莫德村回来了。不过，人们并没有惊慌地窃窃私语，做出各种猜测，看来凯蒂惨遭厄运的消息还没有传开。

“仔细想想，这次下手其实安排得并不巧妙。”罗恩大大咧咧地把一个一年级同学从火边一把好椅子上赶开，自己坐了下来，“那个魔咒连城堡的大门都没能进入，这种安排可不能算万无一失。”

“你说得对，”赫敏说着，用脚把罗恩从椅子上赶走，让那个一年级同学重新坐了下来，“这确实不是一个很周密的计划。”

“马尔福什么时候算得上世界一流的思想家了？”哈利问。

罗恩和赫敏都没有理睬他。

CHAPTER THIRTEEN

The Secret Riddle

Katie was removed to St Mungo's Hospital for Magical Maladies and Injuries the following day, by which time the news that she had been cursed had spread all over the school, though the details were confused and nobody other than Harry, Ron, Hermione and Leanne seemed to know that Katie herself had not been the intended target.

'Oh, and Malfoy knows, of course,' said Harry to Ron and Hermione, who continued their new policy of feigning deafness whenever Harry mentioned his Malfoy-is-a-Death-Eater theory.

Harry had wondered whether Dumbledore would return from wherever he had been in time for Monday night's lesson, but having had no word to the contrary, he presented himself outside Dumbledore's office at eight o'clock, knocked, and was told to enter. There sat Dumbledore, looking unusually tired; his hand was as black and burned as ever, but he smiled when he gestured to Harry to sit down. The Pensieve was sitting on the desk again, casting silvery specks of light over the ceiling.

'You have had a busy time while I have been away,' Dumbledore said. 'I believe you witnessed Katie's accident.'

'Yes, sir. How is she?'

'Still very unwell, although she was relatively lucky. She appears to have brushed the necklace with the smallest possible amount of skin: there was a tiny hole in her glove. Had she put it on, had she even held it in her ungloved hand, she would have died, perhaps instantly. Luckily Professor Snape was able to do enough to prevent a rapid spread of the curse –'

'Why him?' asked Harry quickly. 'Why not Madam Pomfrey?'

'Impertinent,' said a soft voice from one of the portraits on the wall, and

第 13 章

神秘的里德尔

凯蒂第二天就转到圣芒戈魔法伤病医院去了，这时候，她中魔咒的消息已经在学校里传遍，不过大家并不清楚具体细节，除了哈利、罗恩、赫敏和利妮，似乎谁也不知道凯蒂本人并不是那条项链预期的攻击目标。

“噢，马尔福当然也知道。”哈利对罗恩和赫敏说，他俩每次听见哈利提到“马尔福是食死徒”的想法，都只好继续装聋作哑。

邓布利多不知道去了哪儿，哈利甚至怀疑他星期一晚上不能赶回来给他上课。不过既然没有收到取消上课的通知，他还是在晚上八点钟准时出现在邓布利多的办公室外面。他轻轻敲了敲门，里面有声音请他进去。邓布利多坐在那里，显得特别疲惫，那只手还像以前一样焦黑干枯，但是他脸上带着微笑，示意哈利坐下。冥想盆又一次放在桌上，将星星点点的银色光斑投射在天花板上。

“我出去的这段时间，你很忙碌啊。”邓布利多说，“你亲眼看见了凯蒂出事的情景。”

“是的，先生。她怎么样了？”

“情况还很不好，不过还算幸运。她似乎只是一小块皮肤碰到了项链：她的手套上有一个小洞。如果她把项链戴在脖子上，或哪怕是用不戴手套的手拿起项链，她都会死去，也许当场就毙命了。幸好斯内普教授很有办法，阻止了魔咒的快速传播——”

“为什么是他？”哈利立刻问道，“为什么不是庞弗雷女士？”

“没礼貌。”墙上一幅肖像里传出一个轻轻的声音，菲尼亚斯·奈

Phineas Nigellus Black, Sirius's great-great-grandfather, raised his head from his arms where he had appeared to be sleeping. 'I would not have permitted a student to question the way Hogwarts operated in my day.'

'Yes, thank you, Phineas,' said Dumbledore quellingly. 'Professor Snape knows much more about the Dark Arts than Madam Pomfrey, Harry. Anyway, the St Mungo's staff are sending me hourly reports and I am hopeful that Katie will make a full recovery in time.'

'Where were you this weekend, sir?' Harry asked, disregarding a strong feeling that he might be pushing his luck, a feeling apparently shared by Phineas Nigellus, who hissed softly.

'I would rather not say just now,' said Dumbledore. 'However, I shall tell you in due course.'

'You will?' said Harry, startled.

'Yes, I expect so,' said Dumbledore, withdrawing a fresh bottle of silver memories from inside his robes and uncorking it with a prod of his wand.

'Sir,' said Harry tentatively, 'I met Mundungus in Hogsmeade.'

'Ah, yes, I am already aware that Mundungus has been treating your inheritance with light-fingered contempt,' said Dumbledore, frowning a little. 'He has gone to ground since you accosted him outside the Three Broomsticks; I rather think he dreads facing me. However, rest assured that he will not be making away with any more of Sirius's old possessions.'

'That mangy old half-blood has been stealing Black heirlooms?' said Phineas Nigellus, incensed; and he stalked out of his frame, undoubtedly to visit his portrait in number twelve, Grimmauld Place.

'Professor,' said Harry, after a short pause, 'did Professor McGonagall tell you what I told her after Katie got hurt? About Draco Malfoy?'

'She told me of your suspicions, yes,' said Dumbledore.

'And do you –?'

'I shall take all appropriate measures to investigate anyone who might have had a hand in Katie's accident,' said Dumbledore. 'But what concerns me now, Harry, is our lesson.'

Harry felt slightly resentful at this: if their lessons were so very important, why had there been such a long gap between the first and second? However,

杰勒斯·布莱克——小天狼星的曾曾祖父，刚才趴在胳膊上似乎睡着了，这会儿正好抬起头来，“想当年，我可不允许一位学生对霍格沃茨的管理方式提出异议。”

“是的，谢谢你，菲尼亚斯。”邓布利多息事宁人地说，“哈利，斯内普教授在黑魔法方面的知识比庞弗雷女士丰富得多。而且，圣芒戈魔法伤病医院的工作人员每小时都在向我汇报情况，我相信凯蒂很快就有希望完全恢复。”

“你这个周末去哪儿了，先生？”哈利问，他知道自己有点得寸进尺，但他豁出去了，菲尼亚斯·奈杰勒斯显然也觉得哈利太过分了，轻轻地发出嘘声。

“目前我还不想说，”邓布利多说，“不过，以后在适当的时候我会告诉你的。”

“会吗？”哈利惊异地问。

“会，我想会的。”邓布利多说着从长袍里掏出一个装着银白色记忆的新瓶子，用魔杖一捅，拔出了木塞。

“先生，”哈利犹豫不决地说，“我在霍格莫德村看见蒙顿格斯了。”

“啊，是的，我已经发现蒙顿格斯不把你继承的遗产当回事，经常顺手牵羊。”邓布利多微微皱着眉头说，“自从你在三把扫帚酒吧外面跟他说过话之后，他就藏起来了。我想他是不敢见我了吧。不过你放心，他再也不会把小天狼星留下的东西偷走了。”

“那个卑鄙的老杂种竟敢偷布莱克家的祖传遗物？”菲尼亚斯·奈杰勒斯恼火地说，然后大步走出了相框，无疑是去拜访他在格里莫广场 12 号的那幅肖像了。

“教授，”哈利在短暂的停顿之后说，“麦格教授有没有把我在凯蒂受伤后对她说的话告诉你？关于德拉科·马尔福的那些话？”

“是的，她对我说了你的怀疑。”邓布利多说。

“那么你——？”

“凡是在凯蒂事故中有嫌疑的人，我都要对其进行深入细致的调查。”邓布利多说，“可是，哈利，我现在关心的是我们的课。”

哈利听了这话感到有点恼火。既然他们的课这么重要，为什么第一堂课和第二堂课之间隔了这么长时间？不过，他没有就德拉科·马

he said no more about Draco Malfoy, but watched as Dumbledore poured the fresh memories into the Pensieve, and began swirling the stone basin once more between his long-fingered hands.

'You will remember, I am sure, that we left the tale of Lord Voldemort's beginnings at the point where the handsome Muggle, Tom Riddle, had abandoned his witch wife, Merope, and returned to his family home in Little Hangleton. Merope was left alone in London, expecting the baby who would one day become Lord Voldemort.'

'How do you know she was in London, sir?'

'Because of the evidence of one Caractacus Burke,' said Dumbledore, 'who, by an odd coincidence, helped found the very shop whence came the necklace we have just been discussing.'

He swilled the contents of the Pensieve as Harry had seen him swill them before, much as a gold prospector sifts for gold. Up out of the swirling, silvery mass rose a little old man, revolving slowly in the Pensieve, silver as a ghost but much more solid, with a thatch of hair that completely covered his eyes.

'Yes, we acquired it in curious circumstances. It was brought in by a young witch just before Christmas, oh, many years ago now. She said she needed the gold badly, well, that much was obvious. Covered in rags and pretty far along … going to have a baby, see. She said the locket had been Slytherin's. Well, we hear that sort of story all the time, "Oh, this was Merlin's, this was, his favourite teapot," but when I looked at it, it had his mark all right, and a few simple spells were enough to tell me the truth. Of course, that made it near enough priceless. She didn't seem to have any idea how much it was worth. Happy to get ten Galleons for it. Best bargain we ever made!'

Dumbledore gave the Pensieve an extra-vigorous shake and Caractacus Burke descended back into the swirling mass of memory whence he had come.

'He only gave her ten Galleons?' said Harry indignantly.

'Caractacus Burke was not famed for his generosity,' said Dumbledore. 'So we know that, near the end of her pregnancy, Merope was alone in London and in desperate need of gold, desperate enough to sell her one and only valuable possession, the locket that was one of Marvolo's treasured family heirlooms.'

尔福的事再说什么，而是注视着邓布利多把那些新的记忆倒进冥想盆，然后用细长的双手端起石盆轻轻转动。

“关于伏地魔的早期经历，我想你一定还记得，我们上次说到那位英俊的麻瓜——汤姆·里德尔抛弃了他的女巫妻子梅洛普，回到了他在小汉格顿村的老家。梅洛普独自待在伦敦，肚子里怀着那个日后将成为伏地魔的孩子。”

“你怎么知道她在伦敦呢，先生？”

“因为有卡拉克塔库斯·博克提供的证据。”邓布利多说，“说来真是无巧不成书，他当年协助创办的一家商店，正是出售我们所说的那条项链的店铺。”

他晃动着冥想盆里的东西，就像淘金者筛金子一样，哈利以前看见他这么做过。那些不断旋转的银白色物质中浮现出一个小老头儿的身影，他在冥想盆里慢慢旋转，苍白得像幽灵一样，但比幽灵更有质感，他的头发非常浓密，把眼睛完全遮住了。

“是的，我们是在很特殊的情况下得到它的。一位年轻的女巫在圣诞节前把它拿来，说起来那已经是很多年前的事了。她说她急需要钱，是啊，那是再明显不过了。她衣衫褴褛，面容憔悴……还怀着身孕，就快生了。她说那个挂坠盒以前是斯莱特林的。咳，我们成天听到这样的鬼话：‘噢，这是梅林的东西，真的，是他最喜欢的茶壶。’可是我仔细一看，挂坠盒上果然有斯莱特林的标记，我又念了几个简单的咒语就弄清了真相。当然啦，那东西简直价值连城。那女人似乎根本不知道它有多值钱，只卖了十个加隆就心满意足了。那是我们做的最划算的一笔买卖！”

邓布利多格外用力地晃了晃冥想盆，卡拉克塔库斯又重新回到他刚才出现的地方，沉入旋转的记忆之中。

“他只给了她十个加隆？”哈利愤愤不平地说。

“卡拉克塔库斯·博克不是一个慷慨大方的人。”邓布利多说，“这样我们便知道，梅洛普在怀孕后期，独自一个人待在伦敦，迫切地需要钱，不得不卖掉她身上唯一值钱的东西——那个挂坠盒，也是马沃罗非常珍惜的一件传家宝。”

'But she could do magic!' said Harry impatiently. 'She could have got food and everything for herself by magic, couldn't she?'

'Ah,' said Dumbledore, 'perhaps she could. But it is my belief – I am guessing again, but I am sure I am right – that when her husband abandoned her, Merope stopped using magic. I do not think that she wanted to be a witch any longer. Of course, it is also possible that her unrequited love and the attendant despair sapped her of her powers; that can happen. In any case, as you are about to see, Merope refused to raise her wand even to save her own life.'

'She wouldn't even stay alive for her son?'

Dumbledore raised his eyebrows.

'Could you possibly be feeling sorry for Lord Voldemort?'

'No,' said Harry quickly, 'but she had a choice, didn't she, not like my mother –'

'Your mother had a choice, too,' said Dumbledore gently. 'Yes, Merope Riddle chose death in spite of a son who needed her, but do not judge her too harshly, Harry. She was greatly weakened by long suffering and she never had your mother's courage. And now, if you will stand …'

'Where are we going?' Harry asked, as Dumbledore joined him at the front of the desk.

'This time,' said Dumbledore, 'we are going to enter *my* memory. I think you will find it both rich in detail and satisfyingly accurate. After you, Harry …'

Harry bent over the Pensieve; his face broke the cool surface of the memory and then he was falling through darkness again … Seconds later his feet hit firm ground, he opened his eyes and found that he and Dumbledore were standing in a bustling, old-fashioned London street.

'There I am,' said Dumbledore brightly, pointing ahead of them to a tall figure crossing the road in front of a horse-drawn milk cart.

This younger Albus Dumbledore's long hair and beard were auburn. Having reached their side of the street, he strode off along the pavement, drawing many curious glances due to the flamboyantly cut suit of plum velvet that he was wearing.

'Nice suit, sir,' said Harry, before he could stop himself, but Dumbledore merely chuckled as they followed his younger self a short distance, finally

"但是她会施魔法呀！"哈利性急地说，"她可以通过魔法给自己弄到食物和所有的东西，不是吗？"

"嗬，"邓布利多说，"也许她可以。不过我认为——我这又是在猜测，但我相信我是对的——我认为梅洛普在被丈夫抛弃之后，就不再使用魔法了。她大概不想再做一个女巫。当然啦，也有另一种可能，她那得不到回报的爱情以及由此带来的绝望，大大削弱了她的力量。那样的事情是会发生的。总之，你待会儿就会看到，梅洛普甚至不肯举起魔杖拯救自己的性命。"

"她甚至不愿意为了她的儿子活下来吗？"

邓布利多扬起了眉毛。

"莫非你竟然对伏地魔产生了同情？"

"不，"哈利急忙说道，"但是梅洛普是可以选择的，不是吗？不像我妈妈——"

"你妈妈也是可以选择的。"邓布利多温和地说，"是的，梅洛普·里德尔选择了死亡，尽管有一个需要她的儿子，但是，哈利，不要对她求全责备吧。长期的痛苦折磨使她变得十分脆弱，而且她一向没有你妈妈那样的勇气。好了，现在请你站起来……"

"我们去哪儿？"哈利问，这时邓布利多走过来和他一起站在桌前。

"这次，"邓布利多说，"我们要进入*我的*记忆。我想，你会发现它不仅细节生动，而且准确无误。你先来，哈利……"

哈利朝冥想盆俯下身，他的脸扎入盆中冰冷的记忆，然后他又一次在黑暗中坠落……几秒钟后，他的双脚踩到了坚实的地面，他睁开眼睛，发现他和邓布利多站在伦敦一条繁忙的老式街道上。

"那就是我。"邓布利多指着前面一个高高的身影欢快地说，那人正在一辆马拉的牛奶车前面横穿马路。

这位年轻的阿不思·邓布利多的长头发和长胡子都是赤褐色的。他来到马路这一边，顺着人行道大步流星地往前走，身上那件考究的紫红色天鹅绒西服吸引了许多好奇的目光。

"好漂亮的衣服，先生。"哈利不假思索地脱口说道，邓布利多只

passing through a set of iron gates into a bare courtyard that fronted a rather grim, square building surrounded by high railings. He mounted the few steps leading to the front door and knocked once. After a moment or two the door was opened by a scruffy girl wearing an apron.

'Good afternoon. I have an appointment with a Mrs Cole, who, I believe, is the matron here?'

'Oh,' said the bewildered-looking girl, taking in Dumbledore's eccentric appearance. 'Um … just a mo' … MRS COLE!' she bellowed over her shoulder.

Harry heard a distant voice shouting something in response. The girl turned back to Dumbledore.

'Come in, she's on 'er way.'

Dumbledore stepped into a hallway tiled in black and white; the whole place was shabby but spotlessly clean. Harry and the older Dumbledore followed. Before the front door had closed behind them, a skinny, harassed-looking woman came scurrying towards them. She had a sharp-featured face that appeared more anxious than unkind and she was talking over her shoulder to another aproned helper as she walked towards Dumbledore.

'… and take the iodine upstairs to Martha, Billy Stubbs has been picking his scabs and Eric Whalley's oozing all over his sheets – chicken pox on top of everything else,' she said to nobody in particular, and then her eyes fell upon Dumbledore and she stopped dead in her tracks, looking as astonished as if a giraffe had just crossed her threshold.

'Good afternoon,' said Dumbledore, holding out his hand.

Mrs Cole simply gaped.

'My name is Albus Dumbledore. I sent you a letter requesting an appointment and you very kindly invited me here today.'

Mrs Cole blinked. Apparently deciding that Dumbledore was not a hallucination, she said feebly, 'Oh, yes. Well – well, then – you'd better come into my room. Yes.'

She led Dumbledore into a small room that seemed part sitting room, part office. It was as shabby as the hallway and the furniture was old and mismatched. She invited Dumbledore to sit on a rickety chair and seated herself behind a cluttered desk, eyeing him nervously.

是轻声笑了笑。他们不远不近地跟着年轻的邓布利多，最后穿过一道大铁门，走进了一个空荡荡的院子。

院子后面是一座四四方方、阴森古板的楼房，四周围着高高的栏杆。他走上通向前门的几级台阶，敲了一下门。过了片刻，一个系着围裙的邋里邋遢的姑娘把门打开了。

“下午好，我跟一位科尔夫人约好了，我想，她是这里的总管吧？”

“哦，”那个姑娘满脸困惑地说，一边用锐利的目光打量着邓布利多那一身古怪的行头，“嗯……等一等……**科尔夫人！**”她扭头大声叫道。

哈利听见远处有个声音大喊着回答了她。那姑娘又转向了邓布利多。

“进来吧，她马上就来。”

邓布利多走进一间铺着黑白瓷砖的门厅。整个房间显得很破旧，但是非常整洁，一尘不染。哈利和老邓布利多跟了进去。大门还没在他们身后关上，就有一个瘦骨嶙峋、神色疲惫的女人快步朝他们走来。她的面部轮廓分明，看上去与其说是凶恶，倒不如说是焦虑。她一边朝邓布利多走来，一边扭头吩咐另一个系着围裙的帮手。

“……把碘酒拿上楼给玛莎，比利·斯塔布斯把他的痂都抓破了，埃里克·华莱的血弄脏了床单——真倒霉，竟染上了水痘！”她像是对着空气说话，这时她的目光落在了邓布利多身上。她猛地刹住脚步，一脸惊愕，仿佛看见一头长颈鹿迈过了她的门槛。

“下午好。”邓布利多说着伸出了手。

科尔夫人目瞪口呆地看着他。

“我叫阿不思·邓布利多。我给您写过一封信，请求您的约见，您非常仁慈地邀请我今天过来。”

科尔夫人眨了眨眼睛。她似乎这才认定邓布利多不是她的幻觉，便强打起精神说道：“噢，对了。好——好吧——你最好到我的房间里来。是的。”

她领着邓布利多走进一间好像半是客厅半是办公室的小屋。这里和门厅一样简陋寒酸，家具都很陈旧，而且不配套。她请邓布利多坐在一把摇摇晃晃的椅子上，她自己则坐到一张杂乱不堪的桌子后面，紧张地打量着他。

'I am here, as I told you in my letter, to discuss Tom Riddle and arrangements for his future,' said Dumbledore.

'Are you family?' asked Mrs Cole.

'No, I am a teacher,' said Dumbledore. 'I have come to offer Tom a place at my school.'

'What school's this, then?'

'It is called Hogwarts,' said Dumbledore.

'And how come you're interested in Tom?'

'We believe he has qualities we are looking for.'

'You mean he's won a scholarship? How can he have done? He's never been entered for one.'

'Well, his name has been down for our school since birth –'

'Who registered him? His parents?'

There was no doubt that Mrs Cole was an inconveniently sharp woman. Apparently Dumbledore thought so too, for Harry now saw him slip his wand out of the pocket of his velvet suit, at the same time picking up a piece of perfectly blank paper from Mrs Cole's desktop.

'Here,' said Dumbledore, waving his wand once as he passed her the piece of paper, 'I think this will make everything clear.'

Mrs Cole's eyes slid out of focus and back again as she gazed intently at the blank paper for a moment.

'That seems perfectly in order,' she said placidly, handing it back. Then her eyes fell upon a bottle of gin and two glasses that had certainly not been present a few seconds before.

'Er – may I offer you a glass of gin?' she said in an extra-refined voice.

'Thank you very much,' said Dumbledore, beaming.

It soon became clear that Mrs Cole was no novice when it came to gin-drinking. Pouring both of them a generous measure, she drained her own glass in one. Smacking her lips frankly, she smiled at Dumbledore for the first time, and he didn't hesitate to press his advantage.

'I was wondering whether you could tell me anything of Tom Riddle's history? I think he was born here in the orphanage?'

“我信上已经对您说了，我来这里，是想跟您商量商量汤姆·里德尔的事，给他安排一个前程。”邓布利多说。

“你是他的亲人？”科尔夫人问。

“不，我是一位教师，”邓布利多说，“我来请汤姆到我们学校去念书。”

“那么，这是一所什么学校呢？”

“校名是霍格沃茨。”邓布利多说。

“你们怎么会对汤姆感兴趣呢？”

“我们认为他具有我们寻找的一些素质。”

“你是说他赢得了一份奖学金？怎么会呢？他从来没有报名申请过啊。”

“噢，他一出生，我们学校就把他的名字记录在案——”

“谁替他注册的呢？他的父母？”

毫无疑问，科尔夫人是一个非常精明、让人感到有些头疼的女人。邓布利多显然也是这么认为，哈利看见他从天鹅绒西服的口袋里抽出了魔杖，同时从科尔夫人的桌面上拿起一张完全空白的纸。

“给。”邓布利多说着把那张纸递给了她，一边挥了一下魔杖，“我想，您看看这个就全清楚了。”

科尔夫人的眼神飘忽了一下，随即又变得专注，她对着那张空白的纸认真地看了一会儿。

“看来是完全符合程序的。”她平静地说，把纸还给了邓布利多。然后她的目光落在一瓶杜松子酒和两只玻璃杯上，那些东西几秒钟前肯定不在那儿。

“嗯——我可以请你喝一杯杜松子酒吗？”她用一种特别温文尔雅的声音说。

“非常感谢。”邓布利多笑眯眯地说。

很明显，科尔夫人喝起杜松子酒来可不是个新手。她把两个人的杯子斟得满满的，一口就把自己那杯喝得精光。她不加掩饰地咂巴咂巴嘴，第一次朝邓布利多露出了微笑，邓布利多立刻趁热打铁。

“不知道你是不是可以跟我说说汤姆·里德尔的身世？他好像是在这个孤儿院里出生的吧？”

'That's right,' said Mrs Cole, helping herself to more gin. 'I remember it clear as anything, because I'd just started here myself. New Year's Eve and bitter cold, snowing, you know. Nasty night. And this girl, not much older than I was myself at the time, came staggering up the front steps. Well, she wasn't the first. We took her in and she had the baby within the hour. And she was dead in another hour.'

Mrs Cole nodded impressively and took another generous gulp of gin.

'Did she say anything before she died?' asked Dumbledore. 'Anything about the boy's father, for instance?'

'Now, as it happens, she did,' said Mrs Cole, who seemed to be rather enjoying herself now, with the gin in her hand and an eager audience for her story.

'I remember she said to me, "I hope he looks like his papa," and I won't lie, she was right to hope it, because she was no beauty – and then she told me he was to be named Tom, for his father, and Marvolo, for *her* father – yes, I know, funny name, isn't it? We wondered whether she came from a circus – and she said the boy's surname was to be Riddle. And she died soon after that without another word.

'Well, we named him just as she'd said, it seemed so important to the poor girl, but no Tom nor Marvolo nor any kind of Riddle ever came looking for him, nor any family at all, so he stayed in the orphanage and he's been here ever since.'

Mrs Cole helped herself, almost absent-mindedly, to another healthy measure of gin. Two pink spots had appeared high on her cheek-bones. Then she said, 'He's a funny boy.'

'Yes,' said Dumbledore. 'I thought he might be.'

'He was a funny baby, too. He hardly ever cried, you know. And then, when he got a little older, he was … odd.'

'Odd, in what way?' asked Dumbledore gently.

'Well, he –'

But Mrs Cole pulled up short, and there was nothing blurry or vague about the inquisitorial glance she shot Dumbledore over her gin glass.

'He's definitely got a place at your school, you say?'

'Definitely,' said Dumbledore.

“没错，”科尔夫人说着又给自己倒了一些杜松子酒，“那件事我记得清清楚楚，因为我当时刚来这里工作。当时是新年前夜，外面下着雪，冷得要命。一个天气恶劣的夜晚。那个姑娘，年纪比我当时大不了多少，踉踉跄跄地走上前门的台阶。咳，这种事儿我们经历得多了。我们把她搀了进来，不到一小时她就生下了孩子。又过了一小时，她就死了。”

科尔夫人意味深长地点了点头，又喝了一大口杜松子酒。

“她临死前说过什么话没有？”邓布利多问，“比如，关于那男孩的父亲？”

“是啊，她说过。”科尔夫人手里端着杜松子酒，面前是一位热心的听众，这显然使她来了兴致。

“我记得她对我说：‘我希望他长得像他爸爸。’说老实话，她这么希望是对的，因为她本人长得不怎么样——然后，她告诉我，孩子随他父亲叫汤姆，中间的名字随她自己的父亲叫马沃罗——是啊，我知道，这名字真古怪，对吧？我们怀疑她是马戏团里的人——她又说那男孩的姓是里德尔。然后她没有再说什么，很快就死了。

“后来，我们就按照她说的给孩子起了名字，那可怜的姑娘似乎把这看得很重要，可是从来没有什么汤姆、马沃罗或里德尔家的人来找这个孩子，也不见他有任何亲戚，所以他就留在了孤儿院里，一直到今天。”

科尔夫人几乎是心不在焉地又给自己倒了满满一杯杜松子酒。她的颧骨上泛起两团红晕。然后她说：“他是个古怪的孩子。”

“是啊，”邓布利多说，“我也猜到了。”

“他还是婴儿的时候就很古怪，几乎从来不哭。后来长大了一些，他就变得很……怪异。”

“怪异，哪方面怪异呢？”邓布利多温和地问。

“是这样，他——”

科尔夫人突然顿住，她越过杜松子酒杯朝邓布利多投去询问的目光，那目光一点儿也不恍惚或糊涂。

“他肯定可以到你们学校去念书，是吗？”

“肯定。”邓布利多说。

'And nothing I say can change that?'

'Nothing,' said Dumbledore.

'You'll be taking him away, whatever?'

'Whatever,' repeated Dumbledore gravely.

She squinted at him as though deciding whether or not to trust him. Apparently she decided she could, because she said in a sudden rush, 'He scares the other children.'

'You mean he is a bully?' asked Dumbledore.

'I think he must be,' said Mrs Cole, frowning slightly, 'but it's very hard to catch him at it. There have been incidents … nasty things …'

Dumbledore did not press her, though Harry could tell that he was interested. She took yet another gulp of gin and her rosy cheeks grew rosier still.

'Billy Stubbs's rabbit … well, Tom *said* he didn't do it and I don't see how he could have done, but even so, it didn't hang itself from the rafters, did it?'

'I shouldn't think so, no,' said Dumbledore quietly.

'But I'm jiggered if I know how he got up there to do it. All I know is he and Billy had argued the day before. and then –' Mrs Cole took another swig of gin, slopping a little over her chin this time, 'on the summer outing – we take them out, you know, once a year, to the countryside or to the seaside – well, Amy Benson and Dennis Bishop were never quite right afterwards, and all we ever got out of them was that they'd gone into a cave with Tom Riddle. He swore they'd just gone exploring, but *something* happened in there, I'm sure of it. And, well, there have been a lot of things, funny things …'

She looked at Dumbledore again, and though her cheeks were flushed, her gaze was steady.

'I don't think many people will be sorry to see the back of him.'

'You understand, I'm sure, that we will not be keeping him permanently?' said Dumbledore. 'He will have to return here, at the very least, every summer.'

'Oh, well, that's better than a whack on the nose with a rusty poker,' said Mrs Cole with a slight hiccough. She got to her feet and Harry was impressed to see that she was quite steady, even though two-thirds of the gin was now gone. 'I suppose you'd like to see him?'

“不管我说什么，都不会改变这一点？”

“不会。”邓布利多说。

“不管怎样，你都会把他带走？”

“不管怎样。”邓布利多严肃地保证。

科尔夫人眯起眼睛看着他，似乎在判断要不要相信他。最后她显然认为他是可以相信的，于是突然脱口说道：“他让别的孩子感到害怕。”

“你是说他喜欢欺负人？”邓布利多问。

“我想肯定是这样，”科尔夫人微微皱着眉头说，“但是很难当场抓住他。出过一些事故……一些恶性事件……”

邓布利多没有催她，但哈利可以看出他很感兴趣。科尔夫人又喝了一大口杜松子酒，面颊上的红晕更深了。

“比利·斯塔布斯的兔子……是啊，汤姆说不是他干的，我也认为他不可能办得到，可说是这么说，那兔子总不会自己吊在房梁上吧？”

“是啊，我也认为不会。”邓布利多轻声说。

“但是我死活也弄不清他是怎么爬到那上面去干这件事的。我只知道他和比利前一天吵过一架。还有后来——”科尔夫人又痛饮了一口杜松子酒，这次洒了一些流到下巴上，“夏天出去郊游——你知道的，每年一次。我们带他们到郊外或者海边——从那以后，艾米·本森和丹尼斯·毕肖普就一直不大对劲儿，我们问起来，他们只说是跟汤姆·里德尔一起进过一个山洞。汤姆发誓说是去探险，可是在那里面肯定发生了一些什么事。我可以肯定。此外还有许多许多的事情，稀奇古怪……”

她又看着邓布利多，她虽然面颊酡红，目光却很沉着。

“我想，没多少人会舍不得他离开这儿的。”

“我相信您肯定明白，我们不会一直让他待在学校，”邓布利多说，“至少每年暑假他还会回到这儿。”

“噢，没问题，那也比被人用生锈的拨火棍抽鼻子强。”科尔夫人轻轻打着酒嗝说。她站了起来，哈利惊异地发现，尽管瓶里的杜松子酒已经少了三分之二，她的腿脚仍然很稳当。“我猜你一定很想见见他吧？”

'Very much,' said Dumbledore, rising too.

She led him out of her office and up the stone stairs, calling out instructions and admonitions to helpers and children as she passed. The orphans, Harry saw, were all wearing the same kind of greyish tunic. They looked reasonably well-cared-for, but there was no denying that this was a grim place in which to grow up.

'Here we are,' said Mrs Cole, as they turned off the second landing and stopped outside the first door in a long corridor. She knocked twice and entered.

'Tom? You've got a visitor. This is Mr Dumberton – sorry, Dunderbore. He's come to tell you – well, I'll let him do it.'

Harry and the two Dumbledores entered the room and Mrs Cole closed the door on them. It was a small bare room with nothing in it except an old wardrobe, a wooden chair and an iron bedstead. A boy was sitting on top of the grey blankets, his legs stretched out in front of him, holding a book.

There was no trace of the Gaunts in Tom Riddle's face. Merope had got her dying wish: he was his handsome father in miniature, tall for eleven years old, dark-haired and pale. His eyes narrowed slightly as he took in Dumbledore's eccentric appearance. There was a moment's silence.

'How do you do, Tom?' said Dumbledore, walking forwards and holding out his hand.

The boy hesitated, then took it, and they shook hands. Dumbledore drew up the hard wooden chair beside Riddle, so that the pair of them looked rather like a hospital patient and visitor.

'I am Professor Dumbledore.'

'"Professor"?' repeated Riddle. He looked wary. 'Is that like "doctor"? What are you here for? Did *she* get you in to have a look at me?'

He was pointing at the door through which Mrs Cole had just left.

'No, no,' said Dumbledore, smiling.

'I don't believe you,' said Riddle. 'She wants me looked at, doesn't she? Tell the truth!'

He spoke the last three words with a ringing force that was almost shocking. It was a command, and it sounded as though he had given it many

“确实很想。”邓布利多说着也站了起来。

科尔夫人领着他出了办公室，走上石头楼梯，一边走一边大声地吩咐和指责她的帮手和孩子们。哈利看到那些孤儿都穿着清一色的浅灰色束腰袍子。他们看上去都得到了合理的精心照顾，但是毫无疑问，在这个地方成长，气氛是很阴沉压抑的。

“我们到了。”科尔夫人说，他们在三楼的楼梯平台上拐了个弯，在一条长长走廊的第一个房间门口停住了。她敲了两下门，走了进去。

“汤姆？有人来看你了。这位是邓布顿先生——对不起，是邓德波先生。他来告诉你——唉，还是让他自己跟你说吧。”

哈利和两个邓布利多一起走进房间，科尔夫人在他们身后关上了门。这是一间空荡荡的、没有任何装饰的小屋，只有一个旧衣柜、一把木椅子和一张铁床。一个男孩坐在灰色的毛毯上，两条长长的腿伸在前面，手里拿着一本书在读。

汤姆·里德尔的脸上看不到一点儿冈特家族的影子。梅洛普的遗言变成了现实：他简直就是他那位英俊的父亲的缩小版。对十一岁的孩子来说，他的个子算高的，黑黑的头发，脸色苍白。他微微眯起眼睛，打量着邓布利多怪异的模样和装扮。一时间没有人说话。

“你好，汤姆。”邓布利多说着，走上前伸出了手。

男孩迟疑了一下，然后伸出手握了握。邓布利多把一把硬邦邦的木头椅子拉到里德尔身边，这样一来，他们俩看上去就像是一位住院病人和一位探视者。

“我是邓布利多教授。”

“‘教授’？”里德尔重复了一句，露出很警觉的神情，“是不是就像‘医生’一样？你来这里做什么？是不是她叫你来给我检查检查的？”

他指着刚才科尔夫人离开的房门。

“不，不是。”邓布利多微笑着说。

“我不相信你。”里德尔说，“她想让人来给我看看病，是不是？说实话！”

最后三个字他说得凶狠响亮，气势吓人。这是一句命令，看来他以前多次下过这种命令。他突然睁大眼睛，狠狠地盯着邓布利多，而

times before. His eyes had widened and he was glaring at Dumbledore, who made no response except to continue smiling pleasantly. After a few seconds Riddle stopped glaring, though he looked, if anything, warier still.

'Who are you?'

'I have told you. My name is Professor Dumbledore and I work at a school called Hogwarts. I have come to offer you a place at my school – your new school, if you would like to come.'

Riddle's reaction to this was most surprising. He leapt from the bed and backed away from Dumbledore, looking furious.

'You can't kid me! The asylum, that's where you're from, isn't it? "Professor", yes, of course – well, I'm not going, see? That old cat's the one who should be in the asylum. I never did anything to little Amy Benson or Dennis Bishop, and you can ask them, they'll tell you!'

'I am not from the asylum,' said Dumbledore patiently. 'I am a teacher and, if you will sit down calmly, I shall tell you about Hogwarts. Of course, if you would rather not come to the school, nobody will force you –'

'I'd like to see them try,' sneered Riddle.

'Hogwarts,' Dumbledore went on, as though he had not heard Riddle's last words, 'is a school for people with special abilities –'

'I'm not mad!'

'I know that you are not mad. Hogwarts is not a school for mad people. It is a school of magic.'

There was silence. Riddle had frozen, his face expressionless, but his eyes were flickering back and forth between each of Dumbledore's, as though trying to catch one of them lying.

'Magic?' he repeated in a whisper.

'That's right,' said Dumbledore.

'It's … it's magic, what I can do?'

'What is it that you can do?'

'All sorts,' breathed Riddle. A flush of excitement was rising up his neck into his hollow cheeks; he looked fevered. 'I can make things move without touching them. I can make animals do what I want them to do, without training them. I can make bad things happen to people who annoy me. I can make them hurt if I want to.'

邓布利多没有回答，只是继续和蔼地微笑着。过了几秒钟，里德尔的目光松弛下来，但看上去似乎更警觉了。

“你是谁？”

“我已经告诉你了。我是邓布利多教授，我在一所名叫霍格沃茨的学校工作。我来邀请你到我的学校——你的新学校去念书，如果你愿意的话。”

听了这话，里德尔的反应大大出人意料。他腾地从床上跳起来，后退着离开邓布利多，神情极为恼怒。

“你骗不了我！你是从疯人院来的，是不是？‘教授’，哼，没错——告诉你吧，我不会去的，明白吗？那个该死的老妖婆才应该去疯人院呢。我根本没把小艾米·本森和丹尼斯·毕肖普怎么样，你可以自己去问他们，他们会告诉你的！”

“我不是从疯人院来的，”邓布利多耐心地说，“我是个老师，如果你能心平气和地坐下来，我就跟你说说霍格沃茨的事儿。当然啦，如果你不愿意去那所学校，也没有人会强迫你——”

“我倒想看看谁敢！”里德尔轻蔑地说。

“霍格沃茨，”邓布利多继续说道，似乎没有听见里德尔的最后那句话，“是一所专门为具有特殊才能的人开办的学校——”

“我没有疯！”

“我知道你没有疯。霍格沃茨不是一所疯子学校，而是一所魔法学校。”

沉默。里德尔呆住了，脸上毫无表情，但他的目光快速地轮番扫视邓布利多的两只眼睛，似乎想从其中一只看出他在撒谎。

“魔法？”他轻声重复道。

“不错。”邓布利多说。

“我的那些本领，是……是魔法？”

“你有哪些本领呢？”

“各种各样。”里德尔压低声音说，兴奋的红晕从他的脖子向凹陷的双颊迅速蔓延。他显得很亢奋。“我不用手碰就能让东西动起来。不用训练就能让动物听我的吩咐。谁惹我生气，我就能让谁倒霉。我只要愿意就能让他们受伤。”

His legs were trembling. He stumbled forwards and sat down on the bed again, staring at his hands, his head bowed as though in prayer.

'I knew I was different,' he whispered to his own quivering fingers. 'I knew I was special. Always, I knew there was something.'

'Well, you were quite right,' said Dumbledore, who was no longer smiling, but watching Riddle intently. 'You are a wizard.'

Riddle lifted his head. His face was transfigured: there was a wild happiness upon it, yet for some reason it did not make him better-looking; on the contrary, his finely carved features seemed somehow rougher, his expression almost bestial.

'Are you a wizard too?'

'Yes, I am.'

'Prove it,' said Riddle at once, in the same commanding tone he had used when he had said 'tell the truth'.

Dumbledore raised his eyebrows.

'If, as I take it, you are accepting your place at Hogwarts –'

'Of course I am!'

'Then you will address me as "Professor" or "sir".'

Riddle's expression hardened for the most fleeting moment before he said, in an unrecognisably polite voice, 'I'm sorry, sir. I meant – please, Professor, could you show me –?'

Harry was sure that Dumbledore was going to refuse, that he would tell Riddle there would be plenty of time for practical demonstrations at Hogwarts, that they were currently in a building full of Muggles, and must therefore be cautious. To his great surprise, however, Dumbledore drew his wand from an inside pocket of his suit jacket, pointed it at the shabby wardrobe in the corner and gave the wand a casual flick.

The wardrobe burst into flames.

Riddle jumped to his feet. Harry could hardly blame him for howling in shock and rage; all his worldly possessions must have been in there; but even as Riddle rounded on Dumbledore the flames vanished, leaving the wardrobe completely undamaged.

Riddle stared from the wardrobe to Dumbledore, then, his expression greedy, he pointed at the wand.

他的双腿在颤抖。他跌跌撞撞地走上前，重新坐在床上，垂下脑袋，盯着自己的两只手，像在祈祷一样。

“我早就知道我与众不同。”他对着自己颤抖的双手说，“我早就知道我很特别。我早就知道这里头有点什么。”

“对，你的想法没有错。”邓布利多说，他收敛笑容，目光专注地看着里德尔，“你是一个巫师。”

里德尔抬起头。他的面孔一下子变了：透出一种狂热的欣喜。然而不知怎的，这并没有使他显得更好看些，反而使精致的五官突然变得粗糙了，那神情简直像野兽一样。

“你也是个巫师？”

“是的。”

“证明给我看。”里德尔立刻说道，口气和刚才那句“说实话”一样盛气凌人。

邓布利多扬起眉毛。

“如果，按我的理解，你同意到霍格沃茨去念书——”

“我当然同意！”

“那你就要称我为‘教授’或‘先生’。”

里德尔的表情僵了一刹那，接着他突然以一种判若两人的彬彬有礼的口气说：“对不起，先生。我是说——教授，您能不能让我看看——？”

哈利以为邓布利多一定会拒绝，他以为邓布利多会对里德尔说，以后在霍格沃茨有的是时间做具体示范，并说他们眼下是在一座住满麻瓜的房子里，必须谨慎从事。然而令他大为惊讶的是，邓布利多从西服上装的内袋里抽出魔杖，指着墙角那个破旧的衣柜，漫不经心地一挥。

衣柜立刻着起火来。

里德尔腾地跳了起来。哈利不能责怪他发出惊恐和愤怒的吼叫，他所有的财产大概都在那个衣柜里。可是，里德尔刚要向邓布利多兴师问罪，火焰突然消失，衣柜完好无损。

里德尔看看衣柜，又看看邓布利多，然后，他指着那根魔杖，表情变得很贪婪。

'Where can I get one of them?'

'All in good time,' said Dumbledore. 'I think there is something trying to get out of your wardrobe.'

And sure enough, a faint rattling could be heard from inside it. For the first time, Riddle looked frightened.

'Open the door,' said Dumbledore.

Riddle hesitated, then crossed the room and threw open the wardrobe door. On the topmost shelf, above a rail of threadbare clothes, a small cardboard box was shaking and rattling as though there were several frantic mice trapped inside it.

'Take it out,' said Dumbledore.

Riddle took down the quaking box. He looked unnerved.

'Is there anything in that box that you ought not to have?' asked Dumbledore.

Riddle threw Dumbledore a long, clear, calculating look.

'Yes, I suppose so, sir,' he said finally, in an expressionless voice.

'Open it,' said Dumbledore.

Riddle took off the lid and tipped the contents on to his bed without looking at them. Harry, who had expected something much more exciting, saw a mess of small, everyday objects; a yo-yo, a silver thimble and a tarnished mouth-organ among them. Once free of the box, they stopped quivering and lay quite still upon the thin blankets.

'You will return them to their owners with your apologies,' said Dumbledore calmly, putting his wand back into his jacket. 'I shall know whether it has been done. And be warned: thieving is not tolerated at Hogwarts.'

Riddle did not look remotely abashed; he was still staring coldly and appraisingly at Dumbledore. At last he said in a colourless voice, 'Yes, sir.'

'At Hogwarts,' Dumbledore went on, 'we teach you not only to use magic, but to control it. You have – inadvertently, I am sure – been using your powers in a way that is neither taught nor tolerated at our school. You are not the first, nor will you be the last, to allow your magic to run away with you. But you should know that Hogwarts can expel students, and the Ministry of Magic – yes, there is a Ministry – will punish lawbreakers still more severely.

“我从哪儿可以得到一根？”

“到时候会有的。”邓布利多说，“你那衣柜里好像有什么东西想要钻出来。”

果然，衣柜里传出微弱的咔嗒咔嗒声。里德尔第一次露出了惊慌的神情。

“把门打开。”邓布利多说。

里德尔迟疑了一下，走过去猛地打开了衣柜的门。挂衣杆上挂着几件破旧的衣服，上面最高一层的搁板上有一只小小的硬纸板箱，正在不停地晃动，发出咔嗒咔嗒的响声，里面似乎关着几只疯狂的老鼠。

“把它拿出来。”邓布利多说。

里德尔把那只晃动的箱子搬下来。他显得不知所措。

“那箱子里是不是有一些你不该有的东西？”邓布利多问。

里德尔用清晰、审慎的目光深深地看了邓布利多一眼。

“是的，我想是的，先生。”他最后用一种干巴巴的声音说。

“打开。”邓布利多说。

里德尔打开盖子，看也没看一眼，把里面的东西倒在了床上。哈利本来以为里面会有更加令人兴奋的东西，却只看见一堆平平常常的小玩意儿，其中有一个悠悠球、一只银顶针、一把失去光泽的口琴。它们一离开箱子就不再颤抖，乖乖地躺在薄薄的毯子上，一动不动。

“你要把这些东西还给它们的主人，并且向他们道歉。”邓布利多平静地说，一边把魔杖插进了上衣口袋里，“我会知道你有没有做。我还要警告你：霍格沃茨是不能容忍偷窃行为的。”

里德尔脸上没有丝毫的羞愧。他仍然冷冷地盯着邓布利多，似乎在掂量他。最后，他用一种干巴巴的声音说：“知道了，先生。”

“在霍格沃茨，”邓布利多继续说道，“我们不仅教你使用魔法，还教你控制魔法。你过去用那种方式使用你的魔法，我相信是出于无意，但这是我们学校绝不会传授，也绝不能容忍的。让自己的魔法失去控制，你不是第一个，也不会是最后一个。但是你应该知道，霍格沃茨有权开除学生，而且魔法部——没错，有一个魔法部——会以更严厉的方

All new wizards must accept that, in entering our world, they abide by our laws.'

'Yes, sir,' said Riddle again.

It was impossible to tell what he was thinking; his face remained quite blank as he put the little cache of stolen objects back into the cardboard box. When he had finished he turned to Dumbledore and said baldly, 'I haven't got any money.'

'That is easily remedied,' said Dumbledore, drawing a leather money-pouch from his pocket. 'There is a fund at Hogwarts for those who require assistance to buy books and robes. You might have to buy some of your spellbooks and so on second-hand, but –'

'Where do you buy spellbooks?' interrupted Riddle, who had taken the heavy money bag without thanking Dumbledore, and was now examining a fat gold Galleon.

'In Diagon Alley,' said Dumbledore. 'I have your list of books and school equipment with me. I can help you find everything –'

'You're coming with me?' asked Riddle, looking up.

'Certainly, if you –'

'I don't need you,' said Riddle. 'I'm used to doing things for myself, I go round London on my own all the time. How do you get to this Diagon Alley – sir?' he added, catching Dumbledore's eye.

Harry thought that Dumbledore would insist upon accompanying Riddle, but once again he was surprised. Dumbledore handed Riddle the envelope containing his list of equipment, and, after telling Riddle exactly how to get to the Leaky Cauldron from the orphanage, he said, 'You will be able to see it, although Muggles around you – non-magical people, that is – will not. Ask for Tom the barman – easy enough to remember, as he shares your name –'

Riddle gave an irritable twitch, as though trying to displace an irksome fly.

'You dislike the name "Tom"?'

'There are a lot of Toms,' muttered Riddle. Then, as though he could not suppress the question, as though it burst from him in spite of himself, he asked, 'Was my father a wizard? He was called Tom Riddle too, they've told me.'

'I'm afraid I don't know,' said Dumbledore, his voice gentle.

式惩罚违法者。每一位新来的巫师都必须接受：一旦进入我们的世界，就要服从我们的法律。”

“知道了，先生。”里德尔又说道。

很难知道他脑子里在想什么。他把那一小堆偷来的赃物放回硬纸箱时，脸上还是那样毫无表情。收拾完后，他转过身，毫不客气地对邓布利多说：“我没有钱。”

“那很容易解决。”邓布利多说着就从口袋里掏出一只皮钱袋，“霍格沃茨有一笔基金，专门提供给那些需要资助购买课本和校袍的人。你的有些魔法书恐怕只能买二手货，不过——”

“在哪儿买魔法书？”里德尔打断了邓布利多的话，谢也没谢一声就把钱袋拿了过去，仔细地端详起一枚厚厚的金加隆来。

“在对角巷。”邓布利多说，“我带来了你的书单和学校用品清单。我可以帮你把东西买齐——”

“你要陪我去？”里德尔抬起头来问道。

“那当然，如果你——”

“用不着你，”里德尔说，“我习惯自己做事，总是一个人在伦敦跑来跑去。那么，到这个对角巷怎么走呢——先生？”他碰到了邓布利多的目光，补上了最后两个字。

哈利以为邓布利多会坚持陪里德尔去，但事情又一次出乎他的意料。邓布利多把装着购物清单的信封递给里德尔，又告诉里德尔从孤儿院到破釜酒吧的具体路线，然后说道：“你准能看见它，而你周围的麻瓜——也就是不懂魔法的人——是看不见的。打听一下酒吧老板汤姆——很容易记，名字跟你一样——”

里德尔恼怒地抽搐了一下，好像要赶走一只讨厌的苍蝇。

“你不喜欢‘汤姆’这个名字？”

“叫‘汤姆’的人太多了。”里德尔嘟囔道。然后他似乎是如鲠在喉，不吐不快，又似乎是脱口而出：“我父亲是巫师吗？他们告诉我他也叫汤姆·里德尔。”

“对不起，我不知道。”邓布利多说，声音很温和。

'My mother can't have been magic, or she wouldn't have died,' said Riddle, more to himself than Dumbledore. 'It must've been him. So – when I've got all my stuff – when do I come to this Hogwarts?'

'All the details are on the second piece of parchment in your envelope,' said Dumbledore. 'You will leave from King's Cross Station on the first of September. There is a train ticket in there, too.'

Riddle nodded. Dumbledore got to his feet and held out his hand again. Taking it, Riddle said, 'I can speak to snakes. I found out when we've been to the country on trips – they find me, they whisper to me. Is that normal for a wizard?'

Harry could tell that he had withheld mention of this strangest power until that moment, determined to impress.

'It is unusual,' said Dumbledore, after a moment's hesitation, 'but not unheard of.'

His tone was casual but his eyes moved curiously over Riddle's face. They stood for a moment, man and boy, staring at each other. Then the handshake was broken; Dumbledore was at the door.

'Goodbye, Tom. I shall see you at Hogwarts.'

'I think that will do,' said the white-haired Dumbledore at Harry's side, and seconds later they were soaring weightlessly through darkness once more, before landing squarely in the present-day office.

'Sit down,' said Dumbledore, landing beside Harry.

Harry obeyed, his mind still full of what he had just seen.

'He believed it much quicker than I did – I mean, when you told him he was a wizard,' said Harry. 'I didn't believe Hagrid at first, when he told me.'

'Yes, Riddle was perfectly ready to believe that he was – to use his word – "special",' said Dumbledore.

'Did you know – then?' asked Harry.

'Did I know that I had just met the most dangerous Dark wizard of all time?' said Dumbledore. 'No, I had no idea that he was to grow up to be what he is. However, I was certainly intrigued by him. I returned to Hogwarts intending to keep an eye upon him, something I should have done in any case, given that he was alone and friendless, but which, already, I felt I ought to do for others' sake as much as his.

“我母亲不可能会魔法，不然她不会死。”里德尔不像是对邓布利多说话，更像是自言自语，“肯定是我父亲。那么——我把东西买齐之后——什么时候到这所霍格沃茨学校去呢？”

“所有的细节都写在信封里的第二张羊皮纸上。”邓布利多说，“你九月一日从国王十字车站出发。信封里还有一张火车票。”

里德尔点了点头。邓布利多站起身，又一次伸出了手。里德尔一边握手一边说：“我可以跟蛇说话。我们到郊外远足的时候我发现的——蛇找到我，小声对我说话。这对于一个巫师来说是正常的吗？”

哈利看得出来，他是故意拖到最后一刻才提到这个最奇特的本事，一心想把邓布利多镇住。

“很少见，”邓布利多迟疑了一下，说道，“但并非没有听说过。”

他的语气很随便，但却用目光好奇地打量着里德尔的脸。两人站了片刻，男人和男孩，互相凝视。然后彼此松开了手，邓布利多走到门边。

“再见，汤姆。我们在霍格沃茨见。”

“我看差不多了。”哈利身边那位满头白发的邓布利多说。几秒钟后，他们又一次轻飘飘地在黑暗中飞翔，然后稳稳地落在现实中的办公室里。

“坐下吧。”邓布利多落在哈利身边，说道。

哈利坐了下来，脑子里仍然想着刚才看见的一切。

“他相信这件事的速度比我快得多——我是说，当你对他说他是一个巫师的时候。”哈利说，“海格最初告诉我时，我可不相信。”

“是啊，里德尔巴不得相信他是——用他自己的话说——是‘与众不同’的。”邓布利多说。

“那个时候——你就知道？”哈利问。

“我就知道我刚才看见的那个人是有史以来最危险的黑魔法巫师？”邓布利多说，“不，我根本不知道他会成为现在这样的人。不过我确实对他很感兴趣。我回到霍格沃茨后就打算密切关注他，其实本来也应该这么做，因为他独自一人，没有朋友，但是我当时就觉得我这么做不仅是为了他，也是为了别人。

'His powers, as you heard, were surprisingly well-developed for such a young wizard and – most interestingly and ominously of all – he had already discovered that he had some measure of control over them, and begun to use them consciously. And as you saw, they were not the random experiments typical of young wizards: he was already using magic against other people, to frighten, to punish, to control. The little stories of the strangled rabbit and the young boy and girl he lured into a cave were most suggestive … *I can make them hurt if I want to …*'

'And he was a Parselmouth,' interjected Harry.

'Yes, indeed; a rare ability, and one supposedly connected with the Dark Arts, although, as we know, there are Parselmouths among the great and the good too. In fact, his ability to speak to serpents did not make me nearly as uneasy as his obvious instincts for cruelty, secrecy and domination.

'Time is making fools of us again,' said Dumbledore, indicating the dark sky beyond the windows. 'But before we part, I want to draw your attention to certain features of the scene we have just witnessed, for they have a great bearing on the matters we shall be discussing in future meetings.

'Firstly, I hope you noticed Riddle's reaction when I mentioned that another shared his first name, "Tom"?'

Harry nodded.

'There he showed his contempt for anything that tied him to other people, anything that made him ordinary. Even then, he wished to be different, separate, notorious. He shed his name, as you know, within a few short years of that conversation and created the mask of "Lord Voldemort" behind which he has been hidden for so long.

'I trust that you also noticed that Tom Riddle was already highly self-sufficient, secretive and, apparently, friendless? He did not want help or companionship on his trip to Diagon Alley. He preferred to operate alone. The adult Voldemort is the same. You will hear many of his Death Eaters claiming that they are in his confidence, that they alone are close to him, even understand him. They are deluded. Lord Voldemort has never had a friend, nor do I believe that he has ever wanted one.

“你刚才也听见了，对于这样一个年轻巫师来说，他的能力惊人地完善和成熟——而最有趣也最不祥的一点是——他已经发现他可以在某种程度上控制这些能力，并开始有意识地使用它们。正如你看见的，他不像一般的年轻巫师那样毫无章法地胡乱做些实验。他已经在用魔法对付别人，用魔法去恐吓、惩罚和控制别人。那只被吊死的兔子，还有被他骗进山洞的那一男一女两个孩子的故事就很能说明问题……*我只要愿意就能让他们受伤……*”

“他还是个蛇佬腔。”哈利插嘴道。

“是啊，一种罕见的能力，据说跟黑魔法有关，不过我们知道，在伟大和善良的巫师中间也有蛇佬腔。事实上，他与蛇对话的能力并没有使我感到很不安，令我担心的是他明显表现出来的那种残酷、诡秘和霸道的天性。

“时间又在捉弄我们了，”邓布利多指了指窗外漆黑的天空说道，“不过在我们分手之前，我想请你注意一下刚才目睹的那一幕的某些细节，它们跟我们将来要一起讨论的问题密切相关。

“首先，我想你肯定注意到了，当我提到有人的名字跟他一样也叫‘汤姆’时，里德尔是什么反应吧？”

哈利点了点头。

“这显示出，他蔑视任何把他跟别人拴在一起的东西，蔑视任何使他显得平凡无奇的东西。即使在那个时候，他就希望自己与众不同，孤傲独立，声名远扬。你也知道，在那次对话的短短几年之后，他就抛弃了自己的名字，打造出‘伏地魔’这样一个面具，并在它后面蛰伏了那么长时间。

“我相信你同样也注意到了，汤姆·里德尔当时已经极为自负，讳莫如深，而且显然没有一个朋友。他自己去对角巷，不需要别人的帮助和陪同。他什么都愿意自己做。成年后的伏地魔也是这样。你会听见许多食死徒声称他们得到了他的信任，并声称只有他们才能够接近他甚至理解他。其实他们都受了愚弄。伏地魔从来没有一个朋友，而且我认为他从来都不需要朋友。

'And lastly – I hope you are not too sleepy to pay attention to this, Harry – the young Tom Riddle liked to collect trophies. You saw the box of stolen articles he had hidden in his room. These were taken from victims of his bullying behaviour, souvenirs, if you will, of particularly unpleasant bits of magic. Bear in mind this magpie-like tendency, for this, particularly, will be important later.

'And now, it really is time for bed.'

Harry got to his feet. As he walked across the room, his eyes fell upon the little table on which Marvolo Gaunt's ring had rested last time, but the ring was no longer there.

'Yes, Harry?' said Dumbledore, for Harry had come to a halt.

'The ring's gone,' said Harry, looking around. 'But I thought you might have the mouth-organ or something.'

Dumbledore beamed at him, peering over the top of his half-moon spectacles.

'Very astute, Harry, but the mouth-organ was only ever a mouth-organ.'

And on that enigmatic note he waved to Harry, who understood himself to be dismissed.

“最后——我希望你没有因为犯困而忽视这一点，哈利——年轻的汤姆·里德尔喜欢收集战利品。你看见他藏在房间里的那一箱赃物了吧？它们都是从那些被他欺侮过的孩子们那里拿来的，可以说是某些特别可恶的魔法伎俩的纪念品。你记住他这种像喜鹊一样喜欢收集东西的嗜好，这对于将来格外重要。

“好了，哈利，真的该睡觉了。”

哈利站了起来。他朝门口走去时，目光落在上次放着马沃罗·冈特那枚戒指的小桌上，可是戒指已经不在了。

“怎么了，哈利？”邓布利多看到哈利停住脚步，问道。

“戒指不见了，”哈利左右张望着说，“不过我以为你这里还会有那把口琴什么的呢。”

邓布利多笑了，眼睛从半月形的镜片上方望着他。

“眼光很敏锐，哈利，但那把口琴只是口琴而已。”

说完这句令人费解的话，他朝哈利挥了挥手，哈利明白自己应该离开了。

CHAPTER FOURTEEN

Felix Felicis

Harry had Herbology first thing the following morning. He had been unable to tell Ron and Hermione about his lesson with Dumbledore over breakfast for fear of being overheard, but he filled them in as they walked across the vegetable patch towards the greenhouses. The weekend's brutal wind had died out at last; the weird mist had returned and it took them a little longer than usual to find the correct greenhouse.

'Wow, scary thought, the boy You-Know-Who,' said Ron quietly, as they took their places around one of the gnarled Snargaluff stumps that formed that term's project, and began pulling on their protective gloves. 'But I still don't get why Dumbledore's showing you all this. I mean, it's really interesting and everything, but what's the point?'

'Dunno,' said Harry, inserting a gum shield. 'But he says it's all important and it'll help me survive.'

'I think it's fascinating,' said Hermione earnestly. 'It makes absolute sense to know as much about Voldemort as possible. How else will you find out his weaknesses?'

'So how was Slughorn's latest party?' Harry asked her thickly through the gum shield.

'Oh, it was quite fun, really,' said Hermione, now putting on protective goggles. 'I mean, he drones on about famous ex-pupils a bit, and he absolutely *fawns* on McLaggen because he's so well-connected, but he gave us some really nice food and he introduced us to Gwenog Jones.'

'Gwenog Jones?' said Ron, his eyes widening under his own goggles. '*The* Gwenog Jones? Captain of the Holyhead Harpies?'

'That's right,' said Hermione. 'Personally, I thought she was a bit full of herself, but –'

第 14 章

福灵剂

第二天上午，哈利的第一节课是草药课。吃早饭时，他因为怕别人听见，没能把邓布利多给他上课的内容告诉罗恩和赫敏。当他们穿过菜地朝温室走去时，他才把事情的经过一五一十地告诉了他们。周末的狂风终于平息，但是那种怪异的浓雾又回来了，他们用了比平常更多的时间才找到上课的那座温室。

“哇，多么恐怖啊，少年时期的神秘人。”罗恩轻声说，他们围在一棵布满节疤的疙瘩藤的树桩旁，开始戴防护手套。疙瘩藤是他们这学期所学课程的一部分。“但我仍然不明白，邓布利多为什么要让你看这些呢？我是说，有趣倒是挺有趣的，可是有什么用呢？”

“不知道，”哈利说着，戴上一只防护牙托，“但他说非常重要，会帮助我活下来。”

“我认为这很吸引人。”赫敏认真地说，“尽量了解伏地魔这个人是绝对有意义的，不然你怎么能发现他的弱点呢？”

“对了，斯拉格霍恩最近的那次晚会怎么样？”哈利戴着防护牙托口齿不清地问赫敏。

“哦，其实挺好玩的，”赫敏一边戴上防护眼镜一边说道，“我是说，他虽然没完没了地唠叨他以前那些学生多么出名，而且明显是在讨好麦克拉根，因为麦克拉根认识许多头面人物，但他给我们吃了一些很美味的东西，还介绍我们认识了格韦诺格・琼斯。”

“格韦诺格·琼斯？”罗恩说，防护眼镜后面的眼睛一下子睁得老大，“是那个格韦诺格・琼斯吗？霍利黑德哈比队的队长？”

“没错，”赫敏说，“我个人认为她有点儿自我中心，不过——”

'*Quite* enough chat over here!' said Professor Sprout briskly, bustling over and looking stern. 'You're lagging behind, everybody else has started and Neville's already got his first pod!'

They looked round; sure enough, there sat Neville with a bloody lip and several nasty scratches along the side of his face, but clutching an unpleasantly pulsating green object about the size of a grapefruit.

'OK, Professor, we're starting now!' said Ron, adding quietly, when she had turned away again, 'Should've used *Muffliato*, Harry.'

'No, we shouldn't!' said Hermione at once, looking, as she always did, intensely cross at the thought of the Half-Blood Prince and his spells. 'Well, come on … we'd better get going …'

She gave the other two an apprehensive look; they all took deep breaths and then dived at the gnarled stump between them.

It sprang to life at once; long, prickly, bramble-like vines flew out of the top and whipped through the air. One tangled itself in Hermione's hair and Ron beat it back with a pair of secateurs; Harry succeeded in trapping a couple of vines and knotting them together; a hole opened in the middle of all the tentacle-like branches; Hermione plunged her arm bravely into this hole, which closed like a trap around her elbow; Harry and Ron tugged and wrenched at the vines, forcing the hole to open again and Hermione snatched her arm free, clutching in her fingers a pod just like Neville's. At once, the prickly vines shot back inside and the gnarled stump sat there looking like an innocently dead lump of wood.

'You know, I don't think I'll be having any of these in my garden when I've got my own place,' said Ron, pushing his goggles up on to his forehead and wiping sweat from his face.

'Pass me a bowl,' said Hermione, holding the pulsating pod at arm's length; Harry handed one over and she dropped the pod into it with a look of disgust on her face.

'Don't be squeamish, squeeze it out, they're best when they're fresh!' called Professor Sprout.

'Anyway,' said Hermione, continuing their interrupted conversation as though a lump of wood had not just attacked them, 'Slughorn's going to have a Christmas party, Harry, and there's no way you'll be able to wriggle

“这里不许再说话了！”斯普劳特教授厉声说道，她匆匆走了过来，神色很严厉，“你们落后了，别的同学都动手了，纳威已经弄到了一颗荚果！”

他们转脸望去，果然，纳威坐在那里，嘴唇滴着血，半边脸上被挠出了几道血痕，惨不忍睹，可是他手里抓着一个扑扑跳动的令人恶心的绿色物体，有葡萄柚那么大。

“好的，教授，我们这就动手！”罗恩看到老师转过身走了，又低声补充道，“我们应该用闭耳塞听咒的，哈利。”

“不，绝对不行！”赫敏立刻反对，她跟平常一样，一想到混血王子和他那些魔咒就气不打一处来，“好了，快点儿吧……我们最好赶紧……”

她担忧地看了两个伙伴一眼，他们深吸了几口气，便埋头去对付他们中间那个疙里疙瘩的树桩了。

残根立刻活了起来，长长的刺藤从顶上蹿出，在空中甩来甩去。其中一根缠住了赫敏的头发，罗恩赶紧用一把整枝剪刀把它打了回去。哈利总算抓住了两根藤蔓，挽在一起打了个结。这些触手般的枝条中间露出了一个小洞。赫敏勇敢地把手臂插进洞里，洞口立刻像捕鼠夹一样咬住了她的肘部。哈利和罗恩拼命地拖拽、扭动那些藤蔓，让洞口重新张开，赫敏总算把胳膊从里面挣脱出来，手里抓着一颗像纳威弄到的那种荚果。顿时，那些刺藤全部缩了进去，布满节疤的树桩静静地躺在那里，像一截毫无生气的死木头。

“咳，等将来有了自己的房子，我可不想在花园里种这些玩意儿。”罗恩说着把防护眼镜推到额头上，擦了擦脸上的汗水。

“把碗递给我。”赫敏说，她把手里那颗扑扑跳动的荚果举得远远的。哈利递过去一个碗，赫敏把荚果扔进碗里，脸上是一种厌恶的表情。

“别缩手缩脚的，快把汁挤出来，趁着新鲜，质量最好！”斯普劳特教授喊道。

“反正，”赫敏继续着刚才被打断的谈话，就好像没有遭到树桩袭击似的，“斯拉格霍恩还要举办一个圣诞晚会，哈利，这次你可没有办法逃脱了，因为他特意叫我看看你哪一天晚上有空，确保他能把晚会

out of this one because he actually asked me to check your free evenings, so he could be sure to have it on a night you can come.'

Harry groaned. Ron, meanwhile, who was attempting to burst the pod in the bowl by putting both hands on it, standing up and squashing it as hard as he could, said angrily, 'And this is another party just for Slughorn's favourites, is it?'

'Just for the Slug Club, yes,' said Hermione.

The pod flew out from under Ron's fingers and hit the greenhouse glass, rebounding on to the back of Professor Sprout's head and knocking off her old patched hat. Harry went to retrieve the pod; when he got back, Hermione was saying, 'Look, *I* didn't make up the name "Slug Club" –'

'"*Slug Club*",' repeated Ron with a sneer worthy of Malfoy. 'It's pathetic. Well, I hope you enjoy your party. Why don't you try getting off with McLaggen, then Slughorn can make you King and Queen Slug –'

'We're allowed to bring guests,' said Hermione, who for some reason had turned a bright, boiling scarlet, 'and I was *going* to ask you to come, but if you think it's that stupid then I won't bother!'

Harry suddenly wished the pod had flown a little further, so that he need not have been sitting there with the pair of them. Unnoticed by either, he seized the bowl that contained the pod and began to try and open it by the noisiest and most energetic means he could think of; unfortunately, he could still hear every word of their conversation.

'You were going to ask me?' asked Ron, in a completely different voice.

'Yes,' said Hermione angrily. 'But obviously if you'd rather I *got off with McLaggen* …'

There was a pause while Harry continued to pound the resilient pod with a trowel.

'No, I wouldn't,' said Ron, in a very quiet voice.

Harry missed the pod, hit the bowl and it shattered.

'*Reparo*,' he said hastily, poking the pieces with his wand, and the bowl sprang back together again. The crash, however, appeared to have awoken Ron and Hermione to Harry's presence. Hermione looked flustered and immediately started fussing about for her copy of *Flesh-Eating Trees of the World* to find out the correct way to juice Snargaluff pods; Ron, on the other hand, looked sheepish but also rather pleased with himself.

安排在一个你能来的晚上。”

哈利叫苦不迭。罗恩正用两只手按着荚果，想把它的汁液挤进碗里，听了这话，他猛地站起来，使出吃奶的劲儿挤压荚果，一边气呼呼地说：“这个晚会又是专门招待斯拉格霍恩的那些宠儿的吧？”

“对，专门为鼻涕虫俱乐部举办的。”赫敏说。

荚果从罗恩的手里飞了出去，撞在温室玻璃上，又弹回来砸中斯普劳特教授的后脑勺，把她那顶打着补丁的旧帽子打掉了。哈利去捡荚果，回来时听见赫敏在说：“喏，‘鼻涕虫俱乐部’这个名字可不是我发明的——”

“‘鼻涕虫俱乐部’，”罗恩用马尔福特有的那种讥讽口吻说，“真难听。喂，我希望你在晚会上玩得开心。你为什么不跟麦克拉根交朋友呢，这样斯拉格霍恩就能把你们封为鼻涕虫国王和王后——”

“我们还允许带客人去呢，”赫敏说，她的脸不知怎的突然涨得通红，“我正准备邀请你，既然你认为晚会那么无聊，我就不费这个事了！”

哈利突然希望那颗荚果刚才飞得再远一点，这样他就用不着跟他们俩坐在一起了。罗恩和赫敏都没有注意到他，他抓起盛荚果的碗，尽量用最大的声音，以他所能想出来的最卖力气的方式折腾着荚果。不幸的是，他仍然能听清他们俩说的每一个字。

“你本来准备邀请我的？”罗恩问，他的声音完全变了。

“对，”赫敏气冲冲地说，“但是，如果你情愿让我跟麦克拉根交朋友……”

停顿，哈利继续用一把小铲子敲打那颗有弹性的荚果。

“不，我不情愿。”罗恩用很轻很轻的声音说。

哈利一铲子下去没敲中荚果，把碗砸碎了。

“恢复如初！”他赶紧用魔杖捅捅碎片，念了一句咒语，碗立刻自动黏合，恢复了原来的样子。但是，碗被砸碎的声音似乎惊醒了罗恩和赫敏，他们这才意识到哈利的存在。赫敏显得很慌乱，立刻开始在她那本《食肉树大全》里查找给疙瘩藤的荚果挤汁的正确方法。罗恩有点不好意思，但看上去心里美滋滋的。

'Hand that over, Harry,' said Hermione hurriedly, 'it says we're supposed to puncture them with something sharp …'

Harry passed her the pod in the bowl, he and Ron both snapped their goggles back over their eyes and dived, once more, for the stump.

It was not as though he was really surprised, thought Harry, as he wrestled with a thorny vine intent upon throttling him; he had had an inkling that this might happen sooner or later. But he was not sure how he felt about it … he and cho were now too embarrassed to look at each other, let alone talk to each other; what if Ron and Hermione started going out together, then split up? Could their friendship survive it? Harry remembered the few weeks when they had not been talking to each other in the third year; he had not enjoyed trying to bridge the distance between them. And then, what if they didn't split up? What if they became like Bill and Fleur, and it became excruciatingly embarrassing to be in their presence, so that he was shut out for good?

'Gotcha!' yelled Ron, pulling a second pod from the stump just as Hermione managed to burst the first one open, so that the bowl was full of tubers wriggling like pale green worms.

The rest of the lesson passed without further mention of Slughorn's party. Although Harry watched his two friends more closely over the next few days, Ron and Hermione did not seem any different except that they were a little politer to each other than usual. Harry supposed he would just have to wait to see what happened under the influence of Butterbeer in Slughorn's dimly lit room on the night of the party. In the meantime, however, he had more pressing worries.

Katie Bell was still in St Mungo's Hospital with no prospect of leaving, which meant that the promising Gryffindor team Harry had been training so carefully since September was one Chaser short. He kept putting off replacing Katie in the hope that she would return, but their opening match against Slytherin was looming and he finally had to accept that she would not be back in time to play.

Harry did not think he could stand another full-house tryout. With a sinking feeling that had little to do with Quidditch, he cornered Dean Thomas after Transfiguration one day. Most of the class had already left, although several twittering yellow birds were still zooming around the room, all of Hermione's creation; nobody else had succeeded in conjuring so much

“把那个递过来，哈利。”赫敏急急地说，“这上面说，我们应该用尖东西把它们刺破……”

哈利把碗里的荚果递给赫敏，他和罗恩一起重新戴好防护眼镜，再一次埋头对付着那个树桩。

哈利其实并不怎么吃惊，他一边跟一根想要掐住他脖子的刺藤扭打，一边转开了心思。他早就模模糊糊地知道这件事早晚会发生。但是他不清楚自己对此会有什么感觉……如今他和秋·张尴尬得看都不敢看对方一眼，更不用说互相交谈了。如果罗恩和赫敏开始谈恋爱，然后又闹分手，那可怎么办呢？他们的友谊能经得起这番折腾吗？哈利想起三年级时罗恩和赫敏有几个星期互相不说话，他不得不两边周旋，给他们调解，搞得苦不堪言。还有，如果他们最后没有分手呢？如果他们变得像比尔和芙蓉那样，别人在他们面前都会感到尴尬、难以忍受，结果他就只好永远被排斥在外呢？

“抓住啦！”罗恩大喊一声，从残根里拽出了第二颗荚果。这时候赫敏正好把第一个弄开了，顿时，碗里满是蠕动的、像浅绿色毛毛虫一样的小疙瘩。

这节课剩下来的时间里，他们没有再提到斯拉格霍恩的晚会。随后的几天，哈利更加密切地注意他的两位朋友，但罗恩和赫敏似乎没有什么异样，只是相互间比过去客气了些。哈利想，他只能等到晚会举办的那天晚上，看看在斯拉格霍恩房间朦胧的灯光下，在黄油啤酒的作用下，会出现什么情况了。眼下，他还有更加紧迫的事情需要考虑。

凯蒂·贝尔还住在圣芒戈魔法伤病医院里，短期内不会出院，这就意味着，九月份以来哈利精心调教的那支很有希望的格兰芬多魁地奇球队缺少了一名追球手。他迟迟不肯找人替换凯蒂，希望她能回来，可是眼看对斯莱特林的第一场比赛就要临近，他终于不得不承认凯蒂不能赶回来打比赛了。

哈利觉得他再也不能忍受搞一场全院选拔了。一天变形课后，他堵住了迪安·托马斯，心里有一种跟魁地奇无关的沉甸甸的感觉。班上大多数同学都走了，只有几只叽叽喳喳的小黄鸟还在教室里飞来飞

as a feather from thin air.

'Are you still interested in playing Chaser?'

'Wha–? Yeah, of course!' said Dean excitedly. Over Dean's shoulder Harry saw Seamus Finnigan slamming his books into his bag, looking sour. One of the reasons why Harry would have preferred not to have to ask Dean to play was that he knew Seamus would not like it. On the other hand, he had to do what was best for the team, and Dean had out-flown Seamus at the tryouts.

'Well then, you're in,' said Harry. 'There's a practice tonight, seven o'clock.'

'Right,' said Dean. 'Cheers, Harry! Blimey, I can't wait to tell Ginny!'

He sprinted out of the room, leaving Harry and Seamus alone together, an uncomfortable moment made no easier when a bird dropping landed on Seamus's head as one of Hermione's canaries whizzed over them.

Seamus was not the only person disgruntled by the choice of Katie's substitute. There was much muttering in the common room about the fact that Harry had now chosen two of his classmates for the team. As Harry had endured much worse mutterings than this in his school career, he was not particularly bothered, but all the same, the pressure was increasing to provide a win in the upcoming match against Slytherin. If Gryffindor won, Harry knew that the whole house would forget that they had criticised him and swear that they had always known it was a great team. If they lost … well, Harry thought wryly, he had still endured worse mutterings …

Harry had no reason to regret his choice once he saw Dean fly that evening; he worked well with Ginny and Demelza. The Beaters, Peakes and Coote, were getting better all the time. The only problem was Ron.

Harry had known all along that Ron was an inconsistent player who suffered from nerves and a lack of confidence, and unfortunately, the looming prospect of the opening game of the season seemed to have brought out all his old insecurities. After letting in half a dozen goals, most of them scored by Ginny, his technique became wilder and wilder, until he finally punched an oncoming Demelza robins in the mouth.

'It was an accident, I'm sorry, Demelza, really sorry!' Ron shouted after her as she zigzagged back to the ground dripping blood everywhere. 'I just –'

'Panicked,' Ginny said angrily, landing next to Demelza and examining

去，它们都是赫敏的作品。其他同学连一根羽毛都没有变出来。

“你对当追球手还有兴趣吗？”

“什——？有啊，当然有！”迪安兴奋地说。哈利看见迪安身后的西莫·斐尼甘重重地把课本塞进书包，脸色很是难看。哈利之所以不愿意让迪安参加比赛，就是因为他知道西莫肯定会不高兴。然而，他必须把球队的利益放在第一位，而迪安在选拔中飞得比西莫快。

“好吧，你可以加入了。”哈利说，“今天晚上训练，七点。”

“好，”迪安说，“谢谢了，哈利！哎呀，我要马上把这消息告诉金妮！”

他飞快地跑走了，教室里只剩下哈利和西莫两个人，这真是令人尴尬的一刻，赫敏的一只金丝雀正好从他们头顶上飞过，把一滴鸟粪拉在西莫的头上，气氛变得更尴尬了。

哈利选迪安接替凯蒂，对此感到不满的不止西莫一个人。公共休息室里对于哈利挑选两名同班同学入队的事议论纷纷。哈利上学以来忍受过比这糟糕得多的非议，所以并不特别往心里去，但是，他们的压力越来越大，必须保证在即将到来的对斯莱特林的比赛中取胜。如果格兰芬多赢了，哈利知道整个学院的人都会忘记他们曾经批评过他，并且会声称自己早就知道这是一支了不起的球队。可一旦输了……管它呢，哈利苦笑着想，比这更难听的议论他都忍受过来了……

那天晚上，哈利一看到迪安飞起来，就觉得没有理由后悔自己的选择了。迪安跟金妮、德米尔扎配合得十分默契。击球手珀克斯和古特的表现也越来越好。唯一有麻烦的是罗恩。

哈利一向知道罗恩的状态不稳定，他怯场，缺乏自信，不幸的是，本赛季即将到来的第一场比赛似乎把他过去这些心理问题全都诱发出来了。他一连漏了六个球，其中大多数都是金妮打来的，然后他的技术变得越来越没有章法，最后竟然一拳打中了迎面飞来的德米尔扎·罗宾斯的嘴巴。

“怪我不小心，对不起，德米尔扎，太对不起了！”罗恩冲着她的背影喊道，德米尔扎歪歪斜斜地飞回地面，鲜血滴得到处都是，“我只是——”

“太紧张了。”金妮气愤地说，她落在德米尔扎身边，检查她肿得

her fat lip. 'You prat, Ron, look at the state of her!'

'I can fix that,' said Harry, landing beside the two girls, pointing his wand at Demelza's mouth and saying '*Episkey*'. 'And Ginny, don't call Ron a prat, you're not the captain of this team –'

'Well, you seemed too busy to call him a prat and I thought someone should –'

Harry forced himself not to laugh.

'In the air, everyone, let's go …'

Overall it was one of the worst practices they had had all term, though Harry did not feel that honesty was the best policy when they were this close to the match.

'Good work, everyone, I think we'll flatten Slytherin,' he said bracingly, and the Chasers and Beaters left the changing room looking reasonably happy with themselves.

'I played like a sack of dragon dung,' said Ron in a hollow voice when the door had swung shut behind Ginny.

'No you didn't,' said Harry firmly. 'You're the best Keeper I tried out, Ron. Your only problem is nerves.'

He kept up a relentless flow of encouragement all the way back to the castle, and by the time they reached the second floor Ron was looking marginally more cheerful. When Harry pushed open the tapestry to take their usual short cut up to Gryffindor Tower, however, they found themselves looking at Dean and Ginny, who were locked in a close embrace and kissing fiercely as if glued together.

It was as though something large and scaly erupted into life in Harry's stomach, clawing at his insides: hot blood seemed to flood his brain, so that all thought was extinguished, replaced by a savage urge to jinx Dean into a jelly. Wrestling with this sudden madness, he heard Ron's voice as though from a great distance away.

'Oi!'

Dean and Ginny broke apart and looked round.

'What?' said Ginny.

'I don't want to find my own sister snogging people in public!'

'This was a deserted corridor till you came butting in!' said Ginny.

Dean was looking embarrassed. He gave Harry a shifty grin that Harry

老高的嘴唇，“你这个草包，罗恩，你看看她现在的样子！”

“我可以治好。”哈利落在两个姑娘身边说道，他用魔杖指着德米尔扎的嘴，念了一声“*愈合如初*”，“还有，金妮，不许你管罗恩叫草包，这个球队的队长不是你——”

“噢，你似乎太忙了，没工夫管他叫草包，我认为应该有人——”

哈利强忍着没笑出来。

“全体队员，升到空中，我们再来……”

总的来说，这是他们这学期以来最糟糕的一次训练。眼看比赛就要临近，哈利认为实话实说并不是最佳的策略。

“干得不错，诸位，我认为我们准能把斯莱特林打扁了。”他给大家鼓劲儿，因此，追球手和找球手们离开更衣室时情绪似乎都还不错。

“我表现得像一堆臭大粪。”门在金妮身后关上后，罗恩用空洞的声音说。

“不，不是。”哈利毫不含糊地说，“你是我选拔出来的最棒的守门员，罗恩。你唯一的问题就是心理紧张。”

在返回城堡的路上，哈利不断地说一些鼓励的话，最后当他们走到三楼时，罗恩的情绪总算好了一点儿。哈利推开那幅挂毯，想走他们平常走的那条近路去格兰芬多塔楼，却发现迪安和金妮在他们眼前搂抱在一起，如漆似胶地热烈亲吻着。

似乎有个全身长鳞的大家伙在哈利心头突然活动起来，用爪子抓挠他的五脏六腑，热血一下子冲上了他的脑袋，所有的理性都被压制住了，取而代之的是一股强烈的冲动，只想用恶咒把迪安变成一堆果冻。他与这种突如其来的疯狂念头搏斗着，听见罗恩的声音像是从很远的地方传来。

“喂！”

迪安和金妮一下子分开了，扭头张望着。

“怎么啦？”金妮说。

“我不愿意看见我的亲妹妹在大庭广众下跟别人搂搂抱抱！”

“走廊里本来没有人，是你们自己闯进来的！”金妮说。

迪安显得很尴尬。他躲躲闪闪地朝哈利笑了一下，哈利没有理他，

did not return, as the new-born monster inside him was roaring for Dean's instant dismissal from the team.

'Er … c'mon, Ginny,' said Dean, 'let's go back to the common room …'

'You go!' said Ginny. 'I want a word with my dear brother!'

Dean left, looking as though he was not sorry to depart the scene.

'Right,' said Ginny, tossing her long red hair out of her face and glaring at Ron, 'let's get this straight once and for all. It is none of your business who I go out with or what I do with them, Ron –'

'Yeah, it is!' said Ron, just as angrily. 'D'you think I want people saying my sister's a –'

'A what?' shouted Ginny, drawing her wand. 'A *what*, exactly?'

'He doesn't mean anything, Ginny –' said Harry automatically, though the monster was roaring its approval of Ron's words.

'Oh yes he does!' she said, flaring up at Harry. 'Just because *he's* never snogged anyone in his life, just because the best kiss *he's* ever had is from our Auntie Muriel –'

'Shut your mouth!' bellowed Ron, bypassing red and turning maroon.

'No, I will not!' yelled Ginny, beside herself. 'I've seen you with Phlegm, hoping she'll kiss you on the cheek every time you see her, it's pathetic! If you went out and got a bit of snogging done yourself you wouldn't mind so much that everyone else does it!'

Ron had pulled out his wand too; Harry stepped swiftly between them.

'You don't know what you're talking about!' Ron roared, trying to get a clear shot at Ginny around Harry, who was now standing in front of her with his arms outstretched. 'Just because I don't do it in public –!'

Ginny screamed with derisive laughter, trying to push Harry out of the way.

'Been kissing Pigwidgeon, have you? Or have you got a picture of Auntie Muriel stashed under your pillow?'

'You –'

A streak of orange light flew under Harry's left arm and missed Ginny by inches; Harry pushed Ron up against the wall.

因为他内心那个刚刚诞生的怪兽正大吼着要把迪安立刻从球队开除出去。

“嗯……走吧，金妮，”迪安说，“我们回公共休息室去……”

“你走你的！”金妮说，“我要跟我亲爱的哥哥说几句话！”

迪安走了，他似乎巴不得赶紧离开这个地方。

“好，”金妮说着甩去脸上长长的红发，怒冲冲地瞪着罗恩，“让我们彻底把话都说清楚。罗恩，我跟谁好，我跟他们做什么，跟你没有任何关系——”

“不，有关系！”罗恩同样怒气冲冲地说，“你以为我愿意别人说我的妹妹是——”

“是什么？”金妮大喊一声，拔出了魔杖，“是什么？你说清楚！”

“他只是随便说说的，金妮——”哈利下意识地说，而他内心那头怪兽正在吼叫着赞同罗恩的话。

“哼，他就是这么想的！”她突然朝哈利发起火来，“就因为他这辈子从来没有跟别人亲热过，就因为他从小到大只被我们的穆丽尔姨婆吻过——”

“你闭嘴！”罗恩吼道，脸色从红变成了酱紫。

“不，我就不闭嘴！”金妮疯狂般地说，“我看见过你跟黏痰在一起，你每次看见她都眼巴巴地盼着她能吻你的脸，真是可怜！如果你自己也跟某人来点儿搂搂抱抱，就不会这么在乎别人这么做了！”

罗恩也抽出了魔杖。哈利赶紧挡在他们俩中间。

“你知不知道你在胡说些什么！”罗恩嚷道，哈利伸着胳膊挡在金妮前面，罗恩想绕过哈利，把脸正冲着金妮，“就因为我没有在大庭广众——”

金妮发出刺耳的嘲笑，使劲想把哈利推开。

“你是一直在亲吻小猪吗？还是在枕头底下藏了一张穆丽尔姨婆的照片？”

“你——”

哈利的左胳膊下射出一道橘黄色的光，差几寸就击中金妮了。哈利把罗恩顶到了墙上。

'Don't be stupid –'

'Harry's snogged Cho Chang!' shouted Ginny, who sounded close to tears now. 'And Hermione snogged Viktor Krum, it's only you who acts like it's something disgusting, Ron, and that's because you've got about as much experience as a twelve-year-old!'

And with that, she stormed away. Harry quickly let go of Ron; the look on his face was murderous. They both stood there, breathing heavily, until Mrs Norris, Filch's cat, appeared round the corner, which broke the tension.

'C'mon,' said Harry, as the sound of Filch's shuffling feet reached their ears.

They hurried up the stairs and along a seventh-floor corridor. 'Oi, out of the way!' Ron barked at a small girl who jumped in fright and dropped a bottle of toad-spawn.

Harry hardly noticed the sound of shattering glass; he felt disorientated, dizzy; being struck by a lightning bolt must be something like this. *It's just because she's Ron's sister*, he told himself. *You just didn't like seeing her kissing Dean because she's Ron's sister …*

But unbidden into his mind came an image of that same deserted corridor with himself kissing Ginny instead … the monster in his chest purred … but then he saw Ron ripping open the tapestry curtain and drawing his wand on Harry, shouting things like 'betrayal of trust' … 'supposed to be my friend' …

'D'you think Hermione did snog Krum?' Ron asked abruptly, as they approached the Fat Lady. Harry gave a guilty start and wrenched his imagination away from a corridor in which no Ron intruded, in which he and Ginny were quite alone –

'What?' he said confusedly. 'Oh … er …'

The honest answer was 'yes', but he did not want to give it. However, Ron seemed to gather the worst from the look on Harry's face.

'Dilligrout,' he said darkly to the Fat Lady, and they climbed through the portrait hole into the common room.

Neither of them mentioned Ginny or Hermione again; indeed, they barely spoke to each other that evening and got into bed in silence, each absorbed in his own thoughts.

“别干傻事——”

“哈利跟秋·张亲热过！”金妮还在嚷嚷，声音里已经带着哭腔，“赫敏跟威克多尔·克鲁姆亲热过，只有你，罗恩，把这看成一件令人恶心的事儿，那是因为你的经验只有一个十二岁的毛孩子那么多！”

说完，她气冲冲地走了。哈利赶紧放开罗恩。罗恩脸上的表情像是要杀人。他们俩站在那儿，呼哧呼哧地喘着粗气，后来，费尔奇的猫洛丽丝夫人出现在墙角，才打破了这紧张的气氛。

“走吧。”哈利说，他们已经听见费尔奇踢踢踏踏的脚步声了。

他们匆匆上了楼，顺着八楼的一道走廊往前走。“喂，滚开！”罗恩朝一个小女生吼道，那女生吓了一大跳，手里的一瓶蟾蜍卵掉在了地上。

哈利几乎没有听到玻璃摔碎的声音。他只觉得脑子晕乎乎的，找不到方向。被闪电击中的感觉肯定就像这样。*这只是因为她是罗恩的妹妹，他对自己说，因为她是罗恩的妹妹，所以你才不愿意看见她跟迪安接吻……*

可是他脑海里自动浮现出一幅画面：在那条空无一人的走廊里，是他自己在亲吻金妮……他心里的那头怪兽快乐得直哼哼……但紧接着他看见罗恩扯开挂毯帘子，拔出魔杖对准哈利，嘴里吼着一些话，什么“背信弃义”……什么“还说是我的朋友呢”……

“你说，赫敏真的跟克鲁姆亲热过吗？”罗恩突然问道，这时他们已经快要走到胖夫人肖像跟前了。哈利心虚地吃了一惊，赶紧把思绪从那条走廊扯了回来：他幻想中的走廊里没有突然闯入的罗恩，只有他和金妮单独在一起——

“什么？”他慌乱地说，“哦……嗯……”

如果照实回答，应该说“是的”，但哈利不愿意这么说。不过，罗恩似乎从哈利的脸上得出了最坏的结论。

“杏仁鸡羹。”他阴沉着脸对胖夫人说，两人爬过肖像洞口，进入了公共休息室。

谁也没有再提金妮或赫敏，事实上，那天晚上他们几乎没怎么说话，各自想着心事，默默地上床睡觉了。

Harry lay awake for a long time, looking up at the canopy of his four-poster and trying to convince himself that his feelings for Ginny were entirely older-brotherly. They had lived, had they not, like brother and sister all summer, playing Quidditch, teasing Ron and having a laugh about Bill and Phlegm? He had known Ginny for years now … it was natural that he should feel protective … natural that he should want to look out for her … want to rip Dean limb from limb for kissing her … no … he would have to control that particular brotherly feeling …

Ron gave a great grunting snore.

She's Ron's sister, Harry told himself firmly. *Ron's sister. She's out of bounds.* He would not risk his friendship with Ron for anything. He punched his pillow into a more comfortable shape and waited for sleep to come, trying his utmost not to allow his thoughts to stray anywhere near Ginny.

Harry awoke next morning feeling slightly dazed and confused by a series of dreams in which Ron had chased him with a Beater's bat, but by midday he would have happily exchanged the dream Ron for the real one, who was not only cold-shouldering Ginny and Dean, but also treating a hurt and bewildered Hermione with an icy, sneering indifference. What was more, Ron seemed to have become, overnight, as touchy and ready to lash out as the average Blast-Ended Skrewt. Harry spent the day attempting to keep the peace between Ron and Hermione with no success: finally, Hermione departed for bed in high dudgeon and Ron stalked off to the boys' dormitory after swearing angrily at several frightened first-years for looking at him.

To Harry's dismay, Ron's new aggression did not wear off over the next few days. Worse still, it coincided with an even deeper dip in his Keeping skills, which made him still more aggressive, so that during the final Quidditch practice before Saturday's match, he failed to save every single goal the Chasers aimed at him, but bellowed at everybody so much that he reduced Demelza Robins to tears.

'You shut up and leave her alone!' shouted Peakes, who was about two-thirds Ron's height, though admittedly carrying a heavy bat.

'ENOUGH!' bellowed Harry, who had seen Ginny glowering in Ron's direction and, remembering her reputation as an accomplished caster of the Bat-Bogey Hex, soared over to intervene before things got out of hand.

哈利很长时间都没有睡着，他盯着四柱床的帐顶，努力想使自己相信他对金妮的感情完全像哥哥一样。整个夏天，他们不是像兄妹一般生活，一起打魁地奇，一起奚落罗恩，一起嘲笑比尔和黏痰吗？他认识金妮已经好几年了……自然觉得自己有责任保护她……自然想要照看她……想要把迪安撕成碎片，因为迪安竟然敢吻她……不……他必须控制这种特殊的兄长之情……

罗恩发出了呼噜呼噜的响亮鼾声。

她是罗恩的妹妹，哈利坚决地对自己说，*罗恩的妹妹，我不能对她有非分之想*。无论如何不能拿他和罗恩的友谊去冒险。他把枕头拍成一个更加舒适的形状，等待睡意来临，他用全部的力量控制自己，不让思绪游移到金妮那儿去。

第二天早晨，哈利醒来时觉得脑子有点昏沉，晕晕乎乎，因为夜里做了一连串的怪梦，都是罗恩拿着一根击球手的球棒在追他。可是到了中午，他倒情愿让梦里的那个罗恩来取代这个真正的罗恩。罗恩不仅对金妮和迪安满脸阴沉，而且对赫敏也铁青着脸，连嘲带讽，弄得赫敏又委屈又迷惑不解。更糟糕的是，罗恩似乎一夜之间变得像炸尾螺一样敏感易怒，一碰就炸。哈利花了一整天时间在罗恩和赫敏之间调停，都没有奏效。最后，赫敏非常愤怒地回去睡觉了，罗恩气势汹汹地痛骂了几个盯着他看的一年级学生一顿，把他们吓得够呛，然后他怒气冲冲地回男生宿舍去了。

在随后的几天里，罗恩这种火暴脾气并没有缓解，这使哈利感到很沮丧。更糟糕的是，随之而来的是罗恩的守门技术一落千丈，这使他的脾气变得更加暴躁。在星期六比赛前的最后一次魁地奇训练中，追球手打来的球他一个也没有救起，反而朝每个人大吼大叫，还把德米尔扎·罗宾斯给气哭了。

“你闭嘴，别惹她！”珀克斯吼道，他手里拿着一根沉甸甸的球棒，但个头只有罗恩的三分之二左右。

“**够了！**”哈利吼道，他看见金妮气冲冲地瞪着罗恩那边，想起她在施蝙蝠精魔咒方面是公认的一把好手，便急忙飞过去，赶在事态失控之前及时调停，“珀克斯，快去把游走球收拾起来。德米尔扎，打起

'Peakes, go and pack up the Bludgers. Demelza, pull yourself together, you played really well today. Ron …' he waited until the rest of the team were out of earshot before saying it, 'you're my best mate, but carry on treating the rest of them like this and I'm going to kick you off the team.'

He really thought for a moment that Ron might hit him, but then something much worse happened: Ron seemed to sag on his broom; all the fight went out of him and he said, 'I resign. I'm pathetic.'

'You're not pathetic and you're not resigning!' said Harry fiercely, seizing Ron by the front of his robes. 'You can save anything when you're on form, it's a mental problem you've got!'

'You calling me mental?'

'Yeah, maybe I am!'

They glared at each other for a moment, then Ron shook his head wearily.

'I know you haven't got any time to find another Keeper, so I'll play tomorrow, but if we lose, and we will, I'm taking myself off the team.'

Nothing Harry said made any difference. He tried boosting Ron's confidence all through dinner, but Ron was too busy being grumpy and surly with Hermione to notice. Harry persisted in the common room that evening, but his assertion that the whole team would be devastated if Ron left was somewhat undermined by the fact that the rest of the team was sitting in a huddle in a distant corner, clearly muttering about Ron and casting him nasty looks. Finally, Harry tried getting angry again in the hope of provoking Ron into a defiant, and hopefully goal-saving, attitude, but this strategy did not appear to work any better than encouragement; Ron went to bed as dejected and hopeless as ever.

Harry lay awake for a very long time in the darkness. He did not want to lose the upcoming match; not only was it his first as Captain, but he was determined to beat Draco Malfoy at Quidditch even if he could not yet prove his suspicions about him. Yet if Ron played as he had done in the last few practices, their chances of winning were very slim …

If only there was something he could do to make Ron pull himself together … make him play at the top of his form … something that would ensure that Ron had a really good day …

And the answer came to Harry in one, sudden, glorious stroke of inspiration.

精神，你今天表现真不错。罗恩……”他等到其他队员都走远听不见了才说道，“你是我最好的朋友，但如果你继续这样对待别人，我就把你从队里踢出去。”

他本以为罗恩会扑上来揍他，没想到接下来的情况更加糟糕：骑在扫帚上的罗恩似乎完全泄了气，彻底丧失了斗志，他说：“我退出。我糟透了。”

“你没有糟透，你不许退出！”哈利揪住罗恩长袍的衣襟，发着狠劲儿说，“你状态好的时候什么球都能救起，你只是精神问题！”

“你说我有精神问题？”

“对，恐怕我就是这个意思！”

他们互相怒目而视，然后罗恩疲惫地摇了摇头。

“我知道你来不及再找一名守门员了，所以我明天还是参加比赛，但如果我们输了——我们肯定会输的，我就自动离队。”

不管哈利再说什么都无济于事。吃饭的时候，他一直在给罗恩打气，可是罗恩只顾对着赫敏横眉瞪眼，根本没有注意听。那天晚上在公共休息室里，哈利继续鼓励他，一再强调说如果罗恩离开的话，整个球队就完蛋了。可是，其他队员就聚在墙角那儿窃窃私语，显然是在议论罗恩，还不时地朝罗恩投来不满的目光，这使哈利的劝解效果大打折扣。最后，哈利想再发一次脾气，希望用激将法让罗恩进入那种不服输的、频频救球的状态，但看样子这种策略跟给他打气一样没有多少作用。罗恩上床睡觉时还是那样情绪低落，灰心绝望。

哈利在黑暗中躺了很长时间。他不想输掉即将到来的这场比赛。这不仅是他担任队长以来的第一场比赛，而且，他虽然还没能证明自己对德拉科·马尔福的怀疑，但一心想在魁地奇赛场上打败他。可是，如果罗恩的表现还跟最近这几次训练一样，那他们获胜的希望就太渺茫了……

但愿能想出一个办法让罗恩振作起来……让他以最佳状态参加比赛……想个办法让罗恩那一天事事顺利……

突然，哈利脑子里灵光一现，有了答案。

Breakfast was the usual excitable affair next morning; the Slytherins hissed and booed loudly as every member of the Gryffindor team entered the Great Hall. Harry glanced at the ceiling and saw a clear, pale blue sky: a good omen.

The Gryffindor table, a solid mass of red and gold, cheered as Harry and Ron approached. Harry grinned and waved; Ron grimaced weakly and shook his head.

'Cheer up, Ron!' called Lavender. 'I know you'll be brilliant!'

Ron ignored her.

'Tea?' Harry asked him. 'Coffee? Pumpkin juice?'

'Anything,' said Ron glumly, taking a moody bite of toast.

A few minutes later Hermione, who had become so tired of Ron's recent unpleasant behaviour that she had not come down to breakfast with them, paused on her way up the table.

'How are you both feeling?' she asked tentatively, her eyes on the back of Ron's head.

'Fine,' said Harry, who was concentrating on handing Ron a glass of pumpkin juice. 'There you go, Ron. Drink up.'

Ron had just raised the glass to his lips when Hermione spoke sharply.

'Don't drink that, Ron!'

Both Harry and Ron looked up at her.

'Why not?' said Ron.

Hermione was now staring at Harry as though she could not believe her eyes.

'You just put something in that drink.'

'Excuse me?' said Harry.

'You heard me. I saw you. You just tipped something into Ron's drink. You've got the bottle in your hand right now!'

'I don't know what you're talking about,' said Harry, stowing the little bottle hastily in his pocket.

'Ron, I warn you, don't drink it!' Hermione said again, alarmed, but Ron picked up the glass, drained it in one and said, 'Stop bossing me around, Hermione.'

She looked scandalised. Bending low so that only Harry could hear her she hissed, 'You should be expelled for that. I'd never have believed it of you, Harry!'

第二天早晨，早饭还像平常一样热闹。格兰芬多球队的每个队员走进礼堂时，斯莱特林们就大声地喝倒彩，发嘘声。哈利扫了一眼天花板，看见一片清澈、瓦蓝的天空：这是一个好兆头。

格兰芬多的餐桌红彤彤金灿灿的，哈利和罗恩走过来时，同学们热烈欢呼。哈利笑着挥挥手，罗恩勉强做了个鬼脸，摇了摇头。

“打起精神来，罗恩！”拉文德喊道，“我知道你肯定很棒！”

罗恩没有理睬她。

“茶？”哈利问罗恩，“咖啡？南瓜汁？”

“随便。”罗恩愁眉苦脸地说，郁闷地咬了一口面包。

几分钟后，赫敏来了，她因为受够了罗恩最近的古怪别扭，没有跟他们一起下楼吃早饭。她快走到桌边时停住了脚步。

“你们俩感觉怎么样？”她试探地问，眼睛望着罗恩的后脑勺。

“不错。”哈利说，他正忙着把一杯南瓜汁递给罗恩，“给，罗恩，喝了吧。”

罗恩刚把杯子举到嘴边，赫敏突然厉声说道：

“别喝，罗恩！”

哈利和罗恩都抬头望着她。

“为什么？”罗恩说。

赫敏呆呆地瞪着哈利，似乎不敢相信自己的眼睛。

“你刚才往那杯饮料里放东西了。”

“你说什么？”哈利说。

“你听见我说了什么。我都看见了。你刚才把什么东西倒进了罗恩的饮料。现在那瓶子还在你手里攥着呢！”

“真听不懂你在说什么。”哈利一边说，一边赶紧把一个小瓶子塞进口袋。

“罗恩，我警告你，别喝！”赫敏惊慌地又说了一遍，可是罗恩端起杯子，一口喝了个精光，然后说：“你少对我指手画脚，赫敏。”

赫敏看上去又震惊又愤怒。她弯下腰压低声音，为的是不让别人听见：“你会因为这件事被开除的。我真不敢相信你会干出这种事，哈利！”

'Hark who's talking,' he whispered back. 'Confunded anyone lately?'

She stormed up the table away from them. Harry watched her go without regret. Hermione had never really understood what a serious business Quidditch was. He then looked round at Ron, who was smacking his lips.

'Nearly time,' said Harry blithely.

The frosty grass crunched underfoot as they strode down to the stadium.

'Pretty lucky the weather's this good, eh?' Harry asked Ron.

'Yeah,' said Ron, who was pale and sick-looking.

Ginny and Demelza were already wearing their Quidditch robes and waiting in the changing room.

'Conditions look ideal,' said Ginny, ignoring Ron. 'And guess what? That Slytherin Chaser Vaisey – he took a Bludger in the head yesterday during their practice, and he's too sore to play! And even better than that – Malfoy's gone off sick too!'

'*What*?' said Harry, wheeling round to stare at her. 'He's ill? What's wrong with him?'

'No idea, but it's great for us,' said Ginny brightly. 'They're playing Harper instead; he's in my year and he's an idiot.'

Harry smiled vaguely back, but as he pulled on his scarlet robes his mind was far from Quidditch. Malfoy had once before claimed he could not play due to injury, but on that occasion he had made sure the whole match was rescheduled for a time that suited the Slytherins better. Why was he now happy to let a substitute go on? Was he really ill, or was he faking?

'Fishy, isn't it?' he said in an undertone to Ron. 'Malfoy not playing?'

'Lucky, I call it,' said Ron, looking slightly more animated. 'And Vaisey off too, he's their best goal-scorer, I didn't fancy – hey!' he said suddenly, freezing halfway through pulling on his Keeper's gloves and staring at Harry.

'What?'

'I … you …' Ron had dropped his voice; he looked both scared and excited. 'My drink … my pumpkin juice … you didn't …?'

Harry raised his eyebrows, but said nothing except, 'We'll be starting in about five minutes, you'd better get your boots on.'

“是谁在说话呀？”哈利低声说道，“是谁最近给人念了混淆咒呀？”

赫敏气冲冲地走到桌子那头去了。哈利望着她的背影，心里并不感到懊悔。赫敏始终不明白魁地奇是一件多么重要的事情。哈利转过脸来看着罗恩，罗恩正在那里咂着嘴。

“时间快到了。”哈利轻松愉快地说。

他们大步朝体育场走去，霜冻的草踩在脚下，发出嘎吱嘎吱的响声。

“天气这么好，运气真不错，是不是？”哈利问罗恩。

“是啊。”罗恩脸色苍白，好像身体很虚弱的样子。

金妮和德米尔扎已经换上了魁地奇球袍，正在更衣室里等着。

“条件看来很理想，”金妮睬也不睬罗恩，只管说道，“你猜怎么着？斯莱特林的追球手瓦赛——昨天训练时被一只游走球击中脑袋，疼得不能参加比赛了！更妙的是——马尔福也请了病假！”

“什么？”哈利转过身来盯着她，“他病了？什么病？”

“不知道，但对我们来说太棒了。”金妮兴高采烈地说，“现在他们换上了哈珀。他跟我同级，是个大傻瓜。”

哈利淡淡地笑了笑，可是当他套上深红色的球袍时，思路却游移到了魁地奇以外的事情上。马尔福以前也有一次声称自己受伤，不能参加比赛，但那次他是为了改变整个比赛的日程，换一个对斯莱特林更加有利的日子。他这次怎么这样痛快就让替补队员上场呢？他是真的病了，还是装病？

“真可疑，是不是？”他压低声音对罗恩说，“马尔福竟然不参加比赛！”

“这是我们运气好。”罗恩说，似乎有了一些活力，“瓦赛也不来了，他是他们队最好的得分手啊，真没想到——嘿！”他突然叫了一声，呆呆地望着哈利，守门员手套戴到一半停住了。

“怎么啦？”

“我……你……”罗恩放低声音，显得既害怕又兴奋，“我那杯饮料……我的南瓜汁……你没有……？”

哈利扬起眉毛，只说了一句：“五分钟后比赛就开始了，你最好赶紧穿上靴子。”

They walked out on to the pitch to tumultuous roars and boos. One end of the stadium was solid red and gold; the other, a sea of green and silver. Many Hufflepuffs and Ravenclaws had taken sides, too: amidst all the yelling and clapping Harry could distinctly hear the roar of Luna Lovegood's famous lion-topped hat.

Harry stepped up to Madam Hooch, the referee, who was standing ready to release the balls from the crate.

'Captains, shake hands,' she said, and Harry had his hand crushed by the new Slytherin Captain, Urquhart. 'Mount your brooms. On the whistle … three … two … one …'

The whistle sounded, Harry and the others kicked off hard from the frozen ground, and they were away.

Harry soared around the perimeter of the grounds looking for the Snitch and keeping one eye on Harper, who was zigzagging far below him. Then a voice that was jarringly different from the usual commentator's started up.

'Well, there they go, and I think we're all surprised to see the team that Potter's put together this year. Many thought, given Ronald Weasley's patchy performance as Keeper last year, that he might be off the team, but of course, a close personal friendship with the captain does help …'

These words were greeted with jeers and applause from the Slytherin end of the pitch. Harry craned round on his broom to look towards the commentator's podium. A tall, skinny blond boy with an upturned nose was standing there, talking into the magical megaphone that had once been Lee Jordan's; Harry recognised Zacharias Smith, a Hufflepuff player whom he heartily disliked.

'Oh, and here comes Slytherin's first attempt on goal, it's Urquhart streaking down the pitch and –'

Harry's stomach turned over.

'– Weasley saves it, well, he's bound to get lucky sometimes, I suppose …'

'That's right, Smith, he is,' muttered Harry, grinning to himself, as he dived amongst the Chasers with his eyes searching all around for some hint of the elusive Snitch.

With half an hour of the game gone, Gryffindor were leading sixty points to zero, Ron having made some truly spectacular saves, some by the very tips

他们来到外面人声鼎沸的球场上。看台一边是一片红彤彤金灿灿的人海，另一边则是一片绿色和银色的汪洋。许多赫奇帕奇和拉文克劳同学也各有自己支持的球队。在所有这些尖叫声、鼓掌声中，哈利清清楚楚地听见了卢娜·洛夫古德那顶著名的狮子帽的咆哮。

哈利走到裁判霍琦女士面前，霍琦女士站在那里，正准备把球从箱子里放出来。

“双方队长握手。”她说，哈利的手几乎被斯莱特林的新队长厄克特捏碎了，“骑上扫帚。听我的哨声……三……二……一……”

哨声一响，哈利和其他队员使劲一蹬冻得硬邦邦的地面，升上了半空。

哈利绕着球场周围盘旋，寻找金色飞贼，同时警惕地提防在他下面绕来绕去的哈珀。这时，一个跟以往的解说员截然不同的声音响了起来。

“好,现在他们出发了。我想,看到波特这学期拼凑起来的这支球队，大家都会感到吃惊。许多人以为，守门员罗恩·韦斯莱上学期表现时好时坏，大概不会再待在球队了，但是他跟队长私人关系密切，这无疑帮了他的忙……”

这番话赢得了球场那端斯莱特林们的讥笑和喝彩。哈利在扫帚上伸长脖子朝解说员的台子看去。一个瘦瘦高高、金色头发、朝天鼻的男生站在那儿，对着那只曾经属于李·乔丹的魔法麦克风滔滔不绝。哈利认出来了，是扎卡赖斯·史密斯——他非常讨厌的一名赫奇帕奇队员。

“哦，斯莱特林队第一次向球门发起进攻，是厄克特快速飞过球场——”

哈利的心都揪起来了。

“——韦斯莱把球救起，是啊，我想他偶尔也会交点儿好运……”

“没错，史密斯，说得对。”哈利低声嘟囔，暗暗地笑了。他从一群追球手中间俯冲下去，眼睛四处寻找那只行踪不定的金色飞贼的踪影。

比赛进行了半个小时，格兰芬多六十比零领先，罗恩身手不凡，很漂亮地救起了一些险球，有几个甚至是用手套尖扑出去的。在格兰

of his gloves, and Ginny having scored four of Gryffindor's six goals. This effectively stopped Zacharias wondering loudly whether the two Weasleys were only there because Harry liked them, and he started on Peakes and Coote instead.

'Of course, Coote isn't really the usual build for a Beater,' said Zacharias loftily, 'they've generally got a bit more muscle –'

'Hit a Bludger at him!' Harry called to Coote as he zoomed past, but Coote, grinning broadly, chose to aim the next Bludger at Harper instead, who was just passing Harry in the opposite direction. Harry was pleased to hear the dull *thunk* that meant the Bludger had found its mark.

It seemed as though Gryffindor could do no wrong. Again and again they scored, and again and again, at the other end of the pitch, Ron saved goals with apparent ease. He was actually smiling now, and when the crowd greeted a particularly good save with a rousing chorus of the old favourite *Weasley is our King*, he pretended to conduct them from on high.

'Thinks he's something special today, doesn't he?' said a snide voice, and Harry was nearly knocked off his broom as Harper collided with him hard and deliberately. 'Your blood-traitor pal …'

Madam Hooch's back was turned, and though Gryffindors below shouted in anger, by the time she looked round Harper had already sped off. His shoulder aching, Harry raced after him, determined to ram him back …

'And I think Harper of Slytherin's seen the Snitch!' said Zacharias Smith through his megaphone. 'Yes, he's certainly seen something Potter hasn't!'

Smith really was an idiot, thought Harry, hadn't he noticed them collide? But next moment, his stomach seemed to drop out of the sky – Smith was right and Harry was wrong: Harper had not sped upwards at random; he had spotted what Harry had not: the Snitch was speeding along high above them, glinting brightly against the clear blue sky.

Harry accelerated; the wind was whistling in his ears so that it drowned all sound of Smith's commentary or the crowd, but Harper was still ahead of him, and Gryffindor was only a hundred points up; if Harper got there first Gryffindor had lost … and now Harper was feet from it, his hand outstretched …

芬多投中的六个球中，金妮就占了四个。这一下扎卡赖斯收敛多了，不再大声念叨韦斯莱兄妹是因为哈利偏心才进入球队的。他改变目标，开始编派起珀克斯和古特来。

“当然啦，古特并不具备一般击球手那样的体格，”扎卡赖斯傲慢地说，“击球手总的来说肌肉都比较发达——”

“给他一记游走球！”哈利飞过古特身边时朝他喊了一声，古特脸上露出灿烂的笑容，将那只游走球瞄准了正迎面朝哈利飞来的哈珀。哈利听见砰的一声闷响，知道那只球击中了目标，心头暗暗高兴。

格兰芬多队似乎怎么打都顺手。他们一次次进球得分，而在球场的另一端，罗恩轻松地救起了一个又一个球，简直是手到擒来。他现在脸上居然也有了笑容。当他特别漂亮地救起一个险球、观众齐声高唱那首最受欢迎的老歌韦斯莱是我们的王时，他还假装从高处给他们当指挥呢。

“他还觉得自个儿今天是个人物呢，嗯？”一个挖苦的声音说，随即哈珀故意狠狠地撞了过来，把哈利撞得差点儿从扫帚上摔下去，“你那个败类哥们儿……”

霍琦女士背对着他们，下面的格兰芬多们气愤地大声喊叫，可是当霍琦女士转过身来时，哈珀已经迅速飞走了。哈利肩膀生疼，立刻朝他追过去，打定主意也要撞他一下……

“我认为斯莱特林队的哈珀已经看见飞贼了！”扎卡赖斯·史密斯对着魔法麦克风说，“没错，他肯定看见了什么，波特没看见！”

史密斯真是个白痴，哈利想，他难道没有看见他撞自己吗？紧接着哈利的心忽悠一下，简直要从空中沉向地面——史密斯说得对，哈利判断错了。哈珀刚才突然上升不是无缘无故的，他确实看见了哈利没有看见的东西：金色飞贼在他们的高处疾飞，在明朗的蓝天衬托下闪着耀眼的光芒。

哈利立刻加速，风在耳边呼呼地掠过，史密斯的解说声、观众的喧闹声都听不见了，但哈珀还是在他前面。格兰芬多只领先一百分，如果哈珀先飞到那儿，格兰芬多就输了……现在哈珀离飞贼只有几英尺了，他的手向前伸着……

'Oi, Harper!' yelled Harry in desperation. 'How much did Malfoy pay you to come on instead of him?'

He did not know what made him say it, but Harper did a double take; he fumbled the Snitch, let it slip through his fingers and shot right past it: Harry made a great swipe for the tiny, fluttering ball and caught it.

'YES!' Harry yelled: wheeling round, he hurtled back towards the ground, the Snitch held high in his hand. As the crowd realised what had happened, a great shout went up that almost drowned the sound of the whistle that signalled the end of the game.

'Ginny, where're you going?' yelled Harry, who had found himself trapped in the midst of a mass midair hug with the rest of the team, but Ginny sped right on past them until, with an almighty crash, she collided with the commentator's podium. As the crowd shrieked and laughed, the Gryffindor team landed beside the wreckage of wood under which Zacharias was feebly stirring; Harry heard Ginny saying blithely to an irate Professor McGonagall, 'Forgot to brake, Professor, sorry.'

Laughing, Harry broke free of the rest of the team and hugged Ginny, but let go very quickly. Avoiding her gaze, he clapped a cheering Ron on the back instead as, all enmity forgotten, the Gryffindor team left the pitch arm in arm, punching the air and waving to their supporters.

The atmosphere in the changing room was jubilant.

'Party up in the common room, Seamus said!' yelled Dean exuberantly. 'C'mon, Ginny, Demelza!'

Ron and Harry were the last two in the changing room. They were just about to leave when Hermione entered. She was twisting her Gryffindor scarf in her hands and looked upset but determined.

'I want a word with you, Harry.' She took a deep breath. 'You shouldn't have done it. You heard Slughorn, it's illegal.'

'What are you going to do, turn us in?' demanded Ron.

'What are you two talking about?' asked Harry, turning away to hang up his robes so that neither of them would see him grinning.

'You know perfectly well what we're talking about!' said Hermione shrilly. 'You spiked Ron's juice with lucky potion at breakfast! Felix Felicis!'

“喂，哈珀！”哈利孤注一掷地喊道，“马尔福给了你多少钱让你来替他打比赛？”

他不知道自己为什么要说这话，可是哈珀吃了一惊，一下子没有抓牢飞贼，球从他手指间滑脱，他的身子嗖地飞了过去。哈利朝那只扑扇着翅膀的小球猛冲过去，把它抓住了。

“有了！”哈利喊道，他转身飞快地冲向地面，手里高高地举着那只飞贼。当观众们意识到怎么回事时，立刻爆发出一阵震耳欲聋的喧闹，把比赛结束的哨声都淹没了。

“金妮，你去哪儿？”哈利大喊，队员们在空中热烈拥抱，他发现自己被他们挤在了最中间，可是金妮径直从他们旁边飞过，然后哗啦一声，撞上了解说员的台子。随着观众的尖叫声和哄笑声，格兰芬多的队员们降落在那堆被撞得乱七八糟的木板旁，扎卡赖斯在木板下面有气无力地挣扎。哈利听见金妮轻快地对愤怒的麦格教授说：“忘记刹车了，教授，抱歉。”

哈利哈哈大笑着挣脱其他队员，冲过去搂抱金妮，但又赶紧放开了。他躲着金妮的目光，转而去拍打欢呼雀跃的罗恩的后背。格兰芬多的队员们忘记了前嫌，手挽手走出球场，一边朝空中挥舞着拳头，向支持他们的观众挥手致意。

更衣室里一片欢腾的气氛。

“楼上的公共休息室里在开庆功会，西莫说的！”迪安兴高采烈地喊道，“快走，金妮、德米尔扎！”

更衣室里只剩下了哈利和罗恩。他们正要离开，赫敏突然闯了进来。她两只手里绞着她那条格兰芬多围巾，一副心烦意乱、但决心已定的样子。

“我想跟你谈谈，哈利。”她深深吸了一口气，“你不应该这么做。你听见斯拉格霍恩怎么说的，这是不合法的。”

“你准备怎么办，揭发我们？”罗恩问道。

“你们俩在说些什么呀？”哈利问，一边转身去挂他的球袍，这样他们俩就看不见他脸上得意的笑容了。

“你完全清楚我们在说什么！”赫敏声音尖厉地说，“你早饭的时候往罗恩的南瓜汁里掺了幸运药水！福灵剂！”

'No I didn't,' said Harry, turning back to face them both.

'Yes you did, Harry, and that's why everything went right, there were Slytherin players missing and Ron saved everything!'

'I didn't put it in!' said Harry, now grinning broadly. He slipped his hand inside his jacket pocket and drew out the tiny bottle that Hermione had seen in his hand that morning. It was full of golden potion and the cork was still tightly sealed with wax. 'I wanted Ron to think I'd done it, so I faked it when I knew you were looking.' He looked at Ron. 'You saved everything because you felt lucky. You did it all yourself.'

He pocketed the potion again.

'There really wasn't anything in my pumpkin juice?' Ron said, astounded. 'But the weather's good … and Vaisey couldn't play … I honestly haven't been given lucky potion?'

Harry shook his head. Ron gaped at him for a moment, then rounded on Hermione, imitating her voice.

'*You added Felix Felicis to Ron's juice this morning, that's why he saved everything!* See! I can save goals without help, Hermione!'

'I never said you couldn't – Ron, *you* thought you'd been given it, too!'

But Ron had already strode past her out of the door with his broomstick over his shoulder.

'Er,' said Harry into the sudden silence; he had not expected his plan to backfire like this, 'shall … shall we go up to the party, then?'

'You go!' said Hermione, blinking back tears. 'I'm *sick* of Ron at the moment, I don't know what I'm supposed to have done …'

And she stormed out of the changing room, too.

Harry walked slowly back up the grounds towards the castle through the crowd, many of whom shouted congratulations at him, but he felt a great sense of let-down; he had been sure that if Ron won the match, he and Hermione would be friends again immediately. He did not see how he could possibly explain to Hermione that what she had done to offend Ron was kiss Viktor Krum, not when the offence had occurred so long ago.

Harry could not see Hermione at the Gryffindor celebration party, which was in full swing when he arrived. Renewed cheers and clapping greeted his appearance and he was soon surrounded by a mob of people congratulating

“不，我没有。”哈利说着转过去面对他们俩。

“你就是掺了，哈利，所以一切才这么顺利，斯莱特林队员缺赛，罗恩每个球都能救起来！”

“我并没有把它掺进去！”哈利说着，忍不住绽开了笑容。他把手伸进外衣口袋，掏出赫敏早上看见他拿在手里的那个小瓶。满满一瓶金黄色的药水，塞子仍然用蜡封得死死的。“我想让罗恩以为我掺了药水，所以，我知道你在旁边看着，就假装这么做了。”他看着罗恩，“你每个球都能救起来，是因为你自己感觉运气好。你是靠自己的能力做到的。”

他把药水又放回了口袋。

“我的南瓜汁里真的什么也没有？”罗恩大为震惊地说，“可是天气这么好……瓦赛不能来比赛……你真的没有给我喝幸运药水？”

哈利摇了摇头。罗恩呆呆地望了他片刻，然后模仿着赫敏的声音回敬她说：

“你今天早晨在罗恩的南瓜汁里掺了福灵剂，所以他才能救起那么多球！看见了吗！我不用帮助也能把球救起来，赫敏！”

“我从来没说过你不能——罗恩，你自己也以为喝了药水！”

可是罗恩已经扛着扫帚，大摇大摆地从赫敏身边走出了更衣室。

“嗯，”哈利打破突然出现的沉默说道，真没想到他的计划竟然这样事与愿违，“我们……我们上去参加晚会吧？”

“你自己去吧！”赫敏说，她眨眨眼忍住泪水，“眼下我对罗恩感到腻烦了，真不明白我到底做错了什么……”

说完，她也一头冲出了更衣室。

哈利穿过拥挤的人群，走过场地，返回城堡，许多人都大喊大叫地祝贺他，但是他觉得内心沮丧极了。他本来以为只要罗恩赢了这场比赛，罗恩和赫敏肯定会立刻重归于好。他不知道怎么才能跟赫敏解释清楚，她是因为吻了威克多尔·克鲁姆才得罪了罗恩，事情已经过去那么久了，这叫他怎么说呢？

哈利在格兰芬多的庆祝晚会上没有看见赫敏。他赶到时，晚会正在热烈地进行。人们看到他进来，又爆发出一片掌声和欢呼声，祝贺的人群很快就把他团团围住了。他没有能够马上去找罗恩。克里维兄

him. What with trying to shake off the Creevey brothers, who wanted a blow-by-blow match analysis, and the large group of girls that encircled him, laughing at his least amusing comments and batting their eyelids, it was some time before he could try and find Ron. At last, he extricated himself from Romilda Vane, who was hinting heavily that she would like to go to Slughorn's Christmas party with him. As he was ducking towards the drinks table he walked straight into Ginny, Arnold the Pygmy Puff riding on her shoulder and Crookshanks mewing hopefully at her heels.

'Looking for Ron?' she asked, smirking. 'He's over there, the filthy hypocrite.'

Harry looked into the corner she was indicating. There, in full view of the whole room, stood Ron wrapped so closely around Lavender Brown it was hard to tell whose hands were whose.

'It looks like he's eating her face, doesn't it?' said Ginny dispassionately. 'But I suppose he's got to refine his technique somehow. Good game, Harry.'

She patted him on the arm; Harry felt a swooping sensation in his stomach, but then she walked off to help herself to more Butterbeer. Crookshanks trotted after her, his yellow eyes fixed upon Arnold.

Harry turned away from Ron, who did not look like surfacing soon, just in time to see the portrait hole closing. With a sinking feeling he thought he saw a mane of bushy brown hair whipping out of sight.

He darted forwards, sidestepped Romilda Vane again, and pushed open the portrait of the Fat Lady. The corridor outside seemed to be deserted.

'Hermione?'

He found her in the first unlocked classroom he tried. She was sitting on the teacher's desk, alone except for a small ring of twittering yellow birds circling her head, which she had clearly just conjured out of midair. Harry could not help admiring her spellwork at a time like this.

'Oh, hello, Harry,' she said in a brittle voice. 'I was just practising.'

'Yeah … they're – er – really good …' said Harry.

He had no idea what to say to her. He was just wondering whether there was any chance that she had not noticed Ron, that she had merely left the room because the party was a little too rowdy, when she said, in an unnaturally high-pitched voice, 'Ron seems to be enjoying the celebrations.'

弟俩想写一篇极为详细的比赛分析，哈利好不容易才摆脱了他们。接着一大群女生又把他围在中间，不管他说什么没趣儿的话，她们都放声大笑，还一个劲儿地冲他挤眉弄眼，他费了好大工夫才得以脱身。最后，他总算甩掉了罗米达·万尼——她强烈地暗示希望能跟哈利一起去参加斯拉格霍恩的圣诞晚会。哈利躲闪着朝饮料桌走去时，迎面撞上了金妮，侏儒蒲阿囡趴在她的肩膀上，克鲁克山眼巴巴地跟在她脚边喵喵叫。

"在找罗恩？"金妮问，然后嘲笑地说，"他在那儿呢，这个卑鄙的伪君子。"

哈利朝她手指的那个墙角望去。果然，罗恩和拉文德·布朗当着整个休息室的人紧紧搂抱在一起，难解难分，简直分不清哪只手是谁的。

"他好像在啃她的脸，是不是？"金妮冷静地说，"我想他需要提高一下技术。比赛打得不错，哈利。"

她拍了拍他的胳膊。哈利感到心里一阵翻腾，可是接着她就走过去给自己倒黄油啤酒了。克鲁克山颠儿颠儿地跟在她后面，一双黄眼睛死死地盯着阿囡。

看来罗恩一时半会儿还脱不开身，哈利转回身，却正好看到肖像洞口合上了。他心知不妙，因为他好像瞥见一蓬浓密的褐色头发从那里一闪而过。

他赶紧再次避开罗米达·万尼，冲过去一把推开胖夫人的肖像。外面的走廊里似乎空无一人。

"赫敏？"

他试着推开了第一间没上锁的教室，果然看见了赫敏。她独自一人坐在讲台上，一群叽叽喳喳的小黄鸟绕着她的头顶飞来飞去，显然是她刚才凭空变出来的。即使在这样的时刻，哈利也忍不住赞叹她的魔法技艺实在高超。

"噢，你好，哈利，"她用一种冷漠的声音说，"我正在练习呢。"

"是啊……它们……嗯……真不错……"哈利说。

他不知道该对她说些什么。他正猜想她是不是并没有注意罗恩，她是不是因为晚会太吵才离开休息室的，可是，紧接着便听见她用不

'Er … does he?' said Harry.

'Don't pretend you didn't see him,' said Hermione. 'He wasn't exactly hiding it, was –'

The door behind them burst open. To Harry's horror, Ron came in, laughing, pulling Lavender by the hand.

'Oh,' he said, drawing up short at the sight of Harry and Hermione.

'Oops!' said Lavender, and she backed out of the room, giggling. The door swung shut behind her.

There was a horrible swelling, billowing silence. Hermione was staring at Ron, who refused to look at her, but said with an odd mixture of bravado and awkwardness, 'Hi, Harry! Wondered where you'd got to!'

Hermione slid off the desk. The little flock of golden birds continued to twitter in circles around her head so that she looked like a strange, feathery model of the solar system.

'You shouldn't leave Lavender waiting outside,' she said quietly. 'She'll wonder where you've gone.'

She walked very slowly and erectly towards the door. Harry glanced at Ron, who was looking relieved that nothing worse had happened.

'*Oppugno!*' came a shriek from the doorway.

Harry spun round to see Hermione pointing her wand at Ron, her expression wild: the little flock of birds was speeding like a hail of fat golden bullets towards Ron, who yelped and covered his face with his hands, but the birds attacked, pecking and clawing at every bit of flesh they could reach.

'Gerremoffme!' he yelled, but with one last look of vindictive fury, Hermione wrenched open the door and disappeared through it. Harry thought he heard a sob before it slammed.

自然的尖细声音说：“罗恩好像在庆祝会上玩得蛮开心的。”

“嗯……是吗？”哈利说。

“你别假装没有看见他。”赫敏说，“他可没有刻意躲起来，不是吗——”

他们身后的门突然被撞开了。哈利惊恐地看见罗恩拽着拉文德的手，嘻嘻哈哈地走了进来。

“噢。”他看见哈利和赫敏，便一下子停住了。

“哎哟！”拉文德咯咯笑着退出了教室，门在她身后关上了。

教室里一片可怕的、酝酿着惊涛骇浪的沉默。赫敏盯着罗恩，罗恩没去看她，却用一种尴尬的、虚张声势的古怪腔调说：“嘿，哈利！我还纳闷你跑哪儿去了呢！”

赫敏从讲台上滑了下来。那群金黄色的小鸟继续围着她的脑袋叽叽喳喳地飞，这使她看上去像一个奇怪的、长着羽毛的太阳系模型。

“你不应该让拉文德在外面等你。”她平静地说，“她会纳闷你跑哪儿去了。”

她昂着头，很慢很慢地朝门口走去。哈利看了一眼罗恩，罗恩似乎因为没出现更糟的局面而松了口气。

“*万弹齐发！*”门口传来一声尖叫。

哈利猛地转身，看见赫敏正用魔杖指着罗恩，脸上的表情十分激动。那群小鸟像无数沉甸甸的金色子弹一齐朝罗恩射去，罗恩惨叫着用手捂住脸，可是小鸟来势凶猛，在它们够得着的每片皮肤上又啄又挠。

“让它们滚！”他大叫，可是赫敏脸上带着最后一点复仇的怒火，猛地拧开门走了出去。在门砰然关上时，哈利好像听见了一声抽泣。

CHAPTER FIFTEEN

The Unbreakable Vow

Snow was swirling against the icy windows once more; Christmas was approaching fast. Hagrid had already single-handedly delivered the usual twelve Christmas trees for the Great Hall; garlands of holly and tinsel had been twisted around the banisters of the stairs; everlasting candles glowed from inside the helmets of suits of armour and great bunches of mistletoe had been hung at intervals along the corridors. Large groups of girls tended to converge underneath the mistletoe bunches every time Harry went past, which caused blockages in the corridors; fortunately, however, Harry's frequent night-time wanderings had given him an unusually good knowledge of the castle's secret passageways, so that he was able, without too much difficulty, to navigate mistletoe-free routes between classes.

Ron, who might once have found the necessity of these detours a cause for jealousy rather than hilarity, simply roared with laughter about it all. Although Harry much preferred this new laughing, joking Ron to the moody, aggressive model he had been enduring for the last few weeks, the improved Ron came at a heavy price. Firstly, Harry had to put up with the frequent presence of Lavender Brown, who seemed to regard any moment that she was not kissing Ron as a moment wasted; and secondly, Harry found himself, once more, the best friend of two people who seemed unlikely ever to speak to each other again.

Ron, whose hands and forearms still bore scratches and cuts from Hermione's bird attack, was taking a defensive and resentful tone.

'She can't complain,' he told Harry. 'She snogged Krum. So she's found out someone wants to snog me, too. Well, it's a free country. I haven't done anything wrong.'

Harry did not answer, but pretended to be absorbed in the book they were supposed to have read before Charms the following morning (*Quintessence: A Quest*). Determined as he was to remain friends with both Ron and Hermione, he was spending a lot of time with his mouth shut tight.

第15章

牢不可破的誓言

雪花又在窗外旋舞，扑打着结冰的窗棂，圣诞节转眼将至。海格已经独自一人搬来了礼堂里每年少不了的十二棵圣诞树；楼梯栏杆上都缠了冬青和金属箔；甲胄的头盔里闪烁着长明蜡烛，走廊里每隔一段都挂上了一大束一大束的槲寄生。每次哈利从走廊上走过，总会有一堆堆的女孩聚在槲寄生下面，造成交通堵塞。幸好哈利频繁的夜游使他对城堡的秘密通道摸得透熟，能够不太困难地在课间绕过有槲寄生的路线。

这种绕道以前会让罗恩感到嫉妒而不是开心，现在他却只是哈哈大笑。虽然哈利觉得这个嘻嘻哈哈的新罗恩比前几星期那个郁闷、好斗的罗恩好得多，可这种改变却代价高昂。首先，哈利不得不经常看到拉文德·布朗，这女孩似乎觉得一刻不亲吻罗恩都是浪费；第二，哈利再次成了两个似乎决意老死不相往来的人的好朋友。

罗恩手上和胳膊上还带着赫敏的小黄鸟袭击留下的伤痕，他一副防备和怨恨的口气。

“她没什么可抱怨的，”他对哈利说，“她亲了克鲁姆，结果发现也有人想亲我。嘿嘿，自由国家嘛，我没做错什么。”

哈利没有回答，假装专心地看明天上午魔咒课前要读完的那本书（《第五元素：探索》）。他虽然决心继续做这两个人的朋友，但现在很多时候都闭着嘴巴。

'I never promised Hermione anything,' Ron mumbled. 'I mean, all right, I was going to go to Slughorn's Christmas party with her, but she never said … just as friends … I'm a free agent …'

Harry turned a page of *Quintessence*, aware that Ron was watching him. Ron's voice tailed away in mutters, barely audible over the loud crackling of the fire, though Harry thought he caught the words 'Krum' and 'can't complain' again.

Hermione's timetable was so full that Harry could only talk to her properly in the evenings, when Ron was in any case so tightly wrapped around Lavender that he did not notice what Harry was doing. Hermione refused to sit in the common room while Ron was there, so Harry generally joined her in the library, which meant that their conversations were held in whispers.

'He's at perfect liberty to kiss whomever he likes,' said Hermione, while the librarian, Madam Pince, prowled the shelves behind them. 'I really couldn't care less.'

She raised her quill and dotted an 'i' so ferociously that she punctured a hole in her parchment. Harry said nothing. He thought his voice might soon vanish from lack of use. He bent a little lower over *Advanced Potion-Making* and continued to make notes on Everlasting Elixirs, occasionally pausing to decipher the Prince's useful additions to Libatius Borage's text.

'And incidentally,' said Hermione, after a few moments, 'you need to be careful.'

'For the last time,' said Harry, speaking in a slightly hoarse whisper after three-quarters of an hour of silence, 'I am not giving back this book, I've learned more from the Half-Blood Prince than Snape or Slughorn have taught me in –'

'I'm not talking about your stupid so-called Prince,' said Hermione, giving his book a nasty look as though it had been rude to her, 'I'm talking about earlier. I went into the girls' bathroom just before I came in here and there were about a dozen girls in there, including that Romilda Vane, trying to decide how to slip you a love potion. They're all hoping they're going to get you to take them to Slughorn's party and they all seem to have bought Fred and George's love potions, which I'm afraid to say probably work –'

'Why didn't you confiscate them, then?' demanded Harry. It seemed extraordinary that Hermione's mania for upholding rules could have abandoned her at this crucial juncture.

“我从没对赫敏承诺过什么。”罗恩嘟囔道，“我确实要跟她一起去参加斯拉格霍恩的圣诞晚会，可她从来没说……只是朋友……我是自由人……”

哈利把《第五元素：探索》翻过一页，知道罗恩在看着他。罗恩的声音低了下去，在炉火的噼啪声中几乎听不见了，但哈利好像又听到了“克鲁姆”和“没什么可抱怨的”之类的话。

赫敏的时间表太满，哈利到晚上才能跟她正经说上话，反正这时罗恩被拉文德缠得紧紧的，顾不到哈利在干什么。只要有罗恩在，赫敏就不肯坐在公共休息室里，所以哈利一般到图书馆去找她，这意味着谈话要悄悄地进行。

“他爱亲谁就亲谁好了，”赫敏说，图书馆管理员平斯女士正在后面的书架间巡视，“我才不在乎呢。”

她举起羽毛笔，给正在写的字母 i 狠狠加上一点，结果把羊皮纸戳了个窟窿。哈利没吱声，他觉得嗓子一直不用都快要失声了。他把头埋得更低一点儿，继续在《高级魔药制作》永久型药剂一节上做笔记，有时会停下来辨认一番王子对利巴修·波拉奇添加的有用补充。

“顺便说一句，”过了一会儿赫敏说，“你要小心点儿。”

“跟你说最后一遍，”哈利悄悄地说，这是他闷了四十五分钟后第一次开口，声音有点哑，“这书我不还了，我从混血王子这儿学到的比斯内普和斯拉格霍恩——”

“我不是说你那个愚蠢的所谓王子，”赫敏凶巴巴地瞪了他的书一眼，好像它惹了她似的，“我是说刚才，到这儿来之前，我去盥洗室，那儿有一打女孩子，包括罗米达·万尼，都在讨论怎么能让你喝下迷情剂。她们都希望能被你带去参加斯拉格霍恩的晚会，而且好像都买了弗雷德和乔治的迷情剂，我要说的是，恐怕这玩意儿可能会让——”

“你怎么没把那些东西没收了呢？”哈利问，赫敏维护规章制度的癖好却在这节骨眼上松懈下来，他似乎觉得不可思议。

'They didn't have the potions with them in the bathroom,' said Hermione scornfully. 'They were just discussing tactics. As I doubt whether even the *Half-Blood Prince*,' she gave the book another nasty look, 'could dream up an antidote for a dozen different love potions at once, I'd just invite someone to go with you – that'll stop all the others thinking they've still got a chance. It's tomorrow night, they're getting desperate.'

'There isn't anyone I want to invite,' mumbled Harry, who was still trying not to think about Ginny any more than he could help, despite the fact that she kept cropping up in his dreams in ways that made him devoutly thankful that Ron could not perform Legilimency.

'Well, just be careful what you drink, because Romilda Vane looked like she meant business,' said Hermione grimly.

She hitched up the long roll of parchment on which she was writing her Arithmancy essay and continued to scratch away with her quill. Harry watched her with his mind a long way away.

'Hang on a moment,' he said slowly. 'I thought Filch had banned anything bought at Weasleys' Wizard Wheezes?'

'And when has anyone ever paid attention to what Filch has banned?' asked Hermione, still concentrating on her essay.

'But I thought all the owls were being searched? So how come these girls are able to bring love potions into school?'

'Fred and George send them disguised as perfumes and cough potions,' said Hermione. 'It's part of their Owl Order Service.'

'You know a lot about it.'

Hermione gave him the kind of nasty look she had just given his copy of *Advanced Potion-Making*.

'It was all on the back of the bottles they showed Ginny and me in the summer,' she said coldly. 'I don't go around putting potions in people's drinks … or pretending to, either, which is just as bad …'

'Yeah, well, never mind that,' said Harry quickly. 'The point is, Filch is being fooled, isn't he? These girls are getting stuff into the school disguised as something else! So why couldn't Malfoy have brought the necklace into the school –?'

'Oh, Harry … not that again …'

'Come on, why not?' demanded Harry.

"她们没把药水带进盥洗室，"赫敏轻蔑地说，"只是在讨论计策。我怀疑就连混血王子，"她又凶巴巴地瞪了那本书一眼，"也想不出法子同时弄出十几种不同迷情剂的解药，换了我就赶快邀请一个人——这样别人就不会觉得还有机会了。就是明天晚上嘛，她们都急眼了。"

"我找不到一个想邀请的人。"哈利嘟囔道，还是尽量不去想金妮，虽然她总是在他梦中出现，并且出现的方式让他由衷庆幸罗恩不会摄神取念。

"好吧，那你喝东西可得当心，罗米达·万尼看上去可是认真的。"赫敏阴沉地说。

她把那卷长长的羊皮纸朝上拉了拉，唰唰地接着写她那篇算术占卜课的论文。哈利看着她，思绪在很远的地方。

"等一等，"他慢吞吞地说，"费尔奇不是把韦斯莱魔法把戏坊买的东西都禁止了吗？"

"谁在乎过费尔奇禁止什么？"赫敏随口说道，一边还在专心写文章。

"不是所有的猫头鹰都要被检查吗？那些女孩子怎么能把迷情剂带进学校呢？"

"弗雷德和乔治把它们当香水和咳嗽药水送来，这是猫头鹰订单服务的一部分。"

"你知道的真多。"

赫敏凶狠狠地瞪了他一眼，像刚刚瞪他那本《高级魔药制作》一样。

"这些都在他们暑假里给我和金妮看的瓶子背后写着呢。"她冷冷地说，"我可不会在别人饮料里下药……或假装下药，那也一样恶劣……"

"是，好了，别介意。"哈利忙说，"问题是费尔奇给耍了，是不是？这些女孩子把东西伪装一下就可以带进学校！那马尔福为什么不能带项链——？"

"哦，哈利……别又提那个……"

"啊，为什么？"哈利追问。

'Look,' sighed Hermione, 'Secrecy Sensors detect jinxes, curses and concealment charms, don't they? They're used to find Dark Magic and Dark objects. They'd have picked up a powerful curse, like the one on that necklace, within seconds. But something that's just been put in the wrong bottle wouldn't register – and anyway, love potions aren't Dark or dangerous –'

'Easy for you to say,' muttered Harry, thinking of Romilda Vane.

'– so it would be down to Filch to realise it wasn't a cough potion, and he's not a very good wizard, I doubt he can tell one potion from –'

Hermione stopped dead; Harry had heard it too. Somebody had moved close behind them among the dark bookshelves. They waited and a moment later the vulture-like countenance of Madam Pince appeared round the corner, her sunken cheeks, her skin like parchment and her long hooked nose illuminated unflatteringly by the lamp she was carrying.

'The library is now closed,' she said. 'Mind you return anything you have borrowed to the correct – *what have you been doing to that book, you depraved boy?*'

'It isn't the library's, it's mine!' said Harry hastily, snatching his copy of *Advanced Potion-Making* off the table as she lunged at it with a clawlike hand.

'Despoiled!' she hissed. 'Desecrated! Befouled!'

'It's just a book that's been written in!' said Harry, tugging it out of her grip.

She looked as though she might have a seizure; Hermione, who had hastily packed her things, grabbed Harry by the arm and frogmarched him away.

'She'll ban you from the library if you're not careful. Why did you have to bring that stupid book?'

'It's not my fault she's barking mad, Hermione. Or d'you think she overheard you being rude about Filch? I've always thought there might be something going on between them …'

'Oh, ha, ha …'

Enjoying the fact that they could speak normally again, they made their way along the deserted, lamp-lit corridors back to the common room, arguing about whether or not Filch and Madam Pince were secretly in love with each other.

'Baubles,' said Harry to the Fat Lady, this being the new, festive password.

'Same to you,' said the Fat Lady with a roguish grin, and she swung forwards to admit them.

"你看，"赫敏叹了一口气，说道，"探密器能发现恶咒、毒咒和隐藏咒，是吧？它们是被用来探测黑魔法和黑魔法用品的，能在几秒钟内探测到一个威力强大的咒语，比如项链上的那个。但是装错瓶子的东西就检测不出来了——再说，迷情剂不是黑魔法，没有危险——"

"你说得倒轻巧。"哈利嘟囔道，一边想到了罗米达·万尼。

"——所以就要靠费尔奇来发现它不是咳嗽药水了，可他并不是很高明的巫师，我怀疑他并不能区分——"

赫敏突然打住，哈利也听到了，身后阴暗的书架间有人走近。他们等了一会儿，平斯女士那秃鹫般的面孔从拐角露了出来，凹陷的面颊、羊皮纸似的皮肤和长长的鹰钩鼻，被她手里提的灯照得格外分明。

"图书馆该关门了，"她说，"把借的书放回原——你对那本书干了什么？你这邪恶的孩子！"

"这不是图书馆的，是我自己的！"哈利赶紧说，一边从桌上拿起那本《高级魔药制作》，可平斯女士鹰爪般的手已经抓了过去。

"抢劫！"她嘶声说，"亵渎！玷污！"

"不过是在书上写了点字！"哈利辩解着把书从她手里拽了回去。

她看上去就像要发病，赫敏匆匆收拾好东西，抓住哈利的胳膊把他拖走了。

"你要是不小心点儿，她会禁止你进图书馆的。你干吗非得带上那本愚蠢的书？"

"她乱叫乱嚷又不是我的错，赫敏。你说她会不会听到你说费尔奇的坏话？我总觉得他们之间有点什么……"

"哦，哈哈……"

他们很高兴又能正常说话了，于是一边沿着亮灯的空荡荡的走廊往公共休息室走，一边争论着费尔奇和平斯女士是否有私情。

"一文不值。"哈利对胖夫人说，这是节日的新口令。

"你也一样。"胖夫人调皮地笑着，向前旋开把他们让了进去。

'Hi, Harry!' said Romilda Vane, the moment he had climbed through the portrait hole. 'Fancy a Gillywater?'

Hermione gave him a 'What-did-I-tell-you?' look over her shoulder.

'No thanks,' said Harry quickly. 'I don't like it much.'

'Well, take these anyway,' said Romilda, thrusting a box into his hands. 'Chocolate Cauldrons, they've got Firewhisky in them. My gran sent them to me, but I don't like them.'

'Oh – right – thanks a lot,' said Harry, who could not think what else to say. 'Er – I'm just going over here with …'

He hurried off behind Hermione, his voice tailing away feebly.

'Told you,' said Hermione succinctly. 'Sooner you ask someone, sooner they'll all leave you alone and you can –'

But her face suddenly turned blank; she had just spotted Ron and Lavender who were entwined in the same armchair.

'Well, goodnight, Harry,' said Hermione, though it was only seven o'clock in the evening, and she left for the girls' dormitory without another word.

Harry went to bed comforting himself that there was only one more day of lessons to struggle through, plus Slughorn's party, after which he and Ron would depart together for The Burrow. It now seemed impossible that Ron and Hermione would make up with each other before the holidays began, but perhaps, somehow, the break would give them time to calm down, think better of their behaviour …

But his hopes were not high, and they sank still lower after enduring a Transfiguration lesson with them both next day. They had just embarked upon the immensely difficult topic of human transfiguration; working in front of mirrors, they were supposed to be changing the colour of their own eyebrows. Hermione laughed unkindly at Ron's disastrous first attempt, during which he somehow managed to give himself a spectacular handlebar moustache; Ron retaliated by doing a cruel but accurate impression of Hermione jumping up and down in her seat every time Professor McGonagall asked a question, which Lavender and Parvati found deeply amusing and which reduced Hermione to the verge of tears again. She raced out of the classroom on the bell, leaving half her things behind; Harry, deciding that her need was greater than Ron's just then, scooped up her remaining possessions and followed her.

He finally tracked her down as she emerged from a girls' bathroom on the

“嘿，哈利！”哈利刚钻出肖像洞口，罗米达·万尼就说，“要喝一杯鳃囊草水吗？”

赫敏回头向他丢了一个“我说什么来着？”的眼色。

“谢谢，不用了，”哈利忙说，“我不大爱喝。”

“那，拿上这个吧，”罗米达把一个盒子塞到他手里，“巧克力坩埚，里面有火焰威士忌。我奶奶寄给我的，可是我不喜欢……”

“这——好吧——多谢了，”哈利说，他想不出别的话，“哦——我是跟……”

他匆匆跟着赫敏走开了，声音渐渐低下去。

“跟你说了，”赫敏简明地说，“趁早邀请一个人，她们就不会来烦你了——”

她脸上突然变得一片木然，因为她看到罗恩和拉文德正纠缠在一起，挤在一把扶手椅上。

“晚安，哈利。”赫敏说，其实才七点钟，她没再说别的，径自回女生宿舍了。

哈利上床时安慰自己：只要再对付一天的课和斯拉格霍恩的晚会，就可以跟罗恩一起去陋居了。看来罗恩与赫敏不可能在节前和好，但假期也许能让他们俩冷静下来，反省一下自己的行为。

但希望不是太大，第二天他跟那两人一起熬过了变形课之后，觉得希望更渺茫了。他们已经上到人体变形这个特别难的课题。这节课要求对着镜子使自己的眉毛变色。赫敏刻薄地嘲笑罗恩灾难性的第一次尝试——罗恩让自己长出了两撇惹眼的八字胡。罗恩以牙还牙，每次麦格教授提问时，他都惟妙惟肖地恶意模仿赫敏在座位上跳起坐下，拉文德和帕瓦蒂觉得好笑极了，赫敏又差点哭了出来。下课铃一响她就冲出教室，一半的东西都没拿。哈利觉得此刻她比罗恩更需要安慰，便收拾起她的东西追了出去。

终于追到了。赫敏刚从楼下盥洗室出来，旁边是卢娜·洛夫古德，

floor below. She was accompanied by Luna Lovegood, who was patting her vaguely on the back.

'Oh, hello, Harry,' said Luna. 'Did you know one of your eyebrows is bright yellow?'

'Hi, Luna. Hermione, you left your stuff …'

He held out her books.

'Oh, yes,' said Hermione in a choked voice, taking her things and turning away quickly to hide the fact that she was wiping her eyes on her pencil case. 'Thank you, Harry. Well, I'd better get going …'

And she hurried off, without giving Harry any time to offer words of comfort, though admittedly he could not think of any.

'She's a bit upset,' said Luna. 'I thought at first it was Moaning Myrtle in there, but it turned out to be Hermione. She said something about that Ron Weasley …'

'Yeah, they've had a row,' said Harry.

'He says very funny things sometimes, doesn't he?' said Luna, as they set off down the corridor together. 'But he can be a bit unkind. I noticed that last year.'

'I s'pose,' said Harry. Luna was demonstrating her usual knack of speaking uncomfortable truths; he had never met anyone quite like her. 'So have you had a good term?'

'Oh, it's been all right,' said Luna. 'A bit lonely without the DA. Ginny's been nice, though. She stopped two boys in our Transfiguration class calling me "Loony" the other day –'

'How would you like to come to Slughorn's party with me tonight?'

The words were out of Harry's mouth before he could stop them; he heard himself say them as though it were a stranger speaking.

Luna turned her protuberant eyes upon him in surprise.

'Slughorn's party? With you?'

'Yeah,' said Harry. 'We're supposed to bring guests, so I thought you might like … I mean …' He was keen to make his intentions perfectly clear. 'I mean, just as friends, you know. But if you don't want to …'

He was already half hoping that she didn't want to.

'Oh, no, I'd love to go with you as friends!' said Luna, beaming as he had never seen her beam before. 'Nobody's ever asked me to a party before, as a friend! Is that why you dyed your eyebrow, for the party? Should I do mine, too?'

正在胡乱地拍着她的后背。

"哦，你好，哈利，"卢娜说，"你知道你有一根眉毛是金黄的吗？"

"嘿，卢娜。赫敏，你的东西没拿。"

哈利把她的书递了过去。

"哦，对了。"赫敏哽咽地说，一边接过自己的东西，又迅速扭过头去，掩饰她在用文具袋抹眼泪，"谢谢你，哈利。我得走了……"

她匆匆离去，没有给哈利说安慰话的机会，老实讲他也想不出合适的话来。

"她有点儿不高兴，"卢娜说，"起先我还以为是哭泣的桃金娘呢，没想到是赫敏。她提到了罗恩·韦斯莱……"

"是啊，他们吵架了。"

"罗恩有时候说话怪有趣的，是不是？"两人一起走在走廊上，卢娜说，"可是也会有点刻薄，我去年就发现了。"

"是吧。"哈利说，卢娜又像她往常那样——一语道破令人不快的真相，他还真没见过像她这样的人，"你这学期过得好吗？"

"哦，还行。D.A.没有了，有点孤单，但金妮很好。那天她在变形课上制止了两个男生叫我'疯姑娘'——"

"你今晚愿意跟我去参加斯拉格霍恩的晚会吗？"

这句话脱口而出，哈利已来不及阻止，他觉得好像是一个不认识的人在说话。

卢娜那双向外突出的眼睛惊讶地转向了他。

"斯拉格霍恩的晚会？跟你？"

"对，"哈利说，"我们都要带客人，所以我想你也许……我的意思是……"他急于澄清自己的意图，"我的意思是，只是作为朋友，你明白。但如果你不愿意……"

他已经有点儿希望她不想去了。

"啊，不，我愿意作为朋友跟你去！"卢娜笑逐颜开，哈利从没见过她这么灿烂的笑容，"还没人邀请过我参加晚会呢，作为朋友！你是不是为这个还染了眉毛？我也要染吗？"

'No,' said Harry firmly, 'that was a mistake, I'll get Hermione to put it right for me. So, I'll meet you in the Entrance Hall at eight o'clock, then.'

'AHA!' screamed a voice from overhead and both of them jumped; unnoticed by either of them, they had just passed right underneath Peeves, who was hanging upside-down from a chandelier and grinning maliciously at them.

'*Potty asked Loony to go to the party! Potty lurves Loony! Potty luuuuurves Looooooony!*'

And he zoomed away, cackling and shrieking, 'Potty loves Loony!'

'Nice to keep these things private,' said Harry. And sure enough, in no time at all the whole school seemed to know that Harry Potter was taking Luna Lovegood to Slughorn's party.

'You could've taken *anyone*!' said Ron in disbelief over dinner. '*Anyone!* And you chose Loony Lovegood?'

'Don't call her that, Ron,' snapped Ginny, pausing behind Harry on her way to join friends. 'I'm really glad you're taking her, Harry, she's so excited.'

And she moved on down the table to sit with Dean. Harry tried to feel pleased that Ginny was glad he was taking Luna to the party, but could not quite manage it. A long way along the table, Hermione was sitting alone, playing with her stew. Harry noticed Ron looking at her furtively.

'You could say sorry,' suggested Harry bluntly.

'What, and get attacked by another flock of canaries?' muttered Ron.

'What did you have to imitate her for?'

'She laughed at my moustache!'

'So did I, it was the stupidest thing I've ever seen.'

But Ron did not seem to have heard; Lavender had just arrived with Parvati. Squeezing herself in between Harry and Ron, Lavender flung her arms around Ron's neck.

'Hi, Harry,' said Parvati who, like him, looked faintly embarrassed and bored by the behaviour of their two friends.

'Hi,' said Harry. 'How're you? You're staying at Hogwarts, then? I heard your parents wanted you to leave.'

'I managed to talk them out of it for the time being,' said Parvati. 'That Katie thing really freaked them out, but as there hasn't been anything since … oh, hi, Hermione!'

“不用，”哈利坚决地说，“那是个失误。我要请赫敏帮我变回来。那么，我八点在门厅等你。”

“**啊哈！**”头上一个声音怪叫道，把两人都吓了一跳。他们没注意刚才正好从皮皮鬼的下面走过，他倒挂在一个枝形吊灯上，正朝他们龇牙咧嘴地坏笑。

“傻宝宝请疯姑娘去参加晚会！傻宝宝爱上了疯姑娘！傻宝宝爱——上了疯姑——娘！”

他嗖地飞走了，一边咯咯地笑，一边尖叫：“傻宝宝爱上了疯姑娘！”

“这些事最好不要张扬。”哈利说。当然，一转眼的工夫，好像全校都知道了哈利·波特邀请卢娜·洛夫古德去参加斯拉格霍恩的晚会。

“你可以带任何人！”吃晚饭时罗恩不敢相信地说，“任何人！可你偏偏选了疯姑娘洛夫古德？”

“别那么说她，罗恩。”金妮责备道，她刚好从哈利身后路过，去找她的朋友，“我真高兴你要带她去，哈利，她可兴奋了。”

她走过去跟迪安坐在了一起。哈利试图为金妮赞同他带卢娜去参加晚会而感到快乐，可是他做不到。赫敏一个人坐得远远的，拨弄着她的炖菜。哈利注意到罗恩正在偷偷地看她。

“你可以去道歉啊。”哈利直率地提议。

“什么？再让一群小鸟来啄我？”罗恩嘟囔道。

“你干吗要模仿她？”

“她笑我的胡子！”

“我也笑了，这是我见过的最滑稽的事。”

但罗恩好像没听见，拉文德和帕瓦蒂刚刚进来。拉文德挤到罗恩和哈利中间，伸出胳膊搂住了罗恩的脖子。

“你好，哈利。”帕瓦蒂说，她好像跟哈利一样，对两位朋友的行为感到有点儿难堪和厌烦。

“你好，”哈利说，“你好吗？你要留在霍格沃茨？我听说你父母想让你回去。”

“我暂时说服了他们。凯蒂的事着实把他们吓坏了，但因为后来一直没事……哦，嘿，赫敏！”

Parvati positively beamed. Harry could tell that she was feeling guilty for having laughed at Hermione in Transfiguration. He looked around and saw that Hermione was beaming back, if possible even more brightly. Girls were very strange sometimes.

'Hi, Parvati!' said Hermione, ignoring Ron and Lavender completely. 'Are you going to Slughorn's party tonight?'

'No invite,' said Parvati gloomily. 'I'd love to go, though, it sounds like it's going to be really good … you're going, aren't you?'

'Yes, I'm meeting Cormac at eight and we're –'

There was a noise like a plunger being withdrawn from a blocked sink and Ron surfaced. Hermione acted as though she had not seen or heard anything.

'– we're going up to the party together.'

'Cormac?' said Parvati. 'Cormac McLaggen, you mean?'

'That's right,' said Hermione sweetly. 'The one who *almost*,' she put a great deal of emphasis on the word, 'became Gryffindor Keeper.'

'Are you going out with him, then?' asked Parvati, wide-eyed.

'Oh – yes – didn't you know?' said Hermione, with a most un-Hermione-ish giggle.

'No!' said Parvati, looking positively agog at this piece of gossip. 'Wow, you like your Quidditch players, don't you? First Krum, then McLaggen …'

'I like *really good* Quidditch players,' Hermione corrected her, still smiling. 'Well, see you … got to go and get ready for the party …'

She left. At once Lavender and Parvati put their heads together to discuss this new development, with everything they had ever heard about McLaggen, and all they had ever guessed about Hermione. Ron looked strangely blank and said nothing. Harry was left to ponder in silence the depths to which girls would sink to get revenge.

When he arrived in the Entrance Hall at eight o'clock that night, he found an unusually large number of girls lurking there, all of whom seemed to be staring at him resentfully as he approached Luna. She was wearing a set of spangled silver robes that was attracting a certain amount of giggling from the onlookers, but otherwise she looked quite nice. Harry was glad, in any case, that she had left off her radish earrings, her Butterbeer-cork necklace and her Spectrespecs.

帕瓦蒂满脸带笑，哈利看出她是为变形课上笑了赫敏而感到内疚。他扭头一看，赫敏也是一副笑容，如果可能的话，是比帕瓦蒂还要灿烂的笑容。女孩子有时真是很奇怪。

“嘿，帕瓦蒂！”赫敏说，全然不理会罗恩和拉文德，“你今晚去参加斯拉格霍恩的晚会吗？”

“没人邀请我，”帕瓦蒂沮丧地说，“但是我很想去，听起来很棒……你会去吧？”

“嗯，我八点跟考迈克碰面，我们——”

突然一个声音，好像皮搋子从堵塞的水池里拔出来，罗恩浮出了水面。赫敏好像什么也没听见，什么也没看见。

“——我们一起去。”

“考迈克？”帕瓦蒂问，“你是说考迈克·麦克拉根？”

“对，”赫敏甜甜地说，“就是差一点儿——”她格外强调这个词，“——当上格兰芬多守门员的那个。”

“所以你是跟他好上了？”帕瓦蒂瞪大了眼睛问。

“哦——是啊——你不知道吗？”赫敏说着，非常不像赫敏地咯咯笑起来。

“不会吧！”帕瓦蒂看上去对这个消息大为兴奋，“哇，你果真喜欢魁地奇球员，是不是？先是克鲁姆，然后是麦克拉根……”

“我喜欢真正出色的魁地奇球员。”赫敏纠正她说，依旧面带微笑，“好了，以后再聊……得去准备参加晚会了……”

她走了。拉文德和帕瓦蒂马上把脑袋凑在一起议论这个新情况，包括她们对麦克拉根的一切耳闻，以及她们对赫敏的所有猜测。罗恩表情异常麻木，一言不发。哈利留在那儿，思考着女孩子为了报复可以陷得多深。

晚上八点，他来到门厅，发现有异常多的女孩子在那儿游荡。当他走向卢娜时，她们似乎都在怨恨地盯着他。卢娜穿着一套镶着银色亮片的袍子，这引起一些窃笑，但在其他方面她看上去还蛮不错的。哈利很高兴她没戴萝卜耳环、黄油啤酒瓶塞项链和她的防妖眼镜。

'Hi,' he said. 'Shall we get going, then?'

'Oh, yes,' she said happily. 'Where is the party?'

'Slughorn's office,' said Harry, leading her up the marble staircase away from all the staring and muttering. 'Did you hear, there's supposed to be a vampire coming?'

'Rufus Scrimgeour?' asked Luna.

'I – what?' said Harry, disconcerted. 'You mean the Minister for Magic?'

'Yes, he's a vampire,' said Luna matter-of-factly. 'Father wrote a very long article about it when Scrimgeour first took over from Cornelius Fudge, but he was forced not to publish by somebody from the Ministry. Obviously, they didn't want the truth to get out!'

Harry, who thought it most unlikely that Rufus Scrimgeour was a vampire, but who was used to Luna repeating her father's bizarre views as though they were fact, did not reply; they were already approaching Slughorn's office and the sounds of laughter, music and loud conversation were growing louder with every step they took.

Whether it had been built that way, or because he had used magical trickery to make it so, Slughorn's office was much larger than the usual teacher's study. The ceiling and walls had been draped with emerald, crimson and gold hangings, so that it looked as though they were all inside a vast tent. The room was crowded and stuffy and bathed in the red light cast by an ornate golden lamp dangling from the centre of the ceiling in which real fairies were fluttering, each a brilliant speck of light. Loud singing accompanied by what sounded like mandolins issued from a distant corner; a haze of pipe smoke hung over several elderly warlocks deep in conversation, and a number of house-elves were negotiating their way squeakily through the forest of knees, obscured by the heavy silver platters of food they were bearing, so that they looked like little roving tables.

'Harry, m'boy!' boomed Slughorn, almost as soon as Harry and Luna had squeezed in through the door. 'Come in, come in, so many people I'd like you to meet!'

Slughorn was wearing a tasselled velvet hat to match his smoking jacket. Gripping Harry's arm so tightly he might have been hoping to Disapparate with him, Slughorn led him purposefully into the party; Harry seized Luna's hand and dragged her along with him.

'Harry, I'd like you to meet Eldred Worple, an old student of mine, author of *Blood Brothers: My Life Amongst the Vampires* – and, of course, his friend Sanguini.'

“你好！我们走吧？”

“哦，好啊，”她愉快地说，“晚会在哪儿？”

“斯拉格霍恩的办公室。”哈利带着她登上大理石台阶，离开了那些眼光和嘀咕，“你听说了吗？有吸血鬼要去呢。”

“鲁弗斯·斯克林杰？”卢娜问。

“我——什么？”哈利吃了一惊，问道，“你是说魔法部部长？”

“对，他是个吸血鬼。”卢娜十分肯定地说，“斯克林杰刚接替康奈利·福吉的时候，我爸爸写了一篇很长的文章，可是部里有人不让他发表。显然，他们不想泄露真相！”

哈利觉得说鲁弗斯·斯克林杰是吸血鬼太荒唐了，但他习惯了卢娜把她父亲的怪念头当真事讲，便没有说话。斯拉格霍恩的办公室已经近了，笑声、音乐声和响亮的说话声随着他们的脚步而增强。

不知道是本来如此，还是施了魔法，斯拉格霍恩的办公室比一般教师的房间大得多。天花板和墙壁上挂着翠绿、深红和金色的帷幔，看上去像在一个大帐篷里。房间里拥挤闷热，被天花板中央挂着的一盏金色华灯照得红彤彤的。灯里有真的小仙子在舞动，每个小精灵都是一个明亮的光点。远处一个角落传来响亮的、听起来像用曼陀铃伴奏的歌声；几个谈兴正浓的老男巫头上被烟斗的青雾笼罩；一些家养小精灵在丛林般的小腿间吱吱穿行，托着沉甸甸的银制餐盘，盘子把他们的身体都遮住了，看上去就像漫游的小桌子。

“哈利，我的孩子！”哈利和卢娜一挤进门，斯拉格霍恩便声如洪钟地叫道，“进来，进来，有这么多人要让你见见呢！”

斯拉格霍恩戴着一顶带缨穗的天鹅绒帽子，与他的吸烟衫很相配。他不由分说地领着哈利走进人群，把哈利的胳膊抓得紧紧的，好像要带他幻影移形似的。哈利拉住卢娜的手，拽着她一起走。

“哈利，我想让你见见埃尔德·沃普尔，我以前的学生，《血亲兄弟：我在吸血鬼中生活》的作者——当然，还有他的朋友血尼。”

Worple, who was a small, bespectacled man, grabbed Harry's hand and shook it enthusiastically; the vampire Sanguini, who was tall and emaciated with dark shadows under his eyes, merely nodded. He looked rather bored. A gaggle of girls was standing close to him, looking curious and excited.

'Harry Potter, I am simply delighted!' said Worple, peering short-sightedly up into Harry's face. 'I was saying to Professor Slughorn only the other day, *Where is the biography of Harry Potter for which we have all been waiting?* '

'Er,' said Harry, 'were you?'

'Just as modest as Horace described!' said Worple. 'But seriously –' his manner changed; it became suddenly businesslike, 'I would be delighted to write it myself – people are craving to know more about you, dear boy, craving! If you were prepared to grant me a few interviews, say in four- or five-hour sessions, why, we could have the book finished within months. And all with very little effort on your part, I assure you – ask Sanguini here if it isn't quite – *Sanguini, stay here!* ' added Worple, suddenly stern, for the vampire had been edging towards the nearby group of girls, a rather hungry look in his eye. 'Here, have a pasty,' said Worple, seizing one from a passing elf and stuffing it into Sanguini's hand before turning his attention back to Harry.

'My dear boy, the gold you could make, you have no idea –'

'I'm definitely not interested,' said Harry firmly, 'and I've just seen a friend of mine, sorry.'

He pulled Luna after him into the crowd; he had indeed just seen a long mane of brown hair disappear between what looked like two members of the Weird Sisters.

'Hermione! *Hermione!* '

'Harry! There you are, thank goodness! Hi, Luna!'

'What's happened to you?' asked Harry, for Hermione looked distinctly dishevelled, rather as though she had just fought her way out of a thicket of Devil's Snare.

'Oh, I've just escaped – I mean, I've just left Cormac,' she said. 'Under the mistletoe,' she added in explanation, as Harry continued to look questioningly at her.

'Serves you right for coming with him,' he told her severely.

'I thought he'd annoy Ron most,' said Hermione dispassionately. 'I debated for a while about Zacharias Smith, but I thought, on the whole –'

沃普尔是个戴眼镜的小个子男人，他抓住哈利的手热切地握着。吸血鬼血尼又高又瘦，眼睛下有黑圈，他只是对哈利点了点头，一副倦怠的样子，一群女孩站在他旁边叽叽喳喳，好奇而兴奋。

“哈利·波特，我太高兴了！”沃普尔说，一边瞪着近视的双眼仰望哈利的面孔，“我那天还跟斯拉格霍恩教授说呢，我们大家拭目以待的《哈利·波特传》在哪儿呢？”

“呃，”哈利说，“是吗？”

“果然像霍拉斯说的那么谦虚！”沃普尔说，“但说真格的——”他态度一变，突然像谈起了生意，“我很愿意写这本书——人们渴望更多地了解你，亲爱的孩子，渴望！如果你能接受我的几次采访，每次四五个小时，保证几个月就能成书。不会费你什么事，我保证——问问血尼是不是——血尼，别走！”沃普尔突然变得神色严厉，因为吸血鬼朝旁边那群女孩蹭了过去，眼里带着饥饿的光。“给你，吃块馅饼。”沃普尔说着从一个托盘子的小精灵那儿抓过一块，塞到血尼手中，然后又把注意力转到哈利身上。

“亲爱的孩子，你能赚多少钱啊，你想象不到——”

“我实在不感兴趣。”哈利坚决地说，“我看到了一个朋友，对不起。”

他拖着卢娜挤进人群；他确实看到一头浓密的褐色长发，好像消失在了古怪姐妹演唱组的两位成员之间。

“赫敏！赫敏！”

“哈利！你在这儿，太好了！嘿，卢娜！”

“你怎么了？”哈利问，赫敏看上去凌乱不堪，好像刚从魔鬼网中挣脱出来。

“哦，我刚逃脱——我是说，我刚离开了考迈克。”她说，见哈利还在询问地看着她，又解释地加了一句，“在槲寄生底下。”

“谁让你跟他来的。”哈利严厉地说。

“我想他最能惹罗恩生气。”赫敏冷静地说，“我考虑过扎卡赖斯·史密斯，但是我想，总体上——”

'*You considered Smith?*' said Harry, revolted.

'Yes, I did, and I'm starting to wish I'd chosen him, McLaggen makes Grawp look a gentleman. Let's go this way, we'll be able to see him coming, he's so tall ...'

The three of them made their way over to the other side of the room, scooping up goblets of mead on the way, realising too late that Professor Trelawney was standing there alone.

'Hello,' said Luna politely to Professor Trelawney.

'Good evening, my dear,' said Professor Trelawney, focusing upon Luna with some difficulty. Harry could smell cooking sherry again. 'I haven't seen you in my classes lately ...'

'No, I've got Firenze this year,' said Luna.

'Oh, of course,' said Professor Trelawney with an angry, drunken titter. 'Or Dobbin, as I prefer to think of him. You would have thought, would you not, that now I am returned to the school Professor Dumbledore might have got rid of the horse? But no ... we share classes ... it's an insult, frankly, an insult. Do you know ...'

Professor Trelawney seemed too tipsy to have recognised Harry. Under cover of her furious criticisms of Firenze, Harry drew closer to Hermione and said, 'Let's get something straight. Are you planning to tell Ron that you interfered at Keeper tryouts?'

Hermione raised her eyebrows.

'Do you really think I'd stoop that low?'

Harry looked at her shrewdly.

'Hermione, if you can ask out McLaggen –'

'There's a difference,' said Hermione with dignity. 'I've got no plans to tell Ron anything about what might, or might not, have happened at Keeper tryouts.'

'Good,' said Harry fervently. 'Because he'll just fall apart again and we'll lose the next match –'

'Quidditch!' said Hermione angrily. 'Is that all boys care about? Cormac hasn't asked me one single question about myself, no, I've just been treated to A Hundred Great Saves Made by Cormac McLaggen non-stop, ever since – oh no, here he comes!'

She moved so fast it was as though she had Disapparated; one moment she was there, the next she had squeezed between two guffawing witches and vanished.

“你考虑过史密斯？”哈利反感地问道。

“是啊，我现在希望选择的是他，跟麦克拉根相比，格洛普都显得像个绅士。我们到那边去，可以看到他过来，他那么高……”

三人向房间那头挤去，一边抓过几只装着蜂蜜酒的高脚杯，等到发现特里劳尼教授一个人站在那儿时，已经来不及了。

“您好。”卢娜礼貌地说。

“晚上好，亲爱的。”特里劳尼教授费了点劲才看清了卢娜。哈利又闻到了雪利料酒的气味。“最近我课上没见到你……”

“嗯，我今年选了费伦泽的课。”卢娜说。

“哦，当然，”特里劳尼教授带着怒气，醉醺醺地干笑一声，说道，“我喜欢叫他驽马。你们可能以为，我回来了，邓布利多教授会把那匹马打发走吧？可是没有……我们还要分摊上课……这是一种侮辱，说真的，侮辱。你知道……”

特里劳尼教授似乎醉得没有认出哈利。趁着她在激烈抨击费伦泽，哈利凑近赫敏说：“我们现在说清楚，你打算告诉罗恩你干预了守门员选拔吗？”

赫敏扬起眉毛。

“你真以为我做得出那种事？”

哈利目光犀利地看着她。

“赫敏，如果你能邀请麦克拉根——”

“那不一样，”赫敏傲然道，“我没打算告诉罗恩守门员选拔中本来会发生什么，或不会发生什么。”

“那就好，”哈利热切地说，“不然他又会崩溃，我们下一场又完了——”

“魁地奇！”赫敏气呼呼地说，“男孩子就只关心这个吗？考迈克没问过一个关于我本人的问题，一直给我大讲特讲考迈克·麦克拉根的一百个惊险救球——哎呀，他来了！”

她动作快得像幻影移形，前一秒还在这儿，下一秒就从两个大笑的女巫中间钻过去消失了。

'Seen Hermione?' asked McLaggen, forcing his way through the throng a minute later.

'No, sorry,' said Harry, and he turned quickly to join in Luna's conversation, forgetting for a split second to whom she was talking.

'Harry Potter!' said Professor Trelawney in deep, vibrant tones, noticing him for the first time.

'Oh, hello,' said Harry unenthusiastically.

'My dear boy!' she said in a very carrying whisper. 'The rumours! The stories! The Chosen One! Of course, I have known for a very long time … the omens were never good, Harry … but why have you not returned to Divination? For you, of all people, the subject is of the utmost importance!'

'Ah, Sybill, we all think our subject's most important!' said a loud voice, and Slughorn appeared at Professor Trelawney's other side, his face very red, his velvet hat a little askew, a glass of mead in one hand and an enormous mince pie in the other. 'But I don't think I've ever known such a natural at Potions!' said Slughorn, regarding Harry with a fond, if bloodshot, eye. 'Instinctive, you know – like his mother! I've only ever taught a few with this kind of ability, I can tell you that, Sybill – why, even Severus –'

And to Harry's horror, Slughorn threw out an arm and seemed to scoop Snape out of thin air towards them.

'Stop skulking and come and join us, Severus!' hiccoughed Slughorn happily. 'I was just talking about Harry's exceptional potion-making! Some credit must go to you, of course, you taught him for five years!'

Trapped, with Slughorn's arm around his shoulders, Snape looked down his hooked nose at Harry, his black eyes narrowed.

'Funny, I never had the impression that I managed to teach Potter anything at all.'

'Well, then, it's natural ability!' shouted Slughorn. 'You should have seen what he gave me, first lesson, the Draught of Living Death – never had a student produce finer on a first attempt, I don't think even you, Severus –'

'Really?' said Snape quietly, his eyes still boring into Harry, who felt a certain disquiet. The last thing he wanted was for Snape to start investigating the source of his new-found brilliance at Potions.

'Remind me what other subjects you're taking, Harry?' asked Slughorn.

“看到赫敏了吗？”一分钟后，麦克拉根从人堆里挤过来问道。

“没有，对不起。”哈利说完，赶紧转身加入卢娜的谈话，一时竟忘记了她面前的那个人是谁。

“哈利·波特！”特里劳尼教授用带着回响的深沉声音叫了起来，第一次注意到了哈利。

“啊，您好。”哈利冷漠地说。

“我亲爱的孩子！”她说，声音很小，但传得很远，“那些谣传！那些故事！救世之星！当然，我早就知道了……兆头总是不好，哈利……可是你为什么不来上占卜课了呢？对你来说，这门课尤为重要啊！”

“啊，西比尔，我们都觉得自己的课最重要！”一个洪亮的声音说。斯拉格霍恩出现在特里劳尼教授的另一边，他面色通红，天鹅绒帽子有点歪，一手端着蜂蜜酒，一手举着一块巨大的百果馅饼，“可是我想，我从没见过这样一个魔药领域的天才！”他用宠爱的、有些充血的眼睛看着哈利，“有天赋——像他妈妈！我只教过几个天资这么高的学生，我可以告诉你，西比尔——就连西弗勒斯——”

哈利惊恐地看到斯拉格霍恩伸出一只胳膊，像是从空气中把斯内普钩了出来。

“别偷偷摸摸的，来跟我们聊聊，西弗勒斯！”斯拉格霍恩快活地打着饱嗝说，“我正谈到哈利在魔药学上的特殊才能！当然也有你的功劳，你教了他五年！”

斯内普被斯拉格霍恩的胳膊箍住肩膀，动弹不得，他的目光顺着鹰钩鼻子落到哈利身上，黑眼睛眯缝着。

“有趣，我从没觉得我教会过波特任何东西。”

“哦，那就是天才呀！”斯拉格霍恩叫道，“你没看见他第一节课交给我的生死水——从没见过哪个学生第一次能做得比他更好，我想就连你，西弗勒斯——”

“是吗？”斯内普平静地说，眼睛像钻子似的盯着哈利。哈利有点不安，唯恐斯内普追究起他的魔药新才华的来源。

“提醒我一下，你还修了什么课，哈利？”斯拉格霍恩问。

'Defence Against the Dark Arts, Charms, Transfiguration, Herbology ...'

'All the subjects required, in short, for an Auror,' said Snape, with the faintest sneer.

'Yeah, well, that's what I'd like to be,' said Harry defiantly.

'And a great one you'll make, too!' boomed Slughorn.

'I don't think you should be an Auror, Harry,' said Luna unexpectedly. Everybody looked at her. 'The Aurors are part of the Rotfang Conspiracy, I thought everyone knew that. They're working from within to bring down the Ministry of Magic using a combination of Dark Magic and gum disease.'

Harry inhaled half his mead up his nose as he started to laugh. Really, it had been worth bringing Luna just for this. Emerging from his goblet, coughing, sopping wet but still grinning, he saw something calculated to raise his spirits even higher: Draco Malfoy being dragged by the ear towards them by Argus Filch.

'Professor Slughorn,' wheezed Filch, his jowls aquiver and the maniacal light of mischief-detection in his bulging eyes, 'I discovered this boy lurking in an upstairs corridor. He claims to have been invited to your party and to have been delayed in setting out. Did you issue him with an invitation?'

Malfoy pulled himself free of Filch's grip, looking furious.

'All right, I wasn't invited!' he said angrily. 'I was trying to gatecrash, happy?'

'No, I'm not!' said Flch, a statement at complete odds with the glee on his face. 'You're in trouble, you are! Didn't the Headmaster say that night-time prowling's out, unless you've got permission, didn't he, eh?'

'That's all right, Argus, that's all right,' said Slughorn, waving a hand. 'It's Christmas, and it's not a crime to want to come to a party. Just this once, we'll forget any punishment; you may stay, Draco.'

Filch's expression of outraged disappointment was perfectly predictable; but why, Harry wondered, watching him, did Malfoy look almost equally unhappy? And why was Snape looking at Malfoy as though both angry and ... was it possible? ... a little afraid?

But almost before Harry had registered what he had seen, Filch had turned and shuffled away, muttering under his breath; Malfoy had composed his face into a smile and was thanking Slughorn for his generosity, and Snape's face was smoothly inscrutable again.

“黑魔法防御术、魔咒课、变形课、草药课……”

“简而言之，是做一个傲罗需要学的所有课程。”斯内普说，带着微微一丝冷笑。

“是的，我就是想当傲罗。”哈利倔强地说。

“你会成为一名优秀的傲罗！”斯拉格霍恩声音洪亮地说。

“我觉得你不应该当傲罗，哈利。”卢娜出人意料地说，大家都看着她，“傲罗是腐牙阴谋的一部分。我以为大家都知道呢。他们想利用黑魔法和牙龈病从内部搞垮魔法部。”

哈利噗嗤一笑，把一半蜂蜜酒吸到鼻腔里。真的，光为这个带卢娜来也值了。他从杯子上抬起头，咳嗽着，脸上湿漉漉的，依然带着笑，接下来看到的一件事，像是有意要让他兴致更高：德拉科·马尔福被费尔奇揪着耳朵朝这边走了过来。

“斯拉格霍恩教授，”费尔奇呼哧呼哧地说，下巴上的肉抖动着，金鱼眼中闪着抓到学生调皮捣蛋时那种疯狂的光芒，“我发现这个男孩躲在楼上走廊里。他说是受到你的邀请来参加晚会，还说动身时被耽搁了。你给他发请柬了吗？”

马尔福挣脱了费尔奇的手，看上去气急败坏。

“好吧，没邀请我，”他愤愤地说，“我想闯进来，满意了吧？”

“不，我不满意！”费尔奇说，这话与他脸上的得意全然不符，“你有麻烦了！校长不是说未经允许晚上不许乱走动吗？嗯？”

“没关系，阿格斯，没关系，”斯拉格霍恩挥了挥手说，“圣诞节嘛，想参加晚会又不是罪过。这次就算了吧，下不为例。德拉科，你可以留下。”

费尔奇那愤慨和失望的表情自不待说。但令哈利纳闷的是，马尔福为什么差不多同样不高兴呢？斯内普看马尔福的眼神为什么既愤怒又……这可能吗？……有点害怕？

哈利还没来得及弄清眼前所见，费尔奇已经转身拖着步子，小声嘟囔着走开了，马尔福也已经整理出一副笑脸，感谢斯拉格霍恩的宽宏大量，斯内普的表情又平静得深不可测。

'It's nothing, nothing,' said Slughorn, waving away Malfoy's thanks. 'I did know your grandfather, after all …'

'He always spoke very highly of you, sir,' said Malfoy quickly. 'Said you were the best potion-maker he'd ever known …'

Harry stared at Malfoy. It was not the sucking up that intrigued him; he had watched Malfoy do that to Snape for a long time. It was the fact that Malfoy did, after all, look a little ill. This was the first time he had seen Malfoy close up for ages; he now saw that Malfoy had dark shadows under his eyes and a distinctly greyish tinge to his skin.

'I'd like a word with you, Draco,' said Snape suddenly.

'Oh, now, Severus,' said Slughorn, hiccoughing again, 'it's Christmas, don't be too hard –'

'I'm his Head of House, and I shall decide how hard, or otherwise, to be,' said Snape curtly. 'Follow me, Draco.'

They left, Snape leading the way, Malfoy looking resentful. Harry stood there for a moment, irresolute, then said, 'I'll be back in a bit, Luna – er – bathroom.'

'All right,' she said cheerfully, and he thought he heard her, as he hurried off into the crowd, resume the subject of the Rotfang Conspiracy with Professor Trelawney, who seemed sincerely interested.

It was easy, once out of the party, to pull his Invisibility Cloak out of his pocket and throw it over himself, for the corridor was quite deserted. What was more difficult was finding Snape and Malfoy. Harry ran down the corridor, the noise of his feet masked by the music and loud talk still issuing from Slughorn's office behind him. Perhaps Snape had taken Malfoy to his office in the dungeons … or perhaps he was escorting him back to the Slytherin common room … but Harry pressed his ear against door after door as he dashed down the corridor until, with a great jolt of excitement, he crouched down to the keyhole of the last classroom in the corridor and heard voices.

'… cannot afford mistakes, Draco, because if you are expelled –'

'I didn't have anything to do with it, all right?'

'I hope you are telling the truth, because it was both clumsy and foolish. Already you are suspected of having a hand in it.'

'Who suspects me?' said Malfoy angrily. 'For the last time, I didn't do it, OK? That Bell girl must've had an enemy no one knows about – don't look

“没什么，没什么，”斯拉格霍恩一摆手，说道，“毕竟，我认识你的祖父……”

“他一向对您称赞有加，先生，”马尔福马上说，“说您是他知道的最好的魔药专家……”

哈利瞪着马尔福，不是为这马屁而惊奇（马尔福之前都是这样奉承斯内普的），而是马尔福看上去确实有点病态。很久以来他第一次这么近距离地观察马尔福。他发现马尔福眼睛下面有黑圈，皮肤明显有些发灰。

“我有话跟你说，德拉科。”斯内普突然说。

“哎呀，西弗勒斯，”斯拉格霍恩说，又打了一个饱嗝，“圣诞节，别太严厉——”

“我是他的院长，严厉不严厉应由我决定。”斯内普简短地说，“跟我来，德拉科。”

两人走了，斯内普在前，马尔福气呼呼地后面跟着。哈利犹豫地站了片刻，然后说：“我去去就来，卢娜——哦——去盥洗室。”

“好的。”卢娜愉快地说。哈利匆匆钻进人群时，似乎听见她又对特里劳尼教授讲起了腐牙阴谋，特里劳尼教授好像还真感兴趣。

出来之后，哈利从兜里抽出隐形衣披到身上，这样做倒不难，因为走廊上空荡荡的，但是要找到斯内普和马尔福就没这么容易了。哈利跑了起来，斯拉格霍恩办公室里仍在传出的音乐与谈话声掩盖了他的脚步声。也许斯内普把马尔福带到他的地下办公室去了……也许正在把他送回斯莱特林的公共休息室……但哈利还是把耳朵贴到一扇扇门上。当他凑近走廊上最后一间教室的钥匙孔时，顿觉一阵狂喜，他听到了说话声。

“……不能再出纰漏了，德拉科，要是你被开除——”

“那事跟我无关，知道吗？”

“我希望你说的是真话，因为那件事拙劣而又愚蠢，你已经受到怀疑了。”

“谁怀疑我？”马尔福生气地问，“再说最后一遍，不是我干的，

at me like that! I know what you're doing, I'm not stupid, but it won't work – I can stop you!'

There was a pause and then Snape said quietly, 'Ah … Aunt Bellatrix has been teaching you Occlumency, I see. What thoughts are you trying to conceal from your master, Draco?'

'I'm not trying to conceal anything from *him*, I just don't want *you* butting in!'

Harry pressed his ear still more closely against the keyhole … what had happened to make Malfoy speak to Snape like this, Snape, towards whom he had always shown respect, even liking?

'So that is why you have been avoiding me this term? You have feared my interference? You realise that, had anybody else failed to come to my office when I had told them repeatedly to be there, Draco –'

'So put me in detention! Report me to Dumbledore!' jeered Malfoy.

There was another pause. Then Snape said, 'You know perfectly well that I do not wish to do either of those things.'

'You'd better stop telling me to come to your office, then!'

'Listen to me,' said Snape, his voice so low now that Harry had to push his ear very hard against the keyhole to hear. 'I am trying to help you. I swore to your mother I would protect you. I made the Unbreakable Vow, Draco –'

'Looks like you'll have to break it, then, because I don't need your protection! It's my job, he gave it to me and I'm doing it. I've got a plan and it's going to work, it's just taking a bit longer than I thought it would!'

'What is your plan?'

'It's none of your business!'

'If you tell me what you are trying to do, I can assist you –'

'I've got all the assistance I need, thanks, I'm not alone!'

'You were certainly alone tonight, which was foolish in the extreme, wandering the corridors without lookouts or back-up. These are elementary mistakes –'

'I would've had Crabbe and Goyle with me if you hadn't put them in detention!'

'Keep your voice down!' spat Snape, for Malfoy's voice had risen excitedly. 'If your friends Crabbe and Goyle intend to pass their Defence Against the Dark Arts O.W.L. this time around, they will need to work a little harder than they are doing at pres–'

知道吗？那个叫贝尔的女孩肯定有个没人知道的仇人——别那样看着我！我知道你在干什么，我又不傻，可是你不会得逞——我能阻止你！”

停了一阵，斯内普轻声说：“哦……看来贝拉特里克斯姨妈教过你大脑封闭术了。你有什么念头想瞒着你的主人呢，德拉科？”

“我没想瞒着他，我只是不要你插在里面。”

哈利把耳朵贴得更紧一些……是什么使马尔福开始对斯内普这样说话的呢？对斯内普，马尔福可是好像一直尊敬有加，甚至挺喜欢他的啊？

“所以你这学期躲着我？怕我干涉？你要知道，德拉科，如果换了别人，我多次叫他来我办公室而他不来——”

“你就会关禁闭！报告邓布利多！”马尔福讥笑道。

又停了一阵，斯内普说：“你很清楚我不想做这些事。”

“那你最好别再叫我去你的办公室。”

“听我说，”斯内普的声音压得太低了，哈利把耳朵使劲贴在钥匙孔上才能听到，“我想帮助你。我对你母亲发过誓要保护你。我立了牢不可破的誓言，德拉科——”

“看来你必须打破了，因为我不需要你的保护。这是我的工作，他分派给我的，我正在做。我有一个计划，会成功的，只是时间比我预计的要长一些！”

“你的计划是什么？”

“你管不着！”

“如果你告诉我，我可以帮你——”

“我已经有了足够的帮手，谢谢，我不是一个人！”

“你今晚无疑是一个人，这是极其愚蠢的，在走廊里游荡，没有岗哨也没有后援。这些是低级错误——”

“本来有克拉布和高尔跟着我，可是你关了他们的禁闭！”

“小声点儿！”斯内普警告道，因为马尔福这时激动得提高了嗓门，“你的朋友克拉布和高尔这次要想通过黑魔法防御术的 O.W.L. 考试，还得多下点儿功夫——”

'What does it matter?' said Malfoy. 'Defence Against the Dark Arts – it's all just a joke, isn't it, an act? Like any of us need protecting against the Dark Arts –'

'It is an act that is crucial to success, Draco!' said Snape. 'Where do you think I would have been all these years, if I had not known how to act? Now listen to me! You are being incautious, wandering around at night, getting yourself caught, and if you are placing your reliance on assistants like Crabbe and Goyle –'

'They're not the only ones, I've got other people on my side, better people!'

'Then why not confide in me, and I can –'

'I know what you're up to! You want to steal my glory!'

There was another pause, then Snape said coldly, 'You are speaking like a child. I quite understand that your father's capture and imprisonment has upset you, but –'

Harry had barely a second's warning; he heard Malfoy's footsteps on the other side of the door and flung himself out of the way just as it burst open; Malfoy was striding away down the corridor, past the open door of Slughorn's office, round the distant corner and out of sight.

Hardly daring to breathe, Harry remained crouched down as Snape emerged slowly from the classroom. His expression unfathomable, he returned to the party. Harry remained on the floor, hidden beneath the Cloak, his mind racing.

“通不过有什么关系？黑魔法防御术——只是一个笑话，一场戏，对不对？就好像我们中间有谁需要黑魔法防御——”

“这是一场对成功非常关键的戏，德拉科！”斯内普说，“你想想，如果我不会演戏，这些年会在哪儿？听我说！你现在很不谨慎，夜里到处乱走，被人当场抓住，还有，如果你依赖克拉布和高尔这样的助手——”

“不是只有他们，我身边还有别人，更强的人！”

“为什么不能告诉我，我可以——”

“我知道你在打什么主意！你想抢我的功劳！”

又停了一阵，斯内普冷冷地说道：“你说话像个小孩子。我很理解你父亲入狱令你心烦意乱，但——”

哈利几乎连一秒钟的思想准备都没有，就听到马尔福的脚步声在门那边响起。他赶紧闪到一边，门已砰然打开，马尔福大步朝走廊那头走去，经过斯拉格霍恩办公室敞开的门口，转过远处的拐角不见了。

哈利大气不敢出，继续蹲伏着，斯内普慢慢走出教室，表情深不可测，回去参加晚会了。哈利蹲在隐形衣下，脑子飞快地转动着。

WIZARDING WORLD